Studia Fennica
Litteraria 10

ELISE NYKÄNEN

Mysterious Minds

The Making of Private and Collective Consciousness in Marja-Liisa Vartio's Novels

Finnish Literature Society · SKS · Helsinki · 2017

STUDIA FENNICA LITTERARIA 10

The publication has undergone a peer review.

VERTAISARVIOITU
KOLLEGIALT GRANSKAD
PEER-REVIEWED
www.tsv.fi/tunnus

The open access publication of this volume has received part funding via Helsinki University Library.

Publication of the work was supported by the Alfred Kordelin Foundation.

ALFRED
KORDELININ
SÄÄTIÖ

A digital edition of a printed book first published in 2017 by the Finnish Literature Society.
Cover Design: Timo Numminen
EPUB: eLibris Media Oy

ISBN 978-952-222-864-2 (Print)
ISBN 978-952-222-952-6 (PDF)
ISBN 978-952-222-951-9 (EPUB)

ISSN 0085-6835 (Studia Fennica)
ISSN 1458-5278 (Studia Fennica Litteraria)

DOI: http://dx.doi.org/10.21435/sflit.10

A free open access version of the book is available at http://dx.doi.org/10.21435/sflit.10 or by scanning this QR code with your mobile device.

BoD – Books on Demand, Norderstedt, Germany 2017

Contents

To my sisters

Foreword

*M*ysterious Minds is the outcome of my decade-long work with one of the most enchanting figures in Finnish literary modernism, Marja-Liisa Vartio. Vartio's status as an innovator in the portrayal of human consciousness has long been acknowledged. This book is the first study that focuses on the presentation of fictional minds in her novels. By exploring the private and collective dimensions of fictional mind presentation in Vartio's narrative prose, I also attempt to pave the way for a richer account of modernism in literature. This book reassesses the idea of modernism as an "inward turn" by paying attention to the social and intermental aspects of consciousness presentation. Fictional minds are not only introspective, solipsistic, individual, and detached. They are also public, enactive, embodied, and engaged.

I wish to express my gratitude to the Finnish Literature Society for accepting my book to this international publication series. I am especially thankful to the editor, Virve Mertanen, for her cooperation and professionalism. I also wish to thank the two anonymous peer reviewers for their invaluable comments and suggestions. Special thanks are due to the Alfred Kordelin Foundation for funding the proofreading. I feel particularly indebted to translator Jill G. Timbers, who revised the translations of Vartio's texts. I thank Jill for the stimulating conversations we had during my trip to her hometown in Illinois, USA. I owe a great debt also to Glenda Gloss, who revised the English language of the manuscript at different stages of the project. The final choices relating to all translations and revisions remain my own, as do any possible infelicities.

This book is based on my doctoral dissertation, *Worlds Within and Without: Presenting Fictional Minds in Marja-Liisa Vartio's Narrative Prose* (2014). Readers interested in a more theoretically and methodologically oriented approach are welcome to inspect this doctoral dissertation. Earlier versions of parts of this book have also been published in the volumes *Dialogi kaunokirjallisuudessa* (Dialogue in Fiction, 2013) and *Reframing Concepts in Literary and Cultural Studies: Theorizing and Analyzing Conceptual Transfer* (2014).

I hope that readers will find Vartio's fictional minds as captivating and this journey into her narrative worlds as rewarding as I have.

Helsinki, Finland October 2017

8

1. Introduction. Worlds Within and Without

The purpose of this book is to provide a comprehensive account of the narrative tools, techniques, and structures that Marja-Liisa Vartio (1924–1966), the eccentric classic author of Finnish post-war modernism, used to construct fictional minds in her novels. By examining the theoretical challenges of Vartio's modernist narratives, this study makes a contribution to the academic discussion of the formal and thematic features of modernist fiction. I focus on the ways in which fictional minds in Vartio's novels work in interaction and in relation to the imaginary world in which they are embedded. In Vartio's hands, fictional minds are often layered in a challenging manner. Her characters often claim to "know" the contents of other minds, even if they do not know their own. The gradual multiplication of imaginary worlds generates mazes of fictional minds as a result of the characters' increasing fabulation. This complexity of interacting fictional minds is illustrated in Vartio's last novel, *Hänen olivat linnut* (Hers/His Were the Birds).[1] The neurotic widow of a country parson, Adele Broms, opens up to her maid, Alma Luostarinen:

> You have it good, Alma, since you don't grasp everything that's going on in another person's mind. You go through your life with your good sense under control, you suffer less than I do. When I was younger, I couldn't look people in the eye because I always knew what they were thinking and it made me ill, because what I saw they were thinking about me was not always favorable. (*PW*, 222)[2]

Adele's tormented mind perceives other minds full of hostile thoughts as she becomes unable to distinguish between facts and her inflamed, emotional responses to others. In general, the desire of Vartio's characters to know – themselves, other people, and the secret of human existence – pertains to the epistemological problem that enthralled modernist writers. How is an individual, locked in her or his own consciousness, able to obtain knowledge of the enfolding world, of another human being, or even of herself or himself? In this book, the metaphor of a "world" at the center of possible world poetics along with cognitive approaches to literature offer new ways to survey the conventions of modernist fiction. The narrative semantics in Vartio's fiction are related to epistemological world-structures, which I explore by analyzing fictional minds as embodied, emotional, and social entities interacting within her storyworlds. The views of fictional reality are shaped and re-shaped in the interaction between the self, the outer world, and the other minds inhabiting the same storyworld.

My title for this introduction, "Worlds Within and Without," derives from Virginia Woolf's famous definition of the locus of modernist fiction: "[I]llumine the mind within rather than the world without" (Woolf 1958/1929: 121). The discussion of the true focus of modernist writing – whether it is on subjective reality or external objects in the world – has often been related to the question of the "inward turn" believed to be taking place in modernist fiction.[3] Modernist writers themselves often perceived the history of the novel as a move inwards, towards a narrative "with as little admixture of the alien and external as possible," as Woolf (1929: 189) wrote in her essay "Modern Fiction" (1919). As the growing historical distance from the modernist period makes it increasingly possible to re-consider the accounts of contemporary writers and commentators, the claim of an "inward turn" may not turn out to be as great a break from realist tradition as was believed. In this study, I re-consider the modernist move away from the external world to subjective consciousness by analyzing the encounters between fictional minds and worlds in Vartio's novels.

Vartio's oeuvre serves as an interesting point of departure for approaching the schematizations of fictional consciousness. Specifically, her work challenges the scholarly tradition of considering fictional minds primarily in regard to conventions of transparency. In her novels, the duality of fictional minds, both as readable and unreadable entities, constitutes the very spell of her work. My analyses in this study show how Vartio developed as a portrayer of the human mind's complexity, its hidden structures, and its multifold processes related to the modernist epistemology of knowing. Her characters negotiate between the private and the public, the individual and the collective, the conscious and the unconscious, and the rational and the emotional. Vartio offers both internal and external perspectives on these efforts. The characters' actions and interactions revolve around their perceptions and sentiments as well as their dreams, delusions, and esoteric imaginings.

During her career, Vartio published five novels, which comprise the corpus of this study. Vartio's fourth novel, *Tunteet* (Emotions, 1962), was seen as a shift in her style. The critic Timo Tiusanen perceived this shift as originating in Vartio's own voice, which began to sound more forcefully in the novels. Compared to the "steady" and "toughening" female characters in *Se on sitten kevät* (This Then Is Spring, 1957) and in her second novel, *Mies kuin mies, tyttö kuin tyttö* (Any Man, Any Girl, published in 1958), Inkeri, the young protagonist of *Tunteet*, appears "flimsy" and "changeable," resembling the female protagonist in Vartio's third novel, *Kaikki naiset näkevät unia* (All Women Dream, 1960). This portrait of an absent-minded housewife, Mrs. Pyy, prefigures the future developments of Vartio's techniques of constructing fictional minds:

In this way we can divide Vartio's novels into two groups [...] In the newer works, the register has expanded toward increased humor while the vigor and unity have decreased as Vartio has let loose her inclination to spin tales, even to chatter on. It is as if the poetry and intensity that flash forth in specific details of the latest novels had been dammed up in the first two, coloring everything and carrying the whole which remained nonetheless plain, everyday. The central problem for Vartio, this wildly imaginative writer, seems to be dreams and images that do not fit everyday experience, do not take root. (Tiusanen 1962: 19)[4]

The ideas of an increasing amount of scatter and dream were also emphasized by critics of the novels *Kaikki naiset näkevät unia* and *Hänen olivat linnut* published posthumously in 1967. The more unorganized, unconstrained style was considered an indication of the "vivid imagination" of the author herself, which affected the style of writing. The change was not always welcomed. The most critical (and openly misogynist) review was penned by Erno Paasilinna, who considered *Tunteet* an artificial and affected popular romance: "I may be a hater of female writers. Allowing for that, I still argue that our female writers generally do not raise the level of Finnish literature, but rather use it calculatedly. [...] One must take pain not to read them without reservations; we cannot afford to do so." (Paasilinna 1962: 559)[5] Attitudes such as Paasilinna's were reflected in the statements by the fictional character Napoleon in Pekka Kejonen's collection of short stories, *Napoleonin epätoivo* (The Misery of Napoleon), published in 1964, two years after *Tunteet*: "I do not believe a woman is capable of writing even a somewhat sensible novel. You just get things like *Mrs. Dalloway* and other muddled books" (Kejonen 1964: 48).[6]

Some critics shared Paasilinna's views of *Tunteet*. Yet despite their harsh criticism, these reviewers tended to acknowledge Vartio's skill. Even if "ironic distance" and "technical talent" were perceived as distinguishing Vartio from beginning writers, the sentimental content of the novel was considered to have taken a heavy toll. *Tunteet* was more "poorly" constructed than her earlier novels. Vartio, who had previously controlled her material with "austere vigor," had now loosened her grip and brushed on her colors "without a solid drawing plan." The result was "uninteresting," affected by "womanly fuss" and "girlishness." (M. N. 1962: 3)[7] According to Paasilinna (1962: 559), Vartio had calculated with her talent: "[B]ut these emotions, emotions! [...] This 'exuberant' view of life turns out to be merely technique lacking content; and the technique is merely an acquired property that does not necessarily contribute to the content," he wrote; "Even in romance novels one should achieve narrative flow in which expression is expression, not something squeezed into a Venetian corset."[8]

Paasilinna criticized Vartio for succumbing to the trends of women's literature in which the very technique (expression as mere expression) is restricted by the amplitude of emotional content.[9] Softness, passiveness, femininity, effusiveness, and chaos were the metaphors commonly used by Anglo-American Imagists, for instance, to convey the desire to rid poetry of sentimentality. The above-listed attributes were seen as characteristic of symbolist predecessors. They were replaced by "masculine spirit,"

11

hardness, order, and rigor.[10] Sentimental writing ("babble" and "blather") was conceived as being a risk to the intellectual vigor of modern literature, which was forced to confront vulgar, commercial, and simply bad popular writing, like romances (Gilbert & Gubar 1988: 132–135). The fragmentation of narrative coherence and order was often seen in the context of gender, and the emotional was considered equal to the feminine.

While accusing Vartio's *Tunteet* of being sentimental and chaotic, Finnish critics of the time ignored the influence of the Anglo-American modernism on Vartio's work. The first authors to experiment with the new techniques of portraying mental flow, including stream of consciousness, were authors striving to depict the imagination and experience of (female) characters. In an international context authors such as Dorothy Richardson, May Sinclair, Henry James, and D. H. Lawrence were soon followed by writers, now canonized, like Virginia Woolf or James Joyce, who famously portrayed the mental flow of Molly Bloom in *Ulysses* (1922). In the period of modernism in an Anglo-American context, intuition and the unconscious were preferred. It has been claimed that this "inward turn" simultaneously meant a move away from intellect and rationality (e.g. Stevenson 1998: 109). However, as the epistemological world-structures of Vartio's texts demonstrate, the emotional and the rational are complementary rather than exclusive phenomena in the characters' mental actions. Emotions do not defy reasoning, but accompany it.

Some critics have argued that female writers may have felt pressured to conform to the modernist ideals of objectivity and restraint in their work (cf. Clark 1991: 13). The condemnation of Vartio's new style by some critics seems to have originated in the ideals of intellectual discipline and perfection of form that prevailed in Finnish criticism during the 1950s. These ideals survived through the "golden age" of Finnish literature in the 1950s and led even Vartio herself to believe that the accomplishments of her first novel could never be surpassed. While writing *Hänen olivat linnut*, a masterpiece of Finnish post-war modernism, Vartio (1996: 189) confessed in her diary: "I'm a very minor literary talent, no one at all. A couple of poems, a couple of dream stories, 'Se on sitten kevät,' that's all."[11] According to recent biographical writing on Vartio, there are some indications in her manuscripts that her early editor, Tuomas Anhava, and her husband, the poet Paavo Haavikko, suggested some changes to "restrain" her expression and make it more concise (Ruuska 2012: 332). These changes, however, can be considered rather inconsequential with regard to the overall style and composition of Vartio's novels.[12]

Vartio's technique of constructing consciousness in particular, diverges in many respects from the tempered and relatively late Finnish modernist prose, especially in her later novels. Over the years, Vartio forged a style that was completely her own: "[T]here are no tricks supplied, they have to be invented by oneself," she wrote.[13] One of these "tricks" was the technique of embedded fictional minds, which was an innovation in her early novels and elaborated on later. The multiple layering of minds – fictional minds reading other fictional minds potentially rushing into recursive re-readings – is a defining feature of Vartio's novels. As Aatos Ojala (1976: 134) observed,

"Vartio's characters are to each other like 'signs' that they are trying to interpret to the best – or worst – of their ability."[14] The challenging task of tracing the origin of characters' thoughts attaches Vartio's work to the tradition of modernist texts, for instance, Woolf's stream of consciousness novels (cf. Zunshine 2006: 37). The overly self-conscious, affective quest for (self)knowledge by Vartio's characters turns the epistemic worlds into complex and even paranoid constructs.

The tension between the private and the public realms of fictional minds is related to the dream-driven and dark psychology of Vartio's characters. The focus on fabulating, mysterious minds culminates in *Hänen olivat linnut*. The novel shows the delusive quality of human imagination. By and large, the characters' growing imaginations lead to a growing distance from the representation of the external, mimetic worlds. The compact, well-focused composition in Vartio's early, "neutral" narratives was followed by more kaleidoscopic and multilevel world-organizations that reflect the less constrained imaginations of the characters in her later novels. The more convoluted the constructions of fictional minds become, the more sophisticated and innovative are Vartio's tools – and the mastery of her craft.

The Worlds of Modernism(s). The Mind as a Limit

Before I proceed to a more detailed analysis of the construction of fictional minds in Vartio's novels, it is necessary to shed more light on the intricacies of Finnish post-war modernism, which serves as the immediate context for this author's fictional writing. Vartio's career as a professional author began in 1952, when her first collection of poems, *Häät* (The Wedding), was published. Another anthology of poems, *Seppele* (The Garland), appeared the following year. With their fierce, archaic imagery, both collections were seen as continuing the tradition of Finnish-Karelian folk poetry. The poems were perceived as oracular visions with a modernist twist. A collection of short stories entitled *Maan ja veden välillä* (Between Land and Water, 1955) resorts to imagistic narration, fusing the boundaries between poetry and prose. Many of the dream stories in the collection drew on material from Vartio's dreams. Her poems and short stories received critical nods, but *Se on sitten kevät*, published two years later, met with wide approval. *Se on sitten kevät* was considered one of the novels that ultimately launched the renewal of prose fiction in Finnish literature, long after the full bloom of the modernist novel in the Anglo-American context.

Even though Vartio gradually distanced herself from the ideals of restraint and the "unsentimental" poetics of the 1950s, there are certain techniques of detachment that were elaborated in her novels to serve the portrayal of her characters' mental lives. As previous studies on Finnish modernism have emphasized, post-war literature in the Finnish context did not constitute a uniform school of modernism, but diverged into several strands of (modernist) poetics, co-existing simultaneously.[15] Modernism in general has been perceived as consisting of various currents rather than being any single international movement (Whitworth 2007: 4–5; Fokkema

& Ibsch 1988: 1). The following section focuses on the Finnish "new novel," also known as the "new realism." Its principles have been articulated largely in the writings of Tuomas Anhava, a critic and a leading editor in Finnish modernism – the "literary brain" (*kirjallinen aivo*) as Vartio called him.[16]

The atmosphere of Finnish realism in the 1950s has been portrayed as a "no man's land," a metaphor that conveys the feelings of doubt and skepticism which the Finns experienced after World War II (cf. Viikari 1992; Rojola 2008). The country's geographical position between east and west made life particularly difficult during the first and second world wars, as well as during the Cold War that followed. Compared to the more cosmopolitan avant-garde movements and high modernism in Europe, the path chosen by the Finnish "new school" writers was relatively conservative. Finnish modernists pulled away from the chaotic world and retreated to objective, matter-of-fact attitudes and to their reserved and disciplined styles. A neutral and prudent stance was more suitable for wanderers in no man's land, in the space in-between. (Hökkä 1999: 71; Hormia 1968: 73, 80)[17]

The essential aim of the modernists was to create a "new language," a more truthful way of portraying the subjective, immediate experience of changing reality. For Finnish modernists, Wittgenstein's philosophy seemed to offer new methods of approaching the problem of representative language.[18] Wittgenstein's solution was "to bring words back from their metaphysical to their everyday use," to make the words be more at home (Wittgenstein 1958: 48ᶜ). The principles of clarity and empiricism were appealing in a world that was experienced as chaotic and fractured. The practice, that is, the everyday use of language, was the element that seemed to give words their significance. "[W]hat can be said at all can be said clearly, and what we cannot talk about we must pass over in silence," Wittgenstein (1961: 151) wrote, articulating the principle of accuracy. If reality could not be changed, then at least the ways of perceiving it could be.

For Finnish modernists, "conventional" language signified obscurity that could be avoided by relying on restraint and accuracy. By molding conventional language anew – clear, hard, and concrete – authors could make words regain their meaning. The ideals of accuracy and precision resulted in the "odd optimism of communication" (Viikari 1992: 50) manifested in the writings of the period. Finding "one's own voice," "precise expression," or "the eradicative mediation of experience" (ibid.) were clichés that characterized the vocabulary of the time. In his essay "Optimistinen tutkielma" (An Optimistic Study, 1963), Anhava discussed the ideals of preciseness:

> Their [the modernists'] attention focuses primarily on language, not for the language itself but in order to know it at a deep level and train themselves, because their aim is to express their subject as precisely as possible. Which requires personal knowledge not only of the language but also of the subject to be expressed; for this reason they have to limit themselves to their own direct experience. In their work they are completely without any desire to trade it for ideals, truths, and hierarchies, e.g. generalities and systems of generalization, which cannot have exact, personally experienced meaning as anything other

than something to describe, rather than the described thing itself. Instead they expend enormous effort to make their work precisely correspond to what they have experienced of reality and language. (Anhava 2002/1963: 540–541)[19]

The main interest of the modernists, according to Anhava, is language, not for its own sake but because of the need to control the technical tools that aim at precision. His rules of art-making stressed four aspects. The first principle was the sharpened description of experienced reality. Secondly, the new style called for restraint on sentiment in representing subjective experience. Thirdly, the expression had to be precise and austere to convey reality and language as they were experienced by the artist. Fourthly, the exactitude of language required absolute devotion and discipline. Words needed to be studied and practiced, for every artist must know her or his material. Plain diction and clarity were seen as indications of discipline. Obscurity, by contrast, was considered a mask of weakness, a cover-up for a badly constructed work of art (cf. Painter 2006: 96).[20]

As the influences of Wittgenstein's philosophy of language gained more ground in the poetics of the 1950s, fiction-making itself was often conceived as a struggle against "the spell of words" (Viikari 1992: 47).[21] The need to determine foundations for knowledge that were clear and certain defined the climate of post-war culture and made many thinkers of the period wary of the uncontrollable conjectures of mental speculation and forced them to rely instead on knowledge gained by empirical observation (cf. Toulmin 1990: 70). One of these thinkers was Anhava, Vartio's editor. His ideals of emotional restraint and perfection of form stemmed from his interest in the poetic principles of Imagism, the "pure," "hard," and "dry" poetry of Ezra Pound, Thomas Hulme, and early T. S. Eliot. The influence of Asian short poetry, French post-classicism, and paradigms of the New Criticism found their way into Anhava's writings about prose fiction. These influences can be considered among the reasons why the modernist revolution in Finnish narrative prose took such a moderate form. Its main inspirations came from the wing of the modernist movement that Kirsten Blythe Painter has called "tempered modernism" in the context of such poetic schools as Imagism and Acmeism.

Tempered modernism is characterized by three features that distinguish it both from the simultaneous avant-garde movements and from the symbolism that had preceded it. First of all, it is neoclassical in the sense that it stresses the balance of form and content by relying on concision and austerity instead of fragmentation and discontinuity. Its principles include compressed form and clarity. "Perfection of form" is sought by using exact, even laconic, language and simple diction. Second, the tempered modernists' main concern was the sharpened depiction of external reality, the texture of the concrete things of everyday existence. The view of the world derives not from the non-representationalism of avant-garde or symbolist ideal dream worlds, but from rendering the objects of ordinary reality as if seen anew and for the first time. (Painter 2006: 1–3, 8)

Tempered modernists never rejected the traditional idea of using language to represent external reality.[22] The recognition of words' arbitrary and outworn quality resulted in an attempt to create an aesthetic style that at least aimed to generate a vivid illusion of the "thingness of things."[23] The works by tempered modernists often evoke the mundane and commonplace. Depiction of nature still plays a role. Their focus was on objects that the human mind usually encounters habitually without paying much attention to them. The aspiration to render concrete things vividly meant rejecting abstract concepts and explanation. Instead of articulating ideas of the world and processes of perception – in other words, approaching the world conceptually – they sought to capture an illusion of the experience of the perception itself in their texts (cf. Painter 2006: 113–115).[24] Third – and here we come to the focal point of this study – the tempered modernists represented the self as subdued and oblique. The impersonal, objective style rejects precise explanation, sentiment, and the outpouring of subjectivity.

Even if the expression is subtle and controlled, the method of detachment does not mean eradication of the self. The goal is to "balance poetic self and concrete thing, so that the latter – the real things of the world – can come to the fore with more clarity" (Painter 2006: 1). The aim is to "offer a way to *see anew*" rather than "insisting on *being new*" (ibid.). The notion of "seeing anew" refers to Wittgenstein's words on empirical knowledge and understanding. He tried to find new perspectives in looking at familiar things. These new ways of seeing are related to the private psychology "as confusion and barrenness." An awareness of the limits of introspection serves as the motivation to restrict the "picture of reality" to the ways in which the mind relates to the world "as it is," as if the subject itself were excluded from that world: "The subject does not belong to the world: rather, it is a limit of the world," Wittgenstein (1961: 117) argued. To illustrate the mind-dependence of the world, he compares the mind to a book in which no subject can be mentioned: "There is no such thing as the subject that thinks or entertains ideas. If I wrote a book called *The world as I found it*, I should have to include a report on my body, and should have to say which parts were subordinate to my will, and which were not, etc. [...] there is no subject; for it alone could *not* be mentioned in that book" (ibid.; emphasis his).

The idea of the private psychology "as confusion and barrenness" is reflected in Anhava's essay "Virginia Woolf." Anhava sets out to examine Woolf's stream of consciousness novels, but ends up producing an introduction to modernist narrative techniques overall. This becomes a rather normative guideline addressed to contemporary Finnish writers:

> Providing an account of one's own stream of consciousness, particularly at greater length, is almost an insuperable task. Presumably, it is even harder to depict the flow of someone else's inner experience. In general, it seems that the fictional rendering of half-conscious experiences, whether they be one's own or someone else's experiences, must of necessity alter their nature, and in many cases, *the only reliable way to render them is to allow them to be intuited from the narrated actions and incidents.* (Anhava 2002/1949: 57)[25]

According to Anhava, "the veracity of the material" in Woolf's fiction – movements of the mind rendered directly, from within – is highly unreliable. He argues for the importance of the intermediary role of the narrator to balance the external world and the inner reality, in other words, to preserve the boundaries between them. Literary texts need to focus on overt behaviors rather than on covert mental states, because the author's attempts to mediate consciousness, especially half-conscious experiences, are destined to fail. Similar ideas characterize Anhava's view of James Joyce's *Ulysses*. Anhava reflects on Alex Matson's insights into Joyce's technique, presented in Matson's *Romaanitaide* (The Art of the Novel, 1947).[26]

> Inner perception [...] has anything but a reliable reputation in a scientific sense. The behaviorists deny its use altogether, and in general psychology as well it has been emphatically argued that it needs support from the detached observation of actions and reactions. But 'Ulysses' and its successors do not settle for stream of consciousness in the first person, but move freely from one consciousness to another and autonomously represent the content of them all for us. And despite this, its users talk in contemptuous tones about the "omniscient" novelists of the past! – No functionalist representation of reality can be talked about, but rather *products of powerful fantasy*, which are at least as *imaginary* as the earlier novels. [...] Nevertheless, from a purely psychological point of view, the one-sided stream of conscious technique can be considered much more subjective than the normal narrative technique based on both on inner and outer observation. (Anhava 2002/1948: 17–18)[27]

Anhava's critique of the stream of consciousness novels culminates in his notion of these novels as "products of powerful fantasy." He stressed the unreliability of interior monologue as a *scientific* method for portraying human psychology. The contents of the human mind, whether of one's own or of another's experience, cannot be known or represented objectively. The most reliable way to portray the mind is to resort to "normal narrative technique," which enables both "inner and outer observation."

In his aesthetic theory, Anhava stressed the method of detachment, which resembles the detached observation of behaviorist psychology. To create a world of one's own, the author of a novel needs to rely on objectivity. Instead of speaking with one's own voice, the author *pretends* to be someone else by impersonating a fictional speaker, the narrator.[28] The impersonating activity results in making an objective form out of subjective reflections, on which every author, like "every observer of life," is dependent. According to Anhava, the process of creation is seen as an interaction between the self and the world:

> In my opinion, it's obvious that current literature does not aim to be any sort of unprecedentedly effective conserving method, with which life could be preserved with its natural color taste smell into jars of words and sentences. Hardly anyone in today's world is unaware of the subjectivity of the human being: and writers are particularly aware that while writing they constantly and only half-consciously make selections, driving events, words and rhythms whatever which way. But this

> striving for reduction is an effort to prevent the selections from being governed by any consciously adopted principles; writing is a kind of encounter in words between events within the self and life. (Anhava 2002/1964: 268–269)[29]

The presence of a narrator – the product of an impersonating act – ensures the needed aesthetic distance. The ideal of objectivity in regard to the representation of a fictional mind, often conceived as the behaviorism of the Finnish new school of modernism, is thus clarified. The direct rendering of human consciousness easily transforms the text into a stream of consciousness on the part of the author. While the material of the real world is being transformed into an artistic form, the principles of reduction and selection are desperately needed, for objectivity equals creativity. In this context Anhava refers to Joyce's famous metaphor for the artist, "like the God of the creation," who "remains within or behind or beyond or above his handiwork, invisible, refined out of existence, indifferent, paring his fingernails" (Joyce 2000/1916: 181).

The idea of the author's impossible task of conveying one or another's consciousness relates to the influence of New Criticism in Anhava's aesthetics. According to the New Critics, a text should be treated as an autonomous aesthetic object rather than as a reflection of authorial intention, moralistic statements, or historical and cultural contexts.[30] The principles of "intentional fallacy" and "affective fallacy" were established to show the readers' inclination to see the text either as a projection of the author's psychology or to confuse a text's effects with the text itself. The reader cannot know the author's mind. The only objectively existing thing is the text itself. According to Anhava, the only form of the author's subjectivity that is acceptable in modernist narrative is allegory:

> [Allegory] is the subjectivity that a naturalist and objectivist cannot escape. But it does no harm; it is precisely what makes verisimilitude possible. As long as there is information – which all naturalists gather – identifying with someone helps one have understanding, helps one see the protagonist's world with one's own eyes. As an artist, a naturalist often operates *just as if* he were creating a world separate from himself by following the general laws and texture of the external world: he makes the transition from "reality" to the world of art as unnoticeable as possible for the reader, presenting even the most interior knowledge "respectfully" [...] confining himself "to external description, dialog and action." (Anhava 2002/1956: 163; emphasis his)[31]

In Anhava's idea of the stream of consciousness novel, the New Critics' protocols for *reading* literature is expanded and applied to the *technique* and *style* of prose fiction, particularly to the means of mediating the fictional experience. Thus, awareness of the limits of knowledge can lead to an attempt to plunge the reader into the "immediate" flow of the human consciousness *as it is*, as happens in stream of consciousness novels. The other option, recommended by Anhava, is to restrict the observation to the ways in which a character's mind relates to the world *as it is*, as if the subject itself were excluded from that world.

However, in the context of the modernist novel in general and Vartio's fiction in particular, a close reading is mind-reading. In her work the urge for stability and certainty that were so eagerly desired by thinkers in the post-war world is shown to be utterly impossible. The certainty of knowledge is constantly deferred by her characters' "affective fallacies" as manifested in the delusive constellations of mind-reading in her novels. We find her characters continuously balancing the two poles of mental existence that result from the division of the mind into conscious, pre-conscious, and unconscious spheres, as well as into inner and outer perspectives on the self. The different techniques developed by Vartio to portray human consciousness both from without and within problematize the possibilities of the human mind to observe the world "as it is," for there is no world that we can know objectively.

In her concise, yet illuminating introduction to Finnish poetics of the 1950s, Auli Viikari listed four key aspects typical of the Finnish new novel that explain many intricacies of reading fictional minds from the reader's perspective. The first aspect is the presence of a narrator in a text that seems relatively traditional, although the tone may be more objective and detached, even "behavioristic," as some critics have claimed. The second aspect Viikari mentioned is the role of the reader. The reader needs to "know by intuition," to "read" the inner processes of characters from the elements of the external world. Readers have to take a more active part in generating meaning as they read the text. This "cooperation principle" between the narrator and the reader is also manifested in the third feature of the new school novels: the abundance of descriptive (visual) representation that is "metonymically related" to the amplitude of embedded storytelling, intertextual hints, and other evocations in the text. These textual elements contribute to the fourth aspect mentioned by Viikari: the use of allegory. (Viikari 1992: 60–65)[32]

In Vartio's texts, the representation of worlds creates a dual or layered ontology similar to the double worlds of allegory. The domain of the actual is split into two balanced, yet sharply distinct domains of existence; the visible world contains the world of the invisible (cf. Pavel 1986; Ryan 1991: 40). The evocative, allegorical techniques of presenting fictional minds challenge the idea of claimed behaviorism of the Finnish new school novel, which has already been subjected to drastic re-considerations (e.g. Makkonen 1992: 108). In so-called neutral narratives such as Vartio's early novels, emotions may not be stated, but they are evoked by the characters' observations of the surrounding world, in their embodied sensations and perceptions, as well as in their dream worlds. Narratives of restraint and precision do not lack emotion; they call for the reader's participation in establishing an emotional component. The pleasures of reading originate from writerly rather than readerly features of the text. As readers are forced to infer the presence of a mind from the detached elements of the text or to trace the source of entangled thoughts and emotions, these narratives trigger a "desperate search for significance" (Fludernik 1996:173).[33]

Reading Fictional Minds. Objectives and Aims, Theoretical Approaches and Previous Studies

Despite Vartio's status as a pioneer of modernist writing in Finnish literature, her work has received relatively little scholarly attention. With regard to the focus of this study, namely, the reading of fictional minds, the most relevant contribution to date is Pekka Tammi's *Kertova teksti. Esseitä narratologiasta* (Narrative Text: Essays on Narratology, 1992). Tammi reads Vartio's short stories and novels from the perspective of classical narratology. He also addresses the embedded, hypothetical structures in presenting the mind in her texts. In a co-authored article, "Dialogi Linnuista: Kokemuksellisuus, kerronnallisuus, luotettavuus ja Marja-Liisa Vartion *Hänen olivat Linnut*" (A Dialogue on Birds: Experientiality, Narrativity, Reliability, and Marja-Liisa Vartio's *Hänen olivat linnut*, 2007), Maria Mäkelä and Tammi discuss Vartio's novel from the vantage point of more recent approaches to cognitive narrative theory. Their article also tackles with the phenomena of mind-reading and the social mind in Vartio's last novel. These readings demonstrate how Vartio's narrative art offers an intriguing playground for testing the formulations of (cognitive) narrative theory.

Two doctoral dissertations on Vartio's fiction have been published. The more recent is Helena Ruuska's monograph, *Arkeen pudonnut Sibylla* (A Sibyl Fallen into Everyday Life, 2010), which deals with the unfolding of the identity of modern woman in Vartio's novel *Kaikki naiset näkevät unia*. Ruuska's study provides insights into the debates concerning modern art and design in the 1950s in the Finnish context. Her close readings also address the protagonist's everyday experience of living in a city and the effects of the urban environment on her mental development. Sirkka-Liisa Särkilahti's earlier dissertation, *Marja-Liisa Vartion kertomataide* (The Narrative Art of Marja-Liisa Vartio, 1973), explores the narrative structure and thematic shifts taking place in Vartio's oeuvre. In addition to these studies and a number of master's theses (e.g. Vesti 2014), a number of articles have been published on Vartio's novels (Alhoniemi 1971, 1972 & 1973; Ahola 1989; Niemi 1995; Rojola 2008, 2013 & 2014; Hakulinen 2013; Ruuska 2013a; Nykänen 2013a, 2013b & 2014), short stories (Karkama 1994; Nykänen 2012), and poetry (Lippu 1985; Hökkä 1989; Kajannes 2000; Karppanen 2012 & 2013; Ruuska 2013b).

In this study, I approach Vartio's work by examining how the internal and external perspectives on fictional minds serve as two cooperating ways of perceiving fictional minds and mental actions from varying distances. Regarding the interaction of fictional minds, my study elaborates on ideas of "mind-reading," "intersubjectivity," and the "social mind" established within post-classical cognitive narratology (Zunshine 2006; Butte 2004; Palmer 2004 & 2010; Abbott 2008). Furthermore, I employ possible world semantics (Ryan 1991; Doležel 1998; Pavel 1986) in addressing the complexity, incompleteness, and inaccessibility of Vartio's epistemic worlds, including the characters' private worlds of knowledge, beliefs, emotions, hallucinations, and dreams. With regard to the emplotment of fictional worlds, I benefit from "affective narratology" (Hogan 2011a), as well as from research influenced by possible world semantics and narrative dynamics, plot theory, and cognitive narratology (Dannenberg 2008; Kafalenos 2006 & 1999).

MODELING FICTIONAL MINDS IN INTERACTION

The discussion of fictional minds has a long tradition in narrative studies. In her seminal book, *Transparent Minds* (1978), Dorrit Cohn considered the ability to "see" inside other people's minds as a rudimentary feature of narrative fiction. The possibility of portraying consciousness, *another* consciousness in particular, has been perceived as distinguishing fiction from other forms of discourse. In post-classical narratology, accordingly, the relation of an actual mind to its literary representations has been a widely discussed topic. Concepts such as "experientiality" (Fludernik 1996), the "social mind" or "intermental thought" (Palmer 2010, 2004), "deep intersubjectivity" (Butte 2004), and "Theory of Mind" or "mind-reading" (Zunshine 2006) have been used to analyze the cognitive urge of both readers and fictional minds to attribute mental states to another mind. Literary scholars have drawn on ideas from the cognitive sciences to examine the folk-psychological practices and cognitive models that help the reader make sense of the fictional minds she or he encounters in a literary text. Furthermore, these models have been employed to examine the fictional minds reading other fictional minds within the fictional universe.

Lisa Zunshine adopts the term "mind-reading" (or interchangeably, "Theory of Mind," *ToM*) from cognitive psychology, whereby the concept is used to describe the human ability to infer people's behavior on the basis of their thoughts, feelings, beliefs, and desires. Because the existence of another mind cannot be perceived directly by looking inside another person's head, human beings develop a theory of mind. It involves the inference that other people have thoughts, beliefs, and feelings, just as we do. (Wilson 2002: 59) Mind-reading refers not only to characters' actions, but also to readers' interpretations of these actions during the reading process. This kind of "captive mind-reading" (Abbott 2008: 463) of fictional consciousness takes place, even when there are only a few clues to suggest the existence of a fictional experiencer in a text. As H. Porter Abbott remarks, during the reading process the experience of the unreadable mind is very hard to maintain, even if certain fictional minds are meant to remain mysterious, unknowable. The reader's tendency to naturalize what is left unsaid explains why unreadability is often unendurable. When emotions and depictions of mental states are lacking in narrative texts, readers tend to supply them.

Cognitive narratology has been criticized for its tendency to concentrate on readers' ability to "make sense of" fictional minds instead of taking account of the particular nature of these minds as textual constructions and conventions. Cognitive narratology has approached fictional minds as if they were actual minds. The resistance to the naturalization of fictional minds has arisen especially within unnatural narratology, which was formulated as a response to the premises of cognitive narratology, particularly Monika Fludernik's influential study, *Towards a 'Natural' Narratology* (1996). Fludernik's work is based on the notion of experientiality, "quasi-mimetic evocation of 'real-life experience,'" as the defining feature of narrative (Fludernik 1996: 12). In trying to make sense of texts, a reader applies to her or his reading the cognitive, "natural" parameters of the real-life world, such as experiencing, telling, viewing, and reflecting. The reader uses these cognitive prototypes to naturalize the strange situations of narrative fiction.

By contrast, the "unnatural" approaches of narrative theory (Alber, Iversen, Nielsen, & Richardson 2010; Alber 2009; Richardson 2006) have emphasized the artificial, non- and anti-mimetic quality of (postmodern) texts. Fictional texts resist the naturalization of narrative situations for the very reason that those situations are strange by nature. The literariness of fiction is thought to derive from the estranging effect (Shklovsky 1965), which challenges familiar interpretive patterns and sense-making capabilities. Quasi-mimetic real-life experience, suggested as the key element in interpreting fiction, therefore undermines the role of conventions and canonical (in this case: modernist) techniques that are either adopted or violated in narratives. The use of certain narrative techniques may generate a more powerful illusion of "raw feels" or *qualia* in the sense of mental simulation and immersion ("how it feels to be someone else"; see Herman 2009a: 152–153 and 2007: 256–257; Damasio 2000: 19). These narrative techniques, however, may also be employed to produce highly artificial constructs of fictional minds that defamiliarize, modify, complicate, or even dispense with assumptions of the "natural" frames of everyday experience.[34]

Both natural and unnatural approaches tend to overlook the huge variety of texts, ranging from more prototypical cases to narratives that consciously test and manipulate cognitive stereotypes. In order to be able to work with all types of texts, a compromise must be made. (See Mäkelä's discussion 2010: 33) My own approach springs from the conception that fictional minds simultaneously *are* and *are not* similar to actual minds.[35] Even if the characters' experiences resemble the actual human mind and its cognitive mechanisms, the resemblance is a result of artificial, conventional ways of representing that mind (cf. Culler 1975: 134–136). Even if the "unnatural" quality of literary techniques is obvious, the fictional mind created in the process has qualities that at least have something in common with actual human experience. The fictional mind is an aesthetic illusion that is constructed, yet recognizable, and as such, is prone to be empathized with or shunned by the reader (cf. Keen 2007: xxv). In this study, the focus is on the conventions and techniques of modernist mind presentation, by which the fictional consciousness is transformed into a narrative form by plotting fictional everyday experience.

In fact, as Mäkelä (2011: 25) observes, the dynamics between fictional experience and its narrativization have already been written into the literary conventions. Characters' attempts to narrativize their own minds and the minds of others are reflected in the text as meta-representations that thematize readers' attempts to read the characters' minds as if they were real, which they obviously are not. The reading process, therefore, resembles the challenging task of an author trying to transform human experience into narrative form. Characters' readings of other fictional minds and the reader's readings of these representations may not replicate real-life cognitive prototypes, but the human urge to imagine and narrativize other minds – and the failure to do so – are constant themes of modernist fiction. Vartio's fictional universes often become aesthetically estranging and "self-conscious" constructs that emphasize the artifice of embedded fictional minds and worlds. In her work, seemingly simple and banal story material is usually combined with complicated strategies of structuring this material (cf. Tammi 1992: 73).

The traditional views of the "inward turn" taking place in the history of the modern novel have been simultaneously reinforced and challenged by literary scholars working in the field of cognitive narrative theory. In Fludernik's natural narratology, the internalization of the modernist narrative is seen as a result of increasing experientiality in fiction (Fludernik 1996: 170). As Cohn (1983: 8) argued in her influential study, modernist writers themselves perceived the history of the novel as a move "inward to greater passivity and complexity." According to her, this very development led to "a gradual unfolding of the genre's most distinctive potential, to its full Bloom in the stream-of-consciousness novel and beyond" (ibid.). The spiral movement of the genre (repeatedly returning to its "inward matrix"), however, suggests that the "inward-turning" of the stream of consciousness novel itself "is not nearly so singular a phenomenon, nor so radical a break with tradition as has been assumed" (ibid.: 9).[36]

In recent cognitive narrative studies, there have been some preliminary re-assessments of the inward turn in the modernist novel. In his article "Re-minding Modernism," Herman questions the acclaimed inward turn in modernist fiction by scrutinizing the neglected aspects of the interplay between the mind and the world. Could the changes in the narrative method best be described as an "exploration of the mind viewed as an interior space" or rather as a "moment-by-moment construction of worlds-as-experienced"? (Herman 2011b: 250) Herman's article draws on insights of post-Cartesian and post-cognitive accounts of the mind as an entity evolving in action and interaction with its environments. Alan Palmer's (2010, 2004) recent work, accordingly, addresses the embodied and engaged nature of human cognition. Palmer criticizes narratological analyses for having focused on private, solitary, and verbalized aspects of thought. According to him, the classical narratologists have primarily been occupied with canonical modernist texts that focus on the characters' inner worlds of solipsism and contemplation. This "internalist" perspective needs to be balanced by an "externalist" perspective on fictional minds: seeing them as *social* fictional minds. (Palmer 2010: 39–40)

Palmer emphasizes the role of traditional discourse forms, such as the thought report (psycho-narration in Cohn's terms), as the most convenient way of showing fictional minds in interaction. Cohn (1983: 56) defines the locus of the modernist novel as a shift "from *inter*personal to *intra*personal relationships, from the manifest social surface of behavior to the hidden depth of the individual psyche."[37] Palmer's re-thinking of her typology, on the other hand, focuses mainly on the thought report as the mode most suitable for presenting intermental thought. In Palmer's later study, *Social Minds in the Novel*, the intramental activity of fictional minds (the inner speech of characters) is defined as "inner, introspective, private, solitary, individual, psychological, mysterious, and detached" as opposed to the intermental activity of social minds, which is "outer, active, public, social, behavioral, evident, embodied, and engaged." (Palmer 2010: 39)

As several of Palmer's critics have argued, the distinction between the internalist and externalist perspectives seems too rigid, even though Palmer, in theory, suggests the relevance of both perspectives (see Herman 2011c: 266; Hogan 2011b: 247–248; Jahn 2011: 251–252). What of the embodied, social, and interactive aspects of characters' intramental processes? Can we really perceive private fictional minds as sealed containers in which the representations of the world and the other minds appear equally as sealed containers? (cf. Fernyhough 2011: 273–274) An externalist account of single, individual minds and, conversely, an internalist account of the processes of social cognition can both be given in fictional contexts. This shows that the distinctions between private/social, intermental/intramental and internalist/externalist do not necessarily coincide.[38] Palmer (2011b: 382) himself acknowledges this fact by pointing out the possibility of rendering intramental thought from an externalist perspective: "[T]he fact that apparently inaccessible private thought is often available to others; the intensely dialogic nature of much intramental thought; and the fact that the presence of intermental thought is often concealed within descriptions of intramental functioning" can be conceived as manifestations of the dialogic nature of private fictional minds.

Palmer's study relates to a scholarly debate concerning the possibility of the existence of social minds in modernist fiction. According to him, the social minds in modernist texts are typically partial, deeply dysfunctional, attenuated, or even absent. This very absence, however, may turn out to be as significant as their presence might have been. (Palmer 2010: 183–184) As this study will demonstrate, social minds as collective, joint units may have become rare in modernist novels, but fictional minds as interacting entities have not disappeared. The distinction between the social fictional mind as an intermental unit (as a representation of collective, joint, and shared "intermental thought") and social fictional minds as interacting minds (as creators of [mis]representations of other minds) becomes relevant in the modernist novel.[39] The social aspects of mind presentation in modernist fiction more often involve processes of not knowing – misrepresentations of the other mind rather than actual intermental understanding.

As Zunshine (2006: 6) observes, mind-reading comprises the mental tools with which characters navigate their social environment, although the attribution of other characters' mental states often proves to be wrong or even hallucinatory. In Vartio's epistemological structures of mind-reading, for instance, the unconscious and pre-conscious aspects of minds are often her focus and present the delusive quality of characters' mental processes, even their paranoia. The concepts of intramental and intermental *thought*, however, emphasize the verbalized aspects of fictional mind presentation. The act of thinking can be considered a relatively conscious, coherent, goal-oriented activity, and as such, always involves language. Because thinking more or less demands verbal articulation, the essential question seems to be:

is it always conscious *thought* we are dealing with in exploring the mental actions between fictional characters?

The insights of Palmer's theory of social minds, but also its problems stem from his conviction that fictional minds (like real minds) can be known, shared, or accessed by way of mental attributions.[40] Compared to fictional minds mediated by their very creator, real minds can never truly "know" anything certain about the contents of the other mind, however intimately they may interact with one another. The epistemological distinctiveness of the embedded structures of narrative fiction was emphasized by Käte Hamburger (1973: 83) in *The Logic of Literature*: "Epic fiction is the sole *epistemological* instance where the I-originality (or subjectivity) of a third-person qua third person can be portrayed." This idea was later elaborated on by Cohn (1999: 16): "In fiction cast in the third person, this presentation involves a distinctive *epistemology* that allows a narrator to *know* what cannot be *known* in the real world [...] the inner life of his figures."

Fictional social minds are certainly central to our understanding of fictional story worlds, but not as much because real social minds are central to our understanding of the actual world, as Palmer (2010: 4) argues, but because they are central to our understanding of *fictional* world-structures. Mind presentation is a part of the process of fictional world-making in which the pre-existing worlds are composed, decomposed, weighted, ordered, deleted, supplemented, and deformed into new worlds (see Goodman 1978, Nünning 2010, Nünning & Nünning 2010, Herman 2009b) – also by fictional characters. The semantic fascination with the representations of fictional minds in modernist fiction stems from the epistemological interplay of "narrative facts, characters' representations of these facts, and their beliefs about other characters' beliefs," as Ryan (1991: 4) has written about the narrative semantics of fictional worlds.[41] The characters' mental activity – their thinking and feeling, believing and knowing, counterfactualizing and (day)dreaming, decision-making and states of indecision – compose a plot formed of a "collection of concatenated or embedded possible worlds" (ibid.), in which the narrator's and the characters' voices (and other characters' voices) meet in a challenging manner.

PLOTTING MINDS, PLOTTING WORLDS. FOUR EPISTEMIC PATHS

The change of focus from the interior of the self to the mental action and interaction of fictional minds takes us to the most persistent myth of modernism re-assessed in this study: the absence of plot. The psychologization of story has been one of the assets of possible world semantics.[42] Instead of treating characters as mere participants (or "actants") subordinated to a succession of events (or as passive inner voices having nothing do with the actions taken within the materiality of fictional worlds), the narrative semantics of possible worlds perceives characters as beings related to the time-space of fictional worlds in multiple ways (cf. Doležel 1998: 55; Palmer 2004: 29–30). Possible world semantics has been previously used to tackle the ontological problems raised by postmodernist fiction (McHale 1987; see also Hägg 2005). In the present study, the focus is on the epistemological worlds of modernist fiction.[43] As Brian McHale has observed, the dominance of modernism is epistemological uncertainty. The epistemic worlds of modernism provoke questions such as "What is there to be known?; Who knows it?; How do they know it, and with what degree of certainty?; How is knowledge transmitted from one knower to another, and with what degree of reliability?; How does the object of knowledge change as it passes from knower to knower?; What are the limits of the knowable?" (McHale 1987: 9)

As opposed to the ontologically distorted, alternative worlds of post-modernism, in modernist narratives the speculative worlds are generated as reflections within the fictional minds. In their search for knowledge, modern characters may gaze on the other side of the ontological border, yet the border is crossed only *virtually*. The contradictory, counterfactual worlds are represented as ephemeral constructs created in the mind of the character, but they do not reject the natural laws of the fictional universe or the laws of logic. The sophisticated use of the "temporal orchestration" of alternate worlds suggests multiple, simultaneously existing versions of events produced by the fantasies, hypotheses, and hallucinations of the characters (cf. Dannenberg 2008: 42, 45). The vacillation between different levels of ontology, however, is caused by the characters' temporary re-organization of the fictional universe rather than the narrative itself being based on several distinct "actualities." In the epistemology of modernist worlds, the mental activities of imagining, speculating, hypothesizing, and counterfactualizing play a significant role.

In this study, I model a typology of four epistemic paths in order to analyze the different strategies of narrative emplotting which Vartio employed in her novels. These paths of female development are influenced by four types of causal alteration, which relate to the challenges of plotting one's life: chance, counterfact, lingering, and digression. All of these plot patterns draw on cognitive metaphors used widely in literary tradition: *time as a path* and *life as a journey*. The idea of life as a movement along a line or a road illustrates the linear-temporal features of narrative, the plotting of time and space in fiction. In the characters' mental constructs of their lives, the passing of time is often spatialized as a path leading through fictional space. (Dannenberg 2008: 66) The causally-altered modernist narratives both evoke and test the foundations of the discussion of narrative itself as a fundamental cognitive sense-making instrument, which enables humans to make their way through "chaotic" reality. Even though the cognitive urge of the human mind is to re-organize the everyday experience into a coherent storyline, the narrative order is continuously deferred because of the mental actions and interactions of the characters within the storyworlds. Instead of one linear route, the life journey offers multiple, forking paths or digressive roads – at least in the mind of the perceiving character.[44]

The spatial metaphor of *life as a journey* illustrates the different kinds of suspensions or "dysfunctions" along the narrative path as they trigger certain mental responses in characters. First of all, life's coincidences and unlikely events can be seen as randomness. *Chances* may be encountered along the journey of an (unfortunate) traveler who is forced to change her or his future plans as unexpected occurrences alter the course of travel.

Likewise, the *counterfactual plot* is allegorized as the image of forking paths, which suggests the multiple possible trajectories of the characters' life paths – life choices made and regretted. The patterns of *lingering* and *digression*, on the other hand, delay the narrative progression by holding off the traveler's arrival to the final destination or denying it altogether. The images of aimless wandering (lingering) and the missteps made along the journey (digression) both refer to the theme of getting lost, but they differ on the basis of the intentional action involved in the process of going astray. The digressive patterns of life are an outcome of an intentional act of decision-making gone (repeatedly) wrong, whereas lingering only hints at a putative decision which is never made. Lingering characters get lost because of the cyclical and regressive patterns in their lives: the continuous considerations and reconsiderations lack a fixed direction, which would guide their way. While digressive paths eventually lead to a journey's final destination, lingering paths never end.

From the reader's point of view, each of the four types of causal inter-connections Vartio used lead to the disruptive effect of the narrative, either by deferring the attainment of a final balance or leaving the narrative path half untraced. By manipulating the functions that direct the interpretation of causal connections, the four patterns of causal interrelations tend to create narrative instabilities and leave them unresolved. The difficulty with deciding and its random effects serve as key elements especially in determining the two patterns of getting lost, lingering and digression. These narrative patterns manifest the two divergent forms of crossroads situations in the characters' epistemic paths. "Lingering" refers to the lack of a final narrative resolution because of a character's avoidance of making a decision; "digression" refers to the delay in the narrative production because of hasty or wrong decisions made: the characters misread themselves and others and get lost. The types of causal alteration differ on the basis of the degree of intentional action undertaken by the character during the process of going astray. In a digressive pattern, a character makes a decision (or a number of decisions), which leads to action that worsens the initial situation. Lingering characters, in turn, get lost because of the cyclical and regressive patterns of their lives.

In recent plot theories, including Emma Kafalenos's study, *Narrative Causalities* (2006), the role of narrative agency is emphasized, both in the representation and in the interpretation of characters' actions within the storyworlds. Causation involves the action by some sort of agent, either intentional manipulation or applied force, which affects the objects and the events taking place. Thus, the interpretation of causal positions in fiction is shaped by the intentional action of a character. The intentionality of the action in turn is connected to the inference of proper intent on the part of the character undertaking the action. The character's intent guides the reader to discern both the upcoming action and the disruptive moment that directs the reader's attention to the state of imbalance, the disruption of balance (or "normalcy") that needs to be changed. (Kafalenos 2006: 63, 69)

In my analyses of Vartio's novels, the focus is on the representation of emotions in the trajectories of female self-discovery. All four types of causal alteration – chance, counterfact, digression, and lingering – are linked to the states of emotional imbalance and transformation and affect the narrative structures of female self-discovery. Conflict and transformation can be defined as seminal aspects of any narrative.[45] However, in the trajectories of female development, the transformation constitutes the major aspect of the process of self-formation, which is triggered by the initial state of emotional imbalance: alienation and self-estrangement. The disruptive moments along the narrative journey, typical of modernist Bildung, exploit the reader's expectations of causal guidance and misdirect the reader to interpret causal relations in a distorted way (cf. Kafalenos 2006: 105, 113). The sequences of cause and effect are frequently modified in alternating periods of action and inaction in the characters' lives, constructed as episodic cycles of balance and imbalance that never end.

The epistemic paths of female self-discovery in Vartio's fiction are closely related to certain literary genres and story patterns that involve conventions of showing emotions and other aspects of fictional (un)consciousness. I investigate the challenges of epistemic mind-reading in regard to the narrative formulae of female development, the romance plot or love comedy, the sentimental novel, and epistolary fiction (I introduce each narrative pattern in more detail in the analyses of the primary texts). "Sentimental modernism" has previously been analyzed by Suzanne Clark (1991) from the perspective of the sentimental unconscious in the rhetoric of modernist texts written by women. The actual manifestation of emotions in the very structure of modernist narratives, however, has not been explored. Furthermore, I examine how the conventional narrative formulae of female fiction are modified and parodied in Vartio's novels to serve the depiction of the mental lives of female protagonists as they travel across fictional spaces and grow increasingly alienated and self-estranged.

Key Concepts

In this section, I briefly introduce the key theoretical concepts used in the analyses of Vartio's novels. I also clarify the changes in my theoretical focus during the investigation of the five primary texts. One of the key concepts in my tool-box is *mind-reading*. This concept constitutes a methodological tool, by which I re-assess the acclaimed inward turn in modernist fiction through analyzing fictional minds as entities operating in interaction. I employ the concept of mind-reading in two different ways. First and foremost, I use the term to refer to the narrative desire of characters to read other fictional minds inhabiting the storyworlds. Secondly, I apply it to the actual reader's desire to read fictional minds (which are reading other fictional minds). In Vartio's early, "neutral" narratives, the reader's ability to infer the characters' mental states is challenged by a restrained style of writing, which triggers strategies of mind-reading primarily on the reader's part. In Vartio's later novels, on the other hand, the characters' growing urge to read the minds of others creates a maze of minds that tests the readers' ability to keep track of the initial source of the thoughts and mental states in the layered structures of mental projection. In both cases, the reader feels the need to naturalize or displace the unreadability of the unreadable mind that "refuses" to be disclosed.

The notion of *embodiedness* serves as the key term in analyzing the epistemic structures of mind-reading throughout the book. In cognitive narratology, the study of storyworlds has been reconsidered by changing the focus from narrativity to experientiality and embodiedness, that is, to the representation of the situated presence of an experiencing mind within the time and space of fictional storyworlds (Fludernik 1996: 30, 172; Herman 2009a: 132; see also Varela, Thompson & Rosch 1993). This approach takes into account not only the narrative modes for presenting consciousness, but also other story elements that contribute to the depiction of the existential experiences of characters, their sense of time, as well as their location within the space of fictional worlds.

In reading Vartio's early narratives, I use the concept of embodiedness to examine the characters' inner action at the "present" moment within the local, emotionally encoded storyworlds. Embodiedness involves, more or less, characters' "core consciousness," those realms of human cognition that evoke the perceptual experience of "being-in the world" here and now, generating embodied pulses of sensing the self (cf. Hogan 2011a: 31). The state of balance involves attachment to certain fictional spaces reflected in the "feeling of being home." The experience of time is also encoded emotionally, manifested in "subjective time" being separate from "clock time." Certain key experiences are compressed, distilled moments that seem to be frozen. These kinds of isolated moments are "incidents," constituting "minimal units of emotional temporality" that are often evoked automatically, beyond the aware mind. (Ibid.: 29–33)

Certain emotional responses, however, affect more long-term trajectories in narratives. In this sense, the notion of embodiedness also serves as the foundation for my analyses of the emotional story structures in Vartio's novels. Emotions are reactions to changes in what is routine, habitual, known, and expected. When anticipations of normalcy in the storyworld are violated, the focus of attention is triggered and emotions activated. If emotional incidents involve more long-term calculations, then these incidents turn into episodes and the episodes turn into stories. (Hogan 2011a: 30, 32–33) I examine the everyday experiences and traumatic responses of Vartio's characters through the functions of emotions in the story structures of her novels. What is more, I investigate the epistemic paths of female development in regard to the characters' emotional responses: their experiences of randomness, their ways of counterfactualizing their traumatic past, their procrastinatory or akratic reactions or indecisiveness. In analyzing the causal interconnections, I use such terms as *chance, counterfactuality, digression,* and *lingering*[46] to explore the epistemic paths of self-discovery in Vartio's novels.

My analyses of the epistemology of world-structures in Vartio's novels take into account two different perspectives debated in possible world theory. One is the *accessibility* of the characters' private worlds, given that accessibility relations are established between the actual and the fictional realms within a text.[47] Accessibility relations involve different types of access, or denial of access, from the realm of fictional reality to the alternative worlds that surround the domain of the actual within the textual universe. The other important aspect of the epistemology of fictional worlds is the *incompleteness* of imaginary entities. The metaphor of a possible world pertains to a threefold modal system involving 1) the actual world (the world we know), 2) the (textual) actual world stipulated by the text, and 3) the textual reference world that is comprised of the representations of the actual textual world. Together the latter two systems form the *textual universe* as the sum of worlds projected by the text. The textual universe also encapsulates the satellite worlds composed of characters' knowledge and wish worlds, their dreams and fantasies, speculations and hallucinations. These private worlds may reflect, but also counterfactualize or even replace the textual actual world at the center of the textual universe. (Ryan 1991: 22–25, 31) I analyze the relations between the actual and the virtual in the characters' mental constructions by using such concepts as *private world* or *alternative world*. Moreover, I employ the terms *fictional world* or *reference world* along with the concept *textual actual world* when examining the domain of the "actual" within the storyworld.

Hypothetical focalization and *hypothetical speech* are among the concepts I use in exploring the perspectival selection and restriction of information in Vartio's novels. The epistemology of perception becomes central in the notion of hypothetical focalization introduced by David Herman into the terminology of narrative theory.[48] In his model, Herman (1994: 231) addresses "the use of hypotheses, framed by the narrator or a character, about what might be or have been seen or perceived – if only there were someone who could have adopted the requisite perspective on the situations and events at issue."[49] In Herman's scheme, the traditional types of focalization (external versus internal) are replaced by the scalar continuum of epistemic modalities, ranging from certainty to radical uncertainty and virtuality. The epistemic categories along this continuum are distinguished on the basis of the (in)congruence between the narrative's reference and expressed worlds (the latter virtualizing or counterfactualizing the former). Hence, the disparity between the expressed and the reference world corresponds to internal focalization associated with restricted knowledge. The congruence between these worlds invokes a faithful representation of a reference world similar to the external focalization and its unselective perspective. (Herman 1994: 231, 233–234)[50]

In addition to hypothetical focalization, I analyze the counterfactual constellations of private worlds through the concept of hypothetical speech. Hypothetical speech includes "references to speech and thought events that are presented as future, possible, imaginary or counterfactual" (Semino, Short, & Wynne 1999: 308). Whereas in everyday storytelling hypothetical mode constitutes innate norm, in fiction the virtuality of speech can be accentuated in many ways. Hence, the hypothetical modes of speech and thought emphasize the idea of speech representation as one rhetorical device in the author's toolbox. Dialogue, for instance, is one of the methods of constructing fictional communication rather than any transparent media of "transcribing" characters' speech (cf. Karttunen 2010: 249).

As mentioned, I employ the concept of mind-reading to refer both to the narrative desire of characters to read fictional minds within storyworlds and to the readers in the actual world to read fictional minds (reading other fictional minds). The concepts of mind-reading and *intersubjectivity*[51] are accompanied by terms such as the *social mind* or *intermental interaction* whenever I find it necessary to refer to a collective complex for performing mental action as a single, intimate unit. My analyses of *Se on sitten kevät* focus mainly on the characters' experiences and sensations as presented through their observations of the fictional world. These analyses emphasize the actual reader's perspective on mind-reading. However, I examine the later novels more in the context of the intersubjective interactions established between fictional minds. In contrast to her early novels, Vartio moved in her later works from the presentation of perceptual or memory-driven experiences to structures of counterfactual, hypothetical thinking. The distance between reality and fantasy grows wider as the perceptions of the external world are replaced by private worlds of imagining and counterfactual thinking, uncontrollable emotions and speculations, even hallucinations and paranoia.

In Vartio's early, neutral narratives, her restrained style of writing triggers strategies that emphasize the reader's role as the "captive reader" of fictional minds. The allegorical techniques of describing the world constitute a method that I call *mental landscaping*. Intermittent structures of allegory generate double worlds of mental projection built up into the everyday texture of fictional worlds, as the depiction of the external world is accompanied by embodied images of the self.[52] The "density" of narrative texture increases as the extended role of certain images triggers the move to allegorical reading (cf. Abbott 2008: 458). Vartio employs the same embodied images (including allusions and similes used as *psycho-analogies*[53]) in repetitions and variations, thereby producing intertextual relations among her texts. Vartio's private symbolism involves archetypical images of selfhood (*anima*), such as trees and birds and other animals that embody the primitive, collective depths of the human mind and simultaneously become symbols of her art.[54] She also uses certain tropes – the "fallen woman," "the absent-minded housewife," "the madwoman" – to stage the troubled quality of the everyday experience of modern female individuals.

Furthermore, I use the concept *embodied image* to analyze the functions of the emotional unconscious in Vartio's presentations of fictional minds. The non-representable quality of traumatic experiences motivates the use of evocative images in Vartio's early narratives, whereas in her later novels the traumatic processes of self-formation are often more explicitly articulated.[55] On the level of poetics, the "split" memory of a traumatized mind is manifested in two types of cognition: literal and figurative. The former refers to the traumatic event and the latter, to the memory of that event established in the split mind. (Hartman 1995: 537) The pattern of gradual suffering is characteristic of traumatic experiences: the initial moment of shock constitutes a non-experience. As Geoffrey H. Hartman describes it, "[s]omething falls' into the psyche, or causes it to 'split'"; something is "lodged too deeply in the psyche as epiphanic word or image." The initial moment becomes "[b]urnt into the brain" as the presence of images that cannot be either remembered or fully forgotten. (Ibid.: 537, 540)

In Vartio's texts, the embodied images serve as means to render the unspeakable within. The wounds of the mind cannot be explicitly stated, but are present by their absence, as silence projected outwards. As Suzanne Nalbantian (2003: 77–78) points out, the absence of war on the level of explicit narration in modernist novels is linked to the representation of the obsession with traumatic past manifested in the flow of words, images, and ideas arising from characters' associative memories. The initial moment of wounding is registered only in the emotional unconscious, stored in the body, but absent from the aware mind. It may be spontaneously triggered by cues that resemble the original event, which re-emerges in flashbacks, hallucinations, and dreams. Typically, it takes the form of uncontrollable, embodied drama, as the person's faculty to verbalize the traumatic experience is injured (Knuuttila 2009: 24).

The repetitions of embodied images of trauma generate networks of motifs and themes elaborated throughout Vartio's prose fiction and poetry. Such tropes as absence or loss of passionate love, fear of rejection, shame, delusion, madness, suffering, and exile (as a result of the distribution of an inheritance) are varied in the depiction of the trajectories of her female characters.[56] The archetypical quality of Vartio's female figures is reinforced by the method of naming she used in her novels.[57] Proper names are often replaced by references such as a "woman" or a "girl" or by labels that hint at the social status of the characters: "a maid," "Mrs. Pyy," or "the parson's widow" (*ruustinna*).[58] The play on proper names generates varying effects of intimacy and distance (Doležel 1983: 515, 519), reflected in the similarities between the life paths of Vartio's characters as they travel through different stages of self-development.

Outline

In the five chapters of analysis that follow, I examine Vartio's novels in chronological order to demonstrate how she establishes and elaborates on certain narrative techniques in presenting fictional minds. In Chapter 2, entitled "Entering the World: The Emergence of the Embodied Mind in *Se on sitten kevät*," I analyze the manifestations of embodiedness in Vartio's first novel. I approach the gradual emergence of the mind into the world by examining the temporal-spatial situatedness of characters within the storyworld, as well as external objects in the landscapes, which are represented as embodiments of mental states. My focus is on the characters' habitual, daily experiences and inattentive observations, which are challenged by random events that cut off the episodic sequences of everyday routine. The affair between the two middle-aged protagonists, Anni and Napoleon, concludes with Anni's sudden death in the middle of the story. The rest of the novel depicts Napoleon drifting into an odd state of insensibility and confusion until he leaves the village, never to return.

I read the emotional story structure of *Se on sitten kevät* in the context of a tragic romance plot, which Vartio modifies in her unsentimental love story. Moreover, I approach the refusal of the closure of romance through Anni's frustrated, detoured Bildung and Napoleon's self-quest.

The third chapter, "The Emotions of the Body: A Lingering Awakening in *Mies kuin mies, tyttö kuin tyttö*," shifts the focus of my analysis from the randomness of external events to the randomness arising from within, that is, the invisible processes of nature taking place in a character's body and mind. Sentimental moods are restricted to a minimum in the story of a young girl, Leena, who becomes pregnant by a married man. Through a convoluted process, she is eventually able to bear responsibility for herself and for the child. I show how the detached, plain evocations of emotions stem from young Leena's inability to recognize her unconscious mind, her struggles to restrain the public expressions of her emotions, and her tendency to misread the minds of others while planning her actions according to the ideas of others. In this seemingly flat love story, the emotional structure involves cyclic patterns of emotional arousal that alternate with periods of drowsiness as stages of Leena's latent maturation. I examine the fluctuations of embodied emotions, on the one hand, by reading the external landscapes as projections of the character's mental states, and on the other hand, by analyzing the scenes with a split mind, as the self is divided into the observing and the experiencing "I." Finally, I approach the lingering awakening of the protagonist in the context of female Bildung and the romance plot.

The fourth chapter, entitled "Cycles of Arousal and Fall: Mirroring the Self in *Kaikki naiset näkevät unia*," explores the overly imaginative, aroused mind of the female protagonist, Mrs. Pyy. The increasing amount of babble, dream, and fabulation in the novel stems from Mrs. Pyy's obsession with reading other people's minds. Her misattributions to the minds of others often lead her to misread her own mind. In the depiction of past traumatic experiences, Mrs. Pyy's mind becomes a split mental space in which there are gaps and dark spots that embody her emotional unconscious. I examine Mrs. Pyy's desire for a less divided self by analyzing her use of different self-mirrors as building blocks of her middle-class identity, including works of art and dream images that reflect her more desirable self. Furthermore, I demonstrate how the cycles of emotional arousal manifest themselves in the story structure of the novel, as Mrs. Pyy's repeated falls and disillusionment follow her every attempt to escape the trap of the everyday. I then approach these story patterns in the context of the novel of awakening and deferred female Bildung.

In the fifth chapter, "From Emotions to Feelings: Self-Conscious Minds in *Tunteet*," I address the battles of the emotional and rational minds by analyzing the mental development of young Inkeri and her fiancé, Hannu. I explore the relations of the self, the world, and the other in regard to the possibilities of true self-expression and mutual communication portrayed in mind-reading scenes between Inkeri and Hannu. The problem of language is connected to the dual quality of sentiments, emerging both as unconscious emotions and conscious feelings.[59] I examine the theme of (not) becoming conscious vis-à-vis the unreliability of introspection and the verbal accounts of one's mental life, the distorted quality of recollection, and the characters' inability to become aware of their emotions, all leading to self-delusion and pretense. Moreover, I read the emotional story structure of *Tunteet* in the context of the love comedy, Bildungsroman, the sentimental novel and epistolary fiction, all of which are parodied in the novel.

The sixth and last chapter of analysis, "In the Mazes of the Wounded Mind: Narrating the Self in *Hänen olivat linnut*," addresses Vartio's last novel, which has been considered her "swan song." The novel was a major test of strength and was almost finished before her untimely death in 1966 at the age of only 42. Her husband, Paavo Haavikko, edited the nearly finished manuscript and wrote additional sequences to join passages together. *Hänen olivat linnut* reflects the multiplication of fictional world-creation as the relations between the actual and the virtual become more complex and convoluted. The novel continues the portrayal of female everyday experience by telling a story of two spinsters – an eccentric parson's widow, Adele Broms, and her servant Alma – who narrate day after day the same oral tales. The layered, maze-like structures of mind-reading are accompanied by self-narratives constructed by the characters to narrativize the wound of their traumatized, split minds. I examine the interplay of dialogues and other narrative sections, including the parts of the novel that present the characters' minds from within, by reading the characters' inner struggles as epistemic quests, namely, the search for the primal cause of an individual's suffering. I address the novel's emotional story structure by analyzing the characters' life paths as a modification of the cyclic patterns of female Bildung. I show how Vartio employs these cyclic patterns both in the novel's frame story and in the characters' self-narratives as represented in their dialogues.

2. Entering the World. The Emergence of the Embodied Mind in *Se on sitten kevät*

Empty, empty is this world.[1]

– Marja-Liisa Vartio: "The Dance"

Se on sitten kevät begins *in medias res*. It opens with the assumption that a certain world exists, a world into which the reader enters as if there were no boundaries between actual reality and the one being read about. The reader is dropped into the middle of a conversation:

> "So here's the room. Do come and have coffee when you have time."
> The farmer's wife was in a hurry to get back. She closed the door behind her so quickly that it banged. The woman standing in the room heard the farmer's wife's steps in the front hall.
> The woman moved from the door to the window. The farmer's wife was running across the yard. She watched her until she disappeared behind the row of spruce. (*S*, 5)[2]

The female protagonist of *Se on sitten kevät*, a milkmaid later identified as Anni, is shown arriving at her new place of service. The novel begins with a sentence by an unidentified person, evoking the illusion of a story that has no frame; it also gives the impression of a framed story that excludes part of the "reality" being depicted. The limits of the fictional world seem to be known even before the world itself has been properly represented.

As the opening of the novel illustrates, Vartio constructs her fictional world (seen through the character's eyes) metonymically. The world is determined by Anni's gaze and her steps as she moves from one place to another in the fictional space. Anni's observation of the landscape from the window and later from within the landscape itself sets off concise or prolonged descriptive sequences, "legitimized" by the length of time certain objects occupy Anni's mind.

In this chapter, I analyze *Se on sitten kevät* from the perspective of embodiedness. My analysis includes an examination of fictional minds interacting as embodied beings within the fictional space. In the first part of the analysis, I approach Anni's relation to the environment by examining her situated presence within the fictional world. I discuss the expository descriptions Vartio provides at the beginning of the novel in the context of a narrative technique called "mental landscaping": creating double worlds of projection by merging the depiction of outer and inner spaces and using similes and other means to suggest latent mental states. Second, I examine the representations of embodied minds in relation to the interactions between the characters and the manifestations of the unspeakable in human relations. This part also includes an analysis of the unsentimental love story between Anni and Napoleon. Third, I read the habitual and repetitive aspects of the storyworld with regard to incidents that stand out as dramatic turning points in the emotional story structure of the novel. These "deviations" from normalcy include the female protagonist's death in the middle of the story, which subverts the conventional patterns of the romance plot. I also discuss the novel's structure with regard to the epistemic path of female development manifested in the portrayal of Anni's life journey.

In Vartio's novels, the patterns of challenging the one-world system are related to the four epistemic paths I analyze in the context of female developmental plots in this book. The typology of plot patterns involves *chance* and *counterfactuality* as well as *lingering* and *digressive* paths that constitute the structuring principles of the journeys of female self-discovery in these novels.[3] In reading *Se on sitten kevät*, I take into account each of these four types of altering causal interconnections in my interpretation of the novel's story structure. However, chance, accident, and randomness become the most relevant aspects of the structuring of Anni's life narrative. In her epistemic path, the ways of distorting, supplementing, or even replacing the causal-linear conventions of narrative are linked to the depiction of modern experience marked by epistemological doubt and uncertainty. Anni's experiences of randomness are related to her alienation in the modern world. Feelings of estrangement also define Napoleon's emotional life after Anni's death.

The causal-linear patterns of narrative are typically modified in the plots of female development, which are frequently built on structures of repetition rather than progression, constituting circular paths of self-discovery (Hirsch 1983: 26). The female versions of the traditional Bildungsroman include two predominant narrative structures. In the first pattern, the story of female apprenticeship is chronological, similar to the linear structure of the traditional male Bildung.[4] Rita Felski (1989: 126) has called this narrative pattern "feminist Bildungsroman." As a reworking of the established form of Bildungsroman, the female Bildung has certain distinctive features that do not conform to the bourgeois male genre.[5] As opposed to young *Bildungshelden*, the female protagonists' journey into the world is marked by acquiescence and dependency. In feminist Bildungsroman (from now on "female Bildungsroman"[6]) the self-development is materialized as a process of moving outward into the public realm of social engagement and activity, even if this process is often problematic and fraught. The resistance to the rationalization of Bildung[7] is manifested in the search for individual freedom and self-knowledge in female characters. They are longing for wholeness and harmony, which is often found in a renewed connection to (one's) nature, outside culture and the institutional cultivation of gender roles. The depiction of the inner life of characters is related to themes that are absent from the classical Bildungsroman. Romantic love, domestic relations, emotional well-being, and the potential of inward or social awakening are constant themes in these novels. (Cf. Castle 2006: 1–2, 21)

The subversive potential of the Bildungsroman in the nineteenth century thrives in the novels written by women.[8] Whereas the young heroes of traditional Bildungsromane often refine themselves through (troubled) romances, the female Bildungsroman requires an explicit refusal of the romance plot, because the process of separation (from a lover or a husband) constitutes the precondition for any path to self-knowledge. (Felski 1989: 124, 126–127) The plots of female development begin with a stage of alienation, which emphasizes the restrictive quality of women's social roles, yet reflects also to the female characters' inner inhibitions as the cause of their traps, confinements, and bindings (cf. Parente-Čapková 2014: 18). In comparison to the male Bildungsroman, the narratives of female development may cover wider range of ages as the self-discovery typically occurs only at a later stage of the heroine's life (Felski 1989: 137). The psychological maturation of the protagonist constitutes the second step in the story pattern of self-discovery. This stage materializes through a confrontation and dialogue with a social environment. The self-revelation occurs either as a sudden illumination or in the form of a gradual insight and leads to the resistance and survival of the heroine. (Ibid.: 130, 135–137)

The second type of female self-discovery, the "novel of awakening," involves a process of *inward* awakening to an already given inner self or mythic identity. The process of self-discovery often occurs in nature or in some symbolic realm, where the social world is excluded. (Felski 1989: 127) The symbolic or literal departure from society is the precondition for the attainment of a meaningful sense of the self, which requires a radical rupture with the heroine's established modes of perception and her past. The withdrawal from society, manifested as temporary solitude or as a final break from the world, is related to the conventions of the romantic self-quest. The process of coming to consciousness involves the move away from a society, a withdrawal (into inwardness or wilderness) followed by a powerful illumination, after which the heroine must decide whether or not to return and pass her knowledge to the community. (Ibid. 133, 143–144) Thus, the identity is not the goal to be worked towards a "civilized self," but towards an inner child, "a point of origin, an authentic and whole subjectivity from which the protagonist has become estranged" (ibid.: 143). Therefore, the second type of developmental plot forms a circle rather than a linear line.

In female developmental plots, the two narrative patterns introduced above – the active self-realization and the inward awakening of the subjective consciousness – are not necessarily mutually exclusive. They may be combined in the representation of female life paths, leading simultaneously to the world and into the self (Felski 1989: 128). This two-way process of self-discovery is manifested, for instance, in the story structure of *Se on sitten kevät*, as my further reading of the novel illustrates. Anni's fate follows the typical paths of modernist narratives of female development, which often constitute a foreshortened Bildung. In these narratives, the flowering of the inner self is actualized through memory and retrospection rather than through the progression from childhood to adulthood. In the modernist novel, the representation of female development often involves embedded story patterns adopted from myths or fairytales (representing the authentic past typical of the romantic self-quest) or emerges as coded memories in the narrative structure. The reader must infer the process of Bildung from present events, flashbacks, or intertexts that narrate and re-narrate the same process of self-formation. (Castle 2006: 193)[9]

In *Se on sitten kevät*, Anni's Bildung is intertwined with the narrative paths of the Anni-Napoleon love story. Anni's death from heart disease constitutes a narrative "hinge" that ends the love plot and splits the novel into two separate, but equal story lines. The second narrative, which follows Anni's death, tells the tale of Napoleon's mental development. In this regard, the novel modifies the pattern of tragic love plots in which the death of the heroine benefits the transcendental self-quest of the male protagonist. *Se on sitten kevät*, like Vartio's other novels, evokes two alternative paths of personal development – self-quest and romance – which are presented as exclusive of one another. These patterns suggest the two usual options for ending female life plots in nineteenth-century fiction and modified in Vartio's works: death or the trap of marriage, leading to deferred or denied fulfillment of personal growth (cf. DuPlessis 1985: 1, 3–4). Thus, Anni's momentary revival in the love affair can be read as a refusal of the closure of the classic romance plot. Anni's awakening to the lack of harmony between her inner and outer selves is triggered by the love affair. The romance leads to her suffering. On the other hand, Anni's feelings of alienation stem not only from the "failed" romance, but also are linked to the existential estrangement typical of modern characters. Anni's feelings of loss and pain – and her momentary flowering in the love affair with Napoleon – are built into the texture of the fictional world, increment by increment, to be "intuitively" sensed by the reader.

In the following analyses, I examine *Se on sitten kevät* mainly through its resistance to mind-reading. The beginning of the novel in particular resorts to techniques of camera-eye and eavesdropping, which catalyze the reading of the unreadable in the text. The neutral camera-eye narration focuses on the depiction of fictional time and space. The detached descriptions of the storyworld draw attention to what is apparently lacking in the story: the consciousness of the distanced character-observer. The existence of "mute" motivations and emotions behind behaviors, actions, and gestures is hinted at by means of images and allusions that generate poetic density in the text. In his article on unreadable fictional minds, Abbott (2008: 453) mentions three default responses triggered by inaccessible minds in readers: the opaque stereotype, the catalyst, and the symbol. In *Se on sitten kevät*, these responses manifest themselves in the interpersonal relations established within storyworlds, but also on the level of reading these fictional worlds. The very mystery of characters' inner worlds entices the reader into "a guessing game" to collect clues to the unreadable minds scattered throughout the text.

In the case of inaccessible fictional minds, the opaque stereotype refers to the tendency of "captive readers" to classify the essence of a person on the basis of what they see on the outside (the predictability of behavior, looks, etc.). The catalyst, on the other hand, is a function of characterization. The character as a catalyst serves as a way of seeing how a captive reader trying to understand "the other" copes with the unreadability of another mind situated within the same storyworld. Typically, these characters "know enough to know that [they don't] know enough" (Abbott 2008: 460). Characters are shown reading other minds as well as their own, sensing that there might be something under the surface, but not knowing exactly what that something is. They are caught in a feeling of perplexity, and as a result, the reader in the actual world is provided with the opportunity to read the mind of the mind-reader. The third strategy mentioned by Abbott is the symbol, which refers to the unreadable as a way of initiating an allegorical reading. Indeed, very often it is hard *not* to read symbolic meanings into veiled minds. (Ibid.: 458, 463) The reader's desperate search for significance leads to the default response typical of allegorical reading: evocations in the text are understood as tying together concrete story elements and abstract ideas (ibid.: 458). In *Se on sitten kevät*, the unreadable becomes readable at another level. The inexplicable evokes wonder, but simultaneously, by maintaining the immediate experience of the characters' detached minds, it stirs empathy, asking for the acceptance of the human unknown.

The Observing Mind. A Woman and a Landscape

In the opening scene of *Se on sitten kevät*, what the protagonist sees establishes the borders of the fictional world. Certain elements of the description seem to demarcate not only the boundaries of fictional space, but also the borders between the fictional and the actual world. The motifs of the slamming door and window, for instance, mark not only the limits of Anni's view and the world as sensed by her, but they also become the framework for the textual universe. Anni enters the room in a way that is similar to the reader's entry into the fictional world. She serves as the reader's eyes and ears within the alternative, fictional reality. The fictional space is represented through Anni's eyes, yet simultaneously it generates the illusion of encompassing the observer's embodied experience. At first Vartio portrays Anni's mind simply by observing the character as if she were only one fictional "object" among other objects. As the story unfolds, however, Anni becomes more familiar with her surroundings, and through the process, the world becomes more and more vivid and full to the reader as well. A fictional world and the mind experiencing it are gradually evoked and replenished.

The introduction of a character within the textual universe is often linked to a baptism. The character is given a specific proper name. In constructing a fictional being, the reader attaches different human traits to a proper name and builds up a more or less coherent picture of the character. The reader collects all the references to the proper name, all the separate descriptions and propositions, and builds up a consciousness "that continues in the spaces between all of the mentions of the character with that name" (Palmer 2010: 10). Palmer calls this aspect of characterization a "continuing-consciousness frame" (ibid.), which is applied by a reader during the reading process. As in Vartio's other novels, in *Se on sitten kevät* the use of the proper name is pushed as far as possible to avoid fixed points in the construction of a fictional being. The landscape is vividly rendered, to the point that even the most trivial details are depicted. The observer, on the other hand, remains nameless, as if she primarily serves as the reader's access into the fictional universe. The story's progress comes to a halt as the observation of the anti-idyllic scenery cuts off the flow of narration. The view seen by the nameless observer is full of waste and trash, trivial items of the everyday environment:

> There were two mountain ash in front of the cowshed. One grew from under the loft stairs, it grew sideways trying to push its branches toward the light. At the base of the tree was an old sleigh without runners and a cart with just one wheel. A kicksled leaned against the wall of the shed. It had no handlebar. There was a cement base in front of the building. The snow had melted off it altogether and bright green moss grew on its surface. In the center of the cement foundation was a birch block with a reddish enamel pot on it, with dead vines hanging from the pot. They rustled slightly, there was a little wind. (S, 11)[10]

While Vartio describes the physical scene in great detail, she leaves the woman a mystery to the reader. She has no proper name, no proper past. She is merely depicted as having such attributes as "observer," "she," or the "woman." The woman seems to be thrown into the middle of an unframed reality, traveling in a foreign land without proper coordinates, just like the reader, who comes to know the fictional space and the mind observing it increment by increment.

Nevertheless, the idea of a story that allows the reader to enter into the midst of its events is deceptive. The function of literary exposition is to introduce an unknown fictional world to the reader. Every narrative requires exposition; it can never be wholly avoided. Before anything truly relevant can be stated about the fictional universe, the characters, places, and states of affairs need to be introduced – at least to the degree that a reader can recognize them. (Bonheim 1986: 115) The reader cannot navigate without a certain amount of knowledge: she or he needs to be informed about the time and place of the events taking place, about the past of the characters, as well as their looks, their habitual behaviors, and the relationships between them. Furthermore, the text needs to specify the characteristics of the fictional world, its limits, and its general laws. What is possible or probable within that particular fictional universe?[11]

In general, the frames of the fictional world in Vartio's novel seem to be "naturalized" by the limitations produced by the "diegetic gaze" (Bal 2004: 347) of the female protagonist – the milkmaid Anni. The amount of knowledge within the reader's grasp is dependent on Anni's ability to perceive the surrounding world. The reader sees only what Anni sees, and what Anni sees is determined by her limited and hypothetical perspective. In the following passages, Vartio portrays Anni's embodied existence as spatial and temporal situatedness within the world. Her perceptions result in a potentially false, or at least partial, image of the world determined by epistemological uncertainty:

1) Under the window was a ditch, a dark groove in the snow. In it was the toe of a black rubber boot, the tip pointing in the direction the road went. Farther on beside the ditch she saw two rusted tin cans and some brown parcel paper. The paper moved, hit by a puff of wind. On the edge of the forest, in the middle of the snowy, open fields, stood a stake, clearly discernible yet somehow unreal. It was evening. And it was March, and soon it would be April. (S, 6)[12]

2) In front of the cowshed lay an open field; in the middle of the field there was a hill; on the hill was a building; one could barely discern it in the darkening night. First she thought it was a barn; it was unpainted, but then she distinguished the windows and the smoke rising from the roof. (S, 11)[13]

Apparently, these descriptive scenes focus on the depiction of the external world, the objects situated "beyond the skin." However, these scenes are monitored from Anni's position, determined by her particular location within a certain, confined space: first the room and then the landscape observed in the dim evening light. Vartio generates the illusion of the protagonist's embodied experience by providing scenic descriptions in which the outer reality is transformed into a depiction of the character's cognitive processes. The borders between internal and external spaces, the world within and without, vanish. In the following quotation, for instance, is it the narrator or the character who is contemplating the passing of time? "On the edge of the forest, in the middle of the snowy, open fields, stood a stake, clearly discernible yet somehow unreal. It was evening. And it was March, and soon it would be April."

In representing an incomplete fictional world, Vartio's novel generates a picture of reality that is seemingly objective, but turns out to render the character's limited and hypothetical perspective. Vartio conveys the interaction between consciousness and its physical environments by combining passages of narrated perception with the narrator's discourse depicting the fictional world.[14] In the first passage, the limited view (combined with a sense of the unreal) complicates the cognitive processes of perceiving. In the second passage, such details as the dusk of evening increase the chance of miscalculation in observing the landscape. Anni mistakes the farmhouse for a barn until she can make out certain details: the windows and the smoke rising from the chimney. The spatial situatedness of Anni as well as of the objects she perceives is evoked by the mention of different distances, which bring the objects of the fictional universe into focus, or conversely, move them farther away on the horizon. The degree of saturation and detail in the fictional world is bound to Anni's perspective and her ability to see.

As Bal points out, *subjectivity* and *chance* are the two aspects of description that distinguish modernist representation from its realistic counterpart.[15] The works of literary modernism tend to maximize the incompleteness, assenting to the ineradicable partiality of fictional worlds perceived by individual minds. The realist novel of the nineteenth century, the main target of criticism in the modernist revolution, endeavored to sustain the illusion of completeness by camouflaging the blanks and gaps within fictional worlds. In realist fiction, the incompleteness of worlds is often veiled by different narrative themes that "justify" the presence of certain descriptive elements within a literary text. Philippe Hamon (1982) distinguishes three types of default strategies that are characteristic of a realist representation seeking to minimize the effect of incompleteness. They involve *seeing, speaking,* or *taking action* as the motivation for descriptive sequences. In the reading of *Se on sitten kevät,* seeing turns out to be the most interesting aspect of Hamon's typology. The elements of the modernist description, such as chance or subjectivity, can be assessed by analyzing the character's vision and its limitations.

According to Hamon (1982: 149), the realist author is tied to the requirements of impersonation and objectivity. Thus the characters' task is to serve as the author's eye within the fictional world. The aim of the text is to preserve the illusion of the character's ability to see, which motivates and naturalizes the existence of description. For this very reason, realist narratives introduce certain themes to legitimize the presence of description. To justify the prolonged, intense gaze of a character or a character's idle moments, the author pleads with the character's will and ability to see. The character is transformed into an anxious "spy," who interests herself or himself in the objects of the modern world. The spy's disguise exists only to legitimize the description; it is not the consequence, but the cause of the enunciation of fictional objects. (Ibid.: 150)

To be able to render the surrounding world, there are certain conditions that the fictional world must fulfill to make the character see. The milieu into which the character is settled needs to be sufficiently well lighted. In a confined, closed space, there has to be a door or a window that guarantees access to the outer world. The observer cannot be near-sighted, let alone blind. In order to justify the existence of a description of the world, texts often provide "plausible padding," which introduces several themes leading to other themes:

> [T]o introduce description D [the author] must introduce character X, who must observe setting S. Thus there must be a view from above, or a light. But it must also be mentioned that this character is interested in setting S, and that he has the time to inspect or scrutinize it. (Hamon 1982: 156)

In addition to the conditions of transparency (embodied by such elements as windows and doors, bright light and panoramic views), there are other requirements for the naturalization of description. These include certain character types, such as artists, aesthetes, idlers, strollers, and characters who are traveling and getting to know new places. Furthermore, descriptions are typically linked to certain milieus or narrative situations: characters wandering in an unknown landscape, waiting for something or someone, walking, resting, or looking through a window. The goal of the narration is to create an illusion of a character so immersed in the act of observation that she or he has lost the sense of time passing. Hence, a description of this type usually prefers narrative situations that emphasize the *inaction* of characters. (Ibid.)

Furthermore, there has to be some kind of *psychological motivation* behind the static moment or idleness of the character. Such motivation can be the absence of mind mentioned above, yet may equally well be the pedantry of the perceiver (resulting in a detailed depiction of certain objects), curiosity, interest, volubility, aesthetic pleasure, inaction, or even the presence of an empty stare that alludes to an automatized, habitual contemplation of the world. All of these themes mark the frames of descriptive passages, their beginnings and endings. Hamon calls these "empty thematics," for they exist only to serve the needs of the author, to prevent the formation of gaps between narrative and descriptive passages, or to fill these gaps in a convincing way. (Hamon 1982: 156–157) As the realist conception of description suggests, a descriptive "standstill" is less disturbing the more embedded it is into the story. Typically, description seeks to dissolve its frames. The less obvious the motivation of a depiction, the more effortless it is to conclude and incorporate into the dynamics of the story (Bal 1991: 116).

The descriptions Vartio provides in *Se on sitten kevät* often violate the ideals of descriptive framing listed by Hamon. Anni's ability to see is questioned several times, which draws attention to the partiality of the perception itself as well as to the incompleteness of the fictional world. Furthermore, the novel stages the "unrealism" of conventional means of omniscient narration. In the next scene, Anni's perceptions of the view outside are accompanied by speculations about what the view *could* look like in the near future:

> Opposite the window grew a dense clump of spruce trees. The observer at the window thought that it would be moist there, even in summer, and in autumn there would be mushrooms, northern milk-caps, gray and cold.
> She looked at the spruce trees, saw green leaves that had survived the winter. She did not see that they were the kidney-shaped leaves of blue windflowers, and even if she had seen them, she would not have recognized them, for where she had come from, blue windflowers do not grow. (S, 6)[16]

The passage emphasizes Anni's restricted view and knowledge about the world. The extract constitutes a case of hypothetical focalization: Anni becomes a hypothetical witness who *might not* have recognized the leaves even *if* she had noticed them. The mode of hypothetical perspectivization operating here features "a speculative counterfactual conditional" (Herman 1994: 244), invoking doubt within doubt. It also denotes complicated epistemic modality when compared to standard cases of hypothetical focalization. Textual passages of this sort are, according to Herman, "overly meaningful" because they constitute belief contravening even paradoxical suppositions (ibid.). The perception itself is a consequence of a speculative counterfactual conditional whose antecedent is a case of direct hypothetical focalization. In other words, both the status of the onlooker's act of perceiving and the perception itself (*if* the act of looking was ever actualized) are placed in doubt.

The epistemic uncertainty of Anni's perception is reinforced by the narrator's gesture of pointing to the inferior knowledge of a character situated within the fictional world. The passage constitutes an interesting exception to the norm of "neutral" narration in the novel by referring to a perception that is shown to be limited, incomplete (cf. Tammi 1992: 31). The case of narrative "intrusion" is later accompanied by another implication of the narrator's superiority (and the limited view of the character), the second and the last instance of this sort. The narrator is able to see what the character cannot: "The woman opened a purse, took out a mirror and a comb. After combing her hair, she glanced in the mirror, quickly, *out of habit, so quickly that she didn't even see the smudge on her cheek*" (S, 10).[17] The automatic quality of Anni's perception, the act performed "out of habit," motivates the narrator's unusual intrusion. The narrator is still needed to mediate those aspects of mental life of which the character herself is *not* aware. Anni's perceptual limitations allude to the fragility of her self-awareness reinforced by the appearance of the mirror motif in the scene. The gaze directed at one's own image evades and escapes. Anni cannot fully see or recognize herself.

The role of the narrator in the above passage raises interesting questions about the ways of portraying fictional experience in so-called "neutral" narratives. In traditional typologies of narratology, the narrative mode most suitable for portraying the nonverbal realms of fictional minds has been considered the narrator's discourse about a character's mind: psycho-narration. The narrator's epistemological superiority makes it possible to portray those mental dimensions that the characters themselves are unwilling or unable to betray and which remain otherwise unverbalized, penumbral, or obscure. In "a narrator's knowing words," psycho-narration is able to portray also "what a character 'knows,' without knowing how to put it into words" (Cohn 1983: 46).[18] In Cohn's classical model of consciousness presentation, the neglect of the narrator's role in mind presentation constitutes one of the central arguments in her critique of focus in stream of consciousness novels. The narrator's discourse about a character's mind has been one of the most ignored techniques in studies of the modernist novel: the psyche in modernist fiction has often been conceived as "com[ing] at the reader directly, without the aid of a narrator" (Cohn 1983: 12). Consciousness, however, is not the whole mind. Modernist authors still need tools to present unconscious and pre-conscious aspects of fictional minds. Among the reasons why psycho-narration still belongs in the toolbox of modernist writers is its stylistic and temporal flexibility. The narrator can draw explicit attention to the subliminal level of the characters' mental processes or their incapacity for self-articulation. Psycho-narration may manifest itself either in the "plainly reportorial, or the highly imagistic ways" of narrating consciousness (ibid.: 11).

In addition to its ability to compress a long time-span, psycho-narration can also expand the instant moment that constitutes a "favorite time-zone of modern novelists" (Cohn 1983: 38). It was in its plainly reportorial manifestation that psycho-narration became relevant to modernist neutral narratives, in which mental states are suggested rather than stated, shown rather than narrated. The characters' actions, speech, and behavior as such become embodiments of their mental states. The physical and mental aspects of action represented in fictional scenes are often so deeply interwoven that they are difficult to disentangle (Palmer 2010: 136). Scenic descriptions may even generate the effect of "physically distributed cognition," which involves inanimate objects that belong to the individual's immediate environment (ibid.: 51). In this way, the outer landscape serves as projection or even as an extension of a character's cognitive functions.[19]

In *Se on sitten kevät*, Anni's inner perspective is the *primus motor* of every scene, however objective and detached these scenes may appear at first. The plain descriptions in Vartio's novel demonstrate how the existence of a fictional being may grow surprisingly vivid, even if there may be a bare minimum of information available in the text. The reader's cognitive tendency to posit a mind behind every observed behavior and to assume that there must be a mental stance behind each physical action explains why readers are so eager to interpret mental states, even if the author has left only a few clues for making such interpretations. The author's decision to under-represent their characters' mental states is thought to illustrate characters' psychic indifference, their inability to face their true feelings, or to understand the actual course of events. (Zunshine 2006: 22–23)[20] The more understated the narration, the more intensely readers look for signs of the characters' mental states, including figures of speech, allusions, and other means of evocation.[21]

Mental Landscaping

Unreadability of the human mind is a theme throughout Vartio's oeuvre. In her early novels, including *Se on sitten kevät*, Vartio generates the unknowable by the density of her narrative texture. Not every aspect of a fictional universe can be described, a situation that enables the existence of covert meanings in addition to overt semantic constituents.[22] These implicit meanings catalyze the process of allegorical reading in *Se on sitten kevät*. The principle of implicitness can be applied particularly to the way the protagonist's mind is represented. On the level of explicit texture, the inner and outer domains are sharply separated. As I will illustrate in the analysis that follows, Vartio's extensive use of simile in her fiction serves as a way of establishing allegorical world-structures that are built on mental projection: the presence of mental content is marked by absence, the unspeakable that underlies the explicit, visible content of the fictional world. The descriptions of the external world and its objects are accompanied by passages of narration that fuse the inner and outer scenes. T. S. Eliot's concept of "objective correlative" plays a significant role here. Inner, inaccessible emotional states are rendered indirectly "by finding an 'objective correlative'; in other words, a set of objects, a situation, a chain of events which shall be the formula of that particular emotion; such that when the external facts, which must terminate in sensory experience, are given, the emotion is immediately evoked" (Eliot 1950/1920: 100; emphasis his).

In literary semantics, the presence of implicit meaning is often thought to be traced from the explicit texture, which is necessary in order to grasp the implicit. The recognition of a hidden meaning is dependent on recognizing certain markers that manifest themselves either as an *absence* (as signs of ellipsis) or conversely, as a *presence* of some signals – hints and allusions that serve as the reader's guideposts. The series of descriptions in the first chapter of *Se on sitten kevät* includes one of the most powerful images in the whole novel. While walking across the courtyard, Anni notices a newly-built road running across the landscape:

> She walked along beside the spruce hedge, looking around. She wondered why the cowshed had been built away from the house and yard, but then she saw that the road had been straightened right at the house and the cowshed had remained on the other side of the road. The new road had taken with it part of the row of lilacs, uprooted lilac bushes still lay beside the road.
>
> Old they were, she thought. Still trying to burst into bloom in spring, but there it is, they realize they are dead. The new road was like a fresh wound on the sandy hill, the roots of the bushes quivered in the wind, the stakes along the road held open the wound edges like tweezers. She thought that it would be many years before the old road behind the barn grew over. (*S*, 10–11)[23]

The descriptive passage includes a triple simile based on a visual parallelism: the new road is "like a fresh wound" ("kuin tuore haava"), the roots of bushes and sprigs "like slashed veins" ("kuin katkotut suonet"), and the stakes on the roadside are "like tweezers" ("kuin pinsetit"). In Anni's mind's eye, the land torn open and the uprooted bushes resemble a wound and human veins. The effect of the simile is reinforced by the image of stakes portrayed as parallel to tweezers. In a verbalized image, the wound is eternally paralyzed in an open position; it cannot heal.

In the depiction of the road, the similes can be read as manifestations of Anni's visual associations as she observes the scene. Even so, from the vantage point of the reader, the figurative language does not refer to any particular object, but to a wholly distinct discourse: literary description itself.[24] The figures of speech do not reaffirm the mimesis of the prescribed world, they *interpret* it. By means of figurative language, descriptive mimesis turns into descriptive semiosis – interpretation of meaning.[25] The similes used in the descriptions in *Se on sitten kevät* work in this way: they establish an anomaly in the mimetic representation of the external world and change the focus of the reading. Through the use of similes, the description turns away not only from narrativity, but also from the depiction of the primary object (cf. Bal 2004: 344). In this sense, the effort made in the novel to "naturalize" description with certain frames is distracted by vertically-arranged descriptions that draw on figurative language. These descriptions withhold narration that seeks to continue and proceed. The figure of the wound, for instance, has connotations of sickness and pain, which suggest the nature of Anni's inner existence within the textual universe. Being in the world is a painful experience that leaves wounds and cuts on the human soul.

In Vartio's novels, "psycho-analogies" of this sort draw on characters' physical cognition, evoking an illusion of embodied experience. The simile is one of the devices of summary psycho-narration Vartio used extensively.[26] Since psycho-analogies are typical of surveys of a temporal span, they often signal the existence of a narrator with a distanced, bird's-eye view and stress the authorial origin of the comparison. However, they may also enter the fictional universe by way of characters' memories, as flashbacks, or as a depiction of a present moment, thereby generating the effect of expanding or arresting time: a mental instant, as in *Se on sitten kevät*. (Cf. Cohn 1983: 36–37, 43) As the result of associative figures of speech, the narration and the figural consciousness seem to merge: "We can never tell with certainty whether the analogical association originates in the mind of the narrator or in [the character's] own," Cohn (1983: 43) writes.

The landscape as perceived by Anni has been interpreted to reflect the human experience after war. It belongs to the imagery of the experience of discontinuity: rifts, gaps, and cataclysms that cut deeply through lives and the consciousness of modern individuals (cf. Kern 2011: 111). In the depiction of Anni's mental landscape, "the road, emblem of communication," Juhani Niemi (1995: 76) maintains, "becomes a dividing factor in the book's world. It is an instrument of the modern efficiency society, an open 'wound' that breaks natural bonds. The road takes away more than it brings, it lets one get away from somewhere and to somewhere else."[27] The impaired rubber boot pointing in the direction of travel refers to Anni's fate as a lonely traveler who moves aimlessly from place to place. The physical reality becomes an image of Anni's mental life as she makes her last journey across the landscape, which has become strange and alienating. The image of the road and the impaired boot are accompanied by other tropes of loss and disorder visible in the landscape. There is the mountain ash growing at an angle by the barn, the sleigh with no skids, and the one-wheeled carriage lying abandoned. The puff of wind stirs the dead plants, which move silently.

Observing the lilacs on the ground, Anni experiences an odd association: "Old they were, she thought. Still trying to burst into bloom in spring, but there it is, they realize they are dead." This sudden thought carries an apparent meaning in the context of the story: it becomes a premonition of Anni's own death. The reference to the lilacs can also be read in the context of the novel's love story. Two middle-aged individuals try to get their last share of human affection, but soon realize that their time has passed. In this respect, the simile of lilac roots realizing they are dead refers not only to Anni's last summer, but also to her love for Napoleon, which is fated to be in bloom only a short time. Given that the reader is able to discern the lacuna, the hidden meaning within the text, the similes open up a whole universe of semantic hints that add to the interpretation of the novel.

The double world established in the representation of Anni's mental landscape is partly based on a formerly stipulated fictional world opening up a whole new context of implicit meanings through allusion (cf. Doležel 1998: 172–173). In the depiction of the new road, Vartio's text alludes to one of the modernists' seminal texts: T. S. Eliot's long poem *The Waste Land* (1922). Eliot's poem begins with the following lines, which belong to the first part of the book entitled "The Burial of the Dead": "April is the cruellest month, breeding / Lilacs out of the dead land, mixing / Memory and desire, stirring / Dull roots with spring rain. / Winter kept us warm, covering / Earth in forgetful snow, feeding / A little life with dried tubers" (Eliot 1962/1922: 29).[28] The first reference to Eliot's poem is provided at the very beginning of the novel, even though the reader is hardly able to recognize the allusion at this point. When Anni observes the landscape exposed under the melting snow, there is a mention of time passing: "It was evening. And it was March, and soon it would be April" (S, 6). The mention of April is easy to trace back to Eliot's poem *after* the appearance of another intertextual hint in the text: the lilacs trying to rise up from the torn land. The trope refers to the dull roots, dried tubers, and lilacs breeding "out of the dead land" in Eliot's poem.[29]

As these distinct references to *The Waste Land* illustrate, the technique of allusion as used by Vartio corresponds to the strategy in portraying Anni's mental space. It is built inconspicuously into the depiction of the fictional world, hint by hint, as an intermittent network of evocations, tropes, and insinuations.[30] Within the textual universe, two co-existing worlds appear: the observable external world of perceived objects (the explicit texture of the text) and Anni's inner world, which is present only implicitly through gaps or allusions. The motifs of infertility and death in Eliot's poem are linked to the "waste land" in the beginning of *Se on sitten kevät* as a depiction of Anni's inner landscape.

The distance from the external world grows in the scenes in which Anni's inner reflections, triggered by the outer landscapes, focus on past views. These mental images include memories and impressions evoked during Anni's journey to the farm. The fused description mixes memory with the depiction of the perceptible landscape Anni sees along the way:

> The road rose through the spruce trees to the hill. First there had been a broad asphalt road, for at least ten kilometers, then an ordinary gravel road. Another five kilometers of a side road, that had been in bad shape. The bus had rocked like a ship, the road hadn't been rolled yet, it had been just made, the building site stakes beside it were still fresh. The old village road had been improved, widened and its worst curves straightened. A car had gone over the river, a couple had gotten off there, the wife had been sick in the car. You couldn't tell from her body yet but her face showed that she was pregnant, there were spots on her cheeks and forehead. (S, 5–6)[31]

The figure standing by the window and the window itself seem to demarcate the beginning of a literary description. Anni sees a typical Finnish landscape: the road, spruce trees, a hill. The description, however, deceives the reader: it ends before it has even properly begun. This strategy is typical of modernist description: it may begin with a "proper frame," yet before long, the description starts to follow the logic of the perceiver's inner associations, and the real object of observation is lost. (Cf. Bal 2004: 349) The perceptions of the outer reality are replaced by the perceiver's mental images.

The depiction of the landscape turns into a flashback that portrays Anni's recent past. The shift of time from the fictive present to the moment right before the narrated time marks a removal to the exposition, the background information concerning the fictional entities. By means of certain descriptive elements of the fictional world (the road and the memories triggered by it), the reader begins to acquire some knowledge of Anni's past and her character. The reader learns that Anni has traveled a long time; she has been waiting at the station for a bus to arrive. She has a daughter living in the city. She wishes she had met her daughter before arriving at the new place of service. After leaving her husband, Anni has drifted from one place of service to another and feels alienated in the unknown landscape. Recalling her journey, Anni's thoughts drift farther into the past:

> She'd been sitting in the waiting room beside the door. People come in and out through the door, the door swings back and forth, it doesn't have time to stop before someone else comes and the door slams and keeps swinging. She sees herself sitting on the bench beside the door. She has traveled a long way by train, carried her heavy luggage from the train station to the bus. She was on her way to her new job. The place was near Helsinki. The hum of talk and the voices from the street blend together, they surround her in her tiredness like something solid pressing her back into the corner of the bench. (S, 7)[32]

Anni's memories serve here as a function of the exposition, revealing what has occurred before the story's timeframe. As Tammi (1992: 41) has pointed out, the mixture of the protagonist's memories and imaginings constitute a peculiar combination of narrative modes, in which there is no linguistic regularity. The visibility of the exposition is covered by embedded, three-layered time structures, including 1) the present moment, which triggers Anni's memories of 2) the present moment of the flashback, alluding to the time spent at the station, which brings forth 3) the third time level actualized in the past: Anni recalls her train journey into the city while still being situated within the world of the second time frame. The distanced view of oneself sitting at a train station frames a memory within a memory as the two scenes of Anni recalling her journey segue one into the other. The effect of balance between external and internal perspectives in the scene is achieved by means of fused description, mixing descriptive and narrative elements. Anni's physical and mental exhaustion is manifested in the association of her feeling as "something solid" ("jokin kiinteä aine") that weighs heavily on her. Anni's passiveness is reinforced by tactile images of the bustle of the city around her: people walking and chatting, doors swinging and slamming.

The distance from the domain of the actual increases, as Anni distances herself from the perceived landscape and begins to contemplate her past experiences.

In modernist fiction the traditional means of exposition are often replaced by a literary mode that Cohn (1983: 128) calls "narrated memories." They constitute flashbacks motivated by the characters' memories and include events that precede the story's timeframe. Anni's layered memories from the station can be read as an exposition within an exposition. The eccentric compound of free indirect and objective style in the passage includes both external and internal perspectives. The result is a curious effect of self-distancing, a mental image of oneself: "She *sees herself* sitting on the bench beside the door." Anni's inner processes are represented as if from an outer perspective, yet paradoxically, they register the character's mental functioning *per se*. As the two voices – the narrator's and the character's – merge into one, Anni adopts the view of the narrator and sees herself as if on the narrator's film record. By the very act of self-distancing, the reader is allowed to sense the world perceived by Anni at the present moment of her experiences, as if from within.

In the passage above, the external point of view is adopted to show the character's inner experience. This sort of self-objectification or *perspectival split in the self* is a trademark of Vartio's fiction, introduced here for the first time and cultivated later in her novels. The technique manifests itself in narration wherein the narrator perceives characters perceiving themselves as if from an outside position, as a distanced object among other objects. Vartio's characters' tendency for self-reflection through objectification is linked to the sense of the constructed self evolving in time and space. In Vartio's neutral novels, this stage of self-awareness is portrayed as the characters' feelings of estrangement, reflected in their instinctive physical responses. In her later novels, on the other hand, self-objectification is related to misrepresentations of oneself and others. The characters do not observe themselves directly but with a "sideways glance," through the imaginary, hypothetical perspective of others (cf. Tammi 1992: 64, Bakhtin 1981: 375–376).

The effect of self-detachment is reinforced by the use of simile to provide a mental association with a character's state of mind – another characteristic feature of Vartio's texts. In her novels, the sensations experienced by the embodied mind are often evoked in the mental associations generated by means of psycho-analogy. In the depiction of Anni's exhaustion, for instance, the abstract feeling is compared to a concrete, "solid substance" embodying the experiencer's mental and physical state. "The hum of talk and the voices from the street blend together, *they surround her in her tiredness like something solid* pressing her back into the corner of the bench.

The opening scene of *Se on sitten kevät* includes several depictions of vague sensations that are triggered in the perceiver by the landscape. Later, when Anni ruminates on her journey, there are similar indefinite sensations that keep occupying her mind: "The woman moved impatiently, *as if* she were flinging something away from her. She felt heartburn. What kind of shortening was in it? she wondered" (S, 7).[33] Anni's impatient move pertains to a distaste that seems not only physical, but also mental. At the station she had eaten Wiener cake, which, unlike Proust's *madeleines*, does not spark an epiphany[34] or reveal something extraordinary through an involuntary memory. Quite the opposite; instead of pleasure permeating her senses, she feels a deep disappointment that seems to reflect the essence of her attitude toward life in general: "She had thought it would taste the same as before. But with the first bite she'd felt disappointment, like a child who'd been deceived" (ibid.).[35] The narrator observes the character from a distant position by comparing her reactions to those of a child.

The mental associations of Vartio's characters often include concise similes that turn the elements of the perceived world into more concrete and tangible "objects." Abstract sensations or feelings are juxtaposed with more physical conditions. The unpleasant memory of how the cake tasted is followed by other memories that refer to the same pattern of disappointment: there have been numerous places and spaces that Anni has inhabited, but felt them to be strange and alienating, including her last place of service: "The household was too modern. In what way, she couldn't have said, she had just felt it like a sickness whose name and precise location you can't specify" (*S*, 9).[36] The psycho-analogy is employed here to capture Anni's mental activity, which escapes self-articulation and self-understanding ("she couldn't have said, she had just felt it"). Only an ill-defined gut feeling seems to penetrate her awareness. The mental representations of a world rendered in similes reflect the function of psycho-analogies as "objective correlatives." These psycho-analogies emphasize the quality of a character's mental states as physically experienced, intuitive emotions rather than self-conscious feelings.

The "symbolic" episodes analyzed above, as well as the observation of objects in the external world, often become manifestations of the intuitive quality of the characters' ways of experiencing and being in the world. The intuitiveness becomes especially crucial in the references to the event that is the novel's turning point: Anni's death in the middle of the story. Expressions such as the "disease whose name and place one cannot specify," as well as the cake that causes the feeling of "heartburn" seem to suggest that the approaching end is half-intuited. In the beginning of the second chapter, Anni consciously reflects on the heart problem the doctor has told her about: "Stale air and the smell of dirt had recently become offensive to her, that, too, stemmed from the sickness, the shortness of breath. The doctor had said her heart was not in good shape" (*S*, 13).[37] The disease is also alluded to in other references, such as the "unknown disease" ("tuntematon tauti") that killed the young shoats on the farm (*S*, 35) or the fierce beating of her heart which Anni senses while she is waiting for Napoleon to come home after his prolonged journey to the city.

Anni's ruminations on the stains and dirt of the external world can be seen as indication of her mental awareness of the processes of decay taking place in her body, but also her alienation from the modern world. The picture of Anni as a homeless traveler is given right at the beginning of the novel as she observes her new environment, like an automaton or a sleepwalker. Anni's downward path has led "[f]rom parlor to living-room and from living-room to outbuilding and from outbuilding to shed" (*S*, 8), like the decorated bed that she had seen in her last place of service.[38] In the modern world, the decorated, bulky beds and lacy bedspreads "are not in fashion [...] not anymore" (ibid.).[39] There are only outworn cots Anni lays herself with distaste. In Anni's case, the avoidance of getting in touch with her feelings is due to the experience of this worldliness, the hardness of life, that makes her wrap herself in passivity and submission. Waiting for the bus, Anni is depicted standing, the worn-out fur collar of her coat "flattened by the sleet" (*S*, 53).[40] Anni's journey to the city is one of those scenes that foreground the coldness of the modern world. In the city she meets her daughter, who barely allows her mother to come in. She wanders the streets, guided only by an old couple who kindly show this stranger the way through the cityscape.

In her plain, undecorated style of writing novels, Vartio endeavored to depict realms of the mind that are difficult to portray. It was precisely these difficulties in representing unconscious psychology that Anhava (2002/1949: 57) addressed when he encouraged Finnish modernists to leave the (half)conscious experiences "to be intuited from the narrated actions and incidents." The characters' mental states must be understood by reader instinct, not explained by the narrator's comments and inferences, which can never reach the inner experience. In *Se on sitten kevät*, among other new school novels, Anhava (2002/1961: 261) finds "symbolic small episodes" ("symbolisi[a] pikku episode[ja]") that portray the fictional reality, not by telling, but by showing – describing life "as it is." In the following analyses of *Se on sitten kevät*, I approach these symbolic scenes from the perspective of Anni's dawning awareness of her emotional and social situation. Vartio renders Anni's gradual withdrawal from the social world by means of symbolic episodes that suggest her alienation. As Hirsch (1983: 23) pointed out, in the narratives of female awakening, the states of sleep and quiescence often represent "a progressive withdrawal into the symbolic landscapes of the innermost self." The following analyses of Anni's mental life and her character serve as the basis for further reading of the novel's emotional story structure.

From "Sleepwalking" to Dreams

In the beginning of *Se on sitten kevät*, Vartio reveals Anni's character through the accumulation of small incidents that form patterns of behavior. The trivial observations and actions – cleaning up the room, the courtyard, and the barn – demonstrate Anni's nature, which is defined by her desire for decency and permanence. Anni's desire to stabilize her life after her arrival at a strange house is illustrated by these actions, which reflect her need to feel more at home, to attach herself to a particular space. The construction of a character is based on the depiction of Anni's habits, her behavior, and looks, which generate an image of a strong, authentic individual. After a day of hard work, the narrator studies Anni in a deep doze. The author draws her portrait with just a few effective strokes. The description is a detailed account of Anni's overt movements and looks. No access to her mind is provided:

> The woman is sleeping on her back, her face illuminated by moonlight. Her hairline is low, her hair is thick and dark, her brow broad and round. Her eyebrows echo the force and blackness of her hair. Her nose is straight. Her lips make a narrow line in her face and the corners of her mouth have a tired, heavy look. Her jaw is strong and broad, it is the jaw that makes her face appear hard when she's asleep. When her eyes are open, her expression is softer.
>
> She turns in her sleep, the cover slips down so that the top of her body is visible. A short neck rises from the neck of the cotton knit nightgown, her breasts are large. Her arms are on top of the cover, they are sturdy, the fingertips are broad. Her face is turned slightly to the side, her expression has changed, now it contains a touch of helplessness. The woman turns again in her sleep and her full braid comes into view, the braid begins wrist-thick at her neck and continues to below her waist, ending the breadth of her little finger. (S, 27–28)[41]

The organization of the literary description simulates human observation. The prolonged gaze lingers on Anni's face and body from hair to forehead, to eyebrows, nose, lips, and chin, from neck to breasts, arms and fingertips, and eventually to the flat end of the braid. The unfolding image of the female body generates an impression of the "purity" of the description. The plainness of the portrayal is emphasized by the neutral reference to the protagonist as "the woman." The gaze belongs to the narrator, who keeps a distance from the object being observed.

The passage constitutes almost an anatomical rendering of the female body as Anni's physique is exposed to the narrator's and the reader's eyes in the moonlight – conveniently accompanied by the removal of the blanket, which reveals more contours of the woman's body for the beholder to see. The robust and hardy (almost manly) quality of Anni's appearance, however, distracts the viewer, who is prone to expect the aesthetic pleasures of the female beauty more typical of the literary genre of *blazon* (cf. Bal 1993: 387). The representation of Anni's ordinary looks defies voyeurism, which is characteristic of many literary depictions of the female body. The composition alludes to a potential power relation between the viewer and the subject viewed, corresponding to the narrative hierarchy in the novel: the observed woman is in an insecure and passive state of unconsciousness, unable to offer resistance to the narrator's intrusive gaze.[42] The narrator's observation, however, never crosses the boundary between inner and outer space. Anni's mind remains intact. Her nocturnal movements are observed as if the narrator were guarding the sleep of an innocent child. The narrator's gaze is marked by gentleness rather than voyeurism, as the exhausted woman is witnessed having fallen into sweet oblivion after a hard day's work.

The depiction of the sleeping woman is one of the first instances of representation in which the narrator's seemingly objective attitude gives way to a more emphatic rendering of the protagonist. Subtle interpretations of what is observed are included, even if the style of writing is restraint and detached: "Her lips make a narrow line in her face and the corners of her mouth have *a tired, heavy look*. Her jaw is strong and broad, it is the jaw that *makes her face appear hard* when she's asleep. When her eyes are open, her expression is *softer*." The narrator's interpretive stance becomes especially clear as Anni's potential vulnerability is addressed: "Her face is turned slightly to the side, her expression has changed, now it contains a touch of helplessness." Anni's authenticity is connected to her melancholy, the experience of world-weariness in her character, which is materialized in her appearance having "a tired, heavy look" and apparent hardness. The drawing of Anni is plain, yet effective.

Anni's character is defined not only by her looks, but also by her actions. During the brisk morning hours, Anni is depicted walking to the cowshed as she sets out on her daily chores. The narrator registers the minutest details of Anni's actions, looks, and gestures, but provides hardly any information about her emotions. When Anni observes a young calf in the shed, a close view of her face implies the existence of muted feelings. However, these feelings are not to be expressed except with a gesture at what lies beyond: "A smile began to rise on her face but stopped abruptly, as if water had been tossed on a fire that was just beginning. Her eyes looked straight ahead, as if staring fixedly at something. Then they turned slightly downwards. In that position her eyes looked cross-eyed" (*S*, 31).[43] The comparison of the vanishing smile to smothered flames establishes a parallel between the characters' expressions and the phenomena in the physical world, suggesting some implicit mental state. The depiction of Anni's vanishing smile alludes to a pleasant vision passing through her mind until she becomes disheartened again.

In many instances in the novel, the narrator's neutral, objective observation of the characters' behavior results in the vagueness of the content of their minds. The narrator may hint at what might be the cause of Anni's actions and gestures: She "seemed to be looking at something, listening to something that she needed to concentrate to hear" (*S*, 32).[44] At times, however, the reader encounters only lengthy passages of detailed descriptions recording Anni's daily actions and habits. As covert mental states, these reports seem excessively banal and insignificant. Before depicting Anni's sudden smile, the narrator portrayed her actions as she prepared for her daily work:

> The milkmaid awoke, lit the light and looked at the clock; there was still some time before she should go to the cowshed. She got up out of bed anyway. [...] The sun was rising behind the spruce grove. She walked to the shed along the edge of the road where the snow had frozen during the night hard enough to bear weight. She paused at the door to the cowshed kitchen and watched the rising sun. It was dim inside, the kitchen smelled bad after the morning air. Three milk jugs lay on their side on the shelf, the milking rags and towels hung drying over the jugs. The shelves were dirty, covered with milk spots. She lifted the top of a pot. The bottom of the pot held rust-colored water. She fetched wood chips from the front hall and lit a fire under the pot. Then she swept the floor and pushed the trash piled beside the stove into the fire. While she filled the pot with water from the hose, she held her hand under the streaming water. It splashed into her eyes and she stepped back quickly and bumped her leg on a bucket. (*S*, 29–30)[45]

Even though the passage contains an abundance of sensory experiences perceived from Anni's point of view, it is hard to find much psychological motivation behind the detailed description. According to Fludernik (1996: 173), in neutral narratives the very act of the reader's recognizing the cloaked mind behind the overt actions naturalizes the lack (or minimum degree) of experientiality, thereby justifying the story's existence. Observations such as Anni's leg bumping the side of the bucket by no means seem to contribute to the "reader's establishment of experientiality." The default response of symbolic reading cannot be applied either. There are no allegorical insinuations to be neutralized at the level of characterization (cf. Abbott 2008: 458).

The concept of *embodiedness*, however, proves to be a useful one in determining the relationship of mental activity and physical sensations in Vartio's representation of her characters' mental states. In recent cognitive narratology, the concept of embodiedness has been perceived as one of the seminal aspects of fictional, particularly modernist, consciousness (cf. Fludernik 1996: 30; Herman 2009a: 132). Knowledge about one's physical presence, the bodily enmeshment in the world, also affects the comprehension of the abstract areas of reasoning, thought, and introspection. Another key concept in this respect is the cognitive unconscious. The notion refers to the ways in which the characters' experiences are reflected in their bodily and sensory reactions to the events and objects of the external world without appearing in the realm of the conscious mind. Vartio's representation of her characters' physical cognition serves as a way to come to terms with the contents of the mind that manifest themselves as automatic responses, beyond conscious awareness.

The amount of sensory perception in *Se on sitten kevät* is linked to Anni's bodily enmeshment in the physical world she encounters. In particular, the passages in the first chapter of the novel seem to evoke an illusion of physical sensations experienced primarily by bodily cognition, as automatically selected physiological stimuli that involve no conscious reflection on one's habitual perceptions. Anni's mental processes do not occur that much in the aware mind, but rather as more or less unconscious cognitive processes of her embodied mind. At the beginning of the novel, as Anni observes her new surroundings, one particular detail in the country landscape catches her eye. The external view stimulates a disordered sensation within her cognition:

> She had come to the steps to the house. Turning to look behind her once more toward the sauna, she noticed a large white object in the snow beside the sauna wall. At first she didn't realize what it was, then she saw that it was a bathtub. She stared so hard at it that when the window rattled open, she jumped as if awakened from a deep sleep. (S, 11–12)[46]

In the first stage, Anni's perception is depicted with a vague notion of "a large white object" ("suur[i] valkea esine"), which implies an indefinite and automatic quality of her vision. Later, the sensation becomes better defined, and the object acquires a fixed name: a bathtub. The passage seems to imitate the nature of physical sensations experienced primarily by the body's cognition, as automatically selected physiological stimuli involving no conscious reflection or articulation of perceptions. Approached from the behaviorist point of view, the physiological mechanisms *equal* mental states. The mind and the body are components of the same entity, and therefore, phenomena related to the former are immersed in the "processes of adaptation" that occur "somewhere between a stimulus and a response" (Richards 1952: 85).

The seemingly "behavioristic" style in the Finnish new novels often stems from a desire to depict fictional world as concrete and tangible, existing within the reach of an eye and a hand (Hökkä 1999: 73). The mental representations of visual, auditory, tactile, and visceral images relate to the character's act of registering and knowing an object "here and now," through sense experience and empirical knowledge. However, the behavioristic aspects of Vartio's fiction-making, both with respect to its technique and its subject matter, is far more complex, more subtle, and more indirect than has thus far been suggested. Vartio's novels seem to address the very issue of human perception, and they do this by using various innovative, complementary techniques to portray the characters' mental processes. Even though the minds depicted may be covert and undetectable, a mental dimension can certainly be found in the texture of Vartio's early novels. Even Anni's mechanized activities rendered in the cowshed scene can be psychologically motivated by insisting that they address the habitual quality of human cognition. The scene seems to imply that Anni performs her daily activities as mechanical, automatized acts without giving much thought to them – in a similar vein as the body's cognitive sensations are passively sensed rather than consciously contemplated. The heightened focus on external behavior seems to generate an illusion of the characters' actions as mere physical responses to the world: either as intense reactions by the body's involuntary functions or as automatic, bodily sensations that the characters themselves are following more or less attentively.

The external perspective on fictional beings in Vartio's early novels pertains to the study of consciousness by its absence, or rather in the specific, external manifestations of the characters' mental states that are identifiable on the basis of their behavior. The concept of "background emotion" can be applied to the interpretation of the emotional story structure of Vartio's neutral narratives.[47] The signals of background emotions explain why the reading process of the characters' embodied experiences is evoked, even if the text provides only depictions of their behavior. By observing the fluctuating states of awareness, attention, and bodily reactions, the reader is able to draw many conclusions about the characters' mental states. Certain objects trigger a character's attention and simultaneously the reader's search for significance. In *Se on sitten kevät*, for instance, the bathtub resembles the surrealists' *hazard objectif*, which symbolizes the unwilled and the unfocused human drives arising from below (cf. Richardson 1997: 36). The bathtub has been interpreted as a symbol of Anni's white coffin, thus serving as an omen of her death.

In fictional scenes, the continuity of background emotions refers to the emotional incidents in the story structure from which the emotional peak moments arise. In fictional texts, those things that draw the characters' attention often become meaningful. Or conversely, the meaning stems from those very aspects that escape the character's awareness. Anni's attention is often directed from external objects toward some internal object causing absent-mindedness, typical of the state of daydreaming. In the following passage, Anni's mind is portrayed from within, in the transitional state of dream and wakefulness:

> She closes her eyes. But the darkness is full of images. The farther the night progresses and the more tired she feels, the clearer the images become. They break away from their surroundings, they're scattered before her eyes like a deck of cards. Someone is moving the images, fast, then the movement ceases, and she has to look at the image before her eyes for as long as it lingers. (S, 13–14)[48]

At the threshold of consciousness, the external world dissociates. As Anni closes her eyes, the reality is replaced by a darkness that is "full of images" of another kind. On the borderland of sleep, Anni's mind fluctuates between perceptions of the outer reality and the phantasmagoric sensations of the inner world, which come back every time she closes her eyes. In the transitional state (when the mind hovers on the edge of dreams), the involuntary mental images keep emerging. Some of the images are fragmentary, still, and flat, whereas others take on a more vivid form, resembling a motion picture alternately freezing or accelerating the pace of the rolling images. Consciousness continuously drifts in and out of sleep: "She turns over, opens her eyes, and looks at the pale spot visible in the darkness; the window is there. She closes her eyes. The image is still before her eyes, unchanged" (S, 16).[49]

The remnants of the day jolt Anni awake and prevent the transition from half-dream into actual sleep. Anni's pre-sleep visions modify and reshape the minutiae of the things she has seen earlier that day. These images imitate the fleeting impressions that are typical of hypnagogic experiences: the figures, sensations, and sounds occurring on the brink of sleep. One of Anni's mental images constitute a flashback showing her having coffee in the main building on the farm. She sees herself immersed in the scene and in discussion with two women: the old matron of the house and her daughter-in-law. "In the image there is a round table; by the table sit three women. She herself is the one who is sitting next to the kitchen door, at the head of the table" (S, 14).[50] The old matron's face is floating in the air like the distant image of something Anni has seen in a book. In Anni's mental image, the old woman's eyes behind her glasses are frozen, as if they were covered with double glass; her stare forces the other person to look in another direction.

On the brink of sleep, the past impressions are converted by the logic of dreams. At the beginning of the novel, Anni's thoughts about the journey evoke an association: "The bus had rocked like a ship" (S, 5).[51] Before falling asleep, she is still feeling the "waves" of the bus in her body: "Images flash past, cars pass, trains pass, the bus rocks, *no, it's a ship*" (S, 18).[52] Gradually, the grip of consciousness fully yields to the logic of dreams. The distinct images finally melt into the color of the water, the water becoming a dream itself: "More images come, people with unreal faces. But they're half dream [...]. The images merge into the color of the water, are water, are a dream" (S, 19).[53]

Vartio's interest in dreams and dream-like states was related to her fascination with the deeper, less rational areas of the mind emphasized in her later writing. Anni's dawning awareness may be interpreted not only as an illustration of primarily physical mechanisms of sensation, but also as a manifestation of the modernists' pursuit, namely, to represent impressions and associations that may be registered unconsciously, but are articulated and modified only after they have occurred. The "delayed decoding" of external objects (to use Ian Watt's expression) illustrates the human mind's tendency to interpret everyday occasions as meaningful only after their initial recording in the unconscious mind (Watt 1980: 175). Cognition involves not only the routine analysis of present sensory perceptions, but also the remembrance of times past, imagined and dreamed objects and the processes of involuntary psychology.

First and foremost, the mental images arising from the dark serve as metaphors for Vartio's poetics of mind-making. The depiction of Anni's pre-sleep state alludes to the "randomness" of the artist's mental images organized in a narrative text. These images are compared to a deck of cards shuffled before the game. The hypnagogic images emerging from the dark resemble Vartio's depiction of the writing process of *Se on sitten kevät*. Just as a poem may take shape in response to an image, so the process of writing a novel is all about images. At first only one image appears, which then invites others to join. Some of these images are clear and persistent; others are vague and fleeting. In the end these images, symbols, start to settle into place, and consequently, "the actions, the lines that rippled in confusedly," take their place in a novel that is seeking its final form (Vartio 1996: 95).[54]

In her matinée talk given after the publication of *Se on sitten kevät*, Vartio compared her mental images to "secret phosphorous lamps" ("salaisia fosforilamppuja") that lighted her way on the dusky path toward the completion of a literary work (ibid.: 96). Vartio defines her novel as a composition based on images "full of sense (mind) and meaning" ("täynnä mieltä ja merkitystä").[55] This expression is later used as a meta-commentary in Paavo Haavikko's long poem *Talvipalatsi* (Winter Palace, 1959). The speaker in the poem declares: "I in this poem am *a mere image of a full mind*" (Haavikko 1959: 25).[56] The verse takes advantage of the ambivalent meaning of the Finnish word *mieli*, which signifies both "meaning" and the "mind." Analyzing Haavikko, Leena Kaunonen (2001: 140) writes:

> *Mieli* indicates meaning, among other things, the content of meaning, that is, significance or meaningfulness as opposed to insanity or insignificance. *Mieli* is also a notion that denotes the existence of ego or consciousness. In defining '*image*' it is possible to combine all these variations of meaning. "Image" conveys the presence of mind, that is, consciousness as pure meaning: as significance, as the full content of meaning.[57]

The poet's role as a *mere* image (a mere presentation) emphasizes the autonomy of an "image" in relation to the poet's personal self-expression. In the context of Finnish modernist poetry, the notion of image was a key concept that carried ambivalent, loaded meanings.[58] As Kaunonen emphasizes, talking of "a *mere* image" does not denote a dismissive attitude: quite the opposite. A poetic "image" having "a full mind" ("täynnä mieltä") is the slogan of Finnish modernist poetry and refers to the ideal of a "pure" representation that aims at exactitude and distance. The word "mere" (in Finnish, *pelkkä*) can be interpreted not only as a particle signifying understatement, but also as an adjective implying absoluteness, simplicity, and clarity as opposed to obscurity and insignificance.[59] The image is pure significance and nothing else: everything futile has been left out.

The opposition between seeing (as perception) and seeing-as (as intuitive or imaginative seeing) sheds light on the aspects of mimesis in *Se on sitten kevät*. Even if the new school writers were committed to representing the sensual, concrete world, they did not seek a direct *imitation* of reality. The worlds portrayed in fiction may have been rendered concrete, tangible, and life-like, yet at the same time they were portrayed from an aesthetic distance – as seen through the mind's eye of the author and the protagonist. In Haavikko's long poem *Pimeys* (Darkness, 1984), the poem's speaker, who has contemplated delusions of seeing and of reality, ends up asking for more darkness for a work of art: "[I]f a work of art is lacking darkness, it lacks everything" (Haavikko 1984: 13).[60] By veiling the reflections of the material, visible world, darkness gives way to creative imagination and relieves it from the constraints of perception: the mind becomes "more accurate than its image" (ibid.).[61] In *Se on sitten kevät*, the depiction of Anni's hypnagogic images, emerging from within the dark, emphasizes the depth and density of the inner worlds streaming behind her closed eyes. The unknowable becomes momentarily knowable as the readers are given an opportunity to see the protagonist's world through her mind's eye.

Reading Silence, Reading Minds. Narrative Landscapes of Romance

Se on sitten kevät also invites the readers to captive mind-reading on another level: by presenting fictional minds reading other people's thoughts, gestures, and actions. The drama of reading and non-reading is manifested especially in the scenes of the romantic encounter between the two protagonists. The love story of Anni and Napoleon modifies the emotional story structure of the tragic romance plot, ending with scenes of separation and loss. A tragic love plot is one of the most famous variants of the classic romantic formula. The illness or death of the loved one leads to sacrifice and suffering.[62] The aspect of loss intensifies the desire, giving a heightened value to the lost object. The closure of the classic romance often leads to the heroine's death or her suffering, which benefits the hero's transcendental quest. The sacrifice of the female character becomes relevant in the narratives of female Bildung. The tension between love comedy (with a happy ending in marriage) and love tragedies (concluding with separation) is often written into the plots of female development. The latter option has been the preferable ending in the trajectories of female self-discovery. In the more optimistic versions of romance, on the other hand, the transformative power of love changes both parties in the love affair. The recognition of the other serves as a catalyst for transformation. The possibilities of change, progress, and escape are exemplified in the idea of romance as a journey into the self – and out of the self. (Pearce & Stacey 1995: 13, 17–18)

The diverse narratives of romance have certain basic story elements that I refer to as the "classic romance plot" in my analyses of Vartio's novels. The traditional trajectory of romance suggests a potential love union whose fulfillment is complicated by a series of barriers and misunderstandings. The quest for love may conclude with attainment or, just as likely, with its tragic loss. Whatever direction the love story takes, it must reach its closure. The conquest of barriers occurs either in the name of love or for the sake of truth, knowledge, or freedom. (Pearce & Stacey 1995: 15–16) The classic romance plot begins with the scene of "first sighting" pointing at the chemistry between the two characters. The barriers to the union comprise a series of obstacles, such as geographical distance or class, national or racial difference, which make the relationship unsuitable; inhibition or stubbornness of the character; a dubious past; the existence of another lover or spouse. The clash of personalities, on the other hand, is related to the delay of attaining a love union. In this narrative pattern, the mutual antipathy (with a sufficient spark) serves as a foil for the power of love, and at the same time, for the "battle of the sexes," as the inevitable encounter between lovers is postponed by different protestations along the way. Sometimes the love union calls for the "taming" of the uncivilized beast within the other person, or securing or regaining the love that has already been achieved and lost.[63] From these obstacles arises the eternal seduction of the romance plot, its narrative tension: "'[W]ill they or won't they', or rather, *how* will they […]?" (Ibid.: 16, 19)

The typical trajectory of romance has been classified by Lynne Pearce and Jackie Stacey on the basis of Janice Radway's model of the stages of romance. The beginning of the love affair, "the encounter," leads to the heroine's loss of social identity in an initial unpleasant encounter with an aristocratic or otherwise powerful man, whose behavior is potentially misunderstood. The next stage includes a stage of "transformation" as each partner is changed by the force of their passion for another. When the initial fascination begins to wear off, a series of stages of hostility and separation follow: each tries to change the other to overcome the mismatch of the romantic ideal and the actual person in the everyday life. The next stage, "negotiation," is often materialized as lovers' dialogues, as they attempt at productive exchange. The moment of negotiation depicts the two parties aware of the power relations at stake, the frustrations and inequalities involving the affair. The lovers are also aware that things may go two different ways. The moment of negotiation may lead either to "reconciliation," to renewed and extended pleasures (and the renewed social identity of the heroine), or to "refusal," loss, pain, and separation. (Pearce & Stacey 1995: 38–41; Radway 1987: 134)

These formulaic stages of romance can be found in *Se on sitten kevät*, even though the love story of the two adults is radically modified, highly unconventional, and mundane. The "first sighting" between Anni and Napoleon occurs the morning after the new milkmaid has arrived at the farm. Napoleon knocks on Anni's door and introduces himself. The scene modifies the stage of "encounter" in the classic romance plot by introducing a figure of a powerful man (who is behaving *like* an aristocrat). Anni is almost intimidated by the man's presence: "'Martikainen,' the woman introduces herself. She notices that she has said her name awkwardly; the man's politeness has made her self-conscious. Besides, there was something pretentious about the situation, introducing oneself this way" (*S*, 25).[64] In the early stages of the affair Anni is puzzled by Napoleon's character. The following discussion between Anni and the young farmer's wife reveals Anni's curiosity about the unknown man she has met in the servants' quarters. Anni carefully observes the reactions of the farmer's wife as she asks about Napoleon:

> "Who's the man who lives in the same building?" she went on, bending over to draw water from the pot.
> "Napoleon," the farmer's wife said. "Have you already met him?" [...]
> The farmer's wife said that the man was very talented. She laughed.
> The milkmaid was just about to ask something else about the man, she wanted to ask whether he was also a renter, as she'd understood from his talk. But she didn't ask.
> "Flinkman," the farmer's wife said. After a short pause she added, "He's lived with us so long, he's like family."
> Without even realizing it, the milkmaid grew cautious. She went back to talking about the cows. (*S*, 36–37)[65]

The previous night Napoleon had introduced himself, and Anni has not made any sense of his name; it started with the letter F. Anni noticed his habit of speaking swiftly and pointedly, searching for words. The discussion between Anni and the young farmer's wife reflects not only Anni's interest in Napoleon, but also her confusion. Napoleon's name and other personal qualities remain vague and unclear, including his social status in the house. Napoleon seems to dwell in the servants' quarters, but he does not behave like a servant. The farmer's wife's ambiguous comment on Napoleon's position in the house confuses Anni even more: he is "like family" ("kuin omaa väkeä"). However, put off by the farmer's wife's ambivalent laughter and the comment about the man's "talents," she hesitates to ask more, as if she intuitively reads the young matron's talk between the lines. A similar pattern of cautiousness emerges when Anni tells about her own past, about being "from a house" ("talosta lähtöisin"). Afterwards, she feels regretful, as she realizes how shameful it must sound, when "one has ended up here" ("kerta nyt oli tässä"). (*S*, 39)

Anni's difficulties in grasping Napoleon's true nature are connected to his function as a symbol of the modern age. Vartio herself, in a letter to Paavo Haavikko, provided the key for interpreting the dynamics between the novel's two main characters, Anni and Napoleon:

> I became powerful and yet unhappy when I realized what symbols they are, A and N. A is a symbol of the original person [...] with healthy instincts, the individualist and other such good things, a strong, good woman, and N is a layabout, a con man who's not at all as simple to define. Just a victim of the

fuzziness of today's world, a ready victim. [...] This Anni is something that represents the old and genuine, so genuine that she does not lose herself in the woolly fuzziness Napoleon represents. [...] And the coffin represents, symbolizes the time, which is also heading for the grave [...] (Vartio 1996: 82).[66]

The couple, Anni and Napoleon, represents the co-existence of two worlds, the old and the modern. Vartio built up Anni's character to signify the original, pure human being, whereas Napoleon represents the modern age, the new man. Vartio, who heard a real-life story of a workman and a milkmaid who died, was particularly captivated by the man's name: "For instance, the fact that the man's name was Napoleon. The name seemed full of peculiar significance to me. [...] I ruthlessly seized on that Napoleon for my own use, and I would not have agreed to change the name to another; I had my own reasons," Vartio (1996: 91).[67] The author did not give her reasons, but the novel itself offers some explanations, which are revealed in the course of the love story.

The beginning of the romance contains several depictions of the flow of daily life, which brings those dwelling in the servants' quarters closer to each other. Napoleon becomes a part of Anni's small, secure world. As the days go by, Napoleon gradually occupies Anni's room and transforms it into his personal space:

> Napoleon is sitting in the milkmaid's room; they have had coffee. A week has passed since the first time they sat at the same table, they have had coffee together every day; the man comes into the woman's room as into his own home, he no longer bows at the door to ask if he can enter, no longer knocks, simply opens the door, sits at the table reading the newspaper or throws himself onto the bed to wait for coffee. (S, 41)[68]

The author depicts a stream of daily activities through iterative narration, providing episodic summaries of everyday incidents taking place in the servants' building and its surroundings. The dull taxonomy of daily events is accompanied by courting patterns that lead to the love union. The gradual process of becoming closer culminates in the scene in which Anni realizes that Napoleon's eyes resemble the eyes of the calf she has caressed in the shed. The calf evokes the vanishing smile on her face. This smile can be read as a sign of the memory of the son Anni lost soon after his birth; the animal is sucking her fingers like a new-born baby. In the later scene, the same image is laden with erotic connotations. Napoleon wants to know why Anni is laughing. When Napoleon approaches her, Anni tries to keep her distance, as though she refuses to understand the meaning of his gestures. Vartio provides a passage of speculative mind-reading to portray Anni's thoughts as she plans her actions according to what she thinks Napoleon thinks. Anni senses intensely the man's touch on her hand: "The woman feels the hand's warmth, feels his hand pressing her hand, but she doesn't pull her hand away, she thinks the man doesn't notice and so she does not move her hand, so he will not think she thinks something" (S, 47).[69]

When Napoleon is later caught openly gazing at her body, Anni responds with a penetrating look, showing openly her antipathy: "Then she turns to look at the man. Her face is calm, the expression cold, almost unfriendly" (*S*, 48).[70] Afterwards, Anni feels regret. Her feelings are expressed directly in a passage of thought report: "The woman remains standing. Her thoughts are anxious, she feels *disappointed* and *ashamed*, she had hoped that the man would not have left already, that the man would have said something" (ibid.).[71] When Napoleon enters her room that night, Anni is waiting. The depiction of their first sexual encounter is marked by unsentimentality, characteristic of Vartio's love scenes. These scenes exemplify the modernist tendency to emphasize erotic desire at the expense of sentiments (Clark 1991: 1).[72] Napoleon is described as wandering across the hall to the other room, as he had done many times, for "there have been milkmaids in the house before":

> He stubs out the cigarette and sits up on the edge of the bed. He leaves his room, walks the familiar route in his underwear; he has walked this way through the hall at night before, too, there have been milkmaids in the house before.
>
> He does not knock at the door to the woman's room. He opens the door, looks toward the bed from the threshold. A head moves on the pillow; the woman has heard the footsteps in the hall.
>
> She pulls herself up to a sitting position, she doesn't say anything. But the man has come to sit on the edge of the bed. The man has lowered his hand onto the woman's hair and said, "I like long hair."
>
> The woman lies back down. The man has lowered himself beside her. The woman lies still, her black hair around her head like a thundercloud. (*S*, 49)[73]

The unromantic tone of the encounter derives partly from knowledge of the repetitive quality of Napoleon's actions as he approaches Anni, just as he has approached many women before. The plain, simple style of reporting reinforces the impression of unsentimentality. The narration lacks any comment on the characters' emotions at the potentially intense moment of sexual desire. Mental content is embodied only in the concise simile that draws a parallel between Anni's hair and the natural forces of a "thundercloud" ("ukkospilvi"). The blackness of Anni's hair seems to allude to the existence of more primitive, deeper layers of the mind rendered by means of simile.

The episode of the spring party serves as a turning point in the narrative landscape of the romance. By then, Napoleon's role as an unreliable workman on the farm has already become clear to Anni. Napoleon has moved into her room. To celebrate the coming spring, Napoleon has decided to organize a house-warming party. He wants to invite the employers, an idea Anni considers inappropriate, but Napoleon remains firm. During the party, the farmer notices that Napoleon is serving cognac with "a good label" ("hyvää merkkiä"); "[t]he farmer took hold of the bottle, spelled out the name on the side of the bottle. He guessed the bottle had cost thousands. But what of them, the poor. 'Napoleon is Napoleon,' he said" (*S*, 85).[74]

In the farmer's comment on Napoleon's name, Anni senses mockery: "Napoleon is Napoleon." Still, she regards Napoleon's Christian name, Nils, as even stranger. "Nils" is Swedish, which explains Napoleon's way of speaking, his search for words: "His real name was Nils Flinkman, but no one remembered that anymore" (ibid.).[75] Napoleon speaks the same language as the young farmer's wife, which reinforces his uncertain social position. Anni's alienation stems from this realization as much as from the farmer's mockery. She feels left out: "Napoleon turned to the farmer's wife, said something in Swedish to which the farmer's wife answered with a laugh, but at the same time, she blushed" (*S*, 84).[76] The ambivalence of the social relationships in the scene is reinforced by the act of mind-reading, which reveals the simultaneous intimacy and distance between interacting minds: "Both women heard the farmer's voice and saw the men's expressions. Anni sensed what the farmer's wife was thinking, and the farmer sensed what the farmer's wife was thinking, and Napoleon knew what the other three were thinking. But no one said a word" (*S*, 81–82).[77] Vartio conveys the intuitive knowing of each person's thoughts through the complex construction of embedded consciousnesses, which becomes more frequent in her later novels. Each character "knows" what the others are thinking, but remains silent.

Vartio's interest in the name by which Napoleon was called and Anni's distaste for it stem from the same source. They relate to the "Napoleon syndrome," the psychological complex named for the French emperor, Napoleon Bonaparte. This syndrome refers to an individual's (especially a man's) need to compensate for short stature or inferior social status with domineering or aggressive behavior. Napoleon's complex in *Se on sitten kevät* is of a social kind, as he is described as being a tall, sizable man. Napoleon's complex is manifested in his need to perform and pose, to be bigger than he is: to serve cognac of the finest quality, to keep company with his employers, to forget his real social status and fantasize about rising above it. His nature is that of a performer. Recalling the times he left the barber shop, he thinks about the impression he made: "And then he had left with his hair shiny and carefully arranged, had bowed in the doorway, and they were left gazing after him" (*S*, 268).[78]

The episode of the spring party illustrates Napoleon's talents as a performer: his wild imagination as he is roused to compete with the farmer in the manly skills of storytelling.[79] The war of words (who knows the horses better?) urges Napoleon to make up a whole scene about the best mount in Finland, and finally, to take the form of a stallion himself. The horse probably does not exist, even though Napoleon claims to own it. The horse turns into Pegasus, an image of Napoleon's imagination that captivates his listeners: "All three of them were silent, as if they had seen a vision, as if the spirit of the horse had entered the man, had blown him from the chair onto the floor, had spun him around and gone away, leaving the flushed man with the gleaming eyes alone" (*S*, 96).[80] Anni is enthralled by Napoleon's imaginative faculty, but she also questions his story when he claims that the horse neighed to its master over the phone. Anni cannot understand Napoleon's performance as being a performance, just as she cannot understand his lies, when his superficial nature is gradually revealed: "[W]hat's the point in being like this and lying like this" (*S*, 135), she asks him.[81]

Vartio portrays the disappointments one after another in Anni's life through the conflicts that comprise the emotional peak moments in the novel's story structure. As Hogan points out, certain key experiences of characters' lives usually stand out as more isolated moments, more compressed and frozen, more meaningful in the structure of a narrative. The temporal landscape of the narrative is uneven, and this unevenness is motivated by the characters' emotional reactions to changes in normalcy and routine. According to Hogan, emotional moments are "incidents," minimal units of emotional temporality that can narrow emotions to almost timeless points in a narrative structure. Incidents serve as nuclei of "events," and events, in turn, compose "episodes" that form "stories." Stories can project the immediate emotional reactions into long-term goals involving self-conscious, rational scripting, planning, and calculation. (Hogan 2011a: 32–33)

In *Se on sitten kevät*, certain emotional peak moments trigger the stages of transformation and negotiation in the romance plot. From the perspective of female Bildung these incidents point at Anni's gradual detachment from the social world. The first move away from normalcy of neutral "occurrences"[82] to emotionally highlighted episodes occurs after the spring party. The conflict between Anni and Napoleon stems from the obstacles of their love union, materialized both as the murky past of Napoleon and the existence of another lover. The information imparted by the young farmer's wife leads to Anni's growing alienation. Napoleon has a wife somewhere, a clutch of unpaid bills, and stolen tools in his possession. The austerity of the narrator's expression in the scenes of recognition coincides with Anni's self-restraint. When she is working, Anni acts like an automaton or a sleepwalker who refuses to become fully aware: "She brushed the cows, even though she had just brushed them that morning; she swept the cow stalls and washed the drinking troughs, even though she had washed them the day before. And while she worked, she sometimes forgot why she was still lingering in the cowshed" (*S*, 107).[83] Finally, Anni is forced to confront her anxiety. Her emotions are reflected in her perceptions and her body's reactions:

> Steam rose from the pot; you could hear the sound of boiling water from under the lid. She remembered that there was only a little water in the pot, the water would boil dry. She stood up, used the hose to fill the pot up to the brim. She added some wood, moved the footstool nearer the fireplace. – She moved, her mouth opened; a voice was heard that was like a sound from the mouth of an animal, like an animal uttering sounds in the dark. She pressed her hand over her mouth. (*S*, 107–108)[84]

Anni is depicted listening to the intensifying sound of water boiling in a pot as if her emotions were arising from within. She runs more water into the pot "to fill the pot up to the brim." By means of concise similes, Vartio juxtaposes Anni's mind with a container that is about to overflow, like the pot filled with water. As the escalating sound from the pot indicates, so too her mind is about to reach a point at which she can no longer control her emotional reactions. The moment of extreme inner pressure and lost self-control is portrayed as the cry of an animal "uttering sounds in the dark."

The simile alludes to Anni's emotions as the instinctive, unconscious reactions of an animal rather than the self-conscious awareness of a human being. The unconscious aspect of emotions is also manifested in Anni's gesture after hearing the sound. She puts her hand to her mouth as if surprised by her sudden, uncontrollable reaction. After the animal outburst, she is depicted going inside and beginning her familiar routines. It seems as if the automatic actions were partly conducted to calm the body and the mind: "And she went through the same motions and did the same things as on any other day, took off her rubber boots, set them side by side outside the door of the room, took off her scarf and work coat [...]" (S, 108).[85] Anni's tendency to stick to certain daily routines, even at a moment of emotional crisis, defines the essence of her earthly character, yet it also relates to the themes of self-knowledge and emotional detachment, appearing elsewhere in the novel. In the passage above, only a quick look in the mirror constitutes a deviation from the pattern of Anni's usual habits: "She combed her hair; the only unusual thing was that she combed her hair in front of the mirror" (ibid.).[86] The motif of the mirror is aligned with the moment of self-recognition, even though the act of mirroring, as well as the moment of self-recognition as such, is half-mechanical and constitutes only a fleeting instant before Anni continues her habitual routines.

Napoleon's confession at the spring party, where he talks about having "drifted onto the wrong track in his life" (S, 97),[87] has provided a premonition of trouble ahead. His "genuine amazement" ("vilpitön hämmästys") as the young farmer asks about the stolen tools makes the farmer hesitate to ask more, "even though he knew for sure; with his own eyes he had seen the man putting away screws and tools with his own supply" (S, 97).[88] The same gesture appears in a later scene, when Anni asks about the legality of Napoleon's alleged divorce: "Legal? Napoleon was *amazed*. His divorce was legal" (S, 114).[89] When Anni expresses her desire to know everything Napoleon is reluctant to talk about any "old things." Words only make everything more complicated. The talk about talk parallels the layered structures of mind-reading: "What should he have said to that? [...] He, Napoleon, considered *talk* and *talk about talk* nervewracking, and why speak about old matters you couldn't do anything about?" (S, 112)[90]

After the first confrontation, the depiction of the couple's daily routines shows their life returning to its normal track. The events of Anni's last summer are condensed into an iterative narration, which portrays the characters' habitual life. Napoleon seems to have changed his ways, as if he had been able to tame his inner beast: "That May, Napoleon built the threshing barn. Anni made a flower bed under the window; Napoleon turned the soil with the shovel and brought leaf mulch to the flower bed from the woods, from under the birches" (S, 116–117).[91] Napoleon is sowing the seeds of a fruitful relationship as he sows grass seeds in the courtyard. His unexpected behavior astonishes those on the farm: "[T]he other people in the house laughed and were surprised that Napoleon stayed home. And the people of the farm knew that twice already Napoleon had refused to drink" (*S*, 117).[92] He has promised to "start a new life" (*S*, 118).[93]

Another move from normality to disruption takes place after the short period of harmony. Anni comes to know the whole truth about Napoleon, even if the reader cannot be sure whether this is the whole truth. When Anni finds out that Napoleon is having an affair with a woman living in the city, she is angry, yet exhausted, tired of feeling anything:

"You are a bastard," Anni said in her calm, even voice.

"What's the matter with you?" Napoleon asked, almost with curiosity. What was wrong with her, standing there in front of him, staring at him as at an object, actually studying him. It made him nervous. He moved away from her, to the side.

"Are you sick? You're so pale. What are you talking about?"

Anni kept staring at the same place where the man had just been standing. The corners of her mouth curved downward. She kept nodding her head, her face, expressionless.

"Crazy. She's crazy," Napoleon repeated to himself. She's crazy, he thought.

"Like hell there's a horse. A whore in Helsinki."

Anni's mouth twisted, her head jerked as if on a rope that was being pulled. She looked at the floor.

She was that way for a minute before she lifted her head and her lips straightened. (*S*, 134–135)[94]

Both Anni's inner tension and her resignation are reflected in the mechanical movements of her body observed by Napoleon. Her head keeps nodding as if it were part of a marionette operated with strings. The comparison alludes to Anni's position as a puppet in a situation that is beyond her control. She feels tired, emptied of any emotion: "Hate? She didn't hate anyone or anything. She felt indifferent to everything. Last night she had still had the idea that she should have stayed in that place where she had been. Life was the same everywhere. 'What can you do about yourself? I can't change you, it's not my business'" (*S*, 136), she says to the man.[95] The episode concludes with a passage of dialogue that suggests the possibility of a productive exchange between the lovers. However, the absurdity of the situation also converts the romantic ideals of the classical love plot. When Napoleon expresses despair about his chaotic life and asks Anni what to do, Anni bursts out laughing: "Should I – am I the one who should know?" (*S*, 140)[96]

Another move from disruption to normality occurs after the couple's second argument, suggesting the stage of "reconciliation" in the romance plot. Anni's narrated memory indicates a change in Napoleon's habits. Napoleon's mistress living in the city no longer disrupts the balance of their lives. In Anni's mind, the conflicts of the past are distant, like a bad dream. The everyday life continues as if nothing had happened: "[T]he result was that they were again living as if nothing had happened. The man could come and go, the woman knew that he would come and go whether she wanted it or not. […] And Anni slept at night in peace" (*S*, 145).[97] The new balance between the lovers stems from Anni's knowledge and her acceptance of Napoleon's weaknesses. She can do nothing to change him.

Anni's inner peace is motivated by a fragile sense of new kind of certainty, which she is unable to fully acknowledge. The narrator articulates Anni's half-intuitive feelings as new routines are established in the relationship. In Anni's mind, Napoleon is like her shadow.[98] She senses his every movement and thought, but at the same time, the man next to her has become so close that it is difficult to see him anymore: "Anni looks at the man. The man does not turn his gaze from the newspaper, does not see the expression on the woman's face. The woman looks but doesn't really look. The man is like her own hand, like a shadow on the wall that is her own shadow. The man's talk is no longer strange to her ears, the man's habits aren't odd to her" (S, 145).[99] The intimacy of minds is reflected in the wordless communication between the couple. Anni can read the physical signs of Napoleon's emotions and she intuitively senses his mental states: "[S]he sensed the restlessness in the man; he wanted to go to the city; she had learned to understand what he was thinking" (S, 77).[100]

The acceptance of the other person "as he is" is also reflected in Anni's thoughts about Napoleon's childlike "whims," which she has learned to handle. The trivial details of the relationship reveal the subtle changes in the power dynamics between the couple. Anni pours milk into the cream Napoleon uses in his coffee, mixes margarine with the butter he puts on his bread, and makes sauce with the cheap sausage he claims he never eats. Previously, she had satisfied Napoleon's every whimsy, but as the relationship proceeds, "she pretends to believe and do what the man says, but she does as she sees fit" (S, 146).[101] The above description of the couple's everyday life includes an image used throughout the novel to depict the different stages of their relationship, namely, drinking coffee (Ahola 1989: 539–540). At apparently banal moments, incidents involving this trope become emotionally charged as they signify Anni's feelings of estrangement. Before leaving her previous place of service, "[s]he had made coffee for herself, and when the coffee was ready, poured it into her cup, and there was nothing except the cup that she squeezed in her hands and in the cup hot coffee, which kept them warm" (S, 45).[102] The coffee in the cup serves as an image of the stability of everyday life that keeps Anni in touch with herself as she keeps moving from place to place, unable to change the direction of her life.

The trope of coffee drinking is used to reveal the relationship between Anni and Napoleon, as Anni becomes gradually aware of the man's true nature. At the beginning of the affair, Anni confesses to the farmer's wife that no man has ever made morning coffee for her. As the couple begins to drink coffee every night in Anni's room, she makes sure that the drink in Napoleon's cup is hot and strong. Later, as the first conflicts arise, Anni puts the coffee cups on the table "like lifeboats on the waves" ("kuin pelastusveneet aalloille"), as if she were trying to save the remnants of her dreams (S, 109). When the coffee in Napoleon's cup gets cold after their argument, Anni pours the chilled drink into her own cup and serves him fresh coffee. In a burst of anger, Napoleon spills the drink. In silence, Anni observes "how the splashed coffee spreads and forks into streams flowing different directions across the red table. The coffee streams onto the floor, the stream turns into the sound of individual drops, the drops become fewer and stop" (*S*, 131–132).[103]

The scene of silencing voices illustrates Anni's alienation. In addition, the coffee (spreading on the table like forking rivers) serves as a figurative way to show the functions of the episodes prior to the turning point in the narrative, namely, Anni's death. The image represents the potential courses of the relationship: the future paths that finally lead to silence. Other incidents and episodes in *Se on sitten kevät* contain similar hints about the course of events. Their relevance becomes important in interpreting the subsequent parts of the novel, especially Napoleon's ambivalent actions after Anni's death. One of these episodes is the "fowling" scene, which, according to Anhava (2002/1967: 275), resembles the "meaningless, absurd episodes" ("'hullunkurinen' merkityksetön episodi") in life that stick in one's mind and are often narrated in everyday conversation: "this is what happened to me back then." However, the episode, which seems detached, depicts the couple's closeness as their minds go wild together. In the fowling scene, Anni and Napoleon are able to show their hysteria, superstitions, and fears openly.

At first, Anni and Napoleon thin the sounds coming from the upper part of the roof are caused by rats. Anni tries to rationalize the sounds, while calming Napoleon down: "It's like they're changing camp" (*S*, 121).[104] But Napoleon refuses to go back to sleep: "Where would they go, the man wondered. To think that he'd landed in a nest." (*S*, 122–123)[105] In addition to rats, there are the sounds of an imagined bird in the scene. In Karelian mythology, the bird is an animal of the anima, a reincarnation of the human soul that crosses the border from this world to the next at the moment of death. The image of the bird augurs Anni's death, but it also alludes to Napoleon's mental life: his feelings of being trapped in his current situation. Like the sounds of the rats' movements, the bird's call echoes the couple's future plans to leave the farm. When Anni suggests that they should build a fire in the stove to get the bird out, Napoleon is shocked: "The bird wouldn't understand what they wanted, that they were trying to save it. The bird would only keep hitting its beak until it bled, beat its wings against the chimney walls till they broke. How could the woman be so cruel, to torment the bird with smoke and fire!" (*S*, 127)[106] Eventually, Napoleon climbs onto the roof to release the bird, which in his imagination has gotten stuck inside the chimney.

The bird in the chimney is an early variation on Vartio's metaphor for her characters – or their imaginative minds – as birds trapped in the material world and a material body. The scene also suggests Anni's position as the motherly stabilizer of Napoleon's life, as his "savior." She is the one who forces Napoleon to see the chaos in his life. The attic space embodies the primitive depths of the human mind, resulting in irrational actions. The entire episode serves as a Jungian image of masculine and feminine archetypes of the collective unconscious.[107] The fowling scene reveals Napoleon's superstitious and fearful nature, which at first makes Anni feel superior: "[S]he, the woman, was not afraid" (*S*, 121).[108] Eventually, Anni becomes equally agitated, as the man's behavior feeds her fear. The next morning, in the light of day, the feeling of fear is replaced by a sense of existential estrangement and wonder. Anni looks at the bucket that has fallen from the roof:

> The woman went outside, stood still in the courtyard. She looked up at the roof, went to the back of the house, stood still at the foot of the ladder. Nettles covered the lowest steps entirely; only because of some broken stems could one believe that the man had been standing on the roof. The bucket had rolled down the heath and stopped against a stone. The woman went to the bucket, turned it over with her foot; there was still a handle left. She looked at the bucket. It was an object fallen from outer space, lost and abandoned. The night was gone. But there, black and bottomless, was the bucket on the flower-covered heath.
>
> That day turned into a hot one. Bees flew from flower to flower and the air hummed. The flowers hastened to bloom. (S, 132)[109]

In the description above, Anni's position seems to correspond to that of the bucket, the banal object "fallen from outer space, lost and abandoned." "Black and bottomless" it is juxtaposed both with the space surrounding the biosphere and with human beings as objects unable to control the number of their days. Like the bloom of nature, the span of a human life is short. Short too is the bloom of adult love, which Anni experiences right before her death.

The fowling scene contains other archaic images related to the portrayal of the collective unconscious. One is the tableau with Anni and Napoleon standing in the courtyard. The tableau draws on the imagery of folktales – the story of an old man and old woman setting out to coat the moon with tar. The movements of the moon and the contrast of light and darkness frame the scene:

> The moon had emerged from behind the cloud. The August night was black and warm. The figure of the man was large and pale against the sky and the forest; the woman on the ground below, her face looking up, a fireweed flower in her hand. Clouds moved across the sky and the moon came and went among them, appeared, slipped into hiding. They were like the old man and the old woman who set out to coat the moon with tar. (S, 129)[110]

The folktale depicts a human desire to get rid of the moonlight in order to perform questionable business without being seen. The irrationality and superstition of the human mind – the mind's dark spots – are reinforced by the reference to the folktale. In addition, the tableau alludes to past and future events in the story. As Napoleon plans to buy furniture, a glass-doored cabinet and a chandelier, for the renovated servants' room, Anni recalls an old nursery rhyme. An image, a riddle, is constructed of words: "[A]n old woman and an old man built a house. The old woman put pine twigs beneath the stairs; the old man did too. The old woman made a window; the old man did too. The old man climbed up on the roof, made a chimney, and the old woman did too" (S, 70).[111] The end of the imagistic riddle, which recalls the lovers' attempts to build a home, parallels Napoleon's actions: "[A]nd then the old man set out to fetch some water, fell into a hole, climbed out of the hole, fell into the hole, – and what was the rest? [–] and then there's a cat" (ibid.).[112]

The true picture taking form in Anni's nursery rhyme is not a cat, but Napoleon, an old man falling into a hole, not once, but twice. From the perspective of the stages of his and Anni's affair, Napoleon's elaborate plans appear to be merely castles in the air. Napoleon, who paints the old furniture in Anni's room red, brings color and vividness to Anni's life, yet his grandiose plans often seem empty, with no basis in reality. When Napoleon finds an announcement for the position of estate manager and cattle tender, he paints a colorful image of their future together: "a large estate, a mansion perhaps [...]" (S, 152).[113] Yet the counterfactual path suggested in the couple's plan to "start everything over from the beginning" (S, 156)[114] never actualizes in the textual universe. After Napoleon receives a letter from a new employer hiring them for the advertised positions, he finds Anni dead. In the dark of an autumn night, Napoleon hears distant voices coming from next door, but enters the room only the next morning – to find out that Anni has already gone.

The temporal landscape of the latter part of *Se on sitten kevät* appears highly uneven. Anni's death is passed over quickly in the narrative structure, almost as if it constituted only one incident among many others. The condensed, detached depiction of Anni's death gives an impression of flatness. This illusion is generated by manipulating the temporal structure typical of modernist narrative: accelerating or leaving gaps in relating crucial events.[115] Vartio uses the flatness of the narrative itself as a way of generating a shock effect. Modernist death scenes usually emphasize the ontological uncertainty of modern individuals. Death ends people's lives, but it does not stop time. Death breaks into the stream of life with no seeming connection to past or future events, generating a shock that is experienced by the readers when they encounter the unsentimental depiction of a character's sudden death, narrated as if in passing (cf. Kern 2011: 109–110).[116]

On the other hand, the characters' emotional reactions after the blow of Anni's death include some isolated, frozen moments that become more meaningful in the structure of the novel. The events immediately after the story's turning point are depicted from the perspective of the young farmer's wife on receiving a message from Napoleon about Anni's death. In the middle of night, she sees Napoleon's face at the window: "Napoleon emerged from the darkness; his face in the window was like a portrait on a black background" (S, 160).[117] The ekphrastic simile serves as a way of showing the mental associations of the farmer's wife. The contrast of dark and light reinforces the unreal atmosphere in the wake of a sudden death on the farm. Napoleon and the farmer's wife are described as acting like sleepwalkers as they enter the room in the servants' quarters. The portrayal of the departed woman parallels the sleeping woman pictured in the novel's beginning. The expression on Anni's face is surprised; her hands refuse to obey the farmer's wife, who tries to cross them over Anni's chest. The part in her hair stands out "like a bright line, like a river in a nighttime landscape" (S, 166).[118] The reader's last view of Anni is of her blackened toenails as the farmer's wife covers her body with a sheet. When the window is opened, the wind blows in and the scent of grass wafts through the air. Napoleon and the farmer's wife switch off the light, walk out of the building, and never look back.

Apart from these temporally highlighted episodes, the storyworld after the protagonist's death seems strikingly familiar. A summary of the events after the milkmaid's death is given from the collective perspective of the people on the farm. Anni's funeral appears to be merely a nuisance to her employers. Anni's daughter arrives to gather her mother's earthly possessions and then disappears. The passing of time is described as the beginning of winter, which brings a new milkmaid to the farm: "It had snowed the last days of November, and even though it had since thawed and the snow had begun to melt, the thaw had lasted only a few days and then frost had come. And it had snowed some more, and the weather had remained bright" (*S*, 271).[119] Whereas the death of the previous milkmaid was an unlucky coincidence, the arrival of the new milkmaid appears to be a stroke of luck, as she has been found "by chance" and sooner than anyone expected: "We only had to go two weeks without a milkmaid" (ibid.).[120] The above thought can be traced to the young farmer's wife, who after Anni's death realizes that she will be forced to go to the cowshed herself.

The co-existence of life and death is suggested also by some symbolic incidents in the latter part of *Se on sitten kevät*. One aftermath to the rupture in the story line is a depiction of the old farmer and his sudden awakening to enjoy his last bloom after the milkmaid's death. This sudden bloom is juxtaposed with the feelings of alienation in the young farmer's wife, as she listens to her distant voice, as if it were someone else's: "She controlled herself, listened to her own voice, her voice had been cracked, high-pitched, it hung in the air, dropped, vanished. No one heard" (*S*, 232).[121] The young woman's melancholic dream after the milkmaid's death serves as an echo of her anxiety. She dreams of traveling to the Riddarholm Church (in Stockholm), where deceased Swedish kings are brought back to life. The dreamer makes her own journey into the self and into the unconscious, but is still able to come back.

Chance and Coincidence. Breaking the Sequence of Everyday Life

In the contemporary readings of *Se on sitten kevät*, Anni's untimely death was often considered a symbol of the transitory nature of human life. In addition to invoking the universal tragedy of fate, the critics interpreted her death as an unfortunate coincidence, a freak of fortune, which cut short the love affair just before its actual fulfillment. The breach of the traditional plot was considered to be motivated by the novel's semantic focus. The "sense of necessity" of Anni's death served as the thematic and formal element enabling the modification of form without causing damage to the coherence of the story. According to Annamari Sarajas (1980/1957: 142), for instance, "[t]he theme of death determines the elements of the narrative, provides a sense of inevitability and unity to the events. The spiraling atmosphere of death determines the preliminary events and afterwards determines the collapse of the man left alone."[122] Hence, should we read the novel as a modification of a tragic love plot leading to the transcendental quest of the male protagonist or as a narrative of female development denying the reward of a happy-ending?

The structure of Vartio's first novel has largely been addressed by speculating on whether the unconventional plot (the "openness" of its form) was Vartio's initial intention or not. The novel's "unusual layout" ("epätavallinen sijoittelu"), with a division into two consecutive narratives, has been examined in conjunction with the novel's editing process, by weighing the potential effects of the added and the eliminated chapters in the final composition (Niemi 1995: 77; Särkilahti 1973: 100).[123] Anhava's commentary on the novel, however, indicates that the protagonist's death was an intended part of the story. Anni's "untimely" death is a key event that creates a "hinge" in the story structure: it reveals the emotional effects that Anni's disappearance from the fictional world has on the other characters or rather, the lack of any such effects (Anhava 2002/1967: 281). From this perspective, the structure of *Se on sitten kevät* seems to constitute a rescripting of the traditional romance plot by refusing to provide either marriage or death as the story's final image. The protagonist's death in the middle of the novel may be considered to reflect the "fictional escape route [...] away from entrapment in the romance of the love plot," as Dannenberg (2008: 228) has analyzed the "women's plots" in the twentieth century novels.

As Anhava emphasized in his commentary on *Se sitten kevät*, the meaning of the text is dependent on the ways in which the reader interprets the functions of its structure. Is Anni's death to be considered a chance event that ends a relationship that is doomed to end anyway, or it is a freak of fortune, separating lovers who are about to find their way in a chaotic world? In his re-reading of the novel, Anhava analyzed his earlier interpretation of the novel, published on the back cover of the book's original edition. The text stressed the turning point – Anni's death – as an event of pure chance, which strikes at the moment when the couple's intentions are finally in accord: "The wildly capricious, irresponsible mind of the unattached man and Anni's heavy earnestness are coming together [...] to construct the hope of a more stable future... It's about to come true when chance hits, as naturally and suddenly as ever in life, and puts an end to that dream."[124] In writing about the novel in 1967, after Vartio's death, Anhava set out to re-consider his former reading and expressed his doubts about the contingency function of the milkmaid's death. There seems to be some "added value" ("lisäarvo") in the novel, he now wrote, which is difficult to identify and explain. *Se on sitten kevät* is not only a sad story about two people "who find each other... too late" (Anhava 2002/1967: 279).[125] It seems to involve a tragedy that is related not as much to the love plot of the novel, but more to the depiction of the characters' mental existence. Only in this way can the relevance of the "second narrative" involving Napoleon be fully explained.

In the contemporary interpretations of *Se on sitten kevät*, two meanings attached to the etymology of "chance" were evoked in the readings of the novel's turning point. Both meanings emphasize the passive status of the characters rather than the intentional actors who could control the course of their lives. The first type refers to "actual" instances of chance, randomness as pure chance. The second type alludes to the presence of some hidden order or knowledge within the plot, an unfortunate coincidence in which fate masquerades as chance. The origins of the word "chance" imply the second meaning. The word derives from the Latin cadere, "to fall," which denotes the nature of fate as something that "befalls" – the result of a throw of the dice of destiny, which "falls" to an individual or an individual "falls" to his fate. This idea of "blind chance" is closely connected with the goddess Fortuna (or Providence), signifying destiny and chance, luck and goodwill apportioned out by some omnipotent being. In the predestined world, every event on a person's path is mapped out and predetermined before birth; everything happens for a reason. In this regard, the notion of "chance" has also been used as a euphemism for ignorance, a state of not-knowing or intentionally obscuring the cause. In literary texts, ignorance often results in tragic hubris or other effortless jousting with windmills.

The causal interrelations and their disruption in modernist narratives, such as Se on sitten kevät, are linked to the characters' thoughts involving chance, both accidental and random. Randomness, contingency, and ignorance are dramatized in the speculation by characters about their freedom of choice in interpreting outer events. These events are seen as resulting either from chance, accident, or fate, and can potentially thwart the outcome of the characters' actions. In the modernist novel, the causal-linear plot is often replaced by the integration of text by probabilistic causality or chance, reflecting the "arbitrariness of human destinies" (Richardson 1997: 42). Chance manifests itself in the denial of superstition and divine hope. Fate is no longer seen as pre-determined by gods, providence, or some other "causal-manipulative deity acting behind events," not even psychological or social explanation of cause and effect, as in realist narratives (Dannenberg 2008: 228). In modernist fiction, the backgrounding of causal explanations reflects the fundamentally random nature of life (Kern 2011: 63). The aversion to grand narratives stemmed from modernists' conception of the causal-linear design as a narrative form that eliminates the free will of the characters. If characters are controlled by omniscient narrators, then there is no room left for chance to occur within the fictional world. (Jordan 2010: 39–40) In this respect, the shift in causal explanation relates to modernist writers' preference for small episodes that "continue" even after the stories end.

The key factor in the coincidental constellations represented in modernist narratives is the human mind, the processes of cognition itself (Dannenberg 2008: 93, 228–229). As chance is liberated from its religious origins, it is often attached to the existentialist dialectics of fate and free will. The freedom of choice generates new kinds of anxieties: detachment and indecision. How does one make decisions in a meaningless universe in which there is no primal cause, only chaos and contingency that thwart one's intentions? (Jordan 2010: xi, 22) The chaos of the world after a war recasts any human endeavors, leading to passive escapes into the comforts of everyday life, habits, and repetition. Self-created patterns bring modern individuals closest to freedom of choice. (Ibid.: 76)

In Se on sitten kevät, Anni's fate oscillates between the "blind" and the "pure" instances of chance. Anni seems to acknowledge her approaching end subconsciously, "as if it were a disease whose place and name one cannot specify." From the perspective of those left behind, on the other hand, a death appears more as pure chance (or tragic coincidence), which strikes unexpectedly. Right after Anni's death, Napoleon travels to the city to buy a coffin. As he sits in the bus, his thoughts and memories are depicted as simultaneously monotonous and streaming – like the events of life itself. Napoleon's flow of thoughts implies his frozen state or inner numbness: something has "fallen on him like rain."

> Napoleon looked out the window. The fields, houses, roads, people were gliding past like a filmstrip that keeps showing the same image. If you turned your eyes away, then back again, it was still the same. Water streamed from the skies, trees roads houses people streamed like water – a middle-aged woman was walking along the road, wearing a dark coat, a bag in her hand. Napoleon looked at the woman – his memory reached for someone who had been wearing a dark coat, someone who had been standing by the road holding a bag. Napoleon turned to the passenger sitting next to him expecting that person to speak, to say something about what *had fallen on him like rain*. (S, 184–185)[126]

The obscure images embody Napoleon's feelings of uncertainty and confusion after Anni's death. His perceptions of the world constitute a stream of images resembling a filmstrip, "showing the same image." The analogy is based on the parallelism between human perception and artistic representation characteristic of Vartio's texts. In the mental stream the images lose their individual character and fuse into a single image. The words signifying the objects of Napoleon's absent-minded gaze are no longer separated by punctuation marks: "Water streamed from the skies, trees roads houses people streamed like water." His mind is full of fleeting images that simultaneously circle around some persistent association: "Napoleon looked at the woman – his memory reached for *someone who* had been wearing a dark coat, *someone who* had been standing by the road holding a bag." Even if the content of the memory evoked by the unknown woman is not explained, the female figure clearly brings to mind memories of Anni and her absence. Anni's earthly journey has ended, but the flow of life keeps moving. Only Napoleon seems unable to continue living. By occupying himself with the arrangements for Anni's funeral, he tries to keep going in a situation that has "fallen on him like rain."

According to Leland Monk (1993: 1–2), chance is always the protagonist's fate: in the narrative design, the plot turns into a character's lot in life. Elaborating on Monk's ideas, Jordan argues that from the perspective of the reader chance does not "'appear from the heavens'; it is embedded in the predetermined narrative structure of the text" (Jordan 2010: viii). However, if *any* narrative defies a true picture of the unpredictable "stuff" of everyday life, the representation of chance may involve something analogous: "[O]ne is never really writing about chance itself, but what chance can tell us through its refracting, distorting lens," Jordan (2010: xii) writes. In the modernist novel, the very acknowledgement of the inability of narrative to re-create chance "with mimetic truthfulness" results in semantic ambivalence. The poetics of chance becomes a part of the fascination of modernist texts: "[I]n its own representations it always contains the knowledge of the impossibility of that representation" (ibid.: viii).

As a predetermined event in the novel's storyworld, Anni's death, of course, is no true chance, but intentionally *written* into the story structure by Vartio. The tension between chance and fate in *Se on sitten kevät* derives from aesthetic "determinism" rather than from a deterministic worldview. As a chance event, Anni's death serves as a hinge that ends the love plot and splits the story into two separate but equal story lines. Before Anni's death, Napoleon is convinced of his ability to change the course of his life. After having drifted too long, Napoleon considers himself as finally being "free." He intends "to do something, for once [...] It's time to get his life in order at last" (*S*, 150–151).[127] Paradoxically, Napoleon's sense of necessity foretells Anni's death, which eventually changes the course of his life – toward the unexpected: "But now it's over," Napoleon assures Anni; "it has to end [...]" (*S*, 151; 157).[128]

Whereas chance is conceived as an event having "no identifiable cause and no particular meaning" (Reith 1999: 157), coincidence can be described as "a constellation of two or more apparently random events in space and time with an uncanny or striking connection," as Dannenberg (2008: 93) defines the concept.[129] In the modernist novel, as in *Se on sitten kevät*, coincidences are often actualized as negative coincidences, in which the intended intersections of objects in the narrative world are randomly thwarted.[130] Negative coincidences always evoke two counterfactual, diverging paths: the actualized and the alternative path, which is never fulfilled. In *Se on sitten kevät*, the unactualized path is related to the couple's potential future together, affecting the interpretation of the entire novel. From the vantage point of Anni's disappearance, the reader may evaluate the real possibilities for the future of the relationship from the past perspective of Anni and from the perspective of the present moment experienced by Napoleon. The story continues as the narrative of his lonely journey. The novel's protagonist needs to exit the fictional world in an untimely way, so that the consequences of her disappearance can be shown in a more illuminating way.

Napoleon's behavior after Anni's death is marked by ambivalence, which relates to the narrative strategy of not letting the reader see inside the man's head. His actions after Anni's death suggest that he is drifting back to his old habits. He is depicted flirting with the new milkmaid, having drinks, and spending money in the restaurant after having borrowed from the farmer to cover the costs of Anni's funeral. The scene in the funeral home is revealing in many respects. Napoleon's experience of a "fall" (as the mortician announces the price of the coffins) suggests the direction of his life: "He stood for a moment as if he had tumbled down from a world that was better than this world, in which he was again, and looked the man in the eye, the man who was a salesman" (*S*, 201).[131] In the scene of mind-reading related to Napoleon's fall, the mortician (the "salesman") realizes that he has offended his customer by letting his doubt show in his voice. Napoleon's performance as being in mourning may be half pretense, but the salesman, the priest, and Anni's daughter, who appear on the scene after Anni's death, all seem hollow, lacking any true compassion for Anni.

In *Se on sitten kevät*, the construction of "open form" as an ambivalence of meanings is related to Napoleon's inexplicable behavior in the randomness of his actions. Probable cause in the modernist novel often involves disinterested acts that are poorly or incompletely explained, if explainable at all. However, even if the reasons for the man's actions are not foregrounded, the reader's cognitive desire for causal explanation brings in strains of causality. In this respect, the actions depicted in narrative can never be acts motivated by "nothing." The unreadable in Napoleon's character evokes wonder in the readers and holds them captive. Why is Napoleon acting like he is? In analyzing the novel after a ten-year hiatus, Anhava acknowledged a particular detail in the description of Napoleon's mental state after Anni's death. Napoleon has become mentally paralyzed, escaping painful reality by lapsing into a state of sleep and oblivion. Until he becomes aware of his numbness: "But he already knew that *the sorrow* he would have liked to feel and that he nevertheless feared *did not exist*" (S, 237).[132]

Anhava (2002/1967: 280–281) considered Napoleon's recognition of his own lack of sorrow as a sign that he realizes his loss, which he acknowledges now after Anni has gone. True affection had been within his reach. The cut-off roots that "realize they are dead" can therefore be read as an indication of Napoleon's final realization of his hollowness. The long period of waiting that follows Napoleon's seemingly unmotivated actions parallels the "sticky feeling" that spreads and contaminates his whole being and the surrounding world: "And he had been overtaken by disgust, he felt disgust because nothing came, nothing happened, a sticky feeling just spread over everything, it had spread all around, into things, into his thoughts, into his own body" (S, 236).[133] The mental experience of flatness is compared to a physical sensation of stickiness that intensifies and reproduces itself with every movement of the body. Paradoxically, the feeling of flatness is revealed to be the very thing that Napoleon tries to suppress, making him escape painful reality: "He didn't exist to himself as he lay silent" (ibid.).[134]

Napoleon's indecision is reinforced by his actions, as he tries to get back on his feet and get to work again. His despair shows in his attempts to repair the stall door. Napoleon's hammer strikes are uncertain and the nails are skewed. He straightens a nail, and strikes again with anger, but the nail is "hopelessly skewed" (S, 241).[135] All of his actions seem to make the situation even worse: "He looked at the last piece of board he had nailed. The board made the whole stall look confusing, as if he should have kept going, or as if something had broken off." (S, 243).[136] Napoleon's every attempt to go back to his old routines seems to fail. After Anni's death, something has broken in him, and Napoleon doesn't know how to fix it.

In the later part of the novel, Napoleon's future paths are suggested in several images of silent and empty landscapes. He feels the road freezing and hardening under his feet, "the road replies to [his] steps" (S, 256).[137] The same image returns later, when Napoleon escapes into the dark: "[The new milkmaid] stood up, came to the window, but Napoleon was already walking along the road, not looking back, he felt the night air in his nostrils" (*S*, 270).[138] The trope of the road draws in the themes of leaving and not looking back that presage Napoleon's actual departure at the novel's end. The act of leaving is a conventional sign that indicates that the story has reached its end. Napoleon's disappearance is made definite by different variations on the "never-looking-back" motif, which has a long history among the conventions of ending a narrative. Attached to negation – he *never* came back – it becomes a *topos* typical of the modernists' "open form" (Bonheim 1986: 140).

In addition to Anni's death, the trope of leaving is among those compositional aspects that led to the search for the novel's original design. According to Niemi (1995: 77), the manuscript may have been meant to end with chapter 22, the depiction of Napoleon walking in the bright, freezing night. The motifs of a journey and a road seem to mark the point at which the novel is "empt[ied] of meaning, freez[ing] the world" ("tyhjenee merkityksistä, pysäyttää maailman"). Accordingly, Anni's death was pushed to a later, more conventional point in the story. In the final design, the play with the conventions of closure generate the "second narrative," which, in Niemi's interpretation, does not provide any variation on the first narrative: the second part of the story provides only "fragments of the eternal incompleteness of experience" ("fragment[teja] kokemisen ikuisesta keskeneräisyydestä"). (Ibid.)

Vartio's *Se on sitten kevät* is one of those novels that, according to Anhava, demonstrates the ideal design of the modernist narrative, the "open form" in its structure. In his essay "Kohti avointa muotoa" (Towards an Open Form, 1959), Anhava elaborated on his concept. The open form is an artistic composition that has "no clear situation of beginning or end, no causal plot" and has "an ambivalence of meaning" (Anhava 2002/1959: 249).[139] Even if the novel is made of seemingly traditional story elements, the "reality being constructed by the mind in Vartio's novel" ("Vartion romaanista mieleen lukeutuva todellisuus") is something unique:

> The coming together and parting of Anni and Napoleon leave the reader to wonder a long time. Both of their pasts and one of their futures are completely open, and in the end it is hard to say which is gone, the woman who died or the man who remains in life. Perhaps the most defining sign of the open form in this book is the fact that, although the reader can clearly see the author's sympathy toward the woman, she does not oblige the reader to feel the same way nor does she in any way strive to elevate the woman or explain the man or assess the causes and relative importance of events: the world is not this or that, it just is. (Anhava 2002/1967: 250)[140]

The idea of truthfulness, in Anhava's conception, seems to refer to the vividness of form, but as much to the vividness of the worldview constructed in the text. Anhava emphasized the importance of the artist's own vision with regard to the portrayal of the world "as it is." After having refused to give any fixed explanation of his concept of "open form," Anhava ended up clarifying his ambivalent definition by providing a passage from a discussion between a Chinese skeptic, the philosopher Chuang Tzu, and the logistician

Hui Tzu. The openness of form in *Se on sitten kevät* resembles the effect that this parable has on the reader:

> Chuang Tzu and Hui Tzu were strolling along the dam of the Hao River when Chuang Tzu said, "See how the minnows come out and dart around where they please! That's what fish really enjoy!"
>
> Hui Tzu said, "You're not a fish – how do you know what fish enjoy?"
>
> Chuang Tzu said, "You're not I, so how do you know I don't know what fish enjoy?"
>
> Hui Tzu said, "I am not you, so I certainly don't know what you know. On the other hand, you're certainly not a fish – so that still proves you don't know what fish enjoy!"
>
> Chuang Tzu said, "Let's go back to your original question, please. You asked me *how* I know what fish enjoy – so you already knew I knew it when you asked the question. I know it by standing here beside the Hao."[141]

Chuang Tzu's "illogical" answer, which challenges the logical thinking of the person asking the question, can be interpreted as the foundation of the open form itself as an image of pure, boundless consciousness. Sensing the emotions of other sentient beings is possible only by looking at them as they evoke recursive, responding emotions in us. This intuitive "knowing," however, simultaneously shows us the limits of our knowledge as other living beings are potentially only artifacts of our subjective, delusive minds.

Instead of proposing rational, logical thinking as the key to the problem of knowledge, the parable invites the reader to *feel* with the other, or even more radically, to *become* the other. Vartio's novel, accordingly, challenges the readers' routine ways of looking at things by inviting them to experience "how it feels to be someone else." Open form means that the reader is left amazed by "Anni's 'truth'" ("Annin 'totuus'"): "Don't ask me what it is. It is that I felt myself more real while reading Anni," Anhava (2002/1967: 282–283) observed.[142] With the power of a concrete example, Anhava tried to explain the quality of open form itself as a composition defying any articulated, fixed meaning.[143] The "spell" and "truth" of Vartio's novel is its ability to transcribe the silence, the ambiguous quality of human life. Her novel challenges the readers' habits of looking at things by making the readers feel that the reality is more real than before: "The novel is truly an open form, it can be interpreted many ways and carries the mind in many directions, in spite of its seemingly clear story line that ends with the finality of death" (ibid.: 282).[144] The reader is given the possibility of reading and sensing the character's world, her or his microcosm, as it is, as an alternative, possible world.

In the end, both Anni and Napolepon's detoured awakenings are dominated by "structures of repetition rather than structures of progression." The structural "deviations" in *Se on sitten kevät* illustrate the cyclic, eternal recurrence of human existence, which brings coherence to the novel's composition, itself forming a full circle. Whereas the story begins as Anni arrives at a strange house, it ends as Napoleon leaves behind the very same landscape. In the final scene, Napoleon returns to the farm, settles his debts, and disappears again: "He spent his night in the room and left for the city in the morning; he never came back" (*S*, 279).[145] The themes of homelessness, detachment, and estrangement are reinforced by the fluctuation of leaving and returning, fulfilling and emptying, life and death reflected in the novel's structure and its imagery. This double-faced quality of life is signified by the still-life composition embedded in the representation of Anni's observations the first time she enters the farmhouse. On the porch are pieces of a slaughtered animal and baked cheeses steaming near the window: "A cow had calved" (*S*, 12).[146] The *vanitas* composition becomes an artistic reminder of the inevitability of death and the dawn of new life manifested in the novel's design.

3. Emotions of the Body. A Lingering Awakening in *Mies kuin mies, tyttö kuin tyttö*

> There's a mirror in my hand, but it doesn't show
> my face.
> That mirror doesn't give me my face.
> When I raise it to eye level,
> I see only a landscape[1]
>
> – Marja-Liisa Vartio: "A Woman and a Landscape"

In *Mies kuin mies, tyttö kuin tyttö*, the "typical" story of a young girl becoming pregnant by a married man is narrated in an understated, almost unemotional way. This novel too begins in medias res, in the middle of the story. Leena has met a man (sometimes referred to as "K"), and she already knows what the reader does not: that the man has a wife and two daughters. At the beginning of the novel, the image of a bough (a frequent motif in Imagist poetry) is used to introduce the fictional world and its two inhabitants who are interacting within the fictional space:

> The man broke a branch from the tree, swung it and dropped it onto the ground. The branch caught and rocked on two dry brown grass stalks. The man moved his leg, the grass shifted, and the branch fell out of sight. The girl had followed the pointless series of motions with her gaze. (*MT*, 5)[2]

The depiction of the man playing with the bough illustrates how Leena's "pointless" motions are portrayed in the novel as she wanders from one life crisis to another. The novel's overall tone reflects young Leena's way of being in the world. She observes the events of her life from a distance, as if everything were happening to someone else. Even when Leena is aware of her inner states, she often ends up falling silent, unable to articulate or express her deepest feelings. To show Leena's aimless wandering on her way to self-determination, Vartio resorts to subdued narration, but the novel's acclaimed "dryness" or "asceticism" (Laitinen 1965: 623–624, Holappa 1959: 34) is not because of the subject matter. It turns out to be a question of technique together with an objective style of writing, which Vartio uses to portray the ambivalence of Leena's inner life. The tone of the characters' voices in the novel may be reserved and silenced, but there is still an emotional component. The novel portrays Leena's powerful, sometimes even overwhelming, inner pains and desires, which are difficult for her to perceive or control.

Knowledge of the man's prior commitments is the first complication in the relationship, and there is more to come. After a long period of indecision over the future of their affair, Leena discovers that she is pregnant. All the key experiences in Leena's life – the adulterous affair, her sexual maturity, recognition of the pregnancy and its progression – are portrayed as if Leena does not fully grasp what is going on. She is depicted drifting in an odd state of indecision as if she were asleep – awake, yet unaware of her actual situation. These periods of unawareness and apathy alternate with phases of rapidly changing emotions, as the tension between the self and the constraints of the outer world grows too strong to bear. As the pregnancy proceeds, Leena leaves home, moves to the city and gradually learns to see her situation and herself more clearly. Leena's epistemic path involves her awakening that occurs both outwards and inwards. This journey into the social world and into the self, however, is structured as a circle rather than as a linear-causal line of progression. Leena's self-revelation actualizes as a gradual, lingering awakening, but finally leads to her resistance and survival, characteristic of the endings in the twentieth-century female Bildungsromane (cf. Felski 1989: 130).[3]

Leena's journey to self-determination oscillates between the lingering and digressive paths of self-discovery. As in Vartio's other novels, the sequences of cause and effect are frequently materialized as alternating periods of arousal and passivity, which leave open the possibilities for a final self-resolution. A character's intermittent withdrawal from the world is typical of Vartio's young characters, who are still in the process of growing: their regression is parallel to the behavior of children who choose to live in their imaginary worlds while escaping painful realities. In contrast to the life paths of Vartio's full-grown characters, however, the cyclic patterns of Leena's life seem to conclude with a more optimistic view on the possibilities of personal freedom and self-determinacy.

In this chapter, I approach *Mies kuin mies, tyttö kuin tyttö* by examining Leena's embodied emotions as manifestations of the random processes of nature taking place within, beyond her full cognition and control. First, I analyze the "natural forces" of physical emotions in the context of Leena's relation to the man. These embodied sensations are linked to the classic romance plot, which provides the foundation for the novel's emotional story structure. Leena is unable to explain her feelings and she struggles to control her emotions in public. The resulting compositions of mind-reading involve strategic planning and rational calculation, which contrast with the latent processes of the embodied mind. Second, I examine these inaccessible processes in scenes of mental landscaping by analyzing psycho-analogies and other evocations. They add to the allegorical reading of Leena's evolution: her withdrawal to the inner self and nature, characteristic of the narratives of female self-discovery. Moreover, I read these projections of the self in relation to the split in the self, with Leena's mental space portrayed from within, divided into two realms. Finally, I explore the cyclic patterns of the emotional story structure in the context of Leena's detoured Bildung, and then, with regard to the characters' life paths, as modifications of the typical paths of "any girl" and "any man."

A Cold Fog Rising. Veiled Minds in Interaction

In the following discussion of the emotional story structure of *Mies kuin mies, tyttö kuin tyttö*, I examine the processes of mind-reading, both through the actual readers' readings of Vartio's enigmatic characters as well as the characters' readings of the other minds they encounter within the storyworld. The mechanisms of mind-reading in *Mies kuin mies, tyttö kuin tyttö* serve as an illuminating example of the mental functioning that contributes to the configuration of the plot. From the perspective of the characters, the goal of the narrative "game" is to alter the relations between worlds in order to make the private worlds (wishes, fantasies, and knowledge) coincide with the actual world to the highest possible degree. The possibility of private worlds to reflect other private worlds can lead to infinite recursive embeddings, as the characters try to reason their actions according to the plans they read in the minds of others. They try to predict the alternating curves in others' plans and adapt their own actions to correspond to these changes. (Ryan 1991: 119–120) [4]

In the depiction of Leena's mental life, the epistemological effects of temporarily or permanently missing information affect the interpretation of the unreadable that Vartio establishes in her storyworld. These epistemic gaps affect the way the reader perceives the chronological and causal chains of mental events and actions involving the affair.[5] The first cause of Leena's emotional distress – the adulterous quality of her affair – is revealed to the reader only by the gradual exposition of Leena's thoughts. At the beginning of the novel, the origin of the uneasiness between Leena and the man is implied, but not explained: "They had come once again to *that thing* which always silenced them when they remembered *it*, and raised something like a cold fog between them" (*MT*, 51).[6] The unspeakable, "that," is later revealed to be the man's marriage. The impenetrability, or rather the selectiveness, of Leena's mind here serves the purpose of suspense. In the narration, there are gaps marked by Leena's busy thoughts about the man's tendency to fall silent and distant on occasion. Toward the end of the second chapter, Leena's intuitions finally coalesce into more definite ideas in the depiction of her thoughts. These ideas materialize as rhetorical questions embedded in a narrated monologue: "But the girl wondered why the man did not want to talk. Was he ashamed of something? Was he ashamed of himself, the fact that he was married, his wife? Whenever they were talking and found themselves brushing against the man's marriage, he fell silent or began to talk about something else" (*MT*, 53).[7]

In her second novel, Vartio uses both techniques of mind presentation, namely, understatement and the drama of mind-reading, to portray the interactions between the characters' private worlds. Leena sees her own insecurity and emotional hesitation mirrored in the man's behavior. The lack of genuine communication forces her to guess the contents of the man's mind. Likewise, the reader is forced to become a "captive mind-reader," both with regard to Leena's veiled mind as well as to the man's. Leena declares a desire for pure, raw communication. She wants to "show that he could talk straight with her, with no embroidering" (*MT*, 58).[8] Yet in the end, she considers the relationship a game that requires deceit to be played successfully. First, she acts indifferent, then she withdraws when the man tries to approach her, and later she speculates about his lost affections when he becomes distant. The dynamics of the relationship as a game are embodied in a playful battle acted out between the two characters in the novel's third chapter. The episode illustrates what Vartio (1996: 40) called "erotic play of distancing and coming nearer" ("erootti[nen] etääntymisen ja lähentymisen leikki"). Leena coaxes the man to dance with her, and later the dance turns into a physical struggle:

> The girl tried to get free of his hands, she wanted to win, even though it was just a game. They struggled, each looking at the other, and the girl strained to get free, winning had become important, her body was tense. But his hands held her tightly though she slyly pretended to have given in, lay still in place, and then suddenly tried to wrench free; and this continued until the girl started laughing and relaxed. (*MT*, 66–67)[9]

Leena plays the game as if she were testing the man, trying to pit herself against his strength. The motions of the body correspond to the fluctuations of her mental state as they move back and forth. Even if Leena refuses to be the "prey" ("saalis"), which finally stops "pulling" away from the man's hands (as the narrator suggests), on some unconscious level she seems to want the game to turn into something more earnest and bare. She challenges the man to tell her who she really is: "What, what am I then? What am I like, tell me?" (*MT*, 21)[10] The man, however, is unable to give an answer. His lack of determination (not the marriage itself) seems to be what bothers Leena the most. She "knows" the man is unable to tell her who she is and who they are, which results in her own indetermination.

The approaching and distancing results in cyclic patterns of indecision that serve as the structural pattern of the love plot. The intermental breakdowns of the romance plot typically involve misreadings resulting from the lovers' lack of knowledge of one another's state of mind. Another cause for misunderstanding is the characters' misreading of their own minds, not realizing their affection for each other. These traditional love patterns are modified in *Mies kuin mies, tyttö kuin tyttö*, in which the reader witnesses the strategic play, but is rarely informed about the true quality of the characters' emotions.[11] The game played in a love affair demands strategic movements, yet Vartio's players are stuck in their positions: "It was like they were moving pieces back and forth on a game board [...] One of them moved a piece from a black square to a white, and the other moved it back again" (*MT*, 230).[12] The words are "like pawns on the game board" ("kuin pelilaudan nappuloita"), passed from one to another, "empty and light" ("tyhjinä ja kevyinä"), because they have become devoid of meaning (ibid.). The obstacle to the love union materializes in the existence of another lover, the man's wife. The unspeakable haunts Leena, who feels the presence of the man's wife as if she were actually standing between them, as if she "were looking contemptuously at her and holding tight to the man" (*MT*, 53).[13] Leena's mental image of the man's wife is an untouchable, yet still materialized "substance" that embodies the mental barrier between the lovers. Both words and silence constitute a screen, a "cold fog," that blocks true communication. The unspeakable is reflected in the depiction of their physical expressions: "They sat in silence, avoiding looking at each other" (*MT*, 10).[14]

The characters' craving to read the unreadable minds of others catalyzes the reader's reading of these readings. Thus, the drama of non-reading becomes a function of characterization: the reader has an opportunity to read the mind of the captive would-be reader (see Abbott 2008: 451). Vartio portrays Leena's emotional life mainly through her responses to the man's actions and reactions. On the other hand, the novel's scenes of mind-reading stem from the secrecy of the affair, as both Leena and the man speculate on who knows what only they are supposed to know. The man says of his wife: "I don't *know* what she *thinks*, but she already *knows*, at least something" (*MT*, 140).[15] Leena in turn tries to figure out what her family knows. Her gestures are planned to make her sister speak: "[Leena] turned around to look at her and gave a laugh to get the other to talk more, for she wanted to *know* if she *knew* something, and what" (*MT*, 95).[16] The sister's answer indicates that she may indeed know something, but Leena does not know how much her parents know: "I did guess, but you guess what they'll say when they find out" (ibid.).[17] The speculative structures of mind-reading are connected to the rational planning of one's actions. These speculations are needed, for the relationship needs to be concealed from others.

The constellations of mind-reading pertain to potential social stigmas related to the adulterous affair. The social ambivalences are manifested in the tension between the private emotions and their public expressions, since the individual and the collective perspectives on the affair differ dramatically. The tension is also reflected in the misreading between the lovers: "I do *know* what you *are thinking*," Leena says, as she claims to know the man's mind: "Do you *think* that I *don't understand*? [...] you are just wondering how to get rid of me" (*MT*, 62).[18] The man has tried to explain his reasons for keeping the relationship secret. He addressed the stereotype of an innocent young girl being seduced by an older man by invoking the collective prejudice: "There was no point in giving people something to talk about for nothing. The girl was so young that she didn't yet understand what people were really like. No one would understand anything else about them being together, only that he had seduced a young girl [...]" (*MT*, 63).[19]

The interpretation of Leena's subdued mental life is complicated by her tendency to struggle to disguise the public expressions of her emotions. Leena's "sideways glances" – her awareness of the man's eyes on her as she tries to hide her emotions – manifest her fears and insecurity with respect to him: "She didn't dare look to the side so as not to reveal herself, reveal that she was hoping the man would touch her" (*MT*, 47).[20] While hypothesizing and speculating on the man's intentions, Leena becomes estranged from her own inner voice. Every now and then, the narrator lets the reader see the motivations behind Leena's changing moods. And not only are the emotions articulated, but also her struggles to repress them. Her inner voice tells her to "feel nothing," to control her emotions: "The man's helplessness made the girl laugh, and she didn't feel anything, *didn't want to feel anything* but that the man was helpless, he liked her and he didn't know what to do" (*MT*, 71).[21]

The difficulties of mind-reading on the part of the reader derive from the challenges of keeping track of Leena's fluctuating emotions. The fleeting quality of her thoughts is manifested in the narrator's references to her mental content. After the sexual encounter, Leena's mind is full of unspecified impressions: "When they had finished, *this* and *that* came to mind" (*MT*, 69).[22] Leena's changing moods vary from apathy to affection and revulsion, which make it harder to grasp her true intentions. From time to time, Leena does not feel affection, but rather disgust and contempt for the man: "The girl wondered whether she was the one who should decide something. And for a moment the man was almost repulsive to her" (*MT*, 22).[23] The man's indecision makes Leena second-guess her own feelings: "But the girl had already felt that the man's hand in her hand felt foreign, as if it were only there because she was holding onto it" (*MT*, 44).[24]

The intensity of emotions, ranging from ardor to apathy, affects narrative semantics, because passions are more likely to lead to action than are "weak emotions," even though some characters tend to control their passions more diligently than others (Doležel 1998: 68). In *Mies kuin mies, tyttö kuin tyttö*, the very thought of the man's inability to make any real decision makes Leena cautious and on guard. She is unable to let herself fully experience any devotion to the point of denying that her emotions even exist. When the man asks whether Leena wants him to get a divorce, she reads his unconscious intentions as if she were able to "hear" thoughts that he himself is unaware of:

> She didn't answer. She had scarcely understood the meaning of the words. And even though she herself had wanted to bring the man to say those words, now that they were spoken she couldn't answer, because she didn't know what she should say.
> She could feel that the man was making another turn. And she knew that the words just spoken had not meant what the man thought he was saying, and it occurred to her that the man might also feel bad at times. (*MT*, 70–71)[25]

Leena's attributions to the man's mind resemble the mechanisms of her self-restraint encountered by the reader as her motivations gradually become visible. Here, however, Vartio represents Leena's reflections in the course of mind-reading, as she realizes the difficulty of the man's situation and identifies with his inner pain: "the man might also feel bad at times." Leena considers the man to be unaware of the real motivations affecting his decisions: he is being pulled in opposite directions. Guilt leaves no room for other feelings. As an outside observer, Leena may be able to evaluate the man's true emotional state more accurately than the man himself.

In the unsentimental scenes of romance, Vartio addresses the different perspectives on the self, on the other, and on the world. The man's observation about photography at the beginning of the novel turns into a metafictional commentary on the manipulation of views of the world: "The man explained that one can do many things with photography just by taking the picture from a particular angle" (*MT*, 13).[26] Leena's vivid imagination enhances her ability to empathize: she is able to see the world from the man's perspective. Her imagining, however, becomes one of those aspects that also challenges the true understanding between the lovers. Imagining and spontaneous empathizing are related to Leena's immaturity, at least from the man's perspective: "The man didn't understand her imaginings, but treated them like the talk of a child" (*MT*, 18).[27] Leena naivety in the man's eyes, however, is potentially only Leena's speculation as the passage of narrated monologue does not specify the source of the original thought. The aspect of imagining is linked to the difference in the couple's ways of seeing the world, illustrated by their conversation in the forest. There are stakes that, according to the man, look like soldiers; according to Leena, they are "like big birds" ("kuin suuria lintuja"). The man laughs shortly and then looks at the stakes again: "[H]e changed his mind: you could think them birds, if you looked at them that way and wanted to see them as birds" (*MT*, 46).[28]

The man's laughter signals his amusement, as Leena confesses her childish ways of "seeing" things that do not exist. Thus, the trope of birds, the most prominent image in Vartio's oeuvre, serves here as a symbol of excessive imagining. However, the ability to step into another person's skin and change perspective is also the key to human understanding: "I think I see in you the same thing you see in me," Leena tells the man (*MT*, 64).[29] At the beginning of their affair, Leena has been able to touch him, to share his inner pain. The association of stakes with soldiers relates to the man's "scar," which was caused by a flying object in a war. As an embodied war wound, the scar is manifest in the man's silence, which is shared with the girl: "And the pain surged anew because of those hands and that scar; she had found them while touching the man in the dark" (*MT*, 55).[30] The glimpse of Leena's thoughts offers essential information about the psychological motivation behind her varying impulses: she is afraid that the man does not truly care for her.

Later on, Leena's states her doubts frankly when the man finishes a job and prepares to return to his family. The discussion preceding the lovers' separation illustrates the differences in their views on human relations and life in general. The couple's discussion modifies the classical scenes of dialogues between lovers at the stage of negotiation, leading either to reconciliation or separation:

> "Do you think something of us will be left behind in this place? Do you think that when other people are living here and everything is different, something of us will remain? […]"
> "Do you think nothing will be left behind?"
> "I don't know, I can't answer."
> "But say something… Don't you believe that this stone and the rocks and that water and the moon, won't some part of me remain in them, since I want it to?"
> "What do you think?"

"I'm certain of it. And then other people will sit here, on this very stone, and they will wonder who sat here before them."

"Yes, the world doesn't end here if you think about it like that. I guess people always feel the same things in the same way."

"But I feel like you don't really care for me at all; you only think you do."

The girl didn't remember who was sitting next to her. When a match illuminated the man's face, she saw it. The man disturbed her; she didn't want to hear any more. (*MT*, 78)[31]

Leena can see the man's face by the light of the match for only a second, just as she can see only glimpses of man she recognizes and can relate to: "When a match illuminated the man's face, she saw it." Both the mystery of the man's inner world and the intuitive "knowledge" of his mind evoke wonder and anxiety in Leena. At the moment of goodbye, Leena projects her personal feelings onto the man by reflecting on the material world on a more general level. The eradication of personal feeling serves as Leena's way of addressing her worries about the future of their affair. She wants to know whether a part of her will remain in the man's memories. Her questions seem to arise on the spur of the moment, as if in the course of being spoken. By saying what she says, she does not seem to be clear, even to herself, about what she really means, which enhances the possibilities for misunderstanding. In Leena's mind the man's words ("I guess people always feel the same things in the same way") are manifestations of his lack of emotion: "But I feel like you don't really care for me at all; you only think you do." Leena finally expresses the thoughts that have been weighing on her mind right from the beginning.

The darkness surrounding the man illustrates "the known unknown" established in the constellations of mind-reading: Leena intuitively senses she does not know enough. The potential mirroring of minds is expressed in Leena's earlier words, which seem to be the source of the thoughts expressed by the man: "Perhaps I see in you the same thing as you see in me." Paradoxically, the mirroring of minds is actualized not as like-mindedness, but as a behavioral pattern of continuous misunderstandings. Leena adopts the potential "insensitivity" of the man, either intentionally or unintentionally, in order to cope with the painfulness of the situation. She builds an emotional wall to minimize the risks of losing in the game of love.

As the above analyses have demonstrated, the love plot in *Mies kuin mies, tyttö kuin tyttö* is deferred and complicated by Leena's lingering awakening to her true self. The ambivalence of feelings is itself the predominant theme in the novel and serves as the foundation for the cyclical story patterns. Leena tosses and turns and drifts from restlessness to grief and tranquility – as if unable to recognize her emotional impulses. Like Leena's physical maturation, her emotional life involves covert processes, which are reflected in the emotional structure of the story, not only with regard to the romance plot, but also with regard to her personal development. Whereas her (in)actions vis-à-vis the man are mainly portrayed from without, the scenes of Leena's sudden moments of self-awareness are often represented from within and show the reasons for her emotional conflict. These heightened moments of self-awareness are accompanied by embodied scenes that reveal the latent processes of growth taking place beyond her aware mind.

The Split Mind and the Emotions of the Body

Vartio renders Leena's journey of self-recognition as a series of experiences that are more or less latent. The sensations of the body cannot always be recognized by the conscious mind. Leena's estrangement is manifested in the embodied images of the split in the self, the division of the mind into a more articulate, conscious part and inarticulate sensations arising from the body: the involuntary and uncontrolled processes of maturation and pregnancy. On the one hand, Vartio generates the aesthetic illusion of Leena's detachment by portraying mental processes that are transmitted and reflected on the level of physical, tangible reality as biological, cyclic processes similar to nature. The author conveys these embodied experiences by means of mental landscaping, by using psycho-analogies, allegorical descriptions of fictional space, cognitive metaphors, and other techniques of subtle evocation. On the other hand, distanced, embodied scenes alternate with scenes in which Vartio represents Leena's mind from within, by providing interior and narrated monologues. These passages dramatize the tension between the conscious and the unconscious realms of her mind.

In neutral narratives, the characters' emotional responses are often related to the repetitions of background emotions that guide the reader to keep track of the characters' emotional fluctuations. The arousal continuum of background emotions ranges from the character being unconscious, to asleep, to awake but drowsy, to alert, to emotionally aroused. In *Mies kuin mies, tyttö kuin tyttö*, Vartio represents the more conscious end of the scale by combining the external and internal views of Leena's mind, especially in the peak emotional moments involving her sexual awakening. The split in the self is actualized for the first time in the novel's first love scene as Leena's mind divides into two. The pronoun *hän* ("she") refers to the objective, conscious awareness of the self observing the more passive, experiencing *minä* ("I"). In the tradition of female fiction, this technique of portraying consciousness is typically employed to generate an impression of the divided, inner and outer, parts of the self (Felski 1989: 130).[32] Leena's arousal – her heightened attention – is reflected in her physical reactions; her eyes are now "wide open":

> It was my jacket; it fell on the floor.
>
> Her eyes were wide open and fixed on the ceiling. There were two light brown patterns on the ceiling and she thought that the roof had leaked.
>
> Then she said to herself: It's me; it's me who is here.
>
> And after a moment she asked herself: Is it me lying here?
>
> Leena. She thought her name: Leena.
>
> And as the hand searched for her waist and unfastened the hooks of her skirt, she thought:
>
> My hand is helping to open the hooks.
>
> And she raised herself up again so that her back was arched like a bridge during the time it took for the man to pull the skirt down from her hips and down her legs. And the hand lowered the skirt to the floor. (*MT*, 23–24)[33]

The man's distanced presence in the scene is evoked by the synecdochic image of a hand, accompanied by an image of Leena's hand assisting its moves. The unsentimental focus on such a small image emphasizes the act of love, not as the fulfillment of a love affair, but as a rudimentary event in Leena's development. The boundary-crossing quality of the event is expressed by Leena's inner voice repeating her own name: "Leena. She thought her name: Leena." ("Leena. Hän ajatteli nimensä: Leena.") Before the love scene, Leena is depicted writing her name in the margin of a newspaper as if practicing her signature, the designator of her identity. The deictic expressions of Leena's speech addressed to the self ("Is it me lying here"; "Olenko minä se, joka makaa tässä") emphasize the experiences happening "here and now," but also the unstable quality of self-identity. At the moment of "here and now," something is happening to her rather than being enacted by her. In the scene, her body is observed from a distance as if a self-sustained entity making its own decisions.

> I'm stripped now. This is happening to me. Now.
> And then she thought: Is that my voice saying no, no?
> Is it me saying I don't want to, I don't dare, and even so helping the hand that is undressing me now?
> Is this what it's like? This thing that is about to happen to me, this is it, now.
> And she was scared and said in a loud voice, "No!"
> But she couldn't do anything anymore to get up, to leave.
> Am I a fallen woman, now? (*MT*, 24)[34]

The contrast between "event" and "action" is stressed in the scene that dramatizes the split in the self into a more rational, aware mind and the primitive drives and impulses arising from within. In a paralyzed state of inaction, Leena's body seems to be reluctant to obey the voice of reason heard in her audible words ("And she was scared and said in a loud voice: 'No.'") This voice of internalized social order is foregrounded in the final passage of the interior monologue: "Am I now a fallen woman, now?" The scene of the split in the self seems to stage the double function of interior monologue both as associative and as rational thought. The division of the self into two voices thematizes the layered quality of the fictional mind, which is "spontaneously" experiencing and distantly observing itself – even if the silencing of the self-address in modern interior monologues has been considered as reflecting a less rational and less rhetorical quality of self-communion (cf. Cohn 1983: 12).[35]

In studies of modernist mind presentation, the analysis of the unconscious has involved many misconceptions. As Cohn (1983: 77–78) points out in her critique of the focus on stream of consciousness novels, "[t]he phenomenon that interior monologue imitates is, contrary to its reputation, neither the Freudian unconscious, nor the Bergsonian inner flux, nor even the William Jamesian stream of consciousness, but quite simply the mental activity psychologists call interior language, inner speech, or, more learnedly, endophasy."[36] Endophasy involves those contents of the mind that can be called associative, flowing, impulsive, or spontaneous. However, it does not involve those mental processes that remain unconscious, beyond the reach of self-articulation. Rather, in addition to freely associative patterns, it pertains to psychic facts, logical and rational thinking, calculation, and conscious decision-making: emotions, sensations, and associations that come into awareness as more or less articulated, conscious thoughts or feelings.

Thus, how to approach the representation of (unconscious) emotions in modernist novels such as *Mies kuin mies, tyttö kuin tyttö*? Or more specifically: how to delineate the spectrum of mental phenomena in a fictional setting? This is a case in point, since emotions have long been considered to be phenomena too personal, fleeting, and difficult to be approached academically, including in literary studies. Various reasons have been proffered for the neglect of emotions in literary theory. In story pattern analyses, emotions have been excluded as belonging to the character paradigm, and characters, in turn, have been conceived as mere actants. In structuralist narratology, on the other hand, the concept of emotion has not fit into the debates on speech categories or other linguistic models. In addition, the influence of psychoanalysis (emphasizing such concepts as "pleasure" or "desire") has been identified as a factor resulting in the gap of affective theory in narrative studies. (Palmer 2010: 156; Hogan 2011a: 15)

Human cognition has traditionally been associated with such conscious processes as thinking and reasoning. Mental activities like introspection, analysis, reflection, perception, memory, decision-making, speech, and other operations involving language can be added to the list. In Lubomír Doležel's terminology, the operations of the "practical mind" (such as rational planning, reasoning, calculation, or scripting) are classified as "mental acts" that are intentional – contributing to the configuration of the plot. "Mental events," by contrast, are unintentionally, spontaneously – and often more locally – generated. Traditionally, these aspects of the human mind have been considered as the main focus of mind presentation in modernist fiction. Mental events include the mental processes of the "contemplative mind," such as automatic mental images, associations, obsessive thoughts, beliefs and emotions, daydreaming, and dreams. Mental events are like uncontrollable natural forces, deeply rooted in the biological processes of the physical body. This is why it is so difficult for the conscious mind to detect and control them. (Doležel 1998: 73)

Whereas mental acts relate to the action mode that Doležel calls rational action (guided by reason, control, and cognitive motivations), mental events relate more often to actions that diminish or flout rationality: impulsive, akratic, or irrational modes of action that are triggered by a highly emotional mind. This distinction between passion and reason, feeling and thinking, emotion and cognition has a long history, starting with Plato's conception of passions as wild horses that must be reined in by the rational intellect. The struggle between sense and emotion, the primitive and the more sophisticated realms of the mind has been portrayed as an inner battle for control of the human psyche. Impulsive acting has been perceived as stemming from drives. It is spontaneous, unpremeditated, and often reflexively stimulated. Under impulsive drives, the character's control over her or his acting is minimized. A character's emotionally aroused actions typically fluctuate between the rational and the impulsive modes. An akratic mode of action is linked to "weakness of will," also called "the Medea Principle": a person knows the rational path, but does not follow it because she or he is being led by a drive or a passion and thus ends up performing an incorrect action. Madness, in turn, means a total lack of intentionality, as the possibilities for practical reasoning are deprived. (Doležel 1998: 71–72)

The polarity between intentional acting and spontaneous generation can be understood as corresponding to the distinction between the practical and the contemplative mind and thereby between the conscious and the unconscious processes of fictional minds, although not necessarily (Doležel 1998: 73). Even cognitive processes, such as memories, sensory perceptions, or thoughts, can be spontaneously generated. Many cognitive processes (e.g. memory, among others) are related to involuntary psychology. Moreover, emotions, mental images, and different modes of counterfactual thought involve highly sophisticated processes of the human intellect, such as, for instance, rationalizing and entertaining oneself with possibilities. Emotions can serve as motivations for rational planning and calculation. Reasoning and thinking, by contrast, can be frenetic and disorganized, even irrational (cf. LeDoux 1998: 35–36). Hence, the division of mental functioning into a practical and contemplative mind seems to be inadequate. Both *cognitive* and *emotional* unconscious are relevant from the perspective of modernist mind presentation, in which the "dark places of psychology" (Woolf 1929/1919: 192) are often the focus of interest.[37]

In *Mies kuin mies, tyttö kuin tyttö*, the darker, unconscious aspects of emotional life are related to the embodied images that Vartio uses to portray the social stigmas of the affair. These images are introduced before the actual love scene in the episode in which Leena climbs into the man's room. The visual contrast of light and shadow frames the space in the stairway. In the evening light, Leena's climb turns into something sacred and pure, reinforced by the detail of the pure carpet. This virginal purity is contrasted to the darkness rising from below, as if from the instinctive spheres of Leena's and the man's minds. Leena hesitates:

> The girl had stopped. The top of the staircase glowed gold, the evening sun reached to the upstairs hall window and lit the stairs from above, but the lower part was dim. The carpet on the stairs was a light color and clean.
>
> The girl started to go up. Two stairs up, she stopped.
>
> "Take a look: are my shoes clean?"
>
> She lifted her foot, held it up. The man coming behind her saw the grooves of the rubber sole at eye level.
>
> "They're clean." The girl felt the man's fingers squeezing her ankle.
>
> "Let go, I'll fall!" She hopped on one leg and tottered.
>
> Without glancing behind her, she continued to climb the stairs. She heard the man's voice behind her, "You won't fall. I'll catch you." (*MT*, 7)[38]

Other images of purity follow as Leena steps into the room. She observes the rag carpet on the floor "as clean as if no one had ever walked on it" (*MT*, 10).[39] Leena's future "fall" is embodied in the scene with the reference to her new shoes, which are clean at the moment of her climb, but later, at home, Leena notices dirt on them: "What was it she'd stepped into?" (*MT*, 32)[40] The motif of shoes (thrown away as they gradually become completely outworn) reflects the social stigmas of adultery and extramarital pregnancy, as Leena's future fall is written into the embodied scenes before it materializes in the storyworld. In the end, the man never catches her, mostly because Leena never lets him get involved.

After the first sexual experience, Leena feels she has changed in a fundamental way. She is afraid that the inner change can be observed by others. That familiar trope of self-recognition, a mirror, appears in the scene of Leena's self-examination. The memories of the encounter with the man lead to a full and complete awareness of her body:

> She took a mirror from her pocket and saw in it a pale patch and two darker spots.
> Those are my eyes. The same eyes, even though the thing had happened that she feared could be seen from her face.
> With her hand she touched her neck and cheeks, and when she let her hand drop limply, it brushed against her breast and flashed away as if it had touched a burning object. *The touch had awakened full, clear knowledge of what had happened.*
> Breasts. Their name. Round bits that had traveled with her till now like a hand, leg, any body part. They had a name: breasts. She was a woman. They were a woman's breasts. (*MT*, 31)[41]

In Leena's initial state, the objects – the body parts – cannot be identified. Breasts are only separate "round bits" that have been carried along as if unnoticed. They have no specific meaning. After being recognized as objects of a sexual being, the breasts are given their name. The process corresponds metonymically to Leena's own position. The sexual awakening changes her identity, perceived mainly in relation to her bodily experience. The half-blurred image of her face and eyes ("a pale patch and two darker spots") is accompanied by an indolent, habitual gesture of her hand (parallel to the man's hand) and then comes a moment of sudden self-recognition, The sense of the embodied self is evoked by the touch on the breasts: "The touch had awakened full, clear knowledge of what had happened."

In *Mies kuin mies, tyttö kuin tyttö*, Vartio renders the moments of Leena's self-awareness as brief flashes of knowledge, which, however, manifest themselves as embodied sensations rather than as awareness ranging over longer periods of time. At the moment of Leena's self-indulgence, her feeling of the self stems from self-objectification. By closing her eyes, she is able to "see" more clearly:

> I am smiling like this, she felt. And she closed her eyes as if with closed eyes she could see her own face. She raised her hand slowly, touched her cheek as if the smile had been an object whose shape she wanted to know. She ran her finger over her lips tracing their outline. [...] The man had come out from hiding; his eyes followed the movement of her hand, the hand dropped out of the air onto her face, pressed the eyes as if wanting to prevent her from seeing. [...]

"This is what I'm like," the girl said. "Look, like this." She turned from side to side on the bed in satisfaction, stretched her arms and legs as if she had only now realized what she was like. "This is what I'm like," she said again, this time as if surprised and asking herself something. At the same time she smiled again and stretched out her arms as if she no longer knew how she should be just then.

"Yes." The man didn't smile.

She saw the man against the darkness. (*MT*, 67–68)[42]

The process of becoming aware involves Leena's pre-conscious thoughts rendered by psycho-analogy: "*as if* surprised and asking herself something." With her eyes closed, Leena distances herself from the perceptions of the external world. The trope of closed eyes refers to mental images arising in the mind when it is detached from the distractions of the material world (similar to the flood of images in Anni's mind, as her consciousness is monitoring the dark). On the other hand, the comparison of Leena's smile to an "object" or a "form" alludes to the character itself as a fictional construct composed of words. While Leena is getting to know her body, its parts are described one by one as part of the rhetoric of the "character," as fictional objects integrated with names.

Leena's mind behind her closed eyes concentrates on the sensations of the body, the physical touch of a hand, which she senses as more tangible and real in this way. Even if words have become empty and meaningless, the man's touch has an enormous impact on Leena. The "darkness" is an element that encourages Leena and the man to encounter each other exposed and bare. In the dark they "see" each other, which, according to Leena, is the most frightening aspect of the contact: "[H]e has seen me" (*MT*, 24).[43] The physical, uncomplicated understanding between the lovers is illustrated by the trope of "play" typical of Vartio's love scenes. At best, the encounter between a man and a woman is simple, as is everything else in nature: "It made them feel like laughing, as if they were playing without anyone seeing them and they realized they fit together well in the game, they understood each other from the slightest movement" (*MT*, 68).[44] However, the man's role in restraining Leena's maturation is also suggested: his hand prevents Leena from "seeing." By employing mental landscapes as a device to demonstrate Leena's latent development, Vartio shows how the female Bildung requires an explicit refusal of the romance plot. Separation from a lover and withdrawal into the inner self are the preconditions for any path to self-knowledge.

The Cycles of the Moon and the Embodied Maturation

While portraying Leena's gradual awakening to see the bindings of the social world, Vartio employs techniques of mental landscaping that draw from the reader's craving to read allegorical meanings into the elements of the storyworld. In symbolic episodes, the character's experiences are allowed "to be intuited from the narrated actions and incidents," as Anhava (2002/1949: 57) described the focus of the Finnish new novel. Vartio depicts Leena's maturation with sets of embodied images clustered to portray Leena's sexual awakening, the growth of her self-recognition, and the processes taking place in her body and mind during her pregnancy. The most prevailing of these images is the path, which leads to the lovers' secret meeting place in the forest. The path is seen for the first time just after the novel's opening scene: "It was a shortcut, almost overgrown; it branched off from the road and led through the alder grove and across the heath, forked here and there, and ended at a fence" (*MT*, 6).[45]

The image of the forest path catalyzes an allegorical reading of Leena's experiences written into the repetitive scenes of encountering and parting. These cyclic patterns resemble the pattern of emotional approaching and distancing in the relationship. At the beginning of the novel, the image of the path illustrates the many possible trajectories the affair might take just as everything is about to begin. It serves as an image of the affair's early stage, which is never represented in the "real" time-frame of the novel. Leena looks back at the walk she has taken with the man: "They had climbed over the fence, the road was barely visible behind the fence, the forest was so dense, only the wooden gate in the middle of the fence let you guess that a road ran there" (*MT*, 6).[46] Vartio represents this scene through hypothetical focalization, as if Leena was seeing the view from a potential witness's perspective. Only the wooden gate that separates the path from the forest would inform a hypothetical observer that there might be a road leading to the place of their secret encounters protected from the gaze of outsiders.

The path, the road, and the fence serve as border markers that frame Leena's experiences of crossing boundaries. After her first sexual experience, Leena crosses the road as if traversing some symbolic boundary: "A little before the gate, the girl said again that she would go alone now. [...] She stood still at the edge of the road and looked both ways. She ran across the road as if across a border" (*MT*, 29).[47] Crossing the highway becomes an image of breaking the limits of the small world that constitutes Leena's customary domain of existence. The forest path is varied in many of the novel's scenes. In rendering Leena's embodied processes, Vartio also employs other images that are mostly familiar from the narratives of female development, such as the moon, water, and its fluctuations. In the fourth chapter, the moon illuminates the scene by the lake at the lovers' secret meeting place. Leena and the man discuss the details of the physical world as they observe the scene: "[A]nd the ebb and flow of the tides, they change with the cycle of the moon" (*MT*, 74), the man says.[48] Leena is enchanted by the beauty of the moon: "When I look at it, I want to start running or shouting or jumping or hide somewhere, or just watch and never stop watching" (ibid.).[49] The effect of the moon is felt as restlessness in the body. The ebb and flow of the tides resemble Leena's embodied emotions. As the water obeys nature's call by alternately rising and falling, Leena's inner impulses vary from restlessness to reserve and tranquil affection.

The changes within Leena's body and mind are often actualized as latent processes, as instinctive "knowledge" of nature. Her barely sensed inner motions are juxtaposed with the movements of the moon, which reflect the fluctuating process of her self-recognition. The moon's movements also capture the relativity of perception: the worlds are seen from different perspectives by Leena and the man. The moon brightens the scene, as the couple say their goodbyes:

> "Can you wait?" the man asked. "It may be a while before I can come again." He fiddled with a small white stone.
>
> The girl looked at the man's hand, reached out her hand, took the stone, and dropped it into her pocket.
>
> The moon was in the sky. It always kept moving, but you might not notice that even if you looked constantly. But if you turned your eyes away and happened to look at it after a while, it was in some other place. And it kept on moving.
>
> "I suppose I can't do anything else." (*MT*, 79)[50]

Leena's self-restraint is embodied in the white stone, which simultaneously serves as an image of the poetic principles of Vartio's early work: hardness and restraint. The style and technique with which she portrays the movements of emotions in the scene parallel the movements of the moon, which are almost invisible, yet nevertheless exist. These movements also allude to Leena's physical experience, the invisible processes taking place in her body. The materiality of being in the world is emphasized in the hardness of the stone, which in turn emphasizes the hardness of Leena's emotional situation. She cannot do anything but wait.

Another embodied scene illustrating the processes of maturation involves Leena's narrated memory. She once dived into the water and hurt herself. The wound on her head "had bled" (*MT*, 75).[51] The figures of blood and the leap into water belong to the cluster of embodied images that imply the processes of sexual maturation. When Leena prepares to step into the lake by the forest, she hears the man's warnings: "Don't swim that distance yet. […] It's not yet time for swimming; wait a bit" (*MT*, 76).[52] But Leena's feet are already in the water: "You don't have to come. It's not yet time for swimming. But I'm going to swim" (ibid.), she calls.[53] Before taking the dive, she had pictured how the experience would feel. Leena's thoughts are described as hypothetical, future sensations: "It would feel bad to let go of the rock and throw herself into the water; under her legs it would be deep and her arms would curve in a quick stroke and her legs would straighten" (*MT*, 75).[54] Defying the man's warnings, Leena dives into the cold water, even if she feels terrified. At first, the water's coldness takes her breath away. She cannot "get the scream out of her mouth" (*MT*, 76).[55] Her limbs, however, answer the call instinctively, just as she has expected: "But her arms were already opened and her feet sprang to push and she swam as if she were in cold gold. Her limbs had already accepted the cold; they curved and straightened, and she turned onto her back, she wanted to wet her hair completely" (ibid.).[56] Leena's limbs feel young and strong, and she imagines herself swimming to the other side of the lake: "The reflection of the moon on the water was like a road across the lake, and the moon was above the rock to which she would swim" (ibid.).[57]

The allegorical scenes with clustered images trigger mind-reading from the reader's part: the fictional time-space begins to represent Leena's inner space. The notion of throwing oneself into the unknown takes the form of a lake, a space with invisible depths and great distances, like those beyond Leena's customary world. Her swim anticipates her future journey. The swim refers to her growing maturity as something that is mostly dictated by nature and only partly initiated by herself. The man's role in the process, on the other hand, is almost purely instrumental. He serves as a catalyst, a helping hand that sets the process in motion. Later, he is unable to do anything except stand by and watch. Leena's push, her scream, and her dive into the deep all portray the young girl's indulgence and the (sexual) self-knowledge she has acquired. Furthermore, the embodied imagery anticipates the childbirth and the forthcoming emotional distress, symbolized in the images of a bleeding wound and the risky dive. Leena waves her hand and dives deep: "See, I'm drowning" (*MT*, 77), she teases the man who is scared and angry.[58]

The wave reappears later in the scene as the man prepares to leave for the city. The ambivalence of Leena's feelings is emphasized in the depiction of the lovers' meeting. During Leena's last self-surrender, the rain is dripping against the window and darkening the room where the pair has gone to escape the downpour. The rain and the darkness make Leena feel secure and anguished at the same time. The contrasting emotions are manifested in a psycho-analogy symbolizing Leena's muted feelings. The window outlines the landscape as Leena observes it: "The rain pattered against the window, and the room had grown as dark as if night had fallen. She saw the tops of the trees, they were like someone standing in the middle of the water wildly flailing his arms and signaling to the shore" (*MT*, 60).[59]

The image of the human figure in peril at sea is later accompanied by another image that anthropomorphizes objects in nature. Leena compares the trees with living creatures that are trying to hide their true qualities as living beings. This belief, which originated in Leena's childhood, is reflected in her perceptions: "The heaven was as black as if ink had been splashed over the world. The girl raised herself so that she could see out into the yard, she saw grass, and the trees in full. *They were thrashing in the wind as if trying to rip free from their roots*" (*MT*, 61).[60] The jerking trees correspond to Leena's desire to be free of her roots, to see and experience the world. When the man tells about having been at sea, Leena expresses her hunger for new experiences and her desire to get away from home: "She had started to feel that her life was going to waste" (*MT*, 17).[61] The idea of a wasted life is related to the theme of female Bildung, a theme that Vartio elaborates on in her later novels. Like Vartio's other female figures, Leena yearns for change. Leena's father had taken her out of school, unsatisfied with her mediocre grades: "I have never been anywhere or seen anything […]. If I had been in school," she began, agitated, then stopped as if to ask herself something" (*MT*, 19).[62] From the man's perspective, Leena's expectations are shown to be naïve and overly optimistic. Listening to Leena, the man laughs: "Oh, come on. Do you really think it's any better elsewhere?" (*MT*, 17)[63]

The man's role as the restrainer of Leena's development is connected to the themes of individual freedom and integrity, which are relevant to Leena's personal growth. As Leena leaves the man's rented room for the last time, her fierce departure resembles the trees thrashing in the wind – as a picture of her inner restlessness and her desire to leave her familiar world behind. Just as she once climbed up to the man's room, now she is coming down:

> They came down the stairs.
>
> When they had gotten across the yard to the edge of the forest, the girl said she would go on alone, and ignoring what the man was saying, she broke into a run. When she stopped to wave, the man had already turned away. The girl stood there until the man had disappeared behind the house.
>
> Water dripped onto her face. She looked up; the drops of water had fallen from the tree branches. She stood in the dense alder grove. She ought to go down by way of the fence, the path was that way. But she started to run straight through the woods, not caring about or dodging the branches that whipped her face and hair, so that when she came out on the heath, she was completely wet. (*MT*, 72)[64]

At the moment of parting, Leena refuses to listen to the man's words and starts to run. However, as if undecided, she turns, looks back, and waves her hand. The man, however, has already gone. Leena's wave corresponds to the wave of a human in peril at sea, as if she were about to drown. As Leena stands still, drops of water fall from the boughs of the tree, as if reflecting her inner anguish. The next scene shows her repressed emotions bursting forth in a fierce run. Leena's race through the forest leaves her completely wet. The image following the running scene, however, alludes to a different state of mind, relief and inner stoicism. As she arrives home and steps into the courtyard, she thinks about the spring that will soon arrive: "When the lilac bush next to the wall begins to bloom, it will produce a white flower" (*MT*, 73).[65] The hypothetical lilac blossoms contrast with the novel's opening scene, in which the aimless motion of the bough is enacted by the man. Now Leena moves the bough: "She swung the branch with her hand; it moved and stopped, and rose higher with the weight of water on its leaves gone" (ibid.).[66] Something seems to have been resolved. As Leena opens and closes the door of her home, so this chapter in the novel closes a chapter in Leena's life: "She climbed the stairs, opened the door and went in" (ibid.).[67]

The permanent effect that people have on each other and on their surroundings is discussed several times in the novel. These discussions are related to the different emotional peak moments and stages of negotiation in the romance plot, as the couple is constantly oscillating between reconciliation and parting. Leena often pictures the potential traces she has left on the world. The idea of a "trace" relates to two different frameworks introduced in the novel. The first concerns the future paths of the adulterous affair and the resulting social stigma. The concrete cause of Leena's "stain," the "dirt" on her shoes, is the forest path that leads to the man's rented room. At the staircase are the two doors; Leena chooses the "wrong" one as she walks along the clean carpet and allows the man's hand to guide her way. The second framework pertains to Leena's pregnancy and the continuity of life: the child as the "trace" of the affair. Leena's gradual awakening to reality relates to the process of becoming aware of the effects of her previous decisions. The extramarital pregnancy makes her see the constraints related to her dawning womanhood.

Expanding Eyes. From Sleep to Arousal

Leena's growing state of numbness intensifies after she finds out that she is pregnant. Soon after the man's departure, she realizes that some part of the man has endured within her and continues to grow. Leena's recognition of her pregnancy is portrayed as a latent, dawning awareness of which she becomes conscious only gradually. She tries to postpone the inevitable by counting the days since her last period, as if trying to erase the inerasable with the power of her thoughts, namely, her "spell" of repeated numbers: "It couldn't be that, it couldn't. […] She began again from the beginning, whispering numbers and the names of the days as if reciting a spell" (*MT*, 80).[68] Gradually, the state of denial turns into painful awareness, but Leena does not know how to act. Even if her mind screams for action, another part of her is unable to think clearly, much less do anything: "She knew there was no time to waste, and she felt that if she'd just think hard, she'd come up with a solution. But she always fell asleep the moment she climbed into bed" (*MT*, 80–81).[69]

The attempted abortion is one of the emotional peaks in the novel. Leena has a detailed plan that allows her to bathe in privacy in order to rid herself of the fetus. She takes poison, throws water on the stove, and pours cold water on her stomach. In a half-conscious state, she is struck by the fear of death. These extreme measures result in ringing in her ears and the feeling of fiery hoops encircling her heart:

> Her ears were ringing. They are ears, they're ringing. Ringing like electric wires.
> And then she heard jingling as if a small bell had been rung beside her ear and the sound grew and resounded as if the small bell had turned into a big bell. The echo was inside her head and drumming against it to get out.
> As if her brain were boiling.
> Now I'll stand up to throw more water on the stove. But her limbs would not obey. She tried to draw breath, she thought she was suffocating, yet she could only gulp small breaths of the fiery air. […]
> I'm dying. What if I die of this?
> Her heart was drumming as if a fiery hoop had encircled it so fast that the movement was imperceptible.
> Down, I need to get down. (*MT*, 87–88)[70]

In the scene, the interaction of mind and body is rendered as a combination of objective and subjective awareness of the self. The effect is achieved by the transitions between pronouns *hän* ("she") and *minä* ("I"). Leena's body does not obey the orders of the rational mind. The pronoun "she" refers to the Leena's physical sensations and reflect the body's refusal to carry out the plan intended by her conscious mind. The pronoun "I" denotes Leena's awareness of the situation, her determination and will, which are overcome by the limitations of her body. The mind is forced to surrender: "What if someone comes? But the thought didn't make her get up, nor think what to say if someone came and saw. If someone came and asked something, she wouldn't even open her eyes" (*MT*, 89–90).[71]

One of Leena's eye-opening moments, however, is her recognition that the abortion has failed. The inarticulated feeling suddenly leaps from the realm of pre-consciousness into awareness and into her verbalized speech. "Nothing will come of it. And she realized she had said aloud what she *had till now not dared even to think through*" (*MT*, 96).[72] The reader – like Leena's sister, who is listening to her – is prompted to consider Leena's realization as an invitation to speculate and second-guess the girl's pre-conscious thoughts in relation to the future of her affair. At a later point, however, the thing that she fears to acknowledge turns out to be the long-wished-for miscarriage that seems to have failed. The recognition of the fetus still growing inside her makes Leena burst into tears through pure exhaustion: "She wasn't crying because she thought her sister would tell their father, nor crying about what she had feared week after week and now knew to be true. She was tired" (*MT*, 99).[73] Leena's exhaustion stems from the biological changes taking place in her body, which is full of aches and pains. Her body feels strange, as if occupied by some alien force. Her mental image of her body is a map, a body landscape, resembling Mother Earth:

> The veins criss-crossed, they started dark at the neck and branched around the breast.
> The image of a map rose before her eyes. The rivers criss-crossed, all the big rivers of the world.
> She looked at her nipple; it was dark brown like a big eye.
> She let go of her breast, and it was like a rock.
> She carried the breasts like two rocks. They hurt.
> She buried her teeth in her arm, bit it.
> I'm going mad, I'm going mad.
> She hated her body, the parts of her body that were growing and swelling and whose aches and pains she had to bear. (*MT*, 119)[74]

The depiction of Leena's self-hatred contrasts with the previous moment of self-indulgence. Her self-estrangement stems from her notion of the child as an intruder who has taken over her body and turned it into a strange, aching, and swelling thing. Her breasts are like huge mountains, heavy and sore. Leena's alienation culminates in her urge to hurt herself by biting the parts of her body that she has loved and now hates – as if she wants to take revenge on the aches the body makes her bear. Leena's thoughts of going "mad" reflect her split self, her heightened awareness of emotional distress caused by the materiality of the body, which seems to deprive her of her identity. Leena considers natural laws to be constraints on the female body. The humiliation and rage of having to bear the consequences of the love affair are expressed in thoughts of herself as an animal, "[l]ike a cow, like a cow with a lead around its neck" (*MT*, 138).[75] This association returns later as the distant voice of an unidentified woman heard in the hospital. The voice is compared to the sound of "an unknown animal in the forest" (*MT*, 265).[76]

The description of Leena's bodily experience harks back to Vartio's early poem, "Nainen ja maisema" (A Woman and a Landscape, 1952), which draws parallels between the female body and a material landscape. The repressed rage of the female figure is unraveled in her fantasy worlds. Rage is expressed in aggressive moves in the landscape, which embodies the entrapment of the speaker in her body. The bodily existence is pictured as a sweeping and soaring landscape scarred by thunder and eruptions: "There is no step, no step as light / that wouldn't leave a mark on me" (*Häät*, 17),[77] the speaker of the poem declares. Rage is suppressed by conventional roles, which are reflected in the images of the mirror and combing the hair that frame the poem: even when the mirror is broken, the hand absent-mindedly rises to repeat its brush strokes. The growing sense of tension between the mind and the body reflects the tension between the privacy of the inner world and the pressures of the outer world.

Leena's alienation is expressed more explicitly as she "literally" distances herself from her body. She "steps" out and sees herself as if she were two. In the scene that follows, the sudden, feral outburst reflects Leena's loss of self-control. Her fatigue seems to be both mental and physical. Her whole body collapses at the moment of extreme inner pressure. She observes herself, her eyes widening ("silmät laajentuen") at this moment of sudden epiphany:

> And suddenly she went motionless and watched, her eyes widening. She stood up and saw herself as a double, as if she had stepped outside herself to watch.
>
> And she saw: her face was black, her arms black and her legs up to the knees black, and everything else white. And in the middle of the whiteness were two black circles.
>
> And she felt pity for what she saw.
>
> Her cry was like the wail of an animal; overwhelming pain shook her, and she tried to ease it by moving her limbs, her hands jerked up, to the sides, down, her body twisted and turned, her neck extended as if there were a hoop around it from which she was trying to get free. (*MT*, 119)[78]

The powerful image of being trapped in one's body is evoked as Leena feels herself being strangled by the "hoop" ("vanne") around her neck. Leena feels pity for her embodied being, which is unable to escape the situation. What does she "see" at this moment of self-revelation? The two black circles of the nipples seen in the whiteness of the rest of the body resemble Leena's eyes in her reflection in the mirror. Simultaneously, they become the child's eyes, staring out from the depths of her body, accusing her of what she has done. In either case, the scene seems to refer to another episode: Leena's vision, during which she sees the figure of a woman in the garden in the novel's eighth chapter. The vision constitutes the third key scene that involves the image of breasts:

> The cut leaves and torn roots lay scattered around.
>
> She raised herself up to continue the work, but sat back down on the ground. Her breasts hurt. She touched them with her hand. She closed her eyes.
>
> She shouldn't be in the sun, she should have remembered how easy it was to get a headache from the sun. And fiery sparks started to fly before her eyes and green lightning and patterns that resembled something, she didn't know what.
>
> It was indeterminate in shape, but she knew it was a woman. And it was skinny and brown and dressed in rags. Its face – she didn't know whether it had a face,

but she knew its face was terrible to look at: she didn't know whether she had seen its eyes, but they were terrifying and they stared. And it had breasts and milk in them. (*MT*, 130)[79]

The woman figure embodies Mother Earth, which feeds every living being with its huge breasts. The vision serves as an image of collective womanhood. The milk in the woman's breasts is juxtaposed with the milk of dandelions, which leave brown stains on Leena's hands as she weeds them from the garden: "Had she hurt her hands on its breasts, hurt her hands on them without noticing and torn them, and the milk wouldn't leave her hands? She had lifted it against herself. And she had thought, or had she heard the words as if someone had spoken them: plague, poverty and death" (*MT*, 131).[80]

The act of weeding is depicted as a violation of the laws of nature juxtaposed with Leena's attempt to rid herself of the fetus. Leena's struggles to weed out the dandelions and other wild plants growing in the garden are compared to the failed abortion. The plants "offer resistance" as if they had "teeth in their roots" (*MT*, 128).[81] The view of cut leaves and torn roots lying on the ground invoke unpleasant associations in Leena's mind. The greenness of the leaves conjure up associations with poison and snakes, which allude to the potion she had taken while trying to get rid of the fetus. The fiery sparks and green lightning caused by the sunstroke resemble the ringing bells and fiery hoops caused by her violent bath in the sauna. When Leena picks up a thistle and throws it on a stone where it has no chance of putting down more roots, she says aloud: "You, at least, are going to die" (ibid.).[82]

During the sunstroke, Leena sees "patterns that resembled something, she didn't know what." These figures refer to an earlier scene in which the nipples of her breasts are pictured as two staring eyes in Leena's body. The image of Leena's body as the map of a landscape symbolizes her as an incarnation of female fertility, creativity, and the continuity of life. Leena's own aching breasts are compared to the breasts of Mother Earth, the source of life itself: "Her breasts hurt. She touched them with her hand. She closed her eyes." Leena becomes the giver and sustainer of life who nurtures the living. The vision of the woman in rags, with milk in her breasts can be understood as representing women in general, who possess the creative power of life and an obligation to protect it. The awareness of the tension between the role of motherhood and Leena's reluctance to obey the demands of nature are reflected in her aggressive bodily reactions. Leena ends up pouring calmness over her body like cold water. She is forced to accept her situation:

> And her sobs gradually quietened, and she stretched out on the bench, stayed there. Then she shifted, stood up. Her feet pressed against the cold floor, stepped calmly, and the girl went to the pot, raised the cover, and ladled out water.
>
> She sat on a footstool and started to drizzle water on herself. She poured the tepid water over her breasts, poured water over her body like coolness. Her hand brushed her stomach. And she understood the meaning of her hand's movement.
>
> She pressed her hand against her stomach again, let it rest there; but suddenly she startled and took it away.
>
> Whose body was this? Not hers, anymore. (*MT*, 119–120)[83]

Leena's hand, which has previously touched her cheek like some distinct object, now touches her stomach where unfamiliar life is growing. She feels alienated as she realizes "the meaning of her hand's movement." The movement seems to happen instinctively, following the orders of her body as if the orders were given by someone else. Leena's growth to motherhood is a gradual and lingering path that does not come out naturally. It involves self-doubt and fear, but still, also instinctive reactions that seem to stem from the realm of the unconscious shared by all women.

In depicting Leena's awakening, Vartio uses the tropes of sleep and quiescence (often used in narratives of female self-discovery) to show the protagonist's emotional denial and state of indecision. After having tried to abort the fetus, Leena becomes totally paralyzed, as if she can do nothing but wait passively for what lies ahead. The trope of sleep reappears in the series of episodes that portray the reactions of Leena's family to her pregnancy, as knowledge of her state reaches them. In the opening scene of the tenth chapter (in which Leena's conflict with her family escalates), Leena reveals her pregnancy in an effort to make her mother "see" what she has refused to see for a long time. The trope of looking out through the window frames the scene, as if drawing the borders between Leena's perceptions of the external world and her private world of silent contemplation:

> The girl was beside the window. Standing was like standing while asleep and gazing, like gazing while asleep. Two apple trees, the shed wall, a scythe on the wall. She had looked at those and while looking had heard three different sounds.
> First had been a slammed door.
> Mother came inside.
> Then there had been the clatter of pots and pans and she had heard her mother asking her something. But she was so immersed in herself and in just being that she had not replied.
> Then there had been silence.
> Mother stopped behind me.
> And she knew the meaning of the silence. It was so her mother would see. She did not even draw breath so as not to prevent what was about to be revealed.
> She turned, and, turning, knew what she would see: the eyes, the mouth that had opened but could not get a sound out.
> She gazed calmly in front of her and then back at the window. (*MT*, 146)[84]

Leena's attentiveness to the sounds and visions of the external world vary, as if following the fluctuations of her inner sleep as she is "immersed in herself and in just being" ("uponnut omaan olemiseensa"). The view from the window frames the scene: staring at a static scene with empty eyes is like being immersed in the inner worlds of dream and sleep. The slamming of the door and the voices denoting her mother's presence evoke a sudden awareness during which Leena's passive revelation takes place. The heightened moment in the quotation begins with a portion of Leena's interior monologue as she senses her mother standing behind her, watching: "Mother *stopped* behind *me*. And she knew the meaning of the silence. It was so her mother would see. She did not even draw breath so as not to prevent what was about to be revealed." Leena relies on the same strategy as the text itself: showing instead of telling, providing mute, embodied images instead of (inner) speech. Not a single word is uttered, but the mother still understands.

While witnessing the social drama caused by the adulterous pregnancy, Leena distances herself from the events of the external world. Having looked her mother straight in the eye, she turns away to stare at the view from the window, as if the dramatic events were not related to her in any way. The reluctance to communicate is marked by Leena's empty stare, which denies the meaning of silence: "She turned away as if she had just turned her head only to hear what the burst of noise behind her was, and after seeing it was nothing important turned back to the window: the shed wall, the scythe on the wall, two apple trees" (*MT*, 148).[85] Leena's gestures seem to suggest that her "intentional" action was rather automatic, half-conscious, and unintentional in nature. The expressions chosen to depict Leena's awareness at the moment of self-revelation indicate that she is observing herself too, as if not wholly aware of her actions. Even if she states she knows, she seems to have only a distant feeling: "And she knew the meaning of the silence. It was so her mother would see."

Fictional consciousness can be said to derive from the characters' *focused attention*, which is needed in order to know what happens, including conscious problem solving. Leena's thoughts about her situation, however, are implicit and dormant, as if they are not available to her consciousness. The state of being drowsy also defines Leena's concrete physical state. At the moment of exposed truth, Leena experiences neither emotional arousal nor fear, which she had expected. She feels only a tiredness that invites her to immerse herself in the comforting oblivion of sleep. While observing her father's rage, she is half-dozing:

> She would have left, she wanted to sleep. What did they want?
> What were they saying? Didn't they understand that there was nothing for her and them to do with each other?
> Her eyes had blurred, and even though she was still standing, she knew she had almost been asleep for a moment. (*MT*, 156)[86]

Leena feels indifference and disgust at the outburst of emotions that have flared up around her. Her sleep is disrupted: "Then she heard crying behind her, and she felt irritation, as if her sleep had been disturbed, as if she had been woken up violently" (*MT*, 147).[87] The endless questions from her family make her furious. They keep bringing her back to the present moment, which is confusing and full of difficult decisions to be made. In Leena's eyes, her mother, overcome by her emotions, appears insane. The excessive emotions are like some tangible substance that penetrates her consciousness and calls instantly for her attention: "It was all the same. And she wanted to laugh, laugh straight in her face, to be mean. [...] That was her mother, that one there, acting like a crazy person. And a feeling of disgust rose within her, the voice coming from the bedside seeped into her consciousness like some revolting substance" (ibid.).[88]

In a similar vein as Anni's mental life in *Se on sitten kevät*, Leena's emotions are sensed more or less through the cognition of the body. The associative nature of these bodily emotions are rendered by means of psycho-analogy: "She didn't know what had happened for her to feel like this, now. Everything seemed heavy and repugnant, *as if* she had eaten something inappropriate and then begun to feel ill" (*MT*, 258).[89] Leena's disgust (compared to a concrete sensation of some "revolting substance") stems from emotional distractions, which in turn derive from Leena's alienation from everything familiar around her, her wish to be free of her roots. The inclination to distance herself emotionally from the family is one aspect of Leena's maturation. The endless questions from her mother, father, and sister do not reach her, for words do not penetrate her inner walls: "She didn't make any effort to answer, didn't really even hear what was asked and by whom. The words didn't come close enough for her to reach them, or they, her" (*MT*, 155).[90]

Leena's estrangement and her "hard-heartedness" are explicitly thematized in the novel. Leena considers herself an outsider and feels alienated from people's interest in her pregnancy. She prefers to be invisible, among other strangers: "It felt good to be among strangers; you didn't have to wonder what people around you were thinking when you knew it made no difference" (*MT*, 229).[91] Leena, who appreciates a matter-of-fact style when talking about pregnancy, openly mocks the traditional roles of motherly affection: "She couldn't stand how the women babbled at the doctor, talking about babies and pattering about all important, it wasn't any miracle, this is what women were made for, why start on the whole thing if you had to make it into such a production. She didn't like the false faces of the women when they smiled" (*MT*, 228).[92] However, even while having these thoughts, Leena feels hurt after the man calls her childish for feeling this way, for "she had thought that herself, wondered whether there was something wrong with her" (ibid.).[93]

Leena's refusal to accept the traditional roles of womanhood questions the naturalness and instinctive quality of her maturation and pregnancy, at least in terms of showing emotion. Leena's self-restraint is compared with her father's "cold-heartedness." When she reveals the pregnancy to her mother, Leena refuses to listen to her mother's pain. She hears her mother's voice from a distance as she cries over her daughter's indifference: "Now the voice accused her of being insolent, of having always been hard-hearted, claimed that nothing softened her heart, that she was like her father" (*MT*, 148).[94] Leena's father, on the other hand, treats his daughter like the son he never had. According to him, "Leena pitches hay like the best of men" (*MT*, 80).[95] For Leena, haymaking offers a route to escape the painful reality. After a day of hard work in the field, she falls into deep sleep, as if she were intentionally trying to tire out her body.

The scene following Leena's argument with her parents emphasizes the function of sleep as her way of escaping reality into an inner land of slumber. After everything has come to light, she finally feels able to breathe freely again. She is depicted walking out of the house "[a]s if she had gotten out from somewhere dark and narrow and was seeing the world again after having forgotten how everything really looked" (*MT*, 160–161).[96] She enters the drying barn after having roamed around "without thinking" ("ajattelematta") and lies quietly on her back in the dark, listening to the scratching sounds coming from the upper roof. Leena's interior monologue captures her desire for a short moment of rest beyond any emotional distraction: "I feel sleepy, I'll sleep here" (*MT*, 161).[97] The next two paragraphs, as concise as they are, render Leena's dozing and sudden awakening. No access to her inner space is provided: "She drowsed and started awake. She stood up and walked out" (ibid.).[98]

After this rapid awakening, Leena decides to leave home. Her first step toward self-reliance involves her journey to the city, where she begins working as a servant in a bourgeois family. The landscape with the forest path is shown for the last time as she is sitting in the car on her way to the city. The familiar view is seen only in Leena's mind's eye, for she does not look back: "She didn't turn to look out the back window at the receding road, back where the path cut across the road and continued on the other side and led into the forest and on to the gate" (*MT*, 186).[99] Leena feels pleased to be leaving everything behind. "She saw in her mind's eye the gate and the path and then forgot them as the car drove on and she felt good" (ibid.).[100]

Patterns of Lingering Awakening

In *Mies kuin mies, tyttö kuin tyttö*, narrative closure and causal explanation are deferred by cyclic patterns that serve as the basis for the aesthetic design of the story of any girl and any man. The novel both evokes and subverts the plot pattern typical of naturalist and realist narratives in which young innocent girls, having been seduced, are destined for social ruin, madness or death by the end of the story.[101] Vartio's early plan was to write Leena's death at the close of the novel, as the culmination of the story of a young girl drifting into the trap of extramarital pregnancy. The aesthetic, higher "order" written into the story structure, however, was invalidated by the author's decision to change her plan and leave her character alive.[102] The future paths suggested for Leena seem to remain open, as if Vartio herself were reluctant to provide any ready-made answers to her situation. In the final version of the novel, however, hypothetical death still appears to be a counterfactual trail suggesting an alternative closure that is never actualized in the story. Hypothetical death looms, for instance, in the scene of the failed abortion: "I'm going to die. What if I die from this?" Later, Leena "foresees" her death during the delivery of the child, as if it is a realization of the prophecy of death she had heard in the garden. Her regret leads to superstitious interpretations, as if her death were a punishment predetermined by nature itself.[103]

Leena's superstitious fears are motivated by her pregnancy. These fears involve her thoughts of destiny and chance as determining the course of her life. Leena's employer in the city considers the girl's thoughts typical of "every pregnant woman" (*MT*, 236).[104] The employer has helped other girls in the same situation. She reflects on the laws of the fictional world: the paths of one's life are made of one's own choices, but the outcomes of one's actions are never fully predictable. The employer considers the world a strange place, in which "everything doesn't always go the way it should, something always turns out differently than expected" (*MT*, 254).[105] Marriage, according to the woman, is always "a matter of chance" (ibid.).[106] The employer addresses Leena's need to make her own decisions. The reliance on freedom of choice is not the easiest path, but it is the only way out: "Nothing helps a person; you have to help yourself, and it isn't always easy" (*MT*, 253), she says.[107] Speculating on the end of her relationship, Leena has finally realized that in order to "get free," one needs to "see things as they are" (*MT*, 55).[108] The women's discussion turns to the complications of communication between Leena and the man:

"But has Leena actually told him about her doubts concerning marriage? Shouldn't she do so, she should speak frankly, sometimes things get better with talking about them. She supposed Leena could speak to him."

"But I myself don't even know. And besides, if he could understand then I'd think he should have already understood by now that I don't understand anything, anymore."

"Hmm. That is complicated. Or actually, very clearly spoken." (*MT*, 258)[109]

Leena's "complicated" construction of mind-reading, said to be "very clearly spoken," demonstrates the aesthetic principle of open form, namely, complication in clarity. Leena's employer concludes the discussion by implying that possibilities are opened up by such a state of undecidedness: "It will work out. And there are many chances in life, aren't there" (*MT*, 259).[110] The employer's words about randomness as something that "turns out differently than expected" may be seen in the context of Vartio's change of plans for the novel's ending: her intention to culminate Leena's tale in death was never actualized. Thus, many chances for the protagonist's future life remain open.

The tension between emotional, automatic responses and the planning of voluntary actions becomes relevant in regard to Leena's personal development, especially with regard to her chances to make her own decisions. Whereas physical and mental *acts* (such as Leena's rational speculations on the affair) are intentional, the psychic and mental *events* (such as the biological processes occurring in her body) are non-intentional. They are natural forces that happen to her whether Leena wants them or not.[111] In order to make rational decisions on the basis of one's emotions, bodily sensations need to be transformed into conscious feelings. The relations between intentional agency and chance are addressed in *Mies kuin mies, tyttö kuin tyttö* at the point when Leena thinks back to her first encounter with the man. The convergence of their paths has resulted from a random meeting on the road: "The girl had walked along the road *by chance*, remained looking for a while and then left home" (*MT*, 18).[112] The idea of the relationship as the result of chance recurs when Leena perceives her presence in the man's rented room as a result of chance: "They had set out to walk along the path, *by chance* along the very path that led to this house. The girl thought about that; she had actually come to this room *by chance*" (*MT*, 16).[113]

However, afterwards Leena blames herself, as if she had intentionally guided their way: "[S]he was the one who *had led* them to this" (*MT*, 27).[114] Later, as the man's commitments start to trouble her, she keeps recalling the moments of their encounter in the dark, when Leena found and touched the man's scar:

> She recalled the first time they sat close together in the dark car. She had been the one. She had pressed herself against the man pretending to be scared of the approaching car; she had thrown herself against the man's shoulder and as if by accident put her hand on his knee. If she had taken her hand away immediately – would she be sitting here right now?
>
> But she had let her hand be.
>
> And when they had come to the crossroads, there where she had stepped out of the car on previous nights and where they had parted with a simple "good night," the man hadn't stopped the car, not until many kilometers farther on. (*MT*, 55)[115]

While Leena weighs the alternative possibilities of past events, the presence of decision-making is suggested by another image relating to the forking paths: "And when they had come to the *crossroads*." The metaphor of crossroads alludes to Leena's contemplation on the alternative branch of her life while she is already located on the present, actualized trail. The mention of the crossroads refers back to Leena's recollection: the man's truck standing "at the crossroads in the dark," resembling "an animal, a dreadful beast" (*MT*, 18).[116] The truck signifies Leena's mixed feelings of fear and desire. Leena's counterfactual accounts of the events generate uncertainty, stemming from her emotional conflict. Has everything happened "by chance" or "by accident," as she claims? Or has she approached the man by "offering" herself, as she wonders after a moment? (*MT*, 54)[117]

In *Mies kuin mies, tyttö kuin tyttö*, the characters' emotional conflicts typically result from a fusion of two distant emotions – such as affection and disgust or terror and desire – that generate "imperfect" blends as they trigger conflicting responses. Incompatible, mixed emotions toward the same object generate motivational conflicts. Their power is particularly relevant in narrative situations in which characters are "pulled in opposite directions." Motivational conflicts are related to characters' intentions and involve impulsive drives and rational calculation. As emotions drift into conflict, they typically affect the characters' ability to make decisions and take action. The ensuing action is either temporarily deferred or permanently denied. (Doležel 1998: 63–64; 69) Cognitive planning allows a shift from emotional *reactions* to *actions*. Leena's emotional reactions involve emotional plans that, however, never turn into emotional *actions*.

Leena's inaction in relation to the man can be considered "passive moves" or "deliberate nonaction," involving some degree of intentionality, since her goal is to "let events follow their course," even though she is in a position to prevent certain developments (cf. Ryan 1991: 132).[118] Leena's preference for waiting relates to her belief that providence is guiding her way. When she notices an advertisement in the newspaper for the position of housemaid, she considers it a signal from above: "For a moment she thought about the word 'providence.' She thought how pointless it was to worry; everything works out, takes its own course, if you just have the patience to wait" (*MT*, 170).[119] However, in the causality of the storyworld, the functions of waiting are related to latent processes in Leena's growth. The sudden clarity of decisions is explained by the deferred quality of her unconscious processes rather than as a result of guidance from some divine deity acting behind events.

Leena's lingering path to "full, complete knowledge" is manifested in her reluctance to think further: "I just get nervous, I blank when I try to think" (*MT*, 252), she claims.[120] Leena is tired of words, of continuously thinking and talking about love, pregnancy, and the future of her affair. She prefers to wait: "I'm just tired of the whole thing; I don't have the energy to think about it anymore; I guess I've already thought about it enough. I have said that it's best for him to wait, because it seems to me it's better to do nothing now" (*MT*, 208–209).[121] Leena's employer in the city is the first person with whom she is able to talk about the affair. The momentarily intimacy between the two women forces her to articulate her ideas. Whereas the community of bourgeois women, gathered in the employer's parlor to help the "fallen" girl, is depicted as a hypocritical collective of misjudging eyes, the employer is able to ask Leena the right questions. Toward the end of the novel, Leena seems to acknowledge the causes for her indecision more clearly. These ideas reach her awareness as pre-conscious feelings of her emotions: "He's so different from me, the girl said and listened to what she had said. But the voice was gone, she couldn't bring it back to her ears anymore" (*MT*, 255).[122]

Leena's pre-conscious state in the process of self-discovery is manifested in symbolic scenes and allusions that serve as indicators of her inner happenings. The trope of sleep reappears in the scene in which Leena enters a dimly lighted cellar, an embodied space signifying her pre-conscious. When she returns upstairs, the feeling of the unreal remains: "And even after rising in the elevator and opening the door and arriving in the kitchen, it was as if she were asleep, as if she had drifted off and objects wouldn't stay in her hands, as if her hand didn't really know what it held or what was supposed to be done with each thing" (*MT*, 219).[123] Leena feels exhaustion that "had fallen upon her like a cloth flung over her eyes" (ibid.).[124] The comparison of tiredness with cloth that prevents her seeing refers to Leena's inability to attain full knowledge of her situation.

In the later part of the novel, Leena's half-conscious state is evoked by allusions that dramatize her tangled relation to the man. Before the childbirth, Leena is shown wondering whether to continue her needlework. Its tangled threads signify the complicated relationship. As she looks at her knitting, she realizes she has made a mistake and considers unraveling the whole work: "She wouldn't weave it, she couldn't. It was for nothing; she'd never get it finished; once a pattern tangled, it would stay tangled, the model was too complicated and the thread was stained, and it was too thin to stand the unweaving and weaving, back and forth. Or then it should be cut off" (*MT*, 222).[125] The constant unweaving and weaving obviously refer to Leena's thoughts as she ponders the future paths of an affair that has been damaged by the constant state of indecision of all parties in the triangle: Leena, the man, and his wife. Leena's needlework illustrates the continuous oscillation between the stages of negotiation and refusal in the romance plot, suggesting the beginning of the end of the affair.

Unable to disentangle the stained threads, Leena runs across the road to the movie theater. The movie is Jean Cocteau's *Orfeus*. Leena is unable to understand the story: "They talked about Orfeus, Orfeus, Orfeus was a man who wandered through empty houses and leafed through papers; they were searching for a name and talking about some woman. [...] The film ended, but she didn't understand what she had seen" (*MT*, 223).[126] The reference to the film can be seen as reflecting the triangle of Leena, the man, and his wife. While married to Euridice, Orfeus falls fatally in love with Death, becoming "the servant of Death" ("kuoleman palvelija"). Euridyce, who is killed on the very day of her marriage, is dependent on Orpheus's help to escape from the underworld. Orpheus's backward glance, however, condemns her to eternal stay in the underground world. Leena's half-conscious attempt to find a way out of the trap of the possible marriage is suggested in the journey portrayed in the film. The drama of adultery is implied in other allusions too. In the café, Leena sees a modern painting in which there are "different-colored patterns and lines" and "two triangles" that are "slanted" (*MT*, 224).[127] The slanted triangles as well as Orfeus's journey to the underworld reflect Leena's mental state as she talks about her future with the man, who at that point is still planning to get a divorce. The motifs of visual art and film are accompanied by Leena's own performance, as she acts out her role of a willing wife-to-be so animatedly that "she herself even believed what she was trying to act; that they were an ordinary married couple who had quarreled, and now everything was fine again" (*MT*, 231).[128]

At the end of the novel, many scenes with roads and forking paths illustrate the alternative paths of Leena's future. After the child's birth, Leena hears that the man has been at the hospital and has asked permission to see her. Through hypothetical focalization, Leena is depicted seeing the man wandering alone in the courtyard. The image of forking roads is accompanied by other familiar motifs, including a nipped-off bough, a variation on the same motif Vartio uses in the novel's opening scene. The man's backward glance resembles the look of Orpheus, but the door closes before he has the chance to enter the building:

[...] And the girl saw the man's face just when he had turned his head and watched the door close.

Maybe he was outside. He would be standing on the stairs or in the yard. In the yard there was snow; he would stand there, black, in the middle of the snow or maybe he was walking; there were paths; they criss-crossed the snow. Maybe he was walking near the spruce trees; he would stop to look, move the bough with his hand so that the snow fell off the branch, or nip off a needle from the top of the branch when no one was paying attention and then throw it away. It was there on the snow, a green spot. (*MT*, 274)[129]

The image of a green needle on white snow becomes a counter-image to the last withering leaves of summer at the beginning of the novel. In addition, the snow falling from the bough is juxtaposed with the image of the lilac leaves relieved of the weight of the water after Leena's run across the heath. The snowy forking paths seen in the cityscape embody the possible trajectories of Leena's and the man's futures. There are other people wandering the same paths:

> They walked on and came to the edge of the park. The paths were white there; it had snowed just enough to cover the ground.
> "Look, these are the first tracks." The girl looked behind her, black spots showed in the snow; it was wet, the ground was not yet frozen.
> "They're not the first. Look, there up ahead there are others." (*MT*, 233–234)[130]

The seemingly light dialogue involves implicit meanings. "The first tracks" seen in the pure white snow obviously allude to the first steps of the child, but also to the steps taken by Leena on her way to motherhood. In the later depiction of Leena's labor, also the motif of the white stone acquires new meanings, particularly in regard to Leena's endurance and her emotional restraint. As she thinks about the forthcoming birth, she refuses to scream – just as when she encountered the water's cold in diving into the deep: "She cried and clenched her teeth, for she would not scream. [...] it doesn't matter whether it's a stone or a frog, as long as I get rid of it" (*MT*, 266).[131] But she screams, loud and hard: "And something came loose" (*MT*, 267).[132] Leena hears the child's screech as if in response to her own scream and a splash of water which parallels with the splash of a pike she has heard in the silence by the forest lake.

The paths taken by many others in the novel refer to Leena and the man's relationship, which resembles so many typical stories of any man and any girl: "They're not the first. Look, there up ahead there are others." A key episode in the interpretation of the story's title is the lovers' dialogue discussed earlier in the context of the lake scene. Leena reads the man's words ("I guess people always feel the same things in the same way") as an indication of his indifference. She is like any girl being abandoned by any man. After losing her virginity, Leena realizes the stereotypical aspects of their love story: "[S]he was horrified when she realized that it had happened to them, that they were just like the other people, anyone, like the ones she had read about and giggled when the girls read" (*MT*, 26).[133] Leena sees herself as a part of a narrative that she cannot control: "The girl thought that everything was happening like in a novel" (*MT*, 200).[134] Later, Leena sees her name written on the man's letter, but cannot recognize it:

> It was her name, that one, on the envelope. The name was an ordinary girl's name. She had seen it written in many different ways, with many different-looking letters. She herself wrote it with big, tall letters.
> She looked again at the name on the envelope: Leena. There, written with elegant, even penmanship, it said Leena. The letters were the same, as big, as even as always.
> And yet when she looked at them, they appeared as if they were full of obscure meaning. Foreign-looking. (*MT*, 276)[135]

The man's letter is a response to her own letter in which she had asked him to wait, to "think it over and defer any decision-making" (*MT*, 277).[136] Leena perceives her name as ordinary, as being shared by many other girls, or alternatively, as being written differently by different people. She pictures the man's hand writing her name on the paper: "And she saw again a hand and a pen in the hand. [...] and a dot appeared on the paper. And the hand wrote the name on the envelope, quickly, distantly, as if it were any name. And sealed the envelope" (ibid.).[137] The sense of closure is reinforced by the mention of the dot and the closing of the envelope. Leena is finally able to admit something to herself: she does not truly love the man. And the man sees it, too: "[H]e had known for a long time, even from the beginning, that I didn't care for him, not the way people care for each other when it's the real thing" (*MT*, 278).[138] Leena pictures the man's future letters, but thinks they will be different. Even if the words remained the same, their meaning has changed: "She remembered something, some words. She remembered that she had said them. But they had come back to her; he had not understood them" (*MT*, 279).[139]

Mies kuin mies, tyttö kuin tyttö concludes with a scene in which Leena observes a girl and a boy sharing a kiss by the movie theater. As Viikari (1992: 60) points out in her analysis of the novel, we witness "a potential beginning of a new novel with the same title" ("mahdollinen alku uudelle samannimiselle romaanille"). The novel's cyclic patterns are modified by providing a variation on the image of a path. Now it's "a boy" instead of "a man" walking beside the girl. The street ends at the edge of forest: "When she looked outside of the window again, they had disappeared from view. Perhaps they had walked up the street. The street ended at the edge of the forest. There were paths among the trees there; she had walked them" (*MT*, 280).[140] The narrative path of *Mies kuin mies, tyttö kuin tyttö*, however, ends with scenes that suggest separation of the lovers instead of reconciliation. Leena's mental image of the man's hand writing her name (like the name of any girl) is followed by another association, one related to Leena's own hand. As she moves her hand, something happens:

> She turned her eyes away, looked now at the objects in the dim room; she moved her hand. It existed because it moved when she thought, I'll move it now. Sleepless night and tiredness, that's what made her feel like this. As if the world around her had become thinner, the objects, made out of nothing, the hands, empty, merely drawn with a stroke. (*MT*, 279)[141]

Leena's vision of the world as an image-like construct evokes associations of the character herself as a fictional object "made of nothing," predetermined by the "strokes" of the author's hand, forcing Leena to wander the well-trodden paths of tradition. Vartio, however, has left many loose ends. Leena's process of taking action seems to conclude in a state of endless lingering, pointing at the openness of the fictional universe. The ultimate self-knowledge attained at the end of epistemic quests typical of classical Bildungsroman is never accomplished. Leena is left drifting in a state of indecision, as if she were given the opportunity to take her fate into her own hands.

4. Cycles of Arousal and Fall. Mirroring the Self in *Kaikki naiset näkevät unia*

Dreams throng about me.
Dreams open gates into me. [...]

And birds burst open their wings,
their wings, black on top, white under, they burst open
flying to the horizon.
One alone, that tripterous one,
falls during the journey,
on the journey always falls dead.[1]

– Marja-Liisa Vartio: "A Woman and a Landscape"

In *Kaikki naiset näkevät unia*, the female protagonist, Mrs. Pyy, looks back at her life. Gazing at herself in the mirror, she imagines her previous self as a young girl wandering along forest paths. The image of the girl is presented as an unfolding narrative – an animated portrait that resorts to the conventions of fairytale. As the fairytale reaches its end, the young girl's bloom turns into a middle-aged woman's decay, and she grieves over her lost self:

> Once upon a time there was a forest and in the forest was a girl, and the girl had a mouth, small and graceful like a flower. And her face, heart-shaped and her chin soft and round, like the tip of a heart-shaped image. [...]
> The smile vanished from the lips, and she sputtered silently: it cannot be true.
> This is a mistake, this is a betrayal. Where was the girl who had stood under the tree, where had she gone, where had she gone when she left the forest? Had she taken the wrong path and gotten lost? Just when had this dreadful change taken place? (*K*, 229)[2]

In Mrs. Pyy's life narrative, the young girl has chosen the wrong path from among the many forking paths in the forest and has gotten lost. The wrong decisions haunt Mrs. Pyy, a troubled housewife living a middle-class life in the suburbs. She is repeatedly lost in speculations about how things might have been, the alternative paths of her life. The fairy tale pattern serves the depiction of Mrs. Pyy's journey into her inner self as she seeks more authentic ways of being. In trying to alleviate the imbalance in her life, Mrs. Pyy resorts to hypothetical, alternative scenarios, which mentally mutate the traumatic situation in which she finds herself. By counterfactualizing, she seeks to "undo" the events in the past caused by her rashly-made decisions and hasty actions. Every attempt to comfort her anxiety – occupying herself with art, taking a lover, building a house – ends in lost illusions and disappointment. The real reason for her anxiety seems to escape her notice.

A female character caught counterfactualizing the missed opportunities of her life is a recurring motif in subgenres and narrative forms, such as representations of female development and romance plots. In these narratives, the female protagonists often muse about what might have been. In nineteenth-century fiction the representations of female development were used to demonstrate the recurring patterns of women's life plots. These life paths were located exclusively within discordant alternate worlds in which closure or happiness were eternally deferred or denied (this discordancy is illustrated by the trope of the "madwoman" employed in fictions dealing with female development). In twentieth-century fiction, counterfactuality becomes a narrative strategy providing contradictory versions of reality, which generate more unconventional patterns of female fiction. The alternative world suggests a fictional escape that finally leads the female protagonists away from the entrapment of the closure of romance. (Cf. Dannenberg 2008: 138, 228)

In *Kaikki naiset näkevät unia*, Mrs. Pyy's escape from her entrapments is both suggested and challenged. The ambivalence of Mrs. Pyy's epistemic path stems from the uncertainty of her ability to regain her "true" self. In narratives of female awakening, the heroine's self-development is often delayed until adulthood by the protagonist's inadequate education. This version of female Bildung is represented in the plot pattern of the novel of awakening, which is modified in Mrs. Pyy's life story. The protagonist grows only after the closure of marriage. Her growth often blossoms only momentarily and then dissolves. (Abel, Hirsch & Langland 1983: 11–12) In general, the spiritual Bildung related to the inward awakening is an ambivalent achievement. Despite its rewards it may also lead to social isolation, madness, or even death. The heroine may learn to see the lack of harmony between her outer and inner self, but is unable to find her way out. (Hirsch 1983: 26; Castle 2006: 225) The optimistic belief in the possibility of female self-discovery defines twentieth-century narratives, even if the plots of inward awakening do not necessarily supply any resolution. These stories often leave open the possibility of the protagonist's final self-recognition.

This chapter examines the ways in which Mrs. Pyy's embodied trauma is implied in her relations to others and to the surrounding fictional world. First, Mrs. Pyy's performative self-image is explored vis-à-vis her tendency to misread others and thereby to misread her own mind. These analyses are followed by readings of Mrs. Pyy's split mind as a layered mental space, an embodied entity interacting with its surroundings. Her mental space contains gaps and blanks that indicate the presence of past traumatic experiences. These experiences are absent from the representation of her conscious thoughts, but they appear in embodied images provided in the text. As evocations of her split memory, these images are examined in relation to Mrs. Pyy's dream worlds. Certain works of art are also analyzed as being among the self-mirrors that she uses while building up her middle-class identity. Finally, the emotional story structure of the novel is explored in the context of the cycles of Mrs. Pyy's emotional arousal, which led to repetitious failures and disillusionment. These structures are then approached from the perspective of the deferred patterns of female self-discovery staging the possibilities of Mrs. Pyy's awakening to herself and reality as it is.

The Deceiving Mind. Looking at the Self in the Mirror of Others

In *Kaikki naiset näkevät unia*, a mind-reading ability becomes one of the survival tools for Mrs. Pyy, who shields herself by reading the minds of other people. "I read people like an open book, and my instinct does not fail" (*K*, 47).[3] Eventually, she is shown to be suffering from serious self-delusion. While Mrs. Pyy tries to find answers to her personal crises, she continuously reflects upon herself through the mirrors of others, builds identities and roles that protect her from intrusions by others, yet simultaneously these maneuvers separate her from real human contact. The beginning of the novel stages this ambivalence of private and public selves with Mrs. Pyy portrayed as peeping from behind curtains as the new neighbor is moving in. Mrs. Pyy critically observes the woman's property and her appearance. Mrs. Pyy considers herself lucky to have been the first to move into an empty row house: "The same old furniture, although the apartment is new, and one has to show one's life to strange people" (*K*, 13).[4]

The friendship and solidarity between women is a common theme in female Bildungsromane. The exploration of the self with a dimension of group solidarity and collective identity typically projects a visionary hope of future change in women's roles (Felski 1989: 139). In *Kaikki naiset näkevät unia*, however, other women reflect the protagonist's deepening sense of self-alienation and resignation. The idea of hostility to other women's thoughts is emphasized in the dialogues between Mrs. Pyy and her husband following the opening scene. Mrs. Pyy describes the women of the neighborhood as "snakes" full of ulterior motives and evil gazes: "If it's possible for a human to have an evil eye, then she has one" (*K*, 47), Mrs. Pyy says of one of the women.[5] Mrs. Pyy tries to convince her husband of the accuracy of the rumors that she has heard the other women spreading about her: "I heard it with my own ears," Mrs. Pyy insists (*K*, 34).[6] But the narrator catches her out in a lie: "She had heard it from the cleaning woman. She had recounted what she had heard the other women talking about" (ibid.).[7]

Rumors are shown to be marked by potential unreliability: the more layered the talk, the more distorted the initial message. The risks for misreading increase if the character listens to others *too* eagerly. The self-deceiving sufferers, such as Mrs. Pyy, tend to deliberately mishear everything others say. When Mrs. Pyy visits an artist with whom she has tried to strike up an acquaintance, she keeps listening to the "true" meaning behind every word: "'No, you don't disturb me, I wasn't doing anything special,' the artist replied. But Mrs. Pyy heard the voice; it answered her: 'Yes, you disturb me, but I don't have the nerve to tell you, because you are tactless enough to ask if you disturb me'" (*K*, 139).[8] Here Mrs. Pyy misreads the exhaustion in the artist's expressions as a personal insult directed at her. She considers her own false attributions as actual representations of the artist's thoughts. The reader, however, can interpret the more likely signs embodied in the artist's gestures: she is exhausted after an intensive period of working.

The Janus-faced ambivalence of intersubjectivity, evoking both yearning and anxiety, is portrayed in the mind-reading sequences when Mrs. Pyy is talking with her old friend Laura. Laura is sharing the experiences of her painful divorce. In turn, Mrs. Pyy makes her own confession that comes as a surprise to the reader. She has had a lover for some time. In the scene, possibilities for empathy and recognition are suggested and simultaneously denied as Mrs. Pyy imagines tears running down Laura's face, "as if Laura had been somewhere and gotten to know something that she was not even going to try to share with anyone" (*K*, 94).[9] Mrs. Pyy understands that one can never truly know another person. A genuine intimacy means an ability to be silent when words are in vain: "Mrs. Pyy understood. She was herself; Laura over there was someone else. They might talk to each other about everything, like before, but they knew not to talk about things they couldn't speak of. This thing that was happening to them right now, there were no words to explain it" (ibid.).[10] The time of unconditional sharing is over: "It wasn't important anymore," Mrs. Pyy claims and gives a sad laugh (ibid.).[11]

The failure to keep track of oneself as the source of the representations of other people's minds particularly characterizes mentally unstable characters. A paranoid quality of mind-reading arises out of the mechanisms of misrepresenting one's own mind. This aspect of mind-reading manifests itself as the characters perceive their own thoughts emanating, not from their own intentions, but from some outer source not under their control (Zunshine 2004: 55). Disembodied voices stem from a mind that loses its ability to keep track of itself as the origin of obsessive thoughts. The delusions of thought insertions and alien control are manifested in Mrs. Pyy's hallucinations after she has escorted Laura back to the train station. After the train has gone, Mrs. Pyy stands watching the tracks that lead to life elsewhere. She imagines the station clock transformed into a huge eye, resembling a surrealist painting (cf. Ruuska 2010: 131). The clock observes her every movement, as if measuring the diminishing time left in her life. When the second hand moves again, she feels "as if she has heard someone taking a big bite and swallowing it – or as if someone had fallen head over heels down into the darkness, and she had heard the fall" (*K*, 96).[12]

The Icarian fall is mentioned for the first time when Mrs. Pyy talks to Laura about the "black region" ("musta alue") into which she has fallen: "You yourself are so sensible and calm; maybe you are not even aware that there is something inside you – how should I put it – a black region into which you fall, or wish to fall [...]" (*K*, 91).[13] The fall becomes an image of the unconscious, the unknown within, which alienates Mrs. Pyy from her habitual self. She stands, paralyzed, at the station. The world turns into a dark and frightening place, even as she struggles to come back into her own skin, "to breathe herself alive again and free, to be again who she was, Mrs. Pyy" (*K*, 99).[14] The mode of narrated monologue is employed to generate an impression of Mrs. Pyy's self-distancing as she pictures herself joining the stream of citizens who know who they are and where they are going and are rationally planning their actions. She is Mrs. Pyy, "who walks forward, opens the door of the hall, opens another door, comes to the stairs of the station and walks down and to a specific platform to wait for a specific bus that will take her to a specific part of the city, and then she would go into a specific building, and into a specific apartment, number A 8. She was Mrs. Pyy" (ibid.).[15]

As Mrs. Pyy's sense of estrangement deepens, the metaphor of "the evil eye" ("paha silmä") takes a materialized form of paranoia. It is reduced to pure delusion: all humans have evil eyes. The conditional source tag in Mrs. Pyy's previous thought – "If it's possible [for a person to have an evil eye]"[16] – disappears. Mrs. Pyy imagines other people as creatures with "feelers" ("tuntosarvet") watching her. She is an outsider who has landed on another planet, an alien who does not belong where she is. Cars turn into living beings with intellects of their own; a bus has thoughts that resemble Mrs. Pyy's own mechanical, automatic thoughts as the bus "opened up, unloaded something, without paying attention to what it was doing, still thinking about the same thing, the same thing, as if continuing the same thought even while it was standing in place" (*K*, 101).[17] Mrs. Pyy keeps counting the dots in an illuminated advertisement. Her mind is mesmerized by the blinking lights that trigger her need to count the number of dots over and over again. Unable to break the circle, she starts from the beginning, even while she is aware of the irrationality of her actions: "The things I count, she mumbled; she became vexed when she realized she had started to count for the third time the red dots blinking in the illuminated advertisement over the door of the restaurant opposite" (*K*, 103).[18]

The cycles of counting resemble Mrs. Pyy's cycles of self-attentive thought, which demonstrate the dangers of an over-aroused mind. Arousal involving the feeling of fear, for instance, locks the mind into its emotional state, causing emotional tension and anxiety in the aroused mind. In the portrayal of Mrs. Pyy's mental actions, the feeling leads into the vicious cycles of pathological arousal as the mind's attention is persistently directed toward the emotional responses rather than the external reality seen "as it is."[19] Mrs. Pyy cannot control her mind. She is obsessed with the irrational thought that someone is observing her with a malicious eye: "She was hiding there on the fringe, observing, but she had been seen; it was known that there was someone strange over there, looking around the way a stranger does; she had woken that person up, over there" (*K*, 104).[20]

Mrs. Pyy's random interpretations of her environment and other people reveal the imaginative mind's tendency to be superstitious, thereby giving birth to circles of fear and desire (cf. Kavanagh 1993: 12–13). For a tragic, superstitious mind, fate becomes an internalized force, manifesting itself as a desire to repudiate chance and see meaning in every event.[21]

The characters' denial of randomness may result in superstitious beliefs or, by contrast, in delusion, as randomness is repeatedly interpreted as meaningful. This kind of "delirium of interpretation" (Bell 1993: 99) triggers a feeling of mysteriousness that does not truly exist. In Vartio's fiction the delusive quality of imagination is also emphasized in the representations of paranoia that stem from an excess of interpretation, "logical thinking gone wild" (ibid.: 98). Even the most minor details of others' behavior become sources of far-reaching conclusions: "Not only is every event down to the most inconspicuous and minor one incorporated into the paranoid's world view, but, in addition, each of those details is enlisted in the service of an explanation meant to prove that malice of some sort is intended toward the paranoid himself or herself" (ibid.).

The delusiveness of the mirroring of oneself in the mirrors of others relates to Mrs. Pyy's self-obsession. Compared to Vartio's early figures, Anni and Leena, Mrs. Pyy is overly self-conscious. She resembles the figure of Napoleon in her tendency to perform and reach for better worlds: "She read the art column and the for-rent ads in the newspaper. She read them line by line as if looking through them into another world, into other environments, as if they provided comfort, encouragement" (*K*, 39–40).[22] While reaching for better worlds, Mrs. Pyy ends up constructing her self-performances in relation to others. Her motivation to look at others is to see others looking back. The characters' attentiveness to versions of themselves is dependent on how confident they are. The less self-assured the character is, the more attentive she or he is as to what others think of her or him. (Butte 2004: 58) Characters such as Mrs. Pyy perceive themselves mostly as imaged through others. They are powerfully aware of others as a mirror in which their own image is reflected.

In the narratives of female awakening, the false roles imposed upon the protagonist are juxtaposed to the more authentic self, which – in the best scenario – comes to light during the course of the narrative (Felski 1989: 132). The making new of Bildung in the narratives of female development is manifested in formal innovations related to the narrative dynamics of self-formation that reflect the new ideas of subjectivity and the artifice of the self. The frustrated and detoured Bildung of modernist novels leads to a "failure" in terms of the traditional form. This very failure, however, illustrates the re-assessed notion of the self as a constructed and reconstructed image, an ego, rather than as a coherent, harmonious identity. (Castle 2006: 27–28, 192–193) The modernist Bildung refers to identities that are hybrid, ambivalent, and may involve traumatic processes of self-formation (ibid.: 64).[23]

In *Kaikki naiset näkevät unia*, the experience of otherness derives from the dichotomization between self-images that problematizes the process of Mrs. Pyy's self-formation. The other women reflect a narcissistic split in her personality. She is captivated by her own image, and for this very reason, is unable to see others as they are. Other people serve only as projections of her emotional responses. Mrs. Pyy's inclination to see herself through the eyes of others, however, is portrayed with special clarity in her relation to her lover. Mrs. Pyy's thoughts about the affair are revealed only at the point the relationship has begun to approach its end. During her last dinner with her lover, Mrs. Pyy analyzes her expectations of the relationship: "She had expected the man to tell her, the woman, who she was. The woman wanted to see herself through the man, as if only through his eyes would she see herself" (*K*, 156).[24]

Even in the middle of an emotional outburst, Mrs. Pyy is constantly aware of the impression she is making on people. Leaving the restaurant, humiliated and furious, she keeps reading the impressions of herself in the people around her: "I'll walk with my back straight. It's important that I walk with my back straight. I'll walk to that door. And she knew that she had gotten free of something, she walked along the carpet and she knew. Tried, that man, tried to prop me up, and that head waiter *looks at me and thinks that I'm someone, someone whom someone has gotten drunk here*" (*K*, 165).[25] In the restaurant episode, Mrs. Pyy splits in two. She sees herself from a distance as if through someone else's eyes.

In Mrs. Pyy's self-reflection, the scripts of the intersubjective – the layerings of gazes and gestures – are gendered in a subtle way (cf. Butte 2004: 111). The lover's act of mirroring, in Mrs. Pyy's mirror, is hostile and critical. She keeps imagining what the lover is seeing, what occurs in his consciousness as he looks at her. "Then she stared at the man with her head high, and it was as if she had seen her own profile from the outside" (*K*, 157).[26] The vision Mrs. Pyy imagines is not a pleasant one: "[A] cruel look in the eyes, head high, hands trembling, she looked at the man and was pleased with herself. Of course, in his eyes I look awful right now, but that's exactly what I want. For once, to be *who I really am*" (*K*, 157).[27] Mrs. Pyy has realized that she cannot hold onto her performance for long. Paradoxically, her affected smile becomes the signifier of her "real" face: "Someday this man too would see this face, this one that she herself saw in the mirror, saw only this face, not her real face, this face that kept smiling and which she offered to the man's eyes, when he looked at her" (*K*, 124).[28]

The mirroring effect is intensified by the use of a mirror in the restaurant scene. As Mrs. Pyy and the lover are leaving the restaurant, they see their reflection in the mirror on the wall of the elevator: "But a woman looked at them from the mirror, and she knew who it was. And behind her, sideways, stood a man. Sideways, so that his face would no longer be next to the woman's face. The man doesn't need to stand sideways. And she turned, and the woman in the mirror turned [...]" (*K*, 165).[29] The couple's composition reflects the change in their relationship – the distance which has grown between them. This distance is reflected in their gestures when they are trapped in the confined space. Mrs. Pyy wants to show the man that she has no romantic expectations, which leads to a loop of mirrorings: "The other surely understood that she wasn't still standing close to him on purpose, her back against his back. For you are a stranger now, but you think that I pushed you because I still want something from you" (*K*, 166), Mrs. Pyy speculates.[30]

Mrs. Pyy's sense of self-identity is being formed as a result of identifying with her own specular image. This mirror shows the reflections of the people around her. It provides imaginary wholeness to a self that is experienced as a fragmentary entity. Self-articulation of this kind implies, of course, a false recognition: the self is a product of a series of misunderstandings. In the restaurant, Mrs. Pyy realizes the performed quality of her identity: "Wouldn't I try to be wiser than I am, to *perform a role* so as not to lose favor in his eyes, even though I am only a dumb little woman. And that's what he wanted of me, a small dumb woman, who has been pleasant and even considerate, at least lately" (*K*, 155).[31] The scenes of self-distancing reflect Mrs. Pyy's ability to see herself anew as she realizes what the man has thought of her: "And it felt as if she had suddenly risen above that man by seeing and understanding herself the way he had judged her" (ibid.).[32]

As Mrs. Pyy begins to see her lover more realistically, she drops the mask she has been wearing. The mask, however, has already become another version of her self-understanding. Mrs. Pyy cannot always be clear to herself (or to her audience) or define where pretense begins and where it ends. The boundaries between performance and performer have disappeared. She performs even if there is no audience, in the privacy of her home:

> She had poured coffee, taken sugar and cream, stirred it with a spoon, had done all that, being careful not to make any sudden movements. She had sat, back straight, held the cup with her little finger extended, had taken tiny sips as if at a coffee party, where the coffee itself is secondary and the main thing is how you drink it and what you talk about while doing so. But she was sitting alone. [...] Who had seen this gracious comportment? Whom had she been trying to impress? (*K*, 17)[33]

Mrs. Pyy's performances exemplify an action type Palmer calls "dramaturgical action." Its defining feature is the character's aim to evoke in the audience a certain image or impression by purposefully *disclosing her or his subjectivity*. Instead of spontaneous, expressive behavior, the subject stylizes gestures, expressions, feelings, experiences, thoughts, attitudes, and desires with a view to the audience. (Palmer 2004: 166) In other words, the character is pretending.

A character's management of other characters' impressions of them has strategic goals. Mrs. Pyy's performances are typically aimed at masculine audiences.[34] With regard to her husband, she sometimes adopts a role of "a clueless little woman" ("pieni ymmärtämätön nainen") who admires manly wisdom (*K*, 191). By acting like "some dependent being" ("joku epäitsenäinen olento"), she is able to get what she wants, even if she is painfully aware of her actual economic and social dependence (*K*, 18). Her "pretense" is a way to connect, to get attention: "Why are you leaving me in the dark? the wife asked after a moment, in a childish voice, as if pretending to be afraid of the dark, as if waiting for the man to join in the game, *to hear her voice* and say something, something similar" (*K*, 42).[35] The husband's answer is silence: "The man didn't answer. His breathing was heard in the dark" (ibid.).[36] Mrs. Pyy ends up seeking attention from a lover's arms, but drifts into a parallel pattern of futile performance, feeling invisible and unheard, falling into the dark arising from within.

As mentioned above, Mrs. Pyy sometimes forgets she is wearing a mask. The performances of femininity often become naturalized to the actor, and the mask begins to deceive the masker (Butte 2004: 195–196). The soft voice of a child-wife comes out accidentally, as if dictated by a bad habit. In the false mirroring of others, the subject is alienated from itself. Mrs. Pyy often describes her life as a play in which she is acting, playing her role like a professional. When Mrs. Pyy and her lover end up spending their last evening at the lover's friend's place, she again hides her true feelings: "And she seized a glass. The world was this, seizing a glass in a certain way, raising it to the lips. It was expected of one to smile at the host, it belonged to good manners. She pasted a smile on her face and kept it there like a mask" (*K*, 169).[37]

Masks are worn to deceive the audience, to disclose subjectivity from others. For the sake of civility and social balance, it is important to learn to cover up one's negative thoughts, at least temporarily. Whether there is a truer or more authentic identity behind the mask is the problem that Vartio plumbs in her novel. At least there are possibilities for healthier performances of a self, the novel seems to suggest. (Cf. Butte 2004: 196) When Mrs. Pyy observes her lover in the restaurant, she longs for her true self as if it were lost for a long time. She calls herself back like a "lonely stray dog" being badly treated (*K*, 157).[38] Mrs. Pyy's regained self-knowledge is shown in her desire to be "for once who [she] really is" in her paradoxical self-acknowledgment as she sees her reflection in the mirror and *knows* who the woman in the mirror is. Mrs. Pyy keeps repeating her womanly role, but at least in a highly conscious manner. The bitter irony in Mrs. Pyy's comment in the restaurant implies her inclination to wear womanliness like a mask *only* to mock the self-image that has been offered her: "'Excuse me,' Mrs. Pyy said. 'I guess I'm really drunk,' she added lightly. 'Two Martinis... they'll knock down *a small woman like me*,' she said and suddenly felt strange, cold rage, and as she felt the rage spreading through her body like a clear, steely substance, she felt pleasure" (ibid.).[39]

Mrs. Pyy's masked performance is no longer guided by the need for approval, but rather by the wish to ridicule the stereotypical behavior of womanhood. However, it is essential to keep in mind that the role of the "clueless little woman" Mrs. Pyy adopts is only a reflection of the thoughts she *suspects* exist in her lover's mind. Is the role really offered to her or has she adopted it as a result of her misappropriation of her lover's thoughts? The lover's embodied perceptions of her perceptions reflect the role that Mrs. Pyy has written for herself as a woman being mistreated by an indifferent lover: "He evidently thinks that I'm not drunk but just pretending, so I can turn to him for help. He *thinks I think that I am always thinking* myself justified in expecting something from him. That I expect him to be chivalrous, the gentleman, in spite of everything, right to the end" (*K*, 166).[40] As Mrs. Pyy's possible misappropriations show, the characters may see only what they want or fear to see. The reflections perceived in the mirror of others are always mediated, often obscured or distorted. The self is a series of fictions evolving in sequences, in narratives of recognition. (Butte 2004: 5–7, 118) Mrs. Pyy keeps on misreading others, thereby misreading herself, and eventually she gets lost in her complex webs of virtual reflections.

The ambivalent function of mind-reading is manifested also in a scene portraying Mrs. Pyy's visit to the psychiatrist's office, an exact replica of an appointment with a psychoanalyst in Freud's *Vorlesungen zur Einführung in die Psychoanalyse* (Introduction to Psychoanalysis, 1916–1917).[41] In his chapter 16, Freud describes the typical behavior of a patient suffering from megalomania, a condition of grandiosity leading to delusional fantasies, overestimation of personal abilities, and arrogance toward the analyst. Mrs. Pyy has difficulty letting her masks drop, as evidenced by her denial of her mental troubles: "[S]he wasn't the sort of person who was written about in women's magazines; she had had good parents, a good childhood. What traumas could she possibly have?" (*K*, 247)[42] And later: "Nothing troubles me" (*K*, 259).[43] Even during hypnosis, she tries to catch the real intentions behind the psychiatrist's professional mask by studying his facial expressions:

> Mrs. Pyy stared at the face on the other side of the desk.
> The eyes had turned away. But she had had time to glimpse the expression on the face before it vanished immediately. First there had been tense, curious anticipation, then – just as her own face had started to twist – as rage had arisen on her face and made her look ugly, terrible – a tense expression like in a card game had appeared on that face, and at the same time, out of her mouth had come that word, the expression changed to satisfaction, it held pleasure. He was satisfied now; it was as if those eyes were saying: just as I thought. (*K*, 261–262)[44]

As "that word" comes out, Mrs. Pyy feels exposed and beaten, like a stray dog or an insect that has been categorized and examined. She views the psychiatrist as an advocate of the devil himself, an emotionless automaton, or a trickster, a mage who has penetrated her soul and left her completely empty. The psychiatrist has asked whether she loves her husband. Her answer is "no" (*K*, 261).

The idea of a patient as the only valid source of (psycho)analysis is emphasized in Mrs. Pyy's therapy session. Mrs. Pyy is shown to know and understand the motivations of her actions herself: "You do understand, because you are reporting them yourself" (*K*, 266), the psychiatrist explains.[45] According to the psychiatrist, Mrs. Pyy is not a hysterical personality, but rather a person who, "under psychic pressure," is prone to "drift into states that resemble hysteria" (ibid.).[46] These states can be considered as the "defense mechanisms of the soul" (ibid.),[47] driving her to "live possessed by her affects, throwing herself from one into another" (*K*, 269).[48] In this respect, Mrs. Pyy's question of whether she is only "a hen that pretends to be paralyzed" (*K*, 266) is revealing.[49] The hen obviously refers to the protagonist's name "Pyy," which in Finnish means "Hazel Hen" (a bird that cannot fly).[50] Mrs. Pyy is puzzled by the psychiatrist's talk, but at the same time she feels satisfaction: "She had only listened – curious, and feeling a certain pleasure, had felt downright satisfaction when so much was said about her. For it must mean that perhaps she wasn't a totally average person" (*K*, 269).[51] Mrs. Pyy compares herself to the analyst. She is convinced of her own skills as a mind-reader:

Mrs. Pyy stopped, said half aloud: "That trickster is a devil." But at the same time she was amused; it felt to her as if she herself were also a devil, come to spy another devil's tricks – and gotten trapped.

But hadn't he said that she had used all that to avenge her own humiliation on other people? Had she? But she had always hated those people. But at the same time, when she thought about it, she wanted to refute it, the claim that she had exaggerated everything. No, that wasn't true. And still she had confessed: "Yes, I guess it is so, then." (*K*, 266–267)[52]

Mrs. Pyy's "tricks" refer to her tendency to misinterpret other people's minds, to see "evil eyes" all around observing her with hostile thoughts. The delusional fantasies of grandiosity and the "narcissistic scar" that causes her sense of inferiority, however, never come up in her conscious self-analysis. She keeps speculating on the psychiatrist's words and eventually denies everything, even after having affirmed the results of the therapeutic talk. However, after the session, Mrs. Pyy bursts into a purifying laughter, laughing both to herself and to the psychiatrist: "Good God, what a fool she had been!" (*K*, 269)[53]

Mrs. Pyy's trauma, her scar, is manifested in the obsessive cycles of action and thought and seems to be related to her self-delusions, her obsession with the self. The tragedy of Mrs. Pyy stems from her tendency to end up performing the self she wishes to be, while seeking a more genuine, undivided self. Mrs. Pyy's last attempts to patch up her selfhood are embodied in her struggle to build a house that is never finished. The apartment in a row house is a "hen coop" ("kanakoppi") that can no longer satisfy her needs (*K*, 26). In the end, the grandiose plan of a detached, spacious house outside the city is destroyed by financial problems. She finds herself living in an old apartment building in the middle of town, walking among the "ruins" of the house of her dreams. The financial fall leads to a furious auction as Mrs. Pyy sells all her personal belongings to other women, as if turning her public humiliation into a performance. This scene resembles "ritual purification" in the plots of female awakening as the protagonist strips of herself clothing and possessions that represent her more civilized self (Felski 1989: 144). In *Kaikki naiset näkevät unia*, however, the repudiation of Mrs. Pyy's past existence is complicated by her tendency to cling on to the objects of the material world instead of investing in her spiritual and emotional well-being. The other women, "those people" that Mrs. Pyy claims to hate, serve as mirrors of herself and the material ideals of middle-class identity that seem beyond her reach.

The Dark Window. Images of the Embodied Self

Mrs. Pyy's detoured awakening is portrayed through a series of embodied images that reflect the problems of her self-formation. The protagonist's traumatic experiences are represented as distant bodily sensations that arise from the emotional unconscious, but never fully emerge in her awareness. At the psychiatrist's office, Mrs. Pyy's hypnosis evokes a recurring image of "a dark window" ("pimeä ikkuna"), which becomes a key element in the interpretation of her mental life. In a house outside the city, it felt as if "a terrible crime had once happened; the window was like that, painted black, an image of a window on the wall" (*K*, 260–261).[54] During the session, Mrs. Pyy feels that there is "something," "someone dead, murdered" in that house (ibid.).[55] According to Mrs. Pyy's self-analysis, the murder is a manifestation of the rejection of love, just as she had "murdered" her "good husband" by denying him (*K*, 268).[56] The trope of murder occurs again in the scene set in the lover's apartment. Mrs. Pyy tries to draw the lover's attention by reading the newspaper aloud: "It seems that they still haven't caught that murderer" (*K*, 134).[57] On her way to her lover's place, Mrs. Pyy experiences a moment of self-revelation that hints at the potential distortion of her introspection: "Something has died inside me" (*K*, 124), she cries.[58] While holding back her anxiety, she feels like she is suffocating, "her throat hurts as if she had drunk too much water" (*K*, 123).[59]

A parallel scene occurs as Mrs. Pyy struggles to hold on to her mask in the presence of her husband. She walks out of the room, silently closes the door, and stands in the dark entrance: "And while she held back sobs, she felt as if her body had been filled with something; she felt like a vessel filled to the brim, and it was as if she had sensed the taste, something cold and bitter" (*K*, 228).[60] By evoking feelings of drowning and lacking air, these psycho-analogies serve as images of embodied symptoms of anxiety. They are motivated by Mrs. Pyy's attempts to understand and articulate her mental states. In the following quotation, Mrs. Pyy's shortness of breath is compared to throwing an empty bucket into a deep well:

> She drew a deep breath, and another, as if sucking air into her mouth, but she couldn't get her breath to flow; it was as if someone had tried to throw a bucket into a deep well, on the bottom of which there was only a little water; when it was pulled up it was empty; and the person tried again, and only after several attempts reached the water so that the vessel was filled. That's what she would tell the doctor, describe her anxiety just like that. (*K*, 248)[61]

Mrs. Pyy's mind becomes a split space depicted as a house or a container. The latter image modifies symbolist compositions in which the mind is pictured as a vessel being filled with inner reflections emerging from behind a person's closed eyes.[62] In Mrs. Pyy's case, however, the inner images are deeply rooted in her material body. From the deep well of the mind arise fear-induced emotions that lead to the vicious cycles of repetition at moments of emotional arousal.[63] Obsessive bodily repetitions are attached to certain situations, which produce fear and anxiety. These situations are meaningless as such; they serve only as reminders of some initial moment of loss.

Mrs. Pyy is said to have read a book written by some psychiatrist, who has claimed that in a person's mind, restored memories may be found from the past, even from the moment of birth.[64] When Mrs. Pyy tried to express these thoughts to someone, she did not manage to find words to explain her feelings. She recalls how her unborn child moved within her body. She was paralyzed, listening "as if she had stood on the shore in the dim light and heard a fish plunge into water somewhere; so that before there was time to turn around and look, the surface of the water was calm; nothing was seen or heard" (*K*, 276).[65] The distant sensations in the body are used to parallel the fragility of Mrs. Pyy's introspection. She does not know the primal cause of her anxious feelings, because they remain deep in her emotional unconscious. Mrs. Pyy, however, remembers one particular moment of inner peace experienced on a ship in the middle of the sea:

> Something strange had happened: she had felt as if she didn't even exist; yet she hadn't been unconscious, it didn't resemble that. Nothing was worrying her: there was no knowledge or memory of anything; she hadn't even realized, hadn't recognized that she felt good. The feeling had been somehow as perfect as if she hadn't known that there was anything else but the dark water around her. (*K*, 275)[66]

A simultaneous feeling of being and non-being captures the blissful moment when Mrs. Pyy is freed from the pressures of memories and self-observation, and is simply floating in the stream of experience flowing moment by moment. The state obviously refers to the initial state of the human being in the comforting warmth of the mother's womb, unconscious of the self, surrounded by the "dark water" ("himmeä vesi"). This primal state resembles the state of pure, boundless consciousness. During her sleepless nights, Mrs. Pyy has tried to calm her mind by bringing back the feeling, but without success. What if it had been only a dream?

Walking through the dark cityscape, Mrs. Pyy is able to capture a similar, brief moment of inner peace. The trees in the park are colored with autumn leaves. She feels a sudden hunger for living: "It had become important to walk in the dark and in the wet wind, to breathe deeply and become filled with this autumn. And the wind: she had stopped and listened to how the forest soughed and became silent again" (*K*, 118).[67] At this very moment, Mrs. Pyy experiences the presence of a masculine spirit resembling a safe father figure (or Father God): "She had closed her eyes, felt right next to her the presence of some mighty being, man-shaped, a man's shoulder to lean against; the man's heavy breathing and the being had been fierce and calm, and yet deeply mournful" (ibid.).[68] The forest space coincides with the warmth of the mother's womb, which is an allegorical image of Mrs. Pyy's regressive patterns. The darkness in the park is comforting rather than frightening. Before the walk in the park, Mrs. Pyy had been standing in front of her own window, looking at the apartment from outside, feeling a "new kind of fear" ("uutta pelkoa"). It involved the awareness "[t]hat she would have to go inside through the door of her home and recognize that her whole life was inside these walls" (*K*, 117).[69] In the cityscape the cold, bluish light contrasts with the warmth of the forest. The artificially lighted road waits for her to continue her journey: "And she had opened her eyes, turned back and come to the lighted road, cold and blue" (*K*, 118).[70]

Mrs. Pyy's disillusionment in relation to her lover and other failed projects of her life is, of course, not the primal cause of her anxiety, because these only constitute actions that seek to resolve the initial cause of her suffering. The search for comfort, security, and authority makes Mrs. Pyy act like a child, especially in relation to the men in her life, including her husband, her lover, and even her psychiatrist. Mrs. Pyy recalls one particular memory from her adolescence. An apple tree once stood in the courtyard of her farm home. Sitting under the tree, she had imagined being "in the womb of the tree," picturing the apples as "dead fetuses, wrinkled and cold" (*K*, 115).[71] And she was able to "see":

> It had been completely quiet. She had remained sitting under the tree for so long that she no longer really knew how to get away from there; it had felt like she couldn't do anything else other than sit under the tree, the green apples lying on the ground around the tree, their skins shimmering like a newborn puppy. And she had touched the trunk of the tree with her hand and been immediately frightened – as if the tree could feel the touch, as if she had secretly touched a naked foreign body. (*K*, 115)[72]

The epiphanic experience that Mrs. Pyy brings back to mind reminds the reader of the fairytale in which the girl is seen standing under a tree in the forest before she disappears. After having crawled out from under the tree, the girl does not know how to continue: "[S]he had looked at the yard and the road as if she had been away for a long time, the world had become quiet and unfamiliar, as if she hadn't known where to go" (*K*, 115).[73] This crossroad experience is later reflected in Mrs. Pyy's conceptions of the tree. The apple tree becomes an image of her aging body, her lost chances for bursting into flower once more. The tree from her childhood had become old and fruitless, and the adults had threatened to cut it down many times. But every summer it had bloomed so lavishly that no one had had the heart to fell it. Just as Mrs. Pyy had felt compassion for the tree as a child, she now feels pity for her withering body: it is "despoiled like the trees" (*K*, 123).[74]

The apple tree stages Mrs. Pyy's need to get back to her roots, to re-connect to her true nature. The cold, dead fetuses are among the images that signify her inner death. Mrs. Pyy's self-discovery is portrayed through her need for a regained connection to animal instincts repressed within and a rediscovery of the fearful, inner child (cf. Felski 1989: 146). The trope of a naked body re-emerges in the scene in which Mrs. Pyy is depicted critically observing her half-dressed husband. Her strange reactions are observed as if they were someone else's: "Her laughter was unexpected, hollow, and strange, she heard it herself, but she kept laughing, she wanted to hear it a second time, she didn't realize it was coming out of her mouth" (*K*, 42).[75] Mrs. Pyy's ambivalent attitude toward sexuality and bodily functions are also shown as she makes her way to her lover's apartment. She keeps recalling the sounds coming from the next door apartment. In the following quotation, the delay in Mrs. Pyy's thoughts (manifested in the figure of *aposiopesis*) implies the existence of an emotional complex in regard to sexuality and the material body: "Behind the wall, in that house, right behind that wall, on this side of which a man and a woman, a man and a woman – and her train of thought stopped. That behind the wall, right where the bed stood, was the neighbor's toilet. And every sound could be heard from behind the wall, right next to one's ear" (*K*, 128).[76] And Mrs. Pyy wonders why she – a grown-up – kept being embarrassed by something that was completely natural.

Another indication of Mrs. Pyy's problematic relation to her embodied being involves the memory of a woman who had once visited their house. While spending the evening at her lover's friend's place, Mrs. Pyy remembers how her husband had brought a friend home. He had been with a woman who had been married to someone else. The unknown woman, who had first resembled a statue made of ivory, had started to dance, moving around like an animal: "Mrs. Pyy saw the woman's feet, the slender legs cloaked in silk stockings, the muscles in her calves, taut, tight [...]. And the muscles relaxed, then tightened again; they were moving under the stockings, it called to mind a predator, a tiger, a panther, eyes closed, the body twisting like that of an animal" (*K*, 178).[77] According to Mrs. Pyy, the woman "wanted to shame the man by showing herself, but the man didn't want to look, or didn't dare" (*K*, 179).[78] Mrs. Pyy mirrors herself in the dancing woman, who is about to be abandoned by her lover. The memory reflects Mrs. Pyy's purely hypothetical, and still growing, sense of certainty: the lover has gotten tired of Mrs. Pyy and is about to abandon her, leave her in the dark, alone, like a stray dog.

Like the dancing woman, other female figures in the novel serve as Mrs. Pyy's mirrors. One of them is the farmer's wife, who is seen stepping into the same train as Laura. While walking through the cityscape, Mrs. Pyy imagines the two women arriving at their homes in the countryside. She pictures them looking at the fields and forests, drawing the curtains across their windows. The image of the farmer's wife, in particular, occupies her mind: "She imagined the farmer's wife arriving home at a farm house and taking off her hat, imagined the farmer's wife sitting down at the table and going to the cowshed early in the morning, across the yard. Silence, darkness; the farmer's wife walked to the shed and opened the door and the sounds the cows made could be heard in the dark" (*K*, 98).[79] As Mrs. Pyy keeps on walking, she can see her own reflection among other reflections of strangers' faces in the window and in the mirror set behind it. She barely recognizes herself: "Mrs. Pyy walked on and saw faces flash past in the glass surface of the flower stand. Behind the glass there was a mirror; in the mirror she had seen a woman's face, and it had been her face, that one she had been looking at" (*K*, 100).[80] Next to the woman's face bloom roses and pinks, but she realizes their existence only after having walked by.

The two women in the episode, Laura and the farmer's wife, serve as mirrors for Mrs. Pyy, who observes herself like a stranger among other strangers in the cityscape. At the end of the chapter, two women are seen walking by as Mrs. Pyy is riding in a bus. There are two women because there are two women within her.[81] The trope of two women is later modified in the scene in which Mrs. Pyy is depicted crying in the privacy of her bathroom. She stares death straight in the eye in her own reflection. The other woman in the mirror keeps smiling and speaking merciless words of self-hatred:

Pity. No one feels pity for you. No one feels pity for me.
  Go on and cry. Cry yourself out of this ugly, shabby, painted bathroom, out of this bleak, old, stinking stone house in the middle of the city; detach yourself

from objects, from children who don't know anything about you; cry yourself away from your husband, who was not the right man, not the right one...

Go ahead and cry a little longer. And when you have finished crying – go rinse your face with cold water, apply some lotion and some powder on your face, arrange your hair, and we are again one, you and I; I will live, you will die. When you no longer hate me, I won't hate you, either. (*K*, 230–231)[82]

The loss of the bloom of womanhood is reflected in Mrs. Pyy's constant fear of rejection, which makes her long for someone else's life. Her self-estrangement is expressed in her thought: "I can't call myself by name. She doesn't exist anymore, the person with that name" (*K*, 128).[83] The lack of a name reflects the lack of an individual identity, because Mrs. Pyy's passion, her inner fire, has become extinct. She has become alienated, deprived of her ability to feel, which typically triggers the inward awakening in the plots of female self-discovery (cf. Felski 1989: 143) The protagonist's first name, "Kaisu," is mentioned only twice. She is only "Mrs. Pyy," a housewife, or "a letter P [...] a capital letter among others" (*K*, 119).[84] The capital letter appears in the list of mothers whose only salary is child allowance. The strategy of naming in the novel foregrounds the collective aspects of mind presentation staged in the novel's title *Kaikki naiset näkevät unia* – All Women Dream (cf. Ruuska 2010: 180). The title refers to Jung's idea of the collective unconscious as one layer of the human psyche:

> But all women do that, have dreams as you do. Their soul moves through the night as a black cat, creeps across rooftops, meows under the window and comes inside through the window and sits down on the left side of your chest. You are like that woman who dreamed a white cow was coming through the door; the cow was mooing wistfully. And in the dream the woman asked accusingly why the cow had not been milked, even though its udders were aching. You are the way women are: they dream, they wake up in the morning, stare with empty eyes and are either disappointed that the dream was not real or thank their lucky stars that what they did in the dream was only a dream. (*K*, 231)[85]

The female soul is pictured as a black cat wandering from house to house at night. The cat becomes an archetypal image of the collective unconscious shared by all women. The cat is accompanied by an image of a cow, another trope denoting the primitive and collective foundation of the human psyche. These animals represent the lost potential in life. The cow is mooing wistfully, its udders aching and full of milk.

In this key passage of *Kaikki naiset näkevät unia*, the meaning of the word "dream" denotes not only the images of one's dormant state, but also daydreams and fantasies that are never fulfilled, either to the dreamer's relief or disappointment. The alienation typical of female developmental plots is personified in the figure of a housewife who suffers ennui and lack of self-fulfillment after the experience of marriage. The trope of absent-minded housewife is employed in *Kaikki naiset näkevät unia* to represent Mrs. Pyy's emotional estrangement: her repetitious, automatic everyday experiences and states of (day)dreaming. These states suggest the potential recovery of the authentic self. Simultaneously, however, they emphasize Mrs. Pyy's tendency to perform absent-minded actions that worsen her situation and result in intervals of paralysis and inflamed emotions. In the following analyses, the possibilities for Mrs. Pyy's self-transformation are approached from the perspective of her actual dreams as one manifestation of her detoured inward awakening.

The Landscape of Dreams

In *Kaikki naiset näkevät unia*, the dream worlds offer escapes from the actual world, but simultaneously they tell the characters something about their real selves (cf. Ryan 1991: 119). The depiction of Mrs. Pyy's states of day-dreaming, fantasies and dreams constitute a private sphere of spontaneous world-creating, but the dreams themselves are narrated and analyzed only afterwards. In the psychiatrist's office, Mrs. Pyy's attention is drawn to the books on the shelf as the analyst asks about her dreams: "[The] names of the books. Freud's works" (*K*, 266).[86] Mrs. Pyy's dreams are not analyzed during the session, but they appear elsewhere in the novel. In chapter 5, Mrs. Pyy is pictured walking through the silent house, feeling cold and vaguely anxious after having had a dream. She wanders to the entrance and finds snow on the threshold. She keeps asking herself why she is acting like this, making sure that the door is closed. She feels fear: "Why am I standing here and doublechecking that the door is closed? Why did I wake up in the middle of night and why am I walking through these rooms as if I am afraid of something?" (*K*, 53)[87]

Mrs. Pyy's actions parallel the unconscious moves of a sleepwalker, automatic and mechanical: "Like asleep, like in the dream houses in which she often is, in her dreams" (*K*, 53–54).[88] Some elements in the houses of the dream resemble real houses, yet they are purely virtual entities belonging to the dream world: "Houses in which she had once lived, but not the same, and sometimes the house was only a square on the ground, a stony foundation fallen into ruin, or a decayed layer of timber, a sign that a house had once stood here, and she was walking among its ruins" (ibid.).[89] Mrs. Pyy compares herself to a stranger who has entered the house by chance. The strange house with closed doors portrays her psyche: "Like I am in a strange house, having gotten in by chance in the middle of the night without remembering who I was, and where I came from; cautiously, as if I had bad intentions, moving through doors silently as if afraid of what's behind them" (*K*, 53).[90]

Mrs. Pyy's thoughts echo the dream she has had right before waking up. It had been "so disturbing that it had forced her to wake up" (*K*, 54).[91] She had experienced three deaths so troubling that she had actually awakened after each one of them.[92] After the third and last awakening, she gets out of the bed "as one rises after receiving an important message" (ibid.).[93] The dream is like "a command" ("käsky") that she needs to share with others, a collective tragedy involving all people. In her essay "Unien maisema" (The Landscape of Dreams), Vartio called these types of dreams Jungian "big sleep" (*suuruni*). Archetypal dreams are those that may cause a strange feeling of melancholy. They trouble the dreamer to the point that "she feels the desire or even the need to share them with other people and to have them interpreted" (Vartio 1996: 134).[94]

In her essay Vartio expressed her fascination with Jung's theory of dreams and archetypes. Jung's influence can be seen in Vartio's idea of dreams as a storage of archetypal images that speak the language of the collective unconscious.[95] Vartio (1996: 133) compared the human unconscious to a *well* from which black dreams spring: "For dreams are messages sent by our subconscious; they tell us something [...] with metaphor, with symbols, something about ourselves; the dream always refers to ourselves; that message that has been dressed in mute, simplified, condensed images, symbols."[96] Even if dreams may seem mystical, Vartio emphasized their quality as products of the dreamer's own mind. Dreams stem from pre-conscious states of intuitive "knowing." They involve something that "the dreamer in a way already knows and senses something, something she has already inferred, but that her conscious self has not recognized by articulating it in thoughts or words; and so the dreamer, rejoicing, says that she has had a premonition" (ibid.).[97]

The archetypal images of dreams serve as guidelines, especially at the moment of mental crisis and imbalance, when one's personality is under extreme pressure. Vartio reflects on Jungian ideas of archetypal dreams as collective visions that emerge at certain critical stages of a person's mental development. Middle age is the time when the individual "re-organizes herself and gathers her strength to take a look backwards at her life [...] her childhood and youth and the dream images arise from there" (Vartio 1996: 139).[98] Vartio wrote about the function of dreams through stating that they tell the truth of the dreamer if she or he is capable of honest self-examination: "A dream tells us what our true state is. It tells us the direct truth; it does not show us as other people see us nor as we perceive ourselves nor as we wish or believe ourselves to be, but exactly as we are" (ibid.: 133).[99] Dreams provide immediate access to a person's mind because they are "primordial, genuine, unique, and true" (ibid.: 131).[100] The image of Mrs. Pyy at the forking paths in the forest is evoked by Vartio's words describing the effect of dreams on the adult dreamer: "Some part of [her] is as immature, as helpless as if she were a small child; in some things she is as indecisive as a small child lost in the forest" (ibid.: 136).[101]

A lost child represents Mrs. Pyy's situation as she contemplates the lost chances in her adult life. On the other hand, the inner child seems to relate to the embodied trauma that is absent in Mrs. Pyy's conscious thoughts, but appears in her dream worlds. Like the possible worlds of fiction, characters' private dream worlds are generated as a recentering of the fictional universe. If the "textual actual world" is considered to be the center of the work's modal system and the satellite worlds revolving around it are viewed as alternative possible worlds, then the textual universe can be recentered around any of these sub-worlds. This reentering happens by making conjectures about what things would be like in a counterfactual reality, including the characters' dream worlds. (Ryan 1991: 22). Mrs. Pyy considers her dream to be an archetypal dream that needs to be shared: it is a tragedy that involves all people inhabiting the fictional universe. She is able to remember the dream in clear, visual images "as if a film had been running before her eyes" (*K*, 56).[102] As she narrates the dream, she brings back these images and tries to verbalize them, to maintain them as they were.[103] In addition to the dreams, the characters' interpretations of them are provided, as Mrs. Pyy's mother-in-law listens attentively to the dream story.

The first part of the dream shows the dreamer seeing herself, having fallen to the ground. In this fictional recentering of worlds, the basic identity of the dreamer is preserved through the relocation (cf. Ryan 1991: 119). The female figure seen from a bird's-eye view is wearing a graduation cap and a trench coat – clothing that can be interpreted as markers of the dreamer's youth, which is the framework for the first part of the dream world.[104] The fall is followed by another image as the dreamer is transformed into a fly, which lands on a workman's earlobe. The dreamer experiences her first death, simultaneously observing herself as a fly and as a woman lying on the ground. The metamorphosis of Mrs. Pyy into a fly refers to the past stages of her personal development, which have not been successfully accomplished. The image of an ear suggests that she is incapable of listening to her inner voice. The fly, an incarnation of her younger self, is whizzing to the workman's earlobe only to find out that she herself is dead.

The key to the interpretation of the dream's first scene is provided elsewhere in the novel. Mrs. Pyy is waiting for her new house to be built while living temporarily in a country house outside the city. This period of waiting can be seen as a stage of withdrawal from the social world. The window of the porch is dense with flies, which have gathered to warm themselves and escape the cold autumn weather outside. Mrs. Pyy feels nauseated: "It gets on my nerves when I think they're dead, and then when I start to sweep them away, they come back to life and fly around in the air, falling into dishes and God knows where" (*K*, 203–204).[105] The fall and the temporary recovery of the flies' "consciousness" reappear in Mrs. Pyy's dream and embody the pattern of the entire novel. Mrs. Pyy's tendency to fall, be revived, and fall again sets the stage for the protagonist to fulfill her potential to develop her personality.[106] The dream's first message seems to relate to her unconscious knowledge of her futile attempts to alleviate the emptiness of her life, because she is locked in her patterns of self-delusion, her "ego trap."

The second part of the dream begins with a change of scene. The dreamer has arrived in the landscape of her childhood in the country. She stands behind a barn. In the house there is "a strange man" ("vieras mies") holding a book of accounts in his hands. She can hear him leafing through it. "Everything is clear, then" (*K*, 57), the man says in a loud voice.[107] The dreamer gives him a scarf, asking if he will give the scarf to her friend Laura "as a memento from me" (*K*, 58).[108] In the next episode, the dreamer is surrounded by a group of women with children, who are asking her to give them a blessing. As she joins her female relatives on their ride in "an icy sleigh over the unfrozen land," "towards death," she hands them another scarf and mittens (*K*, 59).[109] Two distinct images appear along the journey: a broken bike and a monk in a brown cloak.

131

The mother-in-law interprets this part of the dream as a prophecy of her own death, because she is the eldest. Mrs. Pyy, however, keeps wondering about the meaning of the monk. According to the mother-in-law, the figure does not seem to denote anything bad, because the color of his cloak is brown, not black. The monk signifies spiritual soul-searching that constitutes the kernel of Mrs. Pyy's dream. The key to the interpretation of the figure and the other images in the second part of the dream can be found in Vartio's other text, the poem "Arvoitus" (The Riddle, 1953). Mrs. Pyy's dream includes a citation from this poem, which tells of a young man's journey to inquire about his heritage from his kinsmen's distant lands. The journey ends with his mother warning of his death before he leaves: "The last half mile is travelled / in an icy sleigh over unfrozen land [...]" (*Seppele*, 31).[110] When the last half mile begins, the young man drives the horse vigorously, but the reins, the sleigh, and his hair freeze: "A snow-storm arose – / and snow covered their tracks" (ibid.: 40).[111]

The pattern of blindness in Mrs. Pyy's life is varied in the poem, in which the son does not follow his mother's advice, but carelessly refuses to be poor and humble and gets lost on the way to his real destination. The second part of the dream shows Mrs. Pyy's tendency to ease her inner emptiness with material goods as compensation for the land she has lost in the distribution of an estate. The son's refusal to be poor and humble in the poem can be connected to the figure of the monk in Mrs. Pyy's dream: the spiritual void can never be filled with material goods, which offer only empty promises of a higher social status. In Mrs. Pyy's dream, the older women remind the dreamer of the passing of time and the mortality of all human beings. This part of the dream represents the next stage of the dreamer's life as a married woman and a mother. Among the gifts for the women in the sleigh are a scarf and mittens, which, in "Arvoitus," are given to a gypsy woman, who delivers the prophecy of death to the young man, like his mother.

The third part of the dream depicts the woman standing once again in the landscape of her childhood. The dreamer enters a house in which she finds the strange man. In the middle of the floor is a hayrack. The man gazes at her and replies: "The enemy is behind the lake, the Russians are behind the lake. They've sent negotiators. With wise and understanding talk we may get the enemy to retreat" (*K*, 60).[112] There is also another house: an old barn with "one door" and "a threshold up high" (*K*, 61).[113] In the dream world, the barn has taken the place of an apple tree that had been growing in the courtyard in her childhood. The woman enters the barn and climbs up to the attic. The space is filled with sawdust, and the dreamer knows that there are children hidden beneath. Otherwise the house is empty, for the enemy is approaching. Only the strange man is there, and a large wooden woman standing by the barn, talking in a deep voice and claiming to be the ancestress of the dreamer's kin. In the third part of the dream the prophecy of Mrs. Pyy "big sleep" echoes the voice of the past that is delivered through the dreamer's unconscious to the present moment.

The image of the house was already established in Mrs. Pyy's recollection of the "houses of dreams" while she was awake, which suggests the importance of this image in the dream world. The house becomes an image of the anima, the selfhood. It refers to the woman's associations with the "dark window" merging with her conscious mind during the psychiatrist's appointment. The dark window seen by her is not a real window, but a painted representation: "an image of a window" ("ikkunankuva"). It does not serve the usual functions of an aperture: one cannot see through it; it is a mere optical illusion. In the context of Mrs. Pyy's dream, the terrible crime, the murder, which has happened in the house, serves as an allegory of the dreamer's inner death pictured three times in the dream, in three different variations.

The image of the house is modified in the portrayal of the barn, which signifies the different layers of the dreamer's psyche. The barn has only one door and a threshold that is difficult to step over. The image of a threshold also appears at the beginning of the dream chapter, when Mrs. Pyy almost falls down while wandering in the inattentive state of "sleepwalking." She never remembers the two steps in the space between the living room and the dining room: "In the darkness she often stepped into nothingness there" (*K*, 52).[114] The inner emptiness of the dreamer is reflected in the notion that the dream house is empty, even if there is something hidden in the attic. The image of the hayrack, in turn, involves connotations of captivity, something held in control. The man's words about "the enemy" suggest that the collisions may still be prevented if wise choices are made.

In the beginning of the third part of the dream, the house has disappeared. It is a hazy summer morning. The dreamer stands on the grass lawn, sees a stone foundation on the ground, and realizes that a house once stood there a long ago. This image is the trigger that brings the whole dream to Mrs. Pyy's mind right after she wakes up. She feels like walking among the ruins of the houses of her dreams and experiences the same melancholy as in the dream. Suddenly the dreamer begins to fly. She has turned into a bird, a skylark:

[S]he was a skylark, rising ever higher, flying high above, and as she flew ever higher she knew she was, for the third and last time, conclusively dead. [...] when she remembered what there was on earth, she started falling like a stone; she wasn't a bird anymore, just falling toward the ground, but she fought for her life and was able to rise again. But she wasn't a bird anymore, even though she was floating in the air: she was kicking the air like water. And in the sky some object was moving; it was coming closer, moving fast [...] and she saw that it was an enormous ear, and she knew that it was the ear of God. And she wanted to touch it, for she knew that if she managed to touch it, even lightly, everything would become clear to her, and she would understand what life was, and death. (*K*, 62–63)[115]

The final scene of the dream world emphasizes the significance of the closure of the dream: it carries the most important message for the future of the dreamer and of mankind. The character's knowledge of her future is thus extended by the message sent by a dream from "a sacred layer of reality" in this temporary recentering of the fictional universe (cf. Ryan 1991: 119). The metamorphosis of Mrs. Pyy into a bird has many counterparts in Vartio's novels, the most spectacular, of course, being Adele's transformation into a swan at the end of *Hänen olivat linnut* (to be considered in chapter 7). The bird rising higher and higher signifies Mrs. Pyy's grandiose fantasies, until she falls back into reality. In the dream, the image of the woman floating in the air generates associations of herself as a fetus in the womb. She tries to fly, but is unable to rise on her wings.

The conclusion of the dream enlarges the scale of images that appeared in depicting the dreamer's first death. A fly has been transformed into a bird, a workman's ear has been transformed into the enormous ear of God, which the dreamer wants to touch in order to become conscious, to know life and death. The omnipotent ear reflects the woman's obsessive beliefs in her abilities to "hear" the thoughts of others, to read them like an open book. The last images in the dream, however, suggest the limits of her (self) knowledge: "And she gathered all her strength and thought she touched the ear – but it disappeared, vanishing into space. And at that moment the stars in the sky went out, and it turned dark, and watery snow began to fall" (*K*, 63).[116] The ending of the dream refers to the close of the poem "Arvoitus," in which traces of the young man's hubris are covered by falling snow. At the same time, the dream scene points at the myth of Fall. As a degeneration from an original state of innocence and spiritual grace, the myth of Fall is often thematized critically in the plots of female awakening (Felski 1989: 145). In *Kaikki naiset näkevät unia*, the motif of Fall is re-assessed in the episodes that take place in the Vatican. The touch of God reappears in the ekphrastic sequences addressed in the later analyses of the novel.

After her awakening, Mrs. Pyy finds snow on her doorstep. The snow has swirled into the house and made the floor freezing cold. Standing in the entrance, she looks at her feet and pictures her toes as two homeless creatures, cats coming in from the cold and the dark, and continuing their journey in the cold and the dark. The synecdochic image of Mrs. Pyy's cold feet reveals her need to guard her privacy, which is reflected in the depiction of her unconscious reflexes: "An almost gentle smile appeared on her face. Immediately her expression changed and she glanced behind her, as if afraid: what if someone had been standing behind her and had seen" (*K*, 53).[117] The close of the chapter emphasizes Mrs. Pyy's desire to withdraw to her inner space: "Mrs. Pyy stood by the window and was pleased that it was snowing. The drifts piled up before the door and under the window; they would justify staying inside today, sheltered amid the snow" (*K*, 63).[118]

The defense mechanisms of the self often lead to the flight of cold and painful reality. As an embodied image of the selfhood, the house sheltered with snow indicates Mrs. Pyy's tendency to regress into the passive states of an inner freeze, suggesting that she has never truly awaken. The periods of paralysis are followed by periods of inflamed emotions, which result in the next fall. The houses of Mrs. Pyy's dreams allude to Uuno Kailas's poem "Talo" (The House, 1932), in which the speaker's house is said to have risen "in a single night" ("yhdessä yössä"), made of timber shaped by "that Black Carpenter" ("Musta Kirvesmies"): "Its cold windows face / Nightwards: mine's a chill place. / An icy fire, desperate, / Burns in the grate. / No friends, no guests call / At my house at all. / Two doors are all I have: Two: to dreams and death."[119] The fire of aroused emotions burns in Mrs. Pyy's house, but those flames do not give any warmth, for they are the flames of the icy fire of desperation.

Building the House of Dreams. From Artek to van Gogh

Among the first measures Mrs. Pyy takes to change her life is to decorate a bourgeois home to reflect the self she wants others to see. The most private place of all, a home, becomes a part of the setting constructed for this display of the self. In *Kaikki naiset näkevät unia*, the use of visual clichés of art and design closely relate to how Mrs. Pyy's mental processing and self conceptions are represented. As the visual clichés are clustered and linked, they build up a network of ekphrastic allusions that serve to reflect Mrs. Pyy's ways of perceiving reality. Despite her fantasies, Mrs. Pyy never becomes an artist, not even a dilettante. The theme of failed artistry refers to the narratives of aesthetical female Bildung, which usually conclude with the heroine's madness and self-destruction (see Hirsch 1983: 28, also Rojola 1992). In *Kaikki naiset näkevät unia*, however, the path to artistry is never represented as an actual alternative for the protagonist. Mrs. Pyy's attempts to create something new are stereotypical hobbies suitable for middle-class women, serving as elements of Vartio's parody. In the beginning of the novel, Mrs. Pyy engages in porcelain painting along with other middle-class women in the neighborhood. She had tried to do ceramics before, but soon realized her lack of talent. Her career as a porcelain painter also turns out badly, and she ends up in arguments with the other women.

In Vartio's texts, allusions to visual art often take the form of ekphrastic similes. These are based on visual clichés, similar to the models of roses the bourgeois women used in their porcelain painting. The use of visual stereotypes guarantees that the reader will recognize the artistic topos, theme, or motif being referred to. A general allusion does not demand an excessive amount of knowledge of the visual or plastic arts, but rather it requires an ability to visualize the work of art on the basis of the clichéd model (Yacobi 1995: 628–629).[120] The pictorial models used in the novel show Mrs. Pyy's desire to gain access to the world of genuine art. Her "artistic" work, however, seems to be motivated mainly by her need to impress and belong. After recognizing her lack of talent, Mrs. Pyy focuses on becoming a patroness of art, a specialist who buys modern art and socializes with artists. She tries to generate an impression of herself as a member of a cultivated community of educated, middle-class women, but ends up failing for reasons of economic limitations (cf. Rojola 2011: 80). The ambitious pursuit of the lifestyle and identity she has dreamed of finally leads her family to bankruptcy.

The social climb in the hierarchy of taste is enacted through social mimetism in the sense of Pierre Bourdieu's theory of class distinction (cf. Ruuska 2010: 136, 162). Mrs. Pyy tends to look for objects of comparison in the realm of art as she tries to make sense of the things seen and imagined, including the self. Art serves as one of her self-mirrors, a potential path to self-recognition. However, her tendency to remain blind to the primitive art of dreams suggests that she may not find what she is looking for. Her taste is defined by the stereotypical clichés of art, copies of which are sold to the modern masses, as well as objects of design that signified the ideals of home décor in the 1950s: "And then she had gone to the Artek store, and that fabric had just arrived; it was spread out on the table – large sunflowers on a white background. Like a van Gogh painting" (*K*, 226).[121]

The ekphrastic simile juxtaposed the fabric in Artek (a brand favored in the Finnish design in the 1950s) to Vincent van Gogh's still life *Zonnebloemen* (Sunflowers, 1888), rendered by the artist in many versions. The paintings all share the same theme: yellow sunflowers in a vase.[122] The still life has become an emblem of van Gogh's art and technique. In Vartio's novel, the painting serves as a visual source that Mrs. Pyy can easily recognize and use to build up the stage decor for her self-performance. She is shown going for a walk simply in order to see how the curtains look in the window of their apartment in the row house: "She had thought that no one else in the building had such beautiful curtains" (*K*, 227).[123]

The reference to Artek evokes associations with Finnish art and design, which was flourishing in the 1950s (see Ruuska's analysis 2010). Mrs. Pyy's conceptions of Artek's fabric belong to the discourses of design, art, and home decoration that determine how objects of art are perceived in Mrs. Pyy's fictional reality. A contrast between the world of art and the world of home decoration is generated in the analogy involved in Mrs. Pyy's perceptions. The rustic cabinet from her childhood home is compared to a modern, non-representational sculpture: "She took a few steps back, stopped and looked at the cabinet with her head tilted, as if the cabinet were a sculpture, modern, the kind you can't tell what it is. The cabinet was next to the door. It was painted a pale color" (*K*, 11).[124] The description of the cabinet's plainness implies the simplicity of the furniture itself and alludes to the plain, abstract contours of a modern sculpture. The analogy seems strange, because it contrasts the new to the old, the rustic to the urban.[125] If the ekprastic simile is taken in its literal meaning, however, it draws a parallel between the rustic object and the *manner* in which Mrs. Pyy looks at it: "a sculpture, modern, *the kind you can't tell what it is.*"

The contrast between something natural and something artificial is dramatized by the ekphrastic similes employed in the novel. The cabinet represents Mrs. Pyy's past, her childhood in the countryside. The old piece of furniture had been abandoned in the attic of the cowshed before she saved it from the same destiny as the apple tree pictured in her dream. In Mrs. Pyy's perception of the fictional world, objects of nature are seen as representations rather than as pure nature, thereby suggesting the fragility of her self-identification. For instance, in planning the location of the windows in her new house, Mrs. Pyy juxtaposes the imagined view of a large painting with nature: "And [in the house there would be] a large window; the forest is like a framed painting; when you have a big window, no other painting is needed. I can look at nature from morning till evening" (*K*, 193).[126]

Paradoxically, in the view from the window, the art is nature itself. The outside landscape generates a genuine aesthetic experience, unlike art, which is only capable of "imitating" nature, producing artificial copies. The windows in the new house are contrasted to the "dark window" in the house imagined by Mrs. Pyy during her appointment with the psychiatrist. The painted window provides no view, but rather implies the blind spots in Mrs. Pyy's self-analysis. As Mrs. Pyy begins to realize that she and her husband are lacking the money needed to build the house of her dreams, she can see herself by the "ruins" of that house. She pictures herself through the eyes of a stranger, (a hypothetical witness in her virtual construction of the self) while she is struggling to place the windows in a house that does not even have proper walls. The unfinished building is surrounded by snow: "And she began to see herself – the way she thought the person she was imagining would have seen her: face frenzied, bare-headed, in a building surrounded by thick piles of snow, face framed by the window, wearing a black fur coat, bare-headed" (*K*, 267).[127]

Mrs. Pyy's desire to return to the landscape of her childhood and youth is illustrated in the imagined view from the window of her dream house. As in the ekphrastic simile, however, "nature" is juxtaposed with an artistic representation that exists only as an artifact, as a constructed entity. The forest scene visible through the window frame is simultaneously living and frozen, actual and imagined. In thinking about the painting of nature framed by the window, Mrs. Pyy foregrounds certain details: "[T]hose two pine trees that were growing on top of the rock would be seen in their entirety from base to crown, like in a large painting" (*K*, 193).[128] From her imagined window, Mrs. Pyy can see the rock's "tones of color" ("värisointuja"), which resemble the tones chosen by an artist from her palette. These details of the "painted landscape" – two pine trees and the rock – have associations with her childhood landscape, which Mrs. Pyy can sense vividly as she drifts through her fantasies: "She had seen in her mind's eye how she would sit in an armchair and look at the trees. They were just like two pine trees on a different rock that she used to dive off as a child" (*K*, 193–194).[129]

In recalling the hypothetical view from her new house, Mrs. Pyy can imagine the rock, the pine trees, and the water into which she had jumped off as a child, feet first. She can imagine the boats brought to the shore, the mid-summer bonfire, and the fire dying out: "Only bitter black smoke rose and the rock hissed, spit and cracked" (*K*, 194).[130] The sensual and vivid world in Mrs. Pyy's memories is no longer present. The dying fire signifies her inner death experienced in the urban environment. Nature, compared to a framed painting, has turned into scenery, into something which with the human being can no longer connect. The childhood landscape has gone, and when the drawings of the new house are ready, the large, picturesque window has turned into a small window with a view of the courtyard: "And now they had done the same thing to the house that the sexton had done to the painting: turned it around" (ibid.).[131] The grandiose, large windows fantasized by Mrs. Pyy are getting smaller until they become only "dark windows," mere images painted black.

The discrepancy between the real and the artificial is related to Mrs. Pyy's futile attempts to look for meaning in art that she is barely able to understand. Mrs. Pyy pretends to understand the codes and conventions of visual and plastic art, but confuses these ideas by applying them in the wrong contexts. No matter how hard she tries to look at art, she is unable to truly "see," because it is not art itself that interests her, but the way art serves as a path to her desired self-identity. Art becomes primarily a tool for molding social status. The cabinet is only a special "old thing" among other (modern) things in the décor of a bourgeois home, part of the setting for a self-performance.

Ekphrastic descriptions are typically linked to the ability of literary characters to talk about the objects of art they are looking at. The cultural competence of the characters or their lack of knowledge is often emphasized in scenes involving representations of art. The characters' interpretations of artistic objects, on the other hand, are determined by such factors as class or level of cultivation. Classical examples include Emile Zola's or Honoré de Balzac's descriptions of the encounters between peasants and art. In these encounters, the ignorance of the observers shows an inability to understand the collectively-shared cultural inheritance. Characters parallel to Mrs. Pyy are half-educated people who know art to the degree that they realize its value. However, they do not possess the vocabulary needed to discuss art in a more refined manner. (Cf. Doody 1997: 392–393)

The art-related debate of the middle-class group can be followed in the sixth chapter of *Kaikki naiset näkevät unia*, where Mrs. Pyy has organized a party to introduce her newest purchase – a modern, abstract painting. The painting has been placed in the most visible location in the house to attract as much attention as possible. At first the party-goers focus on discussing the right way to hang the painting until the mother-in-law asks the hostess:

> "But Kaisu, tell me what that really represents?"
> "Dear Granny, there are color surfaces, different color surfaces. It doesn't represent anything; it can't be explained."
> But her mother-in-law didn't understand what kind of thing doesn't represent anything, she felt it had to represent something. And she started to talk about Vyborg again and she asked her son whether he remembered the painting that his father had bought from a real artist, the one that showed a boat on the shore, of the one about which his father used to say that whenever you looked at it in dim light, you always wanted to go rowing on a moonlit sea. (*K*, 67–68)[132]

In explaining the characteristics of the painting, Mrs. Pyy resorts to a general depiction of its non-representational quality. She speaks of "another style" ("toista tyyliä") and "color surfaces" ("väripintoja"), thereby revealing that she is unable to define that "which cannot be explained" ("ei sitä voi selittää"). She can only repeat the words which she has heard said about abstract painting in general, but nothing about this particular painting, The irony related to the reception of the modern painting (and modern literature) is emphasized in the depiction of the onlookers' behavior when they look at the painting: "'It's a beautiful picture.' Mrs. Viita looked at the picture *as if* examining it carefully" (*K*, 65).[133] The debate refers back to the analogy with modern sculpture, which emphasizes Mrs. Pyy's identical confusion in looking at modern, non-representational art that speaks with figures and forms rather than with "pictures" of reality.

In the discussion between Mrs. Pyy and the mother-in-law, two distinct conceptions of art collide. Non-representational modern art aims at plain forms and abstraction, whereas naturalistic and realistic art involves a preference for mimetic vividness: an exact representation of reality. The mother-in law does not consider the painting "with different color surfaces" to be "real" art. In the scene, the older woman talks about paintings that she had seen in Vyborg, an emblematic space signifying nostalgia for past times and lost places. One of the paintings depicts a boat on the sea. It engages the mother-in-law's mind, because it is vivid and generates sensuous, realistic images. In the dim light, the scene seems to come alive so that the onlooker feels like rowing on the sea in the moonlight.

The vividness of pictures is related to another painting mentioned by the mother-in-law. In Vyborg she and Mrs. Pyy's husband, Olavi as a young boy, used to pass by a particular "house of paintings" (*K*, 67). Through the windows of the house, they could see a painting in which the cows were so vivid that little Olavi thought they were real. The mother-in-law mentions having also seen a painting by Ilya Repin in Vyborg. The painting is *Ivan Groznyj i syn ego Ivan* (Ivan the Terrible Killing his Son, 1870–1873), which turned out to be a copy of the original. The "tragic" theme of the painting – a father crying over his murdered son – fascinates the older woman, who contemplates it with deep affection. The ekphrastic allusion can be read as a reference to her son being symbolically "murdered" by his wife.[134] The mother-in-law openly states her folk-like preference for national-romantic and realistic art and thinks back with nostalgia to paintings with golden frames. The modern painting, which is framed only with modern, wooden molding, violates the aura of the old aesthetics. Even if Mrs. Pyy feels embarrassed because of her mother-in-law's nostalgic recollections in the presence of her guests, the difference between the two women is not as great as it seems. The debate on modern art refers to the most elemental ekphrastic sequence in the novel: Mrs. Pyy's visit to the Sistine Chapel in Rome to see the treasures of Renaissance painting.

Mrs. Pyy and Delphica

While planning a trip to Italy, Mrs. Pyy browses though guidebooks of art history. When she sees a picture of the Delphic sibyl, the youngest of the sibyls of the Sistine Chapel (whom Vartio calls here "Delphica") she becomes frightened. She looks at the picture for a long time until finally she takes the book to her husband: "'Do you recognize this picture? Do you see that it resembles a particular woman?' And the man looked at the picture, laughed, pushed the book away and said, 'Who else could it be but you yourself?'" (*K*, 285)[135] Recalling this scene in the Vatican, Mrs. Pyy sees herself as from outside her body, as a parallel figure to the woman in the fresco: "For it was true, it was coincidence and not in any way her fault that the youngest of the sibyls, Delphica, resembled this woman who was standing right here, by the door of St. Peter's Basilica" (ibid.).[136]

Mrs. Pyy mirrors herself in the woman in the painting. She compares the book in her hand to the roll of parchment in Delphica's hand and her yellow dress to the clothing of the sibyl "who looked so much like her that they could have been sisters" (*K*, 285).[137] Among the other female prophets, Mrs. Pyy recognizes the sibyl Cumea, who resembles her grandmother. The trope of two women is also evoked in her memories of her grandmother as a fierce woman in the fields cutting oats: "And the grandmother had straightened her back, raised one hand to shade her eyes, stood holding a sickle in her other hand and looked forward. A large face, like a man's, and the eyes, gloomy and stern" (*K*, 294).[138] On the one hand, the similarities generate pictorial relations between the "real" human beings and objects of art within the fictional actual world of the novel. On the other hand, the husband's ambivalent laughter generates uncertainty. Does the sibyl really resemble his wife, or is the act of mirroring only another sign of her self-obsession?[139]

The theory of ekphrasis has tended to distinguish representations of imagined art objects from those in which the pictorial source can be traced to some recognizable, "actual" work of art.[140] In addition to representations of purely imagined or unrecognizable works of art, the "actual ekphrases," such as Michelangelo's frescoes in *Kaikki naiset näkevät unia*, are never "copies" of a pictorial object turned into a verbal form.[141] Rather, they present certain selected details, which are determined by the way in which the onlooker interprets the picture and relates her interpretation to other interpretations. (Cf. Yacobi 2004: 73–84) The dramatization of the act of looking is also emphasized in the encounter between Michelangelo's frescoes and Mrs. Pyy.

The Delphic and Cumean sibyls are depicted in the Sistine Chapel frescoes by Michelangelo. The details of these frescoes are presented in the novel only through Mrs. Pyy's perceptions and thoughts. As she tries to recall what was written about the frescoes in the guidebooks, the paintings are reduced to a list of the names: "[T]he pictures from the books rose before her eyes as she listed them: The Creation – The Creation of Adam – The Creation of Eve – The Expulsion from Paradise – The Story of Noah – the Great Flood – The River of Sins – and the prophets – seven in all. And the sibyls: Libica – Cumea – and Delphica, the youngest. There were five of them" (*K*, 284).[142] Just as Mrs. Pyy has seen the frescoes only as copies in the guidebooks, her interpretation of them is also based on ready-made definitions. While struggling to understand the figure of Delphica, which appears particularly meaningful to her, she resorts to the depiction she learned by heart from a book by the Finnish art historian Onni Okkonen, entitled *Renessanssin taide* (The Art of the Renaissance, 1947): "The youngest is Delphica; the model is apparently the same maiden portrayed as Eve in 'The Creation of Adam' in the shelter of God's arms. Delphica demonstrates how different emotions can be read in the faces of Michelangelo's portraits: here [it is] unself-conscious yearning and intuitive insight into what is to come –" (*K*, 285–286).[143]

In representing Mrs. Pyy's thoughts, Vartio cites a passage from Okkonen's *Renessanssin taide* word for word.[144] Writing about the frescoes in the Sistine Chapel, Okkonen briefly analyzes the fresco with the Delphic sibyl. Vartio appropriated his analysis and placed it directly in her own novel, linking it to the fictional character's actions and thoughts. Vartio's decision to insert the quotation is partly motivated by the character of Mrs. Pyy, her inability to understand herself except through different ways of self-mirroring.[145] Nevertheless, the essential purpose of the citation seems to suggest the importance of Okkonen's *interpretation* of Delphica. Not only does the picture of the sibyl relate to Mrs. Pyy's (false) self-recognition, but so too does the interpretation of this figure as a prophet or a seer signifying an "intuitive insight." Paradoxically, the model for Mrs. Pyy's self-identification is a sibyl with the ability to channel and interpret visions that affect the collective community. Mrs. Pyy's inability to read her dreams, however, suggests that she has no such talent. Yet why has the verbal description of the fresco with Delphica stayed so vividly in her mind that it follows her all the way to the Vatican?

In *Renessanssin taide*, Okkonen identifies two features that characterize Delphica. First of all, he links this figure to Eve, the woman who, according to Christian tradition, brought sin into the world and who is portrayed in another painting in the Sistine Chapel, *The Creation of Adam*. The woman who was Michelangelo's model for both figures evidently looked a lot like Mrs. Pyy. Second, Okkonen's interpretation of Delphica's portrait emphasized this figure as an example of Michelangelo's technique of portraying emotion. The characters signify certain mental states or moods. In Okkonen's book, Delphica is said to express "unself-conscious yearning" and "intuitive insight into what is to come." At first glance, both of these epithets seem distant from the character of Mrs. Pyy. This endlessly self-regarding, neurotic woman has come to Italy with her husband because she does not know how to go on with her life. Her psychiatrist has advised her to have a change of scene. The journey to Italy serves as the last chance for self-recognition, yet still holds out the promise of seeing oneself more honestly.

At the doorstep of St. Peter's Basilica, on her way to the Sistine Chapel, Mrs. Pyy is about to become conscious of her distant feelings: "She had come to seek – to seek something; the thought vanished, and once again gone from her mind were what she had believed and imagined she would feel in front of this door, and what she had just been about to capture. But it had vanished" (*K*, 288).[146] Mrs. Pyy's vanishing insight is accompanied by her perception of two women who are about to enter the Vatican, just as she saw two women in the urban environment back home. In Michelangelo's sibyl, Mrs. Pyy finds an object suitable for self-identification through which to reflect her own personal development. The feelings of "unself-conscious yearning" and "intuitive insight into what is to come" are related to this new stage in the process of becoming aware, the pre-state of knowing.

The encounter between Mrs. Pyy and a work of art is a turning point, but in a very different way than she expected. Having waited impatiently to see the masterpieces of Renaissance art, Mrs. Pyy is once again disappointed. The faded ceilings do not inspire feelings of strength and peace, "turning the soul into something new" as she had expected (*K*, 300).[147] She is even about to pass by the frescoes without recognizing them – still another indication of her blindness. After having wandered around aimlessly among a group of tourists, Mrs. Pyy finally understands that she is right there, surrounded by the frescoes. She can hardly distinguish the painted figures from the faded ceilings: "Where were the sibyls? She looked for them on the walls, on the ceiling, and found them. So small and black" (*K*, 299).[148] The great works of Renaissance art do not evoke the cathartic experience of purification that she has been expecting. Mrs. Pyy had imagined she would see *The Creation*

141

full of vivid, primitive power, giving her the ability to know, as in the dream in which she tried to touch God's enormous ear: "She would see how God had created the world; she would see the picture in which God is turning around as he separates darkness from light [...]. Hadn't she thought she heard a great swirl of wind when she had looked at that picture in the book? And now she would see it" (*K*, 293).[149]

In her encounter with the treasures of the art world, Mrs. Pyy acts like the tourists whose company she has tried to avoid while walking in the Eternal City.[150] Compared to the bright images given in the guidebooks, the chapel is dark and shadowy, like a catacomb. Looking at *The Creation of Adam*, Mrs. Pyy tries to concentrate as if to bring the picture to life. She waits for it to touch her soul as powerfully as God's hand, which is giving life to a human being: "She looked for Adam on the ceiling, tried to tune in to something, like a prayer, to stretch her forefinger to touch the spark of energy, the spirit that was streaming from God's finger into Adam's finger, turning him into the image of God. But the picture was only a picture. Adam was a naked man on the ceiling" (*K*, 300).[151]

Paradoxically, Mrs. Pyy expects the art to generate the same emotional effect of vividness that she refuses to feel when she listens to her mother-in-law's aesthetic ideals. The works of art in the Sistine Chapel do not meet her expectations of the sublime effects that she has imagined art would produce. The pictures appear banal and even more so when Mrs. Pyy compares them to things she has seen back home. The serpent of Eden turn into a common viper and the chapel into a sauna building with blackened walls. Furthermore, the descriptive techniques and the *topoi* of Renaissance painting are satirized in Mrs. Pyy's parody as she realizes she almost made a fool of herself by asking the way to the Sistine Chapel: "If she had asked. She could hear how the people would have burst out laughing around her. And the guide, that fool, would perhaps have suppressed her laughter, because of her position, but she wouldn't have been able to hide a smile [...]" (*K*, 301).[152] In the guide's hypothetical speech, the stylistic features of Renaissance art are transformed into banal stereotypes:

> [I]t's over here, Ma'am. Here in front, all this is the river of sin. Up there you can see God, though only dimly. The sibyls are in the corners, the prophets in other corners, those sullen gentlemen, and Adam over there, a handsome man, don't you think? Good muscles, a vital-looking gentleman, don't you think? And there the fall, over here the serpent, over there Eve – quite a fleshy old maid – don't you think? (*K*, 301)[153]

In the guide's hypothetical talk, the physical amplitude of the female figures and the masculine anatomy of the males are turned into clichéd images, even if the parody itself stems from a source familiar with the conventions of art and even able to carnevalize them. In this respect, the narrator's voice seems to mingle with Mrs. Pyy's self-distanced voice. The parody is aimed at the tourists who are absent-mindedly looking at the art and less at the style of the paintings.

After having lost her great expectations, Mrs. Pyy focuses on grieving for her loss. She forgets Delphica, who appears only as a tiny, distant figure among the other sibyls. She never finds what she has come to seek. Instead of Delphica, Mrs. Pyy sees "The River of Sins" ("Synnin virta"): "And there was the Son of Man, that naked one, with his hand raised. And bodies entangled with each other, the uppermost one looking like a crossbreed. She had thought it was one-eyed, but evidently it had two eyes after all; it had covered the other eye with its hand" (*K*, 299).[154] In Michelangelo's fresco *The Last Judgment*, Mrs. Pyy's attention is drawn to a detail that shows a human figure waiting for Christ's judgment. Looking at the painting, Mrs. Pyy realizes that she has perceived the painting in the wrong way. The figure waiting for the judgment is not one-eyed, but has covered one eye. Her thought wanders comically – and revealingly – to her own diagnosis, the refractive error in her sight mentioned by the doctor, until she remembers to bring her thoughts back to more sublime ideas. She faces a painful realization: "The things she was thinking about, here! She concentrated on studying The River of Sins. She moved sharply; a mortifying thought had crossed her mind. She was ashamed" (*K*, 300–301).[155]

Instead of catharsis, Mrs. Pyy feels ashamed as she stands before "The River of Sins." Mrs. Pyy feels remorse because of her blindness, which almost leads her into a humiliating situation before the other tourists whom she had observed with a feeling of superiority. Later, she laughs at her husband's ignorance: "We nearly didn't see The River of Sins. I, at least, realized it in time, but you just stood gaping and didn't understand a thing, even though it was right before your nose" (*K*, 303).[156] In the sequence that takes place in the Vatican, the pattern of wasting one's life is modified in different ways. While focused on constructing her grandiose fantasies and grieving over the flatness of everyday life, Mrs. Pyy loses the chance to experience the here and now. Mrs. Pyy's "refractive error" ("taittovirhe"), reflected in Michelangelo's *Last Judgment*, is turned into an image of the human tendency to escape a reality that seems too painful, which in turn prevents a person from seeing the true quality of life. "I, at least, realized it in time," Mrs. Pyy thinks after having walked by Delphica without paying her any attention.

The real, pre-conscious cause of the shame involved in the act of looking, however, can be traced back not only to Michelangelo's *Last Judgment*, but also to another fresco, *The Temptation and Expulsion*. By means of a verbal representation of Delphica, Mrs. Pyy identifies herself with Eve, and also with another figure of a "sinful" woman, Mary Magdalene. This female figure is portrayed in a work of art mentioned in the same episode: a wooden statue that resembles the ancestress of Mrs. Pyy in her dream.[157] The ekphrastic allusions attached to the novel's Vatican episode add to the prime cause of her shame: her adulterous affair. Before of "The River of Sins," Mrs. Pyy displaces her feelings of shame onto another object to avoid acknowledging the true reason for her emotion (cf. Ervasti 1967: 66). Instead of the sibyl, the seer, the real object of Mrs. Pyy's identification is Eve who, after having succumbed to the lure of the serpent, is able to see, "to know good and evil like God."

143

Images involving the biblical depiction of the Fall reappear in the novel's final scene. Mrs. Pyy and her husband follow the group of tourists to the local marketplace. Mrs. Pyy silently observes, shocked, as her husband and a local stallholder trick the two female tourists into buying overpriced, worthless jewelry. The Italian stallholder becomes the seducer into whose trap the two women fall: "The Italian turned to look at them, Mrs. Pyy and her husband; he cast a glance that was beyond words. His tongue had popped out of his mouth, he'd licked his lips as quick as lightning – and Mrs. Pyy felt like she had seen the tail of a serpent flit by in the grass so quickly that she didn't know whether it was a snake or what – in the grass no movement was seen" (*K*, 308).[158]

In this scene, Mrs. Pyy is once again watching herself in the figures of two women who serve as an image of her divided self. She seems to recognize that something terrible is going on, but she cannot act – or is not willing to act – to prevent the fraud from happening: "Mrs. Pyy realized that she would have been mad if she had deprived those poor people of that bliss, mad, if she had revealed to them the truth. How did she know what the truth was, here?" (*K*, 310)[159] Mrs. Pyy leaves the marketplace with her purse filled with the jewelry that the stallholder has given her as a reward for her husband's services. Instead of the touch of God, Mrs. Pyy's journey ends with the feeling of the faked cameos in her fingers. The fall from the grandiose fantasies into the flatness of everyday reality happens once again. The episode includes a concise, meaningful image: the stallholder wraps the woman's fingers around the jewelry "like petals of a flower [folding] back into a bud" (*K*, 311).[160] The closing of the petals of the bud suggests that Mrs. Pyy has a chance to start from the beginning. The novel concludes with Mrs. Pyy's words, as she realizes that she has forgotten to thank the man, who eventually helped her to see: "And I didn't even think to say thank you. Grazie, thank you" (*K*, 312).[161]

The novel's ambiguous ending has raised questions about whether Mrs. Pyy could really change the direction of her life. The closing offers two possible routes for Mrs. Pyy's development: a mute, regressive withdrawal or a social enactment, seeking a true connection with others. The life plot of Mrs. Pyy seems to oscillate between two patterns of female self-discovery: the one constituting the more optimistic path of female Bildungsroman and the other concluding with social isolation more typical of the novel of awakening. In the narrative pattern of female Bildungsroman, the figure of the absent-minded housewife is often employed to portray the protagonist's awareness of her subordinate role. The heroine's awakening to the social world finally leads to confrontation, resistance, and survival. Accordingly, the novel of awakening typically begins only after the fulfillment of marriage, the traditional closure of a romance. After realizing that the fairytale expectations of living "happily ever after" have no basis in reality, the protagonist awakens to see the limitations of her life. In the novel of inward awakening, however, the epistemic path of self-discovery does not necessarily lead to any resolution. The state of emotional imbalance remains. (Rosowski 1983: 49)

In *Kaikki naiset näkevät unia*, originally entitled *Rouva Pyy* (Mrs. Pyy) and then *Kaksikymmentä lukua rouva Pyyn elämästä* (Twenty Chapters of Mrs. Pyy's Life),[162] the decisive moments of Mrs. Pyy's awakening are depicted episode by episode as the possibilities for her flowering are represented as two alternative paths: digression or lingering. Mrs. Pyy is one of Vartio's full-grown characters, who keep falling into regressive traps and lose their sense of the crucial distinction between the virtual and the actual. In the representation of Mrs. Pyy's mental crisis, her inner wound leads to cyclic patterns of regression characteristic of both lingering and digression. Whereas in digressive paths decisions lead to actions that worsen a character's situation and result in intervals of paralysis, in lingering patterns the character's situation worsens while she or he remains undecided, unable to decide whether to act or not. What are Mrs. Pyy's real chances of finding her way after having gotten lost in the forest?

Getting Lost. Digression and the Lingering Paths of Awakening

Already at the beginning of the novel, possibilities for Mrs. Pyy's development are staged, as she is seen observing a new neighbor moving in. The portrayal of Mrs. Pyy arranging flowers by the window alludes to her patterns of accidental, unmotivated, and gratuitous acts. While focused on evaluating the neighbor's taste and furniture, she is depicted performing absent-minded acts: "Maybe it would be better to let [the withered flowers] be, there seemed to be no new buds in the plant. But she nipped off one branch and saw that she had broken off a branch that did have buds on it. Mrs. Pyy noticed that her fingers had gotten moist; she had crushed the flower's branch" (*K*, 6–7).[163] The "fateful" pinching off a branch still in bloom depicts Mrs. Pyy's habitual behavior. In a similar vein, the "dreadful change" ("hirveä vaihtuminen") Mrs. Pyy sees in the mirror is caused by the carelessness of the girl in getting lost in the forest: "Had her attention slipped for a moment – and this happened at that time [...] and the girl had kept on going without knowing that a betrayal had taken place" (*K*, 229).[164] The girl had chosen the wrong road as if by accident (without a conscious decision being made) and remained unmindful of the fatefulness of her actions – a recurring pattern that seems to have become a vicious circle in Mrs. Pyy's life.

The different stages of decision making, illustrated in the passage above, demonstrate the complexity of causal interactions employed throughout the entire novel. The absent-minded acts may have unexpected, far-reaching consequences, as patterns of cause and effect are generated randomly and proliferate against all odds. The difficulties of interpreting causal interconnections in *Kaikki naiset näkevät unia* derive from two strategies used in narrating Mrs. Pyy's story. First of all, Mrs. Pyy's actions are generated by her inability – and consequently, the reader's inability – to discern causal connections, because of a lack of Mrs. Pyy's innermost intention to act, the absent cause for her trauma. In narrative fiction, the interpretation of causal positions is usually determined by the "coming-into-being intent" of the character. This intent leads to the character's decision to undertake action and gives the reader information about what is going to happen and why. Information about intent guides the reader's attention, both to the upcoming action and to the state of instability, which needs to be corrected. (Kafalenos 2006: 69)

Second, the uncertainty in Mrs. Pyy's life plot is caused by the manipulation of causal interactions generating hypothetical, virtual worlds that exist simultaneously with the textual actual world. Mrs. Pyy is constantly lost in alternative worlds, which challenges the reader's ability to distinguish between "real" intents and virtual intents expressed by Mrs. Pyy as hypotheses, lies, fantasies, and other counterfactual accounts. Instead of one chronological sequence, the reader is given alternative sequences with two sets of events: the factual set and its hypothetical other (Dannenberg 2008: 63). Getting lost is caused by Mrs. Pyy's inclination to misread the functions of her actions, whether by misinterpreting her own intentions or escaping into hypothetical realities, which give her momentary liberation from the feeling of suffering.

The modal semantics of possible world theory involves operators of necessity and possibility that, in Marie-Laure Ryan's model, include the subworlds created by the *mental activity* of characters. The opposition of the real world and the possible world is established within the plot of the narrative text in a way similar to the way fictional worlds relate to the actual existing world. Alternative worlds are created by the mental acts of the characters, who manipulate possible worlds through mental operations[165]:

> [T]heir actual world is reflected in their knowledge and beliefs, corrected in their wishes, replaced by a new reality in their dreams and hallucinations. Through counterfactual thinking they reflect on how things might have been, through plans and projections they contemplate things that still have a chance to be, and through the act of making up fictional stories they recenter their universe into what is for them a second-order, and for us a third-order, system of reality. (Ryan 1991: 22)

The fictional world-systems involve not only actual, but also faked and pretended worlds. The characters' private domains are simultaneously authentic and inauthentic constructs, containing "beliefs and mock beliefs, desires and mock desires, true and faked obligations, as well as genuine and pretended intents" (Ryan 1991: 118). In *Kaikki naiset näkevät unia*, the challenges of reading Mrs. Pyy's mind stem from the presentation of her private worlds of delusions and faked beliefs, which do not always align with the textual actual world at the center of the work's modal system.

The narrative path of Mrs. Pyy's epistemic quest is mainly portrayed through *counterfactuals*, her speculations about alternative paths to her life. Counterfactuals create links between decisions made in the past and their consequences, which have far-reaching effects on the present situation and evoke feelings of regret or relief. Counterfactuals are created as the characters look back and revive the life paths they once rejected. These unactualized counterfactual roads often look greener than the paths actually chosen. (Dannenberg 2008: 71) Coincidences often result in the need for counterfactual "replotting" – speculations by the characters on what might have been without the bad timing and the missed connections. They involve speculations about alternative life paths. The causal connections within counterfactuals are realized as a relation between the *antecedent*, which refers to a point in the past at which reality is altered and a new hypothetical version of events created, and the *consequent*, which renders the result of that alteration further down the counterfactual time path. Counterfactual thinking therefore creates cogent causal connections within narrative sequences, but at the same time frustrates the reader's desire for causal-linear clarity by suggesting more than one possible version of events. (Ibid.: 45, 111) Counterfactuals create links between decisions made in the past and their consequences, which have far-reaching effects on the present situation.

Characters' thought experiments about "what might have been" generate altered outcomes and alternative life stories. These alternative scenarios produce patterns of diversification and multiplicity that undermine the causal-linear teleology of events. The fork metaphor (embodying the cross-road situations in life) is actualized in counterfactual life plots involving two different stages in a decision-making process. While the first stage portrays a character contemplating two or more unactualized future alternatives (expressed in the idea of decisions as junctions in the road), the second stage of the process describes a situation in which the unactualized path has already become the alternative branch now being contemplated by the character located on the other, actualized trail. (Dannenberg 2008: 1–2, 71) Counterfactuals, or the "disnarrated,"[166] pertain to narrative patterns involving unrealized possibilities: "one does not do what one intends," "one loses what one has," "one does not obtain what one expects," or "one is not what one seems to be or could be." By suggesting alternatives to the written narrative, counterfactuals present *nonaction, loss, absence,* and different *negatives* (Mosher 1993: 418).

The plot pattern of female Bildung is evoked as Mrs. Pyy counterfactualizes her lost chances for education and a profession. The recurring theme of this story type, namely, the quest for identity being repressed by marriage, is subverted by Mrs. Pyy's counterfactuals, which insert a new line of causation into the story and make it difficult to infer the real causes and consequences of her deferred Bildung. While counterfactualizing her life choices, Mrs. Pyy repeatedly accuses her husband of preventing her from fulfilling her potential. According to Mrs. Pyy, it is her husband who has "cut [her] wings" ("leikannut [...] siivet") and forced her to "let everything pass her by" (*K*, 26)[167]:

> "I certainly have had to pay dearly for this education. If I had known then what I know now, would I have gotten married and had children in such a hurry? Certainly not. I would have continued my studies and I would have a career now."
>
> "You should have looked farther ahead and married a rich man. You knew that I had no money."

"That's not what I mean." Mrs. Pyy stared ahead. And the man asked whether she was now thinking about where she would be if she weren't here. [...] Nowadays you talk about that all the time and even when you don't, you walk around looking like you're always wondering what landed you here. If it's not too late, turn your life around. (*K*, 198)[168]

Mrs. Pyy often represents herself as a victim of circumstances that have nothing to do with the situation she has gotten into. While crying over her lost chances in life, she projects her self-hatred onto the people around her: "She hated her husband and her mother-in-law, hated her whole life, hated it. Her skin had become old, ahead of time, but it wasn't her fault, but the fault of those who had forced her to live these years the way she had had to live them." (*K*, 123)[169] The protagonist's negative affects, her resentments and obsessions, comprise a private world that conforms to fictional reality only to some extent. In brief moments of self-revelation, however, Mrs. Pyy can see that the tragedy of her life is partly of her own making. In one of these moments, Mrs. Pyy reveals her thoughts to the artist, whom she wishes to know more intimately:

> Sometimes I do such precise work that I have no peace if even one match is left on the bottom of the trash bucket [...]. And then I let everything go for weeks. I just sit there like you are doing right now, and wait for someone to come and nudge me into motion. [...] and then I hate doing anything again, as if I had a bad conscience because everything I do is useless and done wrong and I should be doing something else, and I just keep waiting until I figure out what I should do and then I don't do anything anyway. (*K*, 147–148)[170]

The passage demonstrates the blend of two strategies that alter causal relations, namely, digression and lingering, which generate alternating periods of passive waiting and hyperactive decision-making in the novel. These patterns add to the emotional fluctuation typical of Vartio's self-suffering characters. In the novel of awakening, the disparity between dream and reality serves as a state of imbalance that causes Mrs. Pyy to break out of her passivity and take action, which, however, results in failure and another period of stasis, a frozen condition.

Mrs. Pyy's inclination to construct alternative life paths generates repetitious patterns of narrative branching, which illustrates the human mind's tendency to feel regret over what a person didn't do rather than what she or he did. As mentioned, Mrs. Pyy often resorts to hypothetical, alternative scenarios, which mentally mutate the "traumatic" present in which she finds herself. By counterfactualizing her life choices, she struggles to "undo" the events of the past caused by her rashly made decisions. Alternative life scenarios are formulated especially at times of personal crisis in reviewing a life's trajectory. The long-term feelings of loss over the roads not taken are typically triggered by dramatic or exceptional life situations that cause negative or traumatic outcomes. The more abrupt and discontinuous the changes are, the more persistently the human mind tries to explain the departure from normalcy by counterfactualizing alternative, more conventional scenarios. (Dannenberg 2008: 111)

Two counterfactual emotions, satisfaction and regret, refine the emotional story structure of Vartio's novel.[171] These two directions are illustrated in *Kaikki naiset näkevät unia* with a reference to the title of the novel. Awakening to reality – pictured as the shared experience of all women – has two directions, for better or for worse: "You are the way women are: they dream, they wake up in the morning, stare with empty eyes and are either disappointed that the dream was not real or thank their lucky stars that what they did in the dream was only a dream" (*K*, 231).[172] The upward counterfactuals stimulate feelings of regret as they construct a better possible world of the actual outcome of events, whereas the downward counterfactuals create an alternative state of affairs that is worse than the actualized state and therefore brings satisfaction and relief. Thought experiments that either improve or worsen reality are both based on the contrasting relationship between a "real" event belonging to a "factual" world and an alternative version of reality that counters the events of the factual one. (Dannenberg 2008: 112, 119) As stated, the human mind is more inclined to change the course of the actual events to a better direction, to feel regret over the unactualized life paths that now look more promising than the one once chosen.

In Mrs. Pyy's life story, the downfall plot pattern – the accumulative decision-making situations that repeatedly lead to failure – generate upward counterfactuals, which alternate the outcome of events in a better direction. Upward counterfactuals juxtapose a desired, positive version with an undesired, negative version, which becomes the actual narrated story in Mrs. Pyy's life. Towards the end of the novel, it becomes increasingly clear that Mrs. Pyy will not become what she wanted or expected to be. The alternative worlds she has created for herself result in inaction and loss, emptiness instead of fulfillment. One by one she loses the things she has managed to gain, which underlines not only the inefficiency of her actions, but also indicates the temporality of the comfort brought by these accomplishments. The things she achieves are not enough to solve her problems.

The question of whether Mrs. Pyy is a victim of blind chance or a perpetrator of her own tragedy is a crucial factor in discerning the causal interactions in the novel. From the external perspective, statistically unlikely events and (negative) coincidences generate causal uncertainty, which affects the character's life path: familiar causes fail to produce their anticipated effects. Causation involves action by some sort of intentional agent, either the characters themselves or some higher power steering the course of events. Causation also reflects pro-generative paths by which things spring from one another. Often it is the linear progression of events that is interrupted as the causal-linear patterns of narrative are called into question (cf. Richardson 2005: 51). Moreover, causation can be conceived as being necessary, with sufficient conditions having to be fulfilled in order to set the cause of a certain effect in motion. Before a particular outcome can be realized, all the components of the result must converge in the space and time of the fictional world. In mistimed tragic plots, the convergence of the different components produces negative outcomes and unfortunate coincidences. Characters are in the wrong place at the wrong time (or in the right place at the wrong time or vice versa).[173]

Mrs. Pyy's conviction of herself as a victim of circumstances (and other people's hostility) gives rise to further elaborations on her careless actions and her contemplation of unhappy coincidences in her life. Accidents are failures having either sad or happy consequences. They are "incursions of randomness into the realm of purposefulness" (Doležel 1998: 61). While Mrs. Pyy's actions are not intentional in the full meaning of the word (since their *causes* are not intended), they are still the direct causes of her actions.[174] Mrs. Pyy is constantly making decisions, all of which lead to action and worsen the situation in which she finds herself. The action modes of irrationality and impulsion stem from Mrs. Pyy's emotional perseverance. Lost in the mazes of her conditioned fear, she is unable to break the cycles of her behavior, is predestined to follow the old, rigid and inflexible rules, even if she is often aware of the more rational ways of behaving. Irrationality culminates in Mrs. Pyy's states of "madness," which is the most extreme manifestation of the pathological impact of nature on a person. (Ibid.: 71–72, 78)[175]

Counterfactual agency dealing with the question of whether the character can be seen as a perpetrator of circumstances (self-focused counterfactuals) or as a victim (externally-focused counterfactuals) directs the interpretation of the causal connections linking the antecedent to the consequent in counterfactual speculations. (Dannenberg 2008: 112) In counterfactual plots, the speculations about possible life trajectories are often caused by difficulties faced during the decision-making process. It is the characters' inability to make reliable decisions that leads to their thought experiments about how their lives might have developed differently. "For me, the decision-making has always been the hardest part" (*K*, 274), Mrs. Pyy confesses.[176]

As a counterfactualizing agent, Mrs. Pyy does not want to accept the role of an intentional perpetrator. By consciously or unconsciously misreading the people around her and laying the blame for her problems on them, she can still nourish to some degree the false fantasies about her great talent had she had a chance to become something other than an ordinary housewife. While remaining passive, Mrs. Pyy keeps waiting for someone to come and awaken her, as if she is unable to resolve her own anxieties. By evoking the fairytale of sleeping beauty (who waits to be rescued by a prince), Mrs. Pyy's life story draws attention to the contradiction between her desire to be rescued and at the same time become a rescuer who takes fate into her own hands. Indeed, Vartio's storyworlds are often ruled by chance, but most often the actual reason for the experience of contingency is found in the characters' deluded ways of seeing and "knowing" the world. The tendency of the human mind to lie to itself suggests that the experience of contingency stems from the inner chaos projected into the external world rather than from the actual randomness affecting an individual's life choices. The vast, dark regions of motivations are related to the human desire to erase contingency and impose form on life. Moreover, the interpretation of chance as providence or fate pertains to the denial of intentional agency:

unhappy consequences can be attributed to destiny rather than to oneself. (Jordan 2010: 122, 133)

Mrs. Pyy's futile attempts to fill the emotional void in her life can be interpreted in the context of a novel of awakening in which the protagonist – though drifting into futile, wasted battles – remains essentially passive. The narrative tension of this novel type results from the reader's awareness of the impossibility or even the undesirability of the protagonist's efforts, exemplified particularly well by the classic representative of this novel type, Gustav Flaubert's *Madame Bovary*. Emma Bovary's actions are measured not by what she will "bring about," but "by the extent to which she awakens to impossibilities." (Rosowski 1983: 50) In a similar way, Mrs. Pyy can be held responsible for the choices she makes, although she is blind to the real effects of her decisions. The real challenge of her life is whether she is able to awaken and see the impossibilities and limitations in her actions. Rather than blind chance taking control of her life, Mrs. Pyy is a victim of her own blindness. The narratives of female Bildung often critically underline the heroine's ignorance that lead to regret and self-estrangement. In Vartio's novel, the discrepancy between the protagonist's insufficient knowledge of events and the narrator's superior understanding (Felski 1989: 136) is generated in many scenes that involve both empathy and irony, resulting from the use of certain narrative techniques such as narrated monologue.

The novel of awakening typically turns into a novel of adultery. After the all-embracing expectations of marriage have failed, the novel's protagonist tries to find value in life in an extramarital romance (Abel, Hirsch, & Langland 1983: 12). The novel of awakening depicts a break from marital authority, and thus, knowledge (rather than sexuality) plays a dominate role in the process of self-discovery through the loved object (cf. Felski 1989: 131). The self-realization characteristic to the awakening of the heroine is connected to the desire for another, or rather, to the lost illusions as the feeling of desire is revealed to be only a symptom of discontent with the self and marital life (Pearce & Stacey 1995: 13). In *Madame Bovary*, the conventional downfall plot pattern of adultery concludes with degradation and punitive death. By contrast, in Mrs. Pyy's life story the conventional narrative closure is dramatically modified. The narrative sequence of her affair is represented only backwards (from its end to its beginning) and constitutes only one minor strand of the depiction of Mrs. Pyy's deferred Bildung. Ironically, there is no true passion in the adulterous relationship either. The lover finds more interest in his books than in his female companion. The option of choosing another life is rendered only in Mrs. Pyy's counterfactuals, ending in a decision not to take the last decisive step: "[S]he thought back to those days when she had looked at her home and children and thought… She had truly thought what things she would take with her, what to leave behind. […] But it wouldn't happen, no, it wouldn't" (*K*, 125).[177]

As demonstrated in the previous analyses in this chapter, the initial cause for Mrs. Pyy's emotional struggles is never explicated in the novel. It is only suggested in the narrator's depictions of what Mrs. Pyy does *not* fully grasp. The emotional wound is manifested in her inarticulate, burning desire for change: "[…] as if she were waiting, waiting for something, waiting to figure out what she should do so she would finally *feel alive*" (*K*, 148).[178] Mrs. Pyy's traumatic experiences seem to be re-worked especially in her relation to the lover. While walking to her lover's apartment, Mrs. Pyy feels afraid, as if vaguely aware of a distant knowledge of something that never emerges into her conscious mind: "But why, when she looked at the house and walked towards it, why did she feel fear? She had walked here before, without feeling anything except that she would soon be there" (*K*, 129).[179] As she goes in the door, the intuition grows stronger: "Where had it come from, this silence, the knowledge that she should not be standing here, that she shouldn't have come at all?" (*K*, 130)[180]

The cause for the anxiety is revealed later as Mrs. Pyy begins to "foresee" the undesired outcome of the visit. Mrs. Pyy both fears and expects the worst – the lover's rejection: "Hadn't she prepared herself for the humiliation and withdrawal? Hadn't she taught herself what to say when it happened? She would just stand up and say: Okay, so this game's over. Thank you, I had a great time. I feel refreshed" (*K*, 124–125).[181] The conditional phrases used in the passage generate epistemic uncertainty. Is Mrs. Pyy consciously planning her future actions or is she only counterfactualizing, constructing imaginary hypotheses? (Cf. Tammi 1992: 40) The illusion of knowing the lover's mind and calculating its next moves reflects the bad habits typical of Mrs. Pyy. She keeps building paranoic scenarios, which result in her irrational, akratic decisions: "She would say it as if in passing, laughing so unaffectedly that this man, at least, would pause to think. To think that she, the woman, had indeed been the one for whom it had all been just a game" (*K*, 125).[182] Mrs. Pyy has to remind herself that the events have taken place only in her mind, not in reality: "But it hadn't happened yet. Of course, it would happen this way. If she had, perhaps, thought something, waited for it, she knew now that nothing was going to come of this" (ibid.).[183]

The same pattern occurs in the lover's apartment, when Mrs. Pyy remembers the fish, a pike, lying in her purse. She had planned to prepare a meal for the man. She pictures herself pulling the pike out of the purse, cleaning and serving it to her lover. She feels a similar shame to that experienced in the Sistine Chapel at a later point in the story: "She tried not to think about it, that same thing all the time. Because it hadn't even happened; why was she tormenting herself with something the mere thought of which was so embarrassing that she shifted even just remembering it" (*K*, 135).[184] Mrs. Pyy imagines herself holding the fish in her hand, with a humble expression on her face, cleaning the pike and cutting its stomach open "with a blunt knife," pulling out the "bloody guts and gills – and scales" (ibid.).[185] The hypothetical scene with scales flying is a reflection of Mrs. Pyy's feeling of fear as she anticipates the end of the affair. The scales are parallel to the angel's wings that Mrs. Pyy sees in the picture hanging on the wall in the lover's kitchen. Mrs. Pyy tries to focus on counting the quills in the angel's wings, thus *substituting* one obsessional idea for another. But the image of the fish pushes into her awareness, reminding of her potential humiliation.

The tragedy of Mrs. Pyy is juxtaposed with the destiny of such classical figures as Don Quixote or Emma Bovary, who become victims of their own fantasies, fighting the windmills of their own minds. In contrast to Vartio's early novels, *Kaikki naiset näkevät unia* moves from the perceptual or memory-driven experience to counterfactual, hypothetical thinking enacted on the level of the mental functioning of the characters. Emotional operations of imagination enable hypothetical views of possible future situations. However, they also enable obsessive patterns of self-observation, calculation, and endless imaginings of such unstable characters as Mrs. Pyy. The challenges of figuring out Mrs. Pyy's true intent (which guides the interpretation of her actions and the causal connections of the novel) derive partly from her tendency to misread her own mind, a result of her tendency to misread other minds. However, the unconscious conflicts that cause the symptoms of Mrs. Pyy's condition are difficult to discern, not only because of her failure to grasp the prime cause of her anxiety, but also because of the novel's refusal to pursue conventional closure.[186] The unspeakable within is portrayed as Mrs. Pyy's lack of knowledge about her anxiety. By omitting the emotional motives of Mrs. Pyy's actions (which would provide information about the emotional, "disruptive moment" that needs to be corrected), the novel's narrative sequences are left incomplete.

The representation of Mrs. Pyy's unrepresentable trauma is reflected in the cyclic structure of the novel, in the patterns of repetition and variation used as narrative strategies to portray her mental life. In Italy, Mrs. Pyy keeps anticipating the moment of departure, mourning the cyclic paths of the future, which are waiting for her back home: "And everything would begin again from the beginning – everything" (*K*, 293).[187] The difficulty in interpreting the causal chains of the novel is caused by the reader's inability to gauge where an individual sequence begins and ends.[188] The novel begins after the onset of the disruption of normalcy and drops the reader in the middle of Mrs. Pyy's personal crisis. Also, the end of the novel is left open. The omission of a concluding segment that would reveal whether or not the final mental balance is achieved affects the interpretation of the final outcome of Mrs. Pyy's deferred Bildung. Thus, should we interpret the life plot of Mrs. Pyy as moving upward, from disruption to final balance and a state of emotional stability, or downward, from a state of balance to an endless series of disruptive moments worsening the instability of her life? The novel's problematic ending oscillates between the causal patterns of lingering and digression, which determine whether or not the traveler is able to arrive at the final destination of her journey.

The question of failure and success as the result of personal growth is exceeded in the novel of awakening, in which female development is often delayed and deferred. Instead of proceeding toward a fully accomplished development, the process of female self-discovery is compressed into brief epiphanic moments, flashes of recognition. The potential flowering of the inner self is actualized through memory and retrospection: as a foreshortened Bildung embedded into the story. (Abel, Hirsch, & Langland 1983: 12) In *Kaikki naiset näkevät unia*, Mrs. Pyy's endless drifting seems to remain ineffective, yet it serves as a way to portray her delayed, gradual process of soul-searching. Mrs. Pyy seems to be left lingering in a state of imbalance, in preparatory functions instead of primary endeavors, which, according to

Kafalenos, emphasizes the modernist view of personal growth and develop-ment. The incomplete narrative sequences of lingering portrays a character "who continually grows, but never projects that growth into accomplish-ment" (Kafalenos 2006: 113).

The narrative strategy of lingering and the classic trope of the madwoman modified in *Kaikki naiset näkevät unia* challenge the captive reading of Mrs. Pyy's mind: the character's "truth" remains vague and unresolved even when the story ends. In this respect, the character's "hysterical" self-quest becomes one form of resistance. Even though the never-ending path of suffering may entail a tragic entrapment in one's mind, it simultaneously enables the avoidance of conventional closure and causal explanation. In the novel's concluding scene, the stallholder hands the cameos to Mrs. Pyy and bends her fingers around them "like petals of a flower [folding] back into a bud." As many times before, Mrs. Pyy is at a crossroads in her life. Whether her development is nipped in the bud, however, remains to be seen. The "prophecy" of her dream suggests that the flower's bloom might never begin, as the snow starts to fall.

5. From Emotions to Feelings. Self-Conscious Minds in *Tunteet*

> [...]
> only a voice
> like the scream of a bird:
>
> that bird from a foreign land
> when a flood rises
> it flies ahead, flees
> it may fly over
> may fly over, tired,
> blood in its feathers [1]
>
> – Marja-Liisa Vartio: "The Flood Rises"

In the novel *Tunteet*, the female protagonist, Inkeri, is observing her feelings: "[S]he listened to herself: it was as if her whole body were black flowing lava with red flames curling through it; she had never experienced this feeling before, and it brought her a curious pleasure which she let continue" (*T*, 308).[2] The emotions Inkeri feels in her body are compared to "black flowing lava" and "red flames" as she self-consciously observes something she has never experienced before. These bodily emotions evoke "a curious pleasure," and Inkeri lets herself fully indulge in the feeling. This example of emotional observation lays bare the novel's focus: reading human emotions. In *Tunteet*, the protagonists, Inkeri and Hannu, keep close track of their embodied emotions and observe the public expressions of each other's feelings.

In Vartio's story, Hannu becomes Inkeri's personal Latin teacher, then her fiancé, and eventually her husband. The characters' intersubjective breakdowns generate the fluctuations of successes and failures in mind-reading typical of a love comedy, usually ending with a happy union of lovers.[3] The gaps in communication stem from the lovers' blindness: they are in love, yet unable to express their feelings or read the public expressions of each other's emotions. The fulfillment of the couple's love is complicated by constant disagreements and reconciliations. These complications (that constitute the stages of "transformation" and "negotiation" in the classic romance plot) are related to the characters' personal development, as both are in the process of getting to know themselves and each other. The battle between sense and emotion, rational intellect and imagination, genuine self-expression and pretense leads to breaks and misconnections in Inkeri and Hannu's communication. Their marriage, the eventual outcome of their rocky path together, appears to be unhappy and emotionally unsatisfying, resembling the situation in which we found Mrs. Pyy at the beginning of *Kaikki naiset näkevät unia*.

In this chapter, the relations of the self, the world, and the other are examined in *Tunteet*, in which questions of language and communication become the focus of a meeting of minds. First, the different uses of language are explored in regard to the battle between sense and sentiments actualized within and between the characters' minds and reflected in the constellations of mind-reading in the novel. Second, the difference between mental imaginings and the perceptions of the world are approached in relation to pretense and make-believe, which play out in the relationship between Inkeri and Hannu. Third, the unreliability of introspection and of verbal accounts of the mental life of human beings, the distorted quality of recollection, and the characters' inabilities to recognize their emotional motives are addressed by reading the characters' letters as manifestations of their self-delusion and pretense. These analyses are followed by a discussion of the novel's emotional structure from the perspectives of Bildungsroman, sentimental novels, and epistolary fiction.[4] The last part of the chapter focuses on the conventions of showing emotions in the modernist novel.

Reining in Emotions. Sense and Sensibility

One reason for the series of misunderstandings between Inkeri and Hannu is the difference in their social background, speech, and behavior, which is touched upon already in the opening scene. The encounter of Inkeri and Hannu introduces the theme modified during the novel: idealizations and false expectations that result in the complications of the love affair. The door pane frames a vision of a young girl meeting her future husband for the first time: "At the door stood a soldier" (*T*, 7).[5] The soldier has been sent from a nearby military camp to teach Inkeri Latin. Her perception of the young man standing on the threshold is shared by the other members of the family who are gathered in the room. Inkeri observes the encounter from a position of distance. She adopts the soldiers's vantage point and listens to her relatives talk as if she were an outsider. She realizes how curious they must sound to him: "And the soldier looked at Inkeri and heard her speaking the same way as the others, with a broad country accent" (*T*, 21).[6] Inkeri gives an embarrassed laugh meant to elicit understanding, which Vartio depicts as potential mind-reading: "[H]e *must understand* that she *understood* how comical this kind of talk must sound to the stranger's ear and that she was not as simple-minded as these people" (ibid.).[7]

In *Tunteet*, Vartio employs certain patterns of the romance plot, but the conventional formulae of lovers' discourse (typical of sentimental fiction and epistolary mode) are subverted and parodied as they are rewritten into the plot of female development. The first sighting between the lovers modifies the stage of encounter: the meeting of a heroine and an aristocratic (or aristocratically behaving) man, which leads to the heroine's loss of social identity (cf. Radway 1987: 134).[8] Hannu's refined manners draw Inkeri's attention: "In the dining room sat a soldier, a gentleman" (*T*, 18).[9] Inkeri feels excited. She considers the young man's arrival as a welcome deviation from the routines of the farm. The narrator mediates Inkeri's inarticulate emotions, which are felt, but not thought: "And suddenly it felt good, something had begun, you could have called it an adventure, but *she didn't wonder what it was*. It was enough that after a so long time something had happened; this something which you might call an event [...]" (ibid.).[10]

Hannu, conversely, feels confusion as he meets Inkeri and her family. He observes Inkeri's looks and behavior and finds her attractive, yet unrefined and rustic. There is also something defiant in her behavior: "[H]e had watched the girl as she walked across the room towards the kitchen, her head high and her chin up, her hair loose [...] the soldier thought she was an angry-looking girl" (*T*, 15).[11] Hannu has trouble making sense of the "chaotic" speech of Inkeri's relatives. He tries to listen carefully to every word they say. The uncle, Eemeli, keeps talking about the broken phone, and for a while Hannu wonders whether they think he is a repairman: "But now they were talking about the phone, nothing about Latin" (*T*, 12).[12] The grandmother keeps asking about a pig that has escaped from the shed. As Inkeri threatens to let the pig loose on purpose, if she continues to talk about it, Hannu's surprised reaction makes Inkeri self-conscious of her own way of speaking. Hannu is described as listening politely to the stories, to which everyone else knows to give only half an ear. The soldier certainly had "a good education; you could see that in everything [about him]" (*T*, 10).[13]

The beginning of the actual romance is deferred as the third stage of the romance plot – the mismatch of the romantic ideal and the actual person – complicates the affair right from the beginning (cf. Vesti 2014: 22). In Hannu's opinion, Inkeri lacks cultivation: "The girl had not gotten a proper education; at times her behavior was downright coarse" (*T*, 30).[14] Inkeri represents wild nature that needs to be cultured and educated. She is a *tabula rasa*, a canvas awaiting the artist's brush. The idea of Inkeri as an object of Hannu's study and refinement is manifested in the Pygmalion motif employed in the novel. The figure of Pygmalion has its origin in Greek mythology. As related in Ovid's *Metamorphoses*, Pygmalion is a talented sculptor who creates a statue of a perfect ivory maiden and prays to Venus to bring the creature to life for him to marry. Pygmalion has become a symbol of a man who wants to mold his wife into his ideal of womanhood.[15]

The contrast between culture and nature is manifested in the very language of Latin that Hannu is trying to teach his student. The ancient, classical language becomes the signifier of cultivation, intellect, and order, which demand self-discipline in order to be mastered: "And then [Hannu] had spoken at great length about learning Latin in general, the certain unavoidable mechanicalness and precision of the basics of Latin" (*T*, 31).[16] The strictness of grammar refers to the standards of the Finnish modernist poetics of the 1950s (discussed in the later analyses of the novel). Inkeri grows bored and reluctant exactly because Hannu is strictly focused on the business at hand, showing no sign of feeling or personal interest: "He hardly notices that I'm here, Inkeri thought; he seems to think I'm the echo of his voice" (*T*, 27).[17] In Inkeri's mind, the correct forms of Latin and the clear articulation of words begin to represent the teacher himself. She feels warded off by Hannu's impersonal, ironic tone. She interprets his formality and distance as contempt, which results in her struggle to hide her feelings.

The beginning of the romance in *Tunteet* is postponed by the lovers' mixed feelings, leading to anger and resentment. Inkeri is shown figuring out how she should act in order to avoid being caught up in these feelings: "She mustn't let them see, no, she had made it clear to herself [...]: from here on just Latin, so that no one, least of all that boy, would know how her heart pounded, what had happened to her. Crazy, she'd been crazy, but now that was over" (*T*, 38–39).[18] As Inkeri considers what others might think of her, we witness a case of mind-reading. Inkeri imagines Hannu potentially guessing her feelings: "[I]f he had supposed something, he would see that his suppositions were for nothing" (*T*, 39).[19] The representation of Inkeri's thoughts also involves aspects of collective, shared thought. In addition to Hannu's mind, Inkeri's mental suppositions imply the presence of the collective mind of the villagers, including possible rumors about her. Inkeri intentionally plans her future actions in order to clip the wings of any speculation. Like the "social mind" of Inkeri's family observing Hannu's arrival at the farm, the collective mind of the villagers serves as a third, collective pair of eyes watching the couple's moves in the game of love.

As the result of emotional complicacies, the couple is stuck reading and misreading each other's physical expressions. Due to emotional inhibition, they are unable to express their feelings. When they meet for the first time, each experiences a fierce beating of the heart. Both are afraid that their uncontrollable bodies will betray their emotions, which – like their bodies – seem to have a "will" of their own:

> How calm a moment ago, how charming, and now again: clumsy, restless, unnerving. Why doesn't she stay still for even a minute? And the soldier's heart had started to pound so hard he was afraid it could be heard; he was afraid the shabby gray coat of his uniform was moving right where his heart beat beneath it. And he didn't know the girl was listening to her heart, too, that the girl was also afraid that he'd see how her heart was beating, for it had only thin, red-flowered cotton for cover, and it felt to her as if the flowers over her heart were bouncing, betraying it. (*T*, 38)[20]

Vartio depicts the thoughts, emotions, and the physical sensations of both characters from within. The perspective shifts from Hannu's inner realm to Inkeri's mind, simultaneously revealing that Inkeri is in fact listening to her own pounding heart. Paradoxically, even if the minds remain unaware of the reactions caused by one's body in another body, it seems as if the bodies themselves "know."

The scenes analyzed above demonstrate the complex nature of emotions, both as private and public phenomena. Emotions as bodily reactions are observable to others. In fictional scenes they are manifested in the external descriptions of physical actions, facial expressions, and other gestures containing emotional display (external focalization) or as characters' perceptions of other characters as "mediated" by the narrator (internal focalization). The term "feeling," on the other hand, can be reserved for those mental experiences of emotions that are private and mostly unobservable. In fictional scenes, they are typically represented from internal perspectives, or interchangeably, as direct reports of the characters' mental states. This tension between emotions, manifesting as both private and public phenomena, is closely related to rational calculation and decision-making in scenes in which the characters are struggling to control the public expressions of their emotions. Spontaneous expressions of emotions (blushing, crying, facial expressions) are involuntary. Sometimes, however, it is possible to control these expressions in order to disguise them. In these instances, intentional decisions can be made about how to behave. (Cf. Palmer 2010: 163)

The emotional landscpace of *Tunteet* involves motivational conflicts that lead to the characters' attempts to control and repress their emotions. The characters' tendency to withhold (verbal) expression leads to continuous misunderstandings that generate the intersubjective breakdowns typical of a love comedy. In this sense, the tension between emotions as public expressions and feelings as private experiences is the defining factor in the novel's emotional story structure. Furthermore, in the beginning of the novel, the moral dilemma of Hannu's role as a teacher is a source of motivational conflict. Hannu emphasizes his responsibility as a teacher is to be "business-like and strict" ("asiallinen ja tiukka") because his student lacks self-discipline (*T*, 32). He finds Inkeri stubborn and moody, not easily managed: "The girl never looked him straight in the eye unless she had to, when he, in his capacity of teacher, insisted she pronounce the declension clearly so that he could hear whether each form was correct" (*T*, 30).[21]

In the highly emotional scene when Inkeri is speculating on Hannu's speculations as well as on the collective mind of the villagers, her thoughts involve conscious decision-making: "[S]he had made it clear to herself [...]; from here on just Latin." Reading *Tunteet*, we can observe how the distinction between irrational passions and calculated reasoning is continuously questioned. The emotional and the rational minds are working in cooperation. As illustrated by the scene of the two pounding hearts, for instance, the struggle between emotion and sense is not so much about the difference *between* Inkeri's and Hannu's minds, but about the struggle *within* them. Inkeri's "animalism" attracts Hannu more than he is willing to admit. His eyes are continually drawn to her body, even though he struggles to focus on her mind. Hannu's associations of Inkeri with contrasting emotions are revealed when he is unable to fall asleep: Hannu looks "into the darkness" ("pimeään") (*T*, 30) as if trying to detect his unconscious emotions. He feels increasingly disturbed. He rationalizes to himself that he is upset because of Inkeri's lack of restraint during the lessons. However, one particular rumor comes to mind: he has heard that Inkeri attended a secret ball in a barn with the other soldiers. His dream afterwards reflects his mixed feelings about Inkeri. In the dream, "the girl is running ahead and he's trying to catch her, but he can't run fast enough, and he's angry at himself; he has to catch the girl. But the girl is running ahead and laughing, a loud mocking laugh" (*T*, 32).[22] The dream suggests that Inkeri is unruly, ungovernable – and highly intriguing.

Hannu finally loses his self-control the next day when he catches Inkeri cheating, looking up verbs in a book. She is supposed to spell an inflection of the Latin verb *amo*, "to love." Hannu shouts at her, but afterwards, tries to regain his self-control. It is jealousy, a burning passion, that makes him shout and also makes him swallow his anger afterwards: "It felt to the soldier as if he was slowly swallowing something hot and burning. When it was gone, he thought: I'm crazy" (*T*, 34).[23] Hannu considers emotions to be a madness that needs to be controlled. As involuntary impulses, emotions are difficult to rein in – like Inkeri herself. The actual cause of Hannu's blow-up is revealed in his narrated memory, which illustrates the conflict in his emotions: simultaneous attraction and disdain. For a second, the vision of Inkeri standing by the fire makes his heart race: "When he'd come into the main room of the farm house, the girl had been standing by the stove with the glow of the fire around her uncombed hair, her lips slightly parted, like that, just like now, with in her eyes the same expression as in those of an animal frozen in place to listen" (ibid.).[24] The glow of light around Inkeri's "uncombed hair" ("kampaamaton pää") is like a halo of sacred, pure girlhood. In Hannu's eyes, her calm is animal-like, a natural grace that lacks any pretension. The illusion of harmony in the image, however, vanishes as fast as it appeared. "Away with the vision, away with the girl beside the fire, there was a girl, her mouth filled with empty girl talk, where nothing was less than wonderful or terrible – away with the vision that had made his heart pound" (ibid.).[25]

The emotional intensity in many scenes stems from the characters' tendency to attentively read each other's behavior to determine how much the other person knows about what they themselves know. This tension between the private and the public realms is evoked through a wide range of techniques that represent the minds both from within and from without. The following passage starts off as a description of Inkeri's body language and gradually proceeds to her self-conscious thoughts about how she appears in Hannu's eyes: "And the girl shrugged her shoulders, moved her hands as if shaking off something, rubbed her knuckles on her knees – and became thoroughly depressed when she realized she looked ridiculous" (*T*, 40).[26] In her emotional desperation, Inkeri forgets to control her physical reactions. In the following interior monologue, she sees herself through Hannu's eyes and claims to *know* his thoughts: "Go ahead and look at me. I *know* what you're *thinking*, you're thinking I'm a country hick, go ahead, think whatever you want, believe all the gossip, but don't think I'll cry" (*T*, 40–41).[27] The last thought reveals that Inkeri is about to burst into tears, but she still manages to hold them back.

The depiction of Hannu's mind in the following passage shows one of the functions of the novel's shifting perspective, a way of portraying the failures of mind-reading and showing a lack of real communication. The narrator mediates what Hannu *actually* thinks, but also what he *cannot* read in Inkeri's behavior: "The soldier followed the girl's expressions, saw the confusion, saw the bad mood, saw the haughtiness the girl was wrapping herself up in while turning her eyes back to him" (*T*, 41).[28] Hannu attentively reads the changes of mood expressed by Inkeri's body, her indecisiveness and the manifestations of "bad mood" and "haughtiness" on her face, but he does not manage to figure out the real reasons for these embodied emotions. The mutual misreading is followed by Hannu's sudden question that surprises the young man himself: "Are you in love? the soldier asked cynically. And he got scared: that was the last thing he had meant to say" (ibid.).[29]

The unintended question indicates Hannu's inability to identify and control his emotional impulses. First, the reader is informed about the feelings that Hannu himself is conscious of, including his humiliation and desire for revenge.[30] The narrator is needed to "mediate" those motivations that Hannu himself is not able to articulate or even recognize. He is still convinced that his motives for determining whether Inkeri is in love with "that stupid Wasström" ("typerä Wasström") stem from curiosity alone. The scene's tension between the "silent" and the audible voices is illustrated by the contrast between the quiet raving in the privacy of Inkeri's mind and the coldness of her rhetorical question to Hannu: "With whom, the girl asked coldly and raised her chin. And raged to herself: Now he'll guess, he'll think I'm in love with him, when I ask 'with whom' in that tone" (*T*, 41).[31] As Inkeri eventually bursts into tears, Hannu is left puzzled by her reactions. Has he offended the girl? The lack of true communication never resides, which emphasizes the function of the romance plot in the novel's narrative structure and its semantics. The other person is seen through the refractive lens of self-reflection, not as she or he is. The stage of transformation in the love plot steps in right from the beginning.

In *Tunteet*, communication problems are a prominent theme, one that complicates the relationship and generates the fluctuations in the story structure characteristic of a romance plot. As in *Mies kuin mies, tyttö kuin tyttö*, so too in Vartio's fourth novel the patterns of romance are disrupted by the depiction of a young girl's development. The process of growth, however, is now portrayed more clearly as a two-way exchange of intermental meanings attached to the lovers' discourse. By showing the characters both from within and without, by swiftly shifting perspectives from one to the other, the author portrays the rich complexities of human nature. In the end, the parody and irony used in the characterization result in tragicomedy, as the characters are shown being particularly human, vulnerable, and flawed, unknown even to themselves. The scenes of mind-reading portray the initial cause for the misery in the marriage at a later point, as the love comedy turns into a personal tragedy.

The problem of language in the communication between Inkeri and Hannu is related primarily to the contrast between imagination and rational logic, reflecting the discrepancy between the lovers' expectations and their different ways of speaking, seeing, and being in the world. Inkeri is learning to master a language that feels strange, different from her changeful and dialectical mother tongue (Viikari 1992: 66). In addition to spoken language the words need to be occupied to understand one's inner voice, to verbalize one's thoughts and emotions. In novels such as *Tunteet* (or *Mies kuin mies, tyttö kuin tyttö*) the young women are struggling to learn a language that feels like a language of a foreign land. The double bind of socialization and the denial of individual self-expression are emphasized in Viikari's (ibid.: 66–67) analysis of Vartio's novels:

> One's own speech is fragmented and ever shifting, dialectal; the common language that "every man" speaks is the language prescribed by the society. Vartio's women are aware of their position in this inter-world. The space for their own immediate experience is societally mute; in the language of society, woman is an object that is defined from without. But having learned the rules of the common language, this agent of no man's land hears the strange voice in her own speech, her own ambivalence.[32]

Difficulties in communication penetrate all human relations, but the most vulnerable of relations is the connection between women and men. According to Viikari (ibid.: 65–66), especially Vartio's technique of narrated monologue[33] is reined in to serve as a "tool to analyze language, power and the relations of sexes" in the space inbetween, on "the stage of dialogic language."[34] In a similar vein as the soldiers on the scene of war, the female speakers in everyday talk are trained to be attentive, to "hit" the target on the battlefields of power. Her characters are well tuned in to listen to the speech beyond: under what is said, another thing is being said (ibid.: 66).[35] The problem of language leads to the split in the self, which is rendered in Inkeri's thought of becoming "the echo of [Hannu's] voice." The compositions of mind-reading involve Bakhtinian "sideways glances," as Inkeri observes herself while observing Hannu's reactions to her: "But with one eye she kept an eye on Hannu's expressions, all the while thinking to herself was it the devil or what that had made her once again so sweet and calm, just the way Hannu over there liked" (*T*, 111).[36] In the following analyses, the complexities of the relationship are approached from the perspective of make-believe, logic, and affective immersion that reflect the couple's different world-views.

Make-Believe, Logic, and Affective Immersion. A Maiden and a Weeping Willow

Hannu considers Inkeri's reckless behavior a manifestation of her lack of intellectual discipline. Inkeri's mind is constantly being overtaken by her emotional whims, as reflected in the uncontrolled movements of her body:

"You are restless, said Hannu, emphasizing the words 'you are' as if he were teaching grammar" (*T*, 76).[37] Inkeri's imaginative faculties are the focus of the episode portraying the couple's visit to Olavinlinna (the Castle of Olavi) in eastern Finland. In the romantic setting, Inkeri's imagination runs riot. She imagines having seen a water mistress's daughter in the whirlpools of the stream running by the castle walls. Hannu encourages Inkeri to continue her story. He mistakenly thinks that Inkeri has read a narrative or perhaps a folktale: "Tell me – have you read about it?" (*T*, 100)[38] Inkeri goes on, but does not get very far, when the young man cuts in: "'Do you know something?' he asked. 'You certainly have imagination and you also know how to tell a story, but why do you shrug your shoulders? Look, like this.' And Hannu imitated her" (*T*, 101).[39]

Inkeri's story pleases Hannu, yet her manner of talking draws his attention. Inkeri's restless body seems to affect the structure of her narrative that is as spontaneous and disorderly as her embodied being. Hannu suggests that Inkeri should "start from the beginning": "'Keep going,' he said. 'But speak calmly. Your voice is perfect for telling that kind of story, just don't interrupt the whole time. Okay, start from the beginning, I want to hear it again from the beginning. So the daughter of the lady of the waters was sitting on a rock combing her long hair...'" (*T*, 101)[40] But Inkeri feels offended. There is no "beginning." She has only told something that she has heard someone talk about like any other matter. Inkeri suspects Hannu is examining her, as if testing her intelligence: "[M]aybe Hannu was testing how intelligent she was, had deliberately led her to talk like this and then wondered if she was really that simple-minded" (ibid.).[41] "[S]oon he'd be having her conjugate some verb," Inkeri mocks him in her thoughts (*T*, 101–102).[42] Inkeri is irritated, but at the same time she fears that Hannu will think of her as a foolish, childish creature who really believes in such things as the ladies of the waters and their daughters with golden hair.

The contrast between written and oral traditions becomes a way of reflecting the distinction between the two minds. Hannu's claims to "speak precisely" do not end with his attempts to teach Inkeri Latin. The cultivation of her mind also involves weeding out her preference for folk beliefs, which feed her romantic whims. The idea of Inkeri's over-imaginative mind reappears later, when she articulates another image that comes to mind: "Look, there's a mountain ash in that wall [...] It has grown from tears" (*T*, 103).[43] Inkeri's notion of the mountain ash corresponds to her previous perception of the river whirlpool, which she pictures as being caused by the lady of the waters. The mountain ash is an element of a romantic story that Inkeri has heard people talking about. The story refers to the ballad of Olavinlinna that was varied in many folktales and composed into a song (performed by Annikki Tähti) in the 1950s. There was a maiden who fell in love with a Russian soldier. The maiden was said to have been buried alive within the castle wall for her crime of loving the enemy. Provoked by Hannu's dismissive reaction to her words, Inkeri insists the story might even be true:

"But I feel pity," said Inkeri, and sighed.

"What are you feeling pity for – do you really believe that the mountain ash has grown from tears?"

"I didn't say that! I do know that no mountain ash or spruce tree grows out of a tear."

"Then why do you say from a tear? Speak precisely. You just admitted that no tree grows out of a tear, however hard your maiden cries, yet you are talking about the tear again – don't say that the mountain ash grew from the tear, say that it is said, it is told, it is thought, it is believed. Speak precisely." (*T*, 106)[44]

The conflict between Inkeri and Hannu springs from their different views of the use of language and stories. Hannu wishes to make Inkeri see the difference between *reality* and *make-believe*, perceptions and beliefs, observation and imagination. "It's just an image,"[45] Hannu says as Inkeri asks him to salute "the protector of the castle" ("linnan suojelijaa") – in reality, an empty suit of armor standing at the castle entrance (*T*, 96).

Hannu's demands for precise use of language derive from his preference for logic and intellect over emotion and imagination. Inkeri, by contrast, experiences stories empathically, *as if* they were true. Regardless of whether the story is actual or imaginary, Inkeri experiences it with strong emotions: with the pity or love the person within the storyworld feels. In this respect, *Tunteet* modifies the frequent theme of classical Bildungsromane, in which the process of self-cultivation involves aesthetic sensibility in addition to rational faculties. One's nature (not only self-education) plays an important part in the process of development, by giving a seed for an individual's growth to be turned into a full bloom. (Castle 2006: 41–42) In the story of the mountain ash, Inkeri identifies with the maiden, experiencing the maiden's love as fierce and unconditional. Her tears may not have turned into mountain ash, but such love may truly exist. Hannu's disbelief appears to Inkeri as an indication of his lack of empathy. He does not truly know how to feel with others. Hannu's behavior at the castle, when he calls for the oarsman to row them across the moat without giving any thought to the fact that the man might be old and tired, sparks Inkeri's anger: "For a moment, she hated Hannu" (*T*, 94).[46]

Inkeri is entranced by stories in a way that is characteristic of fictional immersion. Affective immersion is based on the double logic of both acknowledging the ontological ambiguity of imaginary beings and simultaneously empathizing with the beings as if they were real.[47] The imagined world evokes affections that are very similar to actual emotions (excitement, pity, fear) felt in reality, even if the person experiencing them is fully aware of the fictional quality of the "reality" represented in the story (Ryan 1991: 21–23). This sort of affectional immersion feels completely strange to Hannu, who seems to believe that Inkeri truly believes in these stories. Hannu perceives the story elements of folktales as formal motifs of folklore:

"But dear child," said Hannu. He came over to Inkeri and fixed her cap, which was once again about to fall off. "Why do you get angry with me?" said Hannu. "It doesn't diminish the beauty of the legend to view it through the prism of reason. Legends are born from the very fact that human nature is prone to imagine things like a mountain ash born from the tears of some unhappy maiden. It's a perfectly typical legend; there are lots of trees that have grown on graves like that." And Hannu talked at length about different legends that circulated around the world in different versions, but were fundamentally the same... (*T*, 107–108)[48]

Hannu's conception of folktales corresponds to ideas of modern folklore and literary studies, which classify both oral and written stories on the basis of their variation of certain story subjects.[49] Hannu perceives the tales through the lens of the intellect ("through the prism of reason"). However, as for the tendency of human nature to imagine and tell stories, he finds no need to explain such an inclination. Tales may include motifs like the daughters of the lady of the waters and mountain ashes growing from tears. Their elements, however, should be considered as story motifs from oral tradition, not as something to be affectionately stirred and moved about.

Hannu considers Inkeri's romantic caprices as a manifestation of her immaturity. She is "a dear child," who does not yet fully recognize the differences between a percept, the certainty of knowledge gained through perception (the world "as it is"), and a mental image, including the beliefs created by the imaginative mind. In Hannu's view, the maturation of Inkeri's imaginative mind is still in progress. Inkeri needs to be able to control her mental images and place them under her conscious will. This is the very first step on the journey of becoming a fully conscious being. These images should not be believed in; they should be separated from beliefs and conceptually differentiated from perceptions. A matured person who is fully conscious of herself must be aware of whether one is imagining or perceiving. (Cf. McGuinn 2004: 121) Inkeri's inclination to talk about the motifs of folktales as if they were real appears to Hannu as a sign of her ignorance. Inkeri does not know how to express the difference between a perception and a mental image: "Don't say that the mountain ash grew from the tear, say that it is said, it is told, it is thought, it is believed. Speak precisely."

The conflict between human imagination and logic demonstrates the differences in how the two minds perceive human relations in general. Inkeri's inclination to "believe" in imaginary things is contrasted with Hannu's conception of emotions as "madness." For Inkeri, the story of the buried maiden signifies the power of love, which exceeds all matters of formality: "Madness, of course," Inkeri says, anticipating Hannu's disapproval. "But it wouldn't be a question of reason and madness, but of love" (*T*, 109).[50] Hannu considers Inkeri's talk of the enemy as being an indication of her childlike sentimentality, which may have dangerous consequences in time of war: "[D]on't play with matters that are serious" (ibid.), he warns.[51] Inkeri's inclination to "play" coincides with her reckless nature; her imaginative whims are things that that she needs to learn to control.

To provide a warning example of what happens to people who give in to their emotions, Hannu tells a real-life story. There was a woman whose hair had been cut off because she had indulged in a relationship with the enemy. Before telling the story, Hannu cautions Inkeri that it is better to think twice before she speaks: "[D]o you know, Inkeri, you have the sort of hair that makes me want to go under it and hide there, but why do you say things that aren't smart, don't you see that it's not appropriate to talk about those kinds of things?" (T, 111)[52] Inkeri's big, uncombed, and unruly hair signifies her unruly nature, which Hannu is trying to temper. The story, however, does not have the effect Hannu has hoped for. Inkeri immerses herself in the world of the real-life narrative in a manner similar to the worlds of romantic folktales. She imagines herself being in the position of the woman Hannu has told her about: "And Hannu didn't know where all Inkeri had traveled during the few minutes his story had lasted, didn't know what all Inkeri had had time to experience: shamed, her hair cut off at the scalp, Inkeri had wandered through dark forests, but she had loved" (T, 111–112).[53]

Inkeri's unwise talk is considered in relation to social norms, particularly in the context of madness as a form of socially abnormal behavior. Hannu's talk alludes to the trope of the hysterical woman or "madwoman" employed in Vartio's other novels. He guides Inkeri to adopt a civilized way of speaking. Inkeri's talk resembles the language of mad(wo)men: "'Don't you understand how strange that sort of talk sounds?' asked Hannu. 'You aren't crazy; why then do you talk about those sorts of things, don't you know that people with mental disorders have hallucinations, and particularly of mice?'" (T, 184)[54] Hannu perceives Inkeri's romantic caprices as social transgressions, but also as the childishness of a school girl who can still be subdued with proper education. Hannu, however, fails to see that Inkeri's inclination to imagine (to "see hallucinations") is a character trait that is inseparable from her personality and self-expression. Inkeri's mind is not the rich ground for the seeds of cultivation that he has expected. Her wild nature fights back.

LET'S IMAGINE!

In the depiction of Inkeri's romantic self-quest, the folktales represent her child-like nature – her spontaneous ways of being – which are connected to her imagination and compassionate feelings for others. Seeing things, such as mice, refers to an episode in which Inkeri is again depicted playing a game of make-believe. In chapter 6, a flashback shows Inkeri and Hannu arriving in a café after their engagement. The café becomes crowded, and an unknown lieutenant joins their table. During the conversation, Inkeri observes the kitchen door swinging back and forth. She envisions a mouse on the doorsill and suddenly screams:

> "[...] Of course, it wasn't a mouse; something just flashed before my eyes," said Inkeri.
> The lieutenant had burst out laughing, and Inkeri had also started to laugh; she and the lieutenant had laughed together, and the lieutenant had started to tease her:
> "What kind of a mouse – black, white, big, little?"
> "A little black mouse."
> "But was it a real mouse, exactly the kind that all women are scared of? (T, 185)[55]

The episode demonstrates the relations of perception and mental imagining, sensory illusion and hallucination touched upon in the previous dialogues between the lovers. According to Inkeri, she is having a sensory illusion ("something just flashed before my eyes"). According to her fiancé, on the other hand, she behaves as if she were hallucinating, seeing "things" like a madwoman. She is making a hysterical scene, and Hannu feels ashamed. His face turns deep red, and with a quiet, "mean voice" he asks whether she has "talked about it enough" (*T*, 185).[56] He considers Inkeri's behavior a breach of social order that makes her appear mad in the eyes of others.

Inkeri's performance raises questions about the real cause of Hannu's anger. Walking into the café, Inkeri feels tired, because she had argued all night with her fiancé. She starts to feel alive again in like-minded, "handsome" company: "[T]he lieutenant was fun, much more fun than Hannu" (*T*, 184).[57] The stranger instantly understands the playful manner of her expression. The unknown soldier even engages in the game: he may not *see* the mouse, but he can *imagine* it. The lieutenant can also recognize the stereotype of all women screaming and being scared of mice, which Inkeri seems to be impersonating in her "womanly" performance. After the discussion with her fiancé, however, Inkeri starts to have second thoughts. What if the lieutenant had only been laughing at Inkeri, not with her? The lieutenant had talked about the human mind's tendency to see illusions in a state of exhaustion, but Inkeri starts to second-guess his sincerity, re-reading the stranger's mind: "Inkeri felt bad. She herself was already beginning to think that the lieutenant had thought her crazy" (ibid.).[58]

The argument following the scene continues the couple's discussion they had on the castle walls of Olavinlinna. Hannu blames Inkeri for not having learned anything about the "precise" use of language. Whether or not Inkeri really knows the difference between perceptions and mental images, she acts as if she does not. The discrepancy between "seeing" (perception) and "seeing-as" (as a sensory pretense of imagining something) forms the basis of the couple's disagreements. Inkeri confesses to having had a sensory illusion. Yet she begins to *talk about* the mouse as if she had truly perceived it. Inkeri's blending of reality and fantasy frustrates Hannu. Inkeri may not know how to control her sensory illusions, but she could rein in her imagination and the ways of expressing herself. The products of imaginative seeing are not like hallucinations or delusions run riot. They can be subjected to conscious will and be forcibly controlled.

Inkeri's ability to imagine alternative worlds reflects her inclination for counterfactual thinking, entertaining herself with possibilities. Even if the mental image of a mouse is conjured up, the movement of a door is still the door's movement and nothing else; the act of imagining is not bound to any truth conditions. Inkeri's anger stems from Hannu's attempts to control her every move and word. In her emotional outburst, Inkeri distorts the words she hears from Hannu. She interprets him as monitoring not only the manner of her speaking, but also her freedom to *think* spontaneously. "You can disapprove of my behavior, but you can't forbid me from thinking," Inkeri rebels in her thoughts (*T*, 183).[59] Inkeri's idea of her imaginings as *thoughts* reveal that she herself considers her "romantic whimsies" as a source of the pleasures of thinking about the world differently: seeing and feeling it from alternative positions, from within the skin of others.

The differences in the couple's use of language reflect the polarity of world-views that alienates Inkeri from Hannu, and vice versa. Expressing one's emotions is impossible without a shared language, and the couple seems to lack an understanding of each other's words. On the castle walls, Hannu invites Inkeri to play another game of make-believe. Hannu resorts to an act of cognitive imagining while counterfactualizing the possible paths of the future. Hannu pictures two paths: one secretly fantasized by Inkeri and the other representing the sensible path she knows she is expected to take:

> "Let's imagine," Hannu began. "Let's imagine," he repeated after thinking a moment, "that we, you and me, are on a journey and we're hungry. We're somewhere abroad, and there are two restaurants side by side – one, known to be fancy, favored by tourists, but expensive, of course, and the other one less fancy but cheaper; it wouldn't have an orchestra and such, for instance, but the food would be good, prepared hygienically and nourishing." Inkeri had already gotten excited, had begun to listen like to a fairy tale, had seen herself and Hannu abroad in front of a romantic restaurant, when Hannu asked:
> "Which one would you go to, which one would you choose?"
> "The cheaper one, of course."
> "You are a sensible girl," said Hannu.
> Inkeri felt that she was starting to become very sensible. (*T*, 114)[60]

Inkeri has enough time to imagine herself abroad with Hannu, entering a fancy restaurant. The fairy tale, however, comes to an end even before it has started, as if Inkeri were turned away at the restaurant door. The thought experiment ends in disappointment. Likewise, the couple's future marriage corresponds to the more prosaic scenario, which becomes the actualized path of Inkeri's life. Becoming "sensible" means adopting certain social rules and abandoning old ones, manifested in Inkeri's symbolic loss of her unruly hair. The marriage means the end of the childish games of make-believe. Life is about to turn into a very serious business.

The Smothered Flames of Love. Introspection and Self-Analysis

In the previous studies of *Tunteet*, the relations of word and world have been perceived mainly by viewing language as the source of Inkeri's alienation. The problem of language in the young couple's relationship has been understood to reflect the estrangement of a female subject in the modern world. More specifically, the novel has been understood as a rescripting of the ideals of empiricism and a comment on the struggle for a "new language" in Finnish modernist aesthetics (Rojola 2008, 2013). The novel has also been read as reflecting the difficulties of a female author trying to grasp the conventions of a male-dominated culture. According to Pertti Karkama (1995: 150), in Vartio's diaries spontaneous thoughts, experiences, emotions, perceptions, and sensations disrupt the chronological order that represents "the feminine logic." In this way, we may perceive what the novel *Tunteet* is about: "It is about growing into a woman, about how a woman gradually has to submit, both sensually and bodily, both emotionally and intellectually to the laws of the masculine culture, and how the amortization of self-expression is finally the only way that offers a chance to survive" (Karkama 1995: 162).[61] As Karkama observes, only self-conceit and repressed desire remain.[62]

Previous scholarly studies on the novel, however, have paid less attention to Hannu's ambiguous relationship to language. In Lea Rojola's (2013: 216) reading, Hannu is considered as being the one who "knows language" ("osaa kieltä"). Despite his difficulties in expressing his emotions, he still manages to achieve his goals by using the old language. (Ibid.: 217, 221) Esko Ervasti, accordingly, considers Hannu an individual in the stage in-between, still operating with the old language of the community.[63] On the other hand, Ervasti emphasizes the problematic aspects of language from the perspective of Hannu's characterization. Hannu has lost his belief in conventional forms of language, but has not yet found a new language to replace them. Inkeri has already discovered a new way of thinking. Whereas Inkeri has alienated herself from the conventional language (or has come to feel alienated from it through her ambivalent relation to the socially acceptable norms), Hannu is only half aware of its problems. Inkeri seems to be more apt to cross the gulf between the word and the world, as her ability to read the signs at the entrance to Olavinlinna demonstrates. She already knows that the message that guides visitors to ring the bell is as outdated as messages of this sort often are: "[T]hey didn't mean anything; only crazy people followed their instructions" (*T*, 93).[64] (Cf. Rojola 2013: 217–218)

The problems of language portrayed in *Tunteet* relate closely to the interplay of the characters' conscious, preconscious, and unconscious processes. The gap between minds and words seems to have grown. Human communication, including self-expression, involves words. Language divides the human mind into "two different selves," into the conscious part still somewhat visible and the unconscious part beyond the reach of words altogether (Stevenson 1998: 183). In *Tunteet*, the problem of language, with regard to the potential for expressing and recognizing one's emotions, is actualized in Hannu's letters embedded within third-person narration. The inability of conventional words to convey profound feelings, such as love and yearning, results in Hannu's alienation from words, his search for "wordless words" (*T*, 153).[65] Inkeri, however, is capable of adding to the reality by means of imaginative language, at least until she loses her ability to speak "adolescent language" (*T*, 355).[66]

In addition to employing the narrative patterns of female developmental plot, *Tunteet* examines the possibilities for Hannu's awakening to see the world anew. In the following analyses, I approach the problems of language from the perspective of Hannu's development. First, I analyze the interplay of unconscious, conscious, and preconscious processes in relation to certain embodied images that Vartio uses to portray those realms of Hannu's mind that he is unable to articulate or comprehend. Then I discuss the unreliability of introspection and self-analysis by exploring the presentation of Hannu's thoughts as verbalized in his letters to Inkeri. Finally, I examine Hannu's letters in the context of misreading one's own mind, which reflects Hannu's inability to keep track of his emotional impulses and motives. Hannu's experiences of being-in-the-world are marked by a growing feeling of unreality, which problematizes his relation to language and its use in human communication.

Hannu's inward awakening is represented in the scenes following the episode of Olavinlinna. After the couple's first kisses on the castle walls, the lovers are physically separated. Hannu is forced to leave Inkeri's home village, as he awaits the command to go into battle. The stage of potential transformation steps in as the geographical distance makes the lovers see another in a more nuanced manner. In another village Hannu rents a room from a farm to be able to study and write. He feels alienated from his habitual self. He is unable to concentrate, because Inkeri's image follows him wherever he goes. This image fills him with inner strength and peace, yet at the same time it observes his every move and thought like an omnipotent, god-like eye. Hannu's alienation is reflected outwardly in the village scenes. Time seems to stop, and soon Hannu realizes that his watch is broken. The farmhouse is pictured as a space divided into two distinct realms, which serve as a projection of Hannu's mental space. He is suddenly surrounded by darkness: "And after opening the door, he had found himself in a dark space, in a hall that divided the house in two down the middle [... he had] seen two doors, one before him, the other behind him" (*T*, 137).[67]

The dream-like atmosphere intensifies as Hannu finds a shop in the village. Its name is hardly legible: "Toiviainen's Jewelry and Watches" ("Kulta- ja Kellosepänliike Toiviainen"). Hannu looks at the writing over the door and can hardly make sense of the letters: "It was smeared in white, the paint was peeling, some of the letters had worn off altogether. If he hadn't known the language, he could not easily have guessed the missing letters or deciphered the name" (*T*, 125).[68] As Hannu is about to enter the shop, he sees his reflection in the empty store window. An odd association passes through his mind: "Wonder what would happen if he threw a stone through that window? The thought was sudden, senseless; and still it felt as if someone in the house sensed that the window was under threat, as if someone were secretly keeping an eye on him from within the house" (*T*, 125–126).[69] The feeling of being observed is reinforced by Hannu's feeling of Inkeri watching him as he enters the shop. He "turned around and looked behind him, toward the tops of the trees, and the image that had moved beside him night and day was now hiding among the leaves, spying on him, observing his every expression and gesture, knowing his thoughts and seeing that there was within him no doubt" (*T*, 126).[70]

The name of the shop is like a sign that Hannu needs to follow. Everything feels strangely meaningful, as if he were seeing the world anew, for the first time: he "saw his own dusty boots, saw the stem of a flower he had trampled under his feet; he sensed everything with a strange clarity, and everything seemed to acquire some *significant meaning*" (*T*, 126).[71] In the shop the experience of the unreal deepens. The shopkeeper's language boggles Hannu's mind in the same way as Inkeri's relatives' talk had done at the beginning of the novel. The old man's words are as misleading and disconnected as the worn-out writing above the store's entrance. According to the old man, his shop is not a shop at all. He sells neither jewelry nor watches: "[A]ctually, he had nothing to do with this shop; this was not a shop, nothing was sold here" (*T*, 129).[72] Hannu, the expert in logical language, is baffled. To know the language means to be able somehow to understand the words, even if they are partially worn out. However, in the shop, the words seem to bear no fixed meaning:

> [The old man] asked as if in passing what had brought the soldier here. Where had he gotten the idea that rings were sold here? Hannu answered that he had seen the writing over the door, had noticed it by chance while walking by, and had come in.
> "It's still there, the writing, it doesn't mean anything, it's there but everyone knows that there is no shop here." (*T*, 129)[73]

The use of words as the source of meaning is illustrated in the old man's notion of a shop that is not a shop. The meanings of the words are known and distributed by a certain social community, whose members share the rules of a certain language. For a stranger in a strange village, these rules, and thereby the language itself, are puzzling and incomprehensible. Hannu's entanglement emphasizes the problems resulting from the arbitrary quality of everyday speech: how does one know a language based on a mere arbitrary contract of speakers ("everyone knows that there is no shop here").

For Hannu, the existence of "non-language" (the language of negations such as "there is no shop here") comes as a striking revelation. Hannu's experiences in the shop demonstrate the feelings of alienation in a modern individual who encounters the changed world as if he were a stranger arriving in a foreign land. The shopkeeper's words seem empty and senseless, until Hannu realizes the rules of the game. The considerations of war time[74] make the old man cautious, but he is more than willing to sell the ring. The old man rephrases certain expressions in the event someone asks questions: "I didn't sell you anything, you just got it somewhere" (*T*, 135).[75] Hannu realizes he should join in the game: he "said he understood completely that the shopkeeper had not sold him the ring. He had not even seen any ring, he had only stopped in here to buy something: fishhooks – yes, he would remember to say that it was only fishhooks" (*T*, 135–136).[76] The old man keeps asking Inkeri's name for to engrave on the ring, but cannot remember it. In the end, Hannu sends Inkeri an engagement ring in an empty envelope without even writing the sender's name.

The sense of the unreal also characterizes Hannu's experiences in his rented room on the farm, where he tries to focus on reading and writing. The house that had once seemed pleasant and charming turns into a primitive and dreary place. He feels afraid: "Hannu got up swiftly from the bed and went over to the window. His heart pounding, the hand holding the curtains slightly trembling, he looked through the crack in the curtains into the yard" (*T*, 142).[77] He senses that the farmer's wife is spying on him. The robust figure of the woman resembles other archaic, masculine women in Vartio's texts. The woman is compared to a sculpture:

> A big, muscular woman, her hip shaped like a man's. Her braided hair was wound tightly around her head, blond hair, sunburned, her arms dangling and large, the muscles well developed. A handsome woman, Germanic type, thought Hannu. Like a statue, truly like a statue. Dressed up in proper clothes, with a little more intelligence and education: if not a real beauty, still handsome, a Valkyrie. But evidently a terrifying woman, hard and completely unkempt. (*T*, 142–143)[78]

In Scandinavian sagas, the Valkyrie ("the chooser of the fallen'") is a host of winged female beings who decide which soldiers die on the battlefield and which ones live. The Valkyries bear their chosen ones to the afterlife. They are sometimes accompanied by ravens, sometimes by swans or horses. Hannu perceives some likeness between the woman and his fiancée: "I really only noticed her because her hair is the same color as yours, the color of ripe straw" (*T*, 157–158).[79]

The image of a house being spied upon and threatened by an outsider is an embodied image of Hannu's selfhood, which is shattered by the primitive fear of death as he awaits the command to go to battle. In this state of being in-between, Hannu dreams. He is walking in the farmyard and hears clopping sounds: "He saw himself walking swiftly to behind the cowshed and heard behind him the clattering of a horse and knew that the iron bar was pounded deep into the ground, knew that it was sinking deeper as the horse wound the halter around it" (*T*, 141).[80] The horse is about to be strangled by the halter. Hannu knows he should do something, but he walks on by: "[I]t's not his horse" (ibid.).[81] The image of the horse is accompanied by the figure of the farmer's wife in the garden plot, terrifying, like Mother Earth herself, refusing to show her face to the dreamer.

The dream images reveal Hannu's fear and his alienation from his true nature. However, the dream also refers to Inkeri's emotional distress, which had escaped Hannu's awareness, but emerges in the dream. The image reappears in the scene, in which Hannu patrols outside Inkeri's window in the city, "winding like a hoop around a barrel" (*T*, 290).[82] Another reference to the dream appears at the end of the novel. Inkeri sees a horse with a flowing mane as she is sitting in the train: "A horse was walking on the pasture, a flaxen-maned horse; it raised its head and looked straight at the train, and Inkeri felt as if the horse had looked right at her and she wanted to wave to it" (*T*, 352).[83] An image of unbridled passions and imagination, the horse signifies Inkeri's free spirit. The flaxen mane resembles her unruly hair, Pegasus of her imagination, which finally leads her into the deadlock of marriage.

The (self-made) prison waiting for Inkeri is varied in the novel's many images. Among the variations on the formula of captivity are the escaped pig at the beginning of the novel and a butterfly that Hannu sees fluttering against the windowpane. Finally, he opens the window and frees it, following "its flight until it had disappeared from sight" (*T*, 56).[84] In the shop, he listens to the old man talk about flies escaping from the fly-paper. The most crucial of the "echoes" of Inkeri's inner voice, however, is the screech of a bird heard in the woods. In her letter, Inkeri writes about the words she has heard in her dream: "If I were a bird" (*T*, 356).[85] The cry of the bird alludes to

Inkeri's muted voice, which is in danger of becoming an echo of Hannu's: "Somewhere a bird was calling; Inkeri heard it, heard the bird calling *as if giving a signal*: she felt melancholy, there had never been and would never be anything but this constant yearning" (*T*, 79).[86] In the bird's cry, Inkeri hears her future miseries, but she refuses to listen.

In *Tunteet*, first-person epistolary fiction serves as a model of intrigue, based on withheld thoughts and the fabrication of emotions. Vartio's parody of the lovers' discourse, typical of epistolary fiction and sentimental novels, is two-dimensional. The ridicule and mockery pay homage to the antecedent tradition, but simultaneously call "attention to its faults, its aporias, its naïveté" (Castle 2006: 198). In the train, Inkeri writes a letter that is meant to make Hannu see "what kind of girl" ("millaisen tytön") he has lost (*T*, 360). Language serves Inkeri's manipulative ends, as she spontaneously fabricates an emotional letter without thinking about the consequences. The letter sets out a series of events that eventually re-establish the engagement that has already been broken – or has it? As the pretended worlds become more complex, Inkeri loses her sense of what is actually happening to her.

Inkeri's aforementioned letter is an answer to Hannu's previous letters that expounded on his feelings for her. In chapter 5, the reader gains access to Hannu's emotional mind through two letters in which he tries to explain what led him to send Inkeri an engagement ring. The first letter conveys his uncensored, relatively spontaneous thoughts about his experiences after the lovers' sudden separation. The second letter is more analytical, a calculated account of the same mental content. This is the letter that Inkeri finally receives. Hannu's own thoughts about the first letter are revealed when he reads it analytically. These thoughts are then reflected in the contents of the second letter in which Hannu's spontaneous emotions are filtered through his conscious, more "sensible" second thoughts. By contrast, his ideas in the first letter correspond more closely the confessions in a diary, even if its contents were originally addressed to the girl.

Hannu spends two nights in a row trying to write the first letter. His mind is "full of words and images" ("täynnä sanoja ja kuvia"), yet he seems unable to convey his feelings: "[H]e would have liked to draw or write, once he had begun a letter, but left it after a couple of sentences; he had begun to fear he would lose something, he'd been jealous of the words; once uttered, they would no longer exist" (*T*, 123).[87] Hannu has tried to draw a picture of Inkeri, but has been unable to capture her gist in the drawing. The difficulty of expressing oneself is accompanied by the popular songs that Hannu is forced to listen to everywhere he goes. He considers the songs sugary and pathetic, even revolting. As folktales and beliefs, they seem to be products of collective human transport rather than individual innovation. During an evening walk, he hears the sound of a gramophone playing in a nearby coffee shop. For a while, Hannu manages to capture the feeling he pictures in his mind to explain people's fascination with these songs: "Those words and tones were necessary for people who didn't have other words to interpret their feelings and moods" (*T*, 121).[88] For once, Hannu can identify with the emotion expressed by the lyrics: "And the words from the song coming from the coffee shop, words about love, yearning, desire – words he had considered tacky, that he could barely tolerate, now captivated him" (ibid.).[89]

One of the tunes that Hannu hears is the same song he has whistled on the walls of Olavinlinna: "Äänisen aallot" (The Waves of Lake Onega). Hannu's whistling on the castle walls is his response to Inkeri's tale of the mountain ash. Inkeri perceives his gesture as an expression of mockery. The song "Äänisen aallot" was one of the most popular Finnish songs during World War II and the years immediately following. Its first lines are quoted in the novel when the record starts to play. The lyrics portray the victorious battles of the Finnish army as witnessed by the waves of Lake Onega in the war against Russia. The second stanza, about the longing of a human being, is not quoted in the novel. However, a reader familiar with the rest of the song will recognize Hannu's reference to the feeling of longing: "Silently, Ääninen lulls her waves / making them crash on the shore / the shore of a fairy-tale island. / Here, my love, / I keep dreaming about you – / someday I will carry you / to the boat of our happiness."[90] In the episode at Olavinlinna, the reference to the "boat of our happiness" is clearly used ironically.

Music as the source of conflict is found already in the novel's opening scene. Hannu is asked to play the piano, which stands unused in the parlor of Inkeri's home. No one in the house knows how to play the instrument, and they want to hear "something happy" (*T*, 23).[91] First, Hannu considers playing Chopin, then suddenly, he starts to play something more unrefined:

> But his fingers seemed to want to play something else, he was suddenly fired up about something, and he started to play, he played and, while playing, smiled a bit mockingly at himself, at his fingers that were playing something quite different – and he stopped abruptly without finishing, banged his palms on the keys, and the piano let loose a sound that was heard, and the old matron in her bedroom thought: now he's stopped. [...]
>
> "That was 'Rustle of Spring,' did you recognize it?"
>
> "Yes, I did," said Inkeri without enthusiasm. He plays well, she thought. But 'Rustle of Spring' – this much she knew – did not say much for the taste and the intellectual level of the player; or had he chosen the song according to the intellectual level of the listeners? That must be it. (*T*, 24)[92]

The meaning of the scene is ambiguous. It is not clear whether, in playing the piano, Hannu is mocking himself or the people of the house, as Inkeri believes. His conscious mind makes the decision to play Chopin. His fingers, however, seem to have a will of their own. Instead of a sophisticated waltz, he starts to play a tune that falls out of the category of classical music: *Frühlingsrauschen* (Rustle of Spring). The popularity of the solo piano piece by Christian Sinding is based on its entertainment value, its ability to impress. Even if its rapid tempo calls for talent and skill, it is easier to play than it sounds. Hannu may be mocking his listeners, but, above all, he seems to be mocking himself in his sudden agitation that forces his fingers to make their own decisions. Inkeri herself becomes the wild "rustle of spring," the embodiment of the excited restlessness that takes over Hannu, as if against his conscious will.

The battle between emotion and intellect is manifested in popular songs that seem naïve, childish, and vulgar to Hannu – like Inkeri's mind sometimes. His musings on the popular songs emphasize his amazement that people actually believe these songs express something meaningful, something real. The music heard in the café brings to mind one particular childhood memory. As a child, Hannu had wondered why the gramophone never got tired, even when it played the same songs time and time again: "He had played one and the same record over and over again and gotten angry when the singer's voice had betrayed not the slightest trace of weariness, not even a sigh that would have shown that the singer was exhausted and wanted to express he couldn't continue anymore" (*T*, 120).[93] The child's way of mingling the voice heard on the record with the immediate voice of a human being corresponds to the simplemindedness of people who listen to popular songs. It is as if they were mixing the reality of human emotions with the representations of those emotions in popular music.

In Hannu's childhood memory, the idea of the relationship between reality and representation is portrayed as the simpleness of an immature being. In Hannu's opinion, the soldiers whistling and singing the songs endlessly, "all in earnest" ("vakavissaan") show the same lack of sophistication. As Hannu listens to the popular songs played by the gramophone, another association comes to mind. The song begins to depict the attitudes of rural people: "Those tunes, those words now spilling over the countryside – the record had been changed – it was like seeing rural folk decked out in their Sunday best, completely inappropriately dressed, stepping stiffly along the road, their faces solemn, heading to a celebration..." (*T*, 121)[94] In Hannu's mental image, the song reflects the naïve beliefs of an old world that still has faith in the ability of language to represent reality. At the same time, however, the lyrics reflect the genuineness of their gesture and pose: the solemnity that seems archaic and strangely appealing.

While trying to phrase his own emotions in written words, Hannu realizes the ambiguous quality of these songs. He recalls "the clichés, the dreadful clichés" ("klisheitä, hirveitä klisheitä") that he has seen in the letters Inkeri received from unknown soldiers on the frontline (*T*, 122). Inkeri had laughed in showing the letters to him and then tore them to pieces. Hannu claims he had not taken the trouble to be jealous, for he knew the content of the letters was always the same: naïve and tacky. Only now does he understand why the letters had been like that, full of quoted love-song lyrics and pathetic patriotism. What else could a young man holding a pen for the first time after school decide to do than resort to these words familiar from popular songs? "Hadn't the same hit tunes stuck in his mind, too? There were enough of them; they came to one's aid, whatever the situation" (ibid.).[95] The words from the songs feel pretentious, outworn, and vulgar, yet there seem to be no other words to replace them. These songs reflect a human need to express emotions that are difficult to convey. They provide the foundation for the collective unconscious: "Maybe it was like that: all the songs in the world sprang from one and the same source, all the songs and poetry in the world, from people's longing... solemn and naïve, distasteful, shudder-inducing, all at the same time" (*T*, 121).[96]

Hannu's struggles to express himself are shown to pertain not only to the clichéd quality of words, but to his inability to identify his own emotions. When Hannu reads his first letter, he senses a vague feeling of dissatisfaction that he cannot explain. The state of (almost) becoming conscious is described in the following passage of narrated monologue[97]: "He could no longer sleep at night, but just kept thinking incessantly about *something, like a solution to something – to what?*" (*T*, 123).[98] By the light of day, the written words sound pretentious and empty. Hannu can hardly recognize the things he has written down: "He could barely remember that all that was true, that it had happened to him, that they were his own experiences" (*T*, 145).[99] As he glances through the letters, he thanks himself for coming to his senses: "And he told himself: how fortunate that I came to my senses. And he stopped to think about something. To my senses – I came to my senses? What do I mean by that?" (ibid.)[100]

This passage of interior monologue portrays Hannu's distanced self-observation, as he struggles to figure out his emotional, unconscious motivations. Hannu reads his own text "as if trying to hold on for a moment to something that was irretrievably gone, vanished" (*T*, 150).[101] It was as if he was about to arrive at some important conclusion here, but the association does not spring to his conscious mind. He decides to read the letter through as if it were a text written by "an outsider," as if it were "a writing exercise" (*T*, 145) that must be graded.[102] Hannu keeps reading the letter and crossing out details that seem redundant or sentimental. There is one paragraph that he considers particularly strange, as if it had been written by someone else:

> "The train moved forward through the night," he read, and erased the unnecessarily repetitive phrase "the train moved forward" "[…] At every stop, on every platform I looked for you, I turned my face toward every woman I saw, looking for you in each of them, your essence, and once I saw one who resembled you but she didn't turn and I didn't have time to see her face before the train left again."
>
> Was that true? he thought. It was and it wasn't. But he crossed out all of it and kept reading, and when he had again reached the end of the page, he said aloud: What rubbish. But he kept reading as if in defiance: […] (*T*, 148–149)[103]

Hannu keeps reading in defiance – of what? A painful self-revelation? His visualization of Inkeri at the station is followed by another depiction of his experiences, which frame Hannu's search for the girl in a more obvious manner. The most revealing part of the text is still to come. Hannu describes a moment of intense emotion experienced on the train as he leaves Inkeri's home village. He perceives the world as an image that keeps growing boundlessly, reaching up to the forests and the skies. Hannu imagines himself immersed in that very image: "[E]verything in me stretched toward it, blended into and consolidated in that image" (*T*, 149).[104] The "real" world appears to him flat, as if it were merely a set piece, beyond which the actual reality exists. From the train's window,

I looked at the landscapes and houses, and it was as if the houses flashing by were not real, but the real ones were behind them, and it was those I was seeing. And I wanted to tell everyone, to proclaim: the world is not what it appears; I know now that everything is completely different; behind these landscapes are the real landscapes, behind the words that you and I speak are the real words – and the train kept going, we were there, in the place where we were being put up for a time. But my mood was still the same, for I knew that your image was walking beside me wherever I went, it heard my words, saw every expression and gesture and filled me with strength and a feeling of peace. (*T*, 150)[105]

Hannu's epiphany on the train corresponds to Vartio's own experience of seeing reality anew: "People don't know how to look at things – underneath it all is another world that I can see directly, I don't even have to imagine it," she wrote in a letter to her husband.[106] Behind the visible worlds and the spoken words are words and worlds that appear more genuine and meaningful. "The world in all its unreality felt more real than ever before" (ibid.), Hannu reads at the end of his letter.[107]

While mulling over these words, Hannu begins to have second thoughts. He tries to evoke the image of Inkeri, following her by pressing both hands to his face: "[W]hen he opened his eyes, he saw before him flashes of green and white – a face, a huge face, before him, in the air. Did it exist? If it existed, it was formless, forced, conjured up by force – an image of a statue made of stone" (*T*, 150–151).[108] The simile of an "image of a statue made of stone" ("kivestä tehdyn veistoksen kuva") obviously refers to the Pygmalion motif in the novel. Moreover, the colors of green and white are associated with the archaic women portrayed in Vartio's fiction, similar to the terrifying figure of Mother Earth appearing in Hannu's dream. Hannu's image of Inkeri is a fading illusion that escapes his grasp, just like the faceless woman at the station. Hannu realizes "he had not used Inkeri's name in the letter even a single time, even though the image had been Inker's face and even though – he remembered this now – he had repeated her name in the dark carriage" (*T*, 151).[109]

The emotional cause for the intensified moment is explained in the letter: Hannu is certain he will die on the battlefield. When the train arrives at its destination, he still sees everything around him in a different light, as if his eyes had been opened. The sudden fear of death experienced on the train makes Hannu "see," able to capture the arbitrary quality of words: they do not express the real. Hannu's alienation from words and the world drives him to search for other worlds behind the visible worlds and words, as if there were another, more real "reality" behind them. Inkeri too is revealed to have been only a personification of a transcendent idea of love or pure womanhood. In the end, the man at the station has not been looking for the girl. He has been looking for the ideal woman in her, constituting a tantalizing and terrifying mystery to him.

Hannu's experiences of the unreal on the train, and later in the shop, seem to result in his decision to send the ring without any inscription or message attached. Even the image of Inkeri observing his every move seems to be nameless, anonymous. "[D]on't you understand: the *wordless words* are the most beautiful," Hannu says as he tries to explain his anonymous proposal. "Would you have wanted me to kneel clumsily before you as in bad chivalry novels – or what would you have wanted me to do?" (*T*, 153)[110] From Hannu's perspective, the words of popular songs, romantic letters, and "bad chivalry novels" nourish something that does not exist, "neither the individual nor the body." Only truth exists: "How foolish is it then to do something as worthless as nourish something that does not exist, something conventional that is neither the individual nor the body. And because of this, I can't produce a letter for you, I cannot speak of anything but what is true" (*T*, 156), he writes.[111]

After the revelation on the train, Hannu becomes acutely aware of the problems related to the forms of language he has tried to teach Inkeri. The ambiguity of words is reflected in the status of Latin as a dead language. Latin is known and used only in special contexts and in written form. As an ordinary, spoken language, it has become extinct; it does not serve everyday communication. Conventional words, such as a "letter" or "shop" or "love," have lost their meanings. A letter is not a letter; the shop is no longer a shop. The formal lists of words (like *amo, amas, amat*) are useless, for they may be learned, but never spoken. "Should he write Inkeri about all that? Should he say: I love you, I miss you. No. No words like that – not any letter until he can convey everything just as he felt it" (*T*, 123–124).[112] The "revolting sentimentality" of the first letter makes Hannu feel ashamed. He tears the letter to pieces and throws the pieces of the torn paper into the river. Inkeri's image breaks into pieces as he attempts to identify his ideas of her, and accordingly, it starts to grow back together when he tears up the letter: "[A]nd the image that he was now tearing up watched from somewhere again, it was whole again, and it was watching him, from a distance, without arousing in him pain or fear, peace or anything else. It simply existed and followed him, but his mind was his own again, all was as it had always been" (ibid.).[113] Hannu wants to maintain the image of the girl as it is: as a distant idea that causes no emotional tumult or anxiety.

With only simple, austere words at hand, Hannu cannot say much to please the girl's romantic expectations. The only way to maintain the vividness of ideas is to keep them moving: "I cannot guarantee you anything eternal, for the only thing I consider almost certainly, eternal, is development, energy, movement. The spirit is too individual a concept to be eternal" (*T*, 153–154).[114] Even these ideas are copies of someone else's: "That much I have managed to get hold of what I feel: slow, clumsy, colorless thoughts that have the additional problem that they are probably an echo of something I have read" (*T*, 154).[115] Indeed, Hannu's thoughts of energy and movement seem to coincide with the ideas of the energies of self-development portrayed in Goethean Bildungsromane. These ideas are both acknowledged and parodied in Vartio's novel, which provides two trajectories of personal development: the one seen from a young man's perspective and the other, from a young woman's point of view.[116]

In his second letter, Hannu struggles to clarify his thoughts about the human intellect and emotion, the mind and the body. He forces himself to write determinedly, without any embellishments. He has decided to tell the truth: "I know that you can give and get satisfaction from direct, clear emotions that surpass conventionality" (*T*, 154), he writes in explaining the unsentimental tones of his letter.[117] His "truth" involves an idea of himself as a mind and an individual spirit. The intellectual mind, his spirit, needs solitude and peace. It is distracted by emotional tumult and primitive sensations. The flesh loves everything that can be sensed immediately and palpably, yet the mind seeks contemplation: "The senses get satisfaction from the stationary, the tangible; the individual, from solitude" (*T*, 156), he explains.[118] Hannu's disgust with the words of romantic letters derives from this very preference of mind over body and sense over emotion: "In a letter like this, I can't offer or receive what is cheap: the body; nor can I relinquish what is indivisible: the individual, my spirit" (ibid.), he writes.[119] In his moment of self-recognition, Hannu becomes aware of his inclination to perceive Inkeri as a reflection of his own ideals: "But sometimes I wonder whether you are to me just the personification of love, at this time – perhaps I have taken what is You in You for love, and as for love itself, perhaps I have attached it, fused it into you" (*T*, 152–153), he confesses while expounding on his abstract ideas of love.[120]

Hannu acknowledges the potential unreliability of his introspection and verbal accounts of his feelings. His perceptions of Inkeri are based more on later contemplation and recollection than on immediate observation: "I have had to form my opinion of you – not so much on the basis of direct observation, but by contemplating you afterwards, relying only on memories – and thus I have surely wronged you, having only seen you mostly in the light of my own world view" (*T*, 155).[121] Nevertheless, Hannu suggests that for this very reason, he might be more apt to guess Inkeri's true motivations – as an outside observer he can more accurately infer her emotional states. Hannu perceives the girl as an individual who is still fighting the primitive demons of her body. There is a potential "woman's individuality" ("naisen yksilöllisyyttä") in her, even if she does not yet realize it:

> You are the type of person who lives powerfully in the current moment and in your immediate environment and whose dreams' fulfillment relies more on chance than on persistence. You don't know it yourself, yet – maybe I am very different from you precisely because I know that about you. […] There is courage in you. You are a woman who has a woman's particular individuality, an extravagant femininity more than a feeble body can bear, and against that background I understand your seemingly odd mood swings: your individuality is striving to separate from your body, and this leads to the concept of the double being; it is what you sometimes complain about, that you yourself don't understand why you do what you do. The body, your body, is striving for balance, for experiences as strong as the individual in you. (*T*, 155)[122]

The concept of a "double being" manifests itself in the battle of body and mind, which – in Hannu's opinion – characterizes the particularly feminine existence. Inkeri's female body is too feeble and weak; it does not have the strength to overcome the weight of bodily emotions that distract the development of her individuality and rational mind. Inkeri "lives powerfully in the current moment" and her "immediate environment," unable to detect consciously her "odd mood swings." The inner battle between emotion and reason is connected to the aspect of Inkeri's growth: becoming conscious of one's feelings – and oneself.

All these complications involving the lovers' individual development contribute to the misunderstandings portrayed in *Tunteet*. Hannu and Inkeri cannot differentiate the apparent reasons from the real causes of their emotional reactions, owing to the unconscious quality of these emotions. This is manifested, first of all, in Inkeri's inability to understand the true cause of her feelings and emotions, as Hannu claims. However, it appears that Hannu himself is equally unable to discern his emotional motivations. He considers the human spirit – individuality – as an "indivisible" and private realm. Paradoxically, the primitive impulses of his behavior stem from this individual, embodied self that is formed primarily in interaction with others. The conflict of sense and emotion, as well as mind and body, seems to represent Hannu's tendency to suppress some realms of his mind that are too indefinite and frightening to be acknowledged. His ideas about Inkeri's body, as presented in the letter, are revealing in this respect: "A woman's body, your body, Inkeri – I long for it; its closeness will be heavenly and its possession will be happiness – yet the most perfect satisfaction does not derive from that, but from emotion, intellect, energy, motion – all that approaches the eternal more than does the decaying body" (*T*, 154).[123]

Hannu's withdrawal to the world of books and contemplation points at the dangers of suppressing either one of the two aspects of the human existence: intellect or emotion, introspection or social activity, the spiritual or the material. The idea of Hannu as a cultured mind and spirit (the masculine) and Inkeri as a body (the feminine) is shown to be a mere delusion. Hannu's inner tension is manifested already in the scene of playing "Rustle of Spring." After having observed Inkeri, her legs and breasts, Hannu chooses to play the wilder tune.[124] The discrepancy between Hannu's words and his actions is emphasized also in the couple's encounter in Hannu's rental room after they have shared their first kiss on the castle walls. Hannu's sexual awakening is triggered by Inkeri who sets free his inner beast, without knowing it. Hannu is unable to control himself: "You're a beast," Inkeri cries while defending herself against Hannu's sexual harassment: "Hannu had pulled and tugged like a madman, twisted her arms so hard that they hurt" (*T*, 177).[125]

Hannu's self-analysis emphasizes his need for self-determination and self-control. He feels vulnerable in facing his primitive responses. Even though Hannu is prone to analyze Inkeri's blind spots, he seems to be half-blind to his own emotional motives. The fear of death makes Hannu hungry for life, and Inkeri represents "the truth of living" ("elämisen totuu[s]") for him (*T*, 154). As an ideal of womanhood and feminity, Inkeri becomes the force of nature that defies the deadening effect of formality, education, and convention. At the same time, however, Inkeri appears to be a threat to his individuality. Love and sexual desire are too self-consuming, and Hannu fears losing himself: "I have a dim feeling that I should keep love outside of my true self, in other words, I am afraid it will destroy my true self, my personality. What it is, I don't yet know. I only know that when love is within me, I no longer exist, there's only love" (*T*, 152).[126] Hannu's fear coincides with the common fear involved in intersubjective relationships. Even if the pleasures of intimacy and affection seem tantalizing, an individual feels the need to protect himself or herself from the invasions of others.

In his letter Hannu claims that he can understand the cause of Inkeri's strong will and her stubbornness. He reflects on his own need to guard his integrity in Inkeri: "I need someone exactly like you, a comrade in battle – how I love you, the you I saw in you, the overflowing and – I hope – also enduring courage that is the beginning of courage in all of life. Someone may think of it as stubbornness, but I would say it is armored sensitivity, the instinct for the self-preservation of one's personality, at least in my case" (*T*, 154).[127] However, Hannu does not seem to consider any harm in his attempts to guide Inkeri to be "the you I saw in you." There are some aspects of her personality that prevent the fulfillment of her personality: "Your nature is genuine and brave, with the exception of – please forgive me – the deftly feminine, very obvious and sometimes even annoyingly visible superficiality. But I think you will shed that with age" (*T*, 157), he writes.[128] Vartio's parody arises from the analysis of the mindblindness of the characters that culminates in Hannu's struggles to understand the "feminine" aspects of Inkeri's personality: "[M]aybe those aspects in you that at times irritate me, like the above-mentioned superficiality, are precisely what make you, you" (*T*, 157).[129]

The characters' desire towards counterproductive dialogue is complicated by "the battle of sexes" typical of romance plots (cf. Pearce & Stacey 1995: 16). Even though Hannu tries to see Inkeri "as she is," he often manages to capture only an image constructed in his own mind. Instead of feeling with the other, he is thinking, building rational categories. Unable to convey his feelings in a more refined manner, he ends up proposing Inkeri with harsh, clumsy words: "I don't know and I don't want know anything other than to see you as my bride, my wife. Are you happy now? Now you have been proposed to with the appropriate ritual" (*T*, 153).[130] Hannu's reluctant proposal epitomizes the difference in the characters' ideals of love. The emotional story structure of *Tunteet* relates in numerous ways to this difference and other misunderstandings between the lovers. For Inkeri, Hannu's reluctance to perform chrivalric rituals appears as insensitivity and coldness. Inkeri's mental impulses, imaginings and emotions, on the other hand, appear as pretense, hysteria, or madness in Hannu's eyes. In the following analyses, I discuss *Tunteet* in the context of the school novel, Bildungsroman, the sentimental novel, and epistolary fiction. Each of these genres serves the representation of the characters' affective fallacies, both with respect to the self and to the other.

Figurative Masks, Self-Performances. From Lingering to Digression

The female developmental plot in *Tunteet* is composed of emotionally-encoded episodes and incidents that draw from the heroine's affective self-quest. Inkeri is among those figures in Vartio's fiction that tend consciously to indulge themselves in their affective fallacies. Like other Vartio characters with over-active imaginations, Inkeri is easily lost in the mazes of her mind. Hannu analyzes the ability of the human mind to produce delusive fantasies. He tries to keep his head clear in Inkeri's company: "[E]verything is make-believe, everything, the product of one's imagination" (*T*, 35).[131] Inkeri's tendency to give in to her emotions is pictured in the novel, when Inkeri observes her bodily emotions and compares them to "black flowing lava" and "red flames curling through it." The circularity of emotions, on the other hand, is manifested in the depiction of the cycles of bodily emotions that generate more emotions: "And she thought: I blushed, of course. And then she blushed because she had blushed" (*T*, 74).[132] Inkeri's thoughts are "rushing to and fro" (*T*, 39)[133] in a frantic manner, which often results in impetuous actions.

The spontaneous, unpremeditated, and reflexively stimulated actions result in an emotional story structure with repetitive stages of separation and negotiation. In Olavinlinna, Inkeri and Hannu's journey together is juxtaposed with the boat, drifting down the river without a guiding hand: "They were at the vortex – and now with the current, oars raised – and it felt as if the boat had taken off and the oarsman could no longer control it, as if someone had grasped the bottom of the boat, spun it around and taken off with it – and then it was over, the oars in the water, the boat at the castle pier" (*T*, 95).[134] The drifting boat becomes an image of a relationship guided by irrational impulses as the characters lose control of their emotions. Hannu's feelings of indecision are reflected in his thoughts after his spontaneous proposal. He feels the need to think rationally, to withdraw into solitude: "What was Inkeri expecting from him now? Hannu felt as if everything had been a dream, as if he had just snatched that girl with him without knowing where he was heading on his journey, and now he didn't know where to take her" (*T*, 113).[135]

In *Tunteet*, the loops of bodily feedback generate cyclic patterns of arousal and passivity, which refer to both lingering and digressive paths. For Inkeri, the world often appears to be a chaotic and evil place. At times, she imagines herself dead, falling into a stupor: "Inkeri closed her eyes, opened them again, and the willow was still blooming and said to her: look at me and you will forget what you don't understand, you will forget how evil the world is. And then Inkeri relaxed into deep, vast, perfect loneliness" (*T*, 313).[136] Inkeri's contemplations of happiness are often related to undefined feelings of yearning embodied in the bird's call. She tries to explain these distant sensations of existential estrangement to Hannu: "Sadness? There had been sadness, sometimes so much that she had wanted to die. 'Happy.' 'Happy?' Yes, she supposed so – probably she was. 'How about you?' Yes, of course, she believed it, and from now on they would be sensible, they would talk about everything, directly and sensibly" (*T*, 175).[137]

Inkeri's alienation stems from the experiences of the self as being divided in two, in the material body and her soul being trapped inside. This self-estrangement is reflected in her perceptions that Hannu is ignoring her melancholy and focusing on her body. The gazes of men make her lose her sense of self: "[A]s if she'd been nothing but hips and breasts, good thing he even remembered her name anymore" (*T*, 162).[138] Inkeri's association of the bed shared with Hannu with "a coffin" ("arkku") represents her emotional void, which is related to Hannu's refusal to engage in a playful game of romantic love, or rather, his tendency to approach her roughly, without any shared emotions. Inkeri's melancholy emerges when she realizes that she needs to play alone: "'Come here,' said the girl under the tree. [...] Her voice was like the voice of a child calling another child to come play with her, because it's lonely and there is no one to play with" (*T*, 78).[139]

The images of embodied being and the coffin are also employed in depicting one of Inkeri's emotional peak moments. This moment occurs at the end of the first part of the novel, on the threshold of Inkeri's Bildung. Before she leaves home to begin her studies, she is walking around in the train station. She sees seven coffins on the platform and notices the name of a young man who had once worked on her home farm. Now he is lying dead in a coffin. And right there, surrounded by death, Inkeri experiences everything around her as simple and perfect, exactly as everything should be. There is no past, no future, only the present moment and she herself, Inkeri, who is filled with a sense of belonging, pre-destined to be alive and to be part of the picture:

> Inkeri looked up at the sky. The sky was blue; under the sky were the harvested fields, wide and empty like the skies, as if stretching to infinity. And there was the station platform; seven coffins were in a row. And she, Inkeri. Like a painting, like a picture, like a painting in which there was her image, no one, nothing, come from nowhere, going nowhere, nothing to ask, nothing to fear, everything in place, silent, simple, everything right here for the picture to be perfect. She, Inkeri, also belonged in this picture; it was ordained, it was as it had been and would always be. This picture was also of her, Inkeri, and the sky and the earth and everything were looking at her and she was looking back, not asking or wondering anything, for everything was exactly as it was meant to be. (*T*, 194)[140]

Inkeri merges into her own mental image, like a figure in a painting. The perfect picture serves as a depiction of Inkeri's feeling of being part of the living cosmos: she is Inkeri, who exists, here and now. Inkeri's illumination resembles Hannu's epiphany on the train, yet it triggers the feeling of harmony instead of fear and estrangement. The embodied experience of the world fills Inkeri with joy: "Inkeri had been created to see all this, to walk in this morning, on these legs, wearing this dress, this walk, these jumps from stone to stone beside this fence. And she saw the curve of her hip, pressed her hand against her waist, and joy carried her forward like a wave and she kept saying to herself – dear God, dear God, this morning, this morning [...]" (*T*, 195).[141]

As Auli Hakulinen (2013: 279–280) maintains, the passage evokes an aesthetic illusion of a bird-eye view of a hypothetical observer, who remains "somewhere above" ("jossain yläpuolella"), as inexplicable and unidentified. Simultaneously, the picture of the world, however, is seen from Inkeri's perspective, constituting an intensive, frozen moment in the temporal landscape of the novel. The deictic markers used in the passage emphasize the idea of the tableau as a representation of the character's wordless sensing of the present moment, her existential, embodied and sensual experience:

"Inkeri had been created to see all *this*, to walk in *this* very morning, on *these* legs, wearing *this* dress, *this* walk, *these* jumps from stone to stone beside *this* fence" (cf. Tammi 1992: 44–45). As Inkeri thinks about the future, she imagines hearing distant music, as if "instruments" were being tuned, giving promise of future happiness: "[A]s if she were standing behind a door leading into a great festival hall, as if she could hear the sounds of celebration behind the door and knew: for me – when the door is opened, I will be let in [...] behind the doors great joy, great happiness, were waiting just for her" (ibid.).[142] The tragedy in the scene is related to the "perfect picture" as part of the predetermined story written by Vartio. She is the creator, the "painter" of this very picture. Inkeri's great expectations are contrasted with the feelings of sadness pictured elsewhere in the novel. The bird's melancholic call serves as an embodied image of Inkeri's vague feeling of trouble lying in wait, behind the closed doors that have not yet been opened.

The events leading to the tragedy of marriage are related to the characters' impulsive, akratic, or irrational acts that are triggered by their emotional minds. The engagement that results from Hannu's emotional whim finally turns into chaos. When Inkeri receives the ring from Hannu, she is not sure if it has come to her only by mistake. The sudden proposal is followed by a series of complications. Inkeri receives a letter from Hannu in which he writes about his parents' dissatisfaction with their son's engagement. Inkeri's emotional conflict increases when she reads Hannu's letter, which is "filled with doubts" ("täynnä epäilyksiä"). She compares her fiancé with a lamb, who has no will of his own: "[T]hose were not the kinds of letters that happy people write to each other. What kind do happy people write, then?" (*T*, 191)[143] The couple's constant misunderstandings lead to a situation in which Inkeri does not actually know whether she is engaged or not. Is she even truly in love?

> Hannu wasn't in love – if he was, she should have been able to feel it more clearly. What about her? Yes, she supposed so – but first she had to make sure whether Hannu loved her or not; only then she could know if she loved him. After a moment, the whole issue of loving seemed unimportant, just thinking about it made her tired. But what if she was the kind of woman who only loved the idea of love? She had read in some book that such women exist, women who only loved love. (*T*, 84)[144]

The idea of being in love with the feeling of love evokes the patterns of the novel of awakening, concluding with tragic loss or the heroine's death.[145] "Those kinds of women" who try to live up to their fantasies and end up feeling disappointment allude to Inkeri's potential future, to a combination of passive waiting and emotional arousal reflected in her (in)action. Inkeri's insecurity is emphasized in her feeling of uncertainty about Hannu's feelings, which leads to exhaustion, even boredom. The periods of exhaustion alternate with periods of inflamed passion and desperation.

The patterns of love comedy modified in the beginning of *Tunteet* are transformed into a student novel as soon as the novel's second part begins. Inkeri's move from the country to the city simultaneously signals a move from a romance plot to the formulae of female Bildung and student novels. The second part constitutes the narrative of Inkeri's individual development. At this stage, the figure of lover is replaced by the feminine community, as the process of moving outward into the public realm leads to the mirroring of the self in other women (cf. Felski 1989: 131–132, 139). In *Tunteet*, a decadent landlady, Mrs. Gräsbäck, and the two other girls living under her protection in the city, Turre and Maija, form a bohemian female community that serves as a source of Inkeri's empowerment, but also her alienation and anxiety. The ideals of female friendship and intimacy (frequently depicted in the narratives of female development) are simultaneously evoked and subverted in Vartio's novel (cf. Vesti 2014: 36–57).

In Finnish literature, the genre of student novel typically depicts the arrival of a provincial character in the capital, Helsinki, to pursue her or his studies.[146] As a subgenre of Bildungsroman, the student novels in Finnish naturalist literature usually end with the moral fall of the protagonist. This pattern of reversed Bildung is also suggested in *Tunteet*. When Hannu comes to visit Inkeri in Helsinki, he observes her changed appearance: "But that artificial voice, that indifferent expression [...] there was none of the healthy country girl left in her. Hannu decided that the city had corrupted Inkeri; her expression and gestures now contained something learned" (*T*, 267–268).[147] The ability to pretend, to hide one's emotions, and to manipulate others are key themes in the episodes that take place in the urban environment. The idea of personality as a performance is manifested in the metafictional references to drama and theater. When Hannu comes to visit Inkeri, he feels as if he has ended up in "some unreal world, the back room of a theater," seeing "the set and other stage equipment" (*T*, 259).[148] The curtain behind which Inkeri observes Hannu as he stands guard under her window is compared to "the stage curtain" (*T*, 285).[149] At this stage, Hannu has turned into a troubadour of love, courting devotedly his Dulcinea.

The degenerating effect of city life and the bohemian female community is fleshed out in Inkeri's relationship to Turre, one of Inkeri's roommates in Helsinki. Turre's life choices make a counterfactual path to Inkeri's life. The "ruin" of Turre, as she becomes pregnant and then has an abortion, is transformed into a play by Turre herself. She performs the clichéd role of a fallen woman who turns into a madwoman: "Turre knew that when a woman is pregnant and unwilling to give birth to a child out of wedlock, she becomes desperate and in her desperation drowns herself in a lake or takes poison or throws herself under a train ... after all, she has lost her mind" (*T*, 326–327).[150] Inkeri's tendency to enter into a hypnotic-like state while watching Turre's performances dramatizes the power of affective immersion. According to Inkeri, "great art [is] witchcraft and hypnosis" (*T*, 331).[151] As a student at the theater academy, Turre is a master of disguise. Turre is said to be the most genuine when she is acting. In Inkeri's mind, she is "such a good actor that she almost knew how to stop acting for a moment" (ibid.).[152] One of the "plays" performed by Turre is Inkeri's visit to Turku, where she meets Hannu's parents for the first time. Inkeri's role is that of a tragic bride:

> [...] What's to be done with you? There should be a play written about you.
>
> Inkeri was deeply flattered by this talk; she herself had started to believe that her engagement was indeed suitable for the plot of a play, and what had really happened had begun to merge in her mind with the imagined; she herself almost believed that things had happened the way Turre wanted them to have happened. [...]
>
> Turre, though, wanted to turn Inkeri's engagement into a comedy at which people would laugh their heads off. Inkeri wanted more genuine feeling in it, tragedy; for she had also felt love, at least at some point, and been unhappy. (*T*, 244)[153]

Turre's play modifies Inkeri's journey to Turku as depicted in the beginning of the novel's second part. Turku, the old capital of Finland, serves as a symbol of the alienating, bourgeois stiffness that Inkeri senses in Hannu's family, especially in his mother. Inkeri cannot recognize herself in the sad girl she sees in the student photograph placed on view by Hannu's parents. She struggles to behave and be "sensible" during the visit, but, one after another, her attempts fail. She keeps listening attentively to the hidden meanings behind every word: "'Is it nice out?' Inkeri asked and turned her back and looked outside" (*T*, 220).[154] Hannu's mother's actual answer merges with Inkeri's interpretation of the conversation as she keeps (mis)reading the other's mind: "And she got an answer that meant yes it is, there's no need to ask, you know it anyway, but *I'm interested in knowing what the air is like inside here*" (ibid.).[155] In the representation of Inkeri's thoughts, the difference between the actual references of speech and imaginary reconstructions of them disappears. Inkeri does not only predict the future trajectories of the other people's talk, but fabulates purely hypothetical versions of them (cf. Hakulinen 2013: 269–271; Tammi 1992: 112)[156] Inkeri senses the parent's disdain in every expression and word she sees or hears. She feels like "a cow being led to market" (*T*, 223).[157]

Inkeri's friend Turre, on the other hand, serves as the figure of a female friend that functions as a symbol of the affirmation of the self, of gendered identity (cf. Felski 1989: 138). Turre represents the hidden, repressed "shadow" of Inkeri's personality. Revealingly, it is Turre who foresees the miseries of Inkeri's marriage: "You've got a lot going for you, but I don't see you succeeding in a bourgeois marriage. No, nothing will come of it; mark my words" (*T*, 248).[158] According to Turre, Inkeri is too naïve to be able to "mask [her] true feelings" (ibid.).[159] Even if she "know[s] how to narrate and even to act" (*T*, 244), she can do it best when she is not conscious of herself acting.[160] Turre pictures Inkeri's future as a bride suffering from shortness of breath, "like being in a cage" (*T*, 245).[161] At the end of the novel, these predictions turn into reality (and the reality turns into a play), as Inkeri's relatives witness the final act before Inkeri and Hannu are secretly married: "Look, they're all standing at the window like in a theater" (*T*, 373), Inkeri says to her groom.[162]

In *Tunteet*, the two mythic stereotypes of womanhood, angel and devil (cf. Beauvoir 1980/1949: 224), are simultaneously evoked and subverted in the characterization of Inkeri and Turre. Hannu sees similarities between these two girls, even if they do not actually resemble each other: "Hannu looked at Turre and wondered what about her had brought to mind Inkeri's image. That girl was totally different, tall and with a refined manner; there was something cold in her voice, and an indifferent tone in her every word" (*T*, 301).[163] Neither one of the stereotypes, an angel or a devil, seems to fully suit to describe Inkeri. In his letter, Hannu compares her with Fyodor Dostoevsky's two female characters that modify the division of women into Madonnas and whores: "There is in you the humility of Sonya and the fire of Nastassya Filippovna" (*T*, 190).[164] The second, devilish image of womanhood, *femme fatale*, is personified in Turre's performance of Sándor Petőfi's poem "Az Őrült" (The Maniac, 1869). The last stanza of the poem (quoted in the novel) introduces the figure of a beautiful beast, driving men crazy:

> For woman attracts as naturally the man
> As foaming oceans draw the rivers' flow.
> Wherefore? In both events to suck them dry!
> A pretty thing, a creature soft and sweet,
> A lovely form, but deadly too for sure;
> A golden goblet full of venomed drug.
> And I have drunk thee deep, oh Love![165]

The beast within Turre is evoked by the female rivalry as described in the later scene when Turre and Maija are escorting Hannu in Helsinki. Inkeri is present only as an image in Hannu's mind as he imagines seeing reflections of Inkeri's face on the other girls' faces. Turre keeps observing the strange behavior of Maija, who is portrayed elsewhere as a modest and reserved girl but who now appears to feel envy and contempt towards the other girls: "I didn't expect Maija to be such a performer; she was walking beside Inkeri's fiancé, looking as if it were perfectly natural to walk there. [...] Turre felt a bit displeased. Inkeri's former fiancé had focused all his attention on Maija and was talking only to her; he hadn't even noticed [Turre]" (*T*, 296).[166]

Inkeri's social alienation stems from the female rivalry as manifested in the triangle of Inkeri, Turre, and Maija. The rivalry is triggered by the idea of bourgeois marriage as the final goal in a woman's life. Turre is shown counterfactualizing her life, picturing herself as marrying Hannu. She feels able to play a happy wife in a bourgeois marriage. The married life, however, is only a second option for Turre. She states her desire to focus on her career. Turre is portrayed as an exceptional woman, who is forced to transgress the social boundaries to be (sexually) active and independent.[167] Turre manages to survive by breaking the rules of the community. In her desire for power and admiration, however, she alienates from other women. On the other hand, the female rivalry is linked to the potential sexual attraction between the girls. When Turre pretends to be a "jap" who takes Inkeri to dance, both of them feel "quivering in their bodies" (*T*, 240).[168]

Inkeri's self-alienation in respect to Turre is demonstrated in the power struggle between the girls as Inkeri is unwilling to except the role of a weak-willed admirer written by Turre for her. The cruelty and disappointment experienced in the female friendship eventually drives Inkeri back to

Hannu. In this sense, the fulfillment of Inkeri's dreams seems to rely "more on chance than on persistence" as Hannu analyzed her fiancée's behavior. In Inkeri's world, external events seem chaotic and irrational, because her inner confusion is projected onto the outer world. Inkeri pictures herself as the choir in a Greek tragedy, unable to change the irrational course of events. Inkeri's "weakness of will" (also known as the "Medea principle") is demonstrated in her relation to Turre's impulsive actions: "Inkeri was only accompanying [Turre], like the choir in a Greek tragedy, explaining to the invisible audience that she couldn't do anything with her, that her voice wasn't heard, whether she cried or swore, refused or gave in" (*T*, 316).[169] Inkeri can only wait for some higher power to intervene, to show that things are no longer under Turre's control.

The impulses of the unconscious mind are difficult to discern, which makes them seem as if they were caused by some changeful, god-like creature playing with the characters' destinies. This chaos, however, is "predetermined" by the author, Vartio, her intention being to include fluctuations of the mind in her depiction of a fictional universe, as shown in the episode at Olavinlinna. The fascination of imaginative storytelling is best served by defying the order, the world "as it is." In archaic oral stories, there is no fixed "beginning," and the rituals of narrating are always subject to the narrator's memory and variations. In Olavinlinna, Inkeri is depicted cursing a mad seamstress who has ruined her new dress by sewing its parts together all wrong: "The dress of green silk, black swallows on a green base – a mad seamstress cut the printed fabric all wrong, sewed the pieces so that the swallows were hanging upside down in the front, but on the sleeves and in the back with their heads up, a mad seamstress" (*T*, 102).[170] The "mad seamstress" is obviously Vartio herself. The swallows in the dress portray Inkeri's changeable nature, her thoughts swooping here and there. The girl's carefree attitude is projected in her observations on the flock of swallows circling right above her head as if illustrating her darting thoughts.

At Turunlinna (the Castle of Turku) Inkeri is seen observing a dress that had belonged to Kaarina Maununtytär (Karin Månsdotter).[171] Looking at the dress, Inkeri imagines the fabric moving with the rhythm of the human breath, as if the woman who once wore the dress was suddenly brought back to life. Inkeri's illusion of the past coming alive in the old fabric refers to works of fiction as being re-worked rather than newly made material. The patterns of the fabric and the stitches in the dress are still visible: "[T]he dress had been sewn exactly as nowadays, needle and thread through the fabric [...] one stitch after another, and the stitches were visible there, were still there, and the dress was still there under the glass" (*T*, 224).[172] The patterns of the fabric of fiction – the craft of archaic tales – may be varied and modified over the ages, but the tales themselves are still generated like they used to be, "exactly as nowadays, needle and thread through the fabric [...] one stitch after another."

The swallows' frantic flight in Inkeri's dress and the dress of Karin Månsdotter demonstrate Vartio's aspiration to generate literary forms in which archaic motifs can still be found embedded in the composition of a modernist novel. Like the parts of the green dress, the parts of Vartio's story are also attached to each other in an unconventional manner. As an image of literary production, the act of sewing emphasizes the linear quality of the narrative (Lat. *linea* = cotton, line), the interweaving of the narrative threads into a linear continuum. In the image of the mad seamstress, however, this sort of linearity vanishes. Not only the text, but also the texture of the mind constitutes a web-like, fragmented fabric in which the strings holding the entity together are frail and in danger of breaking off (cf. Kosonen 2000: 16). The image of chaotically-cut fabric refers to the texture of the literary text as the material from which the inner worlds of chaos are fabricated. The very coherence of Inkeri's oral narratives makes Turre suspect dishonesty. If a narrative is too coherent, it may not be true: "When I think about it more carefully it seems to me that everything is too much in place; it occurred to me that when everything is in its place perhaps nothing is in its place at all" (*T*, 231).[173] Later, Turre asks Inkeri to "tell the entire thing exactly *as it is*" so that she is able to "tell the truth about it" (*T*, 241).[174]

At the end of the novel, Inkeri is depicted fabricating her own "truth" in her letter to Hannu. She writes page after page, trying to convince him that she has grown out of a schoolgirl's whimsies. She pretends a meeting of minds and adopts the rules of his language for her own purposes. Inkeri claims to be completely honest in pouring out her innermost feelings. She writes a sentimental depiction of "the spring nights of my youth" ("nuoruuteni kevätöistä") having almost passed by, her inner growth and the "depthless sorrow" ("pohjaton murhe"): "All the time I was waiting for you to share my longing and my sorrow, but you never did, you never said to me, 'Look at the bird fly! Listen to the bird sing!'" (*T*, 358), Inkeri describes her feelings of alienation.[175] She perceives her and Hannu's love story as being a "game played by fate" (*T*, 351).[176] Their romance has been "like a fairy tale with a sad ending, so sad that I don't know even yet how it actually ended" (*T*, 353).[177] The sad ending of the fairy tale (as a freak of nature) serves Inkeri's manipulative ends. However, it simultaneously reflects the feeling of chaos she experienced as she prepares to head back home after her first year of study.

In the train on her way home, Inkeri keeps reading the notes she had taken during the lectures she attended the past year. The notes involve fragmentary ideas of tragedy, the contrast of emotions, the fatal characters and the vengeance of the gods. According to these definitions, tragedy involves a plenitude of external events that, however, need to manifest the inner decisions of tragic characters, their fall and disappointment. Also various literary genres are mentioned. Inkeri projects her life on these literary models: "Picaresque novel, she read, coming-of-age novel, she read. Coming-of-age novel, what was that like? One grew up, came of age, whereas in a picaresque novel one traveled" (*T*, 347).[178] These metafictional references to aesthetic-theoretical models are provided only to show them to be inadequate in the interpretation of this particular narrative: to parody them (cf. Tammi 1992: 81).[179] Inkeri cannot understand the meaning of the words and sentences she has once written, but on the spur of the moment she begins to write a letter. She fabricates a story of her own journey and personal development as if trying to imitate the patterns of the above-mentioned genres: "On the way home, in the train," (*T*, 348) she begins her letter.[180]

189

Like many modernist epistolary heroines, Inkeri transforms writing into means of subversion and revolt, by stealing the hero's words and parodying his style.[181] The sentimental wording of Inkeri's letter can be read as a parody of Hannu's letter, but also as a meta-commentary on the sentimental epistolary novel of the eighteenth century. In her letter, Inkeri mentions Goethe's loosely autobiographical epistolary novel *Die Leiden des jungen Werthers* (*The Sorrows of Young Werther*, 1774), even though she considered the book "boring" and "ridiculous" (*T*, 359).[182] Another Goethe novel, *Die Wahlverwandschaften* (*Elective Affinities*, 1809), is also mentioned: "Maybe you have read Goethe's Elective Affinities? Our story resembles that book in some respects, and if you have read it, you'll understand what I mean: we were not elective affinities" (*T*, 360).[183]

The idea of elective affinities refers to Goethe's notion of a novel as a laboratory of human relations in which different human elements are combined by the author to observe the resulting reaction. The notion of elective affinities is based on the metaphor of human passions being regulated by the laws of affinity, similar to the tendency of chemical species to combine with certain species and substances in preference to others. Whereas some individuals are drawn to each other and unite naturally without losing their distinctive characters, other human beings are like chemical substances that refuse to be combined, or at least, lose their individuality when they attempt to bond. According to Inkeri, the compound of herself and Hannu (like her and Turre) has not been very successful. These references to Goethe's novels can be read as mirroring Inkeri's tragedy as a young person experiencing the world with intense emotions, which are restricted by social norms. However, the sentimental contents of Inkeri's letter are not authentic self-expressions, but rhetoric intended purely to make Hannu look and listen. In her writing Inkeri is mocking Hannu's serious style:

> "[…] But everything that has happened to me has perhaps been necessary. We don't study for school, but for life – this proverb came to mind and I'm starting to believe it now, because I feel as if in spite of everything I have grown and matured, so much so that now, as I return home, I feel as if only now do I see everything clearly and only now do I understand…"
> She stopped to think: what? And continued: [...] (*T*, 350)[184]

Inkeri's "development" is contrasted with the growth of characters in a Bildungsroman in which young male protagonists are capable of resolving the discrepancies between their personal impulses and their social expectations and become full, self-confident members of society. In writing her letter, Inkeri is still unable to discern her true motives: "What do you suppose I mean by that" (*T*, 350).[185] Nevertheless, her imagination is more inventive than ever. As opposed to Hannu's inability to express himself, Inkeri is captivated by the charm of her language. She feels that she is able to master her words: "My Lord, how brilliantly she wrote! How was she able to do so in a way that even she herself was almost moved by her words?" (*T*, 360)[186]

The idea of transformation experienced by the heroine through romance is ironized in Inkeri's Bildung. The use of parody turns the sentimental to banal and transgressive, "contaminating" also the heroine's voice, as the irony is aimed at showing her naïveté and tragic hubris.[187] The theme of idealization of love, typical of popular romance and sentimental fiction, is mocked in *Tunteet* from two different perspectives. On the one hand, the novel ironizes Hannu's patterns of mirroring himself in the other. His struggles to define himself in relation to an idealized image of the other are shown to stem from the lack of this desired object: it is a product of his imagination. On the other hand, the mismatch of the "loved object" and the real human being is represented from Inkeri's perspective, suggesting her obsession for "true romance," an imaginary, culturally constructed story, and thus, showing the impossibility of the realization of her romantic expectations. (Cf. Pearce & Stacey 1995: 30, 37)

Inkeri's letter proves her sovereignty in the most sophisticated art of human intelligence: social navigation. It proves that even a foreign language can be reined in to serve a purpose of one's own, provided you have become skilled enough to use it: "Inkeri stopped the pen and read what she had written last. Was that too much? But she continued on [...]. What else could she come up with?" (*T*, 359)[188] Inkeri's play on words turns tragic-comic as she is portrayed fabricating her own trap. In this sense, the disparity between the perspective of the superior narrator and the naïve protagonist vanishes at the end of the developmental plot, as the knowledge gained by the heroine leads to the convergence of these two perspectives (Felski 1989: 136). Inkeri may have learned to use Hannu's language, but in the process, she has lost herself. The apprehended, cultivated norms of social behavior – the public expression of emotions and the cultured forms of language – are opposed to the natural, more organic language of her body. Separated from its true nature, "the double being" can never become an undivided self. The letter, written as if on a sudden whim, pre-ordains Inkeri's future as one of the trapped birds in Vartio's collection of *rara avis*.

Love comedies typically end in marriage, a happily-ever-after-closure of the romance. However, in Vartio's novel, the endless lingering in the preparatory stages of the complications of the romance does not lead to the happiness of marriage, but to the heroine's emotional void. The last scene of *Tunteet* depicts Hannu and Inkeri mocking and reciting each other's letters, until Hannu buys her wife's silence with banknotes. The bourgeois marriage is shown to be a trade between a man and a woman. The marriage signifies the dullness of everyday life as experienced by Inkeri. Already unhappily married, Inkeri hears Turre's voice in a radio play. Her laughter brings Inkeri back to another time and place. When she wakes up from her daydream and realizes where she is, she feels melancholy and regret over her life choices. Turre has managed to escape the trap of marriage, whereas Inkeri shares the fate of Hannu's mother, gradually turning into a frustrated and dissatisfied housewife. "Like a dream, year after year. Happy, why not? Surely, but when she thought about it, she didn't know whether it was in the right way. What was she missing? Nothing" (*T*, 383).[189] The process of becoming aware, modeled in many scenes of the novel, suggests that there is something hiding under the oblivion. Nothing seems to be missing, but perhaps something is – or everything.

A Parody of Sentiments

From the perspective of Erno Paasilinna's review of *Tunteet* as an "affected romance" it seems paradoxical that in some of the contemporary critics it was said that the novel was not much about emotions. Or at least, the content was not believed to control the method of narration: "*Tunteet* is [...] by no means a sentimental book," Mirjam Polkunen (1962: 20) wrote.[190] Moreover, the critics emphasized that the carefree tone could easily mislead a lazy reader: a novel that seemed to be a sentimental romance was *not* a sentimental romance (Pennanen 1962: 370). In other words, the responses to *Tunteet* depend on the ways in which the novel's genre is perceived. Paasilinna considered Vartio's novel a popular romance. Many critics, however, identified the work as a parody of romantic popular fiction, Bildungsroman, and the sentimental novel of the eighteenth century. The novel was praised by those critics who saw the function of the more ample, redundant manner of narration as a manifestation of innovative tools of portraying fictional consciousness. The technique of changing perspectives, among other things, was conceived as adding to the author's accomplishments in depicting consciousness.

The ambiguous way of perceiving the role of emotions in *Tunteet* is reflected in more recent Vartio criticism. Whether the novel is about emotions or the lack of them has been debated, with claims on the one hand maintaining that there are plenty of fierce, bodily emotions represented therein (Hakulinen 2013: 291–292), while on the other hand, opposing critics emphasize the unromantic, distanced manner of narrating the love story (Ruuska 2012: 347). Be that as it may, the ambivalence of these views demonstrates that, in Vartio's work, the density of emotions is rendered with narrative techniques (such as irony and parody) that we do not usually find in popular romances.[191] In *Tunteet*, seemingly subjective expressions may result from a performance that lacks any true emotional content. Objectivity, in turn, may derive from the inexpressible quality of emotions rather than from their absence. "I have no emotion, I myself am emotion," says the actor figure in Veijo Meri's short story "Suomen paras näyttelijä" (The Best Actor in Finland, 1962).[192] The reserved expression typical of the Finnish new novel does not eradicate emotional content, but rather highlights it (cf. Stevenson 1998: 176).

In *Tunteet*, the battle of minds relates to the battle between old and new aesthetics. This battle is embodied in the figure of the real-life poet V. A. Koskenniemi, whom Inkeri encounters on the streets of Turku in Turre's "play."[193] The target of parody in *Tunteet*, according to Ervasti, is not only the sentimentality of the old literary forms, but also the former aesthetic theories of emotions. Ervasti read Vartio's novel as a reaction to K. S. Laurila's book *Estetiikan peruskysymyksiä* (The Fundamental Questions of Aesthetics), whose first part was published in 1918. Ervasti (1967: 96) argued that the aesthetic emotions are defined by Laurila in the following, tautological manner: "Aesthetic emotions are those emotions that are evoked in us by certain phenomena when we approach them aesthetically." In Laurila's theory, the basis for the aesthetics of emotions consists of the transmission of emotions, which stipulates the reduction of "pure emotions, emotions in the true meaning of the word, emotions *as they are*" (ibid.). Pure emotions can be recognized "beyond doubt" as "an intuitively felt, *certain* matter of fact" (ibid.).[194]

The portrayal of young Inkeri is a result of Vartio's self-distancing and self-irony: the engagement of Inkeri and Hannu resembles Vartio's own unhappy engagement in her youth.[195] The parody in *Tunteet* is aimed at mocking Inkeri's whimsies, self-satisfaction, and insecurity: her "typicalness" as a growing individual.[196] Vartio wanted to capture the typical expression and sensations of a school girl, yet simultaneously she considered these feelings too sentimental, empty, and pathetic. "I don't know how to say it, and if I try to be witty and lessen the pathos that way, I feel tasteless. I am simply unable to mold anything into any shape," Vartio (1996: 30–31) wrote.[197] Vartio's frustration reveals that parody served her goal of writing a fictional form detached from the outpouring of sentimentality in her own youthful diaries. Thus, Hannu's distaste for the sentimentality of words resembles Vartio's attempts to overcome the pathos of sentimentality that complicated her pursuit to get form into her work. This principle of the "purification" of sentiments is portrayed in *Tunteet* when Hannu finds "a geometrical figure, a triangle, and a fragment of the Pythagorean theorem" behind the lovers' note (*T*, 53).[198] Hannu's preference for mechanical, strict forms of language, including the precise language of mathematics, parallels to Vartio's comparison of the pattern of her fiction to geometrical forms or equation in her analysis of writing *Se on sitten kevät*. The irony in Hannu's voice could be seen as a reflection of Vartio's, yet the same irony is employed to portray the character – his stiffness and formality, his conservatism and prejudice. The antidote to pathos and sentimentality was humor and parody, which guaranteed the necessary distance, the "purity" of the aesthetic form.[199]

Hannu's struggle as portrayed in *Tunteet* coincided with Vartio's own struggle with language. On the other hand, Vartio's development as a writer relates to her process of becoming more conscious of the ways in which the portrayal of the human mind could be made possible by means of the "figurative masks" ("kuvanaamio") typical of Inkeri's thinking. In this sense, *Tunteet* can be read as a parody of the overly confined forms of the new novel in Finnish modernism of the 1950s. The shift in Vartio's fiction seeks a new balance between tradition and innovation, the external and the internal, the paternal and the maternal,[200] emotional restraint and spells of the imagination. The figures of Inkeri and Hannu represent different aspects of the human mind drifting into conflict: imagination and logic, affections and reason, the intuitive and the rational, the feminine and the masculine. Only through the union of these principles the experience of wholeness and harmony are possible. The balance leads to clarity of consciousness and to the birth of a truly creative mind. (Cf. Freeman 1988: 49–50, 57)[201]

The final key to the interpretation of the functions of emotions in *Tunteet* can be found in Vartio's essay "Don Quixote," which deals with the trinity of the spirit, the body, and the mind. These aspects of the human existence are composed into character constellations in Vartio's fourth novel and elaborated on in *Hänen olivat linnut*.[202] In her essay, Vartio (1996: 197–198) analyzed the dynamics of the two figures in Cervantes' novel, Don Quixote and Sancho Panza: "Sancho is Cervantes' own body, growing tired, and his mind, and Don Quixote is his spirit. The spirit cannot perform heroic deeds alone without the help of the body and a healthy mind; both must help each other."[203] According to Vartio (ibid.: 199), Cervantes still needed to resort to the concepts of abstract language, "the language of chivalries" ("ritariromaanien käsitekiel[een]"), but he was able to turn his work into a parody of the chivalric novel. While fighting the difficulties of expression, Cervantes was forced to "rush into battle against images created by his own mind." (ibid.: 200)[204] Thus, the principle of balance involves the process of art-making itself: the harmony between the artist's visions and the knowledge of structure. In order to grow into artistry, one has to learn how to rein in one's mental images, to generate artistic forms in order to organize the chaos of mental images.

6. In the Mazes of the Wounded Mind. Narrating the Self in *Hänen olivat linnut*

> At night her mind is tormented by dreams.
> Even if it is autumn, she hears the cooing of black grouse,
> the call of wood grouse
> as if it were the time of melting snow.[1]
>
> – Marja-Liisa Vartio: "The Archer"

The mechanisms of mind-reading are characterized by their labyrinthine-like quality. Characters are often negotiating among other people's guesses of what the characters might feel about what others feel as the navigation mechanisms circles to and fro. In addition to tracing the minds of others, characters often trace other minds tracing other minds. In *Hänen olivat linnut*, the mazes of fictional minds relate to the mazes of storytelling as characters become lost in the fictions generated by their imagination. Two spinsters – a parson's widow, Adele Broms, and her servant Alma Luostarinen – spend most of their time telling narratives of their life experiences. The two women go over the same stories and nothing much seems to happen. As the novel progresses, however, the reader gradually learns to know the tragic events of the women's lives as they mirror themselves in each other's experiences and try to narrativize their painful past. One of the repetitious narratives Adele insists her servant tell again and again is about young Alma. Having left home, Alma has come to ask for a position at the shopkeeper Mikander's. In her second-person narration, Adele guides Alma to say the words she has heard many times before:

> "'Are you selling something, we don't buy anything,' said the shopkeeper when he saw your veneer case.
> "'Need a person to work here?' I said to that, that's right. And he started laughing. He just stands there and looks at me. I guessed. I thought, I sure know what you've got in mind, old man, but you just guess." (*PW*, 140)[2]

In the above scene young Alma responds to the shopkeeper's intrusive (sexual) gaze with defiance. As George Butte (2004: 29) points out, "deep intersubjectivity" resembles *chiasmus,* in which a knot interconnects the two poles of a loop in a constant back and forth motion. In her recollection, young Alma challenges the shopkeeper Mikander to read her mind similar to the way she is reading his: "but you just guess [what I am thinking about you thinking like you are thinking]" (cf. Mäkelä & Tammi 2007: 227–228).

In Vartio's last novel, the complexity of embedded consciousnesses often pushes the reader beyond the "cognitive zone of comfort," (Zunshine 2006: 37), challenging their ability to keep track of who is thinking: the more layered the intersubjective structure, the more convoluted is the actual source of the thought. The more the levels of mind-reading proliferate and the harder the reading gets, the more probable it is that the reader's attention will be drawn to the embedded structures of mind presentation *per se* (ibid.). In *Hänen olivat linnut,* the reflective loops of mind-reading are connected to the bodily loops of an embodied trauma, reflecting the unspeakable in human relations. The conversational storytelling of the two women turns into a "ritualistic dance" (Kendzior 2001: 243), in which each tries to imitate the movements of the other as a mirror image. Being trapped in their past selves, Adele and Alma's self-identities are in danger of becoming paralyzed. Only through the movement of their ritualistic dance they can learn to recognize themselves or figure out who they are not or will not want to become. (Ibid.).

In writing *Hänen olivat linnut,* Vartio articulated her concern about composing a novel based on dialogue. She could "hear" the characters speaking continuously. The auditory images echoing in the Vartio's inner ear correspond to the visual images envisaged in the process of writing *Se on sitten kevät*: "My writing is flowing well, but unfortunately I can only hear speech. I can make the people talk for however long, but I don't suppose a book can be built just out of conversation – or why not, if it is well done?" (Vartio 1996: 194)[3] The disintegrating effect of building a book "just out of conversation" constituted the essence of the problem for some critics, including Rafael Koskimies (1967: 18): "The feeblest [aspect] in the widow's and the servant's tug of war is undeniably the mundane wrangling over insubstantial things: in a genuinely feminine style the author has been apt to well-aimed observation even there, but it is exactly these sequences that tend to drag."[4]

The fact that Vartio heard only conversation, however, suggests that the parts of the novel based on dialogue resulted from a more or less conscious decision to respond to the "voices" echoing in her inner ear. The repetition, replication, and redundancy addressed by Koskimies as "mundane wrangling" ("arkinen kinastelu") are hallmarks of Vartio's fiction. The design of *Hänen olivat linnut* suggests that aspects of redundancy play a decisive role in the semantics of a fictional world composed of several diverging stories. The narrative patterns involving repetition and embedding seem to culminate in Vartio's last novel, in which the fictional structure becomes more complex than ever. In the women's dialogues, the continuity of identity is created in the reflexive activity of narrativizing the self. The formal innovations of the novel are related to the characters' frustrated, modernist Bildung that reflects the artifice of self-identity.[5] The self is a labyrinthine, constructed and reconstructed image rather than a coherent, harmonious entity. The fictional "self-narratives" are fragmented and circular as they renarrate the past lives of the two spinsters who are reworking their trauma through their relation to another. The stories of the past involve dramatic incidents such as suicide attempts, drug and alcohol abuse, sexual assaults and moments of madness that contribute to the themes of loneliness, the desire for sexual fulfillment and love and for connection with others (cf. Flint & Flint 2008: v–vi). The social, psychological, and spiritual relations between the two women are rich in nuance, challenging the reader with intriguing ambiguity.

In this chapter, the multiplication of the fictional worlds in *Hänen olivat linnut* is analyzed from the perspective of the stories embedded in the novel. The functions of the characters' self-narratives are analyzed in the context of building a cyclic, emotional story structure related to the representation of a trauma. First, the loops of intersubjective structures are examined in relation to the problems of human communication as representing the tension between intimate talk and gossip. Second, the interplay of dialogues and other narrative sections, including the parts of the novel that show the characters' minds from within, are approached from the perspective of an embodied traumatic experience. The removal from the public realm to the private domain is analyzed in the context of a growing sense of losing touch with reality. Third, the possibilities and limitations of intimate talk are examined with regard to the projection of the self in the narratives shared by others. Finally, the cyclic structures of the characters' life paths are addressed by discovering the functions of the embedded narratives and their relation to the frame story. The alternative plots of female awakening portrayed in Vartio's last novel are no longer modifications of the classic romance plot, but focus on the relation between two women. The trope of "spinsterhood" appears in the depiction of female development at the later age, as these two women muse about the alternative paths of their lives.

From Intimacy to Fear. Ambivalences of Mind-Reading

Intersubjectivity creates interworlds in which the private worlds of fictional characters interact. The cooperation of minds blurs the boundaries between the self and others, with characters constantly being conscious of themselves being conscious of others. The intersubjective interiority of mind-reading causes ambivalent feelings of yearning and anxiety. The desire for human contact is set against the fear of social humiliation, exposure, and hostility. The social risks involved in mind-reading are distilled in Adele Broms's contemplation of her life story, leading to her loneliness and resentment: "When I was younger, I couldn't look people in the eye because *I always knew what they were thinking* and it made me ill, because what I saw they were thinking about me was not always favorable. [...] People are far worse than you can guess, Alma, no one cares for anyone, don't ever grow fond of anyone or anything" (*PW*, 222).[6]

The skill of mind-reading minds is an ambiguous gift; it is like *pharmakos*, a potion that both heals and poisons (Butte 2004: 113). In an ideal state, a mind-reading ability leads to human companionship, collaboration, recognition, intimacy, or even affection and love. Knowing what others really perceive enhances empathy with others. However, very often mind-reading becomes a medium of exploitation, cruelty, humiliation, submission, and violation. According to Butte (2004: 40), "[i]ntersubjectivity always poses, at some level, questions about power exercised, negotiated, blocked, or embraced between subjects, between consciousnesses occupying some kind of common space or terrain." Human beings try to take control over the most private realms of other minds – and protect themselves from others' invasions. Adele's skill in navigating other minds results in the loss of human affection:

> You know I'm bitter, I'm mean, I am a very bad person, I don't love people. It's true: I've never learned to love anyone [...] What could you be, I said to myself, you, bitter, mean, full of evil thoughts, and how you root around in them, like digging in filth, I dig up everything that's been done to me in this life, in this house, including everything you've said to me, Alma. You don't know how I've dug up even those things you haven't said to me directly but have told other people. (*PW*, 226)[7]

Adele's talent as a mind-reader, or her inclination to read other minds, is emphasized several times in the novel. Her self-analysis, however, also reveals her paranoia. She even digs in "the filth" that she only *suspects* exists in the words of others. Alma describes Adele's mind-reading skills to her employer's sister-in-law, Elsa: "I don't even have to think, I don't dare think. She can even read my thoughts" (*PW*, 97).[8] Alma in turn learns to register the slightest changes in Adele's behavior. Her twisted smile forewarns Alma of a forthcoming outburst of rage and despair: "[A] smile appeared on her lips, you didn't have to see anything else, all you had to see was that smile and you'd just know" (*PW*, 75).[9] When Adele loses her grip on reality, she is depicted as a devil-eyed witch with nearly occult powers: "[T]he widow pursued her, stood in front of her, regarding her with that terrible expression. That look in her eyes. Every time Alma saw it, it got under her skin, made her furious" (*PW*, 31).[10] The staring look in Adele's eyes pains Alma, because it seems to reveal everything that goes through her mind.

The web of consciousnesses generates intersubjective layers of gestures and expressions as characters try to understand each other on the basis of their body language. While Alma tries to figure out what is happening in the mind of Adele's son, Antti, she reads the true meaning of his spoken words from his facial expressions: "Alma didn't look at the boy. 'What about it?' she answered. 'What do you mean?' she asked the boy, knowing perfectly well what he wanted to say, but her common sense refused to answer, refused to explain to the boy that it wasn't what he'd really meant, or what those eyes and that smile meant" (*PW*, 114).[11] To be more exact, Alma tries her best *not* to figure out Antti's true intentions. He has made intimate advances to Alma, who knows perfectly well what the boy means. While trying to ignore his intentions, she keeps avoiding his gaze and his knowing smile as if she is afraid of revealing her thoughts: she does not want the boy to understand that she understands.

Intersubjectivity ranges from a two-layer exchange to multiple negotiations and perceptions. The subject is not only "a hall of mirrors reflecting images of itself and others" (Butte 2004: 5). The subject is always a body and an experience of that body, even if the intersubjective exchange leads to a mirroring of other bodies, gestures, and experiences. The subject revises the image it perceives in others, and also apprehends itself by means of a responding signal and by understanding the implications of its previous appropriation of others. (Ibid.: 65, 70) The self-conscious mind-reading patterns create layered chains of inner thoughts, gazes, and gestures that allow characters (and readers) to hypothesize what other people think and furthermore, what other people think they are thinking of what they are thinking. Zunshine (2006: 28) speaks of these multiple layers of mind-reading as levels of intentionality. In principle, the proliferation of levels could be infinite, but in practice intentionality usually reaches only the fourth level. Adele's above-cited navigation of hostile minds demonstrates two-level intentionality, a prototypical case of mind-reading: she *imagines* what others might *think* about her. Alma's later retrospection, on the other hand, represents a case of three-level intentionality: she *thinks* she *knows* what Mikander *thinks*. The passage, however, has potential to reach the fourth or even the fifth level of intentionality: she *thinks* she *knows* what he *thinks* about what she *thinks* about what he *is thinking*.

In the following passage, Alma tries to grasp her unconscious intentions, and in doing so, she reads her own mind vis-à-vis the reflections of others. Adele has left Alma alone with Antti, and Alma tries to anticipate what is going to happen with the boy:

> And, hadn't she, Alma, hadn't she known this when she'd heard the parson's widow would be going, hadn't she planned for this without thinking so much as a single thought but still knowing exactly how it would turn out? And hadn't the parson's widow known, or planned for it, or allowed it to happen, that which had to happen? Alma understood that was why the widow had gone, and hadn't the boy also known right away? And hadn't she wanted the boy to come, lain awake listening to the boy's movements from above, footsteps on the stairs and in the kitchen. She felt as if she'd wanted to take revenge against the boy for something, anything. (*PW*, 120)[12]

As Alma reads the unconscious motives of herself as well as those of Adele and her son, we encounter a triad of unspoken thoughts and inner voices intermingling with each other. The passage demonstrates three-level intentionality: Alma *suspects* that the boy *knows* what the widow and Alma both *know* (half consciously): Adele has left the house, for she knows that the encounter between her maid and her son is inevitable.

Even if Alma's thoughts (rendered in narrated monologue) remain on the threshold of verbalization, as Cohn (1983: 103) put it, the reader still has access to her perceptions of the thoughts of others (cf. Mäkelä & Tammi 2007: 235). Readers can test their own abilities to read the hidden intentions in Alma's unconscious. The paradoxical reflection – "hadn't she planned for this without thinking so much as a single thought, but still knowing" – refers to Alma's pre-conscious acceptance as she confronts "the inevitable." However, can the reader really trust Alma to be as pure-minded as she misleads herself to believe? The most obvious reason for Alma's assent, namely, sexual desire, is repressed from her conscious thought. In addition, the triangle of intuitive mind-reading can be interpreted as Alma's attempt to justify getting back at Adele through her son. In Antti's eyes, Alma can see his mother staring and provoking her. Even if Alma is unable to recognize her motive as resentment ("of something, anything"), the reader is attuned to perceive the widow as the third part in the relationship of Alma and Antti.

By determining the perceptions mediated by the omniscient narrator, the reader is able to read Alma's mind to some degree (to the point she herself can understand her intentions or reflect the thoughts of others). The layering of multiple consciousnesses, however, often results in the difficulty of tracing who is thinking or feeling. Whose mind are we ultimately reading? The question arises in the following episode, for instance, in which Adele and Alma are caught observing the drunken pharmacist Holger. The husband of Adele's sister-in-law, Teodolinda, Holger has come knocking on Adele's door. Adele and Alma pretend they are not at home and watch as Holger leaves the house: "[T]hey kept peeking through the curtains, the pharmacist heading off with his back straight, looking like that so the village people couldn't say he was drinking, no, when a man had an erect posture no one had any business saying anything" (*PW*, 129).[13] The origin of the last hypocritical comment is unclear. Do we interpret the episode as a case of second- or third-level intentionality? Are Alma and Adele *thinking* that Holger is so naïve as to *think* that holding "an erect posture" might enable him to maintain his dignity in the eyes of the villagers? Or are Adele and Alma *thinking* that the pharmacist *thinks* that the villagers *might think* that Holger is the kind of a man who maintains his mental posture in every situation? (Cf. Mäkelä & Tammi 2007: 233; Tammi 1992: 63–64)

In *Hänen olivat linnut*, the untraceable "noise" of multiple-level intentionality is often caused by the presence of the villagers in Adele and Alma's speech and thoughts. One of the crucial events in the village's history is the fire at the old parsonage, which still continues to trouble Adele. The fire is described three times in the novel. The first time is in the dialogue between Adele and her servant in chapter 1. In chapter 2, the fire appears in the narration of an extradiegetic narrator, while in chapter 21, Teodolinda, mentions the fire a third time as she gives her version of the event. Every time the fire is re-represented, the details of the episode change. The narration gives no reason to doubt the extradiegetic narrator's account. The changing versions of the different characters, represented in dialogues, however, raise questions about the reliability of the characters' consciousness. Whose version of reality actually holds true? The tension between one's "truth" and another's gossip is manifested already in the novel's opening scene. As the women talk, the novel begins:

"Well, let's just not talk about it."

"That's not what I meant," said Alma, the maid.

"How could I have said something so silly?" the parson's widow said. "I'm not like that."

Alma was silent.

"That's just the way it is. If the sexton had only given the alarm right away, the parsonage wouldn't have burned down." [...]

"But it didn't burst out right away. The sexton thought the smoke was only a bit of fog," Alma said.

"Oh, was Alma herself there to see it?" (*PW*, 3)[14]

In the opening dialogue the fundamental dynamic between Adele and Alma is introduced as they argue about the different interpretations involved in the event. The basis for the "mundane wrangling" between Adele and Alma is shown as stemming from problems of remembering and presenting the past, which is pictured differently by different individuals. The contrast between seeing with one's eyes ("Oh, was Alma herself there to see it?") and the unreliability of one's introspection and recollections (including the things said to another person in the past) result in constant arguing about the truth of a given state of affairs.

The conflict between perceptions and false memories is related to the aspect of the fictional mind, which is usually neglected in literary studies, that is, the representation of the collective, social mind. Other minds are reflected and projected in the (inner) talk: the talk is often about others or about perceptions of others and their perceptions of the speaker (Butte 2004: 168). The collective perspective involves not only the characters' intersubjective representations of other minds, but also pertains to the reflections of the characters interwoven into a single, collective mind. In *Hänen olivat linnut*, the representation of the collective gaze and the speech of the villagers accompany the women's conversation. As in Vartio's other novels, the epistemological uncertainty is dramatized by portraying the conflicts between the individual and the collective ways of viewing the world. In her last novel, the multiple story worlds center on the chaotic speculations of the reality as perceived by multiple eyes and ears.

The rumors and speculations evolving around the fire episode complicate the mind-reading process and manipulate the reader's tendency to keep track of *who* thought. Knowing whose thoughts and sentiments are in question usually helps the reader evaluate the source of the fictional statements and their reliability (Zunshine 2004: 47). The aspectuality of each private world within the reality of the textual actual world enables multiple counterfactual versions of events that are occurring simultaneously. The events are experienced differently by different characters. The task of evaluating the truth-value of representation, however, is difficult if the "tag" specifying the source of the information (who thought, who felt, who said) is missing. In *Hänen olivat linnut*, Adele represents her version of the fire as a universal truth, even if she is just as deeply involved in the event as the other villagers. She is about to refuse to continue the conversation because Alma refers to a detail in the story that she has probably heard from Adele before: the sexton at the parsonage woke up and thought that the smoke coming from the rectory was fog. Adele interprets Alma's words as deception. Instead of staying with her account of the events, Alma has been listening to the villagers' stories, which mischievously target Adele and her husband, the late vicar, and blame them for what happened. Adele is convinced that the sexton tried to cover his own faults. While insisting that he thought the smoke was only fog, he makes excuses for why he didn't give the alarm soon enough to save the vicarage. Later, it is revealed that Adele has not actually heard the sexton's story: "I didn't hear that myself; I wouldn't have listened, *but of course I've been told*" (*PW*, 4).[15]

Thus, everything Adele repeats as witnessed by herself amounts only to rumors and speculations heard from others: Adele *says* what others have *said* that the sexton *said*. The layered structures of rumor reflect the embedded quality of all language. The Bakhtinian idea of language as saturated with "the other word," as a mixture of different voices, is illustrated particularly well in Adele's critique of Alma: "Oh, yes, in your voice I hear the sexton's voice and his wife's voice too" (*PW*, 6–7).[16] (Tammi 1992: 58) Moreover, the pluralism of Bakhtin's "character zones" is actualized in the composition of dialogues in the novel, as the characters' (inner) voices are more or less affected by other voices.[17] Because the "tags" pinpointing the original source of the statements are blurred, the absolute truth of who said what and what was actually said never becomes clear.

The capacity of tracking the source of characters' and narrator's representations allows the reader to assign differently weighed truth-values to fictional statements. This includes the ability to store information in case it has to be revised later. In fact, fictional texts may tease the reader by leaving uncertain which representations originating in the characters' minds are reliable. (Zunshine 2004: 56) In the case of *Hänen olivat linnut*, the more the reader gets to know the characters, the more obvious it becomes that their representations of events cannot always be trusted. The inconsistencies in characters' statements often speak for themselves. For instance, as Adele retells the sexton's reports on the events of the fire, she hints that the sexton has told everyone that the late vicar, her husband Birger, had burned trash outside the parsonage at five o'clock on Sunday morning: "He didn't exactly say Birger did that, but what he meant was that *he might as well have*" (*PW*, 4).[18] Adele's habit of insisting on something and then denying what she has just said makes the reader suspicious. She adds details to her stories to make them coincide with her own private worlds of hallucination and make-believe.

Adele's delusions stem from her tendency to lose track of herself as the source of her representations. She fails to monitor herself as the subjective interpreter of other people's minds and claims to "know" the truth of her (wrong) mind-attributions. She misinterprets the feelings and thoughts of people around her and starts to act upon her suppositions as if they were real. For Adele, the most essential part of human talk is readable only between the lines. Obviously, in the realm of the unspeakable, however, the risks for misreading are at their highest. People may express themselves by talking, but the most obvious (and hostile) thoughts are hidden behind the words: "No, not a single bad word, yet there certainly was talk. And thinking. Just as one can hear in your talk, if one is used to listening not only to how people talk but to what they say. And I've sure learned to do that" (*PW*, 6), Adele says to Alma.[19] The need to naturalize or displace the unreadability of the unattanable mind is thematized in Vartio's last novel. The characters feel constant fear of losing the integrity of the self under the spell of others and become obsessed by their need to explain other people's "hidden" intentions, even though these intentions do not truly exist (cf. Abbott 2008: 461).

In Vartio's novels, Adele is among those self-deceiving sufferers who tend to listen to others too eagerly, deliberately mishearing everything, even the silence of others. Adele's paranoia is related to her failure to keep track of herself as the source of the representations of other people's minds, which leads to misrepresentations of her own mind. She perceives her thoughts emanating, not from her own intentions, but from an external, alien source, which is not under her control (Zunshine 2004: 55). When the spirits are on the move, she hears birds screeching as if they were souls lost in hell: "Oh, my, when I listen at night, they scream out when they're coming. They scream" (*PW*, 64), she cries.[20] The sounds of the birds are juxtaposed with the disembodied voices she hears in her head, the "bad spirits" ("pahat henget") of the past, which are generated in her mind as she loses her ability to keep track of herself as the origin of her obsessive thoughts. In the following analyses, Adele's delusions are approached in relation to her traumatic past, re-constructed in the description of the fire and in her talk with Alma.

Spirits of the Haunted House. Going Back to the Past

The tension between confession (intimate, private talk) and gossip (evil talk spreading from person to person) frames the dialogues in *Hänen olivat linnut*. The gossip evolving around the fire represents the most urgent problem of people's past: the wound that stems from lack of human affection and communication. According to Adele, the trauma is collective, even if others do not want to talk about it, even admit it to themselves: "They don't want to see what it all meant. But I have time to think about things" (*PW*, 8).[21] The fire as a turning point in people's lives is manifested in Adele's description of it as "the end of the world" (*PW*, 4).[22] The fire also serves as the beginning of the world, because the reader gets to know it at the very opening of the novel and in the multiple, counterfactual versions narrated thereafter.

In a previous study on this novel, the fire was interpreted as an allusion to the downfall of the last remnants of class society after the Finnish Civil War (Alhoniemi 1973: 177–178). Be that as it may, the fire constitutes the end of Adele's past life as she watches the house burn down. From the ashes of the parsonage rises a strange, wounded bird, which is observed from a distance by the villagers. In the novel's chapter 2, the parsonage fire is depicted in its "real" time frame as a flashback. The collective perspective of the villagers is marked by an odd feeling of the unknowable reflected in their shared memories. The parson's wife claims that she dropped and broke the baptismal font on purpose, which she had first saved from the fire:

> [...] *But then something happened that people couldn't ever figure out, couldn't determine whether it was the truth or a lie, created out of the shocked mind of the parson's wife.* She shouted, her face all twisted: "I, I was the one who broke it. I saved it but it broke. I broke it!" she cried, "I broke it on purpose. I let it fall from my hands, all of you were baptized in it; you, Birger; you, Elsa; you, Teodolinda. I broke it, it didn't just fall. It was no accident! I broke it, I broke it! Do you hear me!" But no one answered, no one said anything to her. They left, leading the parson's wife off between them, and as they drew further away and went out past the gate, the verger's wife turned and followed them with her eyes.
>
> "Where are you going" asked the people who were still on the road, and drew aside as the little group went past them. (*PW*, 25–26)[23]

In the beginning of the novel, Adele's unwillingness to talk stems from the trauma related to certain events of the past, including the burning down of the parsonage. Unable to forget the past, Adele continues to talk and re-live it. She is haunted by the spirits of the house, the rumors and speculations about the events of the village's past and her own involvement in those events. The end of the first chapter presents a problem related to Adele's self-narratives concerning the unspeakable in human relations. The people inhabiting the book – the relatives of the late vicar – are introduced one by one as they emerge in Adele's mind:

> And now, as it always happened when the parson's widow, whose Christian name was Adele, spoke so intimately with Alma, referring to the parson as Birger, to one of his sisters as Teodolinda instead of "the sister of the dear late parson" or "the pharmacist's wife," and to Elsa instead of "the dear late parson's other sister" or "the county doctor's wife," and all together called them "the late parson's sisters." You could hear in the widow's voice that although she had brought them close, right here in the kitchen, they were still unreachable, just as she herself was, even though she was sitting at the kitchen table drinking coffee. But little by little, though she didn't change her manner of speaking, it began to go more easily, and the distance between "the late vicar" and "Birger" slowly wore down.
>
> "But let's not talk about these things. They're long and involved, much too involved," the parson's widow said. "Let's not talk, let's not talk," she repeated, and raised her hand as if to fend off further words, as if to repel someone who was demanding that they talk about them.
>
> "The parson's widow is getting all excited for no reason, and won't be able to sleep," Alma said. "Let's not talk." (*PW*, 10)[24]

At first, Adele has difficulties remembering and talking about the people who are so near, yet simultaneously so distant, just as she herself is. As time goes by, however, the possibilities for intimate discussions emerge. The mental barrier, "the step" (*porras*), separating the formal from the intimate – and the unspeakable – is worn down.[25] The symbiotic cooperation between minds is achieved as Adele and Alma encounter each other as equals rather than as employer and servant. The necessity of talking arises from within, even though Adele initially refuses to listen to this inner voice: "'Let's not talk, let's not talk,' she repeated, and raised her hand as if to fend off further words, as if to repel someone who was demanding that they talk about them." Alma is often reluctant to talk, precisely because she fears stirring up Adele's inner pain. But eventually the talk begins and continues until the very end of Adele's life.

A true meeting of minds, however, is continuously challenged by Adele's tendency to control the discussion, take the floor herself, interrupt, and argue about every detail in Alma's narratives. As the women struggle to put together the pieces of the past, they encounter tangled threads of stories that seem as fuzzy as the minds constructing them. The endless streams of verbalized thought are represented in the dual interaction between the women. Sometimes they have company, as when Holger joins in them as a third party in the communion of the "chattering minds"[26] in the parlor of the manse. Storytelling that races whimsically from present to past and back again finally overtakes the whole story. The main storyline primarily serves as a framework for assembling the storyworlds together. The outer events are reduced to a minimum, and the "orally" narrated stories become the principal material for constructing the plots of the character's lives, the stories of their suffering.

The events of Adele's past are told mainly in dialogues in the fifth and sixth chapters. These dialogues involve events that took place right after the fire or just before it and were related to her unhappy marriage with Birger, the late vicar. Adele's voice in the first-person narratives becomes so dominating that her oral stories resemble soliloquies, spoken monologues rather than dialogues. Her talk is interrupted only by Alma's terse questions encouraging her to continue ("And then?"; "What did they do then?"; "And then?"; "Then?"). (*PW*, 66–67)[27] Even though Alma has heard it all before, Adele expresses a desire to tell her maid everything: "I'll start from the very beginning, you've heard it all but I'll start from the beginning" (*PW*, 65).[28] Long passages of speech follow.

The beginning of the "whole history of [Adele's] suffering" (*PW*, 58) is the beginning of her marriage with Birger.[29] One day "a fine man" "from a fine family" walks into the post office and asks the postmistress, "only a postmistress" (*PW*, 65), to go with him on a bird outing.[30] The fowler, that is, the clergyman, is standing there, holding a dead bird in his hand. A strange chain of events begins as Adele decides to follow him. As they head out on the lake to hunt waterbirds, Birger's sisters row after them, gradually approaching the rock in the middle of the water where the man is standing with his gun: "The rock we were sitting on was very small and the boat kept circling; the circle grew smaller and smaller until the side of the boat brushed the rock where we were sitting" (*PW*, 66–67).[31] The sisters have a message from their mother: Birger needs to return home immediately. The sound of a shot is heard, and then Adele's scream. When Adele finally has the courage to remove her hands from her eyes, she can see the sisters' boat already far away. "I think I hit one, let's row over there" (*PW*, 67), Birger says and Adele rows.[32] She sees a bird floating in the water, dead.

The scene of the circling boat and the first shot symbolize Adele's entrapment in her marriage. Her life is shattered by increasing suffering, as she gradually realizes Birger's true mental state. On the first night, Adele gets "to know the first bird of [her] life" (*PW*, 67).[33] In this short reference, the material, the spiritual, and the erotic are interconnected in the image of birds, the true objects of Birger's desire. Later, Birger and Adele get married, and not a single one of the relatives is present. Before long, Adele begins to see her husband's obsession. Following the wedding, the vicar preaches a fierce sermon about birds in the church: "[T]hat sermon was burned, a beautiful sermon and it flew up into the air as flames" (ibid.).[34] Before the marriage Adele had suspected that the vicar was "speaking in parables" (*PW*, 68).[35] She perceives his sermon of the longing of birds as a confession of his love for her. The villagers, however, consider him mad, a heathen clergyman. Later, the acknowledgment of Birger's madness ("he is always talking about birds") is reflected in Adele's doubts about the depth of her husband's feelings: "Maybe, well… maybe he took me only because of my name. 'Adele, Adelaide, that's what I'll call you,' he said. 'It's like a bird call – Adelaide'" (*PW*, 69).[36]

The stuffed birds serve as an image of the characters' emotional and spiritual void, their trapped souls that cannot fly and escape the material world. However, the birds refer also to the past painful experiences that cause Adele's emotional paralysis. The correspondences between Adele and the birds are elaborated on in the widow's depiction of her married life. Pregnant with Birger's child, Adele feels ill. She begs him to stop shooting birds, which she has to hold against her stomach, simultaneously feeling the movements of her unborn child: "I couldn't bear to look at [the dead birds], there was a churning in the pit of my stomach from morning to night, this very room, small birds in rows on the table, dead, stiff, and the smell in this room. I fled upstairs, the smell penetrated the walls when he prepared them" (*PW*, 59).[37] Adele looks straight into the glass eyes of a stuffed wagtail and talks about the moment of its death:

> "It was a spring evening, not autumn as it is now, it was spring, and the road curved down to the shore through a birch grove. 'I beg you, don't shoot little birds.' Birger was standing on a rock with a gun in his hand, and this very same little bird on the shore, on a rock, on a rock by the shore, a wagtail, with its tail going up, down, up, and Birger standing there, rifle at the ready against his shoulder. I began clapping my hands to scare it away but the bird didn't hear, the shot rang out and Birger went running along the rocks and came back with this little bird dangling from his hand." (*PW*, 59)[38]

Adele perceives the bird as her "mirror image" (*PW*, 61).[39] She considers herself one of the stuffed birds in Birger's collection, still called by its name from beyond the grave. As Adele looks the stuffed wagtail in the eye, she says: "Maybe my brains have turned into bird brains. Maybe you're right, Alma, maybe I am a wagtail. Well, how could I expect people to understand me?" (*PW*, 57)[40] Adele's loneliness is reflected in the dead animals that are mute and paralyzed; she does not know how to make herself heard. The correspondences between Adele and the bird are reinforced as the widow continues her self-narrative. One night, as Birger returns from the shoals with a gun in his hand, she asks him to prepare her like the dead birds he is carrying:

'What if you shot me?' I said. 'I'd like to see which hymn you'd have them sing after you prepared me. Take a look. Wouldn't it be fun to push a metal wire through these, take a look, I'll hold my arms like this and my legs like that. In what position would you set me? I've been thinking about it all night. Would you have me sitting, or standing on one foot, look, like this, or would you lift one arm in the air, or both arms, or an arm along the side, or both arms? I've been expecting you home all night, I've paced back and forth all night and looked at these birds and thought I'm nothing but another bird in your collection. [...]' (*PW*, 60)[41]

Birger has promised not to bring any more birds to the house, but he keeps going off to hunt, obsessed by the avian creatures. "He's a master shot" (*PW*, 59), the sheriff tries to comfort the abandoned wife: "Just think how he can nail any bird with a single shot" (ibid.).[42] Birger seems to have nailed his wife as well, depriving her of her passion for life: "A child was on the way, you don't understand. I would go walking along the shore and I wanted only to die" (*PW*, 46).[43] The dead birds signify Adele's position as a trapped bird among other birds, condemned to live without life, conserved and labeled by her husband:

What name would you give me, *rara avis*, or what? Would you put me up on the highest spot, on top of that case next to the owl, would you make glass eyes for me too, would I be a *rara avis*?' 'Silly, silly, that's what you would be. I'd put a *silly avis* label on your pedestal, don't you get any ideas of being a phoenix, you're just a nervous woman who can't take a normal attitude toward her pregnancy – try to learn from these country women.' And then I shouted the name of the girl they'd taken along with them to row the boat. (*PW*, 60)[44]

The label given Adele, "silly avis," refers to her earlier notion of herself as having bird brains: her silliness and nervousness. The phoenix rising from the ashes signals that the fire at the parsonage was one of the turning points of Adele's life, an event that will determine her further mental development. The influence of this traumatic event (parallel to the burning fire of obsession in her husband) is simultaneously acknowledged and denied by Birger, who considers Adele's pains as the exaggeration of "a nervous woman." Rejected by her husband, Adele is paralyzed in a static position for life: "I feel I haven't had any arms since then, they stayed around his neck, torn off from me, stayed hanging around his neck forever when he pushed me off" (*PW*, 61).[45]

Adele's rejected womanhood is connected to the adulterous aspects of Birger's hunt or rather to the birds as the true objects of Birger's desire. After having confessed to Alma how she loves birds, Adele describes the terror of her marriage, unable to verbalize the most intimate details:

["...] But my husband didn't even love birds, no, you're wrong, he studied them, you don't understand how I felt when, at this very table, he first skinned a bird, a poor little bird, and then, shall I tell you..."

Alma knew what the parson's widow left unsaid: that the husband had wanted to and his wife had refused him. Alma's eyes turned toward the bedroom door and she felt sick – she didn't want to listen and yet she had believed and been horrified. (*PW*, 223)[46]

For Birger, the birds have been merely objects, something to be studied and categorized.[47] The science of taxidermy refers to Birger's talent as a preserver of life. His art relates to the preparing of dead animals for exhibition in a lifelike state (cf. Rojola 2014).[48] Reinforced by the presence of such erotic motifs as rowing, angling, and boating used elsewhere in the novel, the image of the birds refers not only to Adele's, but also to the unknown girl's position as a rower in Birger's boat. The paralyzed birds are a collective image of women: lost souls living trapped in female bodies.

The collection of birds, however, also serves as an image of collective madness, implicit in the novel's title: S/He was the one with the birds (*Hänen olivat linnut*). Birger has inherited the collection of birds from his Uncle Onni, who used to live at the manse: "[H]ere's where he died, and he was the one with the birds" (*PW*, 9).[49] Adele, who considers herself as an outsider in the family, feels she is closer to Uncle Onni than to any other of her husband's relatives. Birger's father is also mentioned: "Birger's father, this sheriff, whom I know you've heard all kinds of things about" (ibid.).[50] The chain of family members ends with Adele's son, Antti, who is mentioned for the first time in the context of the fire: "I've often wondered whether what people say is true – that some events can affect a child even before birth" (*PW*, 8).[51] The house of the county constable, the collection of birds, and the fire are all closely related to the representation of the past and manifested in Adele's wound, which she tries to resolve in talk. The trope of the madwoman employed in the novel is linked to Adele's "hysteria," but also to her future metamorphosis into a bird at the end of the novel.

The Gothic atmosphere evoked in certain scenes in *Hänen olivat linnut* alludes to the presence of the supernatural in the fictional world, even to the unnatural quality of Adele's sensitive mind. The haunted past is embodied in the spirits of the house, Adele's "guests" ("vieraat") which keep her – and the maid – awake at night. According to Adele, the spirit of the house takes hold of every person living under the manse roof. Alma is not sure whether to believe the talk of her Missus. She considers it dangerous to talk about these things in public:

> "But you have heard them yourself. Onni appeared to you, didn't he? And you still won't believe."
> "I believe, all right, but anyway, one shouldn't talk. People wouldn't understand, and besides, I just don't talk about it to people, not even to my own family."
> "Have you heard them now? Have they been moving about?"
> "The last time I'm sure it was the cat. First I thought it was Paananen, when you said that's who it was, but frankly, the next morning I thought it was the cat. I can't believe every noise or I'll go mad." (*PW*, 47–48)[52]

Alma's notion of going "mad" refers to her attempts to keep her mind clear as she is forced to listen day after day to Adele's stories. According to Adele, the creeping steps belong to Paananen, the former owner of the house, who once tried to demand payment for his property. He and his wife had taken everything with them when they left, even the dahlia roots in the garden. He has now returned to make amends for his past misdeeds.

The creeping steps in the house can be understood as voices heard in Adele's mind, the mental echoes of her traumatic past. She can still hear Birger's mother coming down the stairs: "Sometimes at night I think I hear footsteps on the stairs and I think: Birger's mother. The day Birger brought me to this house, that woman came down the stairs, her steps ringing out from above, coming closer and closer. I stood waiting downstairs in the front hall, terrified, but she didn't say a thing" (*PW*, 49).[53] Birger's mother's ringing steps "coming closer and closer" resemble the scene of the bird outing, when the boat bearing Birger's sisters, who are sent by their mother to save her son, draws closer and closer. The disapproving silence still echoes in the empty house as Adele finds herself alone within its walls after all these years: "Could I have guessed I'd end up living in this house, all alone, and that they would all go away?" (Ibid.)[54] The disembodied voices heard in the manse allude to Adele's guilt and loneliness after she has driven people away, one after another. Even if the people are gone, she still feels like an intruder, a lonely spirit wandering in the empty rooms at night:

> I think [Birger's mother] may not have forgiven me even now, and it's as if I heard steps, as if she were descending the stairs, still looking at me. You don't understand, Alma. I'm innocent, but it's still as if I'd done something wrong, as if I were an intruder. Take a look at these rooms now. Are they meant for a person like me? There was an ornamental full-length mirror. I could see all of myself in it, and I thought: who is that person who is so afraid? I looked at my image and thought: who is it who is so afraid, and then I understood it was me. (*PW*, 49)[55]

The spirits "are moving" because the memories of the past still haunt Adele. The house becomes an image of the self that contains unknown spaces parallel to rooms that she believes were not meant for a person like her. The sense of inferiority persists, causing feelings of fear and anxiety aroused by past experiences of being abandoned and rejected. The ornamental mirror has shown "all of myself" ("itseni kokonaan"), but the image has triggered only a sense of self-estrangement: she does not feel at home in her home.

Alma's verbalized thoughts (conveyed in the short passages of narrated monologue) accompany the dialogue and generate a tension between the private and the public talk, representing the different versions of the textual actual world. The motif of the mirror alludes to the refractive errors of introspection: the mirror may reflect, but the image does not conform to reality. Listening to Adele talking, Alma does not know what to believe. Only a moment before, Adele had admitted that the house belonged to Herman, the husband of her sister-in-law Elsa: "[T]he widow's memory was playing tricks on her. Until now, she had talked about the house as her own" (*PW*, 49).[56] Adele's talking is accompanied by Alma's thinking as she keeps listening and simultaneously recalls "another story" about the same events, "the one that people had told her" (*PW*, 50).[57] Adele's private confessions are juxtaposed with speculations of public gossip that the servant, according to Adele, listens too eagerly.

Here and throughout the novel, *Hänen olivat linnut* provides contrasting versions of an event in the fictional world, mixing the factual with fantasy.

The contrast between the real and the virtual is emphasized in sections where the characters' minds are portrayed alternately from within and without, providing both spoken dialogues and passages of a character's inner speech. These narrative sequences typically provide access to delusive or preconscious processes of the characters' minds, shedding more light on the functions of character constellations in the novel. The other characters serve as mirrors of the self through which the (collective) traumas of the past are reflected. The triangles of intimacy are formed in Adele and Alma's relation to two male figures: Antti and Holger. As the following analyses will demonstrate, in these mirrorings the conventional ideas of masculinity and femininity are subverted. The final act in Vartio's oeuvre is revealingly played not between a man and a woman, but between two women. In this sense, the depiction of the symbiosis of Adele and Alma forms a synthesis of Vartio's analysis of human relations in general and bonding between women in particular. Only when Vartio's women are able to connect to other women in an authentic, intense manner, they are able to find an authentic contact to themselves (Kendzior 2001: 248).

Figures of the Divided Self. A Man-Woman and Two Women

In *Hänen olivat linnut*, the traumas of the past (re-lived at the present moment of the story time) are related not only to Adele and Alma's storytelling, but also to some incidents that remind them of the initial moment of their mental wounding. One of the key scenes in the interpretation of Adele and Alma's intermental interaction is provided in chapter 9 when Adele learns that Holger has asked her maid to go row for him. From the window, Adele observes Alma and Holger playing with the fish, feeding the county doctor's cat. These incidents trigger a cycle of irrational acts by Adele. She carries all the china and silver from the dining room cabinet to the kitchen and starts to wash them. All of a sudden, she feels extremely tired. She goes upstairs and listens to the voices coming from downstairs: "For three hours she lay without stirring. She knew that the house was *full of bad spirits*. Downstairs in the kitchen, Alma was moving about and the bad spirit in Alma was singing. She could hear it, a wicked humming that wanted to incite her to greater wickedness" (*PW*, 106).[58]

The trigger for Adele's hallucinatory state is revealed later when the piles of dishes make her burst into tears: she is exhausted, forced to do all the work by herself. Tired of Adele's martyrdom, Alma yanks the plate from her hand and sets to work. Adele feels disgusted when she looks at her robust, "animal" body and her mannish walk:

> But Alma started washing dishes. The parson's widow looked on, trembling from head to toe. She could see Alma's broad, fleshy back, wet armpits; she looked at Alma's open-necked summer dress and was disgusted by her disheveled, indecent appearance.
> "You're going too far, the widow said. "The least you could do would be to cover your arms, cover up your armpit hair."

But Alma went on washing the dishes and singing.

"So you were taking the bream nets out of the lake – I'd rather use another word to describe what you'd have wanted to be doing."

"When the devil gets into a person, human help has no power", said Alma, and continued singing.

"From this day on, you will not touch my things."

"Well if that's the way it is, I won't."

Alma left the dishes and went out. You could see her walking through the yard. Feet pounding the ground like sledgehammers, the widow thought as she watched that disgusting mannish walk. (*PW*, 107–108)[59]

Erotic undertones related to rowing and the outdoor scene are evoked by Adele's words as she watches Alma's "indecent appearance." In her usual way, Adele speaks "in parables." Rowing is compared to sexual acts: "So you were taking the bream nets out of the lake – I'd rather use another word to describe what you'd have wanted to be doing." Adele's words about the plate reflect her feelings of jealousy and her desire to possess things. Being unable to connect with people, Adele has replaced them with objects: "From this day on, you will not touch my things." In a parallel manner, Adele is jealous of Holger and Alma. She feels left out, as she is unable to rival for Holger's attention as a woman. Adele's observation of Alma's fleshy body contrasts with her words about her own withered body in the story of Birger's rejection: "I tried to wrap my arms around his neck, no, not these [...] not these, Alma, these arms are withered. Not these... I was young then and my arms were white and soft" (*PW*, 61).[60]

In Adele's soliloquy that follows, inanimate objects start to represent human beings, in a way similar to the correspondences she sees between people and birds. Adele makes a confession to her china plate: "It isn't you I hate [...] I hate people who want to take all beautiful things away from me. I love objects." (*PW*, 109)[61] Adele's fear of losing material objects is attached to her loss of human affection, touched upon in her soliloquy:

"They have all forsaken me," she said to the plate. "Holger made a point of not taking you because he knows why I'd like to give you to Teodolinda. They've all decided together that none of them will take you so you can torment me for the rest of my life [...]. They're just waiting for me to break you so they can say: now she broke a plate from our grandmother's china service. They remember what I said: 'Take it away so it doesn't break while I have it in my possession.'" (*PW*, 108)[62]

Adele's monologue refers to the incident when she dropped the baptismal font in the ruins of the parsonage. The plate and the other objects manifest Adele's fixation and fetish for things instead of people as the result of past traumatic events. Adele's own hostile thoughts are projected onto the thoughts of other people as she continues to speculate on why Holger has refused to give the plate to its "rightful" owner, his wife Teodolinda. Adele "pretends" to hear "voices" (*PW*, 108)[63] as she imagines Holger and his wife speaking about the plate. Their conversation is presented as a hypothetical dialogue heard in Adele's inner ear: "'Adele offered me that plate again.' 'You didn't take it, did you?' 'Me, I would have been out of my mind to take the plate she offered in a fit of anger'" (ibid.).[64]

In *Hänen olivat linnut*, the hypothetical speech is among those methods, which Vartio uses to portray the hallucinatory "voices" echoing in Adele's head. The meanings implied in the above hypothetical exchange relate to an actual conversation between Adele and Holger. After Adele's death, Alma recalls the drunken talk of the two, keeping watch over them so that no one can witness their madness. Both Adele and Holger cry over their loveless lives:

> But these matters were secret, none but the three of them knew. The pharmacist who, lying on the floor, drunk, weeping over his wife who didn't love him and whom he had never loved. The parson's widow who hadn't loved anyone, only her birds, the widow weeping over being unable to love anyone individually and that she wasn't the kind of person the pharmacist could love. [...] "Do you forgive me for not proposing to you back then? Do you? You see, I could tell right away that you were out of your mind, and I let Birger have you." "But Birger was mad," cried the parson's widow, and then she laughed as though she would burst. "Yes, yes, he was." "And that's why I didn't love him. I knew he was mad, knew it right from the start, from the day he proposed to me and shot at his sisters when we were out on the rocky islet." (*PW*, 241)[65]

In relation to the alternative path of Adele's and Holger's lives – the possibility that Adele and Holger could have become a married couple – Adele's words to the plate become more meaningful. First of all, the plate embodies Holger, who rightfully "belongs" to his wife, Teodolinda. Second, the baptismal font and the plate (with a female and a male figure) represent Adele herself and Birger, who is said to be "broken" by Adele's madness. Birger's family still blames Adele for driving her husband insane: "He preached, he was gifted, exemplary, say the sisters-in-law. What was it that changed him, they ask, and they look at me" (*PW*, 70), Adele tells her maid.[66] Adele's hallucinations of haunted spirits in the house, on the other hand, maintain the opposite. It is Birger who has passed his madness on to his wife.

The grandmother's china signifies the members of the family who have been separated by the distribution of the inheritance. Their desire to possess things alienates them from one another. As embodied images of human beings, material things begin to represent the complicated human relations reflected in the changing ownership of objects. One of the items most argued about is a painting of a warship sinking in a stormy sea. The storm-tossed boat is a typical icon of the romantic painting, symbolizing a man's struggle against fate or nature and his need for salvation (Eitner 1955: 287). The painting had been promised to Teodolinda before her father's death. Teodolinda has no intention of taking the painting as long as it is hanging on Adele's wall. Her sister Elsa, however, carries it to her parlor. As a small girl, Teodolinda had asked her father: "Will all the people drown?" (*PW*, 157)[67] Her question about the sinking ship refers to the future of the manse and the entire family, which is about to end in ruin.

A parallel picture is Adele's painting "Jacob's Dream" made by Birger in his own image. Looking at Birger's self-portrait, Adele can remember his words: "[Jacob] had a great dream and in order to make it come true he used all the tricks he could. He wanted to be somebody and he cheated his relatives. [...] He's a child of God in all his weakness" (*PW*, 28–29).[68] Thus, even if Adele perceives "Jacob's Dream" as the late vicar's self-image, it also represents Adele's self-portrait and the tricks she herself is ready to use to make her dream come true (cf. Alhoniemi 1973: 169).[69] Adele's role is that of a clever Fool, or a trickster, who uses deceit as defense, to survive the challenges of the cold world.[70] The tension between the spiritual and the material, however, is reflected in Adele's obsession with objects. Adele's emotional void stems from the knowledge of the transitory value of her possessions: "[M]oth and dust will corrupt" (*PW*, 145),[71] Adele hears a trumpet blaring in her dream and wakes up in a cold sweat.

Alma becomes Adele's trustee in her attempts to keep all the property away from her husband's relatives. For Alma, the obligation to maintain Adele's possessions is a pleasant task; the farmer's daughter has been forced to leave her own inheritance behind. To amuse herself, Adele plays a twisted game at the expense of her relatives. She gives the family's silver spoons to Alma, puts all the spoons from different sets on the table, and chuckles to herself while guessing what is happening in Elsa's mind while they are drinking tea. "Did you notice? Elsa tried to count the spoons, one, two, three. I saw how she tried to count, and whenever I knew she'd got to three, I said, 'Have some cake, Elsa'" (*PW*, 201), Adele laughs afterwards, giggling like a child playing a funny game.[72] Elsa, however, can read the minds of others to the same degree: "You can't really *imagine* that I *believe* you *don't know*" (*PW*, 84), she says to Alma while questioning what has happened to her mother's silver.[73] Alma acts simple-minded and, piece-by-piece, collects the silver and puts it into her travel bag. Her traveling case is like the "Pantheon," filled with "wedding presents" ("häälahja") from Adele (*PW*, 204). Whereas Adele is a trickster-like figure, Alma resembles *para*, an attendant spirit of a witch, who helps its master to gain material goods. Sometimes *para* is conceived as being a soul of a shaman, appearing as an animal-shaped figure, often as a bird.

The trickster figure is traditionally portrayed as an ambivalent being who has an access to the realm of the sacred. Trickster is simultaneously a villain and a saint, a child and a wise being, a human and an animal, a man and a woman, a poison and a remedy. Adele's role as a trickster, mage, or shaman is emphasized in the scenes, which point at the potential "unnaturalness" of her mental capacities (cf. Mäkelä & Tammi 2007: 236). Adele seems to stare directly into other people's minds, knowing the most secret of their thoughts. Whether or not Adele's mind-reading abilities are seen unnatural (i.e. physically or logically impossible) depends on the strategy adopted while reading certain scenes (cf. Alber 2009: 79–80). For instance, many situations, in which strange incidents occur, can be read as Adele's internal states or reflections of Alma's feelings of fear. Alma is scared, for she *feels* Adele is able to know her every thought:

> Mad, mad, get out of this room. Alma was speaking in her thoughts – it came on like a disease – she would have wanted to beat, tear, smash something to pieces.

She was overcome by pity for herself, to have been put here, to have to live with someone who, with fiery eyes, came on as if to suppress her. [...] And now she was standing before her, her face radiating that disgusting smile that *seemed to know everything.* (*PW*, 220)[74]

The intersubjectivities of control and lunacy are connected to the power relations between Adele and Alma. These instabilities are reinforced by the class distinction between the maid, Adele and her relatives. The submissive forms of mind-reading, however, are two-tailed. Alma has her own ways of exercising power. The stubborn servant refuses to resign herself to her lower position and silently fights back. Over the years, Alma learns to play the social game and protect her own interest in addition to Adele's. In Adele's giggling, we can often hear also Alma's laughter. The late vicar's sister reminds her of her own sister-in-law – the one who married her brother and thus stole Alma and her sister's inheritance.

Adele and Alma's struggling minds often seek chances for adaptation, truce, and loyalty. For them, the true sisterhood (which is only a distant ideal for such characters as Inkeri or Mrs. Pyy) is available, at least in theory. There seems to be an invisible string holding the two women together. The battles between Adele and Alma always settle down and stabilize into an odd symbiosis. Holger considers Alma as Adele's true life companion: "Don't you understand that I admire you, it amuses me that you're the best man Adele has ever had" (*PW*, 176), he says to Alma.[75] According to Holger, Alma is "of good stock" (*PW*, 169).[76] She is "a man-woman" ("miesnainen"), tough like a bear, determined to be an old maid in order to be able to boss Adele around. According to Holger, Alma will live strong and clear-headed, unlike himself and Adele, who are determined to grow old too soon: "Where did you come from? Here, among us weak and miserable mortals?" (ibid.)[77]

Alma's portrayal as a man-woman introduces the archetype of androgyny related also to the trickster figure, suggesting variability in form, gender, and practices of sexuality. The archetype of androgyny is frequently employed in the narratives of female development, in which a woman protagonist may transgress traditional female roles and "pursues diverse outlets for her energy" (Freeman 1988: 56). The androgyny suggests a utopia of an ideal spirit in which the female and the male aspects of the human mind are fused into one, thus suggesting balance between sexes and the new found unity with nature.[78] The archetype signifies the perfection of the self as the masculine and feminine opposites (existing within every human being) are successfully united to achieve the primal state of wholeness: a person is able to come to peace with her/his masculine/feminine side and merge all aspects of the human existence. (Ibid.: 49, 53) The figure of androgyny refers also to Platonian ideal of romantic love or a mystical reunion of lovers.[79] In Plato's *Symposium*, Aristophanes depicts the symbol of a man-woman as a circle, in which the two sexes are united within. The split of the androgynous being into two (as the result of Zeus's anger) leads to the individuals' desire for total merging that is portrayed in literature either as a search for the missing other or as a symbiotic relationship in which "each person fulfills basic needs for the other" (ibid.: 54).

In *Hänen olivat linnut*, the archetype of androgyny is employed to portray the symbiotic relationship between Adele and Alma. These two women form a dualistic unit, balancing each other's extremes and instabilities (Kendzior 2001: 248). Both Adele and Alma reflect their troubled femininity in Holger. The curious threesome made up of Holger and the "vestal virgins" ("Vestan neitsyet") – as Holger calls the two women – constitutes a triangle of "mimetic desire" involving projection and imitation of affection for the other.[80] The affective imitation manifests itself, first of all, in Adele's relation to Holger. As the discussion between them shows, Adele does not truly love Holger. She is not able to love anyone "individually" ("erikseen") as she claims. The social mimetism established in the relationship among the three parallels a children's game in which two players want to play with the same toy. The imitation of desire leads to rivalry, jealousy, and conflict as the object of affection appears more alluring, precisely because it is the object of someone else's desire.

Secondly, the affective imitation is manifested in the relations of Holger and Alma. Even though Holger thinks Adele is the only person who can truly understand him – like his is the "only one who completely understands Adele" (*PW*, 242)[81] – the true object of his and (potentially Adele's) sexual desire is Alma. Holger's relation to Adele is defined by their mutual recognition, but the servant has "the flesh of a real woman" ("oikea[n] naisen lihaa"). "[W]hat tenderloin!" (*PW*, 241), he ridicules Alma's masculine-like femininity.[82] Alma, on the other hand, finds in Holger a man she never had. Perhaps she even projects in him the young farmer she was not allowed to marry once because of her family's disapproval. Marriage, on the other hand, would have been a self-sacrifice for a woman like her. She talks about her sister: "The husband had made her that way, she'd learned to submit to her husband's will" (*PW*, 212).[83] In Adele's house, Alma is able to maintain her freedom. As Adele repeatedly tells Alma, her maid's chief problem is the desire "to be in charge" (*PW*, 124).[84] Even if Alma's family name, Luostarinen, refers to sexual abstention (*luostari* in Finnish means "convent"), Alma is often described as being unable to resist a man's touch. When Holger approaches her intimately, she cannot fight back: "[B]ut right then, hands, *a man's hands, no longer the pharmacist's but a man's,* pushed their way through the neck of her dress and down [...]. As if unconscious, Alma sank to a sitting position when the hands pressed her further, the man kneeling on top of her knees" (*PW*, 181).[85]

Alma's ambivalent role in relation to Holger and Adele is linked to her first name, which alludes to *alma mater*, the archetype of Mother, who gently guides her children. This correspondence seems, at first, rather distant as Alma is depicted as being a mannish, childless, and waspish creature – in this respect similar to her Missus, whose name refers to a gadfly, *broms* in Swedish (Kendzior 2001: 244–245). Holger claims that there is "enough man" (*PW*, 135)[86] in him for two women, but more often he is depicted as "a poor dear child" (*PW*, 239).[87] Alma and Adele look after the crying man after he has attempted suicide in the cellar, where Teodolinda has locked him up, staring at him "like death, like a ghost" (*PW*, 127).[88] Alma's role as the nurturer of her rare children is emphasized in the image of a stuffed owl that is the only bird that Alma has grown fond of. The poor creature resembles her Missus: "[I]ts head was round, it was alive *like a child*, the size of a small child when she took it in her arms" (*PW*, 200).[89]

Holger, on the other hand, serves as one of Adele's self-mirrors, reflecting the self-destructive aspects of her personality. Holger laughs at Alma's attempts to guide these two sinners as he shares his bottles of "medicine" and his bawdy stories with Adele. Like her, Holger considers himself as being a child of God, innocent and hurt: "I'm the only one who can make dear Adele laugh. We are amazing when we're together. God can see, and looks on approvingly. You see, we're God's children" (*PW*, 242).[90] During Adele's lifetime Alma observes this "indecency" with horror. However, after Adele's death Alma learns to drink up the glass Holger hands her: "Now it was to her, just as it had been to the widow in the old days" (*PW*, 240).[91]

Alma's relation to Adele is determined by another triangle of desire: Alma's relationship to the widow's son, Antti. The name of the three characters each starts with the letter A, which alludes to the function of these figures as reflections of each other's personalities. In chapter 10, Alma and the boy meet in the shed where the fish nets are stored. Adele's presence as the third party in the "love scene" is evoked by Alma's associations of Antti's eyes with her mother's devilish eyes: "[T]he boy's eyes, the parson's widow, the parson's widow's eyes, were glinting from the other side of the tub in the dusky shed" (*PW*, 114).[92] Alma tries to adopt the conventional role of a girl, but is unable to play that part. The episode which at first appears as a rape (Alma being the victim), eventually turns into harsh and loveless sexual intercourse as Alma becomes the instructor of the boy:

> When the boy was there, Alma felt that she had always been some kind of victim, and that's the way it had to be. The other one did what he did because he was a man and knew what he was doing and what he wanted to do, and it was his fault. Alma had been a girl, she'd set out to be a girl, or maybe she was like a young cow that turns its head away, eyes rolling. But here was a boy, and now Alma woke as if emerging from a memory. She became conscious; she snarled and took hold of the boy, who was trying to break loose. [...]
>
> And Alma saw herself standing there next to both of them, standing, but it wasn't her alone; it was in one instant a man, a man and a woman at the same time, on edge, and the boy, a whomp of a ruttish bull-calf but not yet a bull, a puppy dog that was giving it a try, looking after its own thing. And unsatisfied, furious, Alma rose from the nets. (*PW*, 112–113)[93]

Alma's mind hovers between a conscious sense of herself "here and now" and her inarticulate, distant acknowledgment of some previous experience that reminds her of how she is supposed to act. The urges of the primitive body seems to challenge the cultural, passive roles of acting like a woman. The actions performed by one's body are perceived from without, as if through the collective eyes of the community. During the scene, Alma is depicted as becoming fully conscious of the situation, realizing that she is the one who needs to take control if she wants satisfaction. The boy's inexperience is portrayed through the comical repetitions that "imitate" the clumsy, groping movements of the bodies (cf. Tammi 1992: 49): "[A]nd the boy, the parson's widow's son, a boy, nobody's son but a bull that was now *poking*, as in its sleep, *shoving, poking* at her belly, holding her by the feet, *jerking*, not knowing how to do anything in particular" (*PW*, 116).[94] While guiding the boy, Alma becomes conscious of herself as a divided being, as if she were a woman and a man simultaneously.

The split in Alma's mind is emphasized in the episodes that follow. After everything is over, Alma listens to the hissing sound of the boy next to her and feels a primitive rage. Her mind is divided into two: one side of her is aware of what has happened, while the other is not grasping. As Alma "recover[s] her voice" (*PW*, 116).[95] she seems to realize the possible consequences of her actions. She hits the boy, threatening to reveal everything to his mother. She hears footsteps behind the shed and is convinced that Adele is standing outside:

[A]nd suddenly, footsteps – footsteps coming from behind the shed. The parson's widow, she knew it right away, was standing still in the dusk outside, ahead of her the wide expanse of lake, fog, an island in the fog, the pharmacist's boat moored to the dock, nets drying, a bird and a bird call that seemed to come from far away but the bird was making sounds nearby, on the roof of the shed, in a tree, in a birch, in an aspen; she thought of trees and a birch and an aspen and knew it was the plaintive cry of the parson's widow sounding in the birdcall, a bird chirping alone and innocent, like the parson's widow. (*PW*, 116–117)[96]

The epistemological status of Alma's perceptions – and thereby, Adele's – is never fully established in the passage. Adele's hypothetical focalization (what she *might* have seen) is pictured through Alma's imagining mind, as Alma conceives Adele as an innocent victim of her revenge (cf. Mäkelä & Tammi 2007: 241). The reader is left wondering whether Adele really was there or whether the image of the widow seeing and listening is only a figment of Alma's imagination. The latter option is suggested in the scene itself. Only a few moments before, Alma had lied to the boy: "Your mother's coming" (*PW*, 116).[97]

As Alma listens to the bird's call, she drifts into an odd state of self-estrangement, as if hearing her inner voice in the bird's voice simultaneously heard as Adele's innocent, childlike voice. Adele and Antti are sitting "in the dark, both pondering who they were and what had happened to them" (*PW*, 117).[98] The existential tones of the unfolding description reflect Alma's feelings of loss and homelessness, as the external space becomes simultaneously Alma's mental space. The narrated memory of Alma's childhood reflects the sense of detachment she feels at the present moment. The feeling of loneliness falls on her like rain falling from the sky, as Alma again becomes a child who was lost in the world:

"Where will I go?" Alma asked. "Where will I go?" she repeated to herself. "Where?" And all at once, feelings of being homeless, an orphan, poured into her mind like rain, stifling all sounds, clouding her eyes, and she remembered a day from her childhood: she was coming in from the drying barn, brown ferns at the edge of the forest, rain, rain, she got up on a rock and looked around her and she felt that she didn't know where she came from, who she was, as if there were no father, no mother, no one in the whole world. The world was fog, dusk, the gray of houses, autumn, the gray of rocks, gray of the drying barn, silence, no one, no knowledge of anyone, no one, nothing, lost, all alone in the world. The boy stirred. Alma heard the boy's voice and saw him go to the door, undo the latch, go out, away, along the shore, his footsteps crackling on twigs. (*PW*, 117)[99]

In Alma's peak emotional moment (resembling Mrs. Pyy's epiphany under the apple tree), the experienced space serves as the bridge between the present and the past, bringing back painful memories of not knowing who the "I" is. The fluctuations of Alma's anxious mind are generated by the use of elliptical, repetitive expressions: "'Where will I go?' Alma asked. 'Where will I go?'" The same pattern is employed in the short passage of interior monologue at the end of the paragraph: "[Alma] heard the rustle of the nets, faint rustling from the roof, and thought: the pharmacist's boat, and then, where will I go, where?" (Ibid.)[100]

Vartio uses temporal orchestration of counterfactual versions of events to portray Alma's private world as her mind is wandering spontaneously from the present to the past and back again. Her half-conscious mind contains black spots that she tries to restore by remembering what has happened in the shed. Alma's memory analyzed above, the analeptic embedding, constitutes the second flashback in the chapter. The first follows right after the depiction of the split in the self when Alma sees herself both as a woman and a man. Alma pictures herself and the boy carrying a tub into the shed where everything happens. This incident is followed by a third flashback as Alma recalls events going further back in time. She cannot remember – or does not want to remember – the details of Antti's arrival on the shore and his first attempts to approach her. The temporal structure makes it challenging for the reader to figure out what has truly happened. Was it Alma who made the first move?

> The wash she had come to rinse, had been sitting on the step in front of the shed; it had started raining softly, then harder. [...] and all of a sudden the wind rose and the boy was at the door of the shed. Alma had no idea when the rain had stopped. The boy had grabbed hold of her; *that's how it must have been*, she thought, without saying a word, and how long it must have gone on! The rain had ended, they had carried the tub inside, the soaking-wet wash in from the rain. *And then she had wanted the boy to be a man.* Now the boy was going away. (*PW*, 117–118)[101]

The epistemological uncertainty of the events is linked to the challenges of keeping track of the fluctuations of Alma's mind involving conscious, preconscious, and unconscious content. The flashbacks as well as the repetitive quality of the events generate a scene lacking explicit temporal borders between different narrative sequences. The temporal break between the present and the past create semantic ambivalence: what happens in the shed and who took the initiative? At times Alma seems to approach the boy herself, and at times to fight back, as if there were two selves within her. These two selves seem to perceive the events from different perspectives. Her conscious mind is willing to adopt the role of a passive victim, conventionally prescribed for women: "The boy had grabbed hold of her; that's how it must have been." The uncertainty concerning the actual events, however, is never resolved.

The ambivalence of the scene is reinforced by the later depiction of Antti's mockery, potentially echoing only in Alma's inner ear: "She heard the boy's mocking voice coming from the other rooms, saying, first you do it yourself and then you turn all virtuous" (*PW*, 121).[102] The temporal structure is modified in Alma's memories of "the last winter" ("viime talvena") when everything began (*PW*, 118). Antti keeps coming to her room and Alma lets him sleep in the same bed, "just like when he'd been a little boy" (*PW*, 119).[103] Antti's visits give Alma nightmares. She is afraid that Adele will find out, hear her talking in her sleep. And suddenly, in Alma's narrated memory, the narrated time reaches the moment of the scene that takes place in the shed: "But one morning, when Alma was still in her nightclothes, Antti came to the door of her room, and *just as he'd done in the shed*, he wrapped himself tightly to Alma's body" (ibid.).[104] Nothing before this has suggested that a shift was taking place from the time frame of "the last winter" to the present moment.

Alma and Adele's encounter after these scenes emphasize the instrumental role of Antti in the intermental relationship between the two women. Antti serves as Alma's tool for revenge as well as a potential source for pleasure. However, Alma ends up feeling unsatisfied, like Adele in her marriage. The episode also reveals Alma's sense of feminine superiority over her Missus. Tired of Antti's constant visits, Alma decides to leave. When Alma is packing her traveling case, Adele enters the room. Alma feels her gaze on her half-naked body. Suddenly she understands why Adele is covering her withered body. It is a woman's shame:

> And now Alma knew that it wasn't only pious modesty but woman's shame, and just a moment ago the parson's widow, eyes focused, had carefully examined her arms, her half-bare breasts, as she sat on the edge of her bed, her neck, her hair, which, black with sweat, was hanging down her back. With her back to the widow, Alma arranged her hair, tied it up quickly, and still with her back to the parson's widow, as a feeling of superiority began filling her limbs, she now turned toward the widow; with her hair in a bun, she regarded the thin, flat-chested figure, who half leaning against the wall with her feet crossed, was examining her with those black, squinting eyes, the boy's eyes, and the smile, the boy's smile, made Alma say, as if someone else had spoken through her mouth, used her tongue, three words that first came clear from her mouth: "I won't stay." And then: "I won't stay among devils." (*PW*, 122–123)[105]

The words coming from Alma's mouth as if from the mouth of someone else emphasize the split quality of Alma's mind. Adele's ability to "see," to understand what Alma sees while seeing her looking, is manifested in Adele's talk. She understands Alma's unconscious motives concerning Antti better than Alma herself: "Don't talk about devils, because you don't know they're speaking through your own mouth. You're not free of temptations" (*PW*, 123).[106] Adele's words are intended to hurt Alma just as Alma has hurt Adele's feminine pride – by referring to her rejected womanhood: "If you'd only get married, but no one will have you, isn't that right?" (ibid.), she says to Alma.[107] Later, Adele tries to amend her harsh words: "You could get married, but maybe you don't want to. You want to be in charge, and that's your fate" (*PW*, 124).[108]

Adele's prayer right after the scene proves that she can truly "see," including seeing her own motives: "I understand everything now, and that's why I hurt her. I could tell what she was thinking as she was looking at me, putting up her hair and that's why I hurt her. Forgive me, God" (*PW*, 123–124).[109] As Alma looks at Adele, who is strangely calm and silent, she suddenly feels unable to say those words she has planned to say: "Alma couldn't get out what she'd first intended to say, that it wasn't her fault. The widow's eyes were staring, and Alma knew there was no point trying to explain" (*PW*, 124).[110] Alma hears Adele's voice, which is humane, as if it is the voice of someone with whom she can truly empathize: "'I do understand, Alma,' that voice said. Alma wanted to hate this voice, the parson's widow. But what was there to hate about her?" (*PW*, 125)[111] The voice asks her to stay. Antti will be sent off to school, and there will be no one else in the house: "There'll be just the two of us here" (ibid.).[112]

With Adele and Alma's duo, another carnevalistic duo, Don Quixote and his squire Sancho Panza, are reincarnated as females. Alma serves as an earthly voice of reason balancing the gap between the "real" world and the delusions of her master, even if the master seems occasionally to "see" more than her servant. Alma's role as "Adele's best man" is related to Vartio's aforementioned essay "Don Quixote," in which Vartio depicts Sancho as Cervantes' body and mind, and Don Quixote as his spirit. Alma is the embodiment of a strong, healthy, and unaffected mind, sorely needed when rushing into battle against figments created by the imagination. These ideas are reflected in Adele's plans to "move in with" Alma at the moment of death:

> "But the parson's widow should go off and rest first."
> "I don't want to... talk with me. Where do you think my spirit will be after I die? If I die before you, I'll move in with you. What do you say? I'll finally move out of this house. But what if Onni and Birger should follow?"
> "I don't know, but why did you go down to the shore last night when it's so stirred up there? They scream like the children of the damned, shouldn't listen, it gets one all worked up. (*PW*, 69)[113]

Adele's mind is haunted by the spirits of Onni and Birger, the men who passed their madness on to her. The collective madness is pictured as the screeching birds that are linked to the image of phoenix used in the novel. Phoenix is a solar bird, eternally arising from the ashes of its predecessor. This fiery bird serves as a symbol of regeneration and a cyclic reborn identity. The words about the "move out of this house" signify the earthly body as the house of Adele's tormented soul, her spirit. The house is the embodied self, which is left at the moment of death: "I'll move in with you," Adele cries out to her servant.

The themes of empathy and understanding are related to the idea of intimate talk and the desire to re-gain the lost wholeness of the self. The transformation of the soul is attached to the symbol of a bird, which serves a key image throughout Vartio's oeuvre. In one scene in *Hänen olivat linnut*, Adele is depicted chattering to a wagtail as if she is talking to her own image. As long as she keeps talking, she knows she is alive: "Look here, if you really are me. They say I am just like you. What if you happen to be me? Then: I am alive. I exist, I talk even though I'm you. And look: you are not dead, not so long as I am talking to you" (*PW*, 61).[114] The chatter here is addressed to the bird and thus, to Adele herself, but the passage suggests that a human being is alive only as long as she or he communicates with others and understands them. "[T]alk with me," she says to Alma. According to Adele, the wagtail will continue her life as long as someone is calling it by name. The bird serves not only her mirror image, but also her successor's: "[W]hen I'm dead, then you will be me even though I can't talk – but if another comes along to whom they say, 'Missus, you're a wagtail,' then you'll carry on my life" (ibid.).[115] Even though the birds are dead, they have become immortal in Adele's mind: "I will die, but the birds will live forever" (ibid.).[116]

In Adele's eyes, Alma in turn is a wood grouse who has been transformed into a woman. The mating sounds of a wood grouse relate to Vartio's depiction of herself as being "a wood grouse in mating season" ("kuin metso soitimella") while she was writing (Ruuska 2012: 313). In this respect, the immortality of the birds refers to the spirit of an artist: to the immortality gained through art in line of cultural heritage. Adele considers Alma the perfect image of a grouse, especially when she is angry: "Look here, I got you to be exactly what I wanted. When you get angry your hair shines so bright that it sparkles, and when you put that lyre comb into the bun at the back of your head [...] you're the spitting image of a wood-grouse cock" (*PW*, 63).[117] The divided, yet balanced quality of Alma's character is emphasized in Adele's conception of her as half human, half animal (like she is half woman, half man): "In your bottom half you're a woman, all right, but in your upper part [...] you're the very image of a wood-grouse cock" (ibid.).[118]

The frequent theme of female Bildung, the gaining of spiritual awakening only through madness and death, is modified in Vartio's novel. In Adele's mind, Alma is the one, who is able to give her the transcendental keys to break the circle of her passive suffering. The paralyzing effect of Adele is signified in her need to control people around her, to "bite" them with her malicious gossips and see them as reflections of the birds. In Adele's hands the birds turn into deadening, "magical" tools that she uses while depriving people of their souls and self-integrity. (Kendzior 2001: 244–245) On the other hand, Adele herself is one of the trapped birds in the collection of lost souls. The wood-grouse cock is related to another grandiose bird, which serves as a key image in the novel: the white swan. Alma had once told Adele about a bird that had been kept under a feathery asparagus plant in the corner of the parlor in their home. Adele becomes obsessed by the bird. She sees herself in the creature that has been abandoned in the attic.[119] The need for the transformation of the soul is manifested in the motif of metamorphosis as Adele first "transforms" into a fiery bird, phoenix, and then, into a swan – a beautiful, pure, and omnipotent creature representing God or creative divinity.[120] The world-creating power of fictional minds, similar to fictional mind-making, is illustrated by Adele's narrative imagining as she constructs alternative universes to resolve her trauma. In the following section, I approach the characters' cognitive strategies of narrativizing by analyzing Adele's story of the swan. Then, I focus on the narrative strategies employed in the characters' self-narratives.

Being in Fiction. The Story of the Swan

After hearing about the swan that was shot by Alma's brother, Adele wants the bird to be a part of her own collection. Intimidated by Adele's insistent demands for the swan, Alma is finally forced to write a letter conveying Adele's wishes to her brother, but she never receives an answer. Later, while visiting her home, Alma discovers that the bird no longer exists: it had become riddled with worms and was disposed of. Unable to tell Adele the truth, Alma declares that the bird never existed, that "she had made up the whole story" (*PW*, 34).[121] Yet when Alma witnesses Adele's desperation, she decides to tell another story. She reassures Adele that the bird "certainly does exist," but she "just do[es]n't know anything more about it" (*PW*, 35).[122] As Alma sinks deeper into her web of lies, she has difficulty tracing the exact source of her memories. Under Adele's warped control, the boundaries between reality and make-believe vanish. Alma has difficulties monitoring her representations: "Alma had felt like writing to her sister: 'Go and see whether [the swan is] in a corner of the parlor, or did I just dream it isn't there and the feathery asparagus neither.' Now that she had told about it, Alma herself sometimes believed the bird was still there" (*PW*, 33).[123]

The story of the swan culminates with Adele waking up in the middle of her dream, her mind on the threshold between wakefulness and dreaming. Out of the darkness, powerful mental images arise: "She stared into the dark and there was an image she now realized she had gazed upon in her dream, in which Alma's brother, as if he were stubbornly rebelling against time, stared back at her with the shadow of the asparagus plant against his face" (*PW*, 159).[124] She can hear the echo of the bird's call, even though it is difficult to trace the initial source of the sound: "And at that very moment the bird call was within her, the one she had heard in the dream, or else she had had a dream about something that had brought out that sound" (ibid.).[125] Adele's dream (or her memory of the dream) continues as a tableau with Alma's brother in a visit to Alma's home. The sounds heard in the dream are the words she uttered to Alma's brother as she keeps asking him to imitate the swan's call: "'What kind of sound was it? Tell me.' 'Kung kung kung kung'" (ibid.).[126] The ending of the dream, however, is never defined, which makes it challenging to decide where the dream actually ends and reality begins. Are we following a virtual, hypothetical dialogue imagined by Adele or are we following her dream or her memories of the events that have taken place in the textual actual world?

Adele's obsession with the swan is manifested in her adamant desire to see Alma acting out how a wood grouse carries on in mating season.

Alma once mimicked her brother's performance, and Adele keeps insisting that she repeat the performance, even if she claims that it must be "only a reflection, a mere suggestion" ("vain heijastusta, vain kuvajaista") of the authentic performance given by her brother. "I've never enjoyed a single theater performance as much as that one" (*PW*, 62), she adds.[127] One of the most ambiguous instances in the novel, one that reveals the dubious nature of Adele's memories, is the very performance that Alma's brother is said to have presented during the visit. Alma's brother has imitated the mating sounds of a wood grouse with such skill and talent that the performance persuades Adele to give her own interpretation of the swan's call. She is still ashamed of herself for having tried to act like a swan right in front of Alma's brother, "the perfect artist":

> She saw herself trying to act out a swan, a swan she had never had a really good look at and then only once, swans high above the house, not making a sound on their way south. Why then, did I pretend, why did I try to act out something I had never seen myself? [...] And she repented: hadn't she sensed the embarrassment and shame on Alma's brother's face as she stubbornly kept repeating to him: "Tell me, show me how." (*PW*, 159)[128]

One of the crucial factors that has an effect on the reader's ability to differentiate real events from imagined ones is the way in which the elements of the swan's tale are distributed in the story. Even if certain temporal sequences assist the reader in grasping the actual course of events to some degree, certain relevant information is missing. There are gaps in the chronology. The events leading to Adele's hypothetical visit are portrayed at the beginning of the chronology in chapter 3, where Adele expresses her desire to buy the bird, or alternatively, to visit Alma's home and see the swan with her own eyes. Alma, however, is reluctant to grant the widow her wish. The bird does not exist: "Alma could just see how the widow – if Alma were to take her to visit her family – would, barely after introductions, start asking about the bird. Of course, right at the parlor door she would look into that corner. And there would be no asparagus plant and no bird" (*PW*, 33).[129]

The representation of Alma's mind from within reveals that there is no solid proof that the visit has actually taken place, at least in the way Adele depicts it (cf. Tammi 1992: 60). Adele's words, however, give the impression that she has witnessed Alma's brother's performance and has actually visited Alma's home. In chapter 17, for instance, Adele recalls the beautiful village road along which she and Adele walked from the pier toward Alma's home. The true ontological status of events is never explicated. Indeed, the parallelisms between the textual actual world and the different versions of virtual "realities" make it difficult to separate fact from fantasy. The process of the subtle move from reality to Adele's fantastic private worlds is manifested in her reflections on the actual events related to the shooting of the swan. She considers how the events might have developed. The virtual, hypothetical state of affairs is distinguished from the facts of the reference world by using indicators of conditionality, such as "maybe" and "if":

> Why had [Alma's brother] taken [the swan] to be preserved? [...] Maybe the one
> who shot the swan had decided to have it stuffed only after he realized that he
> didn't know how to deal with the strange white body, didn't know how to get rid
> of it. Even the dogs avoided it, considered it unfit to eat. Maybe the women of
> the house... Alma's mother, if she had been told, maybe the mother had become
> agitated, been restless after hearing the bird's call in the night, had become
> terrified, maybe the mother had been shown the dead bird, it had been carried
> to her sick-bed in the dim room, a boy carrying a large bird in his arms, dragging
> the big bird by the feet. (*PW*, 162)[130]

Washed by her imagination, the "ifs" and "maybes" in Adele's (inner) dialogue
disappear. The sound of the swan's call echoing in her ears establishes the
rhythm of her fantasies. Adele repeats her failed performance by imitating
the movements of the bird's wings with her hands: "'Kung kung kung.' The
parson's widow had set her arms down along her sides. Wings dragging on
the ground, maybe the neck, she stretched out her neck..." (*PW*, 162)[131] The
conditional speculations gradually turn into mental images and then into
a fantastic tale that Adele spins out of events that actually happened:

> [...] she saw Alma's brother wandering around the darkening yard with the dead
> bird in his arms, looking for a place to bury it, maybe with the cry of the mate
> of the dead bird circling around overhead in the sky, and the slayer – she said it
> aloud: *slayer* – had decided right then what to do with the white body which you
> couldn't bury because there was no place on earth for a bird that belonged in the
> heavens. The parson's widow said it aloud, she was making up a story of a swan
> which, shot down from the sky, had come across her path and into her life by
> such a strange route [...]. (*PW*, 162)[132]

Enchanted by the details of the swan's journey, Adele makes up a story
about the birds' killer by embellishing the facts she knows about the real-
life incident. In her mind's eye, she can see the fowler (Alma's brother
transformed into a mythical hero) regretting his bloody deed, carrying the
body of the swan on his shoulders "like a cross" ("kuin ristiä") or "a white
coffin" ("valkea ruumisarkku") as he boards the ship and travels to the
taxidermist to get the bird preserved (*PW*, 163). According to Adele, the
man has sinned, but God in heaven may reward him with the swan's soul at
the time of his death. The man is a Christ-like figure, who resembles Adele's
husband. Revealingly, these two male figures seem to merge in Adele's mind,
as if the swan itself was related to Adele's trauma, namely, her troubled
sexuality. Like Birger, Alma's brother is a master shot, but simultaneously
a "perfect artist," who has the power to bring the swan's soul back to life
through his performance.

In Karelian mythology, the swan is a holy bird, and anyone who shoots
a swan will be punished by death. The figure of the fowler in Adele's
narrative draws from the Grail legends of Parsifal and the "swan knight,"
Lohengrin, as well as from the myth of Leda.[133] First and foremost, Alma's
brother resembles the figure of Lemminkäinen in the Finnish national
epic *The Kalevala*. Lemminkäinen is demanded to hunt and kill the swan

of Tuonela River in order to get the permission to marry the maiden of Pohjola. In *Hänen olivat linnut*, the slayer of the swan represent an ideal of an artist who is capable of concluding his spiritual journey and finish his aesthetic self-education in the world of art. In this respect, Adele's brother resembles also the poet Orpheus, who travels to the underworld to retrieve his wife, Eurydice. Adele's failed performance of the swan, on the other hand, refers to the tradition of the female spiritual Bildung. The plot of female spiritual awakening frequently constitutes a story of the potential artist who never manages to accomplish her aesthetic journey. Adele resembles Eurydice, who has no voice of her own and who is killed on the very day of her marriage. Marianne Hirsch (1983: 47) analyses Eurydice's muteness: "Orpheus alone has the medium through which he can both enter and return from the world of the dead, both gain insight and express what he has learned. Eurydice might inspire Orpheus's song [...] but she has no voice with which to assimilate and tell her own highly discontinuous story." In *The Kalevala*, however, gender roles are converted. The person to be saved from the underworld is Lemminkäinen himself. His mother rakes the pieces of his body out of Tuonela River and brings her son back to life.

In Adele's obsessive hunt for the swan, Christianity, Gnostic beliefs, and Platonian esotericism are merged in a strange mixture. According to Adele, "[i]t was God's will that your brother raised his hand, God's will that the swan was shot, for me, by the hand of Alma's brother, a message to my heart, to my collection" (*PW*, 166).[134] In Adele's conception of the swan, we may hear echoes of primitive fetishism in which the replacement of a human relationship with an object or a symbol derives from the primitive worship of inanimate objects (totems) believed to contain the essence of God. Alma's brother becomes a mystical figure, who has the swan's immortal soul. He is able to give back Adele passion for life she has once lost. As a symbol of eternal, pure love the swan represents the missing half of Adele's soul. In this respect, the trope of the swan alludes to the representation of mystical love in some symbolist and romantic poems. For instance, in Aarni Kouta's poem "Joutsen" (The Swan), published in the collection of poems *Tulijoutsen* (The Fiery Swan, 1905) the swan is swimming towards the other, waiting its companion to arrive, as pure and luminous. In the swans' union, the co-existence of the spiritual and the erotic is suggested. Heavenly bliss and earthly desire merge into one, resulting in the attainment of the ideal through the material. (Lyytikäinen 1997: 50–51)

Adele feels regret while counterfactualizing the past and thinking about the mis-timed convergence of her and the swan's paths: "[S]hot down from the sky, had come across her path and into her life by such a strange route, and which would now have been a part of her collection if she had known how to proceed the right way and in time" (*PW*, 162).[135] Taken in by her imagination, Adele starts to make up a story of a swan and visualizes the killer coming back relieved and eager to pay for the taxidermist's work, as if having redeemed himself. As a result of Adele's narrative imagining, a whole world of fantasy, a possible world in its material existence, is evoked:

The parson's widow saw Alma's brother go to the taxidermist to pick up the bird he had shot. She saw him stepping into – every room where the swan had ever been was dim in the widow's imagination, so that the bird's whiteness stood out all the more clearly – stepping into the steamy room, covered with snow, frost clinging to his beard, eyebrows frozen, saw his eyes looking to the back wall of the room where the birds were lined up on the shelf: owls, wood grouse, black grouse, some smaller birds among them, beaks all pointing in the same direction, and in the middle of the shelf, above all others, his bird, the large white one, looking as if it were alive, washed clean of blood stains, its neck lifted, straight, waiting for its mate which, out of sight, was eating succulent grass on the shore. (*PW*, 163–164)[136]

In Adele's mental image, the birds are lined up on the shelf with their beaks all pointing in the same direction. In this composition the swan – the grandest and noblest of birds – is placed above all the others. In the visual, dream-like image, the swan – the unattainable object of Adele's desire – appears like a dream itself, pure and white and brought back alive. In this picture, the swan turns into Adele's self-image. The composition resembles Adele's words to her husband: "Would you put me up on the highest spot, on top of the case?" The image also contains another reference to stuffed birds, the curlew on Adele's desk: "Long, pointed bill, the curlew tossed on the desk, its bill hanging over the edge as if it were taking a drink of water, the water of death. And you see, that's how it's been stuffed, in just that position, *as if its bill were trying to reach the water of death forever*" (*PW*, 61).[137] These birds seem to embody Adele's static position as a stuffed bird among other dead birds, as she seeks to escape from her trapped body through her imagination.

As Adele imagines the mind of the fowler and pictures him dreaming, fiction within fiction within fiction is generated: "[...] she could see [the taxidermist's] blackened fingertips, could sense the smell which haunted him even in a dream" (*PW*, 163).[138] The fictional embedding can be interpreted in the above manner as the translators of Vartio's text have done: the narrator narrates Adele imagining what the fowler sees and sensing the smell he senses. Within Adele's private world, we have a reference to the fowler's private world, which constitutes the third-level embedding within her second-level story. However, the gender-neutral Finnish personal pronoun *hän* (which can mean either a female or a male subject, either "she" or "he"), complicates the interpretation of the ontological levels presented above. The real identity of the person who sees, smells, and dreams is left unspecified. The dreamer might be the one who killed the swan, but the experiencer could equally well be Adele herself, sensing what the dreamer in the embedded dream senses ("[...] *she* could see [the taxidermist's] blackened fingertips, could sense the smell which haunted *her* even in a dream.")[139] This interpretation is reinforced by Adele's previous recollection of the smell that penetrated the walls when her husband prepared the birds.

Adele's tendency to reshape and distort details of the reference world affects the way the reader can rely on her version of the represented reality as well. Her imagination transforms the events of the textual actual world into components of virtual worlds that still bear some resemblance to the actual course of events. These fictions of the mind keep her awake as she roams through the rooms like a haunted spirit, re-living the past: "[T]he parson's widow tried to sleep, tried but still the images, that story, the swan's journey from the open water to the hands of taxidermist... should get some sleep, but she couldn't, she couldn't" (*PW*, 165).[140] By ordering and re-ordering the traumatic events of the past, Adele tries to construct the past world into a coherent whole. Lost in the mazes of her mind, Adele finally imagines becoming the very bird she is trying to bring back to life through the powers of her imagination:

> [T]he shame that this memory of the event brought to her was so painful that her body kept repeating those ridiculous bows as if she were punishing herself, arms flailing along her sides with the fingers now spread, now tightly pressed together, back and forth, repeating the movements she had made when she'd been acting out the bird she had never seen. (*PW*, 166–167)[141]

Adele keeps tormenting herself by weighing the possibilities of acting like the bird as she fears she has acted, even if Alma insists that she never performed such shameful moves and sounds. The fluctuations of Adele's mind are manifested in rambling thoughts, captured in their moment-by-moment flow. At first she pleads guilty, then she renounces her convictions: "And she, the parson's widow, a guest who had come to Alma's old home, in the middle of the parlor emitting from her mouth strange gurgling noises, lifting her head, spreading her arms, her fingers" (*PW*, 166)[142] and then, after a second: "But it wasn't true, of course" (*PW*, 167).[143] Sometimes it seems that the difference between a potential act and its execution never matters. Adele shivers, even over a pure thought of what she *might* have done: "[I]f indeed she had even made the attempt, she hadn't, Alma had sworn to that... *but just the fact that she could have*" (*PW*, 165).[144] In moments of desperation, Adele suspects that Alma is the one who is mixing everything up, purposely misleading her and causing her sleepless nights: "Like cattle you sleep you deep sleep, but I stay awake because of your lies, if only you had said to me straight that it was true, that – I'm prepared to confess my performance was below par" (*PW*, 168), she rages to Alma.[145]

Alma's desperation is also seen through her reflections on the present and the future. Her thoughts are depicted as constellations of mental speculations. She hypothesizes in detailed stages what *could* happen and how she *would* react if Adele's outburst were actualized. The following counterfactual scenarios probably exist only in Alma's mind, even though the incidents might resemble the real events of the storyworld:

> Alma had had to test the pulse rate so often that she knew, and she was no longer able to take pity on this woman whose every fit of madness she had had to see over these past years.
> And now she's over behind the sink, she'll talk from there and soon will be pacing around the room and then she'll either burst into tears or she'll just sit there staring ahead of her until Alma can't take it anymore, but in order to keep herself from hitting that creature, she goes out, heads down to the sauna cabin on the shore [...]. Perhaps she too cries: throws herself face down on the sauna benches and cries – for what will become her life when... where would she go, who would she turn to? (*PW*, 221)[146]

The conditional phrase "perhaps" and memories revealing the repetition of events ("so often that she knew," "every fit of madness she had to see over these past years") guide the reader to construe the passage as a hypothetical account of events. These events may have been realized in the past in different variations as they are counterfactualized here. In Alma's contemplation, distinct events turn into a continuous state of events, and the past blends with the present and future. Alma becomes a counterfactual observer, potentially witnessing alternative manifestations of Adele's desperation and rage taking place over and over again.

Whereas to Alma the past appears through her reflections on the present and the future, Adele conceives the past *as* the present. To her, the reflections of the repressed constitute the present, re-lived reality. The self-narratives embedded in *Hänen olivat linnut* are marked by variation, repetition, and redundancy, which are motivated by the wound burned into Adele's emotional unconscious. Adele repeats the painful experiences of the past with exaggerations. She revives these events "with the greatest ingenuity" in the present moment (cf. Freud 1961: 15). The pleasure related to the instinctive patterns of behavior results from repetitions that bring forth a sense of being in charge, being able to control reality. Adele stubbornly adheres to certain patterns, making sure that the experience remains always the same, repeating and requesting the same narratives. Her fixation resembles the delight of a child playing a familiar game – or hearing a familiar story.

The understanding between Alma and Adele often stems from the pleasures of gossip and mutual storytelling that bring in mental relief. Holger addresses their desire to talk: "The two of you here, you women, what do you do here, I'll tell you, you gossip from morning till night" (*PW*, 172).[147] Frustrated by his wife's silence, Holger willingly joins in: "My wife doesn't gossip, no she doesn't. Teodolinda has learned to keep her mouth shut, she's out for revenge, you see" (ibid.).[148] Like the skill of reading others' minds, talk is also *pharmakos* that, when adequately used, heals, but when misused may poison the mind. Holger describes the spells of gossip with the metaphor of a bottle of poison. He talks about his wife Teodolinda and the relatives who bottle up their bitterness: "[P]oison in every bottle but I am a free man, I go to the city, tell them to pull out the cork, see, I talk, I let it out, do you hear me talking" (*PW*, 177–178).[149] Holger warns Alma about the vicious cycles of gossip. In his view, Adele is the most poisonous of all, a real "bottle of poison" ("myrkkypullo") who will poison the maid's mind if she is not careful.

The negative connotations of gossip stem from the exercise of power by means of creating allies, which divides the world into the reality of "us" and the reality of "others" (cf. Hakulinen 1988: 154). Empathy with others arises from a moral superiority felt in regard to a third party. In *Hänen olivat linnut*, the gossip often involves relatives of both women, even though Holger's presence may make the women hold their tongues. The injustices experienced in relation to one's kin serve as the women's common ground, as they find someone else to blame for the misery of their lives. Adele and Alma's oral stories are marked by a tendency to reconstruct reality rather than reflect it "as it is," to mold it to serve their own purposes. The alternative versions of Alma's and Adele's lives are represented as constructs created by their subjective minds. The use of the temporal orchestration of alternate worlds generates multiple, simultaneously existing life paths that are generated in ritualistic storytelling. The mental activities of imagining, speculating, hypothesizing, and counterfactualizing create embedded private storyworlds that reflect the fictionality of the novel itself.

On the Paths of Ritualistic Storytelling

Adele and Alma's storytelling draws attention to the processes of self-formation, but simultaneously to the construction of self-narratives as *narratives*. In this respect, Vartio's novel seems to both testify and challenge the recent cognitive theories that emphasize the narrative form as a mental strategy used by the human mind to structure and make sense of reality. The tendency of Vartio's texts to challenge any theoretical categories employed to their analysis has previously been demonstrated in the readings of her novels in the context of classical narratology (Tammi 1992) and post-classical narrative theory (Mäkelä & Tammi 2007). The embedded structures of self-narratives, accordingly, question the idea of "naturalness" of the oral everyday storytelling constructed in *Hänen olivat linnut* (see Nykänen 2013a). The maze-like structures of self-narratives seem to make these structures appear highly estranging and metafictional. As Adele and Alma frequently end up arguing about the rules of storytelling *per se*, the idea of life as a linear, continuous story line (experienced as a narrative with a beginning, middle and end) is questioned several times. The reader encounters repetitious and non-linear narratives that are shaped into counterfactual and diverging paths of storytelling. These cyclic stories often seem unique, but are revealed to be performed or heard a number of times (Mäkelä & Tammi 2007: 238).

Vartio's narratives of everyday life may be approached from the perspective of the mode of narrativity that McHale (2001) has called "weak narrativity" (cf. Mäkelä & Tammi 2007: 239). It involves stories that are told "'poorly,' distractedly, with much irrelevance and indeterminacy, in such a way as to evoke narrative coherence while at the same time withholding commitment to it and undermining confidence in it; in short, having one's cake and eating it too" (McHale 2001: 162). Ryan's (1992) notion of "diluted narrativity," on the other hand, refers to stories in which the plot competes for attention with extended descriptions, digressions, meta-narrative comments, narratorial and authorial interventions, etc. In *Hänen olivat linnut*, the hypothetical realities represented in the alternative paths of everyday storytelling are often motivated by the characters *attempts* to narrativize their wounded, fragmentary minds. Simultaneously these narratives, however, underline the artifice of the fictional minds as they are shown to be products of Vartio's narrative trickery. The reading process is continuously interrupted by the comments on the process of narrative production as such, which stresses the metafictional quality of the characters' self-narratives (cf. Tammi 1992: 103, Mäkelä & Tammi 2007: 239).

In addition to Adele's stories of her past, the dialogues of the novel are actualized as Alma's self-narratives, which Adele asks her to tell over and over again. These stories involve the events of Alma's life path that are responses to Adele's intimate confessions. One of Alma's stories involves her arrival in the widow's service. Alma's narrative begins with words: "How would I have guessed it that morning when I left home for the harbor" (*PW*, 137).[150] Adele reacts to the beginning of the story ("So, how did it go again"[151]) and, by putting her knitting aside, encourages Alma to continue:

> "Well, how would I have guessed?" Alma sighed.
> "Why do you sigh? You used to say it was divine guidance."
> "I don't know. Or maybe it is. You know, I could have ended up just about anywhere." (*PW*, 137)[152]

Alma's narrative relates to events that are crucial for her further paths. The retrospective perspective on the younger self stems from the superior knowledge of the present self looking back to the young girl, a proud farmer's daughter, who leaves home in haste, having no idea what is in store for her. Alma's interpretation of the events is ambivalent. She does not know whether to feel regret or relief. Has everything truly been divine guidance or rather has it been the result of unlucky coincidences? In going back home, she is reluctant to reveal her actual position: "Could Alma admit she was working at a place where her job consisted of looking after stuffed birds? [...] never would she confess it to her relatives" (*PW*, 35).[153]

Alma's narratives are related to her need to map the alternative and actualized paths of her life and their causal relations. How did everything begin, what happened, why and how did it shape the course of later events? "And that's how it all started" (*PW*, 143),[154] Alma concludes while telling about her journey from Mikander's house to the pharmacist's and finally into Adele's service. Alma's narrative resembles the simulation of alternative and possible life paths typical of everyday thought and oral narratives. The need to narrativize counterfactual situations and speculate on their effect on one's life reflects the basic cognitive functions of the human mind (cf. Bruner 1987: 15, 28). These kinds of simulations evoke either relief or bitterness over life's lost chances. In *Hänen olivat linnut*, the human mind's tendency to produce hypothetical simulations is (tragicomically) exaggerated as Alma is constantly counterfactualizing her life choices: "I wonder where I'd be now if the parsonage hadn't burned down" (*PW*, 56),[155] Alma wonders; "Heavens knows where I'd be now if I'd left that time" (*PW*, 197).[156] Hypothesizing about Adele's potential fit of madness, Alma is depicted crying over her life: "I would like to go and be among people, but I'm a stranger here, a servant, no one cares about me, if I'd stayed home I might now be a farmer's wife – no, no – none of that, not even a thought, all thrust out of her mind" (*PW*, 221).[157]

The dialogic structure based on the characters' self-narratives draws on the reciprocal patterns of conversational storytelling. Oral stories embedded in everyday conversations typically invite other, corresponding stories in response. The life paths of Alma and Adele are linked by inverse parallelism.

They constitute reversed reflections. (Alhoniemi 1973: 171–172) Alma has lost her battle. She has left home, because she cannot stand seeing her sister-in-law as the matron of her home farm: "'Is this really my home?' […] 'Who's giving the orders around here?'" (*PW*, 42),[158] she is mentioned as having asked her sister and mother when the woman is approaching the house. Adele, however, has managed to get herself a huge chunk of her husband's inheritance. Adele is an intruder who parallels Alma's sister-in-law, a cuckoo stealing other's property, whereas Alma ends up being a servant in a strange house, feeling bitterness and loss.

In talking about the past, Alma is emotionally moved by her story: "The parson's widow could see it coming: now Alma would start to wipe under her nose with the side of her palm, always the palm of the left hand, and it happened that way again" (*PW*, 43).[159] The act of storytelling (involving the tragic-comic repetitions of emotional responses) evokes past experiences and brings them back to awareness to be re-lived. Adele also engages in Alma's life stories with strong emotions, projecting her own life path on the other woman's narratives. Adele considers Alma's experiences as resembling her own struggle with Birger's relatives, especially her sisters-in-law: "They're waiting for me to die, they'd like to get their hands on my things. Oh my, oh my, the story you told this morning was very familiar to me, as if I'd been you, Alma, and cried for the land that had been taken away from me…" (*PW*, 65)[160] While immersed in the story, Adele loses her ability to distinguish the actual contrast between her and Alma's paths. In her mind, Alma's sister-in-law is replaced by her own sister-in-law, Elsa, and Adele herself becomes an innocent victim threatened with the deprivation of all things dear to her: "Elsa was doing the same thing. When something's been taken away you can't get it back, though this story of Alma's isn't at all the same thing as what Elsa did to me" (*PW*, 217).[161]

According to Adele, Alma's story defines the speakers' shared values: "[O]h my, this story Alma is telling us here, has such a familiar ring to it. Alma did the right thing" (*PW*, 215).[162] She considers Alma's and her sister's attempts to save the property as a justified act. Things can be taken, even by force, if one has moral ownership of them: "Elsa took something that belongs to Teodolinda and me. Alma and her sister took what was theirs" (*PW*, 217).[163] While engaging emotionally in Alma's narratives, Adele justifies her ownership of the property that she has managed to keep for herself. Adele's tendency to use her servant's stories to serve her own purposes makes Alma even more bitter and angry. Alma's need for control is emphasized in her relations to the sister-in-law: "[B]ecause you and your mother [and your sister] had decided you'd rather tear everything into bits and pieces than *give up any power* to that woman," Adele repeats Alma's words, simultaneously projecting her own emotional motives (*PW*, 210–211).[164]

The issue of control over one's own life narrative is illustrated in Adele's reflections of Alma's experience. The possibilities for genuine, intimate conversation are continuously challenged by Adele's tendency to guide and dominate Alma's storytelling. Adele keeps interrupting, correcting, and giving orders to make the servant's story coincide with their earlier versions. As a result, Alma's genuine experience threatens to get lost in

Adele's corrections and digressions. Adele thinks that she "knows" Alma's experiences better than Alma herself, who is always arguing about the details: "If I say autumn, you'll say summer... I guess I should know better because I carried it on my own back" (*PW*, 206).[165] Alma is here describing how she and her sister carried the bed from the farm in order the save the property from her sister-in-law's hands. At times, Alma's first-person narrative turns into Adele's second-person narrative, which emphasizes Adele's role as the co-narrator of Alma's narrative. The co-narration begins as Alma's brother is being enchanted by a strange woman. He disappears for "nightly outings" ("yölliset retket") and fishing, takes the birds he has killed to another house to be prepared, to be "consumed by better mouths" ("syötiin parempiin suihin"):

> "[...] Tell the pharmacist just the way you've told me. It started with your brother standing in front of the mirror every day, combing his hair, and insisting that *you* get him a clean shirt. Go on."
> "That's right, he demanded a clean shirt."
> "And *you* said he had just now got a clean shirt, and then *your* brother got mad. And that's how *you* guessed."
> "Did I have the strength to wash and iron shirts every single day...?"
> "'Who's doing all the work around here,' *you* said, "the parson's widow went on in a voice that sounded as though she were beating time.
> "Yes, who did all the work if not me?" Alma said bitterly. [...]
> "*You* milked the cows, *you* did all the work."
> "Who was there but me? And I worked, I'd learned to work."
> "And *you* did it willingly because home was still home for *you* then. But go on."
> "She had come to do some sewing. The mistress of the neighboring farm was her aunt."
> "But there were already rumors going around the village. And you guessed.
> (*PW*, 206–207)[166]

Adele's second-person narration gives a familiar rhythm to the story as Adele makes sure that Alma remembers to mention all the necessary details. Typically, both Adele and Alma know each other's life stories so thoroughly that they can guess in advance what the other will say, and they add to each other's narratives, as in the following passage: "'It was lucky you had this house, so you had a place to go.' That's what the parson's widow would always say at this point, but this time Alma got it in ahead of her" (*PW*, 9).[167] The very predictability of the stories becomes the source of Adele's excitement, as well as the cause of the women's banal wrangling. Adele wants the narratives to follow the recognizable patterns of storytelling. Will Alma say exactly those words that the widow has taught her to say? Adele waits nervously for the peak moment in Alma's narrative as she tells about the meeting with the shopkeeper Mikander: "She didn't want Alma to leave out this part of the story: to her it was exactly this part that was so exciting. Would Alma say the sentences that belonged right here, just as she had learned to say them earlier, although it had taken quite a few reminders" (*PW*, 139).[168]

The second-person narration serves as means to defamiliarize the act of storytelling. It highlights the "unnaturalness" of Adele's ways of determining

Alma's self-narratives as her personal experience is lost on the course of coercive storytelling. The hypothetical quality of experiences rendered in the "you" narrative form is emphasized: only a third person narrator may know what is in the minds of others (cf. Richardson 2006: 6).[169] On the other hand, the choice of the "you" also functions as the sign of intimacy, as it typically appears in interrogations, accusations, and guidance typical of everyday speech (cf. Nykänen 2013a: 81–82). In the dialogues, the intimate sharing often turns into rivalry for narrative control. The ambivalence of the ritualistic conversation is manifested especially in those dialogues where the women are accompanied by Holger. The presence of an outside audience makes Adele impatient. She wants to rush to the highlights, while Alma keeps lingering over irrelevant things: "You said that already. Let me tell" (*PW*, 208),[170] she says as she takes command. The "truth" of the stories, on the other hand, is a secondary matter. When Holger wonders why you would carry a bed if you can get a horse, Adele replies: "But no. You see, if the bed had been carried off on a horse cart, we wouldn't have this story" (*PW*, 217).[171]

According to Adele, the oral stories need to be narrated well, giving justice to their beauty and order: "This story has been ruined. But let it be, I don't insist you begin at the beginning" (*PW*, 211),[172] she says to her maid. Adele's sensitivity to other minds makes her a marvelous narrator. Her ability to imagine other minds and alternative realities resembles the imaginative faculties of an author who is able to add to and complete the perceptible world and to construct virtual worlds (cf. Mäkelä & Tammi 2007: 245). The spell of the narratives stems from the listeners' (and the readers') ability to imagine the experience of the other as Adele points out to Holger: "Go ahead and ask Teodolinda *how she felt*" (*PW*, 214–215)[173] or "Holger you must understand *how I felt*" (*PW*, 218).[174] The most enchanting of the narratives is Alma's story of carrying the bed, in which she reflects an understanding of the others' motives:

> "The bed moved along in the night, swaying as if it were being carried by invisible hands. How mystical, how enchanting," said the parson's widow. "But you haven't yet told the pharmacist everything that happened that night. [...] The brothers were on their way home when they caught sight of people coming along the road toward them, and they ducked into the woods. And they looked out from their hiding place and saw what their sisters were up to. [...] This thing with two legs was swaying in the hands of the people carrying it, you can't believe how enchanting I find this point in the story. 'Let's rest,' the brothers hear their sisters say. They recognize the voices and *understand everything*. [...]" (*PW*, 215–216)[175]

The narratives running in cycles and in the loops of mutual reflection serve as the principle of design in *Hänen olivat linnut*. These repetitions and redundancies pertain to the operations of the characters' minds as they seek lost coherence and balance. Narrative coherence is shown to exist only in the storyteller's mind. In life, there seem to be many alternative and divergent beginnings and endings that refuse to be arranged into a coherent causal-linear story. The narrative of carrying the bed is one of Adele's and Alma's co-narrated stories that leads to a dead end. While trying to guide Alma in storytelling, Adele herself gets lost. Where is the beginning and where is the end?

> "What?" asked Holger.
> "Don't interrupt. This is one of those stories that can't bear any interruptions, and you, Alma, begin at the beginning."
> "How do I know what's the beginning!"
> "Why don't you start where you were carrying the bed. That's not the beginning, but if you start with that, even though it's the end of the story, you can get to the beginning. [...]" (*PW*, 205)[176]

Adele and Alma's co-narratives that defy coherence and order reflect the characters' difficulties in constructing coherent, undivided identities. Holger addresses the repetitious structures of thought as he reads Alma's mind. Holger argues that he knows Adele's habits of sharing all the family secrets with her servant, even if Alma thinks he does not know anything about it: "Yes, you *think* I don't *understand* that you *know...*" (*PW*, 172).[177] The infinite flow of the human mind is portrayed in this three-layered structure of mind-reading that reflects the embedded quality of storytelling as the trademark of Vartio's fiction "Shall I tell you what you're thinking? [...] Go ahead and think. It's good to think. There's no end to a thought. When you start at the beginning you won't get to the end, there's plenty of it" (*PW*, 170).[178] The character-narrators of the embedded stories begin to resemble the extradiegetic narrator on the upper level of narration and even the author, holding the threads of the entire patchwork (cf. Tammi 1992: 70).

The fragility of aesthetic order hints at the chaotic nature of the human mind, its tendency to oscillate between madness and creativity. Time and time again, Alma and Adele end up searching for primal causes and the beginnings of their muddled self-narratives: "But I asked you to start from the beginning, and now you've mixed it all up. I said: start telling it from the beginning, from the very start, but now you've got it muddled" (*PW*, 44), Adele complains.[179] "Whatever the beginning may be" (ibid.), Alma wonders.[180] The search for primal causes involves simultaneously weaving narratives, disentangling the threads of one's life, and constructing a more coherent texture of the wounded selves. As Margaret Anne Doody has argued, breaking and mending, wounding and healing are among the most prevalent "tropic topoi" in the ritual act of storytelling in Western literature: they constitute points, places, and moments of intensified meaning (Doody 1996: 305, 309–318). When Adele and Alma are weaving and unweaving the threads of their lives, the knitting needles are clicking: "You're a good knitter" (*PW*, 152),[181] Adele gives Alma credit as she ends one of her stories.

Considered from the perspective of the tellability of oral stories, narratives repeatedly told bring up the question of why certain narratives are re-told if they have no value in novelty or narrative surprise. As mentioned above, the self-narratives may be considered collectively shared rituals that are related to entertaining oneself or constructing commonly shared reality or one's versions of it. Adele's obsessive need to narrate and listen to the repetitive stories, however, can also be interpreted as referring to the cycles of embodied arousal, as a "compulsion to repeat." Adele and Alma's search for primal causes and beginnings correspond to the "magic words" (*syntysana*) of folk tradition that make it possible to trace the origins of evil. The etymology of the Finnish word *syy* ("cause") refers not only to reason, fault, or mistake, but also to thread, texture, and line.[182] In the magic of words, the ability to recognize the primal cause means the ability to take control of things by explaining the "birth" of the elements of the external world. The act of narrating becomes a way to revive the traumatic experiences of the past by bringing the experiences back into the present moment and providing them with new meanings. By means of repetition, the conscious mind seeks to resolve the traumatic experiences that are repressed in the emotional unconscious.

BREAKING THE CYCLE. THE FINALE

The departures from chronological order in *Hänen olivat linnut* are mostly "naturalized" by the characters' spoken narratives. These oral stories capture the paths of the characters' mental development; their deferred, unconventional Bildung. The narrator's aloof recounting is disrupted by the dialogues of Adele and Alma, who shape and structure their spoken narratives as if "independent" of the frame story. The wandering tales of the characters recount events in an order that is ruled by their personal memory or associative connections – in the order in which the events occur in their minds rather than by their successiveness in time. Vartio makes these rambling tales seem more "natural" by creating an aesthetic illusion of the characters themselves telling the stories on their own. Yet the self-narratives are still embedded in the relatively coherent and serial construction of the frame story governed by the extradiegetic narrator.[183]

The frame narrative itself portrays only a handful of outer events, focusing on the repetitions of Adele and Alma's daily lives. These habitual patterns of action are disrupted only by Adele's outbursts and Alma's departures and returns as she tries to start a new life elsewhere. Holger watches Alma leave and come back again: "A strange creature [...] Goes off with her traveling case and comes back with her traveling case" (*PW*, 184).[184] Even though Alma cries over her destiny as the guardian of a madwoman, she is as dependent on Adele as Adele is dependent on her. There is no other home to go to, and Alma always comes back. The short story "Alma käy kotona" (Alma Makes a Visit Home, 1968) describes Alma's feelings of estrangement as she visits her home farm after Adele's death. She avoids looking at the lost land she has cried over many years. She feels no desire anymore. Suddenly Alma can understand Adele. She was the only person, who truly understood life: "Where had it gone. The will, the desire. There was no desire left, no will – she was like the parson's widow, who didn't want anything else but peace, that's right, only peace" ("A," 148).[185]

In *Hänen olivat linnut*, the problem of not belonging, touched upon in Vartio's every novel, culminates in the depiction of Adele and Alma's symbiosis. Both women are trying to find their way home, to find an inner place of security and safety. Whereas Adele finally arrives at destination of her journey, Alma is left lingering on her path. She has time to experience only few moments of belonging. The passing of time makes her wonder about the things that never change. Another winter approaches and Alma is sealing the windows of the house just as she has done many times before: "Fifteen years had passed. [...] Had it been like this, her hands just like this fifteen years ago when she had opened this window for the first time? Fifteen times she had sealed up these very windows while the parson's widow had paced from parlor to bedroom and back again, just the way she was doing now, keeping an eye on her to see that she was stuffing enough cotton batting between the double windows" (*PW*, 200).[186] When Alma looks at the boats passing by, she suddenly feels home, safe within the walls and the sealed windows and the habitual repetitions: "What she had missed most when she was among strangers, she now realized, were these white boats that carried you home and away from home" (ibid.).[187]

In the frame story of *Hänen olivat linnut*, two deaths break the sequence of repetitious everyday incidents and constitute peak moments in the emotional structure of the novel. These deaths follow each other at short intervals. The first peak is the passing of Alma's brother. When the message of his death reaches Adele, the events culminating in Adele's "metamorphosis" are set in motion. Adele feels desperate. Alma has refused to do her performance of the wood grouse, and now it is too late: "If Alma had shown me even once, her brother would go on living through me, but Alma didn't want to and now it's all too late" (*PW*, 234).[188] Adele sees the bird flying through the skies as if crossing the border between this world and the next, waiting for something to be fulfilled:

> When the sun had gone down beyond the grove of firs, the sky had been strangely clear, like a thin stretched-out sheet of copper above the forest on the opposite side of the lake. The parson's widow had seen a bird fly past the tops of the firs, then vanish as if the sky were water into which the bird could dive. And as though the heavens had clanged at the touch of the bird's wing, the clang still hanging in the air like a bird, nameless birds, black bird-shaped images, celestial satraps. (*PW*, 231)[189]

The image of the bird refers to Alma's brother's death, as his spirit leaves its earthly home. The clanging sound, as the bird's wing touches the heavens, alludes to Adele herself as the swan in her future performance. In the ekphrastic simile, the birds turn into "celestial satraps" ("taivaallisia satraappeja"), rulers of the heavens. As images of God, they embody the redemption and forgiveness gained at the time of death, when the curtains close for the last time.

The second death is obviously Adele's disappearance from the scene. After Adele's death (which is never narrated in the frame story), Alma comes back to the village for the last time and hears Teodolinda's "truth" about the past events. Holger's wife finally opens up and shares her views of the events involving the fire at the parsonage. "This is the first time I'm speaking of these matters and I won't speak about them ever again" (*PW*, 247).[190] According to Teodolinda, the talk about the fire had been exaggerated, and Adele had done her share. Teodolinda questions the idea that events after Onni's death had been predestined. Everything has been only empty talk plucked out of thin air, idle gossip, "nonsense" (*PW*, 248), she says.[191] Thus, the theme of getting lost in the mazes of the superstitious mind, portrayed already in *Kaikki naiset näkevät unia* and *Tunteet*, culminates in Vartio's last novel. The human unconscious is the source of the "hypnosis and witchcraft" that generates alternative worlds of art but also the worlds of madness, loneliness, and desperation (cf. Tammi 1992: 71, Mäkelä & Tammi 2007: 248).

Hänen olivat linnut, however, suggests that this "madness" constitutes the only way out. Before her death, Adele has finally experienced an inward awakening: she acknowledges why she must suffer. After having lived through her life suffering, even having attempted suicide, she now realizes that she is "a child of God" (*PW*, 225).[192] Like Jacob, she has sinned, but simultaneously maintained her "pure soul" in God's eyes. At times, Adele can sense the presence of God within her, in the rhythm of cosmic breath: "[W]hen I'm resting on my bed, it's as if it filled me, my body is light, I am as if in the air and I know: now it is in me. God is in me, I am in God [...] at the moments when God is in me, all people, everything that lives and breathes in the world is unspeakably dear to me" (*PW*, 225–226).[193] Even while possessing this secret knowledge of universal love, Adele has no answer to Alma's question, which resembles the question asked by Teodolinda as a girl: "Why is it that some people have to suffer in this life and others just get through it" (*PW*, 223), the servant asks.[194] Adele's answer states only the importance of knowing the cause for one's suffering: "When one knows why, it's much easier, much easier when at least you know, it is easier" (*PW*, 224).[195] At times, Adele still has doubts. She considers herself a fool in the theater of life, standing alone on the stage: "[M]aybe everything is in vain, my struggle, my prayers, just think what theater, what theater all of this is, good God, I say to myself, maybe I'm only acting, *and you all look on and laugh as I'm acting out*, fighting the good fight" (*PW*, 223).[196]

The witchcraft and hypnosis of Vartio's fictional constructs is related to the two-faced polarity of human existence: simultaneous laughter and cry typical of her novels. Even in the darkest moments of desperation, elements of farce and absurdity bring in mental relief to be experienced by the readers. (Havu 1970: viii; Flint & Flint 2008: viii–ix) The tragicomic aspects of *Hänen olivat linnut* as well Vartio's other novels arises out of the misunderstandings that complicate all human relations. The basis of the miscommunication is deeply tragic, but it has its comical effects. Even if laughter punishes, exposes, and humiliates, it can be healing as well. And the reader is invited to laugh along. The figures of the witch, the trickster and the Fool, which all serve as Adele's alter egos, embody the two-faced quality of human existence. According to Monk (1993: 2), the figure of the Fool is "a person on the periphery of an established order, able by his marginality to give expression to alternative modes of speaking and being." The Fool is the other who is needed at times of crisis in the system to "purge itself of those unwanted traits by identifying and containing them in the figure of the Fool and expelling him, usually in a public ritual involving banishment or execution" (ibid.). The triangles of mimetic desire in *Hänen olivat linnut* are accompanied by Adele's "self-sacrifice" in the social drama of hidden aggression as she becomes the surrogate victim, the scapegoat, needed to channel a collective strife (cf. Girard 1995: 4, 77).

Adele's self-sacrifice is embodied in her Christ-like reappearance in Holger's dream after her death. In the communion held in the parlor of the manse, Alma and Holger empty their glasses and drink in the way Adele has told them to do: "Do this in remembrance of me" (*PW*, 241).[197] And whenever it grows dark, Adele is there with them, "a third person in the dark" (*PW*, 239).[198] At the end of the novel the collection of birds is announced as being inherited by Alma, but soon the birds are scattered around the world. The last remnant of the taxidermy collection is the owl, the image of Birger and Adele, which served as a model for "some painter, an artist who looked like an owl" (*PW*, 252) before it disappeared.[199] The co-existence of creativity and madness is suggested in the figure of the artist, whose body becomes the last "dwelling" of Adele's tormented soul.

One of the most enchanting fictions within Vartio's fiction is undoubtedly Adele's metamorphosis into a swan at the end of chapter 19. Alma's resistance finally breaks down and she yields to Adele's submissive power. When Alma performs the mating dance, she collapses, asking forgiveness for her brother's lost soul. Adele turns into a bird-shaped shaman, a healer through whom the pain is transformed into a word.[200] The noises emanating from Alma's mouth are accompanied by the collective voice of the relatives and the villagers as they witness the madness of the "bewitched" woman, reciting spells of cathartic magic:

> Alma's brother had died before Christmas and Alma had returned from the funeral in time for Christmas; she came from the train carrying a suitcase, a small bag, other people said, and it was this bag that she had flung onto the kitchen floor when she saw the parson's widow right in the front of her insisting on the same thing, and Alma, shouting at the top of her lungs, had thumped down, said the son and daughter-in-law of the parson's widow, shouting and stomping they said she had fallen unconscious, others said, hysterical, said Herman, in the grip of senseless hysteria, said Elsa, an old woman tormented in her period of mourning, said the villagers, collapsed right in front of the parson's widow, blood-curdling shouts, a screaming which then turned into howling, barking, ringing, gurgling, as if a cork had been pulled from a bottle, said Antti, a champagne bottle, said Holger, making the most terrible racket, said the doctor's son, she went mad in the company of a madwoman, said the shopkeeper and his wife, touched by God, said the parson [...] (*PW*, 235–236)[201]

Alma's noises are mixed with "fierce fury," concluding with the "screams of one descending into hell" (*PW*, 236).[202] These noises are followed by Adele's final words: "Go to your resting place, soul" (ibid.).[203] The journey into the self ends with an ambivalent "salvation" of the souls as Adele becomes a shaman and a witch, a transgressive woman, who is burned in the flames of rebirth and simultaneously doomed to death (cf. Hirsch 1983: 33–34). In the novel's grand finale, the bottle of poison is finally uncorked. The rhythm of the noise accompanying Adele and Alma's metamorphoses can be understood as the repetitive, shamanist rhythm of a trance, taking the "bewitched" minds to the other side, to the realm of the collective unconscious where the prime cause of the trauma and the healing potion for the mental wounds can be found.

7. Conclusion

> A novel must be a house fit for free characters to live in; and to combine form with a respect for reality with all its odd contingent ways is the highest art of prose.
>
> – Iris Murdoch: "The Sublime and the Beautiful Revisited"

Modernist writers often claimed a desire to turn inward to escape from material reality into the mind's interior spaces, into imagination and dreams. For a long time, the concept of modernism as a detachment from the external world also reigned in narrative studies.[1] In this investigation, I have re-assessed the alleged "inward" turn of modernist fiction by examining the interactions between fictional minds and worlds in Marja-Liisa Vartio's five novels. The analyses of her works show that fictional minds in modernist fiction are not only introspective, solipsistic, emotional, and streaming, but also embodied, rational, and social entities. To analyze Vartio's poetics, I have drawn on postclassical, cognitive narratology, especially on the theories of mind-reading and intersubjectivity, which have facilitated examining the interaction between fictional minds. The poetics of possible worlds, cognitive-based plot theory, and affective narratology have also contributed to readings of the emotional story structures of Vartio's novels. These readings reveal the focus on embodied interactions between fictional minds and fictional worlds in her texts. Moreover, the application of these theories to the analyses of Vartio's fiction has made it clear that there are indeed stories in modernist narratives. The mental activity of characters involves not only the local experientiality of the "here and now" of the material storyworld, but also long-term, rational planning and calculation, which turn incidents into episodes and episodes into stories.

As this study has shown, the mystery of unreadable minds constitutes the most mesmerizing aspect of Vartio's novels. In addition to "thick" intermental life of (temporarily) accessible minds, there are enigmatic characters, such as Adele Broms, who are beyond default reading or categorization. These partly "unnatural" minds can be temporarily captured by reading them as stereotypes such as a madwoman. In the course of reading, however, their transcendent *bizarrerie* starts to reflect the problematic idea of captive reading itself. As Abbott (2008: 464) has maintained, the ethical approach to "otherness" and social marginality constitutes one possible way to explain why unreadable characters began to proliferate only in twentieth-century literature. The reader's "coping mechanism is to absorb the other by incorporating it into the terms of the self's own understanding" (ibid.: 461). In some instances, however, the ethics of narrative suggest the need for humility and respect for a character's insistent unreadability: a full acceptance of the human unknown (ibid.: 463).

Vartio's work has been previously addressed by evaluating the author's position in the canon of Finnish modernism. Vartio has been acknowledged as a successor of powerful female figures of Finnish literature such as Maria Jotuni. Vartio's original style of writing and her abilities as a portrayer of the human mind, however, become more visible if her oeuvre is placed alongside the works of Anglo-American modernism in which the mechanisms of interacting minds were introduced. Such authors as Virginia Woolf influenced Vartio's work, even though the styles of these writers differ dramatically. Woolf's metaphor for memory as being an old spinster who weaves and knits "the cotton wool" (Woolf 1985/1939: 70) of the everyday links Vartio's novels to the tradition of women's writing, both in national and international contexts. The trope of a "quilt," used as an image of female storytelling since Philomela's loom (cf. Clark 1991: 200, Joplin 1985), depicts the alternative voices that weave the texture of the everyday. In Finnish literature, the threads of the quilt proceed from folk tradition to Jotuni and her novel *Arkielämää* (Everyday Life, 1909)[2] and further to Marja-Liisa Vartio's work, which has given inspiration to a new generation of women authors.[3]

Vartio's narratives of everyday experience with their repetitive, cyclic structures defy causal linearity, often dramatizing the mind's split into distinct realms. Her presentations of fictional minds involve not only the conscious, verbalized, and rational consciousness, but also the realm of "wordless knowing," the emotional, unconscious processing of knowledge. The unspeakable and the unrepresentable merge into the textures of her storyworlds as striking images and psycho-analogies that stress the interactions between the world and the mind. In Vartio's early, neutral narratives, *Se on sitten kevät* and *Mies kuin mies, tyttö kuin tyttö*, the technique of mental landscaping evokes an aesthetic illusion of mental interactions by means of similes, allusions, and other evocations that construct networks of intermittent allegories of projection, drawing parallels between the inner and outer landscapes. In her later novels, *Kaikki naiset näkevät unia*, *Tunteet*, and *Hänen olivat linnut*, the epistemic worlds of "knowing" become more complex and kaleidoscopic as the interrelations of fictional worlds and minds become more convoluted and deluded. The embodied loops of interactions between fictional minds lead to over-aroused calculations, hallucinations, and paranoia, which challenge the individual mind's possibilities to see the world, the self, and others "as they are."

One of the most long-lived myths of Finnish modernist poetics of the 1950s has been the assumption that literary representation is "pure" or "mere presentation," a perfection of form that should not be "squeezed into a Venetian corset." Vartio's novels stage the very impossibility of literary representation to generate any worlds and minds as pure – devoid of any affective fallacies and uncontrollable conjectures. In fact, the very fascination of Vartio's texts stems from succumbing to the spells of words and imagination. The gradual removal of the percepts of the external world to the images of the creative mind (triggered by the interaction of worlds and minds) challenges the accounts of contemporary commentators on modernism, both in Finnish and in international contexts. On closer inspection, the picture of reality in modernist novels seems to involve more complexity and variation than either the modernists' programmatic writings or the more recent accounts of modernist fiction have suggested.

In analyzing Veijo Meri's short story "Tappaja" (The Killer, 1956) about a sharpshooter moving effortlessly around a battlefield, Viikari interprets the narrative as an allegory of the debate on Finnish modernist poetics. "Tappaja" satirizes the well-aimed "clarity" of modernist writers as "[n]othing less than perfect results were demanded of him" (Meri 1985/1956: 134).[4] The bullet fired by the marksman hits two soldiers but, paradoxically, "miss[es them] in the head" (ibid.: 140).[5] The well-aimed miss may be a commentary on the discrepancy between the clichés of the poetics of the 1950s and the practices in modernist texts themselves (Viikari 1992: 52–54). Perfection of form often meant carefully-molded imperfection, as principles of dispersion and ambivalence are always composed into the very structure of fiction: "The material is worked till it is ready; in other words, it is brought forth bare, unmolded" (Meri 1967/1963: 32).[6]

The strange, wounded, winged, and trapped birds in Vartio's prose and poetry embody this ambivalence in the author's artistry. The figure of the "poor winged bird" is mentioned as early as Vartio's youthful diary, when the ambitious, but insecure girl compares her poems to crippled birds. She dreams of finding her own voice: "A new language! But what is it? [...] No, nothing can mean more to me than [my poems]. Even if they never grow wings, strong, carrying wings, those poor broken-winged birds, I will always love them anyway!" (Vartio 1994: 313)[7] Those poor broken-winged birds are later transformed into her female characters, or figures like Napoleon, who listen to their inner voices and hear strange, performed, and muted voices. These characters were created, at least to some degree, in Vartio's own image (cf. Särkilahti 1973: 124–125). In her diary Vartio writes:

> I'm tired of seeing through people, I hate looking at everything I see, you know that I'm just as sensitive as a hound that tracks people and it is painful to see so much – I don't have the strength. The most painful thing is that you also see yourself, all your motives and actions and vanity in a bright light. (Vartio 1995: 243)[8]

In Vartio's contemplations we read Adele's sufferings almost word-for-word, and they show up again in the author's description of Mrs. Pyy's vanities and delusions. Vartio's confession resembles the famous words that have been ascribed to Flaubert: "Madame Bovary, c'est moi."[9] The identification of the author with her or his own creation emphasizes the mind's tendency to generate (textual) illusions and phantasms. These illusions reflect the prototypical activity of a human mind, and also, at the same time, the activity of fictional minds as purely artificial constructs. The human inclination to imagine other minds resembles the act of writing fiction: the creation of entire imaginary worlds from reflections of the actual world.

In the grand finale of Vartio's oeuvre, the metamorphosis of Adele into a swan becomes Vartio's own "swan song." Adele's performance before her death turns into an image of creative madness as she sings her last, deluded lament. The bird of Apollo has a long history in literary tradition: it refers to the legend that, after a lifetime of silence, the swan sings a mournful song just before dying. In Finnish tradition, the use of this trope ranges from the Swan of Tuonela in *The Kalevala* to Eino Leino's *Tuonelan joutsen* (The Swan of Tuonela, 1898), Otto Manninen's symbolist poems, and Aino Kallas's *Reigin pappi* (The Priest of Reigi, 1926). In these texts the swan turns into an image of poetic immortality and gradually becomes the object of an obsessive hunt. In *Hänen olivat linnut*, Adele's obsession with the swan stems from her feelings of inferiority and shame over her failed performance witnessed by a great artist, Alma's brother: "[I]n her attempt to best a perfect artist, she who could not even mimic the squeaking of a duck, had been mad" (*PW*, 165).[10] The swans Adele had once seen are mute and silent, contrary to the bugling sounds she has heard in her dreams in imagining the journey of the slayer of the swan.

Adele's failed performance ironically refers to the romantic trope of a poet who compares himself to a modest goose or a swallow, birds that are inferior to the noblest bird of all, the swan. The poet is unable to rise on the wings of inspiration and touches the transcendent ideas of art only from a distance. His short flight ends in melancholy and yearning. In *Hänen olivat linnut*, this romantic figure is alluded to by subverting the trope's conventional meanings. Adele's metamorphosis into a swan is accompanied by the ridiculous sounds of howling, barking, ringing, and gurgling, transforming the sublime dream of romantic and symbolist poetry into a deformed and banal, embodied, and earthly performance. In Paavo Haavikko's *Talvipalatsi*, a programmatic poem of modernist aesthetics, the squeaking of a duck (*sorsien narina*) vibrates on the skin of a woman depicted as the poet's muse.[11] The speaker in the poem talks about writing and asks: "[A]nd why should I try to write poems when I am not Musset?"[12] The noises and disturbances of Adele's metamorphosis embody chaos and ambivalence as mechanisms of innovation. From disorder and mess, muddle and disruption, new forms rise like crippled birds from the ashes of the old world.

Notes

1. Introduction. Worlds Within and Without

1 Except where noted otherwise, translator Jill G. Timbers reviewed and revised all translations: the excerpts from Vartio's texts and the secondary sources. Emphases in all quotations are mine if not indicated otherwise. The title of *Hänen olivat linnut* requires special mention. The Finnish title involves ambivalence. In the Finnish language, the gender of pronouns is not specified. For this reason both variations of the title are possible: Hers Were the Birds or His Were the Birds (cf. Flint & Flint 2008: 255). In this study, I use the title of the novel's published English translation, *The Parson's Widow*, and identify it with the abbreviation *PW*.

2 Sinun on hyvä olla Alma kun sinä et tajua kaikkea mitä toisen mielessä tapahtuu. Sinä kuljet elämän läpi järki kädessäsi, sinä kärsit vähemmän kuin minä. Kun minä olin nuorempi, en voinut katsoa ihmisiä silmiin, kun tiesin aina mitä he ajattelevat, ja siitä minä tulin sairaaksi, sillä se mitä näin heidän ajattelevan itsestäni ei suinkaan ollut aina minulle edullista (*H*, 226).

3 The concept of the "inward turn" of narrative was originally proposed by the literary scholar Erich Kahler (1973: 5) to describe "an increasing displacement of outer space by what Rilke has called inner space, a stretching consciousness" that "brings with it an incorporation, and internalization [*Verinnerung*] of more and more of the objective world."

4 Näin pääsemme jakamaan Vartion romaanit kahteen ryhmään [...] Uudemmissa teoksissa on rekisteri laajentunut, huumoriin päin, voima ja eheys vähentyneet, kun Vartio on ryöpsähdyttänyt valloilleen taipumuksensa fabuloida, laverrellakin. On ikäänkuin se runo ja väkevyys, mikä viime romaaneissa välähtää esiin tietyissä yksityiskohdissa, olisi kahdessa ensimmäisessä ollut padottuna, sävyttämässä kaikkea, kantamassa kokonaisuutta, joka silti oli koruton, arkinen. Vartion, tämän vilkkaasti kuvittelevan kirjailijan, keskeistä problematiikkaa näyttävät olevan unet ja mielikuvat, jotka eivät arkeen mahdu, eivät juurru.

5 Mahdan olla naiskirjailijoiden vihaaja. Senkin uhalla väitän, etteivät nais-kirjailijamme yleensä ottaen nosta Suomen kirjallisuuden tasoa, vaan laskelmoivat sillä. [...] On suorastaan varottava lukemasta heitä vapautuneesti, siihen ei näytä olevan varaa.

6 [M]inä en usko että naisesta on kirjoittamaan mitään edes jonkin verran järjellistä romaania. Tulee kaikenlaisia *Mrs Dalloway*tä ja muita pimeitä kirjoja.

7 The critic of *Ilta-Sanomat* (Finland's second largest newspaper) shared Paasilinna's views. To the reviewer (who used the pseudonym "M.N."), the novel appeared to be an unrealistic representation of wartime seen from a womanly, even embarrassingly ignorant, perspective.

8   [M]utta nämä tunteet, tunteet! [...] 'Rehevä' elämänkuva näkyykin olevan vain
    tekniikkaa, jolta puuttuu sisältö; ja tekniikka on vain hankittu ominaisuus, joka ei
    välttämättä periydy sisältöön. [...] Rakkausromaaneissakin pitäisi päästä vapautu-
    neeseen kerrontaan, jossa ilmaisu on ilmaisua eikä rajoitu venusten korsetteihin
    [...].

9   Attitudes such as Paasilinna's have resulted in feminist readings whereby the search
    for a new language in modernism has been portrayed as a war of words between
    the sexes, a rhetorical battlefield (cf. Clark 1991: 13). The metaphor "no man's land"
    was adopted to position female writers in a literary arena that was built mainly
    on the male tradition of writing. The break from tradition paved the way for new
    techniques often perceived as a "strange disease of modern life" and considered
    a "feminine, chattering, canting age" (Gilbert & Gubar 1988: 130). Gilbert and
    Gubar reflect upon Matthew Arnold's ideas of modern life and Basil Ransom's
    thoughts as represented in *The Bostonians* by Henry James.

10 According to Osip Mandelstam (1997: 83), "[t]he *ideal of perfect manliness* is
    provided by the style and practical demands of our age. Everything has become
    heavier and more massive; thus man must become harder, for he must be the
    hardest thing on earth; he must be to the earth what the diamond is to glass." Also
    Nikolai Gumilev, the founder of Acmeist poetry in Russia, equated hardness with
    masculinity.

11 Olen kovin pieni kirjallinen lahjakkuus, en yhtään mitään. Pari runoa, pari
    uninovellia, 'Se on sitten kevät', siinä kaikki (Vartio 1996: 189).

12 As Painter's study on "tempered modernism" shows, the literary tradition of
    "female hardness" existed before the theories of "hard" poetry were established. The
    Imagist theories were innovations by male figures, but among the first practitioners
    were female writers with stark voices (cf. Painter 2006: 3, 196–197). Painter's study
    includes analyses of the work of such female poets as Hilda Doolittle (H.D.) and
    Anna Akhmatova, whose poems gave inspiration to male theorists with whom they
    were intimately related, namely, Ezra Pound and Nikolai Gumilev.

13 [K]onsteja [ei] ole otettavissa, ne on keksittävä itse (Vartio 1996: 89).

14 Vartion ihmiset ovat toisilleen 'merkkejä', joita he kokevat tulkita parhaansa – tai
    mieluummin – pahimpansa mukaan.

15 The literary canon of Finnish post-war modernism is characterized by being
    relatively moderate in its reshaping of form and narrative structure. The style of the
    more experimental writers of the 1940s and 1950s – Tyyne Saastamoinen, Sinikka
    Kallio-Visapää, Pentti Holappa, and Lassi Nummi among others – was considered
    "un-Finnish" and too foreign (typically too "French") to fit the literary mainstream.
    (Hökkä 1999: 84)

16 The writers of the Finnish "new novel" did not form any organized school of
    writing, but were modernist authors who were influenced by one another and
    ended up applying the same narrative techniques individually. The loose group of
    "new school" writers included such modernists as Vartio, Haavikko, Antti Hyry,
    and Veijo Meri, but also authors who focused on more complex human psychology,
    such as Marko Tapio, Jorma Korpela, and Juha Mannerkorpi (Makkonen 1992: 95).

17 The Finnish literary scene, however, was also open to new ideas from the Anglo-
    American context (including theories of the New Criticism). Translations of such
    modernist classics as Woolf, Joyce, Proust, Mann, and Kafka appeared during this
    period.

18 Wittgenstein's philosophy of language had a major impact on contemporary thinking
    in the Finnish poetics of the 1950s. The most seminal of Wittgenstein's writings,
    Tractatus logico-philosophicus and *Philosophische Untersuchungen* (*Philosophical
    Investigations*), were introduced to Finnish audiences by the philosopher and
    logician Jaakko Hintikka in two essays published in *Suomalainen Suomi* in 1955:
    "Tutkimus filosofiasta" (A Study of Philosophy) and "Tutkimus kielestä" (A Study
    of Language).

19 Heidän [modernistien] päähuomionsa kohdistuu kieleen, ei kielen takia vaan
perehtymisen ja harjaantumisen, koska heidän tavoitteenaan on niin täsmälleen
kuin suinkin ilmaista asiansa. Mikä ei edellytä vain kielen vaan myös ilmaistavan
omakohtaista tuntemusta; sen takia heidän on pakko rajoittua välittömään koke-
mukseensa. Työssään heiltä puuttuu tyyten halu vaihtaa se ihanteisiin, totuuksiin
ja niiden hierarkioihin, so. yleistyksiin ja yleistysjärjestelmiin, joilla ei voi olla oma-
kohtaisesti eksaktia merkitystä muuna kuin kuvattavana kuvattavan seassa. Sen
sijaan he näkevät tavattomasti vaivaa saadakseen teoksensa tarkalleen vastaamaan
sitä minkä he ovat kokeneet todellisuudesta ja kielestä.

20 The conception of art-making as hard, dedicated craftsmanship is illustrated by
Anhavá's following statement from *Toiset pidot tornissa* (The Second Symposia in
the Tower, 1954): "And yet, the Sacred Cause of Literature requires lodging in one's
mind [the idea] that a man of letters, be he writer or critic, must dedicate himself
heart and soul to the work; it is that hard a task: he must eat, drink, and think ink,
and it is ink he must dream about." ("Ja vielä Kirjallisuuden Pyhä Asia edellyttää
sen mieleenpainamista, että kirjallisuusmiehen, oli hän kirjailija tai kriitikko, on
nahkoineen karvoineen omistauduttava työlleen, siksi kova urakka se on: hänen on
syöminen, juominen, ajatteleminen mustetta ja musteesta unta näkeminen"; Repo
1954: 301–302) These demands were met with mixed feelings. Many writers of the
1950s have described cooperation with Anhava with ambivalence, simultaneously
expressing their admiration and anxiety, acceptance and resistance (cf. Liukkonen
1992).

21 According to Thomas G. Pavel (1986: 1), the early stage of the inquiry of fictionality
led philosophers to focus their attention on "freeing rational discourse from the
trappings of ordinary, prelogical language." The pre-logical use of language was
perceived to be populated with "vague, ambiguous expressions" that misleadingly
referred to nonexistent entities. The problem of fictional, representative language
was excluded as a deviant phenomenon by favoring "literal varieties of language
over fictional or metaphorical ones." (Ibid.) Only later did fiction become a testing
ground for the hypotheses of analytical philosophy and models of logic.

22 In tempered modernism, the naturalist poetics of externals was combined
with more anti-mimetic tones of modernism that relied on fragmentation in
representing the fictional world. As opposed to the avant-gardists, tempered
modernists rarely sought to draw attention to the language itself. Instead of rupture,
non-representationalism, and discontinuity, the tools of tempered modernism were
precision and restraint: a poetic method that aimed at "exactitude," "accuracy," and
austerity of expression. (Painter 2006: 3–9, 85–87)

23 The "outworn" quality of conventional words led many modernists to experiment
with techniques analogous to other arts: painting, music, sculpture, film,
architecture, and theatre. The interplay among different forms of art was considered
a tool with which to stage the representation itself, to make the words more tangible
and vivid. As Painter (2006: 96) states, the idea of an author as a *maker* of a concrete
thing was further reinforced by referring to such forms of art as architecture and
sculpture, which illustrated the notion of art as a "difficult craft requiring intensive
labor, precise technique, and knowledge of structure." This notion of art is reflected
in a Poundian metaphor for poetry as the sculpting of words: "It is as simple as
the sculptor's direction: 'Take a chisel and cut away all the stone you don't want'"
(Pound 1971: 91).

24 While explaining the object of his investigations, Wittgenstein (1958: 42ᵉ) stressed
his aim to "*understand* something that is already in plain view" rather than learn
anything new by it (emphasis his). Plain viewing does not find any interest in
something that can be seen *behind* or *underlying* appearances. It aims to captivate
the very "something that lies open to view" (ibid.: 50ᵉ), to take note of the familiar
things right before our eyes and dwell upon them in order to disrupt routine ways

of seeing. "The aspects of things that are most important for us are hidden because of their simplicity and familiarity," he wrote (ibid.). The simplest path is often the hardest: "How hard I find it to see what is right in front of my eyes" (Wittgenstein 1980: 39).

25 Yksilön omankin tajunnanvirran totuudenmukainen selostaminen varsinkin laajempina kokonaisuuksina on näin ollen melkeinpä ylivoimainen tehtävä. Vielä hankalampaa on arvattavasti toisen ihmisen sisäisen elämystenkulun esittäminen. Ylipäänsä tuntuu siltä, että vain puolittain tajuisen, oman tai vieraan elämysvirran taiteellinen esittäminen pakosta muuttaa sen luonnetta ja että monissa tapauksissa *ainoa luotettava tapa kuvan antamiseksi siitä on jättää se normaalisti kerrottujen tekojen ja tapausten takaisena tekijänä vaistottavaksi.*

26 Many prose writers of the 1950s read Matson's book on the theory of the novel and applied his ideas to their literary works (cf. Hökkä 1999: 76).

27 Sisäinen havainto ei [...] ole suinkaan tieteellisessä mielessä luotettavan maineessa. Behavioristit kieltävät sen käytön kokonaan, ja yleisessäkin psykologiassa on painokkaasti todettu sen kaipaavan tuekseen tekojen ja reaktioiden ulkokohtaista tarkkailua yksilöissä. Mutta 'Ulysses' seuraajineen ei tyydy vain minämuotoiseen tajunnanvirtaan, vaan liikkuu vapaasti tajunnasta toiseen ja esittää meille kaikkien sisällystä yhtä suvereenisti. Ja tästä huolimatta sen käyttäjät puhuvat halveksivassa sävyssä entisajan 'kaikkitietävistä' romaanikirjoittajista! – Mistään uusasiallisesta todellisuudenkuvauksesta ei siis voi olla puhetta, vaan pikemminkin vallan *väkevän fantasian tuotteista*, ainakin yhtä *mielikuvituksellisista* kuin entisetkin romaanit. [...] Kuitenkin voi puhtaasti psykologiselta kannalta lähtien pitää yksipuolista tajunnanvirtamenetelmää paljon subjektiivisempana kuin normaalia kertomatekniikkaa, joka perustuu sekä sisäiseen että ulkoiseen havaintojentekoon.

28 Ryan's (1980) model of fictional assertions follows the same path: fictional discourse is a product of impersonation by an author who creates a fictional speaker belonging to the imaginary world. Ryan's theory comes close to Searle's ideas of fictional assertions as pretended speech-acts (see also Pavel 1986: 88).

29 Minun mielestäni on selvää, ettei nykyinen kirjallisuus pyri olemaan mikään ennennäkemättömän tehokas reksaamismenetelmä, jolla elämää säilöttäisiin luonnollisen värisenä makuisena hajuisena sanojen ja lauseiden purkkeihin. Tuskin kukaan enää nykymaailmanaikaan on tietämätön ihmisen subjektiivisuudesta: ja kirjailijat ovat erityisen tietoisia siitä, että oma ominaislaatu kirjoittaessa suorittaa koko ajan puolihuomaamatonta valikointia, ajaa tapahtumia, sanoja, rytmejä milloin mihinkin suuntaan. Mutta pelkistämispyrkimys tähtää siihen, että valikointia ei ennakolta ohjata millään tietoisesti omaksutuilla periaatteilla; kirjoittaminen on eräänlaista minäntapahtumisen ja siitä tarkastellun elämäntapahtumisen kohtaamista sanoissa.

30 If we are to believe the arguments of the latest study, behind the development of New Criticism loom the empirical doctrines of behaviorist psychology. The main principles of New Criticism have been traced back to I. A. Richardson's literary theory as being highly influenced by behavioristic psychology. Even if the New Critics, Brooks and Wimsatt among them, rejected the behaviorist strands in Richardson's writing, these ideas were perpetuated as part of their own theories and still haunt the assumptions and techniques of close reading. On the other hand, the modernist consciousness novel, it has been argued, was started in part as a critical response to the behaviorist trend in the psychology of the 1910s and 1920s. (Cf. Gang 2011: 1–3, 17–19)

31 [Allegoria] on se subjektiivisuus, jota naturalisti ja objektivoija ei voi välttää. Mutta se ei ole haitaksi; juuri se tekee todenkaltaisuuden mahdolliseksi. Kun vain on tietoja – joita kaikki naturalistit keräävät – samastuminen auttaa eläytymään, näkemään päähenkilön maailman omin silmin. Taiteilijana naturalisti sitten toimii *ikään kuin* loisi itsestään erillisen maailman noudattaen ulkomaailman yleisiä lakeja ja

olemusta: hän tekee lukijalle siirtymisen 'todellisesta' taiteen maailmaan niin huomaamattomaksi kuin suinkin, esittää sisimmätkin tietonsa "kunniallisella tavalla" [...] pitäytyen "ulkoiseen kuvaukseen, vuoropuheeseen ja toimintaan." Anhava is here quoting Frans G. Bengtsson.

32 Allegory also involves "allusion and hint" mentioned by Anhava (2002/1952: 95) in the context of Ezra Pound's and T. S. Eliot's poetry.

33 The complication of the interpretive process was an intentional goal of many Finnish writers at the time. Veijo Meri, for instance, explicitly stated his pursuit of relying on objectivity and the dissolution of precise explanation in order to preserve the reader's independence as a co-producer of the text (see Viikari 1992: 64).

34 According to Maria Mäkelä (2011: 57–58), one of these conventions is free indirect discourse that is not "a presentation of something that exists, a *re*presentation," but rather a phenomenon crossing the boundaries between structure, thematic, and interpretation: "In the narrative structure free indirect discourse may be simultaneously a breaking point between different textual consciousnesses – between two characters as much as between the narrator and the character – as well as a threshold leading from mental worlds into other worlds, a transparent seam between the actual and the virtual." ("Vapaa epäsuora esitys ei ole lopulta esitystä mistään olemassa olevasta, *re*presentaatiota [...] Kerronnan rakenteessa vapaa epäsuora esitys voi samaan aikaan olla murtumakohta eri tekstuaalisten mielten välillä – yhtä hyvin kahden henkilöhahmon kuin henkilön ja kertojankin välillä – ja kynnys mentaalisista maailmoista toisiin, läpinäkyvä sauma toden ja kuvitelman rajalla.")

35 The interdependence of actual and fictional minds is suggested both by Palmer (2010: 19) and Mäkelä (2011: 33), but from quite opposite directions, as the discussion below will show.

36 Cohn (1983: 9) considers "Hemingway's school," for instance, an anomaly of the modern novel, a manifestation of the spiral movement of the genre as it may distance itself from its inward matrix to come back again.

37 Emphasis hers. Some of Cohn's analyses, however, imply that she was half aware of the phenomenon of embedded consciousnesses. According to her, the technique of narrated monologue, for instance, "enables a narrator to weave in and out of several characters' minds." It is not clear whether Cohn refers here to multiple focalizations or to the composition of mind-reading, yet a particular excerpt from the analysis of Woolf's *To the Lighthouse* clearly suggests the latter. Cohn (1983: 133) observes that the question Lily imagines running through Mr. Ramsay's mind at the moment ("for after all, what woman could resist him?") can be interpreted as an ironic "narrated monologue within a narrated monologue that in direct quotation would read: (She thinks) He thinks: 'what woman can resist me?'"

38 In Palmer's previous study these sorts of complications are avoided by resorting to a more flexible classification. The following cases of shared thinking are possible: "[A]n individual thinking about another individual; an individual thinking about a group; a group thinking about an individual; and a group thinking about another group" (Palmer 2004: 233).

39 The latter category involves what Palmer calls "doubly embedded narrative" (2004: 15) and later, to avoid conceptual confusion, "double cognitive narratives" (2010: 12).

40 Palmer's theory does not acknowledge the epistemological "privileges" of the (omniscient) narrator as the mediator of fictional minds, which has been a target of justifiable criticism (see the special issue of *Style* 2011 and Palmer's response to the critique, 2011b: 379–381).

41 Emma Kafalenos (2011: 256), accordingly, writes about the semantic fascination of narrative fiction in her response to Palmer's essay on social minds: "In my own experience as a reader, I take pleasure in the delightful interplay among the three

epistemologically different levels: the narrator's statements, which are facts in the fictional world; the characters' judgments, which are merely opinions; and the statements that may or may not be [free indirect discourse], which can be read as either facts or opinions."

42 The narrative semantics of fictional worlds questions the classical distinction between story and discourse that has been a prominent paradigm, both in the story analysis of formalism and in the schematizations of mind presentation in classical narratology. Whereas story analysis has been related primarily to the action structures contained in the story, classical narratology has focused almost entirely on the accompanying consciousness in the discourse without consideration of mental action as a discourse issue (cf. Palmer 2004: 29–31). Bringing together the story and discourse sides of narratology, however, provides a more holistic vision of the composition of fictional minds.

43 Epistemological doubt and skepticism are the main features of modernist worlds, both in regard to *perceiving* and *representing* fictional worlds. The epistemological uncertainty makes both the narrators and the characters second-guess, speculate, and hypothesize about how things present themselves. The narrator is potentially as fallible as the characters. According to Fokkema & Ibsch (1988: 4), modernists were "interested in the various ways in which knowledge of the world can be worded and transmitted, but consider the actual transfer of knowledge as something of secondary importance." This leads to hypotheticality actualized on all levels of narration. The modernist writer has "doubts about himself and about his narrator, who is certainly not omniscient and, in his turn, cannot be sure of the characters he has himself created. [...] When the characters speak, the uncertainty does not disappear. They correct and qualify themselves continuously; their views are reconsidered and subsequently modified." (Ibid.: 34–35)

44 As Hilary Dannenberg (2008: 67) remarks, readers also experience their own journeys through the space and time of the fictional world. The act of reading cannot be perceived as a stationary mental activity, but rather as movement in space. The spatial metaphor *reading as a journey* portrays the cognitive processes of the reader experiencing the pleasurable release or escape from the real world into the fictional worlds while getting "lost" in a book.

45 Causality is often discerned as a *change* in a state of affairs. According to Richardson (2005: 48), "a cause in narrative literature is an action or event that directly or obliquely produces a transformation." To be categorized as a narrative, an event sequence must follow a trajectory leading from a state of balance to some sort of disruptive moment, namely, an unplanned or untoward event, which may be the effect of other participants' intended actions, finally arriving at an endpoint in which balance is regained or at least seems about to be restored (Herman 2003: 3). As Jerome Bruner (1991: 11) observed, "to be worth telling, a tale must be about how an implicit canonical script has been breached, violated, or deviated from in a manner to do violence to [its] 'legitimacy.'"

46 I have adapted the term "lingering" from Emma Kafalenos' inspiring study *Narrative Causalities* (2006), in which she studies the extended functions of narratives, in which the concluding equilibrium is either missing or the narrative resolution is deferred.

47 Epistemological accessibility constitutes the very core of the metaphor of the "possible world," the idea about the infinitude of worlds originating in Leibniz's philosophy.

48 Herman's hypothetical focalization revises the concept of "focalization" established by Genette (1972) and adjusted by the other narrative theorists (Bal 1985, Chatman 1978 & 1990, Rimmon-Kenan 1983) to the analysis of viewpoint or "vision" within narratives. Focalization theory in general and hypothetical focalization in particular are concerned with the perspectival selection and restriction of

information conveyed in narrative. Herman's model (1994, revised version 2002) contributes to the theory of focalization by applying the concepts of possible world semantics to the investigation of narrative virtual perspective.

49 Herman (1994: 237–239) distinguishes two main categories of hypothetical focalization (HF): direct and indirect. The mode of hypotheticality is "direct" if the text explicitly appeals to a hypothetical witness, a counterfactual focalizer. The situation is opposite in indirect modes of HF in which the presence of such an onlooker must be inferred from the text. In addition to the explicitness of the focalizing agent, the mode of HF can be defined on the basis of "strength" or "weakness" of the hypotheticality of focalization. In the strong mode of HF, both the focalizer and the act of focalization are virtual. Alternatively, in the weak mode, only the act of focalization has virtual status within the textual actual world. Hence, the expressed world still matches to some degree the textual actual world as the focalizer remains a part of the reference world.

50 In Herman's model the term "external" is used in Rimmon-Kenan's sense corresponding to Genette's "zero focalization" or "non-focalization": a type of focalization, in which events are narrated from an unrestricted or omniscient point of view (Herman 1994: 233; Genette 1980).

51 Colwyn Trevarthen (1999: 145–146) defines the concept of intersubjectivity as "the process in which mental activity – including conscious awareness, motives and intentions, cognitions, and emotions – is transferred between minds [...] [it] manifests itself as an immediate sympathetic awareness of feelings and conscious, purposeful intelligence in others."

52 As Pavel (1986: 58–59) points out, the construction of links between primary (extradiegetic) and secondary (diegetic) ontology of fictional worlds resembles the methods of allegorical evocation.

53 In analyzing the functions of psycho-narration, Cohn (1983: 36) mentions one "device for vitalizing summary psycho-narration": psycho-analogy as a "striking image" that "often takes the form of a [...] simile."

54 According to Karkama (1995: 151), there are certain images (birds) and spheres of consciousness (dreams) that serve in young Vartio's diaries as a way of rendering the inner existence of the writer. These images are used later as the author's tools in depicting the inner life of her characters.

55 Drawing on Chris R. Brewin's (2005) account, Sirkka Knuuttila (2009: 52) described traumatic memories as being stored in three types of memory reflected in the literary representation of trauma: first, as embodied, visual imagery; second, as strong negative affects, and third, as explicit narrative memory, "which is arduously awakened after a delay by virtue of either spontaneous or triggered imagery."

56 Knuuttila (2009) analyzes similar tropes as an embodiment of trauma of the female figures in Marguerite Duras' *India Cycle*.

57 In regards to the more detailed analysis of the methods of naming in Vartio's novels, see Särkilahti 1973, Niemi 1995, Ruuska 2010 and 2013a, and Nykänen 2013b.

58 In this respect, Vartio's work resembles the method of characterization used by the Finnish author Maria Jotuni: she too often depicted "the same woman" in her texts (Niemi 1999: xii). Like Vartio's later characters, Jotuni's protagonists challenge the stereotypical categories of women being either angel-like victims or destructive *femme fatales*. Jotuni's techniques of self-objectification, rationalization, and self-discipline had an impact on Vartio's narrative style. The attitudes of discipline and detachment stemmed from Jotuni's interest in the way of the Samurai warriors, *bushido*, which emphasizes the importance of mental strength and moral virtues. The strategies of detachment and pessimistic world view in Jotuni's work, however, are refracted by her comedy that often stems from the motherly wisdom of the heart (*sydämen viisaus*). Jotuni's fiction does not openly stage the struggle for the women's rights, but her way of seeing the issue of womanhood from

the larger perspective of humanity profoundly influenced Vartio's techniques of characterization and rhetorical persuasion. (Cf. Rossi 2013: 115, 123–133)

59 In this study, I follow Antonio Damasio's (2008) distinction between emotions as unconscious, bodily sensations and feelings as more conscious awareness of these emotions. In cognitive and affective studies, these concepts are often used interchangeably or even with opposite meanings.

2. Entering the World. The Emergence of the Embodied Mind in Se on sitten kevät

1   Tyhjä, tyhjä on maailma tämä (*R*, 40).

2   – Tässä tämä huone on, kun ehditte niin tulkaa kahville./Emännällä oli kiire takaisin, hän sulki oven perässään niin nopeasti että ovi kolahti. Huoneeseen seisomaan jäänyt nainen kuuli emännän askeleet eteisestä./Nainen siirtyi oven suulta ja meni ikkunaan. Emäntä juoksi pihan yli. Hän seurasi katseellaan kunnes emäntä hävisi kuusiaidan taakse. The English translation of the Finnish word *emäntä*, "farmer's wife," does not convey all the original connotations of the term, which refers to a woman in power, in charge of the house. However, I have used the translation here as there are no alternatives that correspond perfectly to the original.

3   Each of the four types of causal alteration Vartio uses in her novels questions the classical, causal-linear narrative model in which convergence and closure become the requirements for a "well-made" story. These causal alterations are aimed at against the Aristotelian notion of plot as a coherent story line, in which with the beginning, the middle, and the end follow each other, dictated by causal necessity and probability as opposed to purely random events.

4   The plot of classical Bildungsroman begins with the hero's, a young male's, conflict with a social authority, usually a real or symbolic father. In his break from the familiar authorities and the social values the hero seeks an apprenticeship to life through (symbolic) journeys and experiences of love. At the end of his Bildung the young man returns home, and the circle of socialization closes with harmony and reconciliation.

5   The aesthetico-spiritual Bildung, rationalized in the course of nineteenth century, is re-modelled in the modernist Bildungsroman by reinstating the values of individual freedom within the process of self-development. The classical Bildungsroman is associated with the German tradition. Johann Wolfgang von Goethe's *Wilhelm Meister's Lehrjahre* (*Wilhelm Maister's Apprenticeship*, 1795–1796) constitutes a precedent of the thematic of self-development, self-cultivation, and self-formation in the lives of young men, *Bildungshelden*. The English and French equivalents of Bildung, on the other hand, transform the classical form from a genre concerned with spiritual and aesthetic self-cultivation to one concerned with the pragmatics of socialization (as in the English tradition) or with artistic success or failure (as in the French tradition). The modernist Bildungsroman looked first and foremost at the German tradition of aesthetico-spiritual Bildung. (Castle 2006: 1–3, 7–8; see also Moretti 1987, Redfield 1996)

6   There has been some theoretical discussion on the problematic quality of such a term as "female Bildungsroman." The concept has been perceived as carrying too much Goethean baggage and losing the sight of the cacophonous quality of female self-formation (cf. Fraiman 1993: 12–13). However, as Castle (2006: 214–215) suggests, the subgenre of female Bildungsroman can be conceived as being an unique, creative, and critical reaction to the male-oriented discourse of Bildung, which makes possible its analysis in relation to a broader literary historical context.

7   The rupture with tradition is exemplified in the techniques of depersonalization employed by modernist authors to free literary form from the bourgeois notions of the unified, harmonized self and establish new conceptions of self-formation. The depersonalization strategies of modernism emphasize the idea of a subject as a creative project. The modern individual is a spectator who needs detachment and distance to learn to see one's actions as the part of the spectacle of life. This often means assertation of character as pure style or abolishing it altogether. As T. S. Eliot wrote in "Tradition and Individual Talent," "[t]he progress of an artist is a continual self-sacrifice, a continual extinction of personality. [...] But, of course, only those who have personality and emotions know what it means to want to escape from these things." (Eliot 1934/1932: 17, 21; see Castle 2006: 39, 67)

8   In the narratives of female Bildung, "the culture of everyday" (Moretti 1987: 35) is given a new meaning and emphasis that was missing in the Bildungsromane written by male authors. The early representations of female development include, for instance, Jane Austin's novels, the Gothic horror of Brontës (Emily Brontë's *Wuthering Heights* or Charlotte Brontë's *Jane Eyre* and *Vilette*) as well as George Eliot's *Middlemarch* and *The Mill on the Floss*. Such novels as Virginia Woolf's *Mrs. Dalloway*, Kate Chopin's *Awakening*, and *Wide Sargasso Sea* by Jean Rhys represent the later stage of the subgenre.

9   Tensions that affect female development may also lead to "a disjunction between a surface plot, which affirms social conventions, and a submerged plot, which encodes rebellion; [...] between a plot that charts development and a plot that unravels it" (Abel, Hirsch and Langland 1983: 12).

10 Navetan edessä oli kaksi pihlajaa, toinen kasvoi vintin rappusten alta, se oli kasvanut vinoon yrittäessään työntää oksiaan valoon. Pihlajan juurella oli vanha ajoreki, josta jalakset olivat pudonneet irti, sekä kärryt, joissa oli jäljellä yksi pyörä. Navetan seinää vasten oli nostettu potkuri, siinä ei ollut kädensijaa. Rakennuksen edessä näkyi sementtinen kivijalka, lumi oli sulanut sen päältä kokonaan, pinnassa kasvoi kirkkaanvihreää sammalta. Sementtijalan keskellä oli koivupölkky, sen päässä emalinen punertava kattila, kattilasta roikkui kierrekasvien kuolleita varsia. Ne liikahtelivat hiljaa, tuuli hieman.

11 The opening scene of Vartio's novel resorts to a technique that Helmut Bonheim (1986: 94) calls "modal façade " – a dynamic mode of dialogue that produces an aesthetic effect of immediacy in order to disguise any traces of exposition. The different ways of introducing the fictional universe – the definitizing strategies – vary from one literary period to another. The traditional exposition prefers static modes of description and argument as the means of making the unknown world definite. As the beginning of *Se on sitten kevät* demonstrates, the use of description in the exposition has undergone substantial changes in modernist fiction. Exposition has not disappeared, but it is turned into a more concise and camouflaged form: the apparent role of expository description is minimized by cutting it into pieces.

12 Ikkunan alla oli oja. Uoma näkyi lumen keskellä tummana. Ojassa oli musta kumisaappaan terä, sen nokka osoitti suoraan tien menosuuntaan. Kauempana ojan reunalla näkyi kaksi ruosteista peltipurkkia ja ruskea käärepaperi. Paperi liikahti, siihen sattui tuulenhenkäys. Metsän reunassa lumiaukean keskellä oli pystyssä seiväs, se näkyi selvästi ja kuitenkin epätodellisena. Oli ilta. Ja oli maaliskuu, ja pian olisi huhtikuu.

13 Navetan luota aukeni peltoalue, keskellä peltoja oli mäki, mäen päällä rakennus, sitä tuskin erotti hämärtyvässä illassa. Hän luuli ensin sitä ladoksi, se oli maalamaton, mutta sitten hän erotti ikkunat ja katolta nousevan savun.

14 Poetics of this kind resemble the descriptive technique of haiku and Zen analyzed by Auli Viikari (1993: 72) as an embodiment of the "poetics of presence, enacted spatially and mentally at the same time" ("yhtä aikaa tilallista ja tapahtuvaa

läsnäolon poetiikkaa"). The landscape, the action, and the mind are perceived as boundless, as one.

15   According to Bal (2004: 381), the classic critique of the mode of literary description (for instance, Gerard Genette 1982/1966) – of its arbitrary and endless nature – reflects the fear of its detrimental effect on the coherence of the story as a whole: "Descriptions are endless and they betoken the endlessness of the novel. The compulsion to naturalise them through framing is symptomatic of descriptive fear; descriptions must be contained because they are, by definition, boundless." "[B]y binding, description unbinds," she (2004: 382) writes. Modernist descriptions do not serve as representations of a fictional world, but rather as frames that work as a reminder of the meta-deictic quality of all fictional representation. Fictional world-describing can never provide a complete set of attributes because its objects, referents, do not exist outside the textual universe. Descriptive elements emphasize the role of fictional assertions as references to non-existent, and thereby, incomplete entities. (Ibid.: 381)

16   Ikkunaa vastapäätä kasvoi tiheää kuusikkoa. Ikkunasta katselija ajatteli, että kuusikossa vielä kesälläkin olisi kosteaa, ja syksyllä sieniä, haapasieniä, harmaita ja kylmiä./Hän katsoi kuusikkoa kohti, näki vihreitä lehtiä, talven yli säilyneitä. Hän ei erottanut, että ne olivat munuaisenmuotoisia sinivuokon lehtiä, ja vaikka hän olisi ne nähnyt, ei hän olisi tuntenut niitä, sillä siellä, mistä hän oli tullut, ei kasva sinivuokkoja.

17   Nainen aukaisi käsilaukun, otti esille peilin ja kamman. Sukaistuaan hiuksiaan hän katsoi peiliin, nopeasti, *tavan vuoksi, niin nopeasti, ettei ehtinyt edes nähdä poskessaan nokiläiskää.*

18   On the continuum of the levels of consciousness, the most self-conscious processes of fictional minds have been considered the verbalized thoughts "mediated" in interior monologue (cf. Cohn 1983: 76). A verbalized inner voice denotes a more elaborate sense of the self being aware of the present moment of "here and now," but also of its own mental processes. In the more recent re-readings of the linguistic models of thought and speech presentation, the conventional interdependence of narrative realism and the mimesis of consciousness have been re-considered by stressing the impression of the narrative immediacy as an illusion evoked by rhetorical means (Fludernik 1993; see also Mäkelä 2011). The idea of mimetic modes as more direct, empathy-promoting, realistic, distinctive, and more reproductive than the telling mode of diegetic discourse (considered to be marked by impersonation, detachment, compression, and narratorial control) is questioned by Sternberg (1982: 148) in his formulation of the "Proteus Principle": same form of discourse (whether direct or indirect) "may fulfill different functions *and* different forms the same function" (emphasis his). The degree of representativeness or directness of representation depends on the object and the context of quotation, not on the formal features of discourse modes.

19   Narrated (free indirect) perception has been seen as one of those narrative techniques that serve as an interface between the internal consciousness and its external, physical context. It involves those instances in which the characters' perceptions of physical events appear "to be pure narratorial report but that, on reflection, can be read as descriptions of events or states in the storyworld as experienced by a particular fictional mind," as Palmer (2004: 49) notes. Also the combined use of psycho-narration and narrated perception results in the interaction between consciousness and its social and physical environments. In Cohn's (1983: 111) typology the concept of narrated monologue excludes narrated perception (free indirect perception) as a distinct mode: writers use their characters "merely to reflect (but not to reflect *on*) the external events they witness."

20   According to Fludernik (1996: 48-49), it is no coincidence that a neutral narrative

began to develop on the historical stage at a time when the consciousness novel had already established its conventions and readers had become accustomed to them.

21　As Zunshine (2011: 352) argues, figures of speech (or underlying themes, evocations, aphorisms, metaphors, or allusions) may introduce mental states into otherwise reportorial narratives.

22　According to Doležel (1998: 172–173), the interplay of explicit and implicit meaning can be seen as the basis for the interpretation of literary texts: "[I]mplicitness is cultivated, it is a factor of their aesthetic effectiveness."

23　Hän käveli kuusiaidan viertä ympärilleen katsellen. Hän ihmetteli sitä, että navetta oli rakennettu erilleen talosta ja pihasta, mutta sitten hän näki, että tie oli oikaistu juuri talon kohdalla, navetta oli jäänyt tien toiselle puolen. Uusi tie oli vienyt mennessään osan sireeniaidasta, sireenipensaat olivat vielä juurineen revittyinä tien ohessa./– Vanhoja ne olivatkin, hän ajatteli. Yrittävät vielä keväällä työntää lehteä, mutta siihen se jää, huomaavat olevansa kuolleita. Uusi tie oli hiekkaisessa mäessä kuin tuore haava, pensaitten ja varpujen juuret värähtelivät tuulessa kuin katkotut suonet, tien vierelle pystytetyt kepit pitelivät haavan reunoja auki kuin pinsetit. Hän ajatteli, että kestää monta vuotta ennen kuin navetan takana näkyvä vanha tie on kasvanut umpeen.

24　The difference between description and figurative language, referential expressions and tropes, vanishes when literary description begins to employ figures of speech. The reader, who is looking for signs of verisimilitude from a text, expects the figurative expressions to contribute to the mimetic representation of the world. The reader looks for resemblances, similarities between these two distinct systems. Both description and figures of speech refer to a certain object. The referent of description constitutes the primary object, which is compared to the fictional "secondary object" within the framework of figurative language. The reader perceives this secondary object to serve only as a means of rendering the primary object of description, to reinforce the illusion of verisimilitude ascribed to it. The reader interprets both the figurative and non-figurative aspects of the description as referring to the same object. (Riffaterre 1981: 107–108)

25　According to Lyytikäinen (1992: 124), the difference between description and figurative presentation appears in the linear and non-linear translation of meaning: "Description and narration, however, belong to the same level; together they evoke the world of the work, the fictional 'realities' (together they accomplish mimesis). They translate meanings on the linear level. Figurative presentation, on the other hand, transgresses the linear translation of meaning." ("Kuvaus ja kertominen kuuluvat kuitenkin samalle tasolle, ne yhdessä synnyttävät teoksen maailman, fiktiiviset 'realiteetit' (ne yhdessä siis toteuttavat mimesiksen). Ne vievät merkityksiä eteenpäin lineaarisessa tasossa. Sen sijaan kuvallisuus rikkoo merkityksen lineaarisen etenemisen.") Every anomaly within mimesis serves as a sign of semiosis: as a 'breach' through which the meaning escapes by way of connotation (Lyytikäinen 1992: 156).

26　In the similes used by Vartio as psycho-analogies, the analogy of *tenor* and *vehicle* is actualized as the relation of two distinct conceptual domains, usually an abstract emotion and a concrete thing. The emotion (as the target domain) is part of the fictional reality, whereas the "concrete object" (as the source domain) exists only through the comparison, signaled by the copula "as if " (or "like") linked by conceptual blending.

27　Tiestä, kommunikaation tunnuskuvasta, tulee teoksen maailmassa erottava tekijä. Se on modernin tehokkuusyhteiskunnan väline, avoin "haava", joka rikkoo luonnollisia yhteyksiä. Tie enemmän vie kuin tuo, sitä pitkin pääsee jostakin jonnekin pois.

28　The Finnish translation by Lauri Viljanen (1949: 83) goes as follows: "Huhtikuu on kuukausista julmin, se työntää / sireenejä kuolleesta maasta, sekoittaa / muiston ja pyyteen, kiihoittaa / uneliaita juuria kevätsateella. / Talvi piti meidät lämpiminä, kietomalla / maan lumeen ja unohdukseen, kätkemällä / elämän hivenen kuiviin juurikyhmyihin ".

29 The speculation on Vartio's purpose of writing *Hänen olivat linnut* as a sequel to *Se on sitten kevät* (see Ruuska 2012: 448) is supported by an allusion to T. S. Eliot's poem in Vartio's last novel: "Spring is cruel, isn't it?" (*PW*, 65) Adele says to Alma while listening to the scream of the birds. ("[K]evät on raaka, eikö totta"; *H*, 67)

30 On the diffused and dispersive distribution of intertextual signs and allusive hints, cf. Nummi 2008.

31 Tie nousi kuusien välistä mäelle. Ensin oli ollut leveää asfalttitietä, ainakin kymmenen kilometriä, sitten tavallista soratietä. Vielä viisi kilometriä sivutietä, se oli ollut huonossa kunnossa. Linja-auto oli heittelehtinyt kuin laiva, eivät olleet vielä tasoittaneet, tie oli äsken tehty, työmaan jäljiltä olivat seipäät tien vierillä vielä tuoreet. Vanhaa kylätietä oli parannettu, levennetty ja pahimmat mutkat oiottu. Auto oli kulkenut joen yli, siitä laskeutui alas pariskunta, vaimo oli voinut autossa pahoin. Vartalosta ei vielä ollut huomannut mutta kasvoista oli nähnyt, että hän oli raskaana, poskissa ja otsalla näkyi läikkiä.

32 Hän oli istunut odotussalissa oven vieressä. Ihmiset kulkevat ovissa, ovi jää liikkumaan edestakaisin, ei ehdi pysähtyä, kun taas tulee joku ja ovi paukahtaa, jää heilumaan. Hän näkee itsensä istumassa oven vieressä penkillä. Hän on tullut junassa pitkän matkan, kantanut rautatieasemalta raskaat tavarat linja-autolle. Hän oli menossa uuteen työpaikkaan, paikka on Helsingin lähellä. Puheensorina ja kadulta kuuluvat äänet sulautuvat yhteen, ne ympäröivät hänen väsyneen olonsa kuin jokin kiinteä aine, se painaa hänet penkin nurkkaan.

33 Nainen liikahti kärsimättömästi, kuin viskaten luotaan jotain. Hän tunsi närästystä. Mitä rasvaa siinä oli? hän ajatteli.

34 James Joyce's concept of epiphany can be defined as a transcendent moment of understanding, which is marked by an intensified awareness of the self, an opening up to interior states of knowing. In the early version of *A Portrait of the Artist as a Young Man*, entitled *Stephen Hero*, Joyce (1944: 211) defined an epiphany as "a sudden spiritual manifestation, whether in the vulgarity of speech or of gesture or in a memorable phase of the mind itself." In the Christian tradition, epiphany refers to Christ's revelation as a man, his baptism or the three magi's visit to manger.

35 Hän oli luullut sen maistuvan samalta kuin ennen. Mutta puraistessaan ensimmäistä palaa hänelle oli tullut paha mieli *kuin* petetylle lapselle [...].

36 Talo oli liian uudenaikainen. Miten, sitä hän ei olisi osannut sanoa, hän oli vain tuntenut sen kuin taudin, jonka nimeä ja sijaintikohtaa ei pysty määrittelemään.

37 Lian haju ja raskas ilma ovat käyneet hänelle varsinkin viime aikoina vastenmielisiksi, se johtuu sairaudestakin, hengenahdistuksesta, lääkäri oli sanonut, että sydän ei ole kunnossa.

38 Salista tupaan ja tuvasta aittaan ja aitasta halkoliiteriin.

39 [...] eivät enää [...] eivät ole muotia.

40 [K]auluksen karvat olivat lamassa.

41 Nainen nukkuu selällään, ulkoa tuleva kuunpaiste valaisee hänen kasvonsa. Hiusraja on alhaalla, tukka on paksu ja tumma, otsa on leveä ja pyöreä, kulmakarvat myötäilevät hiusten voimaa ja mustuutta, nenä on suora. Huulet näkyvät kasvoissa kapeana viivana, suupielissä on väsynyt, raskas ilme. Leuka on voimakas ja leveä, juuri leuka saa kasvot näyttämään kovilta, kun hän nukkuu. Silmien ollessa auki kasvojen ilme on pehmeämpi./Hän kääntyy unissaan, peitto luisuu alas niin että vartalon yläosa jää näkyviin. Pumpulitrikoisen yöpaidan kaula-aukosta kohoaa lyhyt kaula, rinnat ovat suurikokoiset. Käsivarret ovat peiton päällä, ne ovat tukevat, sormien päät ovat leveät. Kasvot ovat kääntyneet hieman sivuttain, ilme

on muuttunut, kasvoissa on nyt jotain avutonta. Nainen kääntyy vielä kerran nukkuessaan, niin että hiuspalmikko näkyy kokonaan, palmikko alkaa niskasta ranteen paksuisena ja sen pikkusormen levyinen latuskainen pää ulottuu vyötärön alapuolelle.

42 The description alludes not only to the literary genre of *blazon* (the detailed description of a female figure), but also to the composition of visual art. The composition of "sleepwatchers" in visual art shows two figures, one of them in the shadows watching the other one sleeping. According to Leo Steinberg (1972), the composition serves as a means of examining the different states of being, as well as the possibilities of the dreamer to escape the intruder's gaze into the inner worlds of dream beyond the sleepwatcher's reach.

43 Hänen kasvoilleen alkoi kohota hymy, mutta hymy sammui kesken, niin kuin syttyvään tuleen olisi viskattu vettä. Silmät katsoivat suoraan eteen, kuin tuijottaen kiinteästi jotain, sitten ne käännähtivät hieman alas, siinä asennossa silmät näyttivät katsovan ristiin.

44 [...] näytti katsovan jotain, kuuntelevan jotain, jonka kuulemiseen oli keskittäydyttävä.

45 Karjakko heräsi, sytytti valon ja katsoi kelloa: navettaan lähtöön oli vielä aikaa. Hän nousi kuitenkin vuoteesta. [...] Aurinko nousi kuusikon reunan takaa. Hän kulki navetalle tien reunaa pitkin, jossa lumi oli jäätynyt yön aikana kovaksi ja kantavaksi. Karjakeittiön ovella hän seisahtui ja katsoi nousevaa aurinkoa. Sisällä oli hämärää, keittiön haju tuntui aamuilman jälkeen pahalta. Hyllyllä oli kumollaan kolme maitotonkkaa, lypsyrätit ja pyyhkeet riippuivat kuivumassa tonkkien päällä. Hyllyt olivat likaiset, kauttaaltaan maitotahroissa. Hän nosti padan kantta, padan pohjalla näkyi ruosteenväristä vettä. Hän haki karjakeittiön eteisestä lastuja, sytytti tulen padan alle. Sitten hän lakaisi lattian ja työnsi tulisijan vierille kasaantuneet roskat tuleen. Valuttaessaan kumiletkulla vettä pataan hän piti kättään valuvan veden alla, vesi roiskahti silmille, hän peräytyi nopeasti padan luota ja kolautti jalkansa ämpäriin.

46 Hän oli tullut talon portaitten eteen. Kääntyessään vielä katsomaan taakseen, saunalle päin, hän huomasi lumessa saunan seinän vierellä suuren valkean esineen. Hän ei ensin tajunnut mikä se oli, sitten hän huomasi, että se oli kylpyamme. Hän tuijotti sitä niin, että kun ikkuna rämähti auki, hän säpsähti kuin syvästä unesta herätetty.

47 The concept of "background emotions" used in cognitive sciences refers to the emotional responses that are closer to the inner core of life, such as calmness or bodily tension. Background emotions can be detected as subtle changes in the level of alertness, arousal, and overall shaping of an individual's body posture and movements. (Damasio 2000: 51–53)

48 Hän sulkee silmät. Mutta pimeys on täynnä kuvia. Mitä pitemmälle yö kuluu ja mitä väsyneemmäksi hän itsensä tuntee, sitä selvemmiksi kuvat käyvät. Ne irtoavat ympäristöstään, ovat hajallaan hänen silmiensä edessä kuin korttipakka. Joku liikuttaa kuvia, nopeasti, sitten liike pysähtyy, hänen on katsottava silmien eteen jäänyttä kuvaa niin kauan kuin se viipyy.

49 Hän käännähtää, avaa silmänsä ja katsoo pimeydessä erottuvaa vaaleaa kohtaa, siinä on ikkuna. Hän sulkee silmät. Kuva on yhä silmien edessä samana.

50 Kuvassa on pyöreä pöytä, pöydän ääressä istuu kolme naista. Hän on itse se, joka istuu keittiön oven viereisessä pöydän päässä.

51 Linja-auto oli heittelehtinyt kuin laiva [...].

52 Kuvat vilisevät, menee autoja, menee junia, auto keinuu, *ei, se onkin laiva* [...].

53 Tulee vielä kuvia, tulee ihmisiä, joilla on epätodelliset kasvot. Mutta ne ovat puolittain unta [...]. Kuvat sulautuvat veden väriin, ovat vettä, ovat unta.

54 [Kuvien avulla] sekavana lainehtineet toiminnat, repliikit [...] asettautuivat paikoilleen.

55 [Taiteen kuvio] on niin *täynnä mieltä ja merkitystä* että [kirjailijan] on se sanottava (Vartio 1996: 93).

56 Minä olen tässä runossa *pelkkä kuva täyttä mieltä.* The English translation of Haavikko's poem is Herbert Lomas's (1991: 125). Whereas Lomas's translation focuses on *mieli* as mind in the poem's ambiguous line, Anselm Hollo's (1991: 56) translation of the poem, on the other hand, focuses on *mieli* as meaning: "I am in this poem *merely an image, pure meaning.*"

57 *Mieli* tarkoittaa mm. merkityssisältöä eli signifikaatiota tai mielekkyyttä vastakohtana mielettömyydelle ja merkityksettömyydelle. *Mieli* on myös egon ja tietoisuuden olemassaoloa osoittava käsite. '*Kuvan*' määritelmässä on mahdollista yhdistää nämä kaikki merkitysvariaatiot. 'Kuva' välittää mielen eli tietoisuuden läsnäolon täytenä mielenä: mielekkyytenä, täytenä merkityssisältönä.

58 In the Finnish context the "image" is a defining concept that encapsulates many aspects of the modernist poetics of the 1950s. The image has been the subject of an academic discussion in Finnish literary studies (see Hökkä 1991, Kaunonen 1997, Hollsten 2004), but thus far, its role in relation to the poetics of the Finnish new novel has not been scrutinized.

59 In practice, however, the concreteness of "images" in Finnish modernist poems seldom appears as "simple" as it was suggested. They involved "clarity" similar to Wittgenstein's philosophy of language: easy to read, but difficult to understand (see von Wright 2001: 11–12).

60 Jos teoksesta puuttuu pimeys, siitä puuttuu kaikki.

61 [M]ieli kuvaansa tarkempi [...].

62 The tragic love plot is exemplified by such classic works as William Shakespeare's *Romeo and Juliet* or Emily Brontë's *Wuthering Heights.*

63 In Roland Barthes's *A Lover's Discourse* (1977) the formula of love affair is depicted as *figures* that cluster around the climactic moment of falling in love (*ravissement*). These figures involve the progression of romance: absence, waiting, jealousy, declaration, union etc.

64 – Martikainen, nainen esittäytyy. Hän huomaa sanoneensa nimensä kömpelösti, miehen kohteliaisuus on saanut hänet hämilleen. Sitä paitsi tilanteessa on jotain turhanaikaista, esittäytyä näin [...].

65 – Kuka se on se mies joka asuu siinä samassa rakennuksessa, hän jatkoi puhettaan ja kumartui ammentamaan padasta vettä./– Napoleon, emäntä sanoi. Joko tapasitte hänet? [...] /Emäntä sanoi, että mies oli hyvin taitava. Hän naurahti./ Karjakko oli juuri kysymäisillään vielä miehestä, hän aikoi kysyä oliko mies talossa vuokralaisena, niin kuin hän oli miehen puheesta ymmärtänyt. Mutta hän ei kuitenkaan kysynyt./– Flinkman, emäntä sanoi, ja lisäsi pienen taon jälkeen: – Se on asunut meillä jo kauan, on kuin omaa väkeä./Karjakko oli tietämättään käynyt varovaiseksi, hän jatkoi puhetta lehmistä.

66 Tulin voimalliseksi ja toisaalta onnettomaksi kun tiesin mitä symboleja ne ovat, A ja N. A on alkuperäisen [...] tervevaistoisen ihmisen symboli, individualisti ym. sellaista hyvää, voimakas ja hyvä nainen, ja N. on ei suinkaan niin yksiselitteinen retku, huijari. Vaan tämän nykyajan puolivillaisuuden uhri, jo valmis uhri. [...] Tämä Anni on jotain vanhaa ja aitoa edustava, joka aitona ei sulaudu Napoleonin edustamaan puolivillaisuuteen. [...] Ja arkku edustaa, symbolisoi aikaa, joka niinikään on menossa hautaan [...].

67 Esimerkiksi se seikka, että miehen nimi oli Napoleon. Nimi oli minulle omituista merkitystä täynnä. [...] [K]äytin tuota Napoleonia häikäilemättä hyväkseni enkä olisi suostunut vaihtamaan nimeä toiseksi; minulla oli siihen omat syyni.

68 Napoleon istuu karjakon huoneessa, he ovat juoneet kahvia. Siitä kun he istuivat ensimmäisen kerran saman pöydän ääressä on kulunut viikko, he ovat juoneet kahvia yhdessä joka päivä, mies tulee naisen huoneeseen kuin kotiinsa, hän ei kysy enää ovella kumartaen, saako hän tulla, ei koputa, avaa vain oven, istuu pöydän

ääreen lehteä lukemaan tai heittäytyy sängyn päälle pitkälleen odotellessaan kahvia.

69 Nainen tuntee käden lämmön, tuntee että käsi painaa hänen kättään, mutta ei vedä kättä pois, hän ajattelee ettei mies huomaa, ja siksi hän ei likuta kättään, ettei toinen luulisi hänen luulevan jotain.

70 Sitten hän kääntyy katsomaan miestä, hänen kasvonsa ovat rauhalliset, kasvojen ilme on kova, miltei epäystävällinen.

71 Nainen jää seisomaan. Hänen ajatuksensa ovat hätääntyneet, hän on *pettynyt* ja *häpeissään*, hän oli toivonut, ettei mies olisi vielä mennyt, että mies olisi sanonut jotain.

72 In the classic romance plot, sex is either made invisible or sublimated by making sexual encounter the legitimate (but unspoken) goal of romance (Pearce & Stacey 1995: 21).

73 Hän sammuttaa savukkeen, nousee istumaan vuoteen reunalle. Hän lähtee huoneestaan, kulkee alusvaatteisillaan tuttua tietä, hän on kulkenut näin eteisen läpi yöllä ennenkin, talossa on ollut karjakoita ennenkin./Hän ei koputa naisen huoneen ovelle, hän avaa oven, katsoo kynnykseltä vuodetta kohti. Pää liikahtaa tyynyllä, nainen on kuullut askeleet eteisestä./Hän kohottautuu vuoteessa istualleen, hän ei sano mitään. Mutta mies on tullut vuoteen reunalle istumaan. Mies on laskenut kätensä naisen hiuksille ja sanonut: – Minä pidän pitkistä hiuksista./ Nainen painuu takaisin pitkälleen, mies on laskeutunut hänen viereensä, nainen makaa hiljaa, mustat hiukset pään ympärillä kuin ukkospilvi.

74 Isäntä otti pullon käteensä, tavasi nimeä pullon kyljestä, hän arveli pullon maksavan monta tuhatta. Mutta mitä heistä, köyhistä. – Napoleon on Napoleon, hän sanoi.

75 Hänen oikea nimensä oli Nils Flinkman, mutta sitä ei kukaan enää muistanut.

76 Napoleon kääntyi emäntään päin, sanoi ruotsiksi jotain mihin emäntä vastasi naurahtamalla, mutta samalla hän punastui.

77 Molemmat naiset kuulivat isännän äänen ja näkivät miesten ilmeen. Anni aavisti mitä emäntä ajatteli ja isäntä aavisti mitä emäntä ajatteli, ja Napoleon tiesi mitä muut kolme ajattelivat. Mutta kukaan ei sanonut mitään.

78 Ja hän oli poistunut sitten hiukset kiiltävinä ja hyvin aseteltuina, kumartanut ovella vielä niin, että jäivät katsomaan jälkeen.

79 This episode resembles the real-life competitive storytelling between Vartio and the author Kirsi Kunnas. Vartio won this competition by narrating her erotic dream of Marshal Carl Gustaf Emil Mannerheim. (See Saari 2009: 104–105)

80 Kaikki kolme olivat hiljaa, kuin olisivat nähneet näyn, niin kuin hevosen henki olisi mennyt mieheen, puhaltanut hänet tuolilta lattialle, pyörittänyt miestä ja mennyt pois, jättänyt punoittavan, kiiluvasilmäisen miehen yksin.

81 [M]itä kannattaa tällä tavalla olla ja valehdella.

82 "Occurrence" is a "neutral term" that Hogan (2011a: 32–33) uses to refer to the background noise of happenings, from which the "incidents" stand out as more crucial when they arouse emotional responses.

83 Hän harjasi lehmiä vaikka oli aamulla ne viimeksi harjannut, hän lakaisi lehmien pöydät ja pesi juottokupit, vaikka oli pessyt ne edellisenä päivänä. Ja työtä tehdessään hän välillä unohti, miksi yhä viipyi navetassa [...].

84 Padasta nousi höyry, kiehuvan veden ääni kuului padan kannen alta. Hän muisti, että padassa oli vähän vettä, vesi kiehuisi kuiviin. Hän nousi, valutti letkulla pataan vettä kunnes se oli reunojaan myöten täysi. Hän lisäsi puita, siirsi jakkaran lähemmäksi tulisijaa. – Hän liikahti, hänen suunsa avautui, kuului ääni, joka oli kuin eläimen suusta lähtenyt, kuin eläimen, joka ääntelee pimeässä. Hän painoi käden suulleen.

85 Ja hän teki samat liikkeet ja samat asiat kuin minä päivänä tahansa, riisui ku-

misaappaat, asetti ne vierekkäin huoneen oven ulkopuolelle, riisui huivin ja otti yltään työtakin [...].

86 Hän kampasi hiukset, ainoa poikkeava liike oli hiusten kampaaminen peilin edessä.

87 [...] joutunut elämässään väärälle uralle.

88 [...] vaikka hän varmasti tiesi, oli omin silmin nähnyt miehen korjailevan muttereita ja työkaluja omiin varastoihinsa [...].

89 Laillinen? Napoleon *hämmästyi.* Hänen eronsa oli laillinen.

90 Mitä siihen olisi pitänyt sanoa? [...] Hän, Napoleon, piti *sanomisia ja sanomisten sanomisia* hermostuttavana, ja miksi puhua vanhoista asioista, joille ei mahtanut mitään?

91 Sen toukokuun Napoleon rakensi puimalaa. Anni teki kukkapenkin ikkunan alle, Napoleon käänsi lapiolla maan ja kantoi metsästä koivujen juurelta kukkapenkkiin lehtimultaa.

92 [T]oiset talossa nauroivat, ja ihmettelivät, että Napoleon pysyi kotona. Ja talonväki tiesi Napoleonin jo kaksi kertaa kieltäytyneen ottamasta.

93 [...] alkavansa elämän uudestaan.

94 – Sinä olet saatana, Anni sanoi sen tasaisella, tyynellä äänellä./– Mikä sinulla on? Napoleon kysyi sitä miltei uteliaasti. Mikä sillä oli, seisoo tuossa hänen edessään, katsoo kuin mitäkin esinettä, oikein tutkii. Hän hermostui, siirtyi Annin edestä pois, syrjään./– Oletko sinä sairas? Kun olet noin kalpea. Mitä sinä puhut?/Anni katsoi samaan kohtaan, siihen missä mies oli äsken seisonut. Hänen suupielensä taipuivat alaspäin. Hän nyökäytti päätään, kasvoilla ei ollut mitään./– Hullu se on, hullu se on, Napoleon toisti itselleen. Se on hullu, hän ajatteli./– Ja paskat ratsut sillä on, huora Helsingissä./Annin suu meni vinoon, pää nytkähteli niin kuin olisi ollut kiinni narussa, josta vetäistiin. Hän katsoi lattiaan./Hän oli tuokion niin, nosti päänsä, huulet oikenivat.

95 – Vihata? Hän ei vihannut ketään eikä mitään. Hänestä oli kaikki samantekevää. Eilen illalla hän oli vielä ajatellut, että hänen olisi pitänyt pysyä siellä missä oli ollut. Elämä oli joka paikassa samanlaista. – Minkä sinä itsellesi mahdat? En minä sinua voi muuttaa, eikä se minun asiani ole.

96 – Pitäisikö minun – minunko se pitäisi tietää?

97 [T]uloksena oli se, että he taas elivät kuin ei mitään olisi tapahtunut. Mies sai mennä ja tulla, nainen tiesi, että tämä menisi ja tulisi, tahtoi hän sitä tai ei. [...] Ja Anni oli nukkunut yöt rauhallisesti [...].

98 The Platonian image of a shadow (as an idea being projected on the "wall" of the visible world) is related here to the psychology of the characters. "The shadow" is also one of Jung's archetypes that signifies the unconscious, rejected or projected aspects in an individual's personality.

99 Anni katsoo miestä. Mies ei käännä kasvojaan lehdestä, ei näe naisen kasvojen ilmettä. Nainen katsoo eikä kuitenkaan katso. Mies on hänelle kuin oma käsi, kuin seinällä varjo, joka on hänen oma varjonsa. Miehen puhe ei ole enää hänen korvissaan outoa, miehen tavat eivät hänestä omituisia.

100 [H]än tunsi miehessä levottomuuden, mieli teki kaupunkiin, hän oli oppinut jo ymmärtämään mitä tämän mielessä liikkui.

101 [H]än on uskovinaan ja tekevinään niin kuin mies on määrännyt, mutta tekee niin kuin itse parhaaksi näkee.

102 Hän oli keittänyt itselleen kahvia, ja kun kahvi oli valmista, kaatanut sitä kuppiinsa, eikä ollut muuta kuin kuppi jota hän puristi kämmeniinsä ja kupissa kuuma kahvi, joka lämmitti niitä.

103 [...] miten kahviläiskä laajeni ja haarautui pitkin punaista pöytää eri suuntaisiksi joiksi. Kahvi lirisi lattialle, lirinä muuttui tipahtelevien pisaroitten ääneksi, tipahtelut harvenivat, loppuivat.

104 On kuin ne muuttaisivat majaa.

105 Mihin he menisivät, mies puhui. Että hän oli joutunutkin pesään.

106 Ei lintu ymmärtäisi, mitä he tarkoittavat, ei ymmärtäisi että he tahtovat sen pelastaa. Lintu vain hakkaisi nokkansa verille, takoisi siipensä poikki savupiipun seiniin. Että nainen saattoi olla niin julma, ahdistaa lintua savulla ja tulella!

107 In *Napoleon*, the collective unconscious finds expression as an inner feminine personality (the anima), while, in *Anni* it manifests itself in the inner masculine personality (the animus).

108 [H]än, nainen, ei pelännyt.

109 Nainen meni ulos, pysähtyi pihamaalle. Hän katsoi katolle, kiersi talon taakse, pysähtyi tikapuitten juurelle. Nokkoset peittivät tikapuitten alimmat askelmat kokonaan, vaan [sic] joistakin taittuneista varsista saattoi uskoa todeksi, että mies oli seisonut katolla. Ämpäri oli vierinyt pitkin kervaista maata, pysähtynyt kiveen. Nainen meni ämpärin luokse, käänsi sitä jalallaan, ämpärissä oli sanka jäljellä. Hän katsoi ämpäriä. Se oli avaruudesta pudonnut kappale, eksynyt ja hylätty. Yö oli mennyt. Mutta mustana ja pohjattomana oli ämpäri kukkivien kervien päällä./Siitä päivästä tuli helteinen. Mehiläiset lensivät kukasta kukkaan ja ilma humisi. Kukilla oli kiire kukkia.

110 Kuu oli tullut esiin pilven takaa. Elokuun yö oli musta ja lämmin. Miehen hahmo suurena ja vaaleana taivasta ja metsän reunaa vasten, nainen alhaalla maassa, kasvot tähyämässä ylös, horsman kukka kädessä. Pilvet liikkuivat taivaalla ja kuu meni pilvien sekaan, tuli esiin, vilahti piiloon. He olivat kuin ukko ja akka, jotka menivät kuuta tervaamaan.

111 [A]kka ja ukko teki talon, akka pani havuja rappusen eteen, ukko pani myös, akka teki ikkunan, ukko teki myös, ukko nousi katolle, teki savupiipun, akka teki myös [...].

112 [J]a sitten ukko lähti vettä hakemaan, putos' kuoppaan, nous' kuopasta, putos' kuoppaan, – ja mitä kaikkea siinä on ja sitten siitä tulee kissa.

113 [...] suuri tila, kartano kenties [...].

114 [O]li paljon parempi alkaa kaikki alusta.

115 According to Kern (2011: 105), the modernists invented not only with accelerated and decelerated pacing (employed in *Se on sitten kevät*), but also "concurrent multiple pacing, and serial multiple pacing."

116 In Virginia Woolf's novel *To the Lighthouse* (1927), for instance, the second middle section, "Time Passes," depicts the sudden death of the protagonist, Mrs. Ramsay, narrated in an aloof manner.

117 Napoleon tuli pimennosta, hänen kasvonsa olivat ikkuna-aukossa kuin muotokuva mustalla taustalla.

118 [J]akaus näkyi vaaleana viivana, kuin joki yöllisessä maisemassa.

119 Oli satanut lumen marraskuun viimeisinä päivinä, ja vaikka välillä oli ollut suojasää ja lumi alkanut sulaa, niin suojasäätä oli kestänyt vain pari päivää, ja sitten oli pakastanut. Ja oli satanut lisää lunta, ja ilmat olivat pysyneet kirkkaina [...].

120 Kaksi viikkoa vain oli jouduttu olemaan ilman karjakkoa.

121 Hän hillitsi itsensä, jäi kuuntelemaan omaa ääntään, hänen äänensä oli ollut särkynyt, kimeä, se riippui ilmassa, putosi, hävisi. Kukaan ei kuullut.

122 Kuoleman teema on säätänyt kertomuksen osaset, antanut tapahtumiin välttämättömyyden tunnun ja eheyden. Kuoleman tunnelma on keskuksestaan käsin aaltoina säätänyt ennakoivat tapahtumat ja säätää jälkikäteen yksin jääneen miehen taittumisen.

123 A letter sent to Särkilahti by Anhava reveals that the publishing company had asked for some refinements to the manuscript of *Se on sitten kevät*. Vartio added "around ten pages" to the novel. The letter does not explain the actual placement of these pages in the novel's final design. Thus, there is a possibility that in the

interpretation provided by Särkilahti, the placement of the pages at the end of the novel may result from the scholar's conception of the editing process. Be that as it may, the work's final design implies that Anni's death represents one of the most elemental aspects in the semantic structure of *Se on sitten kevät*.

124 Flinkmanin valtoimenaan kuvitteleva, irtonaisen miehen vastuuton mieli ja Annin raskasliikkeinen asiallisuus yhtyvät [...] rakentamaan toivetta vakaisemmasta tulevaisuudesta... Se on toteutumaisillaan kun käy sattuma, luonnollinen ja äkillinen kuin ainakin elämässä, ja tekee lopun tästä haaveesta (Anhava 1957, the original edition of *Se on sitten kevät*).

125 Voisi sanoa, että 'Se on sitten kevät' on surullinen historia kahdesta jotka löysivät ja saivat toisensa... liian myöhään.

126 Napoleon katsoi ikkunasta ulos. Pellot, talot, tiet, ihmiset liukuivat ohitse kuin nauha, joka näyttää samaa kuvaa, jos käänsi silmät pois, käänsi takaisin, edessä oli samaa. Vesi virtasi taivaalta, puut tiet talot ihmiset virtasivat kuin vesi – keski-ikäinen nainen kulki tietä pitkin, yllään tumma päällystakki, laukku kädessä. Napoleon katsoi naista – hänen muistinsa tavoitti jotain, jolla oli ollut tumma takki, jotain joka oli seisonut tien vierellä laukku kädessä. Napoleon kääntyi vierustoverinsa puoleen odottaen, että toinen puhuisi hänelle, sanoisi jotain siitä *mikä oli langennut hänen päälleen kuin sade.*

127 Hän sanoi kerrankin aikoneensa tehdä jotain [...]. Elämä on saatava nyt lopulta järjestykseen.

128 Mutta nyt se on loppu. [...] Siitä oli tultava loppu [...].

129 At times, coincidence has been used more loosely as an umbrella term, a synonym for chance or any other accident or twist of fate. However, I resort here to Dannenberg's more limited definition of the concept.

130 Dannenberg (2008: 104) defines negative coincidence as "an *inversion* of the structure of the coincidental encounter because it involves the *nonconvergence* of an *intended* intersection in space and time that is the result of random circumstances" (emphasis hers).

131 Hän seisoi hetken kuin olisi pudonnut alas maailmasta joka oli ollut parempi kuin tämä maailma, jossa hän jälleen oli ja katsoi silmiin miestä, joka oli kauppias.

132 Mutta hän tiesi jo, *ettei ole surua* jota hän olisi tahtonut tuntea ja jota hän kuitenkin pelkäsi.

133 Ja hän oli joutunut tympeyden valtaan, hän tunsi tympeyttä kun mitään ei tullut, ei tapahtunut, kaiken ylle vain levisi tahmeutta muistuttava tuntu, se oli levinnyt ympäristöön, esineisiin, ajatuksiin, hänen omaan ruumiiseensa [...].

134 Hän ei ollut itselleen olemassa maatessaan hiljaa.

135 [N]aula [...] oli auttamattomasti mennyt vinoon [...].

136 Hän katsoi viimeistä naulaamaansa laudanpalaa, lauta sai koko tallin sekavaksi, niin kuin olisi pitänyt jatkaa eteenpäin, tai kuin jotain olisi särkynyt.

137 Napoleon [...] tunsi maan jalkojensa alla jäätyvän, hiekka oli kovettunut, tie vastasi askeliin.

138 [Uusi karjakko] nousi, tuli ikkunaan, mutta Napoleon meni jo maantiellä, katsomatta taakseen, hän tunsi sieraimissaan yöilman.

139 [S]iinä ei ole selväpiirteistä alku- eikä lopputilannetta eikä syysuhteista juonta, ja se on monitulkintainen.

140 Annin ja Napoleonin kohtaaminen ja erkaneminen jättävät lukijan pitkiksi ajoiksi miettimään. Kummankin menneisyys ja toisen tulevaisuus ovat aivan avoimet, ja on lopulta vaikea sanoa kumpi on mennyttä, nainen joka kuoli vai mies joka jäi elämään. Ehkä karakteristisin avoimen muodon tunnus tässä teoksessa on se, että vaikka lukija selvästi voi tajuta tekijän myötämielen olevan naisen puolella, se ei velvoita asettumaan samalle kannalle eikä tähtää mihinkään naisen korottamiseen tai miehen selittämiseen tai tapahtumien syy- ja arvosuhteiden punnintaan: maailma ei ole sellainen ja sellainen, se on.

141 The English translation of Chuang Tzu's parable is Burton Watson's (1968: 188–189).

142 Älkää kysykö minulta mitä se on. Se on sitä, että minä tunsin itseni todemmaksi lukiessani Annia.

143 In this respect, open form resembles *kōan*, a narrative or a dialogue characteristic of Zen-Buddhist tradition. *Kōan* is a puzzle that is meant to be resolved through intuition, not through reasoning or logic.

144 Romaani on tosiasiallisesti avoin muoto, se on monitulkintainen ja moneen suuntaan mieltä vievä, tarina-aineksen näköjään selväpiirteisestä ja jopa kuoleman umpisukkeloon päätyvästä kulusta huolimatta.

145 Hän vietti yönsä huoneessa ja lähti aamulla kaupunkiin, hän ei palannut.

146 Oli lehmä poikinut.

3. *Emotions of the Body. A Lingering Awakening in* Mies kuin mies, tyttö kuin tyttö

1 Kädessäni on peili, mutta se peili ei näytä / minulle kasvojani. / Se peili ei anna minulle minun kasvojani. / Kun nostan sen silmieni tasalle, / näen siinä vain maiseman [...] (*Häät*, 14). The English translation of the poem is Kirsti Simonsuuri's (1990: 9).

2 Mies katkaisi oksan puusta, heilautti sitä ja pudotti sen maahan. Oksa jäi keinumaan parin ruskean kuivan ruohon varaan. Hän liikautti jalkaansa, ruohot heilahtivat, ja oksa putosi näkymättömiin. Tyttö oli seurannut silmillään tuota tarkoituksetonta liikettä.

3 Some contemporary critics of *Mies kuin mies, tyttö kuin tyttö* addressed the "problem of a lonely mother" ("yksinäisen äidin ongelma"; Holappa 1959: 34) in the novel and read Leena's story as Vartio's commentary on the social issue of extramarital pregnancy and collective prejudice. This kind of reading is problematic, for Vartio's novel, and her fiction in general, involves semantic ambivalence that resists straight-forward ideological interpretations. Even when Vartio uses means of rhetorical persuasion, her novels never become openly political.

4 Characters' relationships among textual story worlds are not static. The conflicts within and between characters' private worlds, as well as the discrepancies between actual fictional worlds and the private worlds, make the stories move and the characters act. The movements establish the story patterns, which we usually call plot. The relations between worlds change continuously, and "[t]he plot is the trace left by the movement of these worlds within the textual universe," as Ryan (1991: 119) put it.

5 According to Kafalenos (1999: 34–35), suppressed or deferred knowledge creates epistemological gaps in characters' worlds and then affects the reader's interpretation of the text. The reader's interpretation may differ from what it would be if deferred or suppressed information were available at an earlier point in the story.

6 He olivat taas tulleet *siihen*, mikä aina vaiensi heidät, kun he *sen* muistivat, ja nostatti heidän välilleen kuin kylmää sumua.

7 Mutta tyttö mietti sitä, miksi mies ei halunnut puhua./Häpesikö hän jotain? Häpesikö hän itseään, naimisissa oloaan, vaimoaan? Aina kun he joutuivat puhuessaan sivuamaan miehen avioliittoa, tämä vaikeni tai alkoi puhua muusta.

8 [... haluten] näyttää, että hänelle saattoi puhua kaunistelematta.

9 Tyttö yritti päästä käsien otteesta, hän tahtoi päästä voitolle, vaikka se oli vain leikkiä. He väänsivät kumpikin katsoen toisiaan, ja tyttö ponnisteli irti, voitto oli

käynyt tärkeäksi, hänen ruumiinsa jännittyi. Mutta kädet pitivät lujasti kiinni, vaikka hän kavalasti teeskenteli jo antaneensa periksi, makasi hiljaa paikallaan, ja sitten äkkiä yritti tempautua; ja tätä jatkui kunnes tyttö alkoi nauraa ja herposi.

10 – Mikä, mikä minä sitten olen? Millainen, sano?

11 Palmer's analyses of Jane Austen's *Persuasion* and Charles Dickens' *Little Dorrit* show that the emotional fluctuation in love plots often stems from intermental breakdowns between characters. In reading these novels, the reader is often able to "be ahead of" the characters "in picking up the clues" about the characters' true feelings. (See Palmer 2010: 125, 154)

12 Oli kuin he olisivat siirrelleet pelinappulaa ruudukolla edestakaisin […] /Toinen siirsi nappulan mustalta valkealle ruudulle, toinen taas takaisin.

13 [H]än tunsi naisen läsnäolon niin kuin tämä olisi seisonut heidän välissään, katsonut häntä ylimielisesti ja pitänyt miehestä kiinni.

14 He istuivat ääneti välttäen katsomasta toisiinsa.

15 [E]n *tiedä* mitä hän *luulee*, mutta kyllä hän jo *tietää*, ainakin jotain.

16 [Leena] kääntyi katsomaan ja naurahti saadakseen toisen puhumaan lisää, koska tahtoi *tietää, tiesikö* tämä jotain, ja mitä.

17 – Kyllä minä *arvasin*, mutta *arvaa* sinä, mitä ne sanovat, kun saavat tietää.

18 Kyllä minä tiedän, mitä sinä ajattelet. […] /Luuletko sinä, etten minä ymmärrä. […] /sinä mietit vain, miten pääsisit minusta irti.

19 Oli turha antaa ihmisille suotta puheen aihetta. Tyttö oli niin nuori, ettei hän vielä ymmärtänyt, millaisia ihmiset oikein ovat. Kukaan ei ymmärtäisi heidän yhdessä olostaan muuta kuin sen, että hän oli vietellyt nuoren tytön […].

20 Hän ei uskaltanut katsoa sivulleen, jottei paljastaisi itseään, paljastaisi sitä, että toivoi miehen koskettavan […].

21 Tyttöä nauratti miehen neuvottomuus, eikä hän tuntenut mitään, *ei tahtonut tuntea* muuta kuin että mies oli tuossa avuttomana, piti hänestä eikä tiennyt mitä tehdä.

22 Kun he olivat lopettaneet, hänen mieleensä tuli *yhtä* ja *toista*.

23 Tyttö mietti, oliko hän se, jonka pitäisi jostain päättää. Ja mies oli hetken hänestä miltei vastenmielinen.

24 Mutta tyttö oli jo tuntenut, että miehen käsi oli hänen kädessään vieras, aivan kuin se olisi pysynyt siinä vain siksi, että hän piteli siitä kiinni.

25 Hän ei vastannut. Hän oli tuskin ymmärtänyt sanojen tarkoitusta. Ja vaikka hän itse oli tahtonut saada miehen sanomaan nuo sanat, niin nyt, kun ne oli sanottu, hän ei osannut vastata mitään, koska ei tiennyt mitä olisi pitänyt sanoa./Hän tunsi, miten mies kääntyi jälleen. Ja hän tiesi, että äskeiset sanat eivät olleet tarkoittaneet sitä, mitä mies oli luullut sanovansa, ja hän ajatteli, että myös miehellä oli ehkä joskus paha olo.

26 Mies selitti valokuvauksella saatavan aikaan kaikenlaisia asioita, kun kuva vain otettiin tietystä kulmasta.

27 Mies ei ymmärtänyt hänen kuvittelujaan, vaan suhtautui niihin kuin lapsen puheisiin.

28 [H]än muutti mieltään: saattoi niitä luulla linnuiksi, jos katsoi sillä mielellä, että tahtoi ne nähdä lintuina.

29 Minä kai näen sinussa samaa mitä sinä minussa.

30 Ja tuska nousi taas noitten käsien ja tuon arven vuoksi; hän oli löytänyt ne koskettaessaan miestä pimeässä.

31 – Luuletko, että meistä jää jotain tähän paikkaan, luuletko että kun toiset ihmiset elävät täällä ja kaikki on toisenlaista, että meistä on jotain jäljellä. […] /– Luuletko, ettei mitään jää jäljelle?/– En tiedä, en minä osaa vastata./– Mutta sano jotain… Etkö usko, että tämä kivi ja kalliot ja tuo vesi, ja kuu, eikö niihin jää minusta jotain, kun minä tahdon niin./– Mitä sinä itse luulet?/– Minä olen varma, minä olen siitä varma. Ja sitten toiset ihmiset istuvat tässä, tällä samalla kivellä, ja ne kysyvät,

kuka tässä on istunut, ennen heitä./– Niin, ei maailma tähän lopu, jos sitä noin ajattelee. Kai ihmiset aina tuntevat samat asiat samalla tavoin./– Mutta minusta tuntuu siltä, että sinä et oikeastaan välitä minusta ollenkaan, sinä vain luulet./Tyttö ei muistanut, kuka hänen vierellään istui. Kun tulitikku valaisi miehen kasvot, hän näki ne. Mies häiritsi häntä, hän ei halunnut kuulla mitään.

32 Randall Stevenson (1998: 45–46) examines the use of the same method in the work of Dorothy Richardson, the first author to have created a stream of consciousness presentation of her characters.

33 Se oli minun takkini, se putosi lattialle./Hänen silmänsä olivat kokonaan auki ja katsoivat kattoon. Katossa oli kaksi vaaleanruskeaa kuviota ja hän ajatteli, että katto oli vuotanut./Sitten hän sanoi itselleen: Minä olen: minä olen se, joka on tässä./Ja hetken kuluttua hän kysyi itseltään: Olenko minä se, joka makaa tässä./Leena. Hän ajatteli nimensä: Leena./Ja käden etsiytyessä hänen vyötärölleen ja avatessa hameen hakasta hän ajatteli:/Minun käteni auttaa avaamaan hakaset./Ja hän kohottautui jälleen niin että selkä oli kaarella kuin silta sen ajan, minkä miehen käsi veti hametta alas lanteilta, ja alas sääriä pitkin. Ja käsi laski hameen lattialle.

34 Minä olen riisuttu, nyt. Minulle tapahtuu. Nyt./Ja sitten hän ajatteli: Onko minun ääneni tuo, joka sanoo: ei, ei./Olenko minä se, joka sanoo: Minä en tahdo, minä en uskalla, ja kuitenkin auttaa kättä, joka riisuu minut nyt./Tällaistako se on. Tämä, mikä minulle pian tapahtuu, on nyt se./Ja hän säikähti ja sanoi kovalla äänellä: – Ei./Eikä hän kuitenkaan voinut enää tehdä mitään noustakseen, lähteäkseen pois./Olenko minä nyt huono nainen?

35 As Cohn (1983: 81) writes: "[I]f some writers employ the monologue technique to demonstrate how the conscious mind habitually fends off disturbing truths, others reserve it for those special occasions when this defense mechanism breaks down in the course of a momentous inner crisis."

36 According to Robert Humphrey (1955: 2–3), for instance, "[s]tream-of-consciousness fiction differs from all other psychological fiction precisely in that it is concerned with those levels that are more inchoate than rational verbalization – those levels on the margin of attention [...] 'prespeech level.'" The terms psyche, consciousness, and mind, respectively are employed as synonymous concepts indicating "the entire area of mental attention" (ibid.: 2) from pre-consciousness to rational, communicable awareness.

37 The concept of cognitive (or adaptive) unconscious used in cognitive sciences differs from Freud's dynamic unconscious, which is a "darker, more malevolent place where emotionally charged memories are shipped to do mental dirty work" (LeDoux 1998: 29–30). The notion of a cognitive unconscious refers to the tendency of mental processes to take place beyond awareness. It involves memory, automatic sensations, wakefulness, and other aspects of attention. The emotional unconscious, on the other hand, refers to "wordless knowing," the embodied processing of knowledge related to intuition and automatic emotional responses. Sometimes the only manifestation of mental content is a physical reaction to the cause, to which the conscious mind has no access.

38 Tyttö oli pysähtynyt. Porrasaukko hohti kullanvärisenä, ilta-auringon valo lankesi yläkerran eteisen ikkunaan ja valaisi portaat ylhäältä päin, mutta alhaalla oli hämärää. Askelmia peittävä lattiamatto oli vaalea ja puhdas./Tyttö lähti nousemaan. Päästyään pari askelmaa hän pysähtyi./– Katso, ovatko minun kenkäni puhtaat./Hän oli kohottanut jalkansa, piti sitä koholla. Jäljessä tuleva mies näki kumisen kengänpohjan uurteet kasvojensa tasalla./– Puhtaat ovat. Tyttö tunsi miehen sormien puristautuvan nilkkansa ympärille./– Päästä irti, minä putoan. Hän hyppi yhden jalan varassa ja oli horjahtamaisillaan./Katsomatta taakseen hän jatkoi nousemista. Takaa kuului miehen ääni: – Et putoa, minä otan kiinni.

39 [...] niin puhdas kuin ei kukaan olisi sen päällä kävellyt.

40 [...] mitä likaa siinä oikein oli ollut, mihin hän oli astunut.

41 Hän otti taskusta peilin ja näki siinä vaalean läiskän ja kaksi tummempaa kohtaa./Ne ovat minun silmäni. Samat silmät, vaikka oli tapahtunut se, minkä hän pelkäsi näkyvän kasvoistaan./Hän kosketti kädellään kaulaa ja poskia, ja kun hän laski käden veltosti putoamaan alas, se hipaisi rintaa ja karkasi pois kuin olisi koskettanut palavaa esinettä. *Kosketus oli herättänyt täyden ja selvän tiedon siitä, mitä oli tapahtunut.*/Rinnat. Niitten nimi. Pyöreät kappaleet, jotka olivat kulkeneet hänen mukanaan tähän saakka niinkuin käsi, jalka, mikä tahansa ruumiinosa. Niillä oli nimi: rinnat. Hän oli nainen. Ne olivat naisen rinnat.

42 Minä hymyilen näin, hän tunsi. Ja hän sulki silmänsä kuin olisi suljetuin silmin nähnyt omat kasvonsa. Hän kohotti hitaasti käden, kosketti poskeaan kuin hymy olisi ollut esine, jonka muodon hän halusi tietää. Hän kuljetti sormeaan huuliensa yli niitten reunaa pitkin. Mies oli tullut piilosta, hänen silmänsä seurasivat käden liikettä, käsi putosi ilmasta hänen kasvoilleen kuin olisi tahtonut estää näkemästä. [...] /- Tällainen minä olen, tyttö sanoi. Katso tällainen. Hän kääntyili vuoteella tyytyväisenä, ojensi kätensä ja jalkansa kuin olisi itsekin vasta nyt huomannut, millainen oli. Tällainen minä olen, hän sanoi uudestaan, nyt kuin hämmästyen ja kysyen itseltään jotain. Samassa hän taas hymyili, ja ojensi kätensä kuin ei olisi enää tiennyt, miten nyt tuli olla./- Niin olet. Mies ei hymyillyt./Hän näki miehen pimeää vasten.

43 [H]än on nähnyt minut.

44 [H]eitä nauratti kuin olisivat leikkineet kenenkään näkemättä ja huomanneet sopivansa leikissä hyvin yhteen ymmärtäen toisiaan jo liikahduksesta.

45 Se oli oikotie, miltei umpeen kasvanut, alkoi maantiestä ja kulki lepikkojen ja kankaan halki, haarautui välillä eri suuntiin ja päättyi aitaan.

46 He olivat nousseet aidan yli, tie tuskin näkyi aidan takaa, metsä oli niin tiheä, vain risuaidan keskellä erottuvasta lautaveräjästä saattoi arvata, että siitä kulki tie.

47 Vähän ennen porttia tyttö taas sanoi, että hän menisi nyt yksin./ [...] Maantien reunassa hän seisahtui, katsoi molempiin suuntiin. Hän juoksi maantien poikki kuin rajan yli.

48 [J]a nousu- ja laskuvedet, nehän vaihtuvat kuun kierron mukaan.

49 – Kun minä katson sitä, minun mieleni tekisi lähteä juoksemaan tai huutaa tai hyppiä tai piiloutua jonnekin, tai vain katsoa eikä lakata katsomasta.

50 – Jaksatko sinä odottaa, mies sanoi. Kestää ehkä ennen kuin pääsen taas tulemaan. Hän sormeili pientä valkeaa kiveä./Tyttö katsoi miehen kättä, ojensi kätensä, otti kiven ja pudotti sen taskuunsa./Kuu oli taivaalla. Se liikkui aina, mutta sitä ei saattanut huomata, vaikka olisi katsonut herkeämättä. Mutta jos käänsi silmät pois ja sattui katsomaan sitä vähän ajan kuluttua, se oli toisessa paikassa. Ja se liikkui koko ajan./- En kai minä muutakaan voi.

51 Päähän oli tullut haava, siitä oli vuotanut verta.

52 – Älä vielä ui tuota matkaa. [...] Ei vielä ole uimisen aika, odota vielä.

53 – Ei sinun tarvitse tulla. Ei ole vielä uimisen aika. Mutta minä uin [...].

54 Tuntuisi pahalta irrottaa kädet kalliosta ja heittäytyä veden varaan, jalkojen alla olisi syvä ja kädet kaartuisivat nopeaan vetoon ja jalat oikenisivat.

55 [V]eden kylmyys salpasi äänen, hän ei saanut kirkaisua suusta ulos.

56 Mutta käsivarret olivat jo auenneet ja jalat ponnahtivat työntöön ja hän ui kuin kylmässä kullassa. Jäsenet olivat jo hyväksyneet kylmän, kaartuivat ja oikenivat, ja hän kääntyi selälleen, halusi kastella hiukset kokonaan.

57 Kuun kuvajainen oli vedessä kuin tie järven halki, ja kuu oli sen kallion yläpuolella, jonne hän uisi.

58 – Näetkö, minä hukun [...].

59 Sade rapisi ikkunaan, ja huone oli pimentynyt kuin olisi tullut yö. Hän näki puitten latvat, ne olivat kuin joku olisi seisonut keskellä vettä ja käsiään hurjasti heiluttaen antanut merkkejä rannalle päin.

265

60 Taivas oli niin musta kuin maailman päälle olisi läikähtänyt mustetta. Tyttö kohottautui niin että näki ulos pihalle, näki ruohon ja puut kokonaan. *Ne tempoivat
tuulessa kuin yrittäen päästä juuriltaan.*

61 Hänestä oli alkanut tuntua siltä, että koko elämä kului hukkaan.

62 – Minä en ole koskaan ollut missään enkä nähnyt mitään [...]. Jos olisin käynyt
koulua, hän alkoi kiihtyneellä äänellä, pysähtyi miettimään kuin kysyen itseltään
jotain [...]

63 – Voi sinua. Luuletko sinä todella että muualla on jotain parempaa?

64 He laskeutuivat portaat alas./Kun he olivat päässeet pihan halki metsän reunaan,
tyttö sanoi menevänsä yksin, ja toisen puheista välittämättä hän lähti juoksemaan.
Kun hän pysähtyi huiskuttamaan, mies oli jo kääntynyt. Tyttö seisoi paikoillaan
siksi kunnes mies oli hävinnyt talon taakse./Kasvoille putosi vettä, hän katsoi ylös,
vesipisarat olivat pudonneet oksilta. Hän seisoi tiheässä lepikossa. Olisi mentävä
alas aidan viertä, polku oli siellä. Mutta hän lähti juoksemaan suoraan lepikon läpi,
välittämättä väistellä oksia, jotka pyyhkivät kasvoja ja hiuksia niin että kankaalle
tullessaan hän oli märkä.

65 Kun sireenipensas seinän vierellä alkaisi kukkia, se tekisi valkean kukan.

66 Hän heilautti kädellään oksaa, se liikkui ja pysähtyi, nousi korkeammalle, kun
veden paino oli sen lehdiltä poissa.

67 Hän nousi portaat, avasi oven ja meni sisään.

68 Se ei voinut olla sitä, se ei voi. [...] Hän alkoi taas alusta kuiskaten numeroita ja
päivien nimiä kuin olisi lukenut loitsua [...].

69 Hän tiesi, ettei aikaa saisi hukata, ja hänestä oli tuntunut, että kun vain ajattelisi,
niin lopulta keksisi jotakin. Mutta hän nukkui aina heti päästyään vuoteeseen.

70 Korvat soivat. Ne ovat korvat, ne soivat. Soivat kuin sähkölangat./Ja sitten hän
kuuli helinän niin kuin olisi soitettu pientä kelloa korvan juuressa, ja ääni kasvoi
ja kumisi niin kuin pieni kello olisi muuttunut suureksi kelloksi. Kaiku oli pään
sisässä ja takoi päätä pyrkien ulos./Kuin aivot kiehuisivat./Nyt minä nousen heittä-
mään lisää löylyä. Mutta jäsenet eivät totelleet. Hän yritti vetää henkeä, koska luuli
tukehtuvansa, mutta tulista ilmaa ei voinut hengittää kuin pienin haukkauksin
suun kautta. [...] /Minä kuolen. Entä jos minä kuolen tähän?/Sydän kumisi kuin
tulinen vanne olisi kiertänyt sen paikalla niin nopeasti, ettei sen liikettä erottanut./
Alas, minun on mentävä alas.

71 Jos joku tulee./Mutta ajatus ei saanut häntä nousemaan, ei miettimään, mitä sanoa,
jos joku olisi tullut ja nähnyt. Jos joku tusi [sic] ja kysyisi jotakin, hän ei edes avaisi
silmiään.

72 – Ei siitä tule mitään./Ja hän tajusi sanoneensa ääneen sen, mitä ei ollut tähän
mennessä *uskaltanut ajatella loppuun.*

73 Hän ei itkenyt sitä, että olisi uskonut sisarensa sanovan isälle, eikä sitä, mitä oli
pelännyt viikosta viikkoon ja minkä tiesi nyt olevan totta. Hän oli väsynyt.

74 Suonet risteilivät, tummina ne alkoivat kaulasta ja haaroittuivat ympäri rintaa./
Silmien eteen nousi kartan kuva. Joet risteilivät, kaikki maailman suuret joet./Hän
katsoi nänniä, se oli tummanruskea kuin suuri silmä./Hän päästi rinnan kätensä
otteesta, ja se oli kuin kivi./Hän kantoi rintojaan kuin kahta kiveä. Niitä vihloi./
Hän upotti hampaat käsivarteen, puri sitä./Minä tulen hulluksi, minä tulen hulluksi./Hän vihasi ruumistaan, ruumiinsa osia, jotka kasvoivat ja paisuivat ja joitten
kivut hänen oli kestettävä.

75 Kuin lehmä, kuin lehmä naru kaulassa [...].

76 Kuului valitus, hän kuunteli sitä kuin olisi kuullut metsästä tuntemattoman eläimen ääntelyä.

77 Ei ole askelta, ei niin kevyttä askelta, / josta minuun ei jälki jäisi. The English
translation of the poem is Kirsti Simonsuuri's (1990: 11).

78 Ja äkkiä hän jäi liikkumattomaksi ja katsoi silmät laajentuen, nousi seisaalleen
ja näki itsensä kuin kahtena, kuin olisi mennyt itsensä ulkopuolelle ja katsonut./

Ja hän näki: kasvot olivat mustat, käsivarret mustat ja jalat polviin asti mustat ja muu valkeaa. Ja valkean keskellä oli kaksi mustaa ympyrää./Ja hänen tuli sääli sitä, minkä oli nähnyt./Hänen itkunsa oli eläimen ulvontaa, ylivoimainen kipu puistatti ja hän yritti helpottaa sitä jäsenien liikkeillä, kädet nytkähtelivät ylös, sivuille, alas, vartalo vääntelehti, kaula ojentui kuin siinä olisi ollut vanne, josta hän pyrki pois.

79   Katkaistut lehdet ja revityt juuret viruivat ympärillä hajallaan./Hän kohottautui jatkamaan työtä, mutta istui takaisin maahan. Rintoja särki. Hän kosketti niitä kädellä. Hän sulki silmänsä./Ei olisi pitänyt olla auringossa, olisi pitänyt muistaa, että auringosta saa helposti päänsäryn. Ja silmissä alkoi lennellä tulisia kipinöitä ja vihreitä salamoita ja kuvioita, jotka muistuttivat jotain, hän ei vain tiennyt mitä./ Se oli epämääräinen muodoltaan, mutta hän tiesi, että se oli nainen. Ja se oli laiha ja ruskea ja ryysyihin puettu. Sen kasvot – hän ei tiennyt, oliko sillä kasvot, mutta tiesi, että ne olivat kauheat katsoa; hän ei tiennyt, oliko nähnyt sen silmät, mutta ne olivat kauheat ja tuijottivat. Ja sillä oli rinnat ja niissä oli maitoa.

80   Oliko hän satuttanut kätensä sen rintoihin, tietämättään satuttanut niihin kätensä ja repäissyt niitä, eikä maito lähtisi pois käsistä. Hän oli nostattanut sen itseään vastaan. Ja hän oli ajatellut, vai oliko hän kuullut sanat niin kuin joku olisi sanonut: rutto, köyhyys ja kuolema.

81   Jokainen juuri tuntui tekevän vastarintaa [... n]iin kuin niillä olisi hampaat juu-rissa [...]

82   – Sinä ainakin kuolet [...]

83   Ja itku vaimeni vähitellen ja hän oikeni penkille, jäi siihen. Sitten liikahti, nousi. Jalat painuivat kylmää lattiaa vasten, astuivat levollisesti ja tyttö meni padan luok-se, nosti kannen, ammensi vettä./Hän istui jakkaran päälle ja alkoi valella itseään. Hän kaatoi haaleaa vettä rintojen yli, valeli ruumiinsa yli vettä kuin viileyttä. Käsi hipaisi vatsaa. Ja hän tajusi kätensä liikkeen merkityksen./Hän painoi käden uu-destaan vatsaa vasten, antoi sen olla siinä; ja samassa säikähti, otti sen pois./Kenen oli tämä ruumis? Hänen se ei enää ollut.

84   Tyttö oli ikkunan ääressä. Seisominen oli kuin unessa seisomista ja katsominen kuin unessa katsomista. Kaksi omenapuuta, aitan seinä, viikate seinällä. Niitä hän oli katsonut ja katsoessaan kuullut kolme erillistä ääntä./Ensin oli paukahtanut ovi./Äiti tuli sisään./Sitten oli kuulunut astioitten kalahtelua, ja hän oli kuullut kysyttävän itseltään jotain. Mutta hän oli ollut niin uponnut omaan olemiseensa, ettei ollut vastannut./Sitten oli tullut hiljaisuus./Äiti on pysähtynyt minun taakse-ni./Ja hän tiesi hiljaisuuden merkityksen. Se oli sitä varten, että äiti näkisi. Hän ei vetänyt edes henkeä, jottei olisi estänyt sitä, minkä oli nyt tultava ilmi./Hän kääntyi ja kääntyessään tiesi näkevänsä: silmät, suun, joka oli avautunut, mutta ei saanut ääntä ulos./Hän katsoi rauhallisesti suoraan päin, ja sitten takaisin ikkunaan.

85   Hän kääntyi pois ikään kuin olisi äsken kääntänyt päänsä vain kuullakseen, mi-kä melu selän takana oli puhjennut, ja huomattuaan ettei se ollut mitään tärkeää kääntynyt takaisin ikkunaan: aitan seinä, viikate seinällä, kaksi omenapuuta.

86   Hän olisi lähtenyt pois, hän tahtoi nukkua. Mitä ne halusivat?/Mitä ne sanoivat? Eivätkö ne ymmärtäneet, ettei hänellä ja niillä ollut mitään tekemistä keskenään?/ Silmissä oli hämärtynyt, ja vaikka hän yhä seisoi, niin hän ymmärsi olleensa het-ken miltei nukuksissa.

87   Sitten hän kuuli takaansa itkua, ja nousi ärtymys kuin unta olisi häiritty, kuin hänet olisi herätetty väkivaltaisesti.

88   Kaikki oli yhdentekevää. Ja hän tunsi halua nauraa, nauraa päin naamaa, olla ilkeä. [...] /Tuo oli hänen äitinsä, tuo tuolla, joka käyttäytyi kuin hullu. Ja hänessä kuo-hahti vastenmielisyys, sängyn reunalta kuuluva ääni imeytyi tajuntaan kuin jokin inhottava aine.

89   Hän ei tiennyt, mitä oikein oli tapahtunut, kun nyt tuntui tällaiselta. Kaikki oli raskaan ja tympeän tuntuista niin kuin hän olisi syönyt jotain sopimatonta ja sitten olisi alkanut pahoinvointi.

267

90   Hän ei tehnyt elettäkään vastatakseen, ei oikeastaan kuullut mitä kysyttiin ja keneltä. Sanat eivät tulleet niin lähelle, että hän olisi ulottunut niihin, tai ne häneen.

91   Oli hyvä olla vieraitten ihmisten parissa, ei tarvinnut miettiä, mitä ympärillä ajateltiin, kun tiesi että oli yhdentekevä.

92   Hän ei voinut sietää kun naiset paapersivat sille lääkärillekin, puhuivat vauvoista ja kulkea hipsuttivat tärkeinä, eihän se mitä ihmettä ollut, sitä varten nainen oli tehty, miksi ruveta koko asiaan, jos siitä piti tehdä sitten sellainen ohjelmanumero. Hän ei pitänyt naisten naamioista, kun ne hymyilivät.

93   [H]än oli ajatellut sitä itsekin, oliko hänessä jokin vika.

94   Nyt ääni syytti, että hän oli röyhkeä, että oli aina ollut kovasydäminen, että hänen sydämensä ei pehminnyt mistään, että hän oli kuin isänsä.

95   Leena nostaa heiniä kuin paras mies.

96   Oli kuin hän olisi päässyt jostain pimeästä ja ahtaasta ulos ja katsellut taas maailmaa, välillä unohdettuaan, miltä kaikki oikein näytti.

97   Minua nukuttaa, minä nukun tähän.

98   Hän vaipui horrokseen, ja havahtui./Hän nousi ja lähti ulos.

99   Hän ei kääntynyt katsomaan takaikkunasta maantien toiseen suuntaan, sinne, missä polku katkesi maantiehen ja jatkui tien toisella puolen ja meni metsään ja siitä portille.

100 Hän näki silmissään portin ja polun ja unohti ne siihen, että auto meni eteenpäin ja oli hyvä olla.

101 In Finnish realist and naturalist literature the destiny of a ruined young girl is portrayed in such novels as Teuvo Pakkala's *Elsa* (1894), Hilda Tihlä's *Leeni* (1907) and F. E. Sillanpää's *Hiltu ja Ragnar* (Hiltu and Ragnar, 1923). The modern version of the story pattern is manifested in Hannu Salama's *Se tavallinen tarina* (The Typical Story, 1961), in which a rural girl, Eeli, becomes pregnant by her boyfriend, and after having been abandoned by him, ends up in a mental hospital.

102 The author's reluctance to predetermine the fate of her characters (cf. Jordan 2010: 41–42) is illustrated by Vartio's comment about Leena's fate in her interview published in *Hopeapeili* (cited in Ruuska 2012: 340): "Let it be then, let her live! Art does not care for calculation. It sends its message much deeper. And if it doesn't, there will be no art." ("Minkäs sille voi, antaa elää! Taide ei välitä laskelmista. Paljon syvemmälle se lähettää viestinsä. Ja ellei lähetä, ei tule taidettakaan.")

103 Other evocative references to the girl's death are also found in the novel, including the mention of Anni Swan's fairy tale "Tyttö ja kuolema" (The Girl and Death, 1917) in the novel's beginning.

104 Rouva oli sanonut, että sellaiset ajatukset olivat tavallisia jokaiselle raskaana olevalle naiselle, että niistä ei kannattanut välittää.

105 Maailma on niin omituinen, kaikki ei käy niin kuin pitäisi, joku kohta menee aina toisin kuin on laskettu.

106 Kun ihminen on nuori ja menee naimisiin, se on sattuman kauppaa.

107 Ihmistä ei auta mikään, itse on autettava itsensä eikä se aina helppoa ole.

108 Kun hän nyt näkisi asian sellaisenaan, hän lopulta suuttuisi itselleen ja pääsisi siten irti.

109 – Mutta onko Leena sitten sanonut hänelle jotain noista epäilyksistä, mitä naimisiin menoon tulee. Eikö pitäisi sanoa, pitäisi toki puhua suoraan, asiat paranevat joskus puhumalla. Kai hänelle voi puhua./– Mutta kun minä en tiedä itsekään. Ja siksi toisekseen, jos hän ymmärtäisi niin kai hänen olisi pitänyt jo ainakin ymmärtää että minä en ymmärrä enää mitään./– Jaa, sepä oli monimutkainen asia. Tai oikeastaan hyvin selvästi sanottu.

110 – Kyllä se selviää. Ja onhan elämässä monta mahdollisuutta [...].

111 As Doležel (1998: 60) writes, the "person's body is the locus of numerous biological [events] and processes that determine his or her very existence – birth, growth,

biological functions, aging, disease, death. Thus, we can say, the most crucial events of the person's life history are outside intentionality."

112 Tyttö oli kulkenut *sattumalta* maantietä pitkin, jäänyt katsomaan hetkeksi ja lähtenyt sitten kotiin [...].

113 He olivat lähteneet kulkemaan polkua pitkin, *sattumalta* juuri sitä polkua, joka vei tähän taloon. Tyttö ajatteli sitä, että oli oikeastaan tullut tähän huoneeseen *sattumalta*.

114 [H]än oli ollut se, joka *oli johtanut* heidät siihen.

115 Hän muisti, miten he ensimmäisen kerran istuivat toisiaan lähellä pimeässä autossa. Hän se oli ollut. Hän oli painautunut miestä vasten muka pelästyen vastaantulevaa autoa, heittäytynyt miehen olkaa vasten ja pannut vahingossa kätensä tämän polvelle. Jos hän heti olisi ottanut kätensä pois – istuisiko hän nyt tässä?/Mutta hän oli antanut kätensä olla./Ja kun oli tultu tienhaaraan, siihen, jossa hän edellisinä iltoina oli astunut autosta pois ja jossa he olivat hyvästelleet sanomalla vain hyvää yötä, mies ei ollutkaan pysäyttänyt autoa vielä, vaan vasta usean kilometrin päässä.

116 Kuin eläin, joku hirmu peto. Kun se seisoi tienhaarassa pimeässä, minua hirvitti.

117 Sitten hän muisti, että oli itse tarjoutunut.

118 According to Ryan (1991: 133), the passive move may correspond to the non-doer's intent or result in a failure. In the latter case, the outcome of non-action is not what was expected or the plan was interfered with by some unforeseen move by another person.

119 Hetken hän ajatteli sanaa johdatus, ajatteli, miten turhaa oli surra, kaikki järjestyi, kulki omaa tietään, kun vain jaksoi odottaa.

120 Minä vain hermostun, tulen ihan tajuttomaksi kun yritän ajatella.

121 Minä olen vain väsynyt koko asiaan, minä en jaksa enää ajatella, kai minä olen ajatellut sitä jo tarpeeksi. Minä olen sanonut, että hänen on parasta odottaa, sillä minusta tuntuu, ettei nyt pidä tehdä mitään.

122 – Hän on niin erilainen kuin minä, tyttö sanoi ja jäi kuuntelemaan, mitä oli sanonut. Mutta ääni oli hävinnyt, hän ei saanut sitä enää korviinsa.

123 Ja vielä noustuaan hissillä ylös ja avattuaan oven ja tultuaan keittiöön hän oli kuin unessa, niin kuin olisi nukuttanut eivätkä esineet olisi pysyneet käsissä, niin kuin käsi ei olisi oikein tajunnut mihin tarttui: ja mitä minkin kanssa oli tehtävä.

124 [V]äsymys oli pudonnut kuin jokin vaate olisi viskattu silmien yli.

125 Hän ei kutoisi sitä, hän ei voinut. Se oli turhaa, hän ei saisi sitä koskaan valmiiksi, kun kuvio oli kerran sotkeutunut, se sotkeutuisi aina, malli oli liian monimutkainen ja lanka nuhraantunut, se oli liian ohutta kestääkseen edestakaisin purkamista ja kerimistä. Tai sitten se pitäisi katkaista.

126 Puhuttiin Orfeuksesta, Orfeus, Orfeus oli mies, joka kulki tyhjien talojen lävitse ja selasi papereita, he etsivät nimeä ja puhuivat jostain naisesta./ [...] Filmi loppui, mutta hän ei ymmärtänyt mitä oli nähnyt.

127 Erivärisiä kuvioita ja viivoja [...] kaksi kolmiota, jotka olivat vinossa [...].

128 [Hän] itsekin uskoi mitä halusi näytellä; että he olivat tavallinen aviopari ja olivat riidelleet ja nyt oli kaikki taas hyvin.

129 [...] Ja tyttö näki miehen kasvot juuri silloin kun tämä oli kääntänyt päätään ja katsonut miten ovi painui kiinni./Hän oli ehkä ulkona. Hän seisoisi portailla tai pihalla. Pihalla oli lunta, hän seisoisi mustana lumen keskellä tai ehkä hän kävelisi, siellä oli teitä, ne risteilivät lumen halki. Ehkä hän kulki kuusien kohdalla, pysähtyi katsomaan, liikautti oksaa kädellään niin että lumi putosi oksalta alas, tai taittoi neulasen oksan kärjestä, kun kukaan ei huomannut, ja viskasi sen lumeen. Se oli lumella, vihreä pilkku.

130 He kulkivat eteenpäin ja tulivat puiston reunaan. Tiet olivat siellä valkeat, illan kuluessa oli satanut lunta juuri sen verran, että maa oli peittynyt./– Katso, nämä ovat ensimmäiset jäljet. Tyttö katsoi taakseen, lumessa näkyi mustia läiskiä, se oli

märkää, maa ei ollut vielä jäässä./– Eivät ne ole ensimmäiset, näetkö, tuolla edessä on toisia.

131 Hän itki ja puri hampaita yhteen, sillä hän ei huutaisi. [...] olkoon kivi tai sammakko, kun vaan pääsen siitä.

132 Ja jotain irtosi.

133 [H]än kauhistui tajutessaan, että se oli tapahtunut heille, että he olivat kuin muut ihmiset, kuka tahansa, kuin ne, joista hän oli lukenut, ja tirskunut tyttöjen lukiessa.

134 Tyttö ajatteli, että kaikki kävi kuin romaanissa.

135 Se oli hänen nimensä, tuo, kirjekuoren päällä. Nimi oli tavallinen tytönnimi. Hän oli nähnyt sen monella eri tavalla kirjoitettuna, monin erilaisin kirjaimin. Itse hän kirjoitti sen suurilla, pystyillä kirjaimilla./Hän katsoi taas nimeä kuoren päällä: Leena. Tasaisella, kaunokirjoitusmaisella käsialalla kirjoitettuna siinä luki Leena. Kirjaimet olivat samat, yhtä suuret, yhtä tasaiset kuin aina ennen./Ja kuitenkin, kun hän katsoi niitä, ne näyttivät siltä kuin ne olisivat olleet umpimielistä merkitystä täynnä. Vieraat.

136 [... pitäisi] harkita ja siirtää päätöksen teot.

137 Ja hän näki taas käden ja siinä kynän. [...] ja paperille tuli piste. Ja käsi kirjoitti nimen kuoreen, nopeasti, vieraasti, kuin minkä tahansa nimen. Ja sulki kuoren.

138 [H]än oli tiennyt sen kauan, jo alusta alkaen, etten minä hänestä välittänyt, niin kuin ihmiset toisistaan välittävät silloin kun on tosi kysymyksessä. The gender-neutral personal pronoun *hän* in the Finnish language generates some ambiguity here. The one who knows about the true condition of Leena's feelings could be the man or Leena herself. However, the context of the passage includes a series of paragraphs which each contain the man as the agent, which suggests that he is the one who knows.

139 Hän muisti jotain, joitakin sanoja. Muisti että hän oli ne sanonut. Mutta ne olivat tulleet hänelle takaisin, toinen ei ollut niitä ymmärtänyt.

140 Kun hän katsoi taas ulos, ne olivat hävinneet näkyvistä. Ehkä ne olivat kulkeneet katua ylös. Katu päättyi metsän reunaan. Siellä oli polkuja puitten seassa, hän oli kulkenut siellä.

141 Hän käänsi katseensa pois, katsoi nyt esineitä hämärässä huoneessa, liikautti kättään. Se oli, koska se liikkui, kun hän ajatteli, että minä liikutan sitä nyt. Valvottu yö ja väsymys, siitä se tuli, tämä olo. Kuin maailma ympärillä olisi ohentunut, esineet olleet tyhjästä tehtyjä, kädet tyhjät, vain viivalla tehdyt.

4. *Cycles of Arousal and Fall. Mirroring the Self in* Kaikki naiset näkevät unia

1 Unet tungeksivat minussa. / Unet avaavat portteja minuun. [...] Ja linnut leväyttävät siipensä, / päältä mustat ja alta valkeat siipensä ne / leväyttävät / ja lentävät taivaanrantaan. / Vain se yksi, se kolmisiipinen, / putoaa matkalla maahan, / putoaa matkalla kuolleena aina maahan (*Häät*, 15–16). The English translation of the poem is Kirsti Simonsuuri's (1990: 9–10).

2 Oli kerran metsä ja metsässä tyttö, ja suu, pieni, siro suu, kuin kukka. Ja kasvot, sydämenmuotoiset, ja leuka pehmeä ja pyöreä, kuin sydämenkuvan kärki. [...] / Huulilta pakeni hymy ja hän soperi ääneti; se ei voi olla totta./Tämä on erehdys, tämä on petosta. Missä oli tyttö joka oli seisonut puun alla, minne oli joutunut, mihin lähtenyt metsästä, oliko mennyt väärää tietä ja eksynyt, missä kohtaa oli tapahtunut tämä hirveä vaihtuminen.

3 Minä luen ihmistä kuin avointa kirjaa ja minun vaistoni ei petä.

4 [S]amat vanhat huonekalut vaikka asunto on uusi, ja pitää näyttää elämänsä vieraille ihmisille.

5 Jos pitää paikkansa että ihmisellä voi olla paha silmä, niin sillä on.

6 – Minähän kuulin sen omilla korvillani […].

7 Hän oli kuullut sen siivoojalta. Tämä oli kertonut mitä oli kuullut rouvien puhuvan.

8 – Et sinä minua häiritse, en minä ollut mitään erikoista tekemässä, taiteilija vastasi./Mutta rouva Pyy kuuli äänen, se vastasi että kyllä sinä häiritset, mutta minä en viitsi sanoa sitä, kun sinä olet niin tahditon että kysyt, häiritsetkö sinä.

9 […] kuin Laura olisi ollut jossakin ja saanut tietää sellaista, mitä ei edes yrittäisi kenellekään puhua.

10 Rouva Pyy ymmärsi. Hän oli hän, ja Laura tuossa oli joku muu. He saattoivat puhua toisilleen kaiken, niin kuin ennen, mutta ymmärsivät olla puhumatta siitä, mistä ei voinut puhua. Se mitä heille molemmille tapahtui nyt, sen selittämiseen ei ollut sanoja.

11 Ei se ollut enää tärkeää –

12 […] kuin hän olisi kuullut jonkin ahmaisevan suuhunsa suuren palan, ja nielaisevan – tai kuin joku olisi syöksynyt päistikkaa alas pimeään ja hän olisi kuullut putoamisen.

13 Sinä olet itse niin järkevä ja rauhallinen, ehkä sinä et ole itse edes tietoinen siitä että sinussa on jokin – miten minä sen sanoisin – musta alue johon putoat, tai haluat pudota […].

14 […] hengittää itsensä eläväksi taas ja vapaaksi, ollakseen taas se kuka oli, rouva Pyy […].

15 […] joka kävelee eteenpäin, avaa hallin oven, avaa toisen oven, tulee aseman portaille ja menee siitä alas ja tietylle laiturille odottamaan tiettyä bussia, joka vie hänet tiettyyn kaupunginosaan, ja sitten hän menisi tiettyyn taloon ja tiettyyn asuntoon, numero on A 8. Hän oli rouva Pyy.

16 Jos pitää paikkansa [että ihmisellä voi olla paha silmä].

17 […] avautui, se purki itsestään jotakin, huomaamatta mitä teki, yhä miettien samaa, samaa, kuin seisahtuessaankin samaa ajatusta jatkaen […].

18 Kaikkea minä lasken, hän mutisi: ärtyi huomatessaan jo kolmannen kerran alkaneensa laskea, montako punaista pistettä oli valomainoksessa, joka vilkkui vastapäätä olevan ravintolan oven päällä.

19 Mrs. Pyy's repetitious actions remind of the pathological state of "repetition compulsion" analyzed in the context of neurotic patients by Freud. The compulsion to repeat is a symptom of instinctual impulses that have been repressed, but force their way through to a performance of painful experiences (Freud 1961: 14, 26). These past experiences become manifest in symbolic, ceremonial actions and are often comprised of harmless, trivial, and tedious tasks (like counting). Like the most primitive human minds with animistic beliefs, obsessive minds too regard thoughts (or words) as equivalent to deeds or facts: if you do something in your ritual repetitions, you may prevent something bad happening. According to LeDoux (1998: 246), the Freudian idea of repression (manifesting itself as compulsive repetitions) may be conceived as a stress-induced emotional response, a result of biological-based learning, conditioning oneself to certain actions that bring mental relief.

20 Hän lymysi tässä laidalla, tähyili, mutta hänet oli nähty, tiedettiin, että tuossa oli jokin outo, tähyilemässä ympärilleen niin kuin vieras tähyilee; hän oli herättänyt tuon tuolla ylhäällä […].

21 In *The Psychopathology of Everyday Life* (1901), Freud denies the existence of chance. Every forgetful or accidental deed or slip is motivated by the unconscious.

22 Ja hän luki lehdestä taidepalstan ja "vuokralle tarjotaan"-ilmoitukset. Hän luki ne rivi riviltä kuin olisi niitten lävitse katsonut toiseen maailmaan, toisiin ympäristöihin, kuin ne olisivat antaneet lohtua, rohkaisseet.

23 Freud's theories of consciousness, the ego and the importance of childhood

experiences influenced the ways in which the self was portrayed in modern literature. The idea of the ego as a layered entity operating as much through unconscious as through conscious processes had an enormous effect on how self-development was reconceived in fiction. (Castle 2006: 67)

24 Hän oli odottanut että mies olisi sanonut hänelle, naiselle, mikä hän oli. Nainen tahtoi nähdä itsensä miehen kautta, kuin vasta tämän silmien kautta näkisi itsensä.

25 Kävelen suorana. On tärkeätä että kävelen suorana. Menen tuota ovea kohti. Ja hän tiesi, että oli päässyt irti jostakin, käveli mattoa pitkin ja tiesi. Yritti, tuo mies, yritti tukea minua, ja tuo hovimestari *katsoo minua ja ajattelee, että minä olen joku, joka on juotettu täällä humalaan.*

26 Sitten hän tuijotti miestä pää koholla, oli kuin hän olisi nähnyt itsensä sivusta, ulkoa päin [...].

27 [I]lkeä ilme silmissä, pää koholla, kädet vapisten hän katsoi miestä ja oli itseensä tyytyväinen. Tietysti olen nyt kauhean näköinen hänen silmissään, mutta sitäpä juuri haluan. Olla kerrankin *se mikä olen.*

28 Jonakin päivänä tämäkin mies huomaisi ne kasvot, ne jotka hän itse näki peilissä, havaitsi vain ne, ei hänen todellisia kasvojaan, niitä, jotka vain hymyilivät ja joita hän tarjosi miehen silmille, kun tämä katsoi häneen.

29 Mutta peilistä katsoi nainen ja hän tiesi kuka se oli. Ja takana sivuittain seisoi mies. Sivuittain, jotteivät hänen kasvonsa olisi enää tuon naisen kasvojen vieressä. Ei miehen tarvitse seisoa sivuittain. Ja hän kääntyi, ja nainen peilissä kääntyi [...].

30 Kai toinen tajusi ettei hän tahallaan seisonut yhä miehessä kiinni, selkä selkää vasten. Sinähän olet vieras nyt, mutta sinä luulet että tönäisin sinua siksi että haluan sinusta vielä jotain [...].

31 Enkö yrittäisi olla viisaampi kuin olen, *näytellä jotakin* jotten vain menettäisi suosiota hänen silmissään, vaikka olen vain tällainen tyhmä pieni rouvasihminen. Ja sitä hän minusta halusi, pientä tyhmää naista; joka on osannut olla niin mukava ja jopa hienotunteinen, ainakin viime aikoina.

32 Ja tuntui kuin hän äkkiä olisi noussut tuon miehen yläpuolelle näkemällä ja ymmärtämällä itsensä sellaisena kuin tämä oli hänet arvioinut.

33 Hän oli kaatanut kahvia, ottanut sokeria ja kermaa, sekoittanut lusikalla, oli tehnyt tuon kaiken varoen äkillisiä liikkeitä, istunut selkä suorana, pidellyt kahvikuppia pikkusormi ojossa, juonut lyhyin, pienin siemauksin kuin olisi istunut kahvikutsuilla, missä kahvinjuonti on sivuasia, pääasia, miten juodaan ja mitä juodessa puhutaan. Mutta hän istui yksin. [...] Kuka oli katsonut tätä kaunista käytöstä, keneen oli yritetty tehdä vaikutus?

34 In her recent study Parente-Čapková's (2014) analyzes the mimetic strategies in L. Onerva's novel *Mirdja* (1908), including the protagonist's tendency to imitate and mirror herself in the male characters. Mrs. Pyy's behavioral patterns can be read in relation to similar themes of female subjectivity and self-formation that are addressed in Onerva's early work (see Ruuska 2010: 120–121).

35 – Miksi sinä jätät minut pimeään, vaimo sanoi hetken kuluttua lapsekkaalla äänellä, kuin olisi leikkinyt pimeänpelkoa, kuin olisi odottanut, että mies olisi yhtynyt leikkiin, *kuullut hänen äänensä* ja sanonut sitten jotakin, jotakin samanlaista.

36 Mies ei vastannut. Hengitys kuului pimeän läpi.

37 Ja hän tarttui lasiin. Maailma oli tätä, tarttumista lasiin tietyllä tavalla, sen nostamista huulille. Kuului tapoihin hymyillä isännälle, käytökseen. Hän otti kasvoilleen hymyn ja piti sitä niillä kuin naamiota.

38 [K]uin yksinäistä kulkukoiraa [...] hän kutsui omaa itseään takaisin.

39 – Anteeksi, rouva Pyy sanoi. – Taidan olla juovuksissa todella, hän lisäsi kevyesti. – Kaksi Martinia... minunlaiseni pienen naisen ne kyllä kaatavat, hän sanoi ja tunsi äkkiä omituista kylmää vihaa, ja tuntiessaan vihan kuin kirkkaan ja teräksisen aineen joka oli äkkiä levinnyt hänen ruumiinsa läpi, hän nautti.

40 Luulee kai että en ole humalassa vaan teeskentelen, jotta saisin vedota hänen

apuunsa, *luulee* minun *luulevan* että minä jatkuvasti *luulen* olevani oikeutettu odottamaan häneltä jotain. Että odotan hänen olevan ritarillinen, herrasmies, kaikesta huolimatta, loppuun asti.

41 Cf. Ruuska's (2010: 150–153) detailed analysis of the correspondences between Vartio's scene and Freud's text.

42 [E]i hän ollut sellainen ihminen, joista naistenlehdissä kirjoitetaan, hänellä oli ollut hyvät vanhemmat, hyvä lapsuus, mitä traumoja hänellä saattaisi olla?

43 Minua ei vaivaa mikään.

44 Rouva Pyy tuijotti kasvoja, jotka olivat pöydän toisella puolen./Silmät olivat kääntyneet pois. Mutta hän oli ehtinyt kuin välähdyksenä nähdä noilla kasvoilla ilmeen, joka oli sammunut samassa. Ensin oli ollut uteliasta, jännittynyttä odotusta, sitten – samanaikaisesti kun hänen omat kasvonsa olivat alkaneet vääristyä – kun hänen kasvoilleen oli noussut viha joka oli tehnyt hänet rumaksi, hirveän näköiseksi – noille kasvoille oli kohonnut jännittynyt ilme kuin korttipelissä, ja samassa, kun hänen suustaan tuli se sana, ilme muuttui mielihyväksi, siinä oli nautintoa. Se oli nyt tyydytetty, kuin nuo silmät olisivat sanoneet: niinhän se oli kuin arvelinkin.

45 Tehän ymmärrätte, koska itse kerrotte ne.

46 [Hänellä on taipumusta] sielullisen paineen alla joutua tiloihin, jotka muistuttavat hysteriaa [...].

47 [Sellaiset tilat ovat] sielun puolustuskeinoja.

48 [Hän] eli affektien vallassa, syöksyi yhdestä toiseen.

49 [O]liko hän sitten kuin kana, joka tekeytyi halvaantuneeksi.

50 Ruuska (2010: 34–35) analyzes the protagonist's name in the context of the intertextual relations between Vartio's novel and the Finnish folk ballad "Minä, pyy, pesätön lintu" ("I, a bird without a nest").

51 Hän oli vain kuunnellut – uteliaana ja jonkinlaista mielihyvää tuntien, oli tuntenut suorastaan tyydytystä, kun hänestä sanottiin niin paljon. Sillä se kai tarkoitti sitä, ettei hän ehkä ollutkaan aivan tavallinen ihminen.

52 Rouva Pyy pysähtyi, sanoi puoliääneen: "Se narri on piru." Mutta samalla häntä huvitti; hänestä tuntui kuin hän itse olisi myös ollut piru, käynyt vain vakoilemassa toisen paholaisen konsteja – ja joutunut satimeen./Eikö se ollut sanonut, että hän oli kostanut sillä kaikella muille ihmisille oman nöyryytyksensä. Oliko hän? Mutta hän oli aina vihannut niitä ihmisiä. Mutta samassa, kun hän ajatteli sitä, hän halusi torjua sen pois, väitteen, että hän oli liioitellut kaiken. Ei, se ei ollut totta. Ja kuitenkin hän oli myöntänyt: "Niin, niin kai se sitten on."

53 Hyväluoja, mikä narri hän oli ollut!

54 [... tuntuu kuin siinä talossa] olisi joskus tapahtunut joku hirveä rikos, ikkuna on sellainen, mustaksi maalattu, ikkunankuva seinässä.

55 [... tuntuu kuin siellä talossa olisi] jotain, joku kuollut, murhattu.

56 [H]än oli surmannut miehensä [...] hän oli kieltänyt ja häpäissyt oman hyvän miehensä [...].

57 – Eivät näy vieläkään saaneen sitä murhaajaa kiinni.

58 Minun sisältäni on sammunut jotakin [...].

59 [K]urkkuun koski niin kuin hän olisi siemaissut liian paljon vettä.

60 Ja pidättäessään itkua hän tunsi kuin ruumis olisi samalla täyttynyt jostain, hän tunsi olevansa kuin astia, joka täyttyi reunojaan myöten, ja oli kuin hän olisi tuntenut maun; kylmää ja kitkerää.

61 Hän veti henkeä, veti taas, kuin riuhtaisten ilmaa suuhunsa, mutta ei saanut henkeäkään kulkemaan; oli kuin olisi yrittänyt heittää ämpäriä syvään kaivoon, jonka pohjalla oli vain vähän vettä, se nousi tyhjänä ylös, ja taas yrittänyt, ja vasta useitten yritysten jälkeen osunut veteen niin että astia täyttyi. Sen hän kertoisi lääkärille, kuvaisi juuri noin miten häntä ahdisti.

62 Riikka Stewen (1996: 18–19) analyzes closed eyes as a characteristic feature of symbolist painting, where this motif is used to depict the mind as a container filled

with inner images. Compositions constituted of mute and plain facial figures that are seen as contemplating the world within.

63 In Finnish poetry, the image of a deep well refers to death or contemplation as a deep sleep. In Kaarlo Sarkia's symbolist poem, "Unen kaivo" (The Well of Dreams, 1936), the speaker drinks from "the charmed goblet of dreams" ("unten velhojuomaa") and declares: "Above my whole life / you are shimmering, a deep well of dreams [...] Shimmer upon my ruins!" ("Elämäni kaiken yllä / päilyt, unen kaivo syvä [...] Päily raunioni yllä!"; Sarkia 1936: 145)

64 Freud, for instance, considered the anxiety of neurotic patients to stem from the traumatic experience of birth. The restriction of breathing forms the basis for the physical experience of Angst: "We believe that it is in the *act of birth* that there comes about the combination of unpleasurable feelings, impulses of discharge and bodily sensations which has become the prototype of the effects of a mortal danger and has ever since been repeated by us as the state of anxiety," Freud (1991: 444) wrote in his *Introductory Lectures on Psychoanalysis* (emphasis his).

65 [Oli tuntunut] kuin hän olisi seisonut rannalla hämärissä ja kuullut kalan pols-kahtavan jossakin, niin että ennen kuin ehtii kääntyä katsomaan, veden pinta on tyyni, ei kuulu eikä näy mitään.

66 Oli tapahtunut jotakin merkillistä, hänellä oli ollut sellainen olo kuin häntä ei olisi ollutkaan; ei hän silti ollut tajuton, ei se olo sitä muistuttanut. Mikään ei painanut mieltä, ei ollut tietoa, ei muistoa mistään, hän ei ollut edes tajunnut, ei ajatellut sitä että hänen olonsa oli hyvä, se tunne oli ollut jotakin niin täydellistä kuin hän ei olisi tiennyt että olikaan muuta kuin vain himmeä vesi ympärillä.

67 Oli käynyt tärkeäksi kulkea pimeässä ja märässä tuulessa, hengittää syvään ja täyt-tyä tällä syksyllä. Ja tuuli; hän oli pysähtynyt ja kuunnellut, kun metsä kohahti ja vaimeni taas.

68 Hän oli sulkenut silmänsä, tuntenut aivan vieressä kuin jonkin mahtavan olennon läsnäolon, miehenmuotoinen, miehen olkapää johon nojata; miehen raskas hen-gitys; ja olento oli ollut väkevä ja tyyni ja silti syvästi murheellinen.

69 Että olisi mentävä kotiovesta sisään ja todettava, että näitten seinien sisällä oli koko hänen elämänsä.

70 Ja hän oli avannut silmänsä, kääntynyt takaisin päin ja tullut valaistulle tielle, kyl-mälle ja siniselle.

71 [H]änestä tuntui kuin hän olisi ollut puun kohdussa ja nähnyt kuolleita sikiöitä, rypistyneitä, kylmiä.

72 Oli ollut aivan hiljaista. Hän oli unohtunut istumaan puun juurelle niin pitkäksi aikaa, ettei hän enää ollut oikein ymmärtänyt, miten pääsisi sieltä pois, oli tuntu-nut siltä kuin hän ei osaisikaan muuta kuin istua puun juurella, maassa ympärillä pudonneet raakileet, joitten pinta himersi kuin vastasyntynyt koiranpentu. Ja hän oli koskettanut puun runkoa kädellään ja samassa säikähtänyt – kuin puu olisi voi-nut tuntea kosketuksen, kuin hän olisi salaa koskenut alastonta vierasta ruumista.

73 [H]än oli katsellut pihaa ja tietä kuin olisi ollut kauan poissa, maailma tullut hil-jaiseksi ja vieraaksi; kuin hän ei olisi tiennyt, mihin oli mentävä.

74 Hänen tuli sääli, sääli tätä naisen ruumista, riistettyä kuin puut. Ruuska (2010: 101) reads the scene in relation to Vartio's poem, "Vihreää sukua" (My Green Family, 1952), in which the female speaker perceives herself as a tree being alienated from her "sisters, trees" ("sisaristani puista"). The bodily, fierce cry constitutes the most primitive form of self-expression that, for a moment, frees the speaker to feel the presence of her nature, her spiritual sisters. The sound of a woman is the sound of a fierce cry, which is accompanied by erotic images of penetration: "Like a rolling stone: / so my cry begins – / but in the middle, at the moment of the deepest sighs, / the blood of my green family rises within me. / My feet split, / my arms stretch out / upwards, stiffly: / a spruce shoots grows arises through me, / a tree top sings and hums: a nesting tree, a nesting tree – a rest for birds – /

bringing spring, spring –" ("Kuin vierivä kivi – / niin minun itkuni alkaa – / vaan kesken sitä, sen syvintä valituksen kohtaa / nousee minussa vihreän sukuni veri. / Jalkateräni repeävät – / käsivarteni ojentautuvat / jäykkinä ylöspäin: / kuusi tunkee kasvaa nousee minun lävitseni./ [...] latva laulaa ja humisee: / Pesäpuu, pesäpuu – lintujen pysähdyspaikka – / kevättä kevättä viemään –"; *Häät*, 22) The English translation of the poem is Kirsti Simonsuuri's (1990: 3).

75   Hänen naurunsa oli odottamaton, kolkko ja outo, hän kuuli sen itsekin, mutta nauroi yhä, halusi kuulla sen toisen kerran, eikä hän tajunnut, että nauru lähti hänen suustaan.

76   [S]einän takana, tuossa talossa juuri sen seinän takana, jonka tällä puolen mies ja nainen, mies ja nainen – ja hänen ajatuksensa pysähtyi. Että seinän takana, juuri vuoteen kohdalla, oli naapurin WC. Ja jokainen ääni kuului seinän takaa korvan juuresta.

77   Rouva Pyy näki naisen jalat, silkkisukkien verhoamat kapeat sääret, pohjelihakset, tiukat ja kireät [...]. Ja lihakset laukesivat, kiristyivät taas, liikkuivat sukkien alla, mieleen muistui petoeläin, tiikeri, pantteri, ja silmät olivat ummessa, ruumis vääntelehti kuin eläimen [...].

78   [Nainen] halusi häpäistä miehen näyttämällä itsensä, mutta se mies ei tahtonut, ei uskaltanut katsoa.

79   Hän oli näkevinään emännän tulevan kotiinsa, maalaistaloon, ja ottavan siellä hatun päästään, oli näkevinään emännän istuvan pöydän ääreen ja lähtevän navettaan varhain aamulla, pihan poikki. Hiljaisuus, pimeys, emäntä käveli navettaan ja aukaisi oven ja lehmien ääntely kuului pimeästä.

80   Rouva Pyy kulki eteenpäin ja näki miten kasvoja vilahteli kukkakioskin lasin pinnassa. Lasin takana oli peili, hän oli nähnyt peilissä naisen kasvot ja nehän olivat olleet hänen kasvonsa, ne joihin hän oli katsonut.

81   Esko Ervasti analyzes the motif of "mirroring beings" (*peili-ihminen*) in the context of Finnish novels in the 1950s. The idea involves the depiction of characters as modern individuals who are splitting into two distinct selves. In analyzing *Kaikki naiset näkevät unia*, for instance, Ervasti (1967: 64) mentions the repeating figure of two women used in the novel: "In certain situations Mrs. Pyy sees [...] two women. There are two of them, because Mrs. Pyy is two [selves], and because this is the issue and the idea of the novel." ("Tietyissä tilanteissa rouva Pyy näkee [...] kaksi naista. Heitä on kaksi, koska rouva Pyy on kaksi ja koska siinä on romaanin problemi ja idea.")

82   Sääli. Ei kukaan sinua sääli. Ei kukaan minua sääli./Itke vain. Itke itsesi pois tästä rumaksi maalatusta rappeutuneesta kylpyhuoneesta, tästä keskikaupungin synkästä vanhasta pahalle lemuavasta kivitalosta, irti tavaroista, irti lapsista, jotka eivät sinusta mitään tiedä, itke pois miehesi luota, joka ei ollut oikea mies, ei ollut se oikea.../Itke; vielä vähän aikaan. Ja kun olet itkusi lopettanut – kas noin, huuhdot kasvosi kylmällä vedellä, levität kasvoille rasvaa ja ihojauhetta, järjestät hiukset, olemme taas yhtä, sinä ja minä. Minä elän, sinä kuolet. Kun sinä et enää vihaa minua, en minäkään vihaa sinua.

83   En voi kutsua itseäni nimellä. Sitä ei ole enää, sen nimistä.

84   [...] P-kirjain [...] iso kirjain muitten joukossa [...].

85   Mutta niin tekevät kaikki naiset, näkevät unia niin kuin sinä, heidän sielunsa kulkee yöllä mustana kissana, hiipii kattoja pitkin, naukuu ikkunan alla ja tulee ikkunasta sisään, istuu vasemman rinnan päälle. Sinä olet niin kuin se nainen, joka näki unessa valkean lehmän tulevan ovesta, lehmä ammui haikeasti. Ja nainen syytti unessa ettei lehmää lypsetä vaikka sen utareita pakottaa maito. Olet kuin naiset ovat, näkevät unia, heräävät aamulla, katsovat tyhjin silmin ja ovat joko pettyneitä kun ei uni ollutkaan totta, tai kiittävät onneaan siitä että se oli unta mitä he unessa tekivät.

86   [K]irjojen nimiä. Freudin teoksia.

87 Miksi seison tässä ja koetan uudestaan, onko ovi kiinni. Miksi heräsin keskellä yötä ja kuljen nyt näissä huoneissa kuin pelkäisin jotain?

88 Kuin unessa, kuin unen taloissa, niissä taloissa, joissa usein oli unissaan.

89 Taloja joissa oli joskus asunut, eivät kuitenkaan samoja, ja joskus talo oli vain neliö maassa, raunioitunut kivijalka tai lahonnut hirsikerros, merkkinä siitä, että siinä oli ollut kerran talo, ja hän kulki sen raunioilla.

90 Kuin vieraassa talossa, kuin sattumalta poikennut sisään keskellä yötä muistamatta kuka ja mistä tullut, varovaisesti kuin pahoissa aikeissa, ovissa hiljaa kuin peläten mitä on takana.

91 [Hän oli nähnyt unta,] niin ahdistavaa, että se oli pakottanut hänet heräämään.

92 The three deaths experienced by Mrs. Pyy in her dream can be compared to the three violent transformations – spiritual, moral, and emotional – experienced by The Beautiful Soul in Goethe's *Wilhem Meister's Apprenticeship*. The story of The Beautiful Soul constitutes a subplot in Goethe's male Bildungsroman and serves as the example of female spiritual Bildung, finally leading to self-destructive isolation and death. (Hirsch 1983: 26–29)

93 [...] niin kuin noustaan kun on saatu tärkeä sanoma.

94 [...] tuntee halua ja suorastaan tarvetta saada kertoa muille ihmisille ja saada niihin tulkinnan.

95 Vartio's idea that dreams are a result of condensation, symbolization, dramatization, and displacement alludes also to the Freudian theory of the interpretation of dreams. As she expressed it, "dreams are great art" ("[u]ni on suurta taidetta"). She compared dreams to charades that pose visual riddles or to allegorical paintings that "display a scene, an episode from a play" ("esittävät jonkin kohtauksen, tilanteen näytelmästä"). The analogies with different forms of art (painting, film, drama) stage the quality of dreams as the primitive, "natural" form of art that arises from within. (Vartio 1996: 132–133, 151)

96 Sillä unet ovat piilotajuntamme meille lähettämiä viestejä, ne sanovat vertauskuvin, symbolein meille jonkin asian [...] meistä itsestämme, uni tarkoittaa aina meitä itseämme, tuo sanoma joka on puettu äänettömään, pelkistettyyn, tiivistettyyn kuvaan, symboliin.

97 [...] unennäkijä jo tavallaan tietää ja aavistaa [asian], jonka hän on päätellyt jo jostain, mutta jota hänen tajuinen minänsä ei ole vielä oivaltanut eikä ajatukseksi tai sanoiksi pukenut, ja niinpä unennäkijä riemuissaan sanoo, että hänpä näki ennusunen [...].

98 [...] järjestää itseään uudelleen ja kokoaa voimiaan silmätäkseen elämäänsä taaksepäin [...] lapsuuteen ja nuoruuteen ja unikuvat nousevat sieltä.

99 Uni sanoo meille mikä on meidän todellinen tilamme. Se sanoo meille itsellemme suoran totuuden, se ei näytä meitä sellaisina kuin toiset ihmiset meidät näkevät eikä sellaisina kuin itse näemme itsemme, eikä sellaisina kuin itse haluaisimme ja uskomme olevamme vaan juuri sellaisina kuin olemme.

100 [U]net ovat aina alkuperäisiä, aitoja, ainutkertaisia ja tosia.

101 Joku puoli hänessä on yhtä kehittymätön, yhtä avuton kuin pienellä lapsella, hän on jonkin asian suhteen yhtä neuvoton kuin olisi metsään eksynyt pieni lapsi.

102 [...] kuin filminauha olisi kulkenut silmien editse.

103 In this sense, Mrs. Pyy's dream story resembles Vartio's own dream stories: "I have used [my own dreams] as material in my book entitled Between Land and Water. But I didn't know then what I do now: if one uses dreams as literary material, their spell often disappears as one tries to stylize them and turn them into literature." ("Olen käyttänyt [omia uniani] sellaisinaan materiaalina kirjassani jonka nimi on Maan ja veden välillä. Mutta en tiennyt vielä sitä minkä nyt: jos unia käyttää kirjallisena materiaalina niitten teho usein katoaa, jos niitä yrittää stilisoida, tehdä niistä kirjallisuutta"; Vartio 1996: 150)

104 Cf. Anita Konkka's (2008) interpretation of Mrs. Pyy's dream.

105 Minun hermoilleni alkaa käydä kun minä luulen että ne ovat kuolleita, ja kun sitten lakaisen niitä ne vielä virkoavat ja niitä lentelee ilmassa ja putoilee ruoka-astioihin ja vaikka mihin.

106 The image of the flies also appears in Vartio's short story "Jäävuori" (Iceberg, 1955), in which the motif becomes an emblem of the existential situation of human beings having been "blessed" with the conscious feeling of themselves. Yet they are still unable to fundamentally know themselves. The protagonist of the story, a little boy, keeps wondering about the futile attempts of flies to escape from their confined space: "The flies were humming in the window; both halves of the window were closed. If only they had figured out they could fly to the other side of the room; there the window was wide open. They did not figure it out, they just kept throwing themselves against the window, over and over again, as if that would make the window go away." ("Kärpäset surisivat ikkunassa, ikkunan molemmat puoliskot olivat kiinni. Kun älyäisivät lentää toiselle puolelle huonetta, siellä ikkuna oli levällään. Eivät ne keksineet, tekivät vain uudestaan ja uudestaan syöksyjä ikkunaa vasten niin kuin ikkuna siitä mihin menisi"; *MVV*, 7)

107 Kaikki on sitten selvää.

108 Anna tämä Lauralle muistoksi minusta.

109 [...] kuolemaa kohti – jäisellä reellä sulaa maata pitkin.

110 Käy viimeinen virsta / jäisellä reellä sulaa maata pitkin [...].

111 [J]a tuisku nousi – / jäljet satoi umpeen.

112 Vihollinen on järven takana, venäläiset ovat järven takana. On lähetetty neuvot-telijoita. Viisaalla ja ymmärtäväisellä puheella vihollinen saadaan ehkä peräyty-mään.

113 [V]anha aitta [...] sellainen jossa on yksi ovi ja kynnys korkealla.

114 [P]imeässä hän usein astui siinä tyhjään. According to Ruuska (2010: 51), the image of the fall refers to Gaston Bachelard's classic text *La poétique de l'espace* (1957), in which the image of "first stairs" is considered as signifying the embodied experience of one's childhood home. This image is registered in an individual's memory as instinctive reflexes of experiencing a once habitual space.

115 [H]än oli kiuru, kohosi yhä ylemmäksi, lensi hyvin korkealle, ja lentäessään yhä ylemmäksi hän tiesi olevansa kolmannen kerran ja lopullisesti kuollut. [...] kun hän muisti mitä oli maan päällä, hän alkoi pudota kuin kivi, hän ei ollut enää lin-tu vaan putosi maata kohti, mutta ponnisti henkensä hädässä ja pääsi taas ylös. Mutta hän ei ollut enää lintu, vaikka leijui ilmassa: hän potki ilmaa kuin vettä. Ja taivaalla liikkui jokin esine, se lähestyi, tuli kovaa vauhtia kohti [...] ja hän näki että se oli suunnattoman suuri korva, ja hän tiesi että se oli Jumalan korva. Ja hän tahtoi koskettaa sitä, sillä hän tiesi että jos hän olisi saanut sitä kosketetuksi tai vain hipaistuksikin, niin hänelle olisi selvinnyt kaikki ja hän olisi ymmärtänyt mitä on elämä ja mitä kuolema.

116 Ja hän ponnisti kaikki voimansa ja luuli ulottuvansa – mutta se kaikkosi, hävisi avaruuteen. Ja samassa hetkessä tähdet sammuivat taivaalta ja pimeni ja alkoi sataa märkää lunta.

117 Hänen kasvoilleen kohosi miltei hellä hymy. Samassa hänen ilmeensä vaihtui ja hän vilkaisi taakseen kuin säikähtäen: jos joku olisi seisonut takana ja nähnyt.

118 Rouva Pyy seisoi ikkunan luona ja oli tyytyväinen, kun satoi lunta. Nietokset ka-sautuivat oven eteen ja ikkunan alle, ne antaisivat hänelle oikeuden istua tämän päivän sisällä, suojassa lumen keskellä.

119 [S]en ikkunat yöhön päin. / Epätoivon jäinen palo / on tulena liedelläin. / Ei ystä-vän, vieraan tulla / ole ovea laisinkaan. / Vain kaks on ovea mulla, / kaks: uneen ja kuolemaan. (Kailas 1931: 20–21) The translation of Kailas's poem is Philip Riley's (1970: 97).

120 In her later article on pictorial models and narrative ekphrasis, Yacobi interlinks the phenomena of ekphrasis to the narrativization of imagistic analogies. References

to more general, pictorial models (as opposed to the specified descriptions of existing works of art) serve as a way to merge the pictorial allusion into the story. As concise, plain similes, they fuse easily into the flow of narration without the "interruptions" and digressions typical of ekphrastic descriptions. Because of its density, the ekphrastic simile often seems trivial and referential, including in relation to the surrounding textual context. As ekphrastic similes become clustered, they may turn into highly multidimensional networks of meanings, constituting a conglomerate of pictorial allusions distributed through the narrative texture. (Yacobi 1997: 42)

121 Ja sitten hän oli mennyt Artekiin, ja tuo kangas oli juuri tullut sinne, sitä oli levällään pöydällä – suuria auringonkukkia valkealla pohjalla. Kuin van Goghin maalaus.

122 The image of sunflowers appears also in Paavo Haavikko's collection of poems *Tiet etäisyyksiin* (Ways to Distance, 1951), constituting the title of the second section. In the cluster of poems in the second section, the house is pictured as a constructed and reconstructed dwelling (of the self): "Every house is built by many and never finished." ("Jokainen talo on monien rakentama eikä koskaan / valmis"; Haavikko 1951: 19) The poem has been translated into English by Anselm Hollo (1991: 10).

123 Hän oli ajatellut ettei talossa ollut niin kauniita verhoja kellään muulla.

124 Hän otti pari askelta taakse, pysähtyi ja katsoi kaappia pää kallellaan, kuin kaappi olisi ollut jokin veistos, moderni, josta ei tiedä mikä se on. Kaappi oli oven vieressä. Se oli vaaleaksi maalattu.

125 The Artek fabric and van Gogh's still life are juxtaposed in Mrs. Pyy's mind as a result of their correspondences: they share the theme of the sunflowers. However, in an ekphrastic simile, the visual source can also be alluded to by means of an analogous contrast: the analogy is based on the discrepancy between the *tenor* (the target) and the *vehicle* (the source, the image) linked in the comparison (Yacobi 1997: 38).

126 Ja [talossa] iso ikkuna, metsä on kuin kehystetty taulu, kun tekee ison ikkunan niin muuta taulua ei tarvitse. Saan katsella luontoa aamusta iltaan.

127 Ja hän alkoi nähdä itsensä – sellaisena kuin hän luuli, kuvitteli sen, joka oli hänet nähnyt, nähneen hänet: kasvot hurjistuneina, avopäin, paksun hangen ympäröimässä rakennuksessa, kasvot ikkuna-aukossa, musta turkki päällä, avopäin.

128 [N]e kaksi mäntyä, jotka kasvoivat kallion päällä, näkyisivät kokonaan, tyvestä latvaan, kuin suuressa taulussa.

129 Hän oli nähnyt silmissään, miten istuisi nojatuolissa ja katselisi niitä puita. Ne olivat aivan samanlaiset kuin kaksi mäntyä eräällä kalliolla, jolta hän oli lapsena käynyt sukeltamassa.

130 Musta kitkerä savu vain nousi ja kallio sihisi ja kumahti ja halkeili.

131 Ja nyt talolle on tehty sama mitä lukkari teki taululle, käännetty ympäri.

132 – Mutta kuule Kaisu, sano nyt mitä tuo oikein esittää?/– Mummo hyvä, siinä on väripintoja, erilaisia väripintoja. Ei se mitään esitä, ei sitä voi selittää./Mutta anoppi ei ymmärtänyt, mitä se sellainen on mikä ei esitä mitään, kai sen jotakin olisi pitänyt esittää. Ja hän alkoi taas puhua Viipurista ja kysyi pojaltaan, muistiko tämä sen taulun, jonka isä osti oikealta taiteilijalta, sen joka esitti venettä rannalla ja josta isä sanoi, että aina kun sitä katsoi hämärässä, teki mieli lähteä soutelemaan kuutamoiselle merelle.

133 – Kaunis tauluhan se on. Rouva Viita mitteli taulua *kuin* olisi tutkinut sitä tarkasti.

134 Ruuska (2010: 164) connects the discussion of art in the novel to the debate on abstract painting in the 1950s in Finland and the status of modernist painting in the middle-class life style. She finds a link between the painting of the cows in the house at Vyborg and Victor Westerholm's painting *Lehmiä koivumetsässä* (Cattle in a Birch Forest, 1886).

135 – Tunnetko sinä tämän kuvan, huomaatko että se muistuttaa erästä naista? – Ja

mies oli katsonut kuvaa, naurahtanut, työntänyt kirjan pois ja sanonut: "Kukapa muu se voisi olla kuin sinä itse."

136 Sillä se oli totta, sattuma se oli eikä suinkaan hänen syytään, että nuorin sibylloista, Delphica, muistutti tätä naista joka seisoi juuri tässä Pietarinkirkon ovella [...].

137 [...] joka oli niin hänen näköisensä kuin he olisivat olleet sisarukset.

138 Ja isoäiti oli oikaissut itsensä, nostanut toisen käden varjostamaan silmiä, seisonut sirppi toisessa kädessä ja katsonut eteen. Suuret kasvot, kuin miehellä, ja silmät, synkät ja ankarat.

139 Ruuska (2010: 120–121) reads this sequence of *Kaikki naiset näkevät unia* in the context of L. Onerva's *Mirdja*, in which the protagonist becomes captivated by Carlo Crivelli's painting *Madonna*: "My God, how beautiful a woman can be!" ("Jumalani, miten nainen sentään voi olla kaunis!"; Onerva 1908: 221) Mirdja begins to copy the painting until she realizes seeing and admiring herself in the painted figure.

140 John Hollander (1988: 209) has called recognizable representations of works of art "actual ekphrasis" as distinguished from imagined "notional ekphrasis." The distinction is problematic in the sense that the verbal transformations of an actual work of art are always far from being exact transformations (cf. Mitchell 1994: 152–154). The pictorial allusions that are faithful to their source are modifications equal to ekphrastic representations, in which we can find selected or added details if they are compared to the "original" works of art.

141 The frescoes depicted in the narrative sequence constitute a "spatio-contextual" type of ekphrasis: a group of works of art situated in the same space and rendered as a cluster linked to each other (cf. Lund 1998: 177).

142 [K]irjojen kuvat nousivat silmien eteen sitä mukaa kuin hän luetteli niitä: Maailman luominen – Aatamin luominen – Eevan luominen – Karkotus paratiisista – Nooan historia – Vedenpaisumus – Synnin virta – ja profeetat – yhteensä seitsemän. Ja sibyllat: Libica – Cumaea – ja Delphica, sibylloista nuorin. Niitä oli viisi. The name "Creation" ("Maailman luominen") used in Vartio's novel refers to the frescoes *The Separation of Light and Darkness*, *The Creation of the Sun, Moon and Earth* and *The Separation of Land and Water*. "The Expulsion from Paradise" ("Karkotus paratiisista") seems to allude to the fresco *The Temptation and Expulsion*, whereas some details of "The River of Sins" ("Synnin virta") are parallel to the fresco *The Last Judgment*. In my analysis of the ekphrastic constellation of frescoes, I have decided to use the name "The River of Sins" given by Vartio, as it is meaningful in the context of the novel. However, I have used quotation marks instead of italics when referring to this "notional ekphrasis."

143 "Nuorin on Delphica, mallina nähtävästi sama neito, joka on esitetty Eevana Aatamin luomisessa Jumalan käsivarren suojassa. Delphica on esimerkki siitä, miten erilaisia tunnearvoja voi lukea Michelangelon henkilökuvien kasvoilta: tässä itsetiedotonta kaihoa, aavistelevaa tulevaisuudennäkemystä –"

144 See Ruuska 2010: 116. Onni Okkonen was one of the author's teachers at the University of Helsinki during her studies in art history.

145 The blend of different "actualities" in the representation and interpretation of "actual" works of art has contradictory consequences. The meta-commentary of Michelangelo's frescoes, embedded in the depiction of the fictional world, simultaneously reinforces and weakens the illusion of verisimilitude in the novel. The commentary emphasizes the illusion of the fictional world as a living "reality," but on the meta-level, it draws attention to the quality of the world as a fictional, artificial construct.

146 Hän oli tullut etsimään – etsimään jotakin; ajatus hajosi, ja hänen mielestään oli jälleen hävinnyt se, mitä hän oli uskonut ja kuvitellut tuntevansa tämän oven edessä ja minkä hän oli juuri ollut tavoittamaisillaan. Mutta se oli hävinnyt.

147 [K]oko sielu muuttuisi toiseksi [...].

148 Missä olivat sibyllat? Hän haki seiniltä, haki katosta, ja löysi ne. Noin pieniä ja mustia.

149 Hän näkisi miten Jumala oli luonut maailman, näkisi kuvan, jossa on Jumala pyörähtämässä erottaessaan pimeyden valkeudesta [...]. Eikö hän ollut uskonut kuulevansa valtaisan humahduksen, kun oli katsonut sitä kuvaa kirjassa. Ja nyt hän sen näkisi.

150 A parallel text to the Vatican section in *Kaikki naiset näkevät unia* is Vartio's short story "Vatikaani" (The Vatican, 1955), analyzed by Ruuska (2010: 186–195) also in relation to Aino Kallas's short story "Lasnamäen valkea laiva" (The White Ship, 1913) – another depiction of female pilgrimage in Finnish literature (see Vuorikuru 2012, Rojola 2011).

151 Hän etsi Aatamia katosta, koetti virittyä johonkin, kuin rukoukseen, tavoittaa etusormeensa kipinän siitä sähköstä, hengestä, joka virtasi Jumalan sormesta Aatamin sormeen ja teki hänet Jumalan kuvaksi./Mutta kuva oli kuva, Aatami alaston mies katossa.

152 Jos hän olisi kysynyt. Hän kuuli korvissaan miten ihmiset olisivat purskahtaneet nauruun ympärillä. Ja opas, se typerys, olisi ehkä hillinnyt naurunsa, virkansa vuoksi, mutta ei olisi kyennyt peittämään hymyä [...].

153 [T]ässä, hyvä rouva. Tässä edessä, tämä kaikki on synninvirtaa. Tuolla ylhäällä näette Jumalan, hämärästi tosin. Sibyllat nurkissa, profeetat toisissa nurkissa, nuo yrmeät herrat, ja Aatami tuolla, komea mies, eikö totta? Hyvät lihakset, vitaalisen näköinen herra, eikö totta? Siinä syntiinlankeemus, tuossa käärme, tuolla Eeva – aika lihava täti, eikö totta –

154 Ja siinä oli Ihmisen poika, tuo alaston, käsi koholla. Ja toisiinsa takertuneet ruumiit, ylimmäisenä se sekasikiön näköinen. Hän oli luullut sitä yksisilmäiseksi, mutta kai sillä oli kaksi silmää sittenkin, oli peittänyt toisen silmän kädellä.

155 Kaikkea hän nyt mietti, ja tässä./Hän keskittyi katsomaan Synnin virtaa./Hän liikahti rajusti; mieleen oli tullut piinallinen ajatus. Hävetti.

156 Synninvirta oli jäädä näkemättä. Minä sentään huomasin ajoissa, mutta sinä vain töllistelit etkä ymmärtänyt mitään, vaikka se oli nenäsi edessä.

157 Mrs. Pyy doesn't remember the name of the sculptor and suspects that he is Michelangelo. Probably the ekphrastic reference in the novel alludes to Donatello's wooden sculpture *The Penitent Magdalene* (1453–1455) (Ruuska 2010: 111).

158 Italialainen kääntyi katsomaan heitä, rouva Pyytä ja hänen miestään, loi heihin katseen, joka oli sanoinkuvaamaton. Kieli oli pistänyt suusta esiin, lipaissut salamannopeasti huulia – ja rouva Pyystä tuntui kuin hän olisi nähnyt käärmeen hännän livahtavan ruohikossa, niin nopeasti, ettei tajunnut, oliko se käärme vai mikä – ruohikossa ei näkynyt mitään liikettä.

159 Rouva Pyy huomasi, että hullu hän olisi ollut, jos olisi riistänyt noilta ihmispareilta tuon autuuden, hullu, jos olisi paljastanut heille totuuden./Mistä hän tiesi, mikä tässä oli totuus.

160 [...] kuin kukan lehdet takaisin nupulle.

161 – Enkä minä huomannut sanoa edes kiitos. Grazie, kiitos.

162 On the edition process of the novel's title see Ruuska 2013a: 198–199.

163 Ehkä olisi parasta antaa niitten olla, kasvissa ei näyttänyt olevan uusia nuppuja. Mutta hän nipisti yhden oksan poikki ja näki, että oli tullut katkaisseeksi oksan, jossa olikin nuppuja./Rouva Pyy huomasi, että hänen sormensa olivat kostuneet; hän oli pusertanut kukan oksan murskaksi.

164 Oliko hänen tarkkaavaisuutensa hetkeksi hervonnut – ja silloin tapahtunut tämä [...] ja tyttö oli kulkenut ja kulkenut, eikä tiennyt, että oli tapahtunut petos.

165 As perceived by possible world poetics, the conditions of fictionality are not dependent on the truthfulness of the propositions made in the semantic domain of fictional worlds. What really matters is the *representation* of these propositions in the textual universe. Therefore, a virtual event existing only in the private domain

of a fictional mind is as much a part of the plot as an event enacted within the fictional actual world. (Ryan 1991: 262) In fact, as Ryan (1991: 156) has pointed out, the diversification of simultaneously existing virtual worlds is the primary factor that constitutes the conditions of the *tellability* of a story. Tellability deals with the potential appeal of a narrative message; it answers the question of what makes the narrative worth telling, of what is the point of the story (Labov 1972; Polanyi 1979). The diversification and richness of private virtual worlds generate logical complexity, which is the fascination of literary texts.

166 The notion of counterfact coincides with Prince's *disnarrated* to give a slightly different perspective on the alternative versions represented in narratives. Disnarrated can be defined as "terms, phrases, and passages that consider what did not or does not take place," or alternatively, as "all the events that *do not* happen but, nonetheless, are referred to (in a negative or hypothetical mode) by the narrative text" (Prince 2004: 299; emphasis his).

167 [Tätäkö minun elämäni on oltava, että] on annettava kaiken mennä ohitse?

168 – Jaa-a, kyllä minä tästä sivistyksestä olen saanut kalliisti maksaa. Jos minä olisin tiennyt sen mitä nyt tiedän niin olisinko minä mennyt naimisiin ja tehnyt lapsia heti ensimmäiseen kiireeseen. En totisesti, olisin jatkanut lukujani ja nyt minulla olisi ammatti./– Olisit katsonut paremmin eteesi ja nainut rikkaan miehen. Kyllä sinä tiesit että minulla ei ollut rahoja./– En minä sitä tarkoita. Rouva Pyy jäi katsomaan eteensä. Ja mies kysyi, miettikö hän nyt sitä, missä olisi ellei olisi tässä. [...] Sinä puhut siitä nykyään aina ja ellet puhu niin kuljet sen näköisenä kuin miettisit koko ajan mikä sinut on tähän tuonut. Jos ei ole liian myöhäistä, niin pyörrä elämäsi.

169 Hän vihasi miestä ja anoppia, vihasi koko elämäänsä, vihasi. Iho oli vanhentunut ennen aikojaan, mutta se ei ollut hänen syytään vaan niitten, jotka olivat pakottaneet hänet elämään nämä vuodet niin kuin ne oli täytynyt elää.

170 Joskus minä teen niin tarkkaa työtä, että en saa rauhaa jos likaämpärin pohjalle on jäänyt yksi tulitikku [...]. Ja sitten annan viikkokausia kaiken olla. Istun vain niin kuin sinä nyt ja odotan, että joku tulisi ja nykäisisi minut liikkeelle. [...] ja sitten taas vihaan tehdä mitään, koska minulla on ikään kuin huono omatunto siitä että kaikki mitä minä teen on turhaa ja aivan väärin tehty, että minun pitäisi tehdä jotain muuta, ja odotan vain että minulle selviäisi mitä minun pitäisi tehdä enkä kuitenkaan tee mitään.

171 According to Hogan, expectations serve to elicit conditions for emotions, both in themselves and in their relation to actual results in a narrative structure. The different emotional responses to expected and unexpected experiences are obvious, especially in the case of such feelings as relief or disappointment, "since these feelings depend entirely upon the contrast between expectation and experience" (Hogan 2011a: 50).

172 Olet kuin naiset ovat, näkevät unia, heräävät aamulla, katsovat tyhjin silmin ja ovat joko pettyneitä kun ei uni ollutkaan totta, tai kiittävät onneaan siitä että se oli unta mitä he unessa tekivät.

173 Dannenberg (2008: 26) refers to these aspects of causation as "causal-progenerative," "causal-manipulative," and "causal-sufficient" forms of causal explanation. My own distinction in the four epistemic paths follows the paradigm presented by Mark Turner (1987), which also serves as a basis for Dannenberg's typology.

174 As Doležel (1998: 60) observes, in narrative semantics the accident always involves a disruption of *intended* action: "If the intended state is achieved, the action is successful. If, however, the agent finds himself or herself in an end state different from the one intended, an accident has happened."

175 According to Doležel (1998: 72), "[o]nly in insanity, where the person's mind is severely impaired or even destroyed, is intentionality null and void. Insane behavior

281

is semantically identical to nature events. When intentionality disintegrates, nature force takes over."

176 Minulle on aina päättäminen ollut vaikeinta.

177 [H]än muisti niitä päiviä, jolloin oli katsellut kotiaan ja lapsiaan ja miettinyt... Hän oli tosiaan miettinyt, mitä tavaroita ottaisi, mitä jättäisi. [...] /Mutta sitä ei tapahtuisi, ei.

178 [...] hän ikään kuin odotti, odotti jotakin, odotti keksivänsä mitä oikein pitäisi tehdä niin että lopulta *tuntisi elävänsä.*

179 Vaan miksi, kun hän katsoi taloa ja kulki sitä kohti, miksi hän pelkäsi? Hän oli ennen kulkenut sinne tuntematta muuta kuin että olisi pian siellä.

180 Mistä oli tullut tämä hiljaisuus, tieto ettei hänen pitäisi seisoa tässä, ettei hänen olisi lainkaan pitänyt tulla?

181 Eikö hän ollut valmistanut itseään nöyryytyksen varalle, perääntymisen varalle. Eikö hän ollut opettanut itselleen, mitä olisi sanottava sitten, kun se tapahtuisi. Hän vain nousisi ja sanoisi: No niin, tämä leikki on sitten lopussa. Kiitos, minulla oli oikein hauskaa. Virkistyin.

182 Hän sanoisi sen niin ohimennen ja niin luontevasti nauraen, että ainakin tämä mies jäisi miettimään. Miettimään, että hän, nainen, olikin ollut se jolle koko juttu oli ollut leikkiä.

183 Mutta eihän se ollut vielä tapahtunut. Tietysti niin tulisi käymään. Jos hän ehkä olikin ajatellut jotakin, odottanut, niin nyt hän jo tiesi, ettei tästä mitään tulisi.

184 Hän yritti olla ajattelematta sitä, sitä samaa, yhä. Sillä eihän se ollut edes tapahtunut, miksi hän kiusasi itseään yhä sillä, minkä pelkkä ajatteleminen teki olon niin piinalliseksi, että hän liikahti kun taas muisti.

185 [...] halkaissut tylsällä puukolla vatsan, vetänyt veriset suolet esiin ja kidukset – ja suomut.

186 The unwritten parts of *Kaikki naiset näkevät unia* represent an instance of the nonnarrated which Harold F. Mosher (1993: 408) calls "repression." Repression is manifested when the characters do not name their psychological problems or cover up what is wrong. Something is absent in reality, but exists in the mind of the character, yet is not accurately named. In defining his concept "nonnarrated" (employed by Mosher in his analysis) Gerard Prince, on the other hand, maintains that nonnarrated (or unnarrated) does not stem from repression, ignorance, or choice. Rather, something is intentionally left unsaid because of "some narrative call for rhythm, characterization, suspense, surprise, and so on" (Prince 2004: 298).

187 Ja kaikki alkaisi alusta, kaikki.

188 According to Kafalenos, narratives tend to begin either at a period of equilibrium just before the narrative is disrupted or at a moment of disruption that marks the onset of imbalance. Therefore, readers initially interpret the opening scene as an equilibrium and expect the story to conclude at or near the end of a sequence when a new state of equilibrium is regained. The inference of causal networks depends on whether the reader is given sufficient information about the character's position in the sequence of functions that constitute a complete narrative sequence. (Kafalenos 2006: 104–106, 113–114)

5. *From Emotions to Feelings. Self-Conscious Minds in* Tunteet

1 [...] vaan ääni / kuin linnun kirkaisu: / se lintu vieraan maan / kun tulva nousee / edellä paeten / voi lentää tästä yli / voi lentää väsyneenä / verta sulissaan" (*Seppele*, 14)

2 [H]än kuunteli itseään: oli kuin hänen koko ruumiinsa olisi ollut jotain mustaa vellovaa laavaa ja siinä kiemurtavia punaisia tulenliekkejä, hän ei ollut koskaan

tuntenut ennen tätä tunnetta, ja se tuotti hänelle uteliasta nautintoa, jonka hän antoi jatkua.

3   Love comedy has often been affiliated with the popular form of romantic fiction as it offers an affirmation of the reader's desire to see "love conquering all" (Pearce & Stacey 1995: 16)

4   The narratives of female development often subvert the narrative strategies of sentimental love plots and epistolary fiction (Clark 1991: 182). After the heyday of epistolary in the late seventeenth, eighteenth, and early nineteenth century, the mode has been favored especially by women authors of the late twentieth century. In these works, epistolary form, however, appears more or less as a mixed mode: the letters written by characters are embedded within a third-person narrative. The dialogic creation of meaning constitutes the focus of epistolary, emphasizing the varied, contradictory perspectives and fragmented forms, which reflect the changed ways of writing romance. (Beebee 2005: 141)

5   Ovella seisoi sotamies.

6   Ja sotamies katsoi Inkeriä ja kuuli tämän puhuvan samalla lailla kuin nuo toisetkin, maalaisesti, leveästi.

7   [K]ai tämä nyt *ymmärsi* että hän *ymmärsi* miten hullunkurisilta nämä tällaiset puheet vieraan korvissa kuulostivat ja ettei hän ole yhtä yksinkertainen kuin nämä.

8   Vesti (2014) reads the romance plot of *Tunteet* as a rescripting of the narrative structure summarized by Janice A. Radway (1987: 134) in a following manner: 1) The heroine's social identity is destroyed; 2) the heroine reacts antagonistically to an aristocratic male; 3) the aristocratic male responds ambiguously to the heroine; 4) the heroine interprets the hero's behavior as evidence of a purely sexual interest in her; 5) the heroine responds to the hero's behavior with anger or coldness; 6) the hero retaliates by punishing the heroine; 7) the heroine and the hero are physically and/or emotionally separated; 8) the hero treats the heroine tenderly; 9) the heroine responds warmly to the hero's act of tenderness; 10) the heroine reinterprets the hero's ambiguous behavior as the product of previous hurt; 11) the hero proposes/openly declares his love for/demonstrates his unwavering commitment to the heroine with a supreme act of tenderness; 12) the heroine responds sexually and emotionally; 13) the heroine's identity is restored.

9   [R]uokasalissa istui sotamies, joka oli herrasmies [...].

10   Ja tuntui äkkiä mukavalta, jokin oli alkanut, sitä olisi voinut sanoa seikkailuksi, mutta *hän ei miettinyt mitä se oli*. Riitti vain se että oli pitkästä aikaa tapahtunut jotain, tämä oli jotain mitä saattoi sanoa tapahtumiseksi [...].

11   [H]än oli katsonut tytön perään tämän kulkiessa huoneen halki keittiötä kohti pää pystyssä ja leuka pystyssä, hiukset levällään [...] sotamiehen mielestä hän oli vihaisen näköinen tyttö.

12   Mutta nyt puhuttiin puhelimesta, latinasta ei mitään.

13   [H]än oli saanut hyvän kasvatuksen, sen näki kaikesta.

14   Tyttö ei ollut saanut kunnon kasvatusta, hänen käytöksensä oli joskus vallan vulgääriä.

15   One of the most famous adaptations of the Pygmalion theme is the popular musical *My Fair Lady* based on George Bernard Shaw's play *Pygmalion* (1912). In the play, the character of Henry Higgins, a professor of phonetics, educates the Cockney girl, Eliza Doolittle, in certain social graces and impeccable speech in order to integrate her into British high society.

16   Ja sitten [Hannu] oli puhunut pitkälti latinan oppimisesta yleensä, latinan alkeitten tietystä välttämättömästä mekaanisuudesta, täsmällisyydestä.

17   Tuskin huomaa että minä olen tässä, Inkeri mietti, luulee kai että minä olen hänen äänensä kaiku [...].

18   Se ei saanut näkyä, ei, hän oli tehnyt asian itselleen selväksi [...]: tästä lähin vain latinaa, ettei kukaan eikä ainakaan tuo saisi tietää, miten sydän hakkasi, miten sen oli käynyt. Hullu hän oli ollut, hullu, mutta nyt se oli lopussa.

283

19 [J]os oli jotain luullut, näkisi, että luulot olivat olleet turhia.

20 Miten rauhallinen äsken, miten miellyttävä, ja taas: kulmikas, levoton, hermostut-
tava. Miksei hän pysy hetkeäkään alallaan? Ja sotamiehen sydän oli alkanut lyödä
niin että hän pelkäsi sen kuuluvan, pelkäsi harmaan, virttyneen asetakin liikkuvan
siltä kohden missä sydän tykytti sen alla. Eikä hän tiennyt että myös tyttö kuunteli
sydäntään, että myös tyttö pelkäsi näkyvän miten sydän löi, sillä sen peittona oli
pelkkä ohut punakukkainen pumpulikangas, ja tuntui kuin kukat sydämen päällä
olisivat hyppineet, kavaltaneet sen.

21 Tyttö ei katsonut häntä koskaan suoraan silmiin paitsi kun oli pakko, silloin kun
hän opettajan ominaisuudessa vaatimalla vaati että taivutus oli saneltava selvästi,
jotta hän kuulisi tuliko jokainen muoto oikein.

22 [...] tyttö juoksee edellä ja hän yrittää perään mutta ei pääse kyllin nopeasti ja
on vihainen itselleen, hänen on saatava tyttö kiinni. Mutta tyttö juoksee edellä ja
nauraa, kovaa ilkkuvaa naurua.

23 Sotamiehestä tuntui että hän nieli hitaasti alas jotain kuumaa ja polttavaa. Kun se
oli mennyt, hän ajatteli: olen hullu.

24 Kun hän oli tullut tupaan, oli tyttö seisonut lieden äärellä tulen kajo kampaamat-
toman päänsä ympärillä, huulet hieman auki, noin, noin juuri kuin nyt, silmissä
sama ilme kuin eläimellä joka on jähmettynyt kuuntelemaan [...].

25 Ja kuva poissa, tyttö poissa tulen ääreltä, oli tyttö, suu täynnä älytöntä tytönpuhet-
ta, missä mikään ei ollut ihanaa tai hirveää vähempi – poissa kuva joka oli saanut
hänen sydämensä takomaan.

26 Ja tyttö kohautti olkapäitään, liikutteli käsiään kuin olisi ravistellut päältään jotain,
hankasi rystysillään polviaan – ja masentui lopullisesti tajutessaan näyttävänsä
naurettavalta.

27 Katso vain, kyllä minä *tiedän* mitä sinä siinä *ajattelet*, pidät minua maalais-
moukkana, pidä vain, ajattele ihan mitä haluat, usko kaikki mitä ihmiset juoruavat,
mutta älä luule että minä sinua itken.

28 Sotamies seurasi tytön ilmeitä, näki neuvottomuuden, näki pahan mielen, näki
ylimielisyyden, johon tyttö verhoutui suunnatessaan silmänsä taas häneen.

29 – Oletteko rakastunut? kysyi sotamies kyynillisesti. Ja säikähti: sitä hän nyt oli
viimeksi tarkoittanut sanoa.

30 The feelings of resentment refer to the emotional story structure of the ideal
romance, in which the heroine responds to the hero's behavior with anger or
coldness, and then, the hero retaliates by punishing the heroine (Radway 1987:
134).

31 – Kehen, tyttö sanoi kylmästi ja nosti leukaansa. Ja raivosi itselleen: – Nyt se arvaa,
luulee että häneen, kun kysyy tuolla äänellä että kehen.

32 Oma puhe on katkonaista ja ailahtelevaa, murteellista; yhteinen kieli, jota 'mies
kuin mies' puhuu, on yhteisön säänneltyä kieltä. Vartion naiset tiedostavat sijansa
näiden välimaastossa. Oman välittömän kokemisen tila on yhteisöllisesti mykkä;
yhteisön kielelle nainen on kohde, joka määritellään ulkoa. Mutta opittuaan
yhteisen kielen tavoille tämä ei kenenkään maan agentti kuulee omassa puheessaan
vieraan kielen, oman kaksiarvoisuutensa.

33 On Vartio's technique of narrated monologue in *Tunteet* see Rojola 2013.

34 [...] Vartion proosassa tämä esitysmuoto saa omanlaisiaan tehtäviä: se on väline
kielen, vallan ja myös sukupuolten suhteiden analyysissä. Se välimaasto jossa nyt
liikutaan on kielen dialogisuuden näyttämö.

35 Rojola (2008: 137–138) compares Vartio's technique to Nathalie Sarraute's "sous-
conversation," a form of dialogue in which two spheres of talk, the one on the
surface of speech and the other underneath it, co-exist.

36 Mutta toisella silmällä hän piti silmällä Hannun ilmeitä ajatellen samalla itsekseen,
oliko se piru vai mikä joka oli tehnyt hänestä taas näin kiltin ja rauhallisen, juuri
sellaisen josta tuo Hannu pitää.

37   – Sinä olet levoton, sanoi Hannu korostaen olet sanaa kuin olisi opettanut kielioppia.

38   – Kerro – oletko lukenut siitä?

39   – Tiedätkö mitä, hän sanoi. – Sinulla on kyllä mielikuvitusta ja sinä osaat myös kertoa, mutta miksi sinä kohauttelet olkapäitäsi? – Katso, näin. Ja Hannu matki.

40   – Kerro lisää, hän sanoi. – Mutta puhu levollisesti, sinun äänesi sopii kertomaan juuri tuollaista, äläkä keskeytä koko ajan. No niin, aloita alusta, haluan kuulla sen uudelleen alusta. Siis, veden emännän tytär istui kivellä ja kampasi pitkiä hiuksiaan...

41   Hannu kokeili ehkä kuinka älykäs hän oli, yllytti tahallaan häntä puhumaan tällaisia, ja sitten ihmettelisi, oliko hän todella niin yksinkertainen.

42   Kohta se tietysti panisi hänet taivuttamaan jotain verbiä [...].

43   – Katso, tuolla muurissa on pihlaja [...]. Se on kasvanut kyynelistä.

44   – Mutta minua säälittää, sanoi Inkeri, ja huokasi./– Mikä sinua säälittää – sinä siis uskot että tuo pihlaja on kasvanut kyynelistä?/– Enhän minä ole sellaista sanonut – tiedänhän minä nyt sen ettei sen enempää kuusi kuin pihlaja kasva mistään kyyneleestä./– Miksi sitten sanot että kyyneleestä – puhu täsmällisesti. Sinä myönsit äsken ettei mikään puu kasva kyyneleestä, itki sinun neitosi vaikka kuinka, ja kuitenkin puhut taas kyyneleestä – älä sano että pihlaja kasvoi kyyneleestä vaan sano että sanotaan, kerrotaan, luullaan, uskotaan – puhu täsmällisesti.

45   – Sehän on vain kuva [...].

46   Hän vihasi hetken Hannua [...].

47   As Paul Gray (1989) points out, literary critics and academicians have been insisting for a long time that characters who appear in fiction do not exist outside words and works that create them. According to Gray, these ideas of literary criticism (similar to Hannu's conception of the motifs of folktales) are "technically right, of course, but imaginatively out to lunch." The human mind is prone to imagine, to picture possibilities: "One of the principal pleasures of reading stems from the illusion of eavesdropping on unguarded lives, of getting to know people better than they may know themselves." (Gray 1989: 66; quoted by Ryan 1991: 21–22)

48   – Mutta hyvä lapsi, sanoi Hannu, tuli Inkerin viereen ja korjasi Inkerin lakkia joka oli taas putoamaisillaan. – Miksi sinä minulle suutut, sanoi Hannu. – Eihän se tarinan kauneudesta vähennä mitään vaikka asioita katsellaan järjen kannalta, tarinat syntyvät juuri siitä että ihmisluonne on taipuvainen kuvittelemaan esimerkiksi sellaista että tuo pihlaja on syntynyt jonkun onnettoman neidon kyynelistä. Aivan tyypillinen tarina, tuollaisia haudalle kasvaneita puita on monta. Ja Hannu puhui pitkälti erilaisista tarinanaiheista, jotka kiersivät ympäri maailmaa erilaisina muunnoksina, mutta ytimeltään samoina...

49   The motif of the weeping willow alludes to Vartio's poem "Itkun synty" (The Birth of Weeping, 1953), in which the elegiac, metapoetic motifs of the grave and a weeping willow are linked to archaic imagery from folk poetry and the medieval legend of Mary Magdalene (on the figure of Mary Magdalene in Vartio's poetry see Karppanen 2012). The weeping willow motif also appears in James Joyce's *Ulysses*.

50   – Hulluutta tietysti, myönsi Inkeri. – Mutta eihän siinä olisikaan kysymys järjestä ja hulluudesta, vaan rakkaudesta.

51   [Ä]lä leiki asioilla jotka ovat vakavia.

52   [T]iedätkö Inkeri, sinulla on sellainen tukka että tekisi mieli mennä sen alle kokonaan piiloon, mutta miksi sinä Inkeri puhut sellaista mikä ei ole viisasta, etkö sinä ajattele ettei sellaista sovi puhua [...].

53   Eikä Hannu tiennyt missä Inkeri oli ehtinyt käydä niitten parin minuutin aikana, jotka hänen kertomuksensa oli kestänyt, ei tiennyt mitä Inkeri oli ehtinyt kokea: Inkeri oli häväistynä, tukka juurta myöten leikattuna oli vaeltanut synkkiä metsiä pitkin, mutta rakasti.

54   – Etkö sinä ymmärrä miten kummalliselta sellainen puhe kuulostaa, sanoi Hannu,
– ethän sinä hullu ole, miksi puhuit sitten sellaisia, etkö sinä tiedä että mielenhäi-
riössä olevat ihmiset näkevät harhoja, ja nimenomaan juuri hiiriä.

55   Ei se tietysti ollut hiiri, minun silmissäni vain vilisi, sanoi Inkeri./Luutnantti oli
purskahtanut nauruun, ja myös Inkeri oli alkanut nauraa, hän ja luutnantti yhdessä olivat nauraneet ääneen ja luutnantti oli alkanut laskea leikkiä:/– Minkälainen
hiiri – musta, valkea, iso, pieni?/– Pieni musta hiiri./– Mutta oliko se oikea hiiri,
juuri sellainen jota kaikki naiset pelästyvät?

56   [Ä]kkiä Hannu oli sanonut [...] ilkeällä äänellä:/– Oletko puhunut siitä jo tarpeeksi.

57   [L]uutnantti oli hauska, paljon hauskempi kuin Hannu [...].

58   Inkeriä harmitti. Hän epäili jo itsekin, että luutnantti oli pitänyt häntä hulluna.

59   Minun käytöstäni saat paheksua mutta sinä et voi kieltää minua ajattelemasta.

60   – Kuvitellaan, aloitti Hannu – kuvitellaan, hän toisti hetken mietittyään että me, sinä ja minä, olisimme matkalla ja meillä olisi nälkä, olisimme jossain ulkomailla ja
olisi vierekkäin kaksi ravintolaa, toinen tunnetusti hieno, turistien suosima, mutta
kallis, tietysti, ja toinen vähemmän hieno mutta huokeampi, siinä ei esimerkiksi
olisi orkesteria ja sen sellaista, mutta ruoka olisi kuitenkin hyvää, siististi valmis-
tettua, ravitsevaa. Inkeri oli jo ehtinyt innostua, oli alkanut kuunnella kuin satua,
oli nähnyt jo itsensä ja Hannun ulkomailla jonkin romanttisen ravintolan edessä,
kun Hannu kysyi:/– Kumpaan menisit, kumman valitsisit?/– Sen halvemman
– tietysti./– Sinä olet järkevä tyttö, sanoi Hannu./Inkeristä tuntui, että hänestä oli
tulossa hyvin järkevä.

61   Kyse on naiseksi kasvamisesta, siitä, miten nainen joutuu vähitellen alistumaan
sekä aistillisesti ja ruumiillisesti että tunteiltaan ja ajattelultaan mieskulttuurin la-
keihin ja miten hänen itsekokemuksensa kuolettaminen on lopulta ainoa tie, joka
tarjoaa mahdollisuuden selviytyä.

62   Karkama's view denotes a one-world frame that stipulates a direct correspondence
between the author's "feminine logic" and the logic of the female character.
This notion is problematic for two different reasons. Firstly, the idea of the
existence of a specific "feminine speech" in women's writing has been questioned
by several feminist scholars. Felski (1989: 66), for instance, emphasizes language
as a playground of intersubjective meanings. Language needs to be understood
as a "form of social activity which is both rule-governed and open, which
does not simply determine consciousness but can also be employed to contest
existing world views and to develop alternative positions." Secondly, can there be
a direct correspondence between a real human being and a creation of her mind,
a construct of fiction?

63   Karkama (1995: 162), however, refers to this aspect of Vartio's novel by stating
that, by comparison with the works of Maria Jotuni, for instance, the orders of
society are no longer only women's problem, but have an influence on both men
and women, since the presence of society is experienced as a third party in erotic
relationships.

64   [...] eivät merkinneet mitään, vain hullut ihmiset toimivat niitten mukaan.

65   [S]anattomat sanat ovat kauneimpia.

66   [M]utta koska olin kasvava, miksen siis olisi puhunut kasvavien kieltä [...]

67   Ja avattuaan oven hän oli joutunut pimeään tilaan, eteiseen, joka jakoi talon
keskeltä kahtia [... hän oli] nähnyt kaksi ovea, toisen edessä, toisen takana.

68   Se oli tuhrittu valkealla, maali oli rapissut, osa kirjaimista kulunut kokonaan pois.
Ellei olisi taitanut kieltä, ei olisi heti arvannut puuttuvia kirjaimia eikä saanut
nimestä selvää.

69   Mitähän tapahtuisi jos hän viskaisi kiven tuohon ikkunaan? Ajatus oli yllättävä,
järjetön; ja kuitenkin tuntui siltä kuin talossa olisi aavistettu ikkunaa uhattavan,
kuin joku olisi pitänyt häntä talosta käsin salaa silmällä.

70 [...] kääntyi ja katsoi taakseen, puunlatvoja kohti, ja kuva joka oli yötä päivää kulkenut hänen vierellään, oli nyt kuin piilossa lehtien lomassa, tähystämässä, tarkastamassa hänen jokaista ilmettään ja elettään, tietäen hänen ajatuksensa ja nähden ettei hänessä ollut epäilystä.

71 [Hän] näki omat pölyiset saappaansa, näki kukan varren jonka oli polkenut jalkansa alle, hän aisti kaiken kummallisen tarkasti ja kaikki tuntui saavan *jotain tärkeää merkitystä*.

72 [H]änellä [ei] ollut tämän kaupan kanssa oikeastaan mitään tekemistä, ei tämä mikään kauppa ollut, ei täällä mitään myyty.

73 [Ukko] kysyi kuin ohimennen, miten sotamies oli tänne osannut, mistä oli saanut päähänsä sellaista että täällä myytiin sormuksia? Hannu vastasi nähneensä oven päällä kirjoituksen, oli huomannut sen ohi kulkiessaan sattumalta, ja tullut sisään./– Se on nyt jäänyt, se kirjoitus, ei se tarkoita mitään, se nyt on siinä mutta kaikki sen tietävät ettei tässä mitään kauppaa ole.

74 At the beginning of the Winter War (as the first part of World War II is known in Finland) an announcement in the newspapers appealed to the Finns to exchange their gold rings for iron rings in order to provide financial support for the Finnish Air Force. The gold was melted into bars, but they were not used for the stated purpose, allegedly remaining instead in the vault of the Finnish National Bank. Many rumors spread about what had happened to the gold, rumors to which the old man in *Tunteet* refers: "The whole cargo of rings lies on the bottom of Lake Onega." ("Äänisen pohjassa koko sormuslasti"; *T,* 128) In fact, the gold bars were apparently moved abroad, mainly to Sweden, for safer storage.

75 – Minä en ole myynyt teille, saitte sen vain jostain.

76 [Sotamies] sanoi täydellisesti ymmärtävänsä, ettei kauppias ollut hänelle sormusta myynyt. Hän ei ollut nähnyt edes mitään sormusta, oli vain pistäytynyt ostamaan tänne jotain; ongenkoukkuja – kyllä, hän muisti kyllä sanoa että ongenkoukkuja vain.

77 Hannu nousi nopeasti ylös vuoteelta ja meni ikkunaan. Sydän hakaten, ikkunaverhoa pitelevä käsi hieman vavisten hän katsoi verhojen raosta pihalle.

78 Suuri ja jäntevä nainen, lantion muoto kuin miehellä. Palmikoitu tukka oli kierretty tiukasti pään ympäri, vaaleat hiukset, auringon polttamat, kädet riippuvat ja suuret, lihakset voimakkaasti kehittyneet. Komea nainen, germaanista tyyppiä, ajatteli Hannu. Kuin veistos, todella kuin veistos. Puettuna oikeisiin vaatteisiin, vähän älyä lisää ja sivistystä: jos ei suoranainen kaunotar niin komea, valkyria. Mutta ilmeisesti kauhea nainen, kova ja tyystin hoitamaton.

79 Huomasin hänet oikeastaan siksi että hänellä on samanvärinen tukka kuin Sinulla, kypsän oljen värinen [...].

80 Hän näki itsensä menevän nopeasti navetan taakse ja kuuli takaansa hevosen tömistelyn ja tiesi että rautakanki oli isketty syvälle maahan, tiesi sen painuvan yhä syvemmälle hevosen kiertäessä riimua sen ympärille.

81 [S]e ei ollut hänen asiansa eikä hevonen hänen hevosensa [...].

82 Heistä tuntui jo kaikista [...] että Inkerin sulhanen kävelisi iankaikkisesti ympäri taloa ja pitelisi heitä talon sisässä, kiertyisi kuin vanne tynnyrin ympärille.

83 Hevonen käveli laitumella, liinaharja hevonen, nosti päänsä, katsoi suoraan junaa kohti, ja Inkeristä tuntui kuin hevonen olisi katsonut juuri häneen ja hänen teki mieli vilkuttaa sille.

84 Hannu alkoi avata ikkunaa ja auttoi perhosta pääsemään ulos, seurasi sen lentoa kunnes se oli hävinnyt näkyvistä.

85 Jos olisin lintu [...].

86 Jossain huusi lintu, Inkeri kuuli sen, kuuli miten lintu huusi *kuin antaen merkin*: oli ikävä, ei ollut ollutkaan koskaan muuta eikä tulisi olemaan kuin alituinen ikävä –

87 [H]än olisi halunnut piirtää tai kirjoittaa, kerran hän oli aloitellut kirjettä, mutta

se oli jäänyt silleen, pariin lauseeseen, hän oli alkanut pelätä menettävänsä jotain, ollut mustasukkainen niistä sanoista, sanottuina ne lakkaisivat olemasta.

88 Nuo sanat ja sävelet olivat tarpeellisia niille, joilla ei ollut muita sanoja tulkitsemaan tunteita ja mielentiloja.

89 Ja kahvilasta kuuluvan laulun sanat rakkaudesta, kaihosta, kaipauksesta – sanat, joita hän oli pitänyt mauttomina, joita oli tuskin sietänyt kuunnella, ottivat hänet valtoihinsa.

90 Hiljaa tuutii Ääninen aaltojaan, / uupuu rantaan / satujen saarelmaan. / Sua kaukaa, armain, / täällä muistelen – / kerran noudan / onnemme venheeseen.

91 – Soittakaa jotain iloista.

92 Mutta sormet tuntuivat tahtovan jotain muuta, hän oli äkkiä kiihtynyt jostain, ja hän alkoi soittaa, soitti ja hymyili soittaessaan hieman ivallisesti itselleen, sormilleen, jotka soittivat jotain aivan muuta – ja hän lopetti äkkiä kesken, löi kämmenpohjat koskettimia vasten, ja pianosta lähti ääni joka kuului, ja vanha emäntä ajatteli kamarissa: nyt se lopetti. [...] /– Se oli 'Kevään kohinaa', tunsitteko?/– Tunsin, sanoi Inkeri laimeasti. – Soittaa hyvin, hän ajatteli. Mutta 'Kevään kohinaa' – sen verran hän tiesi – ei todistanut soittajan mausta ja henkisestä tasosta mitään erinomaista, vai oliko hän valinnut kappaleen kuulijoitten henkisen tason mukaisesti? Niin kai.

93 Hän oli soitattanut loputtomasti yhtä samaa levyä ja häntä oli suututtanut, kun laulajan ääneen ei ilmaantunut pienintäkään väsymyksen oiretta, ei edes huokausta, josta olisi käynyt ilmi, että laulaja oli uupunut ja tahtoi edes jotenkin ilmaista ettei jaksanut enää.

94 Nuo sävelet, nuo sanat, jotka nyt vierivät maiseman yli – levy oli vaihdettu toiseen – kuin olisi nähnyt pyhäasuun sonnustautuneita, aivan sopimattomiin vaatteisiin pukeutuneita maalaisia astelemassa jäykästi, kasvot vakavina tietä pitkin, menossa juhlaan...

95 Eivätkö vain hänenkin mieleensä olleet takertuneet ne samat iskelmät; niitä riitti, ne tulivat apuun, oli tilanne mikä tahansa.

96 Ehkä olikin niin, että kaikki laulut kumpusivat yhdestä samasta lähteestä, kaikki maailman laulut ja runous, ihmisen ikävästä... juhlallista ja naiivia, vastenmielistä, kylmiä väreitä nostattavaa, kaikkea yhtaikaa.

97 The first step into the light of consciousness in fictional scenes involves half-conscious mental processes. The technique of narrated monologue (or interchangeably free indirect speech, *style indirect libre, erlebte Rede*, or emphatic narrative) allows the narrator to follow the characters' thoughts as they drift towards the very "threshold of verbalization," to the edge of consciousness (see Cohn 1983: 103).

98 Hän ei saanut enää öisin unta vaan mietti herkeämättä *jotakin, kuin ratkaisua johonkin – mihin*?

99 Hän tuskin enää muisti että tuo oli totta, hänelle tapahtunutta, hänen omia elämyksiään.

100 Ja sanoi itselleen: mikä onni että tulin järkiini./Ja pysähtyi ajattelemaan jotain./ Järkiini – tulin järkiini? Mitä sillä tarkoitan?

101 [...] kuin yrittäen pidellä kiinni hetken jostain mikä auttamattomasti oli jo mennyt, hävinnyt.

102 Hän [...] alkoi uudelleen lukea uskotellen olevansa ulkopuolinen henkilö. Hän katsoisi tekstiä kuin harjoituskirjoitusta. The process corresponds to a technique Hannu uses in studying. Later he explains to Inkeri how "a text can have a subconscious effect," so that one is able to understand something only after it has appeared in another context. ("Hannu [...] selitti, miten teksti saattoi vaikuttaa alitajuisesi ja [...] miten sanan ymmärsi jostain toisesta yhteydestä [...]"; *T*, 180)

103 "Juna kulki yössä eteenpäin," hän luki ja pyyhki parista kohtaa yli tarpeettomana toistuvan sanonnan "juna kulki eteenpäin" "[...] Jokaiselta asemalaiturilta etsin

Sinua, kurkoitin kasvoni jokaista näkemääni naista kohti etsien jokaisesta Sinua, Sinun olemustasi, ja kerran näin erään joka muistutti Sinua, mutta hän ei kääntynyt enkä ehtinyt nähdä hänen kasvojaan kun juna taas lähti./Oliko tuo totta? hän mietti. Oli ja ei ollut. Mutta hän pyyhki sen kaiken yli ja luki eteenpäin, ja kun oli taas päässyt arkin loppuun, sanoi ääneen: mitä roskaa. Mutta luki edelleen kuin uhalla: […].

104 [K]aikki minussa kurkottui sitä kohti, sulautui ja keskittyi siihen kuvaan.

105 [K]atselin maisemia ja taloja, ja oli kuin ohitse vilahtelevat talot eivät olisi olleet oikeita, vaan oikeat olisivat olleet niitten takana ja olisin nähnyt juuri ne. Ja olisin halunnut kertoa, julistaa kaikille: maailma ei ole sitä miltä se näyttää, minä tiedän nyt että kaikki onkin aivan toisin, näitten maisemien takana ovat todelliset maisemat, niitten sanojen takana joita te ja minä puhutte ovat todelliset sanat – ja juna kulki eteenpäin, olimme perillä, paikassa mihin meidät majoitettiin toistaiseksi. Mutta minun mieleni oli yhä sama, sillä minä tiesin että Sinun kuvasi kulki minun vierelläni sinne minne minä, kuuli sanani, näki jokaisen ilmeen ja eleen ja täytti minut voimalla ja rauhantunnolla.

106 Ihmiset eivät tietäneet, millä silmällä katsella – kaiken alla on toinen maailma, jonka näen suoraan, ei minun tarvitse edes kuvitella. Vartio's letter to Paavo Haavikko, 9 June 1954 (Vartio 1996: 31).

107 [M]aailma kaikessa epätodellisuudessaan oli todemman tuntuinen kuin milloinkaan ennen –

108 [A]vatessaan silmänsä auki hän näki edessään läikehtivän vihreää ja valkeaa – kasvot, valtaisat kasvot, hänen edessään, ilmassa? Olivatko? Jos olivat niin ne olivat hahmottomat, pakotetut, väkisin esiin kutsutut – jonkin kivestä tehdyn veistoksen kuva.

109 [Hän huomasi] ettei hän ollut käyttänyt kirjeessä Inkerin nimeä yhtään kertaan, vaikka kuvalla oli ollut Inkerin kasvot ja vaikka – hän muisti sen nyt – hän oli toistanut Inkerin nimeä pimeässä vaunussa.

110 Mutta etkö ymmärrä: sanattomat sanat ovat kauneimpia. Olisitko halunnut minun polvistuvan kömpelösti eteesi kuten huonoissa ritariromaaneissa – vai mitä olisit halunnut minun tekevän?

111 Miten naurettavaa silloin onkaan tehdä jotakin niin arvotonta kuin ravita jotain olematonta, muodollista joka ei ole yksilö eikä ruumis. Ja näin ollen minulta ei synny Sinulle kirjettä, en voi puhua muuta kuin mikä on totta.

112 Kirjoittaako Inkerille kaikesta siitä, sanoako: minä rakastan sinua, minun on ikävä. Ei. Ei sellaisia sanoja – ei yhtään kirjettä ennen kuin hän voisi ilmaista kaiken juuri niin kuin hän oli sen tuntenut.

113 Ja kuva, jota hän näin repi rikki, katsoi taas jostain, oli taas kokonainen, ja katsoi häneen, loitolta, herättämättä hänessä enempää tuskaa kuin pelkoa, rauhaa kuin mitään. Se oli vain ja seurasi häntä, mutta hänen mielensä oli taas hänen, oli kuten oli aina ollut.

114 En voi taata Sinulle mitään ikuista, sillä ainoa mitä pidän lähinnä varmana ikuisena on kehitys, energia, liike. Henki on liian yksilöllinen käsite ollakseen ikuinen.

115 Tuon verran olen siis saanut käsiini siitä mitä tunnen: hidasliikkeisiä, kömpelöitä ja värittömiä ajatuksia, joita vaivaa kaiken lisäksi vielä se, että ne ovat varmasti kaikua jostain lukemastani.

116 The developmental plots of the two protagonists in *Tunteet* convert the narrative structure of the two embedded Bildung plots in Goethe's *Wilhem Meister*. The classical male Bildung of Wilhelm is accompanied by the "Confessions of a Beautiful Soul" in book 6. Whereas the female spiritual awakening in *Wilhem Meister* is described in terms of contemplation and solitude, the male Bildung is marked by Wilhem's interaction with the social world.

117 Tiedän että Sinä voit antaa ja ottaa tyydytyksen suorista, selkeistä, yli sovinnaisuuden menevistä tunteista […].

118 Aistit saavat tyydytyksen paikalla olevasta, kosketeltavasta, yksilö taas yksinäisyy-destä.

119 En voi näin kirjeessä antaa enkä saada sitä mikä on halpaa: ruumis, enkä myös-kään luopua siitä mikä on jakamatonta: yksilö, minun henkeni.

120 Mutta epäilen, oletko minulle toistaiseksi vain rakkauden personoituma, – mikä Sinussa on Sinua, sen minä olen kenties omaksunut rakkautena, ja mikä taas on rakkautta itseään, sen minä olen ehkä liittänyt, vain sulattanut Sinuun.

121 Minä olen joutunut muodostamaan mielipiteeni Sinusta – en niinkään välittömän näkemisen perusteella kuin katselemalla Sinua perästäpäin, pelkkien muistojen turvin – ja niinpä varmaan olen tehnyt Sinulle vääryyttä, katsellut Sinua etupäässä vain oman maailmankatsomukseni valossa.

122 Olet sitä ihmistyyppiä joka elää voimakkaasti nykyhetkeä ja lähintä ympäristöään ja jonka unelmien toteutuminen on enemmän sattuman kuin kestävän pyrki-myksen varassa. Et tiedä sitä vielä itse – olen ehkä juuri siksi hyvin erilainen kuin Sinä tietäessäni Sinusta tuon. [...] Sinussa on rohkeutta, Sinä olet nainen, jossa on nimenomaan naisen yksilöllisyyttä, tuhlailevaa naisellisuutta enemmän kuin heikko ruumis jaksaa kantaa, ja juuri sitä taustaa vasten ymmärrän Sinun joskus oudoilta vaikuttavat mielialan vaihtelusi: yksilöllisyys pyrkii eroon ruumistasi, ja näin syntyy käsite kaksinaisesta olemuksesta, se on sitä mitä Sinä joskus valitat, ettet itsekään ymmärrä miksi teet mitä teet. Ruumis, Sinun ruumiisi pyrkii tasa-suhtaan, yhtä voimakkaisiin elämyksiin kuin yksilö Sinussa.

123 Naisen ruumis, Sinun ruumiisi Inkeri, – minun on sitä ikävä, sen läheisyys tulee olemaan ihana ja sen omistaminen onni – mutta täydellisin tyydytys ei tule siitä, vaan tunteesta, älystä, energiasta, liikkeestä – kaikesta mikä lähenee ikuista enem-män kuin lahoava ruumis.

124 The hero's (rather than the heroine's) sexual awakening inverts also the formula of the classic romance plot, in which the aristocratic lover is the more experienced partner (see Vesti 2014: 19). The playing of piano has traditionally been considered as being a skill demanded from high class young women, serving as an indication of the cultivation of the heroine in the aristocratic lover's eyes (Launis 2005: 327).

125 [S]inä olet peto. [...] Hannuhan oli riuhtonut kuin hullu, vääntänyt hänen käsiään niin että niihin koski [...].

126 Tunnen hämärästi että minun tulisi pidellä rakkaus todellisen minuuteni ulkopuo-lella, ts. pelkään sen hävittävän todellisen minuuteni, so. persoonallisuuteni. Mikä ja mitä se on, sitä en vielä tiedä. Tiedän vain että silloin kun rakkaus on minussa, ei minua ole, on vain rakkaus.

127 Tarvitsen juuri sellaista kuin Sinä, taistelutoveria – miten pidänkään sinusta, siitä Sinusta jonka näin Sinussa olevan, kuohahtavasta ja – toivon – myös kestävästä rohkeudesta joka on koko elämän rohkeuden alku. Joku voi luulla sitä itsepäi-syydeksi, mutta sanoisin että se on panssaroitua herkkyyttä, persoonallisuuden itsesäilytysvaistoa, ainakin minun kohdallani.

128 Sinun luonteesi on vilpitön ja rohkea, lukuunottamatta – suo anteeksi – ketterän naisellista, hyvin tuntuvaa ja joskus jopa hyvin kiusallisena esiintyvää pintavilppiä. Mutta luulisin sen karisevan Sinusta iän mukana.

129 [E]hkä juuri ne seikat jotka Sinussa joskus minua saattavat ärsyttää, kuten edellä mainittu pintavilppi, tekevät Sinut juuri Sinuksi.

130 [E]n tiedä enkä halua tietää mitään muuta kuin nähdä Sinut morsiamenani, vai-monani. Oletko tyytyväinen nyt? Nyt Sinua on siis kosittu asianomaisin menoin.

131 [K]aikki on kuvittelua, kaikki, mielikuvituksen tuotetta [...].

132 Ja ajatteli: punastuin tietysti. Ja sitten hän punastui sitä että oli punastunut.

133 [H]änen ajatuksensa alkoivat säntäillä edestakaisin.

134 Oltiin pyörteen kohdalla – ja nyt myötävirtaan, airot koholla – ja tuntui siltä kuin vene olisi lähtenyt menemään soutajan voimatta sitä enää hallita, kuin joku olisi

tarttunut veneen pohjalautoihin, kieputtanut sitä, lähtenyt viemään – ja se oli ohi, ja airot vedessä, vene linnan laiturissa.

135 Mitä Inkeri nyt häneltä odotti? Hannusta tuntui kuin kaikki olisi ollut unta, kuin hän olisi vain tempaissut tuon tytön mukaansa tietämättä mihin oli matkalla, ja nyt hän ei tiennyt minne tytön veisi.

136 Inkeri sulki silmänsä, avasi ne taas, ja pajupensas kukki yhä, sanoi hänelle: katso minuun niin unohdat sen mitä et ymmärrä, unohdat miten paha on maailma. Ja siihen Inkeri raukeni, syvään, suureen, täydelliseen yksinäisyyteen [...].

137 Ikävä? Oli ollut ikävä, joskus niin kovasti että olisi halunnut kuolla. – Onnellinen. – Onnellinen? Kyllä kai – kai hän oli. – Entä sinä? Niin tietysti, hän uskoi sen, ja tästä lähtien oltaisiin järkeviä, puhuttaisiin kaikesta, aivan kaikesta suoraan ja järkevästi.

138 [K]uin olisi ollut pelkkää lantiota ja rintaa, vähältä ettei nimeään enää tajunnut. The passage can also be read as referring to the girl's experience; that it is Inkeri who cannot remember her name – or identify herself – anymore: "[...] good thing *she* even remembered her name anymore."

139 – Tule tänne, puhui tyttö puun alta. [...] Hänen äänensä oli kuin lapsen joka kutsuu toista lasta leikkimään kanssaan kun on niin ikävä eikä ole ketään joka leikkisi hänen kanssaan.

140 Inkeri kohotti silmänsä, katsoi taivaalle. Taivas oli sininen, taivaan alla leikatut pellot, avarat, tyhjät kuin taivas, kuin ulottuen äärettömyyksiin. Ja tervattu asemalaituri, rivissä seitsemän arkkua. Ja hän, Inkeri. Kuin taulu, kuin kuva, taulu johon hänet oli kuvattu, ei kukaan, ei mitään, ei tullut mistään, ei menossa mihinkään, ei mitään kysyttävää, ei pelättävää, kaikki paikoillaan, ääneti, yksinkertaista kaikki tässä jotta tämä kuva olisi täydellinen. Hän, Inkeri kuului myös tähän kuvaan, oli määrätty niin, oli niin kuin oli ollut ja tulisi aina olemaan. Tämä kuva oli myös hänestä, Inkeristä, ja taivas ja maa ja kaikki katsoi häneen ja hän katsoi takaisin, ei kysyen, ei ihmetellen mitään, sillä kaikki oli juuri niin kuin tarkoitettu oli.

141 Inkeri oli luotu näkemään tämä kaikki, kulkemaan tässä aamussa, näillä jaloilla, tämä puku yllä, tämä kulku, tämä hyppäys kiveltä kivelle tämän aidan luona. Ja hän näki lantionsa kaaren, painoi kätensä omalle vyötärölleen ja ilo kantoi häntä kuin aalto eteenpäin ja hän hoki itselleen – hyvä jumala, hyvä jumala, tämä aamu, tämä aamu [...].

142 [K]uin hän olisi seisonut äärettömän suuren juhlasalin oven takana, kuullut ovien takaa juhlan äänet ja tiennyt: minua varten, – kun ovi avataan, pääsen sisään [...] ovien takana odotti juuri häntä suuri ilo, suuri onni.

143 [N]e eivät olleet sellaisia kirjeitä, joita onnelliset ihmiset kirjoittavat toisilleen. Millaisia sitten kirjoittavat onnelliset?

144 Hannu ei rakastanut – jos, niin sen olisi pitänyt jotenkin tuntua selvemmin. Entä hän itse? Kyllä, kyllä kai – mutta ensin hänen olisi saatava selvyys siitä, rakastiko Hannu vai ei, sitten vasta hän tietäisi, rakastiko hän Hannua. Hetken kuluttua tuntui yhdentekevältä koko rakastaminen, väsytti koko asian ajatteleminen. Mutta jos hän olikin sellainen nainen, joka rakasti vain rakkautta? hän oli lukenut jostain kirjasta, että oli olemassa sellaisia naisia, jotka rakastivat vain rakkautta.

145 This passage in Vartio's novel alludes to L. Onerva's novel *Mirdja*, in which the protagonist, a decadent *femme fatale*, ponders the true quality of her feelings towards her lover: "She has been in love with love itself, she has been in love with it already for many years, and her imagination has been constructing an image of a troubadour of love in her soul for the same number of years." ("Itse rakkautta oli hän vaan rakastanut, rakastanut jo monta vuotta ja yhtä monta vuotta oli mielikuvitus hahmotellut lemmentrubaduurin kuvaa hänen sielussaan"; Onerva 1908: 16-17)

146 On the genre of the student novel in the context of Finnish literature, see Ameel 2013, Lappalainen 2000. On the possibilities of female Bildung in *fin de siècle* Finnish literature, see Aalto 2000.

147 Mutta tuo selvästi teeskentelevä ääni, tuo välinpitämätön ilme. [...] hänessä ei ollut terveestä maalaistytöstä mitään jäljellä. Hannu ajatteli, että kaupunki oli turmellut Inkerin, tämän ilmeissä ja eleissä oli jotakin opittua.

148 Hannusta tuntui kuin hän olisi joutunut johonkin epätodelliseen maailmaan, teatterin takahuoneeseen ja nähnyt kulisseja ja muita näyttämövarusteita.

149 Rouva [Gräsbäck] tuli ikkunaan, vetäisi verhon kokonaan auki kuin näyttämön esiripun [...].

150 Turre tiesi, että kun nainen on raskaana eikä tahdo synnyttää aviotonta lasta, niin hän tulee epätoivoiseksi, ja epätoivoissaan nainen juoksee järveen, ottaa myrkkyä tai heittäytyy junan alle [...] olihan hän menettänyt järkensä.

151 [S]uuri taide oli noituutta ja hypnoosia.

152 [H]än oli niin hyvä näyttelijä että hän melkein osasi olla hetken näyttelemättä.

153 [...] Mitähän sinulle tekisi – sinusta pitäisi kirjoittaa näytelmä./Inkeriä imarteli kovin tämä puhe, hän oli alkanut jo itsekin uskoa, että hänen kihlauksensa oli todella sopiva näytelmän juoneksi, ja todella tapahtunut ja kuviteltu olivat sekoittuneet hänen mielessään, hän jo miltei itsekin uskoi asioitten tapahtuneen niin kuin Turre tahtoi ne tapahtuneiksi. [...] /Turre tosin tahtoi tehdä Inkerin kihlauksesta huvinäytelmän, jolle ihmiset nauraisivat katketakseen. Inkeri olisi halunnut siihen todellista tunnetta, tragiikkaa; olihan hän ainakin jossain vaiheessa rakastanutkin ja ollut onneton.

154 – Onko ulkona kaunis ilma, Inkeri kysyi ja kääntyi selin, katsoi ulos.

155 Ja hän sai vastauksen joka tarkoitti että kyllä siellä on, turha sitä on kysellä, kyllä sinä tiedät sen ilmankin, mutta *minua kiinnostaa tietää minkälainen ilma on täällä sisällä.*

156 See Auli Hakulinen's (2013) refined analysis of the hypothetical constructs of speech and thought in the novel, including her reading of the affective uses of tempus and personal pronouns in the representation of the characters' fictional experience.

157 [M]inua viedään kuin lehmää markkinoille [...]

158 Sinussa on kyllä ainesta mutta en minä usko että sinä tulet onnistumaan porvarillisessa avioliitossa – ei, siitä ei tule mitään, sano minun sanoneen.

159 Vai olisiko asia niin, että sinä osaat taitavasti naamioida todelliset tunteesi? Ei, sinä et kykene siihen, sinä olet luvattoman lapsellinen [...].

160 [S]inä osaat kertoa ja osaat jopa näytellä, suorastaan hyvin silloin kun et itse tiedä sitä tekeväsi [...].

161 [K]uin häkissä, henkeä ahdisti [...].

162 – Katso nyt, seisovat ikkunassa kaikki kuin teatterissa [...].

163 Hannu katseli Turrea ja mietti, mikä hänessä oli tuonut Inkerin kuvan mieleen. Tuo tyttöhän oli aivan erilainen, pitkä ja huolitellusti käyttäytyvä, hänen äänessään jotain kylmää ja kaikessa mitä hän puhui jokin yhdentekevä sävy.

164 Sinussa on Sonjan nöyryys ja Nastasja Filippovnan tuli...

165 Niin vetää puoleensa miehiä nainen / kuin virtoja meri – / mitä varten? Nielläkseen! / Kaunis peto on nainen, / kaunis ja vaarallinen, / kultamaljassa myrkkyjuoma. / Sua juonut olen, oi lempi! The Finnish translation quoted here is Otto Manninen's (1922: 77). The excerpt provided in Vartio's novel is probably based on this translation, even if there are some differences. Petöfi's poem has been translated into English by Henry Philips (1885: 30).

166 [E]npä aavistanutkaan että Maija on tuollainen tekijä, käveli Inkerin sulhasen rinnalla sen näköisenä kuin siinä käveleminen olisi ollut aivan luonnollista. [...] Turrea jo hieman harmitti. Inkerin entinen sulhanen oli kiinnittänyt kaiken huomionsa Maijaan, puhui vain tälle, ei ollut häntä edes huomannut [...].

167 In this respect, Turre resembles the figure of a decadent female artist, personified, for instance, in the protagonist of *Mirdja*. Mirdja's aesthetic Bildung ends with

madness and death, whereas Turre survives (see Rojola 1992: 54; also Lyytikäinen 1997: 153–175).

168 [H]e olivat eläytyneet osaansa niin että olivat tunteneet ruumissaan väristyksiä. Turre oli olevinaan merimies, jätkä [...].

169 Inkeri vain säesti häntä kuin kreikkalaisen tragedian kuoro, selitti näkymättömille katselijoille ettei hän voinut tälle mitään, että hänen äänensä ei kuulunut, itki hän tai vannotti, kielsi tai taipui.

170 Puku vihreää silkkiä, vihreällä pohjalla mustia pääskysiä – hullu ompelija, leikkasi kuviollisen kankaan väärin, ompeli palaset niin että pääskyset riippuivat etupuolella alaspäin mutta hihoissa ja selässä pää ylöspäin, hullu ompelija.

171 Karin Månsdotter became the Queen of Sweden in the sixteenth century and was held as a prisoner in the Castle of Turku.

172 [P]uku oli ommeltu aivan samoin kuin nyt yhä, noin, neula ja lanka kankaan läpi [...] pisto pistolta, ja pistot näkyivät siinä, olivat yhä ja puku oli yhä siinä lasin alla [...].

173 Kun minä ajattelen tarkemmin niin minusta siinä on kaikki jotenkin niin kuin liian paikallaan, minun mieleeni tuli vain että sellainen asia jossa kaikki on paikallaan, saattaa ollakin niin ettei ole mikään paikallaan.

174 Kerrohan nyt minulle se asia kokonaisuudessaan juuri sellaisena kuin se on niin minä sanon sinulle siitä totuuden.

175 [K]oko ajan odotin sinulta juuri sitä että sinä jakaisit minun ikäväni ja murheeni, mutta sitä sinä et tehnyt, et sanonut minulle koskaan: katso kun lintu lentää, kuuntele kun lintu laulaa [...].

176 [K]oko tämä meidän tarinamme [...] on [ollut] alusta loppuun kuin kohtalon leikkiä.

177 [...] kuin satua jolle tuli murheellinen loppu, niin murheellinen etten vieläkään tiedä miten se oikeastaan loppui.

178 Vaellusromaani, hän luki, kehitysromaani, hän luki. Kehitysromaani, millainen se oli? Siinä tietysti kehityttiin, kuvattiin tietysti kirjan päähenkilön henkistä kehitystä, ja vaellusromaanissa tietysti vaellettiin.

179 As opposed to the episodic structure of the picaresque novel, the classical Bildungsroman builds on a character's entire life path guided by "the seeker's" goal of attaining an authentic way of being, self-knowledge, and education (Bakhtin 1981: 130). Inkeri's fragmentary remarks on these genres could be read as (self)irony on Vartio's part. The coming-of-age novel (or the Bildungsroman) and the picaresque novel were both analyzed in Anhava's essays, "Romaanityyppejä" (Types of Novel, published in 1956 in *Parnasso*). The theoretical introduction of literary genres made Vartio feel desperation as she acknowledged the challenges of writing according to these models (see Vartio 1996: 67).

180 Matkalla kotiin, junassa [...].

181 The modernist mode of epistolary writing in general suggests the gradual death of the genre as a result of technological innovation. Linda S. Kauffman's discussion on the epistolary mode in modernist and postmodernist texts addresses the tendency of these texts to subvert the traditional definitions of "feminine speech" versus "masculine writing" by satirizing the stereotypes of the feminine as subjective, disordered, hysterical, and illogical and the masculine as objective, orderly, rational, and logical. (See Kauffman 1992: 231)

182 [T]uo kuuluisa kirja oli hänen mielestään ikävä ja naurettava [...].

183 Olet ehkä lukenut Goethen Vaaliheimolaiset? Meidän tarinamme muistuttaa jollain tavoin sitä kirjaa, ja jos olet lukenut sen niin ymmärrät mitä tarkoitan: me emme olleet vaaliheimolaisia.

184 "[...] Mutta kaikki mitä minulle on tapahtunut, on ehkä ollut tarpeen. Emme opiskele koulua vaan elämää varten – tuli mieleen sananlasku, ja siihen minä alan

nyt uskoa, sillä tunnen että kaikesta huolimatta olen kehittynyt ja kypsynyt, jopa niin, että palatessani nyt kotiin minusta tuntuu kuin nyt vasta selvästi näkisin kaiken ja nyt vasta ymmärtäisin…" Hän pysähtyi miettimään: minkä? Ja jatkoi: […]

185 Mitähän minä oikein tuolla tarkoitan […].

186 Herranjestas, miten hienosti hän osasi kirjoittaa! Miten hän nyt osasikin näin että aivan heltyi jo kohta omista sanoistaan.

187 In sentimental (educational) novels, the pathos of sentimentality is provided to evoke empathy in the reader (cf. Cohen 1999: 68–69; Isomaa 2009: 9). The very style of parody, however, suggests inversion of the sentimental ethos.

188 Inkeri pysäytti kynän ja luki mitä hän oli viimeksi kirjoittanut. Olikohan tuo jo liian paksua? Mutta hän jatkoi eteenpäin […]. /Mitähän vielä keksisi?

189 Kuin unta, vuosi vuoden perään. Onnellinen, miksei, varmasti niin, mutta kun ajatteli, ei tiennyt oliko oikealla tavalla. Mitä häneltä puuttui? Ei mitään.

190 "Tunteet" on […] kaikkea muuta kuin tunteellinen kirja.

191 Scholars have examined the same phenomenon of seemingly thin, yet simultaneously ample emotional worlds in the works of Jane Austen, one of the first authors to examine complex emotions in social relations (See Palmer 2010: 159). See the reviews of Austen's novels in Anhava 2002/1950, 2002/1952, 2002/1953 and 2002/1954.

192 Minä olen tunteeton, minä olen itse tunne (Meri 1962:106).

193 V. A. Koskenniemi was one of the critics of the modernist poetics and the symbol of the more conservative strand of Finnish literature, thus representing the battle between the new and the old generation in the poetics of the 1950s (Hökkä 1999: 74). In *Tunteet*, Inkeri is said to have plagiarized Koskenniemi's elegy "Yksin oot sinä ihminen" (Lonely are you, man, 1918) in one of her letters to an unknown soldier on the frontline. The poet's elegy is juxtaposed with the sentimentality of the popular songs and patriotic verses Hannu has seen in Inkeri's letters.

194 "Esteettiset tunteet ovat ne tunteet, joita ilmiöt herättävät meissä silloin, kun niihin suhtaudutaan esteettisesti"; "[P]uhtaita tunteita, tunteita sanan varsinaisessa merkityksessä, tunteita semmoisinaan"; "[K]iistämätön, ihan jo tunteenomaisesti varma tosiasia" (cf. Laurila 1918: 18–31).

195 The author had met her former fiancé Horst during her matinée journey in Turku, while planning her next novel (Vartio 1996: 98).

196 Vartio read her diaries amused, thinking back her younger self who tended "to sense everything more immediately – more passionately" ("aistin kaiken suoremmin – kiihkeämmin") and considered herself particularly exceptional creature, different than any other girl (Vartio 1996: 187).

197 [E]n osaa sanoa, ja jos yritän olla vitsikäs ja sillä taittaa paatostani, tunnen olevani mauton. Kerta kaikkiaan olen kykenemätön saamaan muotoa mihinkään.

198 [Kirjeen] takana oli jokin geometrian kuvio, kolmio ja katkelma Pythagoraan teoreemaa […].

199 According to Kenneth Burke (1974/1945: 503), irony functions as one of the "master tropes" of modernist literature. It enables self-critical skepticism and helps to avoid "the sentimental mistake," that is, the dangers of uncritical absorption (Clark 1991: 194).

200 In Vartio's work, the paternal world order is often replaced or complemented with the maternal order manifested in the old folk tradition and primitive rituals. The search for the regained balance between sexes is perfectly illustrated by Vartio's short story "Vatikaani," in which the female protagonist's pilgrimage to the Vatican turns into a quest of the word through four different languages. First of them is the language of the Holy Father, whom the protagonist encounters in the Eternal City. This language represents the language of Christian community: a kind of *patrius sermo* based on Latin. Secondly, there is the language used in the book that is shown only to the protagonist against the Holy Father's permission. It seems to

be based on image-like signs. These letters signify different objects of nature that can be found in the woman's home village: flowers and ears of different grains. The cardinal, who hands the book, speaks also the third language mentioned in the story: the language of the protagonist, "my language." As the result of the cardinal's translation, a fully new, fourth language is created: a language combining the image-like signs and the protagonist's own language, her mother tongue. Thus, from a variety of languages there emerges a new language that is neither an earthly, bodily *maternal lingua* nor a spiritual "father's speech," *logos*, but a hybrid of image-like signs and letters, words and images. The red-dressed woman, who resembles the author in her own dream of Vatican, gets a voice, at least one stammering sentence: "Along the flowers and the ears of corn we return to where we have come from." ("Kukkia ja tähkäpäitä pitkin palataan sinne, mistä on tultu"; *MVV*, 95)

201 In Woolf's aesthetics, for instance, the ideal work of art was androgynous; it captured and harmonized both the masculine and feminine opposites (Freeman 1988: 51).

202 The character constellations and cyclic structures of *Tunteet* and *Hänen olivat linnut* can be linked to Jungian figure of "mandala" analyzed by Vartio in the context of *Don Quixote*. Jung (1985: 169–170) defined the term mandala as "the ritual or magic circle used [… as an] aid to contemplation." Vartio state that Cervantes's novel is full of mandalas, figures of nested wheels and circles or perceptions of macro-worlds in micro-worlds. These figures represent the different incarnations of Dulcinea in Don Quixote's mind, simultaneously symbolizing the artist's battles with writing (Vartio 1996: 196).

203 Sancho on Cervantesin oma väsyvä ruumis ja mieli, Don Quijote hänen henkensä. Henki ei pysty yksin suorittamaan sankaritekoja ilman ruumiin ja terveen mielen apua, kummankin on autettava toinen toistaan.

204 [H]än syöksyi taisteluun oman mielensä luomia kuvia vastaan […].

6. *In the Mazes of the Wounded Mind. Narrating the Self in* Hänen olivat linnut

1 Öisin hänen päänsä on kiusattu unilla. / Vaikka on syksy, kuulee hän teerien kujerruksen / metsojen soiton / kuin olisi sulavan lumen aika (*Häät*, 7).

2 – Oletko sinä kaupalla jotakin, ei meillä osteta mitään, kauppias sanoi kun näki sinun faneeriaskisi./– Tarvitaanko täällä työihmistä, minä sanoin siihen, niin. Ja sitä rupesi naurattamaan. Seisoo siinä ja katsoo minua. Minä arvasin. Ajattelin että kyllä minä tiedän ukko mitä sinä siinä ajattelet, mutta arvaapas sinä (*H*, 143).

3 Taidan olla kovin hyvässä kirjoitusvireessä, mutta valitettavasti kuulen vain repliikkejä, saan ihmiset puhumaan vaikka kuinka pitkälti, mutta eihän nyt kirjaa voine tehdä pelkillä repliikeillä, tai miksei, jos hyvin tekee.

4 Helkointa tässä ruustinnan ja palvelijan köydenvedossa on kieltämättä arkinen kinastelu olemattomista asioista: aito naiselliseen tapaan kirjailija on pystynyt siinäkin tarkkaan havainnointiin, mutta nuo kohdat juuri pyrkivät laahaamaan.

5 According to Anthony Giddens (1991: 52), for instance, self-identity "is not something that is just given, as a result of the continuities of the individual's action-system, but something that has to be routinely created and sustained in the reflexive activities of the individual."

6 Kun minä olin nuorempi, en voinut katsoa ihmisiä silmiin, kun *tiesin aina mitä he ajattelevat*, ja siitä minä tulin sairaaksi, sillä se mitä näin heidän ajattelevan itsestäni ei suinkaan ollut aina minulle edullista. […] Ihmiset ovat paljon pahempia kuin arvaatkaan, Alma, kukaan ei välitä kenestäkään, älä koskaan kiinny kehenkään äläkä mihinkään... (*H*, 226–227)

7   Olenhan minä katkera, olen ilkeä, olen hyvin paha ihminen, en rakasta ihmisiä. Se on totta: minä en ole oppinut koskaan rakastamaan ketään [...]. Mikä sinä olisit, sanoin itselleni, sinäkö, katkera, ilkeä, täynnä pahoja ajatuksia, ja miten sinä niitä kaivelet, minä kaivelen kuin saastaa sitä kaikkea mitä minulle on tässä elämässä tehty, tässä talossa, kaikkea sitäkin, mitä Alma on minulle sanonut, Alma ei tiedä miten minä sitäkin olen kaivellut ja jopa sitä minkä Alma on jättänyt sanomatta minulle mutta on puhunut muille ihmisille (*H*, 230–231).

8   – Minun ei tarvitse edes ajatella, en uskalla ajatellakaan, hän arvaa jopa minun ajatukseni (*H*, 99).

9   [H]änen huulilleen ilmestyi vain hymy, ei tarvinnut muuta kuin nähdä se hymy kun jo tiesi [...] (*H*, 78).

10 [R]uustinna [...] oli taas hänen edessään ja katsoi, silmissä se vastenmielinen ilme, joka, kun Alma sen näki, teki hänen olonsa kiusaantuneeksi, tuo ilme, niin, raivostutti (*H*, 34).

11 Alma ei katsonut poikaa kohti. – Miten niin, hän vastasi. – Mitä sinä oikein tarkoitat, hän kysyi pojalta, hyvin tietäen, mitä tämä halusi sanoa, mutta hänen järkensä kieltäytyi vastaamasta, selittämästä pojalle ettei se ollut sitä mitä poika tarkoitti, sitä mitä tarkoittivat nuo silmät, tuo hymy (*H*, 116).

12 Ja eikö hän, Alma, ollut tiennyt tämän jo silloin kun oli kuullut, että ruustinna menisi, eikö hän ollut suunnitellut tämän valmiiksi silloin, yhtään ajatusta ajattelematta, mutta silti tarkasti tietäen miten tässä kävisi. Ja eikö ruustinna ollut tiennyt, tai suunnitellut, antanut tapahtua sen minkä oli tapahduttava. Alma tajusi, että sen takia ruustinna oli mennyt, ja eikö myös poika heti ollut tiennyt. Ja eikö hän ollut itse halunnut että poika tulisi, oli maannut valveilla, kuunnellut pojan liikkeitä ylhäältä, askelia portaissa ja keittiössä. Tuntui kuin hän olisi halunnut saada pojalle kostetuksi jotain, mitä (*H*, 122).

13 [H]eidän kurkkiessaan salusiinien raosta: apteekkari menemässä pois selkä suorana, sen näköisenä etteivät kyläläiset päässeet sanomaan että hän juo, ei, kun ihminen säilytti ryhtinsä, ei ollut sanomista kenelläkään (*H*, 131–132).

14 – Ei puhuta sitten koko asiasta./– En minä sillä./– Miten minä olisin voinut sanoa jotain noin hupsua, ruustinna sanoi, – en minä niin hupsu ole./Alma vaikeni./ – Siinä se juuri onkin, että jos lukkari olisi heti juossut tekemään hälytystä niin pappila ei olisi palanut. [...] /– Eihän se heti ilmiliekillä palanut. Lukkari luuli savua sumuksi, Alma sanoi./– Voi voi, oliko Alma näkemässä (*H*, 5).

15 En minä sitä ole kuullut, en minä olisi kuunnellut, *mutta onhan minulle tietysti kerrottu* (*H*, 6).

16 Ja minä kuulen Alman äänessä lukkarin äänen, lukkarin äänen ja hänen vaimonsa äänen (*H*, 9).

17 According to Bakhtin (1981: 316), character zones are "formed from the fragments of character speech [*polureč*], from various forms for hidden transmission of someone else's word, from scattered words and sayings belonging to someone else's speech, from those invasions into authorial speech of others' expressive indicators [ellipsis, questions, exclamations]."

18 [E]i hän sanonut että Birger olisi niin tehnyt, mutta hän tarkoitti että *miksei sekin teko olisi rovastilta syntynyt* (*H*, 6). In the original text, the emphasis is not that much on what the late vicar might have done, but rather what he is capable of doing.

19 – Ei, ei pahaa sanaa. Pahaa sanaa ei sanottu, mutta puhuttiin. Ajateltiin. Juuri niin kuin Alman puheista kuulee, jos on tottunut kuulemaan ei vain mitä ihmiset puhuvat vaan mitä he sanovat. Ja sen minä olen oppinut (*H*, 9).

20 Voi voi, kun minä yöllä kuuntelen, ne huutavat kun ne tekevät tuloa, ne huutavat (*H*, 66).

21 He eivät halua nähdä mitä kaikkea se merkitsi. Mutta minulla on aikaa miettiä asioita (*H*, 11).

22 [N]iin kuin hän olisi tullut herättämään meitä ennen maailmanloppua (*H*, 6).

23 [...] *Mutta silloin tapahtui jotain mistä ei koskaan saatu tietää oliko se totta vaiko ruustinnan järkyttyneen mielen synnyttämä valhe.* Hän huusi kasvot vääristyneinä: – Minä, minä sen rikoin. Minä pelastin sen, mutta se meni rikki. Minä rikoin sen, hän huusi, – rikoin tahallani, annoin sen pudota käsistäni, teidät on kaikki kastettu siitä, Birger, sinut, Elsa, sinut Teodolinda. Minä rikoin sen, ei se pudonnut. Ei se ollut vahinko. Rikoin rikoin, kuulitteko. Mutta kukaan ei vastannut, ei sanonut hänelle mitään. He lähtivät taluttaen ruustinnaa välissään, ja sitä mukaa kun he loittonivat, menivät portista, kääntyi suntion vaimo ja seurasi heidän menoaan./ – Minne ne menevät, kysyivät ihmiset, joita oli tiellä, ja väistyivät tien sivuun kun he menivät ohi (*H*, 28–29). Unlike the Flints' translation, in the original text the village people's question (concerning where Adele and the other people are going) is addressed to the other villagers witnessing the event, not to the members of the group leaving: "Where are *they* going?"

24 Ja nyt niin kuin aina kun ruustinna, jonka etunimi oli Adele, puhui näin läheisesti Alman kanssa – sanoi rovastia Birgeriksi, tämän toista sisarta Teodolindaksi sen sijaan että olisi puhunut rovastivainajan sisaresta tai apteekkarin rouvasta, ja sanoi Elsa sen sijaan että olisi sanonut rovastivainajan toinen sisar tai kunnanlääkärin rouva, tohtorin rouva, ja kaikkia yhdessä sanonut rovastivainajan sisariksi – ruustinnan äänestä kuuli että vaikka hän toi heidät näin lähelle, alas, keittiöön, niin he kuitenkin olivat tavoittamattomissa, ja niin oli hän itsekin, vaikka istui keittiön pöydän ääressä ja joi siinä kahvia. Mutta vähitellen kävi niin että vaikka hän säilytti puhetapansa, se alkoi käydä yhä helpommin, ja porras, joka erotti rovastivainajan Birgeristä, kului./– Mutta ei puhuta näistä asioista, ne ovat pitkiä asioita, liian pitkiä asioita, ruustinna sanoi, – ei puhuta, ei puhuta, hän toisti, ja teki kädellä torjuvan eleen, kuin jollekin joka vaati että niistä oli puhuttava./– Ruustinna vain suotta hermostuu eikä saa unta, Alma sanoi. – Ei puhuta (*H*, 12–13).

25 Here the Finnish word "porras" (*a step* or *stair*) has been translated by the Flints into a word "distance," which does not fully convey all the connotations in the original expression. Adele seems to be mentally moving from one space to another, "stepping" from an idea of her husband as the "late vicar" to a more intimate conception of him as Birger, as if her mind was pictured as a container including different spheres.

26 According to Tim Parks (2012), the protagonists of twentieth-century literature are typically "chattering minds," prone to qualification, self-contradiction, and complication, trapped in inaction, running in the cycles of thought. Park's definition can be criticized for ignoring that mental action is *action*. Modernist minds are like vessels threatening to bubble over (See Jabr 2012).

27 Entä sitten?; Mitä he sitten?; Entä sitten?; Entä sitten? (*H*, 68–70)

28 Minä aloitan alusta, sinä olet kuullut jo mutta minä aloitan alusta… (*H*, 68)

29 Tahdotko sinä kuulla koko minun kärsimyshistoriani (*H*, 61).

30 Niin Alma, minä olin pelkkä postineiti, hän oli hienoa sukua, hieno mies (*H*, 68).

31 [K]ivi jolla me istuimme oli kovin pieni, ja vene teki ympyrää, ympyrä pieneni, pieneni, kunnes veneen reuna hipaisi kiveä jolla me istuimme [...] (*H*, 69).

32 Taisinpa osua, soudetaan tuonne (*H*, 69–70).

33 [S]inä iltana opin tuntemaan elämäni ensimmäisen linnun (*H*, 70).

34 [S]e saarna paloi, se oli kaunis saarna ja se lensi tulena ilmaan (*H*, 70).

35 [P]uhuiko hän sittenkin vertauskuvin [...] (*H*, 70).

36 – Ehkä, niin… ehkä hän otti minut minun nimeni takia vain. "Adele, Adelaide, minä kutsun sinua," hän sanoi. 'se on kuin linnun ääni: Adelaide' (*H*, 71).

37 En sietänyt katsoa, sydänalassa velloi aamusta iltaan, tämä sama huone, pieniä lintuja, pöydällä rivissä, kuolleita, kangistuneita, ja haju tässä huoneessa. Minä pakenin yläkertaan, haju tunki seinien läpi, kun hän preparoi (*H*, 61).

38 – Oli kevätilta, ei tällainen syksyinen kuin tämä, vaan kevät, tie kaartoi koivikon

halki rantaan. "Minä pyydän älä ammu pieniä lintuja." Birger seisoi kalliolla pyssy kädessä, ja tämä sama pieni lintu rannalla, kivellä, rantakivellä, västäräkki, pyrstö ylös, alas, ylös, ja Birger seisoi valmiina kivääri olkapäätä vasten. Minä aloin läiskyttää käsiäni vastakkain antaakseni merkin, mutta lintu ei kuullut, laukaus kajahti ja hän juoksemassa rantakiviä pitkin ja palaamassa takaisin riiputtaen kädessään tätä pientä lintua (*H*, 61).

39 [M]inun kuvani (*H*, 64).

40 – Ehkä minun aivoni ovat muuttuneet linnun aivoiksi, ehkäpä. Ehkäpä sinä Alma olet oikeassa, jospa minä olen västäräkki. Kuinka siis voisin odottaa että ihmiset minua ymmärtäisivät (*H*, 60).

41 "Mitä jos ampuisit minut," sanoin. "Tahtoisin tietää minkä virren laulattaisit sen päälle kun olisit preparoinut minut, katsoppas, eikö näitten läpi olisi mukava työntää rautalanka, katsoppas kun minä pidän niitä näin ja jalat näin, mihin asentoon sinä laittaisit minut, minä olen miettinyt sitä koko yön, panisitko sinä minut istumaan, seisomaan yhdellä jalalla, katso näin, vai panisitko näin, käden koholle ilmaan, vai molemmat kädetkö, vai käsi pitkin sivua vai molemmat kädet? Koko yön minä olen odottanut sinua kotiin, koko yön olen kulkenut edestakaisin ja katsellut näitä ja ajatellut että mikäpä muu minä olen kuin lintu tässä kokoelmassa [...]" (*H*, 62–63)

42 Hän on mestariampuja, ajatella että yhdellä laukauksella hän tavoittaa linnun kuin linnun (*H*, 62).

43 – Sinä et ymmärrä, lapsi oli tulossa, et ymmärrä, minä kävelin pitkin rantoja, halusin kuolla (*H*, 49).

44 ["M]inkä nimen sinä minulle antaisit, rara avis vai mitä. Panisitko minut tuonne korkeimmalle paikalle kaapin päälle päälle tuon pöllön viereen, tekisitkö minullekin lasisilmät, olisinko rara avis?" "Hupsu, hupsu sinä olisit, panisin sinun jalustaasi lapun 'hupsu avis,' älä sinä kuvittele olevasi mikään Fenix-lintu, sinä olet hermostunut nainen joka ei osaa suhtautua raskauteensa normaalisti – ota oppia kansannaisesta." Ja silloin minä huusin sen tytön nimen, sen joka oli ollut niillä soutajana mukana (*H*, 63).

45 Minusta tuntuu, ettei minulla ole käsivarsia sen jälkeen ollut, ne jäivät hänen kaulaansa, repesivät minusta irti, jäivät hänen kaulaansa ikuisesti riippumaan kun hän tyrkkäsi minut luotaan pois... (*H*, 63)

46 ... Mutta minun mieheni ei rakastanut edes lintuja, ei, luulet väärin, hän tutki niitä, sinä et ymmärrä, miltä minusta tuntui kun hän tämän saman pöydän äärellä nylki linnun, pienen linturaukan, ja sitten, sanonko minä sinulle.../Alma tiesi mitä ruustinna jätti sanomatta: sitten mies oli tahtonut, ja suuttunut kun ruustinna oli kieltäytynyt. Alman silmät kääntyivät makuuhoneen ovea kohti ja hänen mieltään etoi – hän ei ollut tahtonut kuunnella ja kuitenkin hän oli uskonut ja kauhistunut (*H*, 228).

47 The taxidermist study of birds can be juxtaposed with the medicalization and regulation of female sexuality in the taxonomic study of hysteria as related to the Victorian culture and the trope of the madwoman used, for instance, in the Gothic horror literature. The study of hysteria asked for scientific methods of controlled observation and classification. (See Myers 2000: 300)

48 In her reading of *Hänen olivat linnut*, Rojola emphasizes the quality of birds as animals rather than as literary symbols. The submissive relations between humans and animals epitomize the problematic idea of man as the ruler of the universe. In their desire for knowledge, "human" being are ready to make other sentient beings suffer. (Rojola 2014: 152)

49 [T]äällä hän kuoli, ja hänen olivat linnut (*H*, 12).

50 [...] Birgerin isä, tämä nimismies josta Almakin varmasti on kuullut yhtä ja toista [...] (*H*, 11).

51 Sitä minä olen joskus miettinyt että onko se totta kun sanotaan että jotkut tapauk-set voivat vaikuttaa lapseen jo ennen syntymää (*H*, 10–11).

52 – Mutta olethan sinä itse kuullut, ilmestyihän Onni sinulle. Ja sinä et kuitenkaan usko./– Uskonhan minä mutta silti ei pitäisi puhua, ihmiset eivät ymmärrä, enkä minä ihmisille puhukaan, en edes omille sukulaisilleni./– Oletko kuullut nyt – ovatko kulkeneet?/– Kyllä se oli kissa silloin viime kerralla, ensin minä uskoin että se oli Paananen kun te sanoitte niin, mutta aamulla minä suoraan sanoen ajattelin että kissa se oli, en minä usko jokaista ääntä, siinä menee järki (*H*, 50).

53 – Joskus yöllä olen kuulevinani askelia portaissa ja ajattelen: Birgerin äiti. Sinä päi-vänä kun Birger toi minut tähän taloon, se nainen laskeutui portaita alas, askeleet kuuluivat ylhäältä, lähestyivät. Minä seisoin alhaalla eteisessä, pelkäsin, mutta hän ei sanonut mitään (*H*, 51).

54 [O]lisinko arvannut silloin, että minä joudun yksin asumaan tätä taloa, että he kaikki menevät pois (*H*, 51).

55 Eikä [Birgerin äiti] liene vieläkään antanut minulle anteeksi, on niin kuin yhä kuulisin askeleet, niin kuin hän laskeutuisi portaita alas, yhä katsoisi minuun. Sinä et ymmärrä Alma, viatonhan minä olen, mutta silti on niin kuin minä olisin tehnyt väärin, kuin olisin tunkeilija. Katso nyt näitä huoneita, ovatko nämä minun kaltaistani ihmistä varten, tuossa on trymoopeili, siitä minä näin itseni kokonaan ja ajattelin: kuka on tuo, joka pelkää. Minä katsoin kuvaani ja ajattelin kuka tuolla pelkää, ja sitten ymmärsin, että siinä olin minä itse (*H*, 51–52).

56 [R]uustinnan muisti petti. Tähän asti hän oli puhunut talosta omanaan (*H*, 51).

57 Alma muisteli toista kertomusta, sitä mitä ihmiset olivat hänelle puhuneet (*H*, 53).

58 Kolme tuntia hän makasi liikkumattomana ja tiesi että talo oli *täynnä pahoja hen-kiä*. Alhaalla keittiössä liikkui Alma ja paha henki Almassa lauloi. Hän kuuli sen: se oli ilkeää hyräilyä, se tahtoi yllyttää häntä yhä suurempaan pahuuteen (*H*, 108).

59 Mutta Alma oli asettunut tiskaamaan. Ruustinna katsoi ja vapisi kauttaaltaan. Hän näki Alman leveän, lihavan selän, märät kainalokuopat, näki Alman avonaisen kesäpuvun ja inhosi Alman siivotonta siveetöntä asua./– Sinä menet liian pitkälle, ruustinna sanoi. – Sinä menet liian pitkälle. Voisit edes käsivartesi peittää, voisit kainalokarvasi peittää./Mutta Alma tiskasi ja lauloi./– Lahnaverkkoa sinä siis olit kokemassa – mieleni tekisi käyttää erästä toista sanaa siitä mitä sinä olisit mielinyt olla tekemässä./– Kun piru riivaa ihmistä, ei siinä ihmisen apu auta, sanoi Alma ja lauloi./– Sinä et koske minun tavaroihini tämän päivän perästä./– Ka, kun kerta en niin en./Alma jätti tiskit sikseen ja lähti ulos. Hänen menonsa näkyi pihalla. Jalat jumpsuttaen maata kuin moukarit, ajatteli ruustinna, tuota vastenmielistä miesmäistä käyntiä kulkien (*H*, 109).

60 Yritin kietoa käsivarteni hänen kaulaansa – en näitä [...] en näitä Alma, nämä ovat kuihtuneet. En näitä... minä olin nuori silloin, käsivarteni olivat valkeat, pehmeät [...] (*H*, 63).

61 – En minä sinua vihaa [...] minä vihaan ihmisiä jotka haluavat ottaa minulta kaik-ki kauniit esineet pois. Minä rakastan esineitä (*H*, 110).

62 – Kaikki ovat siis hyljänneet minut, hän sanoi lautaselle. – Holger jätti tahallaan sinut ottamatta, koska tietää miksi haluaisin antaa sinut Teodolindalle. He ovat kaikki yhdessä päättäneet ettei kukaan heistä ota sinua, jotta sinä kiusaisit minua lopun elämääni [...]. He odottavat vain sitä että minä särkisin sinut saadakseen sanoa: nyt hän särki meidän isoäitimme serviisilautasen. He muistavat mitä minä sanoin: ottakaa se pois ettei se säry minun hallussani (*H*, 110).

63 [H]än oli kuulevinaan äänien puhuvan [...] (*H*, 110).

64 "Adele tarjosi minulle taas sitä lautasta." "Ethän vain ottanut." "Minäkö, olisinko niin järjiltäni että ottaisin hänen kiukunpuuskassaan tarjoamansa lautasen." (*H*, 110)

65 Mutta nämä asiat olivat salaisia, niistä ei ollut tietoa kenelläkään muilla kuin heillä kolmella. Apteekkarilla joka lattialla juopuneena maaten itki syntejään, itki

vaimoaan joka ei rakastanut häntä ja jota hän ei ollut koskaan rakastanut. Ruustinnalla joka ei ollut rakastanut ketään, vain lintujaan, ruustinnalla joka itki ettei kyennyt rakastamaan ketään erikseen ja sitä ettei ollut sellainen jota apteekkari olisi voinut rakastaa. [...] "Annatko anteeksi etten minä sinua aikoinani kosinut, annatko? Katsos, minä näin jo silloin että sinä olet hullu, ja annoin Birgerin ottaa sinut." "Mutta Birger oli hullu," itki ruustinna ja nauroi sitten katketakseen. "Niin, niin oli." "Ja siksi minä en rakastanut häntä, minä tiesin että hän oli hullu, tiesin alusta alkaen, siitä päivästä alkaen kun hän kosi minua ja ampui luodolla sisariaan kohti." (*H*, 245)

66   Hän saarnasi, hän oli lahjakas, esimerkillinen, sanovat kälyt. Mikä hänet muutti, he sanovat ja katsovat minuun (*H*, 72).

67   'Hukkuvatko kaikki ihmiset?' (*H*, 160)

68   [Jaakobilla] oli suuri unelma, toteuttaakseen sen hän käytti kaikkia niitä keinoja joita osasi, hän tahtoi olla jotakin ja petkutti sukulaisiaan [...] hän on Jumalan lapsi kaikissa heikkouksissaan (*H*, 32).

69   "Jacob's ladder" refers to the dream described in the Book of Genesis. The character of Jacob is one of the first tricksters in the ancient tradition of the ambivalent figure of the Fool. The son of Isaac gains social and material advantages by resorting to deceit. His ingenuity, however, is meant to be received with laughter rather than with moral outrage. In her essay "Unien maisema" ("The Landscape of Dreams"), Vartio writes about this biblical story in the following manner: "Jacob dreamed, saw ladders leading to the heavens, and this one, single dream gave him immense strength of faith and the knowledge that a great mission had been prepared for him in particular." ("[Jakob] näki unen, näki portaiden vievän taivaaseen, ja tämä yksi ainoa uni antoi hänelle suunnattoman uskon voiman ja tiedon että juuri hänen kohdalleen on määrätty suuri tehtävä"; Vartio 1996: 140)

70   The figure of a trickster or a devil appears also in Vartio's short story "Suomalainen maisema" (A Finnish Landscape, 1955), in which the sad figure known from Hugo Simberg's naivistic paintings, Poor Devil, serves as a self-image of the protagonist: an artist who falls down from the sauna bench, that is, from the heights of his fantasy worlds (see Nykänen 2012).

71   [H]erään tuskan hiessä ja ikään kuin pasuuna olisi huutanut minun korvaani "koi syö, ruoste raiskaa" (*H*, 148).

72   Huomasitko? Elsa laski lusikoita, yksi, kaksi, kolme, minä näin kun hän yritti laskea ja aina kun tiesin hänen päässeen kolmeen, minä sanoin: "Ota kakkua, Elsa." (*H*, 205)

73   [E]t kai sinä *luule* minun *uskovan ettet* muka *tiedä* (*H*, 86).

74   Hullu, hullu, mene tästä huoneesta pois. Alma puhui ajatuksissa – se tuli kuin tauti – hän olisi halunnut lyödä, repiä, paiskata jotakin rikki. Hänen tuli niin sääli itseään, kun hänet oli pantu tähän, kun hänen oli elettävä ihmisen kanssa joka silmät leimuten tuli ikään kuin lannistamaan häntä. Tuollaiselleko hänen piti tehdä työtä, tuollaiselle [...] Ja nyt seisoi hänen edessään, kasvoilla tuo vastenmielinen hymy joka *tuntui tietävän kaiken* (*H*, 224–225).

75   [E]tkö sinä ymmärrä että minä ihailen sinua, minua huvittaa, kun sinä olet Adelen paras mies (*H*, 180).

76   Sinussa on rotua, nainen [...] (*H*, 173).

77   [M]istä sinä olet tänne ilmestynyt, meidän heikkojen ja vaivaisten keskelle (*H*, 174).

78   The archetype of androgyny is exemplified in Finnish-Swedish poet, Edith Södergran's, poem "Vierge Moderne" (1916) that emphasizes an individual's need for authentic selfhood and freedom: "I am no woman. I am a neuter. / I am a child, a page-boy, and a bold decision, / I am a laughing streak of scarlet sun... / I am a net for all voracious fish, / I am a toast to every woman's honor, / I am a step

toward luck and toward ruin, / I am a leap in freedom and the self..." ("Jag är ingen kvinna. Jag är ett neutrum. / Jag är ett barn, en page och ett djärvt beslut, / jag är en skrattande strimma av en scharlakanssol... / Jag är ett nät för alla glupska fiskar, / jag är en skål för alla kvinnors ära, / jag är ett steg mot slumpen och fördärvet, / jag är ett språng i friheten och självet..."; Södergran 1916: 24–25) The English translation of the poem is Stina Katchadourian's (1992: 29).

79   Cf. Parente-Čapková's (2001) analysis of androgyny in L. Onerva's early work and her reading of the "mystical marriage" of Mirdja and her husband Runar at the end of *Mirdja* (Parente-Čapková 2014: 164–168).

80   René Girard's (1976: 2–3) idea of "triangular desire" involves the relation of three, in which either two members of a love triangle are vying for the favors of the third member, or each member is vying for the favor of the next one over.

81   [V]ain minä ymmärrän tämän Adelen [...] (*H*, 246).

82   [M]ikä sisäfilee (*H*, 246)

83   Mies oli sen jo sellaiseksi tehnyt, se oli oppinut alistumaan miehensä tahdon alle (*H*, 216).

84   [S]inä haluat määrätä ja se on sinun kohtalosi (*H*, 126).

85   [M]utta samassa kädet, *miehen kädet, eivät enää apteekkarin vaan miehen,* työntyivät hänen pukunsa kaula-aukosta sisään ja alemmaksi [...]. Kuin tajuttomana Alma käsien painaessa häntä yhä lattiaa kohti vaipui istualleen, ja mies polvillaan hänen polviensa päällä (*H*, 185).

86   Minussa riittää miestä teille kummallekin (*H*, 138).

87   [...] ja lapsihan hän oli. Ruustinnan ja Alman yhteinen lapsi, lapsiraukka (*H*, 243).

88   [H]än vain katsoo, kuin kuolema, kuin aave (*H*, 130).

89   [S]en pää oli pyöreä, se oli elävä kuin lapsi, pienen lapsen kokoinen kun sen nosti syliin (*H*, 203).

90   [V]ain minä osaan puhua niin että tämä Adele nauraa. Me olemme ihmeellisiä kun me olemme yhdessä, Jumala näkee, näkee varmasti, katsoo hyväksyvästi, näetkös, kun hänen lapsiansa ollaan (*H*, 246).

91   Nyt hänelle, niin kuin ennen ruustinnalle (*H*, 244).

92   [P]ojan silmät, ruustinna, ruustinnan silmät, hämärässä vajassa kiiluen [...] (*H*, 116).

93   Kun poika oli siinä, Alma muisti että oli ollut aina kuin uhri, ja niin sen piti olla, että toinen teki, koska oli mies ja tiesi mitä teki ja tahtoi, ja sen oli syy. Alma oli ollut tyttö, hän rupesi tytöksi, tai oli kuin nuori lehmä joka kääntää päänsä pois, silmät mullillaan päässä. Mutta nyt tässä oli poika, ja nyt Alma heräsi kuin muistosta, tajusi, murahti, otti kiinni pojasta joka yritti erota. [...] /Ja Alma näki itsensä seisomassa heidän molempien vierellä, seisomassa, mutta ei se ollut yksin hän, se oli samalla mies, yhtä aikaa mies ja nainen, ja ärtynyt, ja poika oli häränpurrikka, kiimassa mutta ei vielä härkä, koiranpentu joka yritti, hoiti oman asiansa. Ja tyydyttämättömänä, raivoissaan Alma nousi verkoilta (*H*, 114–115).

94   [J]a poika, ruustinnan poika, poika, ei kenenkään poika vaan härkä joka nyt töykki, kuin unissaan, *iski, töykki, iski, töykki,* päällä hänen vatsansa alaosaa, mahaa, puski vatsaa, piti häntä jaloista, riuhtoi, osaamatta tehdä mitaan määrattya (*H*, 118).

95   [K]unnes hän tajuten mitä oli tapahtumassa sai äänen [...] (*H*, 118).

96   [J]a samassa askeleet – vajan takaa askeleet. Ruustinna, hän tiesi sen heti, seisoi ulkona hämärässä, liikahtamatta, edessä järven selkä, sumu, saari sumussa, apteekkarin vene laiturissa, verkot kuivumassa, lintu ja linnun ääni joka tuli kuin kaukaa mutta lintu äänsi lähellä, vajan katolla, puussa, koivussa, haavassa, hän ajatteli puut ja koivun ja haavan ja muisti ruustinnan, ja tiesi että kuin se olisi ollut ruustinnan valittava itku, linnun huudossa, yksin lintu visertämässä, viaton kuin ruustinna (*H*, 119).

97   – Äitisi tulee (*H*, 118).

98   He istuivat pimeässä kuin miettien kumpikin keitä he olivat, mitä heille oli tapah-
     tunut (*H*, 119).

99   – Minne minä menen, Alma kysyi, – minne minä menen, hän toisti puhuen it-
     selleen, – minne? Ja äkkiä kodittomuus, orpous valui hänen mieleensä kuin sade
     maailman ylle tukahduttaen äänet, sumentaen silmät, ja hän muisti päivän lap-
     suudestaan: hän oli tulossa riiheltä, metsän reunassa ruskeita sananjalkoja, sade,
     sade, hän nousi kivelle ja katsoi ympärilleen ja oli sellainen olo kuin ei olisi tiennyt
     mistä tuli, kuka oli, ei olisi ollut isää, äitiä, ei ketään koko maailmassa. Maailma oli
     sumu, hämärä, rakennusten harmaus, syksy, kivien harmaus, riihen harmaus, ää-
     nettömyys, ei ketään, ei tietoa kenestäkään, ei ketään, ei mitään, eksyksissä, yksin
     maailmassa. Poika liikahti, Alma kuuli pojan äänen ja näki miten hän meni ovelle,
     avasi säpin, meni ulos, pois, rantaa pitkin, askelet ratisivat risuissa (*H*, 119).

100 [Alma] kuuli verkkojen kahinan, pienet rasahdukset katolta, ajatteli: apteekkarin
     vene, ja sitten: minne minä menen minne minne (*H*, 119).

101 Pyykkejä hän oli tullut huuhtomaan, istunut verkkovajan porraspuulla, oli alkanut
     sataa vettä, hiljaa, sitten kovemmin. [...] ja äkkiä nousi tuuli, ja poika oli vajan
     ovensuulla. Milloin sade oli lakannut, Alma ei tiennyt. Poika oli käynyt häneen
     kiinni, *niin sen täytyi olla*, Alma mietti, mitään sanomatta, ja miten kauan sitä oli
     kestänyt. Sade oli lakannut, oli haettu saavi ulkoa, läpimärät vaatteet suojaan sa-
     teelta. *Ja sitten hän oli tahtonut että poika olisi mies.* Ja nyt poika oli menossa pois
     (*H*, 119–120).

102 Hän kuuli pojan ilkkuvan äänen joka puhui huoneista että ensin sinä itse ja sitten
     sinä äkkiä rupeat niin helvetin siveäksi (*H*, 123).

103 [Alma] oli antanut pojan tulla vierelleen kapealle vuoteelle, kuin pikkupoikana (*H*,
     121).

104 Mutta yhtenä aamuna Alman ollessa vielä yöpukeissa Antti tuli hänen huoneensa
     ovelle, ja *niin kuin verkkovajassa* sotkeutui sitkeästi hänen vartaloonsa [...] (*H*,
     121–122).

105 Senkin Alma nyt tiesi, ettei se ollut jumalisen ihmisen kainoutta vaan naisen
     häpeää, ja vielä äsken ruustinnan silmät olivat tarkentuneina tutkineet hän käsi-
     varsiaan, hänen puolittain paljaita rintojaan, kun hän istui sängyn laidalla, hänen
     niskaansa jossa hiukset mustina nyt hiestä kosteina valuivat selkää pitkin. Selin
     ruustinnan Alma korjasi hiuksiaan, sitaisi ne ylös, ja yhä ruustinnaan selin, nyt jo
     ylivoiman täyttäessä jäsenet hän kääntyi ruustinnaa kohti, hiukset nutturalla hän
     katsoi tuota laihaa, litteärintaista hahmoa, joka jalat ristissä puolittain seinään
     nojaten tutki häntä mustilla, kieroilla silmillään, pojan silmillä, ja hymy, pojan
     hymy sai Alman sanomaan kuin joku olisi puhunut hänen suullaan, käyttänyt
     hänen kieltään, kolme sanaa, ne tulivat hänen suustaan ensin selvinä:/– En rupea
     asumaan. Ja sitten: – En rupea asumaan paholaisten seassa (*H*, 124–125).

106 – Älä puhu paholaisista, sillä et tiedä että ne puhuvat sinun oman suusi kautta. Sinä
     et ole kiusauksista vapaa [...] (*H*, 125).

107 Menisit naimisiin, mutta sinua ei kukaan huoli, niinkö? (*H*, 125).

108 – Kyllä sinä Alma pääset naimisiin, mutta sinä et ehkä itse sitä tahdo, sinä haluat
     määrätä ja se on sinun kohtalosi (*H*, 126).

109 Minä ymmärrän nyt kaiken, ja juuri siksi minä loukkasin häntä, minä tiesin mitä
     hän ajatteli katsoessaan minuun kun hän solmi hiuksiaan, ja siksi minä loukkasin
     häntä, anna anteeksi Jumala [...] (*H*, 126).

110 Alma ei saanut sanotuksi niin kuin oli ensin aikonut, että se ei ollut hänen syy-
     tään. Ruustinnan silmät katsoivat, ja hän tiesi että oli turha ruveta selittämään [...]
     (*H*, 127).

111 – Kyllä minä ymmärrän Alma, se ääni sanoi./Alma halusi vihata tätä ääntä, ruus-
     tinnaa. Mutta mitä vihaamista hänessä oli (*H*, 127).

112 Me jäämme kahden (*H*, 127).

113 – Mutta ruustinna menee nyt ensiksi lepäämään./– Minä en tahdo... puhele mi-

nun kanssani. Missä sinä luulet minun henkeni olevan kun minä olen kuollut. Jos minä kuolen ennen kuin sinä, minä muutan sinun luoksesi. Mitäs sanoisit. Muutan tästä talosta lopulta pois. Mutta jos Onni ja Birger tulevat perässä./– En tiedä, mutta miksi te menitte viime yönä rantaan kun siellä on niin levotonta, huutavat kuin kadotuksen lapset, ei pitäisi kuunnella, se niin kiihdyttää (*H*, 71).

114 – Katsos, jos se onkin niin että sinä olet minä. Ne sanovat että minä olen niin kuin sinä. Entäpä jos sinä oletkin minä... siis: minä elän. Minä olen olemassa, minä puhun vaikka olen sinä. Katso: sinä et ole kuollut, et niin kauan kuin minä puhun sinulle [...] (*H*, 64).

115 [...] kun minä olen kuollut, sinä olet silloin minä vaikka et puhu – mutta jos tulee toinen jolle sanotaan "te olette västäräkki," niin sinä jatkat minun elämääni (*H*, 64).

116 [M]inä kuolen, linnut eivät (*H*, 64).

117 – Katsos nyt, nyt minä sain sinusta sen minkä halusin. Kun sinä suutut, sinun tukkasi kiiltää niin että se ihan säihkyy, ja kun sinä olet pannut nutturaasi tuon lyyrakamman [...] sinä olet ilmetty teerikukko (*H*, 65).

118 Alapäästä sinä olet nainen mutta yläpäästä [...] ilmetty teerikukko (*H*, 65).

119 The stuffed swan that served as a model for the swan portrayed in the novel, belonged to one of Vartio's uncles. It was abandoned in the attic after the distribution of an inheritance. (Ruuska 2012: 454)

120 In the Eastern imagery, swan (or goose) is conceived as being the Hamsa bird, representing perfect union, purity, and the oneness of the human and the divine. It refers to cosmic breath, illumination, and the escape from the cycle of regeneration.

121 Ja Alma päätti valehdella keksineensä koko asian (*H*, 38).

122 [Onko minun siis sanottava että] kyllä se on, mutta minä en tiedä siitä sen enempää [...] (*H*, 38).

123 [Alman] oli tehnyt mielensä kirjoittaa sisarelleen: mene ja katso onko se salin nurkassa vai näinkö minä unta ettei se siinä enää ole eikä unelmakaan. Mutta kerran kerrottuaan hän joskus itsekin uskoi sen vielä olevan siellä [...] (*H*, 36–37).

124 Hän tuijotti pimeään, ja oli kuva jota hän nyt tajusi katselleensa unessa, jossa Alman veli kuin itsepäisesti aikaa uhmaten katsoi takaisin asparaguksen varjo kasvoillaan [...] (*H*, 162).

125 Ja samassa ääni oli hänessä, se jonka hän siis oli kuullut unessa, tai hän oli nähnyt unta jostain joka oli tuonut äänen (*H*, 162).

126 "Minkälainen ääni se oli, sanokaa minulle." "Kung kung kung." (*H*, 162)

127 [En] minä ole yhdestäkään teatteriesityksestä nauttinut niin kuin siitä (*H*, 65).

128 Hän näki itsensä yrittämässä näytellä joutsenta, joutsenta jota ei itse ollut koskaan kunnolla nähnyt, vain kerran joutsenet korkealla talon yllä, äänettöminä etelää kohti. Miksi siis teeskentelisin, hän ajatteli, miksi yritin näytellä sellaista mitä en ollut itse nähnyt. [...] Ja hän katui: eikö hän ollut tajunnut kiusaantunutta häpeän ilmettä Alman veljen kasvoilla toistaessaan tälle itsepäisesti: "Kertokaa, näyttäkää miten." (*H*, 162)

129 Alma näki jo silmissään, miten ruustinna – jos hänet ottaisi mukaan kotiin käymään – tuskin ehdittyään kunnolla perille, tuskin tervehdittyään alkaisi kysyä lintua. Tietysti heti salin ovelta katsoisi sitä nurkkaa kohti. Eikä nurkassa olisi asparagusta eikä lintua (*H*, 36).

130 Miksi [Alman veli] oli vienyt [joutsenen] preparoitavaksi? [...] Ehkä ampuja päätti antaa joutsenen täytettäväksi vasta sitten kun tajusi ettei osannut kohdella tuota outoa valkeaa ruumista, ei tiennyt miten päästä siitä eroon. Koiratkin sitä kaihtoivat, siitä ei ollut niiden ruoaksi. Ehkä talon naiset... Alman äiti, jos se oli hänelle sanottu, ehkä äiti oli kiihtynyt, ollut levoton kuultuaan linnun äänen pimeässä illassa, kauhistunut, ehkä äidille oli näytetty kuollutta lintua, se oli kannettu hänen sairasvuoteensa ääreen, hämärässä tuvassa poika kantamassa sylissään, jaloista roikuttaen suurta lintua (*H*, 165).

303

131 Kung kung kung. Ruustinna oli asettanut kätensä pitkin sivuja. Siivet laahaten maata, ehkä kaula, hän ojensi kaulaansa... (*H*, 165)

132 [...] hän näki Alman veljen harhailemassa pimeää pihaa kuollut lintu sylissä, etsimässä paikkaa mihin hautaisi sen, ehkä vielä silloin taivaalla ympyrää lentäen kuolleen linnun puolison huuto, ja surmaaja – hän sanoi sen ääneen: surmaaja – kuin murhamies päätti juuri silloin, mitä tehdä valkealle ruumiille jota ei voinut haudata koska maan päällä ei ollut paikkaa taivaan linnulle. Sen ruustinna sanoi ääneen, hän sepitti ääneen tarinaa joutsenesta joka taivaalta alas ammuttuna oli tullut hänen tielleen, hänen elämäänsä niin omituisia teitä pitkin [...] (*H*, 165).

133 In Greek mythology, Leda was the daughter of the king Thestius, who was seduced and raped by Zeus, disguised in the form of swan. In art, Leda is often seen in paintings and sculptures as caressing the swan that is wrapped tightly around her body.

134 "Oli Jumalan tahto että sinun veljesi käsi nousi, Jumalan tahto että joutsen ammuttiin, minua varten, viesti Alman veljen käden kautta minun sydämeeni, minun kokoelmiini" (*H*, 169).

135 [T]aivaalta alas ammuttuna oli tullut hänen tielleen, hänen elämäänsä niin omituisia teitä pitkin, ja joka – jos hän olisi osannut ajoissa menetellä oikein – olisi nyt hänen kokoelmissaan [...] (*H*, 165–166).

136 Ruustinna näki Alman veljen tulossa noutamaan ampumaansa lintua preparoitsijalta. Näki hänet astumassa sisään – jokainen huone jossa joutsen oli, oli ruustinnan mielikuvituksessa hämärä, jotta linnun valkeus näkyisi sitä selvempänä – astumassa lumisena, parta jäässä, kulmakarvat jäätyneinä huuruiseen huoneeseen, näki silmien katsovan kohti huoneen peräseinää jossa linnut olivat rivissä hyllyllä, pöllöt, metsot, teeret, pienempiä lintuja joukossa, nokat samaan suuntaan ojennuksessa, ja keskellä hyllyä ylinnä muita hänen lintunsa, valkea suuri, kuin elossa, veritahroista pestynä, kaula koholla, suorana, vartomassa puolisoa joka sen takana näkymättömissä söi rannalta mehuista ruohoa (*H*, 166–167).

137 Pitkä suippo nokka, kuovi viskattuna nokka riippuen pöydän reunan yli, kuin juomassa vettä, kuoleman vettä, ja näetkö, niin se on myös preparoitu, samaan asentoon, *kuin iankaikkisesti tavoittamaan nokallaan kuoleman vettä* (*H*, 63–64).

138 [...] hän näki tämän mustuneet sormenpäät, tunsi tuon hajun joka vainosi häntä vielä unessakin (*H*, 166).

139 The translator's annotation in the novel includes a comment on the role of the gender of pronouns in Finnish: "Most often, a Finnish reader would have no trouble identifying a character's gender, and in the few instances where there is ambiguity, that was clearly the author's intent" (Flint & Flint 2008: 255). The translation renders the narrative situation in a manner that follows the first type of rendition I have provided here. The passage, however, could also be translated in another way: "[...] *she* could see [the taxidermist's] blackened fingertips, could sense the smell which haunted *her* even in a dream" or "[...] *he* could see [the taxidermist's] blackened fingertips, could sense the smell which haunted *him* even in a dream." The original version and its immediate context goes as follows: "Laiva oli jäässä, joutsen jäässä, sen kantajan käsiä paleli, jäiset rukkaset pitelivät lintua kiertyneinä valkean kaulan ympäri, höyhenissä tahroja, kuivunutta jäistä verta, likatahroja, jotka preparoitsija... hän näki tämän mustuneet sormenpäät, tunsi tuon hajun joka vainosi häntä vielä unessakin. Ruustinna näki Alman veljen tulossa noutamaan ampumaansa lintua preparoitsijalta" (*H*, 166).

140 Ruustinna yritti nukkua, yritti, mutta yhä mielikuvat, tuo tarina, joutsenen matka sulasta vedestä, hämärästä talvi-illasta preparoitsijan käsiin ... piti nukkua, mutta ei voinut, ei voinut [...] (*H*, 168).

141 [H]äpeä jota tapauksen muistaminen hänelle tuotti oli niin piinallinen että hänen ruumiinsa toistamiseen toisti noita naurettavia kumarruksia ikään kuin hän olisi

tahallaan rangaissut itseään... yhä, yhä hänen kaulansa kiertyi ylös, alas, käsivarret heiluivat sivuilla sormet vuoroin hajalla vuoroin tiiviisti yhdessä, edestakaisin, toistaen liikkeitä joita hän oli tehnyt näytellessään lintua jota ei ollut koskaan nähnyt (H, 169–170).

142 Ja hän, ruustinna, Alman kotitaloon tullut vieras keskellä salia päästelemässä suustaan omituisia kurluttavia ääniä, päätään nostaen, käsiään levittäen, sormiaan [...] (H, 169).

143 Mutta eihän se ollut totta (H, 170).

144 [J]os hän nyt oli edes yrittänyt sitä, ei ollut, Alma oli sen todistanut... *mutta juuri se että hän olisi voinut* [...] (H, 168).

145 – Kuin nauta sinä nukut yösi sikeää unta mutta minä valvon sinun valheittesi takia, jos sinä olisit sanonut minulle suoraan että se oli totta, että – minä olen valmis tunnustamaan että minun esitykseni oli ala-arvoinen [...] (H, 171).

146 Alma oli saanut koetella pulssia niin monta kertaa että hän tiesi, eikä hän kyennyt enää säälimään tuota ihmistä, jonka jokaisen hulluudenpuuskan hän oli näinä vuosina joutunut näkemään./Ja nyt tiskipöydän takana, puhuu sieltä ja kohta kulkee ympäriinsä huonetta ja sitten joko purskahtaa itkuun tai jää istumaan tuijottaen eteensä kunnes Alma ei enää kestä vaan hillitäkseen itsensä lyömästä tuota oliota menee ulos, menee vaikka rantasaunalle [...]. Ehkä hänkin itkee: paiskautuu suulleen lauteille ja itkee – sillä mitä on sitten hänen elämänsä... minne hän menisi, kenen puoleen kääntyisi (H, 225).

147 Te kaksi naista, mitä te täällä teette, minä sanon sen, te juoruatte aamusta iltaan (H, 176).

148 Minun vaimoni ei juorua, ei. Teodolinda on oppinut pitämään suunsa kiinni, hän kostaa, näetkös (H, 176).

149 [M]yrkkyä joka pullossa mutta minä olen vapaa ihminen, minä menen kaupunkiin, käsken avata korkin, katsos minä puhun, annan tulla ulos, kuuletko sinä kun minä puhun [...] (H, 182).

150 "Olisinko minä arvannut sinä aamuna kun kotoa läksin laivarantaan" (H, 140).

151 – Niin, mitenkä se taas oli (H, 140).

152 – Niin olisinko arvannut. Alma huokasi./– Miksi huokaat? Ennen sinä sanoit että se oli Jumalan johdatusta./– En tiedä. Tai jos lienee. Olisinhan minä saattanut joutua vaikka minne (H, 140).

153 Hänkö tunnustaisi olevansa paikassa, jossa hänen tehtävänään oli topattujen lintujen hoitaminen. [...] sukulaisille hän ei ikinä tunnustaisi [...] (H, 38).

154 Ja siitä se kaikki sai alkunsa (H, 146).

155 – Missähän minä olisin jos pappila ei olisi palanut [...] (H, 58).

156 – Jos minä olisinkin silloin lähtenyt, tiedä missä nyt olisin (H, 201).

157 [H]aluaisin mennä ihmisiin mutta täällä minä olen vieras, olen palvelusihminen, kukaan ei minusta välitä, jos olisin jäänyt kotiin, olisin ehkä talonemäntä – ei ei – siitä ei mitään, ei ajatustakaan, pois kaikki mielestä (H, 225–226).

158 "Onko tämä koti" [...] "Kuka tässä määrää?" (H, 45)

159 Ruustinna näki: nyt Alma alkaisi kämmensyrjällä, aina vasemman kämmenen, pyyhkiä nenänjuurtaan, ja niin tapahtui (H, 46).

160 [M]inun kuolemaani he odottavat, tavaroita he minulta himoitsevat, voi voi, se kertomus jonka sinä minulle aamulla kerroit oli minulle tuttu, ikään kuin minä olisin ollut sinä Alma ja itkenyt maata joka minulta oli viety... (H, 67)

161 Saman teki myös Elsa. Kun tavara on viety ei sitä takaisin saa, vaikka tässä Alman kertomuksessa ei ole kysymys siitä asiasta minkä Elsa teki minulle (H, 221).

162 [V]oi voi, tämä kertomus jota Alma kertoo tässä, on niin tuttu minulle, Alma teki oikein (H, 219).

163 Elsa otti sellaista mikä oli Teodolindan ja minun. Alma ja hänen sisarensa ottivat mikä oli heidän (H, 221).

164 [K]oska te, äitisi ja sinä ja sisaresi, olitte päättäneet ennemmin repiä kaiken kappaleiksi kuin *antaa valtaa* sille naiselle (*H*, 215). Alma's sister is not mentioned in the Flints' English translation.

165 – Jos minä sanon että syksy niin te sanotte että kesä… ja kai minä itse sen paremmin tiedän kun omassa selässäni sitä kannoin (*H*, 210).

166 […] Kerro apteekkarille niin kuin olet sen minulle kertonut. Se alkoi siitä että *sinun* veljesi seisoi joka päivä peilin edessä tukkaansa kampaamassa ja vaati *sinulta* puhdasta paitaa, jatka./– Vaati paitaa, niin./– Ja *sinä* sanoit että vastahan sinä sait päällesi puhtaan paidan, ja silloin *sinun* veljesi suuttui. Ja siitä *sinä* jo arvasit./ – Jaksoinko minä joka päivä paitoja pestä ja silittää… /– Kuka tässä työt tekee, *sinä* sanoit, ruustinna sanoi äänellä joka oli kuin tahdin lyönti./– Kuka ne teki niin, jos en minä, Alma sanoi, äänessään katkeruus. […] /– *Sinä* lypsit lehmät, kaikki työt sinä teit./– Kuka sitten jos en minä. Ja minä tein, olin oppinut tekemään./– Ja teit mielelläsi koska koti oli vielä *sinullekin* koti silloin. Mutta jatka./– Oli tullut ompelemaan, naapuritalon emäntä oli sen täti./– Mutta kylällä liikkui jo huhuja. Ja te arvasitte" (*H*, 211).

167 – Olihan teillä onneksi tämä talo, että oli joku paikka. Niin ruustinna aina sanoi tässä kohden, ja Alma toisti sen jo edeltä (*H*, 11).

168 Hän tahtoi ettei Alma jättäisi kertomuksesta tätä kohtaa pois: juuri tämä kohta oli hänestä niin jännittävä. Sanoisiko Alma tähän kohtaan kuuluvat lauseet juuri sellaisina kuin oli ne aikaisemmin oppinut sanomaan, tosin monien muistutusten jälkeen (*H*, 142).

169 On the functions of the second-person narration see Richardson 2006: 28, 35; Fludernik 1996: 229, 232.

170 – Sen sinä sanoit jo. Anna minun kertoa nyt (*H*, 213).

171 – Mutta eihän, jos sänky olisi viety hevosella, olisi koko tätä tarinaa (*H*, 221).

172 – Tämä kertomus on turmeltunut. Mutta annetaan sen nyt olla, en minä vaadi sinua aloittamaan alusta (*H*, 215).

173 – Kysy vaikka Teodolindalta, *miltä hänestä tuntui* […] (*H*, 219).

174 Mahdat ymmärtää Holger *miltä minusta tuntui* […] (*H*, 222).

175 – Sänky kulki yössä huojahdellen kuin näkymättömien käsien kantamana. Miten mystillistä, miten lumoavaa, sanoi ruustinna. – Mutta sinä et ole kertonut apteekkarille vielä kaikkea, mitä sinä pimeänä yönä tapahtui. […] Veljekset olivat tulossa kotiin ja kun huomasivat vastaantulijoita tiellä menivät metsään piiloon. Ja sieltä piilopaikastaan he katsoivat ja näkivät, mitä heidän sisarensa olivat tekemässä. […] Tämä kaksijalkainen huojahteli kantajiensa käsissä, sinä et usko miten tämä kohta tässä kertomuksessa saattaakin minua viehättää. "Levätään," veljet kuulevat sisariensa sanovan, tuntevat heidän äänensä, ja *ymmärtävät kaiken* (*H*, 219–220).

176 – Mikä? kysyi Holger./– Älä keskeytä, tämä on nyt niitä kertomuksia joka ei siedä keskeytyksiä ja sinä Alma, aloita ihan alusta./– Mistä minä tiedän mikä on alku!/ – Aloita vaikka siitä kun te kannoitte sänkyä, se ei ole alku, mutta kun aloitat siitä, vaikka se tosin on tämän kertomuksen loppu, niin pääset siitä takaisin alkuun (*H*, 210).

177 – Kyllä, sinä *luulet* etten minä muka *käsitä* että sinä *tiedät…* (*H*, 176)

178 – Sanonko minä sinulle mitä sinä ajattelet? […] On hyvä ajatella. Ajatus ei lopu, ei lopu, kun alat alusta et pääse loppuun, sitä riittää (*H*, 174).

179 – Mutta minä pyysin sinua aloittamaan alusta, sinä sotkit nyt. Minä sanoin: kerro alusta, aivan alusta, mutta sinä sotkit (*H*, 47).

180 – Mikä lienee alku (*H*, 47).

181 – Sinä olet taitava kutoja […] (*H*, 155).

182 *Etymologinen sanakirja* (*The Etymology Dictionary*) 1987: 298.

183 In analyzing the growing "temporal autonomy" of modernist narrative, Stevenson (1998: 99) examines the transitional role of spoken narratives in the context of Joseph Conrad and Ford Madox Ford's work. According to Stevenson, "departures

from serial, chronological order create highly unconventional novels. Yet these departures are also [...] carefully and plausibly explained: even fractured, wayward forms of construction can seem legitimate, natural, even conventional, if they are seen as aspects of oral narrative." As a result, these works "simultaneously serve propriety and novelty, convention and innovation."

184 – Omituinen olento [...] Lähtee askinsa kanssa, tulee takaisin askinsa kanssa (*H*, 188).

185 Minne se oli mennyt, tahtominen, haluaminen, ei ollut jäljellä edes minkään haluamista, ei minkään tahtomista – hän oli kuin ruustinna, joka ei halunnut muuta kuin rauhaa, niin juuri, rauhaa.

186 Viisitoista vuotta oli kulunut. [...] Näinkö, kädet näin, hän oli viisitoista vuotta sitten ensimmäisen kerran avannut tämän ikkunan. Viisitoista kertaa tilkinnyt nämä samat ikkunat ruustinnan kulkiessa salin ja makuuhuoneen väliä kuten nytkin, katsellen paniko hän tarpeeksi pumpulia (*H*, 204).

187 Eniten hän oli vieraissa ollessaan kaivannut, hän ymmärsi sen nyt, näitä valkeita laivoja jotka toivat kotiin ja kotoa pois (*H*, 204).

188 – Jos Alma edes kerran olisi näyttänyt sen minulle hänen veljensä eläisi minun kauttani mutta Alma ei halunnut ja nyt on kaikki myöhäistä (*H*, 238).

189 Kun aurinko oli laskenut kuusikon taa, oli taivas ollut kummallisen kirkas, taivas kuin ohut pingotettu kuparilevy metsän yllä, järven takana. Ruustinna oli nähnyt linnun lentävän kuusten latvojen ohi, häviävän kuin taivas olisi ollut vettä, johon lintu sukeltaa. Ja kuin taivas olisi helähtänyt linnun siiven koskettaessa sitä, helähdys yhä ilmassa, kuin lintu, linnut nimettömiä, mustia linnunmuotoisia kuvia, taivaallisia satraappeja (*H*, 235).

190 – Minä puhun nyt ensi kertaa näistä asioista enkä minä niistä sitten enää puhu [...] (*H*, 251).

191 In the original text, there is no explicit reference to gossip, but rather to empty talk plucked out of thin air ("tyhjästä temmattua") or that is in some other way suspicious or vague ("epämääräinen puhe"): – Sanalla sanoen kaikki tyhjästä temmattua, niin epämääräisiä puheita että sekään mikä piti paikkansa ei ollut totta (*H*, 253).

192 [...] minä olen Jumalan lapsi (*H*, 230).

193 [K]un olen vuoteella lepäämässä, se ikään kuin täyttää minut, ruumis on kevyt, minä olen ikään kuin ilmassa ja tiedän: nyt se on minussa. Jumala on minussa, minä Jumalassa [...] niinä hetkinä kun Jumala on minussa ovat kaikki ihmiset, kaikki mikä maailmassa elää ja hengittää on minulle sanomattoman rakasta (*H*, 230).

194 – Miksi toisten ihmisten on kärsittävä tässä elämässä niin paljon ja toiset pääsee läpi (*H*, 228).

195 Kun tietää miksi, on helpompi, paljon helpompi, kun tietää edes, on helpompi (*H*, 228–229).

196 [J]ospa kaikki on turhaa, minun taisteluni, minun rukoukseni, ajattele mikä teatteri, mitä teatteria kaikki tämä, hyvä jumala sanon itselleni, jospa minä näyttelen vain, ja *te kaikki katsotte ja nauratte kun minä näyttelen* kilvoittelijaa... (*H*, 227–228)

197 "Tehkää se minun muistokseni" (*H*, 245).

198 Kun oli pimeä, ruustinna kolmantena (*H*, 243).

199 [...] taiteilijalle, joka muistutti pöllöä, ja piti sitä mallina (*H*, 256).

200 Alhoniemi (1973:175) refers to the folklorist Matti Kuusi's (1963: 40) characterization of the shaman: "Among other things the shaman was a person, through whom the pain was transformed into a word: a poet." (Kaiken muun ohessa šamaani oli ihminen, jossa kipu muuntui sanaksi: runoilija.) The Sámi verb *kej* refers both to a mating dance of a wood grouse and to the incantation of a shaman falling into a trance (*langeta loveen*). The intensive and ecstatic "psychosis"

of a shaman falling into a trance is accompanied by the words of his assistant spirit, a guesser (*arvaaja*), who interprets the mysterious hallucinations of his master. (Ibid.: 34–35) The shaman does not die, because his bird-shaped spirit (*kaakkuri*) will return to this world to find a new human dwelling to live in. This chosen one (potentially falling into hysteria, neuroticism, and depression) will finally continue the tradition of the magic of words, after having resigned himself to the curse and gift of his calling (ibid.: 39–41).

201 Joulun alla oli Alman veli kuollut ja Alma palannut hautajaisista jouluksi; hän tuli junalta kantaen matkalaukkua, pientä kassia, sanoivat toiset, ja sen kassin hän oli paiskannut kädestään apteekin keittiön lattialle, kun näki ruustinnan edessään vaatimassa sitä samaa, ja suoraa huutoa tömähtänyt, sanoivat ruustinnan poika ja miniä, huutaen tömähti he sanoivat nauraen, kaatui tajuttomana, sanoivat toiset, hysteerisenä, sanoi Herman, mielettömänä hysterian vallassa, sanoi Elsa, vielä suruaikana rääkättynä vanha ihminen, sanoivat kyläläiset, ruustinnan eteen huutaen suoraa käsittämätöntä huutoa joka muuttui ulinaksi, haukunnaksi, kaakatukseksi, soitoksi, pulputukseksi, kuin pullon korkki, sanoi Antti, kuin samppanjapullon, sanoi Holger, hirveätä ääntä pitäen, sanoi kunnanlääkärin poika, mielipuolen kanssa mielipuoleksi tulleena, sanoivat kauppias ja hänen vaimonsa, Jumalan satuttamana, sanoi kirkkoherra [...] (*H*, 239–240).

202 [R]aivokkaiden vihanpurkauksien seasta [...] Alman jatkuva kirkuva ääni, joka – niin sanoivat kaikki jotka sen kuulivat – oli kuin helvettiin putoavan kirkuna [...] (*H*, 240).

203 "Mene lepoosi sielu" (*H*, 240).

7. Conclusion

1 The predominance of the experience of ordinariness in modernist fiction has traditionally been overlooked because critics have put their emphasis on the modernist endeavor to subvert the conventions of nineteenth-century realism. (See Olson 2009: 3)

2 The existentialism of Jotuni's early modernist work (cf. Rossi 2011) influenced Vartio's fiction. These influences are manifested in Vartio's female vagabonds, who are often forced to settle for less that they have expected from life. While writing about Jotuni's work to the writer Brita Polttila, Vartio confessed that she suffered from serious inferiority: "I read Jotuni yesterday and especially *Arkielämää* depressed me terribly [...] I looked at my own miserable sheets and I felt contempt, fathomless inferiority and the most dreadful disgust. And I said to myself [...] I am just a popular writer, and a bad one, at that [...] Anyway, Jotuni is a hell of a writer, but no realist – though such has been said." ("Luin eilisiltana Jotunia ja erikoisesti *Arkielämää* teki minut ihan synkäksi [...] Halveksien ja täynnä syvintä alennuksentunnetta ja tympeintä inhoa katselin surkeita liuskojani ja sanoin [...] minä olen pelkkä ajanvietekirjailija, huono sellainenkin [...] Jotuni on joka tapauksessa hiton hieno kirjailija, mutta ei mikään realisti – sellaista on sanottu näet"; quoted in Ruuska 2012: 348) Vartio was also inspired by other early modernist writers, such as the Nobel laureate F. E. Sillanpää (see Nykänen 2013b).

3 Vartio's successors include such authors as Kerttu-Kaarina Suosalmi, Marja-Leena Mikkola, Anu Kaipainen, and Raija Siekkinen, among other writers (cf. Laitinen 1981: 565). On the earlier period of women's writing in Finnish literature see Launis (2005) and Grönstrand (2005).

4 Häneltä ei vaadittu muuta kuin täydellistä suoritusta. The English translation of Meri's text is John R. Pitkin's (1978: 255).

5 [...] pään läpi ohitse. Translation by Pitkin (1978: 259).

6   Materiaali työstetään valmiiksi asti eli, niin kuin näyttää, tuodaan esille paljaana, muokkaamattomana.

7   Uusi kieli! Mutta mikä se on? [...] Ei, ei mikään voi minulle koskaan merkitä enempää kuin [runoni]! Vaikka ne eivät koskaan saisi siipiä, voimakkaita, kantavia siipiä, ne siipirikot linturaukat, tulen kuitenkin aina niitä rakastamaan!

8   Olen väsynyt näkemään ihmisten läpi, minua inhottaa katsella sitä kaikkea mitä näen, tiedäthän, että minä olen aivan yhtä herkkä kuin jokin vainukoira haistamaan ihmisiä ja on tuskallista nähdä niin paljon – ei jaksa. Kaikkein tuskallisinta on se, että näkee myös itsensä, kaikkien tekojensa vaikuttimet, kaikki tekonsa ja turhamaisuutensa kirkkaassa valossa.

9   According to Toini Havu, Vartio had once shouted in the middle of conversation about her slightly mad character, Mrs. Pyy: "It's me, it's me!" (Särkilahti 1973: 124–125; Ruuska 2010: 59)

10 [H]än yrittäessään voittaa täydellisen taiteilijan, hän joka ei osannut matkia edes sorsan narinaa, oli ollut hullu (*H*, 168).

11 In the seventh poem of *Talvipalatsi* Haavikko (1959: 42) wrote: "[W]inter, dream, and in summer, the gleam on hair and the squeaking / of ducks, vibrating on the skin, soft is a woman's skin when three unborn ones look out of her eyes [...]" ("[T]alvi unta ja kesällä tukka välkehti ja sorsien / narina väreili iholla, / pehmeä on naisen iho, kun silmistä katsoo / kolme syntymätöntä [...]")

12 [...] ja miksi yrittäisin runoilla kun en ole Musset (Haavikko 1959: 51). The English translation of the poem is Anselm Hollo's (1991: 66).

References

Primary Sources

Works by Marja-Liisa Vartio
Poems, Short Stories, Novels, and Translations

Vartio, Marja-Liisa 1952: *Häät*. [*The Wedding*]. Helsinki: Otava.
— 1953: *Seppele*. [*The Garland*]. Helsinki: Otava.
— 1955: *Maan ja veden välillä*. [*Between Land and Water*]. Helsinki: Otava. [*MVV*]
— 1957: *Se on sitten kevät*. [*This Then Is Spring*]. Helsinki: Otava. [*S*]
— 1958: *Mies kuin mies, tyttö kuin tyttö*. [*Any Man, Any Girl*]. Helsinki: Otava. [*MT*]
— 1960: *Kaikki naiset näkevät unia*. [*All Women Dream*]. Helsinki: Otava. [*K*]
— 1962: *Tunteet*. [*Emotions*]. Helsinki: Otava. [*T*]
— 1966: *Runot ja proosarunot*. [*Poems and Prose Poems*]. Helsinki: Otava. [*R*]
— 1967: *Hänen olivat linnut*. [*Hers/His Were the Birds*]. Helsinki: Otava. [*H*]
— 1968: Alma käy kotona. [Alma Visits Home]. In *Parnasso* 3/1968, 146–151. ["A"]
— 2008: *The Parson's Widow*. Translated by Aili & Austin Flint. [*Hänen olivat linnut*]. Champaign & London: Dalkey Archive Press. [*PW*]
— 1990: My Green Family. [Vihreää sukua]. A Woman and a Landscape. [Nainen ja maisema]. In *Enchanting Beasts. An Anthology of Modern Women Poets of Finland*. Edited and Translated by Kirsti Simonsuuri. London: Forest Books, 3–4, 9–12.

Diaries and Letters

Vartio, Marja-Liisa 1994: *Ja sodan vuosiin sattui nuoruus*. Edited by Anna-Liisa Haavikko. Helsinki: Art House.
— 1995: *Nuoruuden kolmas näytös: Päiväkirjamerkintöjä ja kirjeitä vuosilta 1941–1952 sekä uninovelli Vatikaani*. Edited by Anna-Liisa Haavikko. Helsinki: Art House.
— 1996: *Lyhyet vuodet: Muistiinmerkintöjä ja kirjeitä vuosilta 1953–1966 sekä novelli Marjapaikka*. Edited by Anna-Liisa Haavikko. Helsinki: Art House.

Other Literary Works and Essays Cited

Eliot, T. S. 1962/1922: *The Waste Land and Other Poems*. New York: Harcourt.
— 1949: *Autio maa: Neljä kvartettia ja muita runoja*. Edited by Lauri Viljanen & Kai Laitinen. Translated by Yrjö Kaijärvi et al. Helsinki: Otava.

— 1934/1932: *Selected Essays*. London: Faber & Faber.
— 1950/1920: *The Sacred Wood: Essays on Poetry and Criticism*. London: Methuen & Co.
— 1975: *Selected Prose*. Edited by Frank Kermode. New York: Harcourt & Farrar.

Haavikko, Paavo 1951: *Tiet etäisyyksiin*. Helsinki: WSOY.
— 1959: *Talvipalatsi*. Helsinki: Otava.
— 1966: *Puut, kaikki heidän vihreytensä*. Helsinki: Otava.
— 1984: *Pimeys*. Helsinki: WSOY.
— 1991: *Selected Poems*. Translated by Anselm Hollo. Manchester: Carcanet.
— 1991: Fourth Poem (*Winter Palace*). In *Contemporary Finnish Poetry*. Edited and Translated by Herbert Lomas. Newcastle upon Tyne: Bloodaxe Books, 124–125.

James, Joyce 2000/1916: *A Portrait of the Artist as a Young Man*. Oxford World's Classics. Oxford: Oxford University Press.
— 1944: *Stephen Hero*. A Part of the First Craft of a Portrait of the Artist as a Young Man. Edited by Theodore Spencer. New York: New Directions.

Kailas, Uuno 1931: *Uni ja kuolema*. Helsinki: WSOY.
— 1970: The House. Translated by Philip Riley. In *Ariel* Vol. 1, No. 2, 97.

Kejonen, Pekka 1964: *Napoleonin epätoivo*. Helsinki: Tammi.

Mandelstam, Osip 1997: *Complete Critical Prose*. Translated by Jane Gary Harris & Constance Link. Edited by Jane Gary Harris. Ann Arbor: Ardis.

Meri, Veijo 1967/1963: Käsityksiäni novellista. In *Kaksitoista artikkelia*. Helsinki: Otava, 28–42.
— 1985/1956: Tappaja. In *Novellit*. Helsinki: Otava, 133–140.
— 1962: Suomen paras näyttelijä. In *Tilanteita*. Helsinki: Otava, 102–112.
— 1978: The Killer. Translated by John R. Pitkin. In *Snow in May. An Anthology of Finnish Writing 1945–1972*. Edited by Richard Dauenhauer & Philip Binham. Cranbury, New Jersey: Associated University Presses, 254–259.

Onerva, L. 1908: *Mirdja*. Helsinki: Otava.

Petöfi, Sandor 1885/1869: The Maniac. [Az Őrült]. In *Selections from the Poems of Alexander Petöfi*. Translated by Henry Philips. Philadelphia. Privately Printed, 28–31.
— 1922: *Petöfin runoja II*. Translated by Otto Manninen. Helsinki: WSOY.

Pound, Ezra 1913: Poetry: A Few Don'ts by an Imagist. In *Poetry: A Magazine of Verse*. March, Vol. 1, 200–206.
— 1960/1934: *The ABC of Reading*. New York: New Directions.
— 1971: *Selected Letters of Ezra Pound, 1907–1941*. Edited by D. D. Paige. New York: New Directions.

Sarkia, Kaarlo 1936: *Unen kaivo*. Helsinki: WSOY.

Södergran, Edith 1916: *Dikter*. Borgå: Holger Schildts Förlag.
— 1992: *Love & Solitude: Selected Poems 1916–1923*. Translated by Stina Katchadourian. Seattle: Fjord Press.

Tzu, Chuang 1968: *The Complete Works of Chuang Tzu*. Translated by Burton Watson. New York: Columbia University Press.

Woolf, Virginia 1929/1919: Modern Fiction. In *The Common Reader*. London: Hogarth Press, 184–195.
— 1950/1923: Mr. Bennet and Mrs. Brown. In *The Captain's Death and Other Essays*. London: Hogarth Press, 184–195.
— 1958/1929: Phases of Fiction. In *Granite and Rainbow. Essays by Virginia Woolf*. London: Hogarth Press, 93–145.
— 1978: *The Diary of Virginia Woolf*. Vol 2, 1920–1924. Edited by Anne Olivier Bell. London: Hogarth Press.
— 1985/1939: A Sketch of the Past. In *Moments of Being*. Edited by Jeanne Schulkind. London: Hogarth Press, 64–159.

Secondary Sources

Scholarly Work and Reviews Related to Vartio

Ahola, Suvi 1989: Kuvia hajanaisesta elämästä. In *"Sain roolin johon en mahdu"*: *Suomalaisen naiskirjallisuuden linjoja*. Edited by Maria-Liisa Nevala. Helsinki: Otava, 537–546.

Alhoniemi, Pirjo 1971: Marja-Liisa Vartion Hänet olivat linnut: Aineksia ja rakenteen piirteitä. In *Sananjalka* 13 (1972). Turku, 147–161.

— 1972: Marja-Liisa Vartion Kaikki naiset näkevät unia ja Paavo Haavikon Toinen taivas ja maa rinnakkain. In *Kirjallisuudentutkijan seuran vuosikirja 26* (1972). Helsinki, 9–23, 239.

— 1973: Hänen olivat linnut. In *Romaani ja tulkinta*. Helsinki: Otava, 165–179.

Flint, Aili & Flint, Austin 2008: Translators' Note. In *The Parson's Widow*. Champaign & London: Dalkey Archive Press, 255–256.

Hakulinen, Auli 2013: Puheet, havainnot ja mielen ailahtelut Marja-Liisa Vartion teoksessa *Tunteet*. In *Dialogi kaunokirjallisuudessa*. Edited by Aino Koivisto & Elise Nykänen. Tietolipas 242. Helsinki: SKS, 264–296.

Havu, Toini 1970: Marja-Liisa Vartio. A Foreword in *Valitut teokset*. Helsinki: Otava, iii–x.

Holappa, Pentti 1959: Suoralla tiellä. In *Parnasso* 1/1959, 34–35.

Hökkä, Tuula 1989: Itkun runoa – Marja-Liisa Vartio. In *"Sain roolin johon en mahdu"*: *Suomalaisen naiskirjallisuuden linjoja*. Edited by Maria-Liisa Nevala. Helsinki: Otava, 532–536.

Kajannes, Katriina 2000: Feminiinisen subjektin modernisaatio: Analyysia Helvi Hämäläisen, Sirkka Seljan ja Marja-Liisa Vartion 1950- ja 60-luvun lyriikasta. In *Taasleitud aeg: Eesti ja soome kirjanduse muutumine 1950–1960 aastatel*. Edited by Luule Epner & Pekka Lilja. Tartu: Tartu Ülikooli, 221–232.

Karkama, Pertti 1995: Naiskirjailijan syntymä: Marja-Liisa Vartion päiväkirjat 1939–1941. In *Identiteettiongelmia suomalaisessa kirjallisuudessa*. Edited by Kaisa Kurikka. Turku University. Department of Arts. Series A, No. 33. Turku: Åbo Akademis Tryckeri, 146–167.

Karppanen, Esko 2012: Upea portto Maria Magdalena -aiheesta Marja-Liisa Vartion runoudessa. In *Vartija* 125: 4 (2012), 155–158.

— 2013: Viluista tanssia, huokausten seppeleitä: Marja-Liisa Vartion runoudesta. In *Unohduksen tällä puolen*. Helsinki: ntamo, 73–117.

Kendzior, Nøste 2001: En kvinnelig utopi: An Afterword in *Fuglene var hans*. Translated by Nøste Kendzior. Larvik: Bokvennen Forlag, 242–250.

Koskiniemi, Rafael 1967: Marja-Liisa Vartion viimeinen. In *Uusi Suomi* 22 October 1967, 18.

Lippu, Hilkka 1985: Naisen identiteettikokemus Vartion lyriikassa. In *Noidannuolia: Tutkijanaisen aikakauskirja*. Edited by Auli Hakulinen, Hannele Kurki, Päivi Setälä & Liisa Uusitalo. Helsinki: Gaudeamus, 102–114.

M. N. 1962: Tuskat ja Tunteet. In *Iltasanomat* No. 281, 3.

Mäkelä, Maria & Tammi, Pekka 2007: Dialogi Linnuista: Kokemuksellisuus, kerronnallisuus, luotettavuus ja Marja-Liisa Vartion Hänen olivat linnut. In *Kirjallisia elämyksiä: Alkukivistä toiseen elämään*. Edited by Yrjö Hosiaisluoma, Maria Laakso, Hanna Suutela & Pekka Tammi. Helsinki: SKS, 227–251.

Nykänen, Elise 2012: Far from the Evils of Mankind: Mental Landscapes and National Identity in Marja-Liisa Vartio's short story "A Finnish Landscape." In *Paysages en dialogue: espaces et temporalités entre Centres et Périphéries européens*. Edited by Judit Maár & Traian Sandu. Paris: L'Harmattan, 55 – 68.

— 2013a: Puhuvia päitä: kerrottavuus ja *Hänen olivat linnut*. In *Dialogi kaunokirjal-*

lisuudessa. Edited by Aino Koivisto & Elise Nykänen. Tietolipas 242. Helsinki: SKS, 59–98.

— 2013b: Kansankuvauksesta ihmiskuvaukseen: Marja-Liisa Vartion *Se on sitten kevät* ja karjakon muodonmuutokset. In *KIVIAHOLINNA: Suomalainen romaani*. Edited by Vesa Haapala & Juhani Sipilä. Helsinki: Avain, 175–195.

— 2014: Re-reading (Modernist) 'Fictional Minds' after the Cognitive Turn: Embodied, Social and Emotional Minds in Marja-Liisa Vartio's novel *Tunteet*. In *Reframing Concepts in Literary and Cultural Studies: Theorizing and Analyzing Conceptual Transfer*. Edited by Nora Berning, Ansgar Nünning & Christine Schwanecke. ELCH Series. Trier: WVT, 97–114.

Paasilinna, Erno 1962: Tunteen kehässä. In *Suomalainen Suomi* 1962, 559.

Pennanen, Eila 1962: Jos olisin lintu. In *Parnasso* 8/1962, 370–371.

Polkunen, Mirjam 1962: Nuoruuden komedia. In *Uusi Suomi* 11 November 1962, 20.

Rojola, Lea 2008: Une nouvelle langue pour un nouveau monde: la Littérature Finlandaise des années 1950. In *L'identité? un question de langue? Actes du colloque de Caen (2-4 novembre 2006)*. Caen Cedex: Presses universitaires de Caen, 133–142.

— 2011: Rouva Pyy, pesätön lintu. In *Sanelma: Turun yliopiston kotimaisen kirjallisuuden vuosikirja 2011*, No. 17. Turku: Uniprint, 79–81.

— 2013: Kielten taistelu: Marja-Liisa Vartion *Tunteet* ja suomalainen modernismi. In *Romaanin historian ja teorian kytköksiä*. Edited by Hanna Meretoja & Aino Mäkikalli. Helsinki: SKS, 200–229.

— 2014: Hänen olivat täytetyt linnut. In *Posthumanismi*. Edited by Karoliina Lummaa & Lea Rojola. Turku: Eetos, 131–154.

Ruuska, Helena 2010: *Arkeen pudonnut sibylla: Modernin naisen identiteetin rakentuminen Marja-Liisa Vartion romaanissa* Kaikki naiset näkevät unia. Helsinki: Yliopistopaino.

— 2012: *Marja-Liisa Vartio: Kuin linnun kirkaisu*. Helsinki: WSOY.

— 2013a: Rouva P, rouva Pyy, kaikki naiset: Marja-Liisa Vartion *Kaikki naiset näkevät unia* -romaanin moderni nimileikki. In *KIVIAHOLINNA: Suomalainen romaani*. Edited by Vesa Haapala & Juhani Sipilä. Helsinki: Avain, 196–211.

— 2013b: "Kenkä piirtää ruusunkukkaa, liljankukkaa": Modernin naisen tanssiaskeleita Marja-Liisa Vartion runoissa "Häät" ja "Tanssi." In *Kirjallisuuden naiset: Naisten esityksiä 1840-luvulta 2000-luvulle*. Edited by Riikka Rossi & Saija Isomaa. Helsinki: SKS, 278–295.

Sarajas, Annamari 1980: Modernismin vakiutumista. In *Orfeus nukkuu: Tutkielmia kirjallisuudesta*. Helsinki: WSOY, 140–144.

Särkilahti, Sirkka-Liisa 1973: *Marja-Liisa Vartion kertomataide*. Tampere: Tampere University.

Tiusanen, Timo 1962: Kirpeän-hilpeät tunteet. In *Helsingin Sanomat* 1 November 1962, 19.

Other Works Cited

Aalto, Minna 2000: *Vapauden ja velvollisuuden ristiriita: Kehitysromaanin mahdollisuudet 1890-luvun lopun ja 1900-luvun alun naiskirjallisuudessa*. Helsinki: SKS.

Abbott, H. Porter 2008: Unreadable Minds and the Captive Reader. In *Style* 43.4, 448–467.

Abel, Elizabeth; Hirsch, Marianne & Langland, Elizabeth 1983 (eds.): *The Voyage In: Fictions of Female Development*. Hanover & London: Dartmouth.

Alber, Jan 2009: Impossible Storyworlds – And What to Do with Them. In *Storyworlds* 1.1, 79–96.

Alber, Jan; Iversen, Stefan; Nielsen, Henrik Skov & Richardson, Brian 2010: Unnatural

Narratives, Unnatural Narratology: Beyond Mimetic Models. In *Narrative* 18, 113–136.

Ameel, Lieven 2013: *Moved by the City: Experience of Helsinki in Finnish Prose Fiction 1889–1941*. Helsinki: Unigrafia.

Anhava, Tuomas 2002: *Todenkaltaisuudesta: Kirjoituksia vuosilta 1948–1979*. Edited by Helena & Martti Anhava. Helsinki: Otava.

Bakhtin, M. M. 1981: *The Dialogic Imagination: Four Essays*. Edited by Michael Holquist. Translated by Caryl Emerson & Michael Holquist. Austin: University of Texas Press.

Bal, Mieke 1985: *Narratology: Introduction to the Theory of Narrative*. Toronto: Toronto University Press.

— 1991: *On Story-Telling: Essays in Narratology*. Edited by David Jobling. California: Polebridge.

— 1993: His Master's Eye. In *Modernity and the Hegemony of Vision*. Edited by David Michael Levin. Berkeley, CA: University of California Press, 379–404.

— 2004: Over-Writing as Un-Writing: Descriptions, World-Making and Novelistic Time. In *Narrative Theory: Critical Concepts in Literary and Cultural Studies*. Edited by Mieke Bal. London: Routledge, 341–388.

Barthes, Roland 1979: *A Lover's Discourse: Fragments*. Translated by Richard Howard. London: Jonathan Cape.

Beauvoir, Simone de 1980/1949: *The Second Sex*. Translated and edited by H. M. Parshley. Harmondsworth: Penguin Books.

Beebee, Thomas O. 1995: Epistolary Novel. In *Routledge Encyclopedia of Narrative Theory*. Edited by David Herman, Manfred Jahn & Marie-Laure Ryan. London & New York: Routledge, 140–141.

Bell, David F. 1993: *Circumstances: Chance in the Literary Text*. Lincoln & London: University of Nebraska Press.

Bonheim, Helmut 1982: *The Narrative Modes: Techniques of the Short Story*. Cambridge: D.S. Brewer.

Brewin, Chris R. 2005: Encoding and Retrieval of Traumatic Memories. In *Neuropsychology of PTSD: Biological, Cognitive and Clinical Perspectives*. Edited by Jennifer J. Vasterling & Chris R. Brewin. New York & London: The Guilford Press, 131–150.

Bruner, Jerome 1987: Life as a Narrative. In *Social Research* Vol. 54, No. 1, 11–32.

— 1991: The Narrative Construction of Reality. In *Critical Inquiry* 18, 1–21.

Burke, Kenneth 1974/1945: *A Grammar of Motives*. Berkeley: University of California Press.

Butte, George 2004: *I Know That You Know That I Know: Narrating Subjects from* Moll Flanders *to* Marnie. Columbia: The Ohio State University Press.

Castle, Gregory 2006: *Reading the Modernist Bildungsroman*. Gainesville: University Press of Florida.

Chatman, Seymour 1978: *Story and Discourse: Narrative Structure in Fiction and Film*. Ithaca: Cornell University Press.

— 1990: *Coming to Terms: The Rhetoric of Narrative in Fiction and Film*. Ithaca: Cornell University Press.

Clark, Suzanne 1991: *Sentimental Modernism: Women Writers and the Revolution of the Word*. Bloomington: Indiana University Press.

Cohen, Margaret 1999: *The Sentimental Education of the Novel*. Princeton: Princeton University Press.

Cohn, Dorrit 1978: *Transparent Minds: Narrative Modes for Presenting Consciousness in Fiction*. Princeton: Princeton University Press.

— 1999: *The Distinction of Fiction*. New York: John Hopkins University Press.

Culler, Jonathan 1975: *Structuralist Poetics: Structuralism, Linguistics, and the Study of Literature*. Ithaca, New York: Cornell University Press.

Damasio, Antonio 2000: *The Feeling of What Happens: Body, Emotion and the Making of Consciousness*. London: Vintage.

Dannenberg, Hilary P. 2008: *Coincidence and Counterfactuality: Plotting Time and Space in Narrative Fiction*. Lincoln & London: Nebraska University Press.

Doležel, Lubomír 1998: *Heterocosmica: Fiction and Possible Worlds*. Baltimore & London: The John Hopkins University Press.

Doody, Margaret Anne 1996: *The True Story of the Novel*. New Brunswick & New Jersey: Rutgers University Press.

DuPlessis, Rachel Blau 1985: *Writing Beyond the Ending: Narrative Strategies of Twentieth-Century Women Writers*. Bloomington: Indiana University Press.

Eitner, Lorenz 1955: The Open Window and the Storm-Tossed Boat: An Essay in the Iconography of Romanticism. In *The Art Bulletin*. Vol. 1, No. 4, 281–290.

Ervasti, Esko 1967: *Välivaihe: Poimintoja suomalaisesta nykyepiikasta*. Forssa.

Felski, Rita 1989: *Beyond Feminist Aesthetics: Feminist Literature and Social Change*. London: Hutchinson Radius.

Fernyhough, Charles 2011: Even "Internalist" Minds are Social. In *Style* 45, No. 2, 272–275.

Fludernik, Monika 1993: *The Fictions of Language and the Languages of Fiction: The Linguistic Representation of Speech and Consciousness*. London & New York: Routledge.

— 1996: *Towards a 'Natural' Narratology*. London & New York: Routledge.

Fokkema, Douwe & Ibsch, Elrud 1988: *Modernist Conjectures: A Mainstream in European Literature 1910–1940*. New York: St. Martin's Press.

Fraiman, Susan 1993: *Unbecoming Women: British Women Writers and the Novel of Development*. New York: Columbia University Press.

Frank, Joseph 1963: *The Widening Gyre: Crisis and Mastery in Modern Literature*. New Brunswick, N. J.

Freeman, Alma S. 1988: Androgyny. In *Dictionary of Literary Themes and Motifs*. Edited by Jean-Charles Seigneuret. New York: Greenwood Press, 49–59.

Freud, Sigmund 1991/1916–1917: *Introductory Lectures on Psychoanalysis*. Volume 1. London: Penguin Books.

— 1961: *Beyond the Pleasure Principle*. Translated and edited by James Strachey. New York & London: W.W. Norton & Company.

Gang, Joshua 2011: Behaviorism and the Beginnings of Close Reading. In *English Literary History*. Vol. 78, No. 1, 1–25.

Giddens, Anthony 1991: *Modernity and Self-Identity: Self and Society in the Late Modern Age*. Cambridge: Polity Press.

Girard, René 1976: *Deceit, Desire and the Novel: Self and Other in Literary Structure*. Translated by Yvonne Freccero. Baltimore & London: The Johns Hopkins University Press.

— 1995: *Violence and the Sacred*. Translated by Patrick Gregory. Baltimore & London: The Johns Hopkins University Press.

Genette, Gerard 1980: *Narrative Discourse*. Translated by Jane E. Lewin. Oxford: Blackwell.

— 1982/1966: Frontiers of Narrative. In *Figures of Literary Discourse*. Translated by Alan Sheridan. New York: Columbia University Press, 127–144.

Gilbert, Sandra M. & Gubar, Susan 1988: *No Man's Land: The Place of the Woman Writer in the Twentieth Century. Volume 1: The War of Words*. New Haven & London: Yale University Press.

Goffman, Erving 1981: *Forms of Talk*. Philadelphia: University of Pennsylvania Press.

Goodman, Nelson 1978: *Ways of World-Making*. Indianapolis: Hackett.

Gray, Paul 1989: Telling It Like Thackeray." (Review of A Natural Curiosity by Margaret Drabble.) In *Time* 9/4, 66.

Grönstrand, Heidi 2005: *Naiskirjailija, romaani ja kirjallisuuden merkitys 1840-luvulla*. Helsinki: SKS.

Hakulinen, Auli 1988: Miehiä juoruilemassa. In *Isosuinen nainen: Tutkielmia naisesta ja kielestä*. Edited by Lea Laitinen. Helsinki: Helsinki University Press, 135–156.

Hamburger, Käte 1993/1973: *The Logic of Literature*. Translated by Marilynn J. Rose. Preface by Gérard Genette (translated by Dorrit Cohn). Bloomington: Indiana University Press.

Hamon, Philippe 1982: What is a description? In *French Literary Theory Today*. Edited by Tzvetan Todorov. Cambridge: Cambridge University Press, 147–171.

Hartman, Geoffrey H. 1995: On Traumatic Knowledge and Literary Studies. In *New Literary History*, Vol. 26, 537–563.

Herman, David 2003: Introduction. In *Narrative Theory and the Cognitive Sciences*. Edited by David Herman. Stanford, California: CSLI Publications, 1–30.

— 2004: Hypothetical Focalization. In *Narrative*. Vol. 2, Issue 3, 230–253.

— 2007: Cognition, Emotion, and Consciousness. In *The Cambridge Companion to Narrative*. Edited by David Herman. Cambridge: Cambridge University Press, 245–259.

— 2009a: *Basic Elements of Narrative*. Malden, Mass: Wiley-Blackwell.

— 2009b: Narrative Ways of Worldmaking. In *Narratology in the Age of Cross-Disciplinary Narrative Research*. Narratologia 20. Edited by Sandra Heinen & Roy Sommer. Berlin & New York: De Gryter, 71–87.

— 2011a: Introduction. In *The Emergence of Mind: Representations of Consciousness in Narrative Discourse in English*. Edited by David Herman. Lincoln & London: University of Nebraska Press, 1–40.

— 2011b: Re-minding Modernism. In *The Emergence of Mind: Representations of Consciousness in Narrative Discourse in English*. Edited by David Herman. Lincoln & London: University of Nebraska Press, 243–272.

— 2011c: Post-Cartesian Approaches to Narrative and Mind: A Response to Alan Palmer's Target Essay on "Social Minds". In *Style* 45, No. 2, 265–270.

Hintikka, Jaakko 1955: Tutkimus filosofiasta. In *Suomalainen Suomi* 4/1955, 206–211.

— 1955: Tutkimus kielestä. In *Suomalainen Suomi* 5/1955, 273–277.

Hirch, Marianne 1983: Spiritual *Bildung*: The Beautiful Soul as Paradigm. In *The Voyage In: Fictions of Female Development*. Edited by Elizabeth Abel, Marianne Hirsch & Elizabeth Langland. Hanover & London: University Press of New England, 23–48.

Hogan, Patrick Colm 2011a: *Affective Narratology: The Emotional Structure of Stories*. Lincoln & London: University of Nebraska Press.

— 2011b: Palmer's Anti-Cognitivist Challenge. In *Style* 45, No. 2, 244–248.

Hollander, John 1988: The Poetics of Ekphrasis. In *Word and Image*, Vol. 4, No. 1, 209–217.

Hollsten, Anna 2004: *Ei kattoa, ei seiniä: Näkökulmia Bo Carpelanin kirjallisuuskäsitykseen*. Helsinki: SKS.

Hormia, Osmo 1968: Moderni suomalainen kirjallisuus: Miten siihen on tultu? In *Äidinkielen opettajain liiton vuosikirja XV 1967–1968*. Vammala: Äidinkielen opettajain liitto, 63–89.

Humphrey, Robert 1955: *Stream of Consciousness in the Modern Novel*. Berkeley, Los Angeles: University California Press.

Hägg, Samuli 2003: *Narratologies of Gravity's Rainbow*. Joensuu: University of Joensuu.

Häkkinen, Kaisa (ed.) 1987: *Nykysuomen sanakirja 6: Etymologinen sanakirja*. Helsinki: WSOY.

Hökkä, Tuula 1991: *Mullan kirjoitusta, auringon savua: Näkökulmia Eeva-Liisa Mannerin runouteen ja sen modernistisuuteen*. Helsinki: SKS.

— 1999: Modernismi: uusi alku – vanhan valtaus. In *Suomen kirjallisuushistoria 3: Rintamakirjeistä tietoverkkoihin*. Helsinki: SKS, 68–89.

Isomaa, Saija 2009: Sentimentaalisia juonteita pohjoismaisessa realismissa. In *Avain* 2/2009, 5–20.

Jahn, Manfred 2011: Mind = Mind + Social Mind? A Response to Alan Palmer's Target Essay. In *Style* 45, No. 2, 249–253.

Joplin, Patricia Kliendienst 1985: Epilogue: Philomela's Loom. In *Coming to Light: American Women Poets in the Twentieth Century*. Edited by Diane Wood Middlebrook & Marilyn Yalom. Ann Arbor: The University of Michigan Press, 254–267.

Jordan, Julia 2010: *Chance and the Modern British Novel*. London & New York: Continuum.

Jung, Carl Gustav 1985: *Dreams*. Edited by R.F.C. Hull. London: Ark Paperbacks.

Kafalenos, Emma 1999: Not (Yet) Knowing: Epistemological Effects of Deferred and Suppressed Information in Narrative. In *Narratologies: New Perspectives on Narrative Analysis*. Edited by David Herman. Columbus: Ohio State University Press, 33–65.

— 2006: *Narrative Causalities*. Columbus: Ohio State University Press.

— 2011: The Epistemology of Fiction: Knowing v. 'Knowing.' In *Style* 45, No. 2, 254–258.

Kahler, Erich 1973/1970: *The Inward Turn of Narrative*. Princeton: Princeton University Press.

Karkama, Pertti 1994: *Kirjallisuus ja nykyaika: Suomalaisen sanataiteen teemoja ja tendenssejä*. Helsinki: SKS.

Karttunen, Laura 2010: Hypoteettinen puhe ja suoran esityksen illuusio. In *Luonnolliset ja luonnottomat kertomukset: Jälkiklassisen narratologian suuntauksia*. Edited by Mari Hatavara, Markku Lehtimäki & Pekka Tammi. Helsinki: Gaudeamus, 220–252.

Kauffman, Linda S. 1992: *Special Delivery: Epistolary Modes in Modern Fiction*. Chicago & London: The University of Chicago Press.

Kaunonen, Leena 1997: Heinänkorren tarkkuudella: taiteesta ja näkemisestä Paavo Haavikon Pimeydessä. In *Muodotonta menoa: Kirjoituksia nykykirjallisuudesta*. Edited by Mervi Kantokorpi. Helsinki: WSOY, 226–241.

— 2001: *Sanojen palatsi. Puhujan määrittely ja teoskokonaisuuden hahmotus Paavo Haavikon Talvipalatsissa*. Helsinki: SKS.

Kavanagh, Thomas M. 1993: *Enlightenment and the Shadows of Chance: The Novel and the Culture of Gambling in Eighteenth Century France*. Baltimore: The Johns Hopkins University Press.

Keen, Suzanne 2007: *Empathy and the Novel*. New York: Oxford University Press.

Kern, Stephen 2011: *The Modernist Novel: A Critical Introduction*. Cambridge: Cambridge University Press.

Knuuttila, Sirkka 2009: *Fictionalizing Trauma: The Aesthetics of Marguerite Duras's India Cycle*. Helsinki: Helsinki University Press.

Kosonen, Päivi 2000: *Elämät sanoissa: Eletty ja kerrottu epäjatkuvuus Sarrauten, Durasin, Robbe- Grillet'n ja Perecin omaelämäkerrallisissa teksteissä*. Helsinki: Tutkijaliitto.

Kuusi, Matti 1963: Esisuomalainen runous. In *Suomen kirjallisuus I: Kirjoittamaton kirjallisuus*. Helsinki: SKS & Otava, 31–41.

Labov, William 1972: *Language in the Inner City*. Philadelphia: University of Pennsylvania Press.

Laitinen, Kai 1965: 1940- ja 1950-luvun kirjailijoita. In *Suomen kirjallisuus V: Joel Lehtosesta Antti Hyryyn*. Edited by Annimari Sarajas. Helsinki: SKS & Otava, 589–628.

— 1981: *Suomen kirjallisuuden historia*. Helsinki: Otava.

Lappalainen, Päivi 2000: *Koti, kansa ja maailman tahraava lika: Näkökulmia 1880- ja 1890-luvun kirjallisuuteen*. Helsinki: SKS.

Launis, Kati 2005: *Kerrotut naiset: Suomen ensimmäiset naisten kirjoittamat romaanit naiseuden määrittelijöinä*. Helsinki: SKS.

Laurila, K. S. 1918: *Estetiikan peruskysymyksiä*. Porvoo: WSOY.

LeDoux, Joseph 1998: *The Emotional Brain: The Mysterious Underpinnings of Emotional Life*. New York: Phoenix.

Liukkonen, Tero 1992: Kätilö, paavi vai inkvisiittori? Tuomas Anhava kirjallisena vaikuttajana. In *Avoin ja suljettu: Kirjoituksia 1950-luvusta suomalaisessa kulttuurissa*. Edited by Anna Makkonen. Helsinki: SKS, 192–202.

Lund, Hans 1998: Ekphrastic Linkage and Contextual *Ekphrasis*. In *Pictures into Words: Theoretical and Descriptive Approaches to Ekphrasis*. Edited by Valerie Robillard & Els Jongeneel. Amsterdam: VU University Press, 173–188.

Lyytikäinen, Pirjo 1992: *Mielen meri, elämän pidot Volter Kilven Alastalon salissa*. Helsinki: SKS.

— 1997: *Narkissos ja sfinksi: Minä ja Toinen vuosisadanvaihteen kirjallisuudessa*. Helsinki: SKS.

Makkonen, Anna 1992: Sivullisia ja kokeilijoita: Näkökulmia 1950-luvun proosaan. In *Avoin ja suljettu: Kirjoituksia 1950-luvusta suomalaisessa kulttuurissa*. Edited by Anna Makkonen. Helsinki: SKS, 93–121.

Matson, Alex 1947: *Romaanitaide*. Helsinki: Tammi.

McGuinn, Colin 2004: *Mindsight: Image, Dream, Meaning*. Cambridge & London: Harvard University Press.

McHale, Brian 1987: *Postmodernist Fiction*. New York & London: Methuen.

— 2001: Weak Narrativity: The Case of Avant-Garde Narrative Poetry. In *Narrative* 9.2, 161–167.

Mitchell, W. J. T. 1994: *Picture Theory*. Chicago: The University of Chicago Press.

Monk, Leland 1993: *Standard Deviations: Chance and the Modern British Novel*. Stanford: Stanford University Press.

Moretti, Franco 1987: *The Way of the World: The Bildungsroman in European Culture*. London: Verso.

Mosher, Harold F. 1993: The Narrated and It's Negatives: The Nonnarrated and the Disnarrated in Joyce's Dubliners. In *Style*, Vol. 27 (Fall 1993), 407–428.

Myers, Elyse 2000: Virginia Woolf and *The Voyage Out* from Victorian Science. In *Virginia Woolf: Turning the Centuries*. Edited by Ann Ardis & Bonnie Kime Scott. New York: Pace University Press, 298–304.

Mäkelä, Maria 2011: *Uskoton mieli ja tekstuaaliset petokset: Kirjallisen tajunnankuvauksen konventiot narratologisena haasteena*. Tampereen yliopisto: Tampere University Press.

Nalbantian, Suzanne 2003: *Memory in Literature: From Rousseau to Neuroscience*. Hampshire & New York: Palgrave Macmillan.

Niemi, Irmeli 1999: Vallan rajoilla ja risteyksissä. In Maria Jotuni: *Kun on tunteet. Tyttö ruusutarhassa*. Helsinki: SKS, vii–xvi.

Niemi, Juhani 1995: *Proosan murros: Kertovan kirjallisuuden modernisoituminen Suomessa 1940-luvulta 1960-luvulle*. Helsinki: SKS.

Nummi, Jyrki 2008: Kadotettu ja jälleen löydetty: *Nummisuutarit* ja *Filius Prodigus* -traditio. In *Homeroksesta Hessu Hopoon: Antiikin traditioiden vaikutus myöhempään kirjallisuuteen*. Edited by Janna Kantola & Heta Pyrhönen. Helsinki: SKS, 135–154.

Nünning, Vera 2010: The Making of Fictional Worlds: Processes, Features, and Functions. In *Cultural Ways of World-Making: Media and Narratives*. Edited by Vera Nünning, Ansgar Nünning & Birgit Neumann. Berlin & New York: De Gryter, 215–244.

Nünning, Ansgar & Nünning, Vera 2010: The Ways of World-Making as a Model for the Study of Culture: Theoretical Frameworks, Epistemological Underpinnings, New Horizons. In *Cultural Ways of World-Making: Media and Narratives*. Edited by Vera Nünning, Ansgar Nünning & Birgit Neumann. Berlin & New York: De Gryter, 1–28.

Ojala, Aatos 1976: Kertomuksen struktuurianalyysi: Roland Barthesin menetelmä ja sen sovellutus Antti Hyryn kertomataiteeseen. In *Tutkimus ja opetus: Strukturalismia. Äidinkielenopettajain Liiton Vuosikirja 23.* Helsinki: Merkur, 109–136.

Olson, Liesl 2009: *Modernism and the Ordinary.* Oxford & New York: Oxford University Press.

Painter Blythe, Kirsten 2006: *A Revolution of Precision and Restraint in American, Russian, and German Modernism.* Stanford: Stanford University Press.

Palmer, Alan 2004: *Fictional Minds.* Lincoln & London: University of Nebraska Press.

— 2010: *Social Minds in the Novel.* Columbus: Ohio State University Press.

— 2011a: Social Minds in Fiction and Criticism. In *Style* Vol. 45, No. 2, 196–240.

— 2011b: Enlarged Perspectives: A Rejoinder to the Responses. In *Style* Vol. 45, No. 2, 366–412.

Parente-Čapková, Viola 2001: Kuvittelija/tar: Androgyyniset mielikuvat L. Onervan varhaisproosassa. In *Lähikuvassa nainen: Näköaloja 1800-luvun kirjalliseen kulttuuriin.* Edited by Päivi Lappalainen, Heidi Grönstrand & Kati Launis. Helsinki: SKS, 216–238.

— 2014: *Decandent New Woman (Un)bound: Mimetic Strategies in L. Onerva's "Mirdja."* Publications of Turku University. Series B, Humaniora, Vol. 378. Turku: Turku University.

Pavel, Thomas 1986: *Fictional Worlds.* Cambridge & London: Harvard University Press.

Pearce, Lynne & Stacey, Jackie 1995: *Romance Revisited.* New York: New York University Press.

Polanyi, Livia 1979: So What's the Point? In *Semiotica* 25, 207–241.

Prince, Gerald 2004/1988: The Disnarrated. In *Narrative Theory: Critical Concepts in Literary and Cultural Studies.* Edited by Mieke Bal. London: Routledge, 297–305.

Radway, Janice 1987/1984: *Reading the Romance: Women, Patriarchy, and Popular Literature.* Chapel Hill & London: The University of North Carolina Press.

Redfield, Marc 1996: *Phantom Formations: Aesthetic Ideology and the Bildungsroman.* Ithaca: Cornell University Press.

Reith, Gerda 1999: *The Age of Chance: Gambling in Western Culture.* London & New York: Routledge.

Repo, Eino S. (ed.) 1954: *Toiset pidot tornissa.* Helsinki: Gummerus.

Richards, I. A. 1952/1924: *Principles of Literary Criticism.* New York: Harcourt, Brace & Company.

Richardson, Brian 1997: *Unlikely Stories: Causality and the Nature of Modern Narrative.* London: Associated University Presses.

— 2005: Causality. In *The Routledge Encyclopedia of Narrative Theory.* Edited by David Herman, Manfred Jahn & Marie-Laure Ryan. London: Routledge, 48–52.

— 2006: *Unnatural Voices: Extreme Narration in Modern and Contemporary Fiction.* Columbus: The Ohio State University Press.

Riffaterre, Michael 1981: Descriptive Imagery. In *Yale French Studies* No. 61, 107–125.

Rimmon-Kenan, Shlomith 1983: *Narrative Fiction: Contemporary Poetics.* London: Methuen.

Rojola, Lea 1992: Oman sielunsa hullu morsian: Mirjan matka taiteen maailmassa. In *Pakeneva keskipiste: Tutkielmia suomalaisesta taiteilijaromaanista.* Edited by Tarja-Liisa Hypén. Sarja A, No. 26. Turku University. Department of Arts, 49–73.

— 2011: "And She Felt a Desire to Speak": Aino Kallas, Maie Merits, and the Female Voice. In *Aino Kallas: Negations with Modernity.* Edited by Leena Kurvet-Käosaar & Lea Rojola. Studia Fennica Litteraria. Helsinki: SKS, 36–53.

Rosowski, Susan J. 1983: The Novel of Awakening. In *The Voyage In: Fictions of Female Development.* Hanover & London: Dartmouth, 49–68.

Rossi, Riikka 2011: Vapauden muunnelmia: Naturalismi ja eksistentialismi Maria Jotunin Arkielämää-kertomuksessa. In *Avain* 1/2011, 5–23; 96.

— 2013: Villinainen ja soturi: Alkukantaisuus ja pessimismi Maria Jotunin naiskuvissa. In *Kirjallisuuden naiset: Naisten esityksiä 1840-luvulta 2000-luvulle*. Edited by Riikka Rossi & Saija Isomaa. Helsinki: SKS, 278–295.

Ryan, Marie-Laure 1980: Fiction, Non-Factuals and the Principle of Minimal Departure. In *Poetics* Vol. 9 (4). August 1980, 403–422.

— 1991: *Possible Worlds, Artificial Intelligence, and Narrative Theory*. Bloomington: Indiana University Press.

— 1992: The Modes of Narrativity and Their Visual Metaphors. In *Style*, Vol. 26, No. 3, 368–388.

Saari, Mauno 2009: *Haavikko-niminen mies*. Helsinki: WSOY.

Semino, Elena; Short, Mick & Wynne, Martin 1999: Hypothetical Words and Thoughts in Contemporary British Narratives. In *Narrative* 7: 3, 307–334.

Shklovsky, Viktor 1965/1917: Art as Technique. In *Russian Formalist Criticism: Four Essays*. Edited and Translated by Lee T. Lemon & Marion J. Reis. Lincoln: University of Nebraska Press, 3–24.

Steinberg, Leo 1972: Picasso's Sleepwatchers. In *Other Criteria: Confrontations with Twentieth Century Art*. New York: Oxford University Press, 93–114.

Sternberg, Meir 1982: Proteus in the Quotation-Land: Mimesis and the Forms of Reported Discourse. In *Poetic's Today*, Vol. 3 (2). Spring 1982, 107–156.

Stewen, Riikka 1996: Suljetut silmät. In *Katsomuksen ihanuus: Kirjoituksia vuosisadanvaihteen taiteesta*. Edited by Pirjo Lyytikäinen, Jyrki Kalliokoski & Mervi Kantokorpi. Helsinki: SKS, 17–26.

Stevenson, Randall 1998: *Modernist Fiction*. London: Prentice Hall.

Tammi, Pekka 1992: *Kertova teksti: Esseitä narratologiasta*. Helsinki: Gaudeamus.

Toulmin, Stephen 1990: *Cosmopolis: The Hidden Agenda of Modernity*. New York: The Free Press.

Trevarthen, Colwyn 1999: Intersubjectivity. In *The MIT Encyclopedia of the Cognitive Sciences*. Edited by Robert A. Wilson & Frank C. Keil. Cambridge: MIT Press, 415–419.

Turner, Mark 1987: *Death is the Mother of Beauty: Mind, Metaphor, Criticism*. Chicago: University of Chicago Press.

Varela, Francisco J.; Thompson, Evan & Rosch, Eleanor 1993: *The Embodied Mind: Cognitive Science and Human Experience*. Cambridge & London: The MIT Press.

Viikari, Auli 1992: Ei kenenkään maa: 1950-luvun tropologiaa. In *Avoin ja suljettu: Kirjoituksia 1950-luvusta suomalaisessa kulttuurissa*. Edited by Anna Makkonen. Helsinki: SKS, 30–77.

— 1993: Ancilla narrationis vai kutsumaton haltijatar? Kuvauksen poetiikkaa. In *Toiseuden politiikat*. Edited by Pirjo Ahokas & Lea Rojola. KTSV 47. Helsinki: SKS, 60–84.

Vuorikuru, Silja 2012: *Kauneudentemppelin ovella: Aino Kallaksen tuotanto ja raamatullinen subteksti*. Helsinki: University of Helsinki.

Watt, Ian 1980: *Conrad in the Nineteenth Century*. London: Chatto & Windus.

Whitworth, Michael H. 2007: Introduction. In *Modernism*. Edited by Michael H. Whitworth. Oxford: Blackwell Publishing.

Wilson, Timothy D. 2002: *Strangers to Ourselves: Discovering the Adaptive Unconscious*. Massachusetts: The Belknap Press of Harvard University Press.

Wittgenstein, Ludwig 1961/1921: *Tractatus logico-philosophicus*. Translated by D. F. Pears & B. F. McGuinness. Introduction by Bertrand Russell. London: Routledge & Kegan Paul.

— 1958/1953: *Philosophical Investigations*. Translated by G. E. M. Anscombe. Oxford: Basil Blackwell.

— 1980: *Culture and Value*. Introduction by G. Von Wright. Translated by P. Winch. Oxford: Blackwell, 3–60.

von Wright, Georg Henrik 2001: Saatesanat Ludwig Wittgensteinin teoksessa *Filosofisia Tutkimuksia* [Foreword in Ludwig Wittgenstein's *Philosophical Investigations*]. Helsinki: WSOY, 7–12.

Zunshine, Lisa 2006: *Why We Read Fiction: Theory of Mind and the Novel*. Columbus: Ohio State University Press.

— 2011: Style Brings in Mental States. In *Style* 45, No. 2, 349–356.

Yacobi, Tamar 1995: Pictorial Models and Narrative Ekphrasis. In *Poetics Today* Vol. 16, No. 4, 599–649.

— 1997: Verbal Frames and Ekphrastic Figuration. In *Interart Poetics: Essays on the Interrelations of the Arts and Media*. Edited by Ulla-Britta Lagerroth, Hand Lund & Erik Hedling. Amsterdam: Rodopi, 35–46.

— 2004: Fictive Beholders: How Ekphrasis Dramatizes Visual Perception. In *Iconotropism: Turning Toward Pictures*. Edited by Ellen Spolsky. Lewisburg: Bucknell University Press, 69–87.

Unpublished Sources

Jabr, Ferris 2012: A Contemplation of Chattering Minds. http://thesciencebulletin. wordpress.com/2012/07/01/ [24 February 2014]

Konkka, Anita 2008: Kaikki naiset näkevät unia. http://anita-konkka.blogspot. fi/2008/10/kaikki-naiset-nkevt-unia.html [21 April 2017]

Parks, Tim 2012: The Chattering Mind. http://www.nybooks.com/blogs/nyrblog/2012/ jun/29/chattering-mind/ [21 April 2017]

Vesti, Laura 2014: *Naiskuva Marja-Liisa Vartion romaanissa* Tunteet. Master's Thesis. Tampere University.

Abstract

Elise Nykänen ⓘ http://orcid.org/0000-0001-8812-6510

Mysterious Minds
The Making of Private and Collective Consciousness in Marja-Liisa Vartio's Novels

This study examines the narrative tools, techniques, and structures that Marja-Liisa Vartio, a classic of Finnish post-war modernism, used in presenting fictional minds in her narrative prose. The study contributes to the academic discussion on formal and thematic conventions of modernism by addressing the ways in which fictional minds work in interaction, and in relation to the enfolding fictional world. The epistemic problem of how accurately the world, the self, and the other can be known is approached by analyzing two co-operating ways of portraying fictional minds, both from external and internal perspectives. The external perspective relies on detachment and emotional restraint dominating in Vartio's early novels *Se on sitten kevät* and *Mies kuin mies, tyttö kuin tyttö*. The internal perspective pertains to the mental processes of self-reflection, speculation, and excessive imagining that gain more importance in her later novels *Kaikki naiset näkevät unia*, *Tunteet*, and *Hänen olivat linnut*.

In the theoretical chapter of this study, fictional minds are discussed in the context of the acclaimed "inward turn" of modernist fiction, by suggesting alternative methods for reading modernist minds as embodied, emotional, and social entities. In respect to fictional minds' interaction, this study elaborates on the ideas of "mind-reading," "intersubjectivity," and the "social mind" established within post-classical cognitive narratology. Furthermore, it employs possible world poetics when addressing the complexity, incompleteness, and (in)accessibility of Vartio's epistemic worlds, including the characters' private worlds of knowledge, beliefs, emotions, hallucinations, and dreams. In regards to the emotional emplotment of fictional worlds, this study also benefits from affective narratology as well as the plot theory being influenced by possible world semantics, narrative dynamics, and cognitive narratology.

As the five analysis chapters of this study show, fictional minds in Vartio's fiction are not only introspective, solipsist, and streaming, but also embodied and social entities. In the readings of the primary texts, the concept of embodiedness is used to examine the situated presence of an experiencing mind within the time and space of the storyworld. Fictional minds' (inter)actions are also demonstrated as evolving from local experientiality to long-term calculations that turn emotional incidents into episodes, and episodes into stories. In Vartio's novels, the emotional story structure of certain conventional story patterns, such as the narratives of female development and the romance plot, the sentimental novel, and epistolary fiction, are modified and causally altered in the portrayal of the embodied interactions between the self, the other, and the world. The trajectories of female self-discovery in Vartio's novels are analyzed through the emotional responses of characters: their experiences of randomness, their ways of counterfactualizing their traumatic past, their procrastinatory or akratic reactions or indecisiveness. The gradual move away from the percepts of the external world to the excessive imaginings and (mis)readings of other minds (triggered by the interaction of worlds and minds), challenges the contemporary and more recent accounts of modernism both in Finnish and international contexts.

Index

Studia Fennica Historica

Modernisation in Russia since 1900
Edited by Markku Kangaspuro & Jeremy Smith
Studia Fennica Historica 12
2006

SEIJA-RIITTA LAAKSO
Across the Oceans
Development of Overseas Business Information Transmission 1815–1875
Studia Fennica Historica 13
2007

Industry and Modernism
Companies, Architecture and Identity in the Nordic and Baltic Countries during the High-Industrial Period
Edited by Anja Kervanto Nevanlinna
Studia Fennica Historica 14
2007

CHARLOTTA WOLFF
Noble conceptions of politics in eighteenth-century Sweden (ca 1740–1790)
Studia Fennica Historica 15
2008

Sport, Recreation and Green Space in the European City
Edited by Peter Clark, Marjaana Niemi & Jari Niemelä
Studia Fennica Historica 16
2009

Rhetorics of Nordic Democracy
Edited by Jussi Kurunmäki & Johan Strang
Studia Fennica Historica 17
2010

Fibula, Fabula, Fact
The Viking Age in Finland
Edited by Joonas Ahola & Frog with Clive Tolley
Studia Fennica Historica 18
2014

Novels, Histories, Novel Nations
Historical Fiction and Cultural Memory in Finland and Estonia
Edited by Linda Kaljundi, Eneken Laanes & Ilona Pikkanen
Studia Fennica Historica 19
2015

JUKKA GRONOW & SERGEY ZHURAVLEV
Fashion Meets Socialism
Fashion industry in the Soviet Union after the Second World War
Studia Fennica Historica 20
2015

SOFIA KOTILAINEN
Literacy Skills as Local Intangible Capital
The History of a Rural Lending Library c. 1860–1920
Studia Fennica Historica 21
2016

Continued Violence and Troublesome Pasts
Post-war Europe between the Victors after the Second World War
Edited by Ville Kivimäki and Petri Karonen
Studia Fennica Historica 22
2017

Personal Agency at the Swedish Age of Greatness 1560-1720
Edited by Petri Karonen & Marko Hakanen
Studia Fennica Historica 23
2017

PASI IHALAINEN
The Springs of Democracy
National and Transnational Debates on Constitutional Reform in the British, German, Swedish and Finnish Parliaments, 1917–19
Studia Fennica Historica 24
2017

Studia Fennica Anthropologica

On Foreign Ground
Moving between Countries and Categories
Edited by Marie-Louise Karttunen & Minna Ruckenstein
Studia Fennica Anthropologica 1
2007

Beyond the Horizon
Essays on Myth, History, Travel and Society
Edited by Clifford Sather & Timo Kaartinen
Studia Fennica Anthropologica 2
2008

TIMO KALLINEN
Divine Rulers in a Secular State
Studia Fennica Anthropologica 3
2016

www.ingramcontent.com/pod-product-compliance
Lightning Source LLC
Chambersburg PA
CBHW081401090726
47908CB00012B/2758